I0728830

THE TAGGER HERD
COLLECTION FOUR

From Book One
The phone call that changed their lives forever

The phone was still ringing, so she hit the answer button and raised it to her ear.

"The Stables," she answered.

There was hesitation before the person spoke. When she did, Dru could tell it was an older woman. "Can I speak with the owner please?" She said quietly.

"I am one of the owners, Dru Tagger."

There was more hesitation. "Oh…good. I'm so sorry to bother you."

She hesitated long enough that Dru could add, "No bother at all, how can I help?"

"Well," another hesitation. Even over the phone Dru could tell she was upset.

"I'm not really sure how to start," the woman paused. "My name is Cora Smith and my husband, Wes, passed away a little over three weeks ago."

Well that was a start, Dru frowned. "I'm so sorry."

"Yes, well, thank you. I received a phone call a few minutes ago," she hesitated again, "I'm a bit confused about the call."

"Was it from someone here at The Stables?"

"No, I got your number from a card my husband had in his wallet."

"Do you have horses? Was your husband looking for somewhere to board them?"

"No horses. We sold all our horses a couple years ago."

"OK…" Dru walked away from the arena and the excited chatter from the two teenagers talking about the last day of school.

"That's what's so strange about the phone call I received. The man who called said he would be delivering the hay in the morning."

"Did they call from Tagger Enterprises for the hay?"

"No."

Dru quietly exhaled in rising confusion. "Hay for what?"

"I don't know; we don't have any animals. I canceled the hay order from the man, but now I'm worried," The woman's voice trembled as she continued. "My husband was being very secretive before he died. He even shipped me to Seattle to spend time with my sister for a couple weeks."

Dru still wasn't sure what this had to do with The Stables.

The woman on the phone continued, "We live in Lenore, but I haven't been there since a week before he died."

"Mrs. Smith," Dru leaned against the back of the building. "I'm a bit confused. How can The Stables help?"

The voice let out a frustrated sigh, "I am afraid my husband bought some animals without telling me and they have been at our home in Lenore, unattended, for over three weeks."

Dru slowly stood away from the building, "Horses, sheep, cattle, chickens…a lot of animals can forage for themselves for three weeks."

"Yes," The woman's voice was a little stronger since she had finally voiced her concern. "After my husband died, we had him brought to Seattle and buried here, with family. I haven't been to our home now for over a month. I have no one there to call to go check the property. With your card here… well, I thought maybe he had talked to you about this."

"No, not with me," Dru frowned. "I'll talk to the manager here to see if he spoke with your husband. If not, then we'll take a drive and check." This could be a total waste of time… she HOPED it was a total waste of time. "You have no idea what kind of animals he may have bought?"

"No," she sighed, "I'm just so worried. The man with the hay was so adamant that my husband had bought the hay AND that it was scheduled to be delivered in the morning."

"Did he say how much hay he was delivering?" It was coming on summer when most large animals would be grazing in pastures and not be dependent on hay. The first hay crop was coming off the fields. He could have been stocking up for winter.

"He didn't say."

"OK, I'll go check it out," Her parents and grandparents had taught her to have respect for animals. Something in her gut told her to make the drive. She wouldn't be able to forgive herself if there were animals suffering because she didn't have time to take a drive 30 miles up the river.

This book is fiction. The characters, properties, and dialogues are from the author's imagination and are not to be construed as fact. Any resemblance to actual events or people, alive or dead, is entirely co-incidental.

COPYRIGHT © 2022 BY GINI ROBERGE. All rights reserved. No part of this book may be used or reproduced in any manner whatsoever without written permission from the author except in case of brief quotes.

www.thetaggerherd.com

978-1-7339528-6-6

THE TAGGER

HERD

Collection Four

A Series by

Gini Roberge

The two men below were the first to know the book existed and were the first to read it. Through their encouragement I continued with the series.

Our 'courier' Emily is Ben's wife and now a good friend of mine as well as their daughter Kenzie.

SPECIAL THANKS TO
BEN SMITH, DVM
For Your Input and Editing Expertise
And the courier Emily!
AND
STEVE ROBERGE, BRO
My sounding board, encouraging voice, and special editor

THE TAGGER HERD

SERIES

Josey Franklin

Gini Roberge

CHAPTER ONE

"How long do you think we can sit out here before they come out to see what we're doing?" Josey glanced at Nikki then back to the red building.

"I don't particularly want to find out," Nikki chuckled.

Josey smiled nervously. "Me, either." The clock on the dash of the rental car read 9:55.

"The appointments at 10:00…we need to go in," Nikki turned to her. "Are you sure about this?"

"Yes…you?"

"Yes…but for some reason, I don't think it means as much to me as it does to you."

"That's because of your family."

"They are yours now, too."

"Not all of them," Josey reached for the door handle as Matt's grin flashed in her mind. "I have to do this…" She looked at her sister. "I have to face the past to be able to move on with my life. I want to be strong and take control. Hiding in the shadows? Being too scared? I'm done with it. It's time to move on."

The sisters met at the front of the car, smiled nervously, then stepped toward the building. There were a number of white buildings behind the red one. A tall wire fence surrounded all the buildings except the front of the red building and rolled barbwire was along the top and bottom of the fence.

"I don't think they want anyone to leave," Nikki chuckled nervously.

"I think the word is escape," Josey took a deep breath and gripped the handle of the door with the letters spelling out the Women's Correctional Center.

They silently walked to the check-in counter.

"I'll be with you in a moment," A woman on the phone smiled at them.

The sisters nodded back and turned to each other. They had read the rules of prisoner visitation time after time. They wore no blue clothes…they concluded it was because the prisoners wore blue. Their pockets were completely empty except for the keys and identification which they would leave at the security area. They had on plain casual dress shirts, Nikki's white and Josey's green, tan khaki's, and they stood in plain slip on shoes. Their long dark hair was down and loose.

The woman behind the counter signed them in, took the keys and ID's then led them down a hall and into the visitation room. There were multiple tables setup around the room. It was what they had imagined…just like in the movies.

"Do you think she'll come out?" Josey whispered. She nervously took her seat on the same side of the table as her sister.

"Well, it was a gamble when we requested the visit. She'll probably come out due to curiosity…wondering what we want."

"Or boredom."

They sat quietly and waited; their hands resting on the top of the table…per the rules. A door to the right opened and their heads turned to see a guard walk through; leading Elena.

The woman spoke to the guard then turned to the table; she hesitated when she saw the sisters…her daughters looking nervously at her. Walking straight to the table Elena sat down without a word and looked between Nikki and Josey.

Josey's stomach turned…the last time she had seen Elena the guards in Lewiston were escorting her out of the court house after the judge accepted her plea agreement.

Now she sat across from them, her inquisitive brown eyes turning from one sister to the other. Her dark hair was straight and cut in a bob, just stopping at the top of her shoulders.

"It's a bit bizarre seeing the two of you together," Elena said. "You look more alike than I thought you did."

"Why did you keep us apart?" Nikki asked; her voice shook.

"Because of this…" Elena pointed between the two of them. "I didn't want to be ganged up on."

"Do you think that's what we're doing?" Josey asked with a tilt of the head. She wished her stomach would stop moving.

"Isn't it?" Elena asked pointedly.

"Not really," Nikki answered.

"What would you call it?" Elena asked with a skeptical tone.

"We're not here to accuse you or harass you," Nikki frowned.

"Then why are you here?" Elena continued the shifting of her eyes between the two sisters.

"We just want to know why," Josey answered, she needed to know why…to be able to move on with her life…to get the real Josey back.

"Why what?" Elena raised a brow in curiosity.

"Why all the stealing…extortion…fraud…why?" Nikki asked. Her voice had stopped shaking. It was more firm; confident.

"Why use us? Why couldn't you just be a mother to us?" Josey tried to keep her voice calm. too. She wasn't sure it worked.

"Well, getting right to it," Elena leaned back in her chair and nodded. "Might as well."

The sisters waited. Josey was afraid if she spoke Elena wouldn't talk.

"I am not the motherly type," Elena said bluntly. "I didn't want to be one, but I figured if I had a kid then your fathers would stick with me…I liked the rodeo life." She looked at Nikki. "Yours didn't, he had a more screwed up life than I thought. I learned that at New Year's." She turned to Josey. "Yours tried…that didn't work out. He got hurt, stopped competing, and wanted to settle down so you could go to school. It was massively boring. I didn't like it, so I left."

Josey sat and stared in disbelief. She never dreamed Elena would be open to giving them this much information.

"I also like fine things…stuff. I'm materialistic, but I don't want to work for it…I want it given to me," Elena continued indifferently. She looked back to Nikki, "I thought after your trick with the stable manager, that you were like me. In a way you were."

"What do you mean?" Nikki asked a bit tersely.

"Nick did you a favor by dropping you off with Dru…you want something…they give it to you. You don't have to work for it."

"Of course, I did!" Nikki's back straightened. "I worked at the ranch growing up and at The Stables to work my way through college. If The Stables hadn't been there I would have found somewhere else to work."

Elena stared at Nikki, her eyes narrowing slightly then she nodded, "Nick was like that…always had to be doing something…so you took that from him." Elena sat up straight, leaned her arms on the table and stared at Nikki. "If you wanted something…they gave it to you. Do you deny that?"

"To a point they would," Nikki admitted. "But not anything more than any parent would give their child if they could."

"Not mine," Elena looked to Josey then back to Nikki. "They gave me nothing. I couldn't have anything…not a doll…not a fancy dress…nothing."

"Why?" Josey asked, genuinely curious.

"They thought it would lead to evil things if they gave me everything I wanted…so they gave me nothing I wanted," She grunted. "They were a bit surprised when their whole parenting skill backfired on them."

"You stole from them?" Nikki asked.

"They had nothing to steal or I probably would have," Elena answered honestly. "They were furious when I gave you to Nick."

"Why did you?" Nikki leaned forward.

Elena leaned back…away from Nikki. "Punish my parents by taking away their only chance at a grandchild and to punish Nick for taking me back to them."

"Did you love Nick?" Nikki asked.

"Honestly?" Elena looked emotionlessly at the sisters, who nodded. "I don't think I have it in me to love anyone. I loved the things he bought me…I love things."

Josey was stunned at the woman's honesty. Never would she have dreamed this conversation.

"Why did you use us?" Josey asked, her inner strength growing.

"I'd use anyone to get what I wanted," Elena shrugged.

"Why take my college fund?" Josey leaned forward, matching Nikki's position.

"Why not?" Elena shrugged again. "You didn't work to earn that money…so why should you have it and not me?"

Josey wanted to laugh in disbelief at the woman's reasoning. "Didn't you care about how I would feel about it? What it would do to me?"

"Josey," Elena shook her head with a deep chuckle. "I didn't care…honestly, I still don't care. You're young and can bounce back. I'm not, I wanted the money. I loved the stuff I bought with it but I got bored with it and wanted different stuff."

Josey thought her jaw had literally dropped to the table. She couldn't believe there was anyone as cold and uncaring as this woman. She kept pushing…wanting all the answers and it seemed like Elena was willing to give them.

"Did you really think I would go along with the sexual harassment case against the Taggers?" Josey asked.

Elena sighed with a slight one shoulder shrug, "It was worth the gamble. When I saw Nick's son in front of the hotel, I figured you two were the same age…he was still young…he would make mistakes with girls. He looked so…righteous. I realized then that I could use him to get to his family's money." She shifted and leaned an arm over the back of the chair. "Once I saw the picture of the two of you on top the truck, he had hold of your jeans…" She shrugged. "It was a gamble."

"Why are you talking to us?" Nikki asked; obviously as shocked as Josey was at the conversation.

"We didn't even know if you would come out to talk to us" Josey added.

Elena smiled, an evil smile that Josey frowned at, but it didn't scare her anymore. "My counselor in here told me you had requested a visit. I agreed because I was curious. She informed me that even if the truth made no difference to me, it would make a difference to you," She looked between the two girls. "I still can't say I care, but she said it was the right thing to do and I have to impress her."

Elena turned to the guard at the door and nodded. She stood, "I have nothing to give you…materialistically," Elena added. "But the counselor said I should tell you something that you need, something that would help you and in the long run, it might help me past my issues and, more importantly, out of here," She shrugged again. "I don't know if it will, but I'll do it anyway, consider it an early Christmas gift."

Both girls just stared at her, not knowing what to say or do.

Elena turned to Nikki. "You want to know how I found out about Billings…that the Taggers would be there?"

Nikki nodded.

"I created a fake Facebook page in the name, or close to, one of Reilly's friends. He accepted the friend request, probably not knowing it wasn't his friend…a Mike Ridley…spelled with an L…E…Y, I spelled it without the E. I asked him about the trip when he posted over the winter that he couldn't go and how bummed he was. I confirmed the first of May in a private message and he answered."

Josey turned and looked at Nikki. She was glaring at Elena; probably upset that the woman would use an innocent kid like Reilly.

"And you," Elena said. When Josey turned to her, she continued, "When I met you in Billings, you said your dad had disappeared. You didn't know where he was."

Josey nodded, afraid of what Elena was going to say, but she took a deep breath and tried to prepare herself. Was she going to tell her where he is? Lucas had already offered the information; she didn't need it from Elena. Besides, how would she know?

Elena stared at her. She looked like she was trying to decide something.

"Well," Elena finally blurted. "Greg's not your real father. I was already pregnant when I met him. I don't remember the guy's name…could be a couple different guys…both local bull riders…I like bull riders…" She smirked at her daughters and shrugged when they didn't react. "It was at one of the first PBR events held in Pendleton." Elena reached up, pulled a few strands of hair from her head and placed them on the table. "If I were you, I wouldn't believe me, so you can use these to get a DNA test if Greg will agree to it. Which he probably will. I didn't tell him you weren't his, but I'm sure he knew."

With that, she turned away and walked to the guard.

Josey stared at Elena as she walked away… her whole body tingling from the shock. When the woman disappeared behind the door without a glance back, Josey looked down at the hair on the table. She slowly reached forward and pulled them to her. Twisting them between her fingers, she held them tightly.

"Let's go," Nikki whispered and the sisters stood.

They signed the log, retrieved the keys, and their ID then left the building without saying a word to each other. When they slid into the car they both sat quietly; staring ahead of them.

Josey looked down at the hair in her hand. Opening her wallet she found a piece of paper and folded the hair into it and safely tucked it away. She leaned back, buckled her seat belt and turned to her sister.

Nikki turned and they hesitantly smiled at each other.

"Wow," Nikki finally managed to say.

"Yeah…"

"Well, we got answers."

"More than we thought." Josey bit her lip nervously. "Do you think she was telling the truth…about my dad?"

Nikki shrugged, "Let's see if she was telling the truth about Mike Ridley."

"How?" Josey asked as Nikki typed a message on her phone.

"Leah is at The Stables today. I'll send her a text and ask her to look on Reilly's Facebook page for the name…both names."

"Why would she lie?"

Nikki started the rental car and turned out of the parking lot. They were just outside of Las Vegas and had a flight out that evening to return home.

"I don't know," Nikki answered. "I sure didn't expect everything we got."

"Me, either."

"We'll have to send a thank you card to that counselor," Nikki giggled.

Josey laughed; the tension and the fear she felt when she got up that morning was gone.

"She sure is one cold fish." Nikki chuckled and her phone alert rang out.

Josey picked up the phone and looked at the message.

TEXT FROM LEAH: Both names on his account

TEXT FROM NIKKI/JOSEY: Check private messages with Ridly

They rode quietly. Josey reviewed the conversation with Elena…every word she said.

TEXT FROM LEAH: Nothing but conversation about Billings. Is this what I think it is?

TEXT FROM NIKKI/JOSEY: Yes

"If she told the truth to you," Josey turned to her sister. "She probably told me the truth. So my dad isn't my dad." She wasn't really sure how she felt about that.

"Probably not."

"Then who is?" Josey sighed. The real Josey suddenly seemed farther away than she was before they walked into the building.

CHAPTER TWO

"You realize she didn't ask us one question about our lives or about us?" Nikki asked as they stood in line at the airport security gate. They had both been quiet on the ride to the airport.

"I think she made it pretty clear she didn't care about us," Josey answered. "I'd hate to be like that…not caring about people."

They were quiet again as they made their way through security and onto the tram system that traveled from the terminal to their gate.

Josey thought of the comments that Elena said about her own parents.

"Have you ever thought of looking up her parents?" Josey asked.

Nikki shook her head. "No, I was too afraid they would be like her. I made that mistake once already."

"She said that you were the only chance of her parents having a grandchild. That must mean she didn't have any brothers or sisters."

Nikki nodded.

"I wonder if they are still alive."

"I'm sure Lucas knows…he'll tell us if we ask."

Josey glanced at her sister. She didn't fully understand the information system with Lucas and the Taggers…it seemed odd.

"I don't particularly want to go down Elena's family tree at this point." Josey answered.

The tram stopped and the doors opened. The sisters walked slowly down the corridor to their gate.

"How much time do we have?" Josey asked.

"Two hours."

"I didn't eat last night, or this morning because I was too nervous." Josey sighed. There were times when she was alone in Montana that she would go a day or two with only a peanut butter sandwich for the entire day because she couldn't afford anything more. One loaf of bread and a small container of peanut butter could last her a whole week. She was very thankful those days were in the past. "I'm hungry."

"Me, too."

They took seats in a small café with large windows showing the airplanes flying into the blue sky or crossing on the tarmac.

"You want to try and find out who your father is?" Nikki asked after the waitress brought their food.

"Yes," Josey nodded. She needed all the puzzle pieces of her life together to make her feel whole…make her feel like she was the strong, confident, fierce person Matt deserved.

"Dad was still riding at that time," Nikki told her. "He will be able to help."

Josey nodded, "We'll have to try to find the line up for a March PBR event in Pendleton the year before I was born," Josey chuckled. "That should only narrow it down to about thirty or forty men."

Nikki smiled at her. "I came up with a bunch of different scenarios for the meeting this morning…you coming out fatherless was not one of them."

"Me, either," Josey shook her head while looking out at the planes.

"She gave us some insight as to why she's like she is…and I don't want someone like that in my life."

"Me either. What she did….just using us?" Josey shook her head and sighed. "It didn't have anything to do with us…that we're her daughters…we were just tools…"

"To get 'stuff'." Nikki finished.

Josey watched the workers throw luggage on an escalator that slowly moved the bags into the planes belly. She had always wondered if she had done something wrong to make Elena act like she did towards her. That was what had been bothering her the last couple of years…dragging her down.

The idea to visit Elena came from Grace while they were riding.

"I finally have something to say to help you get rid of your 'Frankie' and move onto just being you," Grace had said. *"Uncle Scott said the past happens so we can help make the future better."*

"How does that help me?"

Grace turned to her with a decisive expression, "You have to face the past, Josey."

"You mean I have to face Elena?"

"You've tried everything else; you're just treading water. You have to take that leap. She can't hurt you anymore, but maybe she can help you understand."

"Understand what?"

"Exactly!" Grace had grinned. "Face your past, that horrible mother head on and find out what you are trying to understand."

Josey chuckled and shook her head, "That doesn't make sense."

"It will when the answers reveal themselves and you…understand."

Grace was right. The answers had helped reveal that none of it was Josey's fault. She now understood that it was Elena's fault not hers. Josey took a deep breath and mentally threw her guilt and doubt baggage on the plane's escalator. Let the plane take it to an unknown destination, she thought. There was nothing more she needed from her birth mother but she needed to give Grace a huge thank you and hug.

"You know," Josey smiled confidently. "I've closed that door."

"Closure with her?"

"Yes, and now I need closure with my dad…or Greg…or whatever he is to me now."

"You want the information from Lucas?"

"Yes, when we get back, I'll call him in the morning."

"DNA test?"

"I'll ask him if he'll do it, just because I don't trust Elena."

"You think he'll do it?"

"Yes. I think he knows…he'll probably want to confirm it in his own mind."

"Did he ever treat you bad?"

"No, just not…well not like Scott and Grayson with the girls…never like that."

"The Cinderella stepdaughter?" Nikki asked with raised concerned brows.

"No," Josey smiled at the thought. "But he was much more loving with his step son then with me. I think he always saw Elena in me," She sighed heavily, feeling the sadness in her heart. "I did think he loved me though."

Nikki nodded, "Nick and Lucas fly in tomorrow morning, we can discuss this with them after they land. It'll be fun to shock them with all this information after a long 20-hour flight from Australia."

The sisters smiled at each other.

No one but Grace and Dru knew they were flying to Vegas to visit Elena. They both supported the trip and offered to come with them but they declined their offer. It was something the sisters needed to do together and they knew both Nick and Lucas would have tried to talk them out of it.

"What about Matt?"

Josey shook her head, "Hopefully this is all done and over by the time he gets home."

"Have you heard from him?"

"Not for a couple of days…you?"

Nikki shook her head, "He only sends a text every once in a while now."

"When he first went overseas, he texted every day," Josey sighed and stood so they could catch their flight. "At least one of us would get a text."

Nikki nodded as she paid for their meal and they walked out of the cafe. "I don't know how to take the decline in communication. It was so weird not having him there for Thanksgiving…first time ever. I can't imagine him not being here for Christmas. Growing up, we were the only entertainment for each other until Grace finally got old enough. We've never been apart this long. I really miss him."

"So do I."

As they walked down the corridor to their gate, Josey thought of the last time she had seen him. It was at the first team penning night of the winter series. They had laughed and teased and at the end of the night he had kissed her softly to say goodnight. When she woke the next morning, she received word that he had gone overseas to help search for victims of an earthquake. He had now been gone for four weeks as he helped with the recovery and cleanup.

Lucas slid the paper across Nick's kitchen table to Josey. With a shaky hand she picked it up and looked at the phone number to her father.

"He's in Florida," Lucas told her. "Are you alright?"

Josey nodded. He had always said he wanted to live somewhere warm. He got his wish.

"I'll wait outside with Nick and Nikki. Just take your time, we'll just be shoeing the horses."

"Thanks," Josey sighed and tried to think of what to say to her dad as she reached for the phone and called the number. When she looked up; Lucas was gone.

"Hello?"

"Dad?"

"Josey?" His voice was hesitant.

"Yes."

"How did you get this number?"

That's the first thing he says to her? It was a punch in the stomach…no…the heart.

"My future brother-in-law," Josey answered tersely; she knew it would confuse him.

"Your what?" He asked in surprise.

"Do you want to know how I am?" She asked coldly.

"Of course…but you don't have any siblings…did you get married?"

"No," She started pacing to release the hurt and rising anger.

"Josey, I don't understand."

"I'll give it to you in a nut shell," Josey stopped pacing and stared out the window. "Elena showed up, told me I had a sister named Nikki, I met Nikki's brother then her. I put Elena in jail last spring, decided to visit her for answers and she informed me yesterday that you are not my father."

She probably could have handled that better.

There was silence, she wasn't sure if he ended the call or not.

"Josey…I don't know what to say."

Josey's mind screamed at him. Tell me that you love me, that you miss me, that you're sorry! Why couldn't he be a father like Jack, Grayson or Scott? Even Nick!

It wasn't just Elena she had needed answers from…but him, too.

"Why did you leave me?" She finally asked.

"You know why…Elena…you couldn't let her go."

"So you let me go? By myself?"

"I had to…it was the only way."

"No, it wasn't," Josey's back stiffened.

Silence again.

"If you loved me like a daughter…you would never have left me," Josey finally admitted it to herself.

"I took care of you after Elena left."

Josey grimaced, "So I take it you knew you weren't my real father?"

"I considered you my daughter."

"Until Elena came back?"

"Josey, I am truly sorry how things worked out," He sighed heavily. "I grew to hate Elena, but I did love you."

"Did?" Again the punch in the heart.

"Do…I do love you Josey but I was afraid you were like Elena. I had myself convinced that you were working with Elena in stealing the money."

"What?" Josey was shocked. How could he think that of her?

"The first time, I knew it was Elena," He sighed. "But when you gave her the college money then came and asked me to help…to give you more…I thought you were working with her."

Josey closed her eyes to keep the tears from escaping. She had never considered what it looked like to him…he had never accused her…he had just left. Running…from her.

"I would never…" She whispered.

"I fought it, Josey. I really did, but I had to protect Kristen and Barry." His voice shook when he spoke of her step mother and brother. She wished she was able to see his face. "I didn't want to hurt you by openly accusing you…so we just left."

"It would have been better if you accused me," Josey's shoulders drooped. "Then I could have understood."

"I'm sorry, Josey. I really am. I didn't know…I didn't know what to do."

She sat back in the chair and let the emotion take over, the tears fell.

"Are you alright Josey? Your sister? Are you with her now?" His voice was full of concern…the concern she wanted to hear when he answered the phone.

"Yes, she has a great family. I'm living on their cattle ranch in Idaho training horses."

"Oh, Josey!" His voice shook from relief and the tears she knew he was letting go, too. "I have thought about you, but I just couldn't reach out. I am so happy for you. That sounds like the perfect life for you."

Josey could feel the anger towards him leave her body and mind.

"It is," She sniffed and tried to wipe away the tears.

"Are you happy, Little Bit?"

Josey's heart constricted. It was the nickname he had called her when she was young. She had missed hearing it and the warm feeling it caused inside her.

"I'm getting there," She said honestly.

She spent the next hour telling him about Nikki, Elena, the Taggers, and all the horses.

"Josey, I knew you weren't my natural daughter, but it didn't matter, you are my daughter."

"Thanks, Dad." Josey felt another round of tears rise. He was back in her life.

"Did Elena tell you anything?"

She told him what Elena had said about her natural father.

"I was a steer wrester, not a bull rider," He reminded her. "But I do remember her saying something about that weekend. I remember her talking about a couple of local bull riders from Pendleton." There was silence. "I know she had seen a guy named Dean and one named…ahhh, what was that name…? Oh yeah…they called him Tigger… after the cartoon character because he used to growl when he rode."

"Growl?" Josey chuckled.

"Yeah, it was weird." He laughed.

It was a laugh she thought she wouldn't hear again; it made her smile into the phone.

"I can't guarantee either one of them would be your natural father, but they are the only two I can think of right now. If I think of anyone else, I'll call you."

"You'll stay in touch now?" Josey hoped.

"Absolutely, Little Bit," He sighed happily. "And I'm going on the computer as soon as we're done and check on The Tagger Herd and look for your pictures."

"Thanks, Dad." Josey smiled.

"I should go but you'll call?"

"Yes. Take care and tell Kristen and Barry hello for me."

"I will, I love you, Little Bit."

"I love you, too." Josey smiled then ended the call.

The door was back open with her Dad. She understood his actions now and that gave her the closure she needed to let the past go and move on to the future.

Now she just needed to follow the clues to find her natural father.

CHAPTER THREE

When Josey walked out of the house, all eyes turned to her. The concerned expressions changed to smiles when she grinned at them. It was so wonderful to have people care about her again. There were so many nights in her past that she cried herself to sleep because she was so alone.

Even now when Jessup would stay with Kate in town, leaving her alone at the ranch, the nights would be so quiet and lonely that the tears would return. A few nights, the past summer, she had slept out in the barn to be close to her horse, Apollo, and not feel so abandoned. The tall palomino gelding reminded her of the fun times in the past. She would look at him and remember all the rodeos and the people in the high school club. That always made her feel better.

"It looks like it went well?" Nikki said hopefully from her perch on the tailgate of Nick's truck.

"It did," Josey nodded as she ran a hand down Blue's neck. The horse turned to her and rubbed his nose on her side. She continued to give him attention. He had the biggest, softest, most gentle eyes she had ever seen on a horse.

"Want to talk about it?" Nikki asked.

Josey shook her head, "Not all…but I do have a question for Nick."

"What's that?" Nick set Bay's hoof back on the ground and stood. He leaned backward to stretch his back muscles causing a low groan to escape.

"I said I'd do that," Lucas grinned.

"Someday…but I'm not that old…yet." Nick returned the grin. "Besides, this way I can talk Tessa into giving me a back rub."

They all laughed.

"I think she probably would anyway," Lucas shook his head.

"What's the question?" Nick asked; leaning against the tailgate next to Nikki.

"Do you remember a bull rider that used to growl when he rode?" Josey asked with a giggle.

"A growl?" Nikki and Lucas asked in unison.

Nick frowned at her, then his face relaxed and a wide grin appeared, "Tigger."

Josey's jaw dropped, "You know him?"

"Knew him," Nick nodded with a laugh. "Why do you ask?"

Josey told them what her dad had said.

"Do you remember what his real name was?" Josey asked.

Nick rolled his lips into a grimace and slowly shook his head. "I would probably recognize it if I saw it. I didn't go back to Pendleton after Nikki was born, for any bull ride, so I don't know if he was there or not."

"What's the second man's name?" Lucas asked.

"Dean…Dad didn't know anything else," She answered.

Lucas nodded, removed his phone from his pocket and headed for the house.

Josey watched him walk away and turned back to the father daughter pair on the tailgate.

"I'll say it again," Nick said. "I wish you two would have told us you were going."

"Would you have tried to talk us out of it?" Josey asked; already knowing the answer.

Nick nodded and walked back to the horse. Josey slid up onto the tailgate next to her sister.

"Have you heard from Matt?" Josey asked him.

"I would tell you if I did," Nick groaned as he reached for the horse's hoof. "We're all worried about him."

"You know…I can shoe a horse too." Josey offered with a wicked grin.

Nick dropped the hoof, stood, and glared at her.

The sisters burst out laughing as he retrieved the hoof again and started filing.

Lucas reappeared just as Nick walked the horses back to their pasture. He handed Josey a sheet of paper.

Eyes wide and jaw dropped, Josey looked at the list of 34 potential fathers. "How did you do that?"

Lucas chuckled, "There was only one PBR event in Pendleton, nine months before you were born. Kind of narrows the search for an expert internet researcher."

Josey nodded and looked down the list of names. There was only one Dean.

"Dean Hayes," Josey looked up at Nick when he returned.

He started nodding, "Yeah, I remember him. Rode with him for years; he was still riding here in the States when I left to Australia. Most of the bull riders that travel to the PBR were from all over the States and international but Dean was from Pendleton, just like Elena said."

"Was Tigger?" Josey asked as she handed him the list.

Nick shrugged, "I don't remember," His head dropped and he reviewed the list.

Josey tried to keep her expectations low, "Just because Dad remembered those names, doesn't mean it will be them."

"But it's a place to start," Nikki smiled.

Josey nodded. She was still a bit stunned with everything happening so fast.

"I recognize most of the names," Nick said thoughtfully. "I'm pretty sure Tigger's real name is Tim Whited."

He handed the list back to Josey.

"Now what?" Lucas asked.

"I don't know." Josey shook her head. "This is just happening so fast." She looked over at him. "What do you think?"

"You can either approach them yourself or I will have someone do it for you," He offered.

"I wouldn't know what to say," Josey admitted. "Do we blindside them with this?"

Nick and Nikki exchange a glance. She turned quickly to her sister.

"This is the dilemma you had with me?" Josey gasped at the realization.

Nikki nodded.

"I made the wrong decision," Nikki reminded her. "When I found out you existed, I didn't reach out to you because I thought you had a happy life and didn't want to interrupt it."

"How do you know? How do I know?" She suddenly felt very confused. Her conversation with her dad flashed through her mind. She didn't look at things from his side; was she doing that again? What would these men think? Want? Would they even want to know they had a daughter?

"Josey?" Nick said.

She turned to him.

"I didn't give Matt and Nikki a choice…we don't know what they would have said. Nikki didn't give you a choice, but we do know what you would have said."

"So I should give them the choice?" Josey asked him.

"If I had to do it over again?" Nick turned to Nikki. "I would have."

Nikki smiled contentedly at him then turned to Josey. "I would have given you the choice."

Josey stared at the list of men on the piece of paper. "How?"

"I'll handle it, if you want." Lucas said softly.

She looked up at him. "How?"

"We'll start with Hayes and Whited," He told her. "I'll have a person approach each of them and let them know they could possibly be the father of Elena's child. We give them the choice to take a DNA test or not."

Josey looked back to the list. That seemed fair…leave it up to them…but what if they weren't good? Like Elena wasn't good. Did she want a male version of Elena in her life?

"What if they aren't ….good?" Josey turned worried eyes to him.

"We don't want another Elena situation," Lucas nodded in understanding. "I have a team that can research them before they are approached."

One last look at the list of names and Josey handed him the piece of paper. "Ok." She whispered, hoping she wasn't making a mistake.

Lucas took the list and turned, phone already to his ear.

Josey watched him until he disappeared into the house and turned back to Nikki. "You ever going to explain all that?"

Nikki chuckled and slid off the tail gate.

"How about I take the three of you out to lunch before you head to Circle 50?" Nick offered.

"The steakhouse?" Josey grinned. "I say yes."

"Sounds good to me," Nikki nodded.

###

"Seriously, Lucas? It's only been two hours," Josey stared at him in disbelief.

"It's just phone calls, Josey," Lucas shook his head at her. "They go pretty quickly."

"And they both said they would take the test?" Her heart was racing but her mind seemed numb.

"Whited was married at the time, he was faithful to his wife but he did give me a couple other names to try." He leaned back in the restaurant chair.

Josey stared at the picture of John Wayne behind Lucas' head.

This was going way too fast! She had barely had a chance to process all the information and consequences of a DNA test. Did she really want this?

All four of their phones alerted them to a text message. They all reached for the phones and read the message at the same time.

TEXT FROM MATT: Been on remote island with no service, sorry, I am fine

"That's it?" Nikki said in surprise. "That's so frustrating."

Josey didn't comment, but she did agree with her sister.

"At least he's alright," Nick nodded.

Josey stared at the message and remembered the last time she had seen him and the sweet kiss they had shared. Someday he was going to come back and she wanted to be ready. So, yes, she did want this to happen as fast as it was…she wanted to know now!

"How long will it take?" She looked up at Lucas.

"There are five men and they all agreed to send the tests tomorrow if we can get it to them…which we will." Lucas smiled wryly. "It takes the lab about 5-10 days to process."

"Do you need the hair Elena gave us?" She asked.

"It wouldn't hurt," Lucas answered.

Josey pulled the wrapped paper out of her wallet and handed it to him. "It's folded in here. So, in five to ten days I'll know if one of those five men is my natural father?"

Lucas nodded.

"One step closer," Nikki smiled.

"So we need to keep my mind busy for that much time," Josey sighed.

"Josey, what do you expect from him…no matter which one it is?" Nick asked.

Josey shrugged. "I haven't had time to expect anything from him…or even know that I want to KNOW him…I just want to…" She grinned. "…know."

***

The air was brisk for a mid-December day. No snow covered the ground of Circle 50 ranch yet but the darkening sky warned of a snow storm headed their way.

Nikki's bay colt with the wide blaze she bought at the auction stuck his nose in the crook of Josey's neck and nestled it comfortably. Josey just giggled and stroked his face. The colt with the crooked blaze had his head tucked under Dru's arm and was soaking in the attention she was giving him.

"You name these two yet?" Dru asked Nikki.

"They are such lovies, I was thinking of Romeo for the crooked blaze." Nikki answered with a loving smile at her two eight month old colts.

"I love that name," Dru ran a gentle hand down his neck.

Nikki laughed, "I haven't decided on the other…something lovey and romantic too."

"Can't get any more romantic than the person that created Romeo," Josey said as she wiggled her head enough the colt's breath stopped sliding across her face and up her nose.

"Shakespeare?" Nikki asked with a grin.

"Perfect!" Dru chuckled.

"I wouldn't be able to think of them as anything different than Shakespeare and Romeo now…so that's their barn names." Nikki nodded then turned back to look at the Circle 50 ranch house that she and Matt owned. The house and ranch had belonged to their neighbor Andy who had died over a year before.

"So…what were you thinking?" Josey asked and looked back to the house.

It was two levels with four small bedrooms upstairs and the downstairs was cramped with a small kitchen, dining room, utility room, office, bathroom, and what they called a living room…which wasn't much bigger than the dining room.

"I never realized how small it actually was." Dru sighed. "I've spent many an hour in the office with Andy."

"You OK with this, Mom?" Nikki turned concerned eyes to her.

She nodded and sighed again. "It's your house now. You need to make it work for you and Matt."

"Andy and Clara made it work for the two of them and three boys." Nikki reminded her.

"But it was meant for one family." Dru argued. "You and Matt decided to remodel for a house to fit both of your future families…a bit of your own homestead."

Nikki and Josey nodded. With Lucas and Matt gone part of the time, it made sense for Nikki and Matt's future wife, whoever it ended up being, to be together; for company and safety.

"This is Dad's fault." Nikki glanced at her mother with a grin.

"If he hadn't decided to remodel his place to fit an office plus Tessa and Alex then Matt wouldn't have thought of it." Dru nodded with an agreeing smile.

"It would have happened sooner or later." Josey pointed out. "What does Matt want?" She silently wished she was more a part of the remodel and future of the house than she currently was. She couldn't help but think of what it would be like to live in the house with Matt…and Nikki and Lucas.

"He doesn't really care, as long as there is one room for his fitness equipment so he can stay in shape during the winter." Nikki sighed.

Dru chuckled, "So what does Lucas want?"

"A bigger bedroom and the same fitness room Matt wants." Nikki answered.

"What does Nikki want?" Josey smiled.

Nikki laughed, "I want to convert the whole lower floor to offices for the rehabilitation business." She turned and looked at the barn. "I've put it on hold to get the ranch back in order, but it's good now. I have six horses I'm taking care of right now and I have just started the advertising. It could grow substantially once we sell Mustang at the horse expo." She glanced at Josey and her mother. "I want the barn to stay the same. It has the 'old west' look and feel to it…and personal history."

"Well, why don't you do that?" Josey asked. The colt moved his nose from her neck to bump her arm for attention. She wrapped her arm around his neck and played with his mane.

"Just add onto the house?" Nikki asked.

"No…" Josey grinned. "Use this house as your business office…so you don't change it…much."

"And build another?" Nikki's eyes grew large and excited.

"That sounds perfect!" Dru nodded and looked back at the house. "You keep the history you wanted and get the new house for everyone. Build fresh instead of trying to make a small one-family house into two."

"That's a fantastic idea." Nikki grabbed Josey's arm and squeezed excitedly. "You're brilliant!"

"I'd like to think so." Josey laughed.

"In the long run, it could be less work and stress than trying to remodel." Dru said.

"I'll still need to remodel," Nikki nodded, her eyes looking at the house in a different light. "But to a lesser extent…and to only what I want for the business!"

"Building a new house and remodeling an old…" Josey grinned. "Sounds like a heck of a winter project."

"Plus, planning a wedding AND starting up a new business." Dru nodded. "You're going to be busy!"

"No," Nikki grinned at Josey. "WE'RE going to be busy."

"I'm all for that!" Josey nodded, she really needed a project to work on. The ranch workload had diminished greatly since winter set in.

"I'll call Dad and see who designed his house." Nikki said and pulled out her phone.

Josey smiled at her sister's 'go for it' attitude. Someday Josey would have that again…she just didn't feel it yet.

"Then you have to decide where to build." Dru pointed out.

Nikki's eyes went wide and worried at the thought.

Josey and Dru gave the two colts attention while Nikki spoke to her dad on the phone.

Josey's phone started ringing and she quickly retrieved it from her pocket but didn't recognize the number.

"Hello?" She answered tentatively.

"Josey?"

"Yeah."

"This is Reece, I climb with Matt."

"Oh, yeah. We've met a couple times." Josey nodded as if he could see her.

"Yeah, I was here the couple times Matt brought you out rock climbing."

"What can I do for you?"

"Well, I was actually looking for Matt. I tried calling the last couple of weeks and he doesn't answer. I just tried Nikki and it went to voice mail."

"Nikki is right here…she's talking on the phone. Matt's helping search and rescue overseas right now."

"Do you know when he'll be back?"

"No clue." Josey sighed and glanced at Dru who was playing with the horses.

"So…he wouldn't be able to help with training next weekend?"

"I'm gonna guess no on that one." Josey smiled.

She would have talked Matt into taking her again. Rock climbing had turned out to be a lot more fun that she expected. She just wished she was better at it so Matt didn't have to help her so much and could enjoy himself more.

"OK, well, if you talk to him, have him give me a call."

"I will," Josey nodded then smiled with a new idea, "Reece?"

"Yeah."

"Do you have any time open that you can train me in climbing while Matt is gone? I'd like to surprise him when he gets back."

Dru's head whipped around with her eyes opened wide.

"Yeah, I've got a couple people on Thursday…I could fit you in."

"What time?" Josey's stomach tightened in anticipation.

"Me, too!" Dru exclaimed and raised her hand, a grin spreading across her face.

"And can Matt's mom come, too?" Josey grinned at her. The thought of climbing with Dru made it that much more exciting.

"Dru? Of course, she can! She can come any time she wants." Reece laughed.

"When and where?" Josey said excitedly.

He gave her all the details and Josey relayed them to Dru who nodded excitedly.

CHAPTER FOUR

With the fireplace roaring and warming the house and a light snow falling, Josey and Nikki sat on the floor and used the coffee table as their drafting table. Lucas was due back from Nick's at any moment.

Josey sat quietly as Nikki drew a square for the common living room, added a kitchen next to it then added a laundry room, fitness room, guest bathroom, and an entry way through a screened in porch. The square became a long rectangular house.

"The fitness room should be to the east so it has the morning sunrise…Matt would like that." Josey said thoughtfully. Nikki smiled and nodded.

"Because of the time difference between here and Sydney, Lucas will often work at night. I don't want him in another room so we can put a small office in our bedroom…which should be on the opposite side of the house so it doesn't get morning light so he can sleep in…but we'll be able to see great sunsets."

"Matt likes mornings. His bedroom should be on the same side of the house as the fitness room so he gets the sunrises."

Again Nikki nodded and smiled to herself.

"I can extend out the rectangle to make our 'wing' of the house." Nikki said as she drew the rooms. "A big master bedroom, a small living room, plus two bedrooms for boys and girls."

"And if you turn Matt's 'wing' of the house, you'll create an L – shape house with his bedroom, 2 kids rooms, and a private living room." Josey pointed.

Nikki nodded and smiled again.

"Ok," Josey frowned. "What's that all about?"

"What?" Nikki giggled.

"You smile every time I say something."

Nikki finished the drawing quietly then stood from the floor. She placed more wood on the fire then sat at the end of the couch with her legs curled under her. Josey stood and sat on the couch opposite of her sister.

"I can't stop myself from thinking we're designing OUR future home; not just mine and Matt's." Nikki sighed.

Josey agreed but didn't say anything.

"When you comment, add Matt's input, what he would like, I just..." Nikki turned and looked at the fire.

"What?"

"... you're getting more of Josey back," Nikki glanced back at her. "And it's that much closer for you and Matt having a chance together."

"Frankie wouldn't have said anything about the house...I do feel stronger. I feel like I'm getting there...just not quite."

"What's holding you back?"

Josey shook her head, "I have to admit that if I was with Matt right now, I would still be standing behind him, not next to him like he wants me to be...and like what I want."

"Why?"

"I don't know," Josey admitted. She'd debated that question hundreds of times.

"How can I help?"

"I don't know." She shrugged. "It's up to me, I feel like I'm close...but I don't know."

"Is it about the DNA test? Who your father might be?"

Again Josey shrugged, "It might be...you said you didn't go looking for your natural mother or Nick..."

"I was never lacking in a mother or a father." Nikki answered. "I had a strong family around me and never felt like I was missing anything. The only thing I needed was to know 'why' from Dad…why did he leave me with Dru…what the whole story of my birth was."

"But you never searched for your natural mother."

"Thought about it…once…but I just never really needed to know about that either. I had Mom, Leah, Jordan, Scott, Grayson…a strong parental group."

"I didn't understand Elena, but she was there. Kristen was never really…loving," Josey sighed. "I thought I had a great relationship with Dad…Greg. But, he abandoned me…even if I was seventeen he should have talked to me. I think I just need to know who my natural father is. I don't know if I want him in my life or not…but I just feel like it's a part of me that's missing."

"I understand that. Hopefully we'll get some answers for you." Nikki glanced down at their drawing of the future house. "I really want this house to be ours."

Josey sighed dramatically with a roll of her eyes, "Me too! Can you imagine if I helped design that house and have to come visit you with some other woman being there as Matt's wife!"

"Unimaginable!" Nikki shook her head and Josey nodded.

***

Jeans, black turtle neck, boots, wet hair pulled back into a pony tail and her black cowboy hat pulled low like normal…simple, quick, and she was ready for the day.

Nikki was in her office working on her equine rehabilitation business plan so Josey plopped down on the couch and picked up the branding picture book for the 1000th time. She teetered her feet on the edge of the coffee table so she could use her lap to hold the book at an angle for easy viewing.

She glanced out the window to look down the road for Grayson's truck. No sign of him yet so she focused on the cover of the book; the group picture taken before the first branding at Circle 50.

A beautiful Hereford calf was surrounded by all the cowboys and cowgirls. It had a bright blue tag with the #1 on it. How she wished she had been there! Instead, about the time they were branding, she was secluded in her small bedroom in the back of the older couple's house. Or she might have been on one of the walks she went on to get out of the house; she had a set of stores and galleries she used to wander through. Either way, she would have been alone.

Josey mentally shook the memories out of her head and looked at the picture. Matt first, a smile crossed her face as she took in his very happy grin; her finger lightly caressed the paper. Then Nikki, just as happy. She was holding Matt's hand but her head was tilted onto Lucas' shoulder. Those two, she'd never seen anyone so head-over-heels as Lucas and Nikki were for each other. Matt had told her it was instant between the two of them.

Her eyes went back to Matt. It wasn't at first sight with Matt; that moment had been way too stressful. She'd seen his picture when she was looking up information on Nikki and thought he was good looking but her focus was on her newly discovered sister.

When she saw him at the stockyards, it was terrifying. The thought of Elena seeing them together had nearly made her physically sick. They had agreed to meet at Trapper's Café and she had driven half way there and stopped to decide if it was the right thing to do. It was so…scary…terrifying…but the need to see Nikki was even stronger so she continued the drive to the café. When she walked into the building and saw Matt in the back, she nearly turned and left but he looked so relieved to see her that she sat next to him.

The conversation was tense at first, all she wanted to hear was information on Nikki but he seemed to draw her own history out of her. She didn't think he was doing it intentionally but after she relaxed she just felt so comfortable with him. There was a moment, when he teased her, wondering if she was the 'right' Frank he was supposed to be looking for…that grin he gave her…that humor in his eyes…her heart had fluttered.

The next day, she and Nikki had been looking for Lucas and Matt at the horse competition when they heard a bang and saw the back door of a horse trailer fly open. The gate hit a very good looking cowgirl and sent her flying right into Matt's arms. Josey was shocked at the strong desire to pull the blonde's hair out by the roots when the cowgirl smiled up at him and rubbed her shoulder with his…and then the girls asked him to join them for a beer! Very much to Josey's surprise, the green monster of jealousy washed over her. That's when she knew.

That night Matt had surprised her, Grace, and Reilly with a trip to the climbing walls. It had shocked her at first that the cowboy she had known for barely 48 hours was also into adventure and fun. There was a moment that night, when she looked up at him and saw just how happy he was, it touched her in a calming way.

But the next day the wall had begun to grow between them. He didn't vote for her to work at Tagger Enterprises because of Elena. At the time it was frustrating but she understood it now because what he and Dru had predicted had come true. They had wanted to protect the family…one she would do just about anything for now.

Josey had found herself looking forward to seeing Matt during the day, even if it was just a moment or two since he seemed to be avoiding her. Until the morning he called about the stock truck in the ditch and the horses inside. His take charge attitude was surprising and even though Jessup and Warren were older and could have taken over the rescue, they had listened to him. It was because of Matt himself…he is a protector and rescuer.

She'd tried to detach her emotions from the event unfolding in front of her until the horse she walked up the hill collapsed to the ground. As much as she loved horses, and hated to see any suffer, it was when she looked up and saw the expressions on Matt and the Trio's faces that she realized the true devastation of the day. Freddy lay dying, the last horse that had carried their mentor and friend Andy to his last days, and there was nothing they could do about it. Tears brimmed Dru's eyes and each brother had reached out to her; a hand to the back and one to her elbow. Their own faces were fighting the emotions.

Matt stood alone, so when Josey rose to make room for the veterinarian to get to the dying horse she had gone to his side to help comfort him. But his arm sliding around her and holding her close…it had caused a relaxation within her body and soul. That moment, he began to heal the part of her that was broken and abandoned.

She'd felt instantly cold when he stepped away from her and knelt at the dead horse's side. She would never forget the feelings he created inside her when she saw his tear filled eyes, the crack of emotion in his voice, and the tender touch of a hand down the shoulder of the horse as he quoted his poem of goodbye. Matt was a man of compassion, of healing, of protection. That is what she needed.

She thought of that moment after the horses were buried when she walked into the barn and saw him…shirtless…as a pinup calendar version of him…she couldn't stop herself from kissing him. He was shocked at first but when his arms tightened around her and he kissed her back. Her heart and soul began to heal.

Then he broke it off and the angry words they said built the wall back up between them. She could see in his eyes it wasn't really what he wanted. She was frustrated and angry at him for pushing her away but she would never be sorry she kissed him.

Although the confrontation in the library over the harassment papers Elena forged cleared the air and began the slow crumbling of the wall, she would never understand the Taggers' fear. There was more to it than money but she couldn't figure out what it was. Something in her gut told her it had to do with Nick even though his name was never mentioned.

Her eyes went to Nick's image on the branding book cover. The mysterious Nick who looked so much like Matt. She lightly traced Matt's image on the cover of the book. A smile crossed her face at the memory of Matt calling her for their first date.

"What are you doing?" Nikki hollered from the back office.

"Guess!" Josey chuckled.

"Looking through the Sadie's branding book again?"

"Yeah," Josey sighed.

"You'll be there this year."

"Yeah…"

"I don't think anyone will be able to keep Sadie out of the branding corral; she's already talking about it."

"She was teaching Cora how to work the camera." Josey flipped through the pages quickly catching all the different pictures. "But it won't be the same."

"Why?"

"It's not the first for Circle 50."

"No…" Nikki said loudly, still sitting at her desk in the back room. "But it's the first year that OUR program comes into play. Last year's calves were from Andy's son's breeding program. Which was basically just throwing any bull in any pasture; they really didn't care. They actually put their biggest bull in with the young heifers! We lost three of those cows to prolapses and had two emergency c-sections due to the size of the calves. This year is our breeding program."

"Just you and Matt did it?"

"Basically, we put the plan together and reviewed with the Trio. Mom and Jessup suggested a couple changes, which we agreed with."

"You need to explain that to me. What made you decide which bull and cow to put together?"

"You have the best teacher out there as a resource…use him."

"Who?"

"Jessup…you won't get a better resource for learning a breeding program. He was the Livestock Supervisor for the ranch he managed in Wyoming before he came to work for Tagger Enterprises. He and the Trio have worked the T3E programs together."

Josey closed the book and looked at the cover photo again. Her eyes moved to the Trio and spouses…Dru and Jack, Grayson and Leah, Scott and Jordan. The Trio had gone through one of the worst things anyone could ever go through and came out strong and together, which was the most important thing. And they had found the perfect spouses.

She sat the book down, glanced out the window, still no silver truck. She leaned her head back on the cushions and thought of Grayson, Scott, Jack, and Nick. The father's in Nikki and Matt's lives. They were a diverse group; Grayson tall, larger than life, leading with a strong hand but with a teddy bear heart. There was a massive soft spot for his wife and girls. Scott, the little brother; compared to his siblings he was more light hearted, more temperamental, but just as loving with his kids. He and Jordan had a more 'firey' marriage but it worked for them. Jack…the handsome Jack. Smart, caring, protective of Dru and Reilly. He was with other people too…but with those two…it was to another level.

Then there was Nick; the mysterious Nick. There was so much more to him then what she had been told but she wasn't sure exactly what. She knew his life in Australia was deliberately not discussed in Idaho but had no clue why. She also knew that Lucas worked FOR Nick and not as co-workers like they implied to the kids. Why would they try to hide that?

The only thing that wasn't a mystery about Nick was his dedication to Matt and Nikki. If they needed him…he was there…no matter what else was going on in the world; business or personal. She knew that Nick had only been back in his kid's life for a couple of years but she didn't know much about his life from before that time.

His love for Tessa and Alex was evident in his devotion to them. His emotions and feelings were open for Matt, Nikki, Tessa, and Alex…and Nora, but everything else about him was shrouded in mystery.

The four men in Matt's life; his four fathers. Thank goodness she liked all of them and the feelings seemed to be mutual. Grayson was very protective of her and had been since the moment they met. In the last seven months he had been more of a father to her than Greg ever had allowed himself to be. Grayson didn't see Elena in Josey…he saw Nikki. Greg saw Elena so there really had never been a chance for them to have the close father and daughter relationship.

The best advice Grayson had given her was to listen to what Matt had requested about her and 'Frankie' because he agreed with him. Take the time now to find herself again and it would change her future forever. He pointed out that she needed to be her own person before she could truly be part of a relationship. She had been struggling with what he meant and how to accomplish that.

Josey picked up the book again, cradled it in her lap and stared at the picture; more specifically the women in the picture.

Dru…so strong. Josey could only dream of someday being as strong as the matriarch of the Tagger family. The woman may work with Grayson and Scott in running the business but they relied on her to lead them. What a lady she was! Strong, independent, loving, and just…fierce.

Leah…a shining example of what a lady and business woman should be. She ran the Barn, Bed and Breakfast with a strong but compassionate hand. She took no guff from customers which made her more likable to them. Not even the broken leg from the accident could slow her down. She knew what she wanted and worked to get it. The little paint colt she'd bought from Nikki was an example of that. Still in a leg cast for the crash down the mountain, Leah had worked day after day to get the colt to come to her and now he ran to her every time he saw her.

Jordan; the no nonsense woman who was the manager and protector of the kids. Such a tiny woman to drive such a huge truck and trailer outfit thousands of miles each rodeo season. Barely five foot tall but no one pushed her around or told her what to do…not even her husband, as if Scott would even try.

Tessa…the battles that woman has fought in her mere thirty some years! She had taken Josey out to lunch and told her of her battle with breast cancer, dealing with Alex's leg issues, the divorce, struggles to find a job to support herself and a son, and then her meeting with Nick. She'd battled through and become such a strong and independent woman.

Cora…it had to be hard to survive losing your husband of 48 years. She not only survived but had adopted the Tagger family as her own. They should all be lucky to live a long, strong life like her.

Nikki…her wonderful sister she'd only known for seven months. They had missed out on so much in life but both were determined to make up for it. Nikki had stood up to Elena from the first time she'd met her, unlike Josey who had let the woman bull doze right over the top of her. Nikki had graduated college, worked hard right next to Matt in getting Circle 50 back into shape AND worked with Dru on running Tagger Enterprises. She was putting together her own business, planning a wedding, and now designing her future home.

Grace, Sadie, and Nora…all so different but all so strong for their ages. Grace was in control; she was determined and had a great business mind as well as an over the top happy personality. She had easily and quickly become Josey's best friend.

Her gentle demeanor was a huge contrast to her sister; the hot headed Sadie. After witnessing a couple of Sadie's 'moments' she had to agree that Lucas had nicknamed her well when he called her a dingo. But as Nora pointed out, it was only when someone tried to take something from her or when they wouldn't listen to her when she knew she was right.

Nora…she was…quiet. Josey had heard someone call Nora an introvert but she didn't really agree with that description. With her family she was very open and seemed to be happy, but when she was in a crowd she was more…in control of her personality? Was that it? She had absolutely no problem spending a complete day by herself with her horses in the barn and arena. But she was also good in a crowd. In her royalty duties, she was very professional and friendly and people liked to be around her.

Even at 17, 15, and 13, all three were…independent…just like their mothers.

That's what Josey was missing! She looked at each one of the women again. As a family they were strong, but each one was independent in their own way. Dru, Leah, Jordan, and Tessa had found the love of their lives but they stood strong and fierce at the men's side…not behind them…not following them…but being equal to them. That was what Matt had pointed out to Josey. He had four women as examples of what he wanted. He'd seen it in her…he knew she could be that woman. Like he'd reminded her… he'd never called her Frankie…the person she had become to hide from Elena and cower from the world.

Josey lowered her feet to the floor and placed the book on the coffee table. Leaning her elbows on her knees, she continued to stare at the picture…at the women in the picture.

Then it dawned on her…she had to become independent, strong, and fierce for HERSELF not for Matt…not for anyone else…for HERSELF. Only then could she walk beside him and not use him as a shield from the world…or rely on him for her own self-worth.

The last five months she had been trying to figure out how to become strong for Matt…not for herself.

Her eyes lifted from the book to out the window as she contemplated how to do just that. How did she become independent like she used to be? Strong, like she used to be before Elena came into her life and shattered her confidence and her world?

A silver truck appeared on the road.

"Nikki! Grayson's here."

"OK, tell him good morning for me." Nikki called out. "Have fun!"

"We're going into town for supplies…how is that supposed to be fun?" Josey said as she slid on a denim jacket.

"Haven't you ever heard that 'life is what you make out of it'?" Nikki called out with a laugh.

Josey laughed with her. "You sure you have everything on the list you need?" She asked as she picked up the paper off the table and stuffed it in her pocket.

"If not, we'll pick it up tomorrow night when we go down to ride with the girls."

Wednesday night barrel riding…she loved and hated all in one. Loved being with the girls and back into racing…hated the way she was treated by some of the mothers and as a reflection of their actions, their daughters treated her that way too.

CHAPTER FIVE

Josey stared out the window, the scenery she normally enjoyed passing unseen.

"Where's your head?" Grayson asked.

"Independence…" She answered without thinking then glanced at him. His blonde hair was just long enough to stick out the bottom of his black cowboy hat and there was always something comforting in his blue eyes when he looked at her.

"As in…?"

"Part of finding me is finding that independent person I used to be."

"What made you so independent?"

"I used to do whatever I wanted to do and when I wanted to…I didn't really wait for permission." She grinned. "That wasn't always a good thing."

"I can imagine," He chuckled. "That would be a nightmare with Sadie. Grace is seventeen and more level headed but I don't think I could handle that from her either."

"She's pretty strong minded and independent."

"She is…" He nodded thoughtfully. "But she has a big family and a Reilly helping her out when she needs guidance."

"I didn't have a Reilly but I had some friends that helped. There were some other barrel racers I enjoyed…plus the rodeo club."

"Your dad and step-mother weren't there?"

"To a point…Dad anyway; Kristen didn't like horses and wouldn't even go to the barn and feed Apollo if I wasn't home. I usually traveled by myself to rodeos or a group of us would go together and share the cost of gas."

"What did you drive?"

"I had an older F150 and a 2 horse slant load trailer. Dad cosigned the loan and I was able to get them paid off quickly with the money I won."

"They sold too?"

"Yeah," Josey sighed as she felt the tears start to return at the memory. "I sold them right after I sold Apollo; paid off the IRS bill and had enough to buy that little truck."

Josey sat up straighter in the truck seat when she realized what she needed…that little bit of independence she had been missing.

"What?" Grayson asked.

"I need my own truck." She looked over at him, hoping he would understand. She had been driving Tagger Enterprises trucks since she moved to Idaho. That made her dependent on them, she needed her own.

He nodded with a grin, "Your own vehicle is the ultimate bridge to independence."

"It's not that I don't appreciate…"

"I understand, Josey." Grayson assured her. "Reilly's driving the truck Jack bought in Montana so Nora is driving the blue Toyota. Which means everyone in the family, that is old enough to drive, has their own vehicle…you don't."

The excitement started to build, "Can we look today after we finish picking up supplies?"

"Don't see why not…what do you want?"

Josey shrugged, "I guess just look to start with…see if something appeals to me."

"I hate to be personal," He glanced at her. "How is your credit?"

It felt like the hopeful balloon that had grown inside her suddenly burst.

"I don't have any bills. The last one I had was the IRS, so I really don't know."

"Let's go to the bank before we head to North 40; get your application in so they can run the numbers and see what happens."

"Ok," She just knew it wasn't going to be good.

An hour later her head ached as they walked out of the bank.

"That wasn't so bad." Grayson chuckled at her.

She tried to smile at him, "I guess I want it so bad that…I just hate that it's up to them and not me."

"Josey," He stopped in front of the truck which made her stop. "You are the one that sold everything to pay off the IRS…you made that decision, no one else."

"I know…"

"So if your credit is good, it's because of you, not them."

"Yeah," She took a deep breath and let it out slowly. "They seemed to feel better after you told them I was family."

"They know you're grounded here and not going to run off and not pay the loan." He walked to the truck and slid in the driver's seat. "I'll co-sign too…you know that."

Josey didn't; hadn't even considered asking. It must have shown on her face when she closed her door.

He laughed, "You're family whether you like it or not, and we help each other out."

"It's supposed to be me getting MY independence," She said.

"You'll be responsible for the loan payment, not me." He argued with a smirk.

Her phone rang as they walked out of the ranch store with the supplies.

"Hello?" She answered, knowing it was the loan officer. She listened carefully…a smile crossed her face as she looked at Grayson. He grinned in return.

"What if Grayson co-signed for me?" She asked.

Quickly grabbing pen and paper she wrote down the numbers and handed it to him.

"Thank you…we'll call as soon as we find one." She ended the call and looked at her boss. "If you co-sign I get a lower interest rate and can either have a lower payment or buy a more expensive truck for the same monthly payment."

She grinned at his grin.

"Very smart," He nodded proudly. "But you can buy on your own credit, you don't need me."

"And that means a lot to me, but you're family!" She reminded him with a chuckle. "I'll let you help save me money."

"Atta girl," Grayson laughed as he drove out of the parking lot and into the first car lot.

Three car dealerships later she walked next to a big red truck and looked inside. It was OK; same as all the others. She wanted something different, something showing her uniqueness, something that let people know it was her pulling into a parking lot. She was done hiding from the world.

She saw a yellow vehicle out of the corner of her eye and looked…then smiled…but it wasn't logical…not appropriate…she turned away and looked into the next truck. Her eyes flickered back over to the yellow one…the pattern was repeated three times.

"Josey?" Grayson was walking patiently behind her.

"What?"

"Any work you do for Tagger Enterprises, you will be driving one of the company trucks."

"OK…"

"If you go to a barrel event…you'll be with family."

"Yeah…Grace or Jordan."

"So go buy the yellow one you can't keep your eyes off of…the only one that's drawn that much attention from you."

"It's not practical!" Josey laughed.

"But it's what YOU want." He argued. "It's fun. I would have wanted and HAD at your age if I could."

"But…" She glanced back at the vehicle in question.

"No buts…just go get it." His big hands clamped on her shoulders, twisted her, then pushed her toward it.

An hour later she slid into the driver's seat of the bright yellow Jeep Wrangler Sahara. The hard top was on but she had also bought the soft cover for summer months…but she couldn't wait until she could take the top off altogether!

She sat quietly in the Jeep and looked around…she felt stronger…empowered. Taking a deep breath, she took in the new car smell; it made her whole body tingle in excitement.

Her phone rang…it was Grayson.

"What?" She asked with a chuckle.

"You've been sitting there for ten minutes…it's yours…you can drive away without them calling the cops on you."

She giggled, "I know…I was just taking a few minutes to appreciate it."

"Feeling independent?"

"Feeling stronger." She admitted.

"Would Frankie have bought it?" He asked.

"No!" Josey laughed. "She wouldn't have…but Josey is LOVING it!"

"Atta, girl," He laughed. "Take your time, show it off. I'm picking up Leah and we're headed to the ranch for the evening. I'll see you there in the morning. Be careful around the corners while you're getting used to driving it."

"Thank you, Grayson." She grinned then ended the call.

She turned the key and listened to the roar of the Jeep engine. It filled her soul with more power. She pulled away from the dealership as the overwhelming sense of independence took over her…a tear escaped.

"No, that's not happening." She said out loud and wiped away the tear…the strength grew that much more.

***

"I hate this." Grace scrunched her face and glared at her.

Josey chuckled, "Not much I can do about it."

"School always seems to get in the way…I want to go with you and Aunt Dru."

Josey shrugged a shoulder and smiled, "I'd let you skip."

"That would be…" Grace started.

"You are not skipping school to go rock climbing with them." Leah strode into The Homestead kitchen.

"But Mom…" Grace whined.

"No, end of story." Leah shook her head.

"I'd skip to go with Mom." Reilly grinned as he trotted down the long stairway.

"No, you're not skipping either." Dru said as she came down the steps right behind him.

"Then why don't you do it on the weekends so we can go with?" Grace pouted.

"Because today is the day Reece has time to take us." Josey answered; starting to feel guilty.

"Besides you're busy on Saturday with your royalty duties at the Christmas Parade." Leah reminded her.

"That's why you can't do the endurance run with Sadie and Mustang on Saturday." Dru said as she poured herself a cup of coffee and brought the decanter over to refill the other coffee mugs.

"Dang!" Grace slumped. "I wanted to ride Cooper doing that!"

"Can't you wait until Sunday?" Josey asked.

"It's supposed to snow Sunday and Monday. The road is clear now but it would be too risky to do it with snow." Dru answered.

"Then worse weather next week. We get farther into winter the less likely we can do the race. Saturday will probably be the last chance in quite some time."

"Hmmmff…" Grace frowned. "It needs to be done…has to be Saturday then."

"So Nora and Grace have royalty commitments and Reilly and Wade will be with Nick and Alex." Leah said. "Who's riding Cooper?"

"We have lots of riders…" Dru started.

"Will you do it, Josey?" Sadie asked as she jogged down the stairs making her long blonde ponytail bounce.

Josey's eyes widened, "Me?"

"Sure, why not?" Sadie chuckled. "You're already up there and you're young and fit…"

"Excuse me?" Dru and Leah stopped in their tracks and turned to the thirteen-year-old.

"Well," Sadie tilted her head to them, her blue eyes trying to look innocent. "It's going to be almost two hours of trotting and cantering. I need someone that's young enough to be able to handle that…you two," Sadie raised her brows and grimaced. "No…you're just too…"

"If you say old, I'm gonna ground you for the rest of your life." Leah said haughtily.

"The heck with grounding, I'll toss you in that cold, dirty water trough outside." Dru glared.

"Do both!" Reilly and Grace exclaimed in unison followed with a laugh.

"Really, Ladies," Sadie sighed dramatically and raised both her hands in the air. "I have to be able to out ride you…I was going to say…you're just too GOOD."

"Excuse me?" Josey's eye brows rose.

"Oh, Sadie…" Leah shook her head with a roll of the eyes.

"Good save," Dru laughed.

"No, it's not!" Josey looked at them in disbelief.

Sadie grinned at her, then put a hand up to her face to block her eyes from being seen by her mother and aunt. She winked at Josey with a giggle.

Josey's head flew back in laughter.

"Oh, young lady!" Aunt Dru took a quick step to Sadie who turned with a squeal and ran down the hallway to the outside door with her aunt right after her.

"We better go." Reilly laughed.

He and Grace waved and left the house as Wade and Nora descended the stairs.

"Why is Sadie outside screaming?" Wade asked.

"She called Dru old." Josey chuckled.

"Well…she is the oldest in the family." Wade grinned with a mischievous glint in his eyes.

"You keep that up, young man," Leah chuckled. "And you'll be screaming outside, too."

The back door opened and the two blondes walked back in…both laughing.

"You going to repeat what you said?" Josey asked with a grin.

Dru looked at him with a raised brow.

"I just said 'How could Sadie insult such a wonderful young woman?'." Wade grinned.

"Yeah, right." Dru laughed and put an arm around his neck to pull him in tightly and kiss his cheek.

"You're quite the charmer." Nora laughed and headed out the back door. "I'm gonna move the horses."

"I'll help!" Josey hurriedly offered.

Once the horses were put to pasture and all kids off to school, Josey reentered the house.

"We need to stop at the B&B for a meeting before we leave." Dru said as she slid on her jacket.

"Ray Sampson?" Leah raised a brow.

"Yeah," Dru grinned and nodded to Josey. "I thought I'd let her sit in."

Leah laughed, "Oh yes! And Tessa too!"

"Who's Ray Sampson?" Josey asked; the looks on their faces made her a little worried.

"He's someone you have to see for yourself." Dru chuckled and they walked out the door. "We're taking your Jeep to meet Reece?"

"Yes," Josey smiled.

A half hour later, she was sitting in the large meeting room at the Barn and Breakfast with Tessa and Dru. Leah was walking down to the registration desk to greet Ray Sampson.

Tessa's curly light brown hair rested gently on her shoulders. She wore a white long sleeve dress shirt and black jeans with knee high boots. She looked professional. Dru had her long blonde hair down and flowing around a navy blue turtle neck she was wearing for their rock climbing and jeans. Josey's hair was in a high ponytail and was dressed with a red turtle neck and jeans. They looked more causal than professional.

"You're in for a treat here ladies," Dru whispered with a glint in her eyes. "Don't react to his words; don't bite your lip, get angry, or gasp. If you feel you need to do something, concentrate on pressing one foot into the ground as hard as you can and keep your face as calm as possible." She glanced at them and they both nodded. "We're meeting at a circular table so it visually puts us on equal ground."

"What did you get us into?" Tessa asked with narrowed eyes.

Josey was a bit nervous, too.

"1965." Dru whispered and stood as she looked at the door.

A short stocky man walked in with a pleasant smile that quickly faded as he took in the three women. He turned to Leah, but she had already left his side.

"Mr. Sampson, good to see you." Dru smiled warmly.

"Mrs. Morgan." He nodded and walked towards them. His voice was low and sounded a bit impatient. Josey guessed his age in the late-sixties and he was wearing black dress pants, white long sleeve shirt, and a slim red tie…very professional.

Dru extended a hand; he hesitated and finally took it for a quick handshake.

"These are my assistants, Tessa Elliot who helps here at the B&B and Josey Franklin, she works at the ranch." Dru motioned to them and the man barely glanced at them.

The first tingle of irritation made its way through Josey but she remained calm with a slight smile frozen on her face.

"Can we get you coffee or water?" Dru asked as she sat down and motioned for him to sit…which he did straight across the round table from her.

"Mrs. Tagger is getting the coffee," He said gruffly. "And I believe her husband."

Dru calmly smiled and shook her head. "Grayson is at the ranch with Scott."

The look of disdain on his face made Josey push her foot into the ground as hard as she could. She was surprised how concentrating on that action made her face remain calm.

"This was supposed to be a productive meeting." He frowned, his eyes boring into Dru.

"It will be," She answered with a slight smile. "As long as we get right to business."

Leah walked into the room carrying a small tray with a coffee carafe and a mug with the T3E brand on it. She smiled brightly and placed the mug on the table and filled it with coffee. She placed the carafe next to him and started to turn.

"Where is your husband?" Mr. Sampson glared at her.

"Excuse me?" Leah and Dru said in unison.

Josey pressed her foot on the ground again and forced herself not to react. It was a much different tone of 'excuse me' than what the two women had with Sadie that morning. Dru looked ticked and Leah look surprised.

"Grayson is at the ranch." Leah looked quizzically at him then to Dru.

"Thank you, Leah." Dru said with a very calm and controlled voice.

Leah nodded and walked out the room. Josey was sure she wanted to stay and hear what was going to happen.

"I told you where Grayson was." Dru said firmly, staring him directly in the eye and letting him know she was pissed. No poker face this time!

He stared right back and didn't flinch. "Mrs. Morgan, I did not come all this way to sit in here with YOU. I expected one of the Tagger brothers; someone that can make a decision on the spot, not have to call someone else."

Dru's poker face returned and she stared at him with steely blue eyes. "Please feel free to leave if you do not want to discuss business with me."

Josey relaxed her leg. She was ticked too and didn't have a problem keeping her face calm. She was well practiced at hiding her anger.

His lips roll into a straight line.

"The ball is in your court, Mr. Sampson." Dru said very calmly, her gaze not wavering.

Josey silently took in a deep breath and let it out. She hoped Dru didn't get mad at her…

She stood without a word and walked to door which they had entered. Along the wall was a display of company flyers and business cards. Taking a card off the rack she walked back to the table and placed it in front of Mr. Sampson. Then she returned to her seat.

Dru's eyes hadn't left his.

He lowered his gaze to the card, leaned over to read it, picked it up, and looked at it closer. His hand shook slightly as it placed it back on the table and he took a deep breath.

He looked up at Dru…and talked business.

Josey knew once he read the card that stated Dru Tagger-Morgan, CEO Tagger Enterprises with the three businesses listed under it, he wouldn't have an issue anymore.

Both Josie and Tessa leaned forward on the table and listened intently as the two of them discussed new legislature being introduced to the Senate concerning restrictions at feed lots.

CHAPTER SIX

"You handled yourself well in there," Dru said as she swiped the keys out of Josey's hand.

Josey laughed and walked to the passenger side of her Jeep. "I was hoping you wouldn't get upset."

"No…it was a good move. It helped him save face without me having to throw out a title and try to sound superior. There aren't very many people like that anymore. He's actually the first one in years I've had to deal with."

"How did you know it was coming?"

"I talked to him at a cattleman's conference in Boise when I was with Jack. Or I should say Jack talked to him."

"Thanks for inviting me…it actually turned out quite interesting. I never really think of the government side of ranching."

"I'll try to include you into more so you get a little bit of experience in all different areas."

"Thanks!" Josey grinned. That sounded fun.

"But for now…no more business…it's time to play!"

"I can't wait." Josey bounced in her seat like Reilly did. It made both of them laugh. "I want Matt to be able to enjoy himself more instead of having to teach me all the time."

"You know he enjoys that part, too."

"Yeah," Josey nodded but crinkled her nose. "I just don't want him to think it's all work when it comes to me."

Dru drove across the blue bridge that took them into Clarkston. Part way through town Josey's phone rang.

"Hello?"

"Josey, it's Reece."

"We're on our way, we'll be there on time." She glanced at the clock, they were actually early.

"I'm at Granite Rock, it's too wet and cold out here."

Josey's mood plummeted, "So…we're canceled?"

Dru glanced at her with a disappointed expression.

"Just for the rock," Reece chuckled. "We can go to Moscow at the U of I fitness center."

"Don't you have to be a student?"

"No…but I am a student, in my senior year." He reminded her. "I'll get you in and it will be much warmer, that way we can play as long as our arms and legs hold out."

"Sounds like fun!" Josey grinned and bounced in her seat again.

They met Reece and the two other student climbers at 1:00 at the large center and were surprised at the amount of equipment he had brought. He had it displayed out on the floor and went through every piece of climbing and rappelling equipment he had. A few university students had wandered over and watched his training and became part of their group. Different types of carabiners, pulleys, ropes, harnesses, helmets, shoes, gloves, edge guards, ascenders, belts, flat webbing, climbing rings, protective eye gear, and more were reviewed. Josey's head was spinning with the amount of knowledge flooding her brain. Then he moved onto the different knots!

Once everyone felt they had a good handle on the equipment, he went through standard safety procedures for climbing or rappelling outside as well as there in the fitness center.

Then they started climbing. For hours their small group went up and down and around the 55ft climbing tower, 24ft instructional wall, and a cave.

After thoroughly thanking Reece and saying goodbye to their group an exhausted Josey climbed into the driver's seat of her Jeep.

"I'm more than happy to let you have your Jeep back." Dru laughed, "My arms are tired!"

Josey grinned at her, "And I'm STARVING!"

"Me too! There's a Hawaiian BBQ place on Main Street that Nikki, Matt, and I used to go to all the time."

"Point the way."

****

Josey sat back from the table and placed a hand over her very full stomach. "Play hard, eat lots." She grinned at Dru.

"Sounds like a good motto."

"You seemed to know most of the equipment Reece was showing us. How long have you been climbing?" Josey asked.

"Couple of years with Matt. This is the first time without him though."

"You start after the plane crash, too?"

"Yes, and I've tandem jumped from planes with him." Dru grinned.

"Oh, that sounds like fun!" Josey laughed. "I'll have to do that too."

"I just don't tell Jack anymore until I get back." She chuckled.

"He's not much of an adventurer?"

"No, it's about the only thing we don't have in common…I really can't think of anything else."

Josey nodded thoughtfully…how much did she and Matt have in common?

"Part of becoming and growing as a couple is finding out what you have in common." Dru said with a knowing smile.

Josey felt the flush rise in her neck, she'd never really discussed Matt with his mom.

Dru leaned back in her chair and crossed her legs; the top leg bouncing slightly. "We've never discussed last spring."

Josey swallowed hard.

"You know I didn't vote for you last spring to work for Grayson." Dru said bluntly.

"I know, but Nikki said you wanted to find me a job over here."

Dru smiled, "From the moment Matt found you in Billings, you were family and I had every intentions of taking care of you."

Josey's jaw dropped, "What? But Elena…"

"You are not Elena." Dru turned and looked at her through narrowed eyes. "When Matt called that morning in Billings and told me about you…what you had gone through…the way he spoke about you? Nikki would never let you stay behind. I was pretty confident you were coming back to Idaho with us. Even if you didn't, I would have made sure you were OK before we left. "

"But…"

"You are Nikki's sister; that makes you family. My protective mother-mode kicked in."

Dru's smile was warm and inviting. It made Josey's heart skip a beat.

"Between your starting work for Grayson and the meeting in the library when Lucas told us about the harassment papers, we had seen each other and worked together a few times a week." Dru said and Josey nodded. "In those times and the way Grayson and Jessup spoke about you, I came to care for you."

"But at the meeting in the library, you were so upset…like everyone else." Josey whispered. She hated that day and the raw emotions that played out. The look of betrayal from Scott, whose vote gave her the job with Tagger Enterprises, was heart wrenching.

Grayson and Nikki had been on her side from the start but Lucas, Dru and Matt had not. She fought hard to make sure they knew she didn't betray them. Matt was in disbelief that it was happening, fear that he would lose his work with the sheriff's office for search and rescue, followed by his anger at Elena. It had forced the issue with her finally stepping up and facing her terrible mother and putting an end to her attacks.

"I was worried about Tagger Enterprises," Dru explained. "That's my job. But even more than that, I could see what it was doing to Matt." Dru leaned against the table towards Josey and looked at her intently. "I am very protective of my whole family, but with my kids; Matt, Nikki and Reilly? It's at a whole new level. They are my heart and soul."

"I never wanted to hurt Matt." Josey said quickly, she had begun to tremble with nerves.

"And YOU didn't, Elena was attacking him through you." Dru said. "That was what Matt and I knew would happen. Scott and Grayson have a belief in the good, Matt is protective of the family, and I am more cynical. I have to be for business. I was as worried about you that day as I was for Matt. I just couldn't believe you would go after Tagger Enterprises, it was obvious that you loved working at the ranch and with Grayson. I also didn't believe you would go after Matt in such a terrible way. There was an attraction between you two from the start."

Josey nodded, still trembling. Where was she going with this conversation? Confusion started making Josey doubt herself again. How could she explain her feelings for Matt to his mother? "Matt is…." She swallowed to get rid of the nerves. "He's…"

"I know," Dru chuckled. "I also know how he feels about you."

Josey sighed and started to relax. "These last couple of months have been really hard."

"And I am very thankful you two slowed the relationship down so you could figure out what you wanted and who you were."

Josey nodded, "I'm getting there."

Dru leaned back in her chair and looked at her thoughtfully, "To be honest, after we setup the time with Reece, I started wondering if you were doing this for you or for Matt."

"What?"

"I was hoping you weren't just climbing because it's what Matt does and what he wants in a woman...someone adventurous. I really want you to be doing it because you enjoy it and want to do it."

Josey nodded, "I understand that…if I only do what Matt wants then I'm not being me, I'd still be in his shadow. But I really LOVE climbing and rappelling. I will do it even if Matt and I don't end up together."

"I could see that," Dru laughed. "There was pure joy on your face when you beat me to the top of the tower."

Josey grinned, "You didn't look too happy about that."

"I've been climbing longer…and have longer legs and arms." Dru laughed. "I should have beaten you!"

"I promise I won't tell Sadie."

Dru rolled her eyes, "That little snot would really give me a bad time about being old."

"She is a treasure."

"Yeah, 'treasure', is a definite way to describe her."

They sat quietly a moment before Dru cocked her head and looked at Josey with amused eyes, "You know I said I am very protective when it comes to my kids."

Josey nodded.

"This morning when Sampson looked at you and gave you that instant look of dismissal?"

"Yeah…it wasn't very pleasant."

"I wanted to haul off and backhand him across the face."

"Seriously?" Josey's jaw dropped. "You looked so in control and calm!"

Dru chuckled again with a gleam in her eyes. "I was pissed. Tessa is older and has gone through a lot in her life, I knew she would let it roll off her back, but you? My protective mode shot through the roof and it was all I could do to keep my face calm."

"But when he asked Leah where Grayson was…"

"I purposely let him see how mad I was. It's one thing to be composed when you're dealing with business and most attitudes, but THAT disrespect was just over the top.   I couldn't allow it to happen or he would think that he could walk all over me."

"Selective poker face," Josey grinned in understanding.

Dru laughed, "Yes, you have to learn when to have it and when to let it go."

They were quiet a moment again…until Josey realized what Dru had actually said, then her eyes widened in surprise. "You were protective of me? Like one of your kids?"

Dru nodded, "From the moment in the library when Matt made it sound like he wanted you to leave town and I hollered 'no'. I knew then, that you were becoming like a daughter to me. I was protecting you from HIM, for goodness sake! I guess it was natural since you are Nikki's sister."

Tears welled in Josey's eyes. This conversation had been so confusing…she never would have guessed, "I don't know what to say. I have so much respect for you and…."

"You don't have to say anything, just know and understand." Dru smiled warmly and she reached across the table to firmly squeeze Josey's hand. "You haven't had much luck when it comes to mothers…so hopefully, if you need something that way, you'll come to me…I will be there for you."

"Oh, Dru…" The tears slid down Josey's cheeks before she could stop them. "I…absolutely…I just love you and your whole family."

"OUR family," Dru chuckled as she stood to leave. "As long as you don't tell Sadie you beat me to the top of the tower…I will continue to love and support you."

They both laughed as they left the restaurant.

***

"Are you ready, yet?" Josey asked Nikki as she shut the back gate of the horse trailer.

"We're taking your Jeep aren't we?" Nikki leaned around the end of the trailer which was parked in The Homestead driveway.

Josey laughed, "Yes, Grace is driving the truck and trailer. Grayson wants her to have as much practice as possible before summer. She and Reilly will be going to a lot of rodeos that Jordan's not going to, so they have to share the driving duties."

"And so we can ride in your Jeep." Nikki grinned and walked to the yellow vehicle.

"Good enough reason for me." Josey waved at Grace, Sadie, and Nora as they stepped out of the back of the house. "We loaded all the horses for you."

"But we wanted to ride in your Jeep!" Sadie yelled and frowned in disappointment.

"Then load up!" Josey shouted. Her new vehicle had gone over well with the entire family.

Sadie and Nora ran to the Jeep while Grace stood next to the driver's door of the truck and frowned at the group.

"Hey...that leaves me by myself." Grace complained.

"It's only five minutes, Grace." Nikki laughed as Josey did a quick turn in the driveway and made her way to the road where she waited for Grace to reach them. Then Josey followed the truck and trailer down the road...for five minutes.

"You're getting good at that." Nikki complimented Grace as the stepped out of the vehicles.

"It's getting easier...and I don't get as stressed out as much anymore when I pull five horses." Grace said. "Dad has me practicing backing up all the time."

"Is Candace coming down?" Josey asked Nora.

"She's already here...she's in warming up." Nora answered.

They quickly saddled their horses and rode into the indoor arena together. Candace and her horse Lola quickly joined them. For a mid-December night the weather was fairly warm and they only wore their Tagger Enterprises jean jackets. Even Candace was wearing hers.

"We look like the Tagger Team." Grace laughed her 'life is good' laugh.

Josey noticed two of the riders mother's off to the side; they heard the comment and smiled as they looked at the group…until they saw her. Then their smiles turned to smirks.

It was a look Josey had been receiving since she joined the Tagger girls in August for their club's barrel racing day. After the first hour that first night, she was ready to go home but the girls wouldn't let her. The women created a tension within her that she couldn't shake…their looks and attitude became more apparent each week. Even their daughters were starting to look at her as if she was an intruder.

She lay in bed many nights wondering what she could do to make these women accept her.

"What?" Sadie had stopped and looked down at the women.

"Sadie, keep going." Josey said in surprise; she didn't want to make a scene and have more people dislike her.

All the other Tagger riders had moved into the arena and started trotting to warm up, unaware of the simmering confrontation.

"No," Sadie turned, her blue eyes flashing in irritation. "They have absolutely no reason to look at you that way. I'm tired of it, and not gonna keep my mouth shut anymore." She glared at the two mothers.

Josey grinned…suddenly feeling protected and loved. She looked at the two women standing with stunned expressions and she realized she didn't need their approval or acceptance to be there. She had family that wanted her there.

"Sadie?" Josey said softly.

Her tone caught the blonde by surprise, "What?"

"I love you." Josey laughed as Sadie's expression went from irritated to humored in a flash.

"And I love you!" Sadie grinned.

"Whatever their problem is…is just that…their problem." Josey said and didn't even bother glancing at the women in question. "We won't let anyone put a negative atmosphere into this fun night ever again. They can glare or smirk, all they want. We're just going to have fun."

Josey nudged her gold gelding, Apollo, forward to move next to the golden Scarecrow. Sadie nodded and took the lead as they walked around the arena.

"You know…I was about to go all Dingo on them." Sadie said with a tilted head, her eyes showing a glint of the dingo look.

Josey's laughter rang out in the building. "I know…but let's go have fun so you can try to keep up with us."

Sadie's eye brows shot up, "You think you two can beat me and Scarecrow?"

"Of course we can," Josey laughed at her protector's devilish grin.

"We'll have to put a wager on that one." Sadie nodded.

"And what do you think that should be?"

"You going to ride with me Saturday morning?"

"The endurance test ride with Cooper and Mustang?"

"Yeah."

"Of course, I am…I told you I would."

"Well, then…winner of two out of three gets choice of horse." Sadie grinned.

"Oh…that's a tough one," Josey grinned. "You sure you want to risk not riding Mustang after you've worked with him so long?"

"Not much of a risk there…" Sadie shook her head with a devilish laugh.

"Oh, you little snot!" Josey laughed. "You're on!"

"Who's calling who little?" Sadie raised a brow in humor; her grin wide. "Maybe you haven't noticed I'm as tall, if not taller than you! And I'm only 13! What do you say to that 'old lady'?"

"Dang girl!" Josey thought Sadie was going to laugh right off the saddle. "You're really pushing it tonight!"

"Maybe we should get you some more fiber so everything goes smoothly for you." Sadie's face was red with laughter…tears starting to form in her eyes.

"You little blonde headed pip-squeak!" Josey gasped between the fits of giggles.

Sadie fell backwards on Scarecrow so her back was arched over the saddle and her head bouncing off the mare's rump. Her laughter was screaming through the building.

Nikki galloped up next to them.

"What's going on here?" She shook her head at Sadie.

Sadie started to rise as she grinned at Josey.

"She's older than me…by YEARS!" Josey pointed to Nikki with a wicked grin. "So what do you call her?"

"A dusty antique!" Sadie gasped as she fell back on the horse in laughter.

Nikki looked at Sadie in false horror, "And I rode up here for this?"

"Do you need a pillow for your hemorrhoids? Maybe denture cream? We don't want your teeth to fall out while you're riding." Sadie gasped as she twisted her head to look at her cousin.

"Sadie," The announcer in the arena said. "How many times have we told you, we don't allow horizontal barrel racing?"

Sadie sat up but fell forward in laughter.

"That's better." Laughter rang out from the intercom system. "Line up ladies and gentlemen, let's get this party started."

Josey and Nikki quickly turned and galloped away from the blonde who turned, saw them galloping, and started laughing louder.

"Speaking of party; don't forget next Wednesday night is our Christmas party pot-luck. Bring food that can be eaten on horseback. No ride in two weeks, we'll start back up the Wednesday after Christmas."

"So any ideas on what to bring next week?" Josey asked Nikki as they took a place in line.

"I thought we'd try something different and unexpected; cannoli." Nikki said.

"Oh, fun. Like the ones Cora did for Nora's birthday. We can dip the ends in different holiday candies like she does."

"Good evening, Ladies." Sadie smiled innocently as she rode up next to them. "Interested in running barrels?"

"I'm interest in running a mustang in an endurance race." Josey smirked at her.

Sadie giggled, "Two out of three."

CHAPTER SEVEN

Sadie was the first of their group to run. Just before she took off, she glanced back at Josie and gave her the devilish grin.

"What did you do to her?" Grace asked as she, Nora and Candace rode up next to them.

"Threatened to ride Mustang on Saturday." Josey chuckled.

"Oohhh, dang." Nora barely had out of her mouth when Sadie took off. "This should be good."

Sadie flew to the first barrel and it was a near perfect turn. She slid around the second barrel as smooth as could be and ran for the third.

"Yee Haw!" The blonde yelled as she turned the third barrel and Scarecrow flew to the end with Sadie riding her like a jockey...and grinning ear to ear.

"15.593 Miss Sadie," The announcer called out. "Something's up your saddle tonight to fly like that."

As Sadie trotted out of the arena she chuckled at Josey.

Josey rolled her eyes and waited patiently for her turn.

Apollo pranced into the arena and Josey stared at the barrels. She was a State Champion barrel racer...on this horse...she knew she could beat Sadie...maybe if she took the barrel at a closer angle...

She turned Apollo to the barrels and they ran at a tight angle...her knee hit the barrel and she reached down and managed to keep it from tipping. She kicked wildly to the second barrel. Another tight turn...this one was good...one of her best...more kicking...turning around the third barrel...at the last second she realized it was too tight and the barrel tipped to its side. She groaned when the announcer called out; "16.525 plus five."

Josey purposely kept from looking in Sadie's direction and she heard no sound from her as she trotted to Candace, Grace and Nikki, who all chuckled.

"Shut up…." Josey whispered which made them chuckle again.

Once everyone made a run, the round was finished and the second round started.

Josey remained quiet when Sadie came into view. Scarecrow trotted into the arena and circled.

Just before they took off, Sadie's laugh echoed in the building. Josey cringed. Tight turns, flying horse, and laughing rider…15.581.

Sadie didn't say anything nor look at her as she trotted out of the arena.

"She's psyching you out." Nikki whispered.

"I know…and it's working." Josey took in a deep breath and let it out.

Nikki, Grace, Nora, and Candace all chuckled again.

"Stop that," Josey tried to glare at her sister and friends but it just made them giggle again.

She trotted into the arena while reminding herself that she and Apollo have numerous saddles, championships, and dozens of buckles because she remained calm and level headed. Sure Apollo was nearing twenty but the horse had been running barrels since before Josey had owned him…which was now twelve years. They were both experienced and were a great team…she just had to concentrate.

Just as she started to turn the gelding to the barrel she glanced up and saw Sadie…grinning…that little devilish grin. Then the laugh… 'I'm happy and gonna win, Old Lady!' laugh.

Josey turned Apollo too tight and made the horse stumble as he dug in to run to the first barrel. They were at a bad angle and nearly ran right over the top of the barrel and it tumbled down. Josey just about screamed! Second barrel was wide, third barrel…didn't really matter so it was perfect. She didn't even bother to push the horse to the end and waited patiently for Sadie's laugh…but it didn't come.

Josey trotted up next to Nikki, Grace, Nora and Candace again, who were all holding back grins. They didn't speak, they just waited.

Josey watched the next rider race around the barrels until she saw Scarecrow's head appear to her right…just to her knee. Josey tried hard to ignore it but her eyes kept flicking down to the golden nose. Scarecrow took two more steps and she could see the horse's long neck. Josey stared in front of her; gritting her teeth to keep from reacting.

Another palomino step… she could see Sadie's knee. Josey's body was starting to tremble…another palomino step…Josey turned her head slightly away…a low giggle reached her and Josey threw her head back and laughed. "I hate you, Sadie Tagger!" She yelled up at the ceiling.

Everyone around her started laughing but not as loud as the blonde-headed pip squeak at her side.

"But you just said you loved me." Sadie whined through her laughter.

Josey turned and looked at her; she was still grinning ear to ear. Right behind Sadie, on the bleachers watching, were the two mothers that had glared at Josey but were now laughing right along with everyone else.

"How are you so good at only 13?' Josey chuckled.

"I have a secret." Sadie said with a tilt of the head and her eyes twinkling mischievously.

"Scarecrow is no secret." Josey pointed out the obvious reason why.

Sadie shook her head slowly and leaned towards her.

Josey leaned to the blonde and as low as possible, so she wasn't overheard, Sadie whispered in her ear. "I ride for fun."

Josey leaned back and looked at her in surprise.

"Try it some time." Sadie giggled.

And so she did; on the third round of barrels Josey entered the arena with nothing more on her mind than enjoying her horse and the people around her. She did a near flawless ride and rode in with a 15.974.

***

"We'll be checking on you throughout." Grayson told Josey and Sadie. "When you see Dr. Mark, you dismount a good distance in front of him then jog the horses in so he can check them."

"We will, Dad." Sadie nodded from the back of Mustang. "It's only twenty-five miles today so they should be OK."

"I'm not concerned about Cooper, he's in pretty good shape but that's still a good distance for Mustang. We don't want to push him too soon or too hard."

"I know, Dad. I did my research." Sadie said patiently. "We have the heart monitors on them and will be watching the rates closely." She held up the wrist monitor that wirelessly read the heart rates from the adapter under the saddle pad.

"We're only going twenty-five miles today." Josey repeated. "That's pretty short for an endurance race."

"We'll be done in less than two hours…if I calculated everything right." Sadie told him.

"I'm sure YOUR calculations are just spot on." Jessup chuckled.

Grayson nodded, already knowing their plans. He ran a hand down the black horse's neck, patting him gently. "Maybe, Cooper, you'll finally get a run in that satisfies you."

"He does like to run!" Sadie smiled. "This should be a good test to see if he can compete in endurance races too."

"He already does cutting, team roping, team penning, calf roping, barrels, poles, and goat tying…and ranch work!" Josey laughed. "How much more does he need to do?"

"He is an all-around competitor." Grayson nodded with a smile and affectionately patted the horse's rump. "Off you go."

Sadie and Josey started at a trot away from the barn at the Tagger ranch house and toward the fall branding corrals.

She was used to riding many different horses but mainly her own horse Apollo. Cooper was just an inch or two shorter than Apollo but his body was broader with a bulldog conformation. Josey decided they both had a very comfortable trot. She kept herself even with Mustang.

"He looks comfortable," Josey said to Sadie.

"He is," Sadie hollered back. "We should be able to go a good pace, just watch the heart monitor. If it flattens out without raising too much, then we'll move to a longer trot."

"Do you want to stay together or separate if one needs to get their rate up more?"

"Separate…we want to do a good test on what they can do on their own and not predicated on what each other can do."

Josey checked the monitor. Cooper's heart rate was elevated but not too bad. A mile in, she pushed him to a little faster trot and Sadie followed suit.

They were riding a large loop between the multiple ranches. All the neighbors had been alerted to the race and would be watching out for them if they were driving on the roads. The route Sadie chose included flat roads, slight inclines, and one good hill about three quarters of the way to really test the horses.

They had placed mile markers on the road to keep track of their progress and know when to push the horses and when to lighten up.

At the third mile marker, Josey's mind started to wander. It went to Matt first, wishing he was there to see them run. Then she thought of Nora and Grace who were upset they couldn't be at the run, or even ride it. She smiled at the image of the two of them, plus Candace, in their sparkling shirts, sashes, and their black hats with the crowns. They were disappointed not to race but excited about the parties and parades they were attending.

Josey checked the monitor. His heart rate had increased but not even close to what Sadie had decided was his high end.

"How is Mustang doing?"

"He's good, tipping to the top. Cooper?"

"Still really good. I'm going to take him out a little faster and test the heart rate."

Sadie nodded and Josey nudged Cooper into a faster pace. The horse responded immediately and picked up his energy; he seemed to be enjoying himself. Josey leaned forward and ran a hand down his neck. His sweat covered her hand which made her giggle to herself as she wiped it off on her leggings. After doing research, she and Sadie decided to wear leggings instead of jeans so they didn't get sores on their legs from the seams.

Checking the heart monitor again; a little rise, but not too a bad…the pace was good for him.

Her mind wandered again…to her dad…Greg. She'd spoken to him a number of times now and they seemed to be in a good place. Then there was the DNA test. It had been five days; they should get the results soon. What then? What to do…

They passed the sixth mile marker; heart rate was good, her mind continued to wander. Would she look like her birth father? She looked like Nikki and Elena, except for the eyes and the jaw line.

What if she didn't like him? Was he married? Would he have other children? Did she have more family…half-sisters and brothers that she didn't know about? Last year she had no one, now she had Nikki and the possibility of so many more.

She checked the heart monitor again as she approached the tenth mile marker. Dr. Mark was sitting on the tail gate of his truck with Dru at his side. She slowed Cooper to a walk and dismounted a hundred yards out then jogged alongside of him.

"How's he doing?" Dru asked as she smiled proudly at the sweaty black horse.

"Really well, I think he likes this." Josey smiled as she loosened the cinch so the vet could quickly examine him.

"Take some water while Dr. Mark checks him out." Dru handed her a bottle.

Josey looked back down the road she had just traveled to see Sadie a few minutes behind her.

"He's doing real well," Dr. Mark patted the horse then he too wiped his hand off on his jeans.

"I'm curious how Mustang is doing." Josey tightened the cinch then remounted.

"We'll do a drive by and tell you once we check on him." Dru said.

"Next time we should have walkie-talkies." Josey pushed Cooper into a trot.

Ten miles down…fifteen to go.

Her mind went back to the DNA test. If she could choose a father, what would she want? Greg probably wasn't the best example, having abandoned her and all. Of all the fathers she has seen she would want Grayson to be her dad. Nothing against the rest of them…it's just he had been such a supporter of her from the moment they met. He was a great teacher, confidant, and mentor to her. Sadie and Grace were so lucky.

Dr. Mark's truck pulled up next to her.

"Mustang is doing very well," Dru told her. "Sadie may have been holding him back so she's going to push him a little more. We'll check them at mile eighteen."

"OK!" Josey nodded with a grin.

"You're having fun?" She asked.

"I love riding," Josey laughed.

"OK…we'll see you in a bit." Dru waved as they drove away.

Mile twelve went by, just over half way through. Heart rate check; it was a little high. Knowing the hill was coming up she slowed him to a jog to get the heart rate down.

Lifting one arm at a time she stretched her arms over her head and behind her then rolled her neck. This was tough on the rider too.

She glanced back and could see Sadie and Mustang had closed the gap. Good for Mustang! He was a wonderful horse; great disposition and beautiful. He was the first mustang she had been around and had really impressed her and everyone else. Nora was doing a fantastic job in training him and Nikki's feeding program was working; evident in his noticeable weight gain in the six weeks since they won him at the auction.

Josey wished she'd been there. Although she was taking care of Nikki's rehab horses, Jessup had offered so she could go but she said no. It was the cousin's project…not hers. Admitting it to herself, she had still been hiding at the ranch at the time. She'd never let that happen again and miss out on such a fun day.

At mile fifteen, his heart rate had lowered maybe a little too much, she increased the pace again.

Not wanting to leave everything to the heart monitor, she stopped thinking so hard and listened to Cooper's breathing. It was heavy; she could hear and feel every breath but he didn't seem stressed. Out of curiosity she released the tension on the reins to see what he would do. He broke into a canter!

Josey giggled and reined him back down. He was enjoying himself.

Dr. Mark's truck appeared as she rounded a corner so she slowed down, dismounted then jogged in again.

Coming to a halt, she took the water bottle from Dru.

Sadie reached them just as Josey was remounting.

"How is he?" Josey asked with a grin.

"He was pissed when you got ahead of him." Sadie laughed, her eyes shining. "He's a bit competitive."

"That's good." Dru smiled.

Josey took off at a trot.

That was mile eighteen…only seven more to go.

She and Cooper rounded another corner and passed Warren, the foreman from the neighboring ranch. She waved and smiled. Another corner and the hill came within sight so she slowed the pace down to prepare for the strenuous incline.

Looking back, she saw Sadie and Mustang right behind her.

Fifty yards from the base of the hill, she increased the pace. He tried moving faster but she held him back.

Half way up the hill they passed mile marker twenty.

Three quarters of the way up and his heart rate was good so she let him have his lead and go up the hill at his own speed. He took off!

Josey was breathing heavy as they made it to the top of the hill. She reined him in at the top expecting Dr. Mark to be there but there was a hundred yards of road before going around a corner. She couldn't see anything but trees.

Heart monitor check…just at the high end so she brought the pace back down.

Sweat was dripping down her forehead and her back…that climb may not have exhausted Cooper but it took its toll on her! She looked back just before they rounded the corner. Sadie and Mustang were just coming over the top of the hill.

When she rounded the corner, Dr. Mark's truck came into view, as well as Grayson's. He, Scott, and Jessup had joined Dru and Dr. Mark.

She slowed down, dismounted, and then jogged in with a grin on her face.

"Well, look at you!" Josey teased.

"We were a bit curious." Jessup grinned.

"How's he doing?" Scott asked.

"He's still full of energy!" Josey laughed and took the water bottle from Dru. "I gave him his head coming up the hill and he nearly sprinted up the whole thing."

"His heart and lungs sound good." Dr. Mark announced and looked behind her.

Sadie was approaching on the very sweaty dark brown mustang.

Josey stepped back in the saddle, "I don't want him to cool down too much. See you at the end…have water and aspirin."

She waved at Sadie then took off at a fast trot.

What if her actual father didn't like her? Josey shook her head at the thought. Where did that come from and why wouldn't he like her? Why did she always doubt herself? The four men she just rode away from liked her…so why wouldn't he? What if she didn't like him or his family?

He was originally from Pendleton, would he still be there? Curiosity had gotten the best of her a couple of nights before and she had to Google how far it was from Lewiston; only a three hour drive.

Mile marker twenty two went by and she could just barely make out the ranch in the distance.

Monitor check; he was holding steady. Hearing test; he was breathing hard but not bad. She increased the pace and watched the ranch buildings as she got closer.

Dr. Mark and Grayson's trucks drove by her and she waved.

At two hundred yards away from the ranch his heart rate and breathing were good so she let him have his lead. He took off again.

She past the larger corral on the left, then the barn…the bunkhouse to the right and the ranch house to her left. Everyone was standing in front of the barn and waved, whooped, and hollered as she past them.

She reined Cooper in and trotted down the road then turned to trot back to the buildings. Sadie was cantering in; grinning from ear to ear.

They continued to trot the horses until their heart rates lowered, then they walked in circles until they were back to normal.

"That was fun!" Sadie declared.

Josey nodded, "I agree."

When they slid off the horses, Grayson and Scott removed the tack so Dr. Mark could check on the horses again.

"We'll wipe them down and get their blankets then keep them in the barn out of the weather." Dru told them.

"Get the ligament on their legs to help them recover." Dr. Mark called out.

Josey nodded and walked to Cooper's head. He still looked excited as she ran a hand down his nose and up his rounded jaw. He tipped his head to her and ran his ears from her hip, across her belly and to her shoulder; leaving a wet sweat streak right across her jacket. She just laughed.

After the horses were taken care of and placed in the barn, the group moved to the ranch house for lunch. They discussed the endurance test and all decided to run it again in January or February, depending on weather, and compare the mustang's results.

"I can't believe how hungry I am." Sadie laughed then half her hamburger disappeared in her mouth.

"Sadie!" Grayson frowned in disgust. "Ladies don't shove their food in their mouths."

Sadie grinned, "Cowgirls do though." She squeezed out around the food.

They all chuckled.

"Well, I think Cooper deserves a night off from team penning." Dru said.

"Well, Jack's been saying he wanted to use Chevy this year too." Scott said of one of the three horses bought at the Billing's auction for Nora to train.

"He's a nice horse. Nora did a good job with him." Dru nodded.

"If Josey, Lucas, and Jessup are a team…who's riding for Matt with Nick and Nikki?" Sadie asked.

"I am," Dr. Mark grinned.

"Oh, fun!" Sadie grinned at him. "A whole day with you!"

"Well, why don't you finish up there, and you can ride with me back down off the mountain." He smiled behind his mustache.

Sadie shoved the other half of her hamburger in her mouth and tried to grin at her dad.

CHAPTER EIGHT

Josey slid her phone in the pocket of the Tagger Enterprises jeans jacket she wore over a black hoody. Her hair was loose down her back with the cowboy hat pulled low to keep it in place. The sun had set and the evening had begun to get chilly.

She lifted her saddle onto Trooper's back. He was about the same size as Apollo and Cooper so she didn't have to adjust the cinches. As she retrieved the bridle from the horse trailer an odd feeling passed over her. Hesitantly, she looked around the rodeo grounds. All the cowboys and cowgirls were in different stages of saddling their horses or already riding toward the indoor arena. She saw no one actually looking at her.

Josey shrugged off the feeling…the worse it could be was Elena and she was still in prison.

"Ready?" Nikki asked as she rode Harvey next to her.

"Yep," Josey smiled and stepped into the saddle of the large brown horse.

She liked riding Trooper; it made her feel closer to Matt.

As they walked into the arena to warm up, one of the competitors trotted by and nearly ran them over.

"Hey!" Nikki and Josey called out in unison.

"Sorry." He mumbled and trotted away from them.

Josey glared at him as she watched him trot around the arena. He nearly ran over three more people. A few months before she would have ridden off without saying a word, but now?

"Is he drunk?" Josey asked.

"He has been before," Nikki nodded. "We had some real issues with him last year."

The odd feeling passed over Josey again and she looked around. No one was looking at her.

The drunk rider came by them again…close enough he brushed her leg even though there was plenty of room around them.

"Knock it off!" She yelled at him.

He turned, gave her a half-smile and kept on moving.

"I'm getting pissed." Josey turned to her sister. "We're here for fun, not to deal with that."

"I agree," Nikki sighed. "I'll see if I can find Roger…he hosts the night."

She turned away and trotted across the arena.

As Josey was just under the announcer's booth, the drunk rider trotted right up to her and stopped in front of Trooper. The horses nearly collided.

"What's your problem?" She asked angrily.

"You're really pretty." He grinned.

Josey impatiently exhaled but didn't say anything. She wasn't fond of dealing with drunk idiots.

"You're pretty…I like your hair." He tried to flirt but his words were a bit slurred.

"Why don't you go out to your truck and sleep it off…then come back in a bit and have a good ride?" She asked trying to be polite.

"Why don't you come out to my truck with me?" His smile was more of a leer.

"Really? Seriously?" She shook her head. "Your drunken riding and that stupid line is supposed to make me attracted to you?"

Her comment caught him off guard and his smile slowly faded.

"It's very insulting to come to a family evening like this and have someone say something like that…no woman would want to be with you after that."

His jaw had dropped and he just stared.

"How would you feel about someone that said something like that to your daughter?" Josey asked…not knowing if he had a daughter or not.

His eyes moved over to the bleachers where the families of the riders were sitting. All the Tagger's, that weren't riding, were currently sitting front and center on the bleachers.

"I wouldn't." He finally looked back to her. "I'd probably knock them off their horse."

"Well?" Josey said, not really knowing what she wanted him to do, except leave her alone.

He sighed and turned away from her and trotted across the arena and out the back.

Nikki rode up to her. "Where did he go?"

Josey shrugged, "We better get warmed up."

After a few more laps around the arena, they moved into the competitors section and watched the 15 steers being pushed into the arena. They wore plastic chains around their necks. Three had blue, three with red, three with yellow, three with white, and three with green chains.

The announcer called out the first team to run; Scott, Grayson, and Jack.

All three men trotted across the arena towards the cows. Chevy, the gruella Jack was riding, seemed to dance in excitement.

"Men, you're looking for blue." The announcer said.

They moved a little faster with Grayson and Eli plunging into the middle of the herd and pointing out the three steer with the blue chains. Each man took charge of a steer and cut them from the herd without any of the buddies following. The cut steers were herded across the arena and quickly pushed into a small round pen. Grayson reached up and rang the bell indicating the end of the ride.

"Good job!" The announcer yelled over the cheering crowd. "Forty-five seconds. You set a challenge for the night."

Grayson and Scott pushed the steers back to the herd and remained by them to make sure they stayed together for the next team. Jack rode Chevy out of the arena and toward a very proud Nora; the pair high-fived with a laugh.

"Next riders; Josey, Lucas, and Jessup"

Josey and her teammates walked into the arena together and slowly walked to the herd while waiting for their color to be called out.

"You're looking for yellow."

Grayson and Scott rode away from the herd and out of the arena.

Josey pushed Trooper into a trot toward the steer on the right end…it had a yellow chain. She quickly cut it away from the herd and across the arena toward the small pen. She turned and looked at her teammates…Jessup and Dollar were right behind her with a second steer, she slowed down so the calf would group with hers. Both steers went into the round pen…they turned to Lucas and his horse, Bay. The steer was running up the side of the arena but just as it looked like it was going right into the pen, the steer stopped, turned quickly then it headed back to the herd.

"Geez, Lucas…do I have to do everything?" Josey called out with a grin as she and Trooper ran across the arena to block the calf.

"Just get your butt over there." Lucas laughed as they cut off the steer again. The two of them pushed the steer toward Jessup, and the older man came around to join them to push it in the pen. Once the steer was in and all three riders together, Jessup rang the bell.

Josey felt the odd feeling again. As she walked through the gate she looked around…no one out of the usual. Then, she spotted him standing under the announcer's stand. He was leaning against the wall, hat low and the collar of his jacket up. He was nearly unrecognizable… but she knew it was him.

Her heart raced as she smiled at all the competitors and walked to the back corner. She was directly across the arena from him.

With a shaking hand, she reached in her pocket and withdrew her phone. She pushed the button and looked across the arena to see him lift his phone to his ear.

"Hello, Beautiful."

Her insides melted from the sound of his voice and his words. She had to tip her head down so her hat would block her glistening eyes and flushed skin from the crowd around her.

"Matt…" Her voice was low…breathless. "What are you doing?"

"Watching the most beautiful woman I have ever seen ride my horse."

His voice was warm and loving; her heart and mind tingled.

"How long have you been back?"

"About an hour."

"Does anyone know you're here?"

"No, just you…how did you know?"

"I just had a feeling I was being watched. I saw this creepy man in the corner and figured it had to be you." She giggled.

He laughed softly and her heart trembled at the sound, she had missed it so much!

"It was more like staring…ogling…ravishing you with my eyes." He whispered.

Her face flushed.

"Next riders; Nikki, Nick, and Dr. Mark" The announcer called out.

Josey lifted her head to watch them ride.

"So…Dr. Mark replaced me."

"No one can replace you." She sighed.

He chuckled but they didn't speak until the riders had penned their steers.

"So, Beautiful…would you like to go out to my truck?" He chuckled again.

"You heard that?" She grinned.

"Yeah, do you know who he is?"

"No, clue."

"That's Marla's dad."

"Reilly's on again, off again girlfriend?" She asked in surprise.

"Yeah…so your comment probably really hit home."

"I didn't even know if he had kids."

"Must have been women's intuition."

Josey giggled softly as she watched another team try to corral their three steer.

"The kids are going to be really upset with you." She told him.

"Why?"

"Because they were expecting a Christmas morning miracle of you walking in while everyone was opening presents."

"Well, I could hide out somewhere for the next two weeks."

"And I know just exactly where," She giggled and heard him laugh. "But could you imagine what would happen if your family found out I was hiding you for two weeks?"

"Heads would roll!"

"Yeah…I'm sure they would want to see you now…rather than wait."

"You've changed."

"Yes…I believe I have." She said proudly.

"So what happened while I was gone?"

"There's just so much…"

"What's the biggest…what caused Josey to come out?"

"Next riders: Dru, Jordan, and Leah." The announcer called.

They remained quiet while the three women trotted into the arena.

"Mom looks great…Leah's out of her cast and back riding…everyone else OK here?"

"Yes, and your mother is the best."

"I agree."

"We went climbing together the other day."

"Really?"

"Yeah, Reece called about your helping with training this weekend and I talked him into helping me, so I could surprise you. Of course when Dru heard she came with me. We were going to climb Granite Rock first, but it was too cold and icy. So Reece took us into the U of I fitness center and we climbed on the wall for hours."

"Just the two of you?"

"Sort of, there were some other people that joined in but we had a blast…I can't wait to show you everything I learned."

"Good run, Ladies! You beat your husbands by three seconds!" The announcer informed them.

There were whoops and laughter ringing out through the building.

"I've missed this." Matt whispered.

"Are you OK? With everything over there?" She asked worriedly. "I watched the news and saw all the destruction. It was just awful. You're OK?"

"Yeah…I will be…I…" His voice trailed off.

"Matt?"

"I'm just tired…exhausted really. I didn't sleep much over there…it was pretty hard physically as well as mentally." He sighed. "I couldn't sleep on the plane back; which took forever. So I just need sleep then I'll be OK."

Another team entered the arena.

"So what else happened while I was gone?" He asked.

"Are you sure you don't want to wait until later?"

"Once everyone knows I'm here, it will be awhile before just the two of us will be able to talk like this."

"That's true." Josey nodded.

"Josey! Who are you on the phone with…everyone's here!" Nikki called out.

"Busted…" Josey giggled and waved at her sister.

Another team entered the arena.

"Tell me something, Josey…talk to me…I want to hear your voice."

She loved hearing him say her name.

"Last Saturday, Nikki and I flew down and visited Elena in Nevada."

"Seriously?"

She gave him a quick version of everything Elena told them.

"Your dad isn't your dad? I can't believe that."

"Yeah, it was a bit shocking."

"Next riders; Grayson, Scott, and Jack again; they'll try to get the lead back from their wives." The announcer called out.

"You're up next…call me back."

"I will."

She ended the call and slid the phone back in her jacket.

As casually as she could, she joined her sister.

"Who was that?" Nikki asked.

Josey was saved from answering when laughter erupted from the building and they turned to see the three men racing the steer across the arena. Two of the steer went right in the pen…the third took a sharp left and jutted around the fence and headed back to the herd. It took them another thirty seconds to get him back.

"Oh, so close men…well, actually not." The announcer laughed.

Josey met up with Jessup and Lucas just inside the arena. Her eyes shot to Matt against the wall and she grinned. It was exciting to be the only person to know he was there.

"You have red this time…red." The announcer told them.

"Let's get it done, men." Josey called out and cantered to the first red chain she could see…as luck would have it, two of them shot out the side and down to the corner to her left. She just needed to show Trooper which ones to go after and he took off. The two steer tried to shoot to the inside of the arena but Trooper cut them off and kept them along the fence…they ran right into the small round pen.

Josey whipped around and looked at her partners. They were guiding the lone steer straight at her. Trooper backed out of the pen so the calf could get in, which it did quickly and Josey slapped at the bell.

"There you go! Lucas…Jessup…nice of you to handle that one little calf for Josey. That was 28 seconds." The announcer laughed.

Josey grinned at her teammates who just shook their heads at her.

They pushed the three steer back to the herd and waited until the colors were announced for the next team then trotted out of the arena. She waited long enough for everyone to joke and tease her then turn their attention back to the next team. She quietly made her way to the back corner and pulled out her phone.

"Wow…that was awesome." He answered.

"I had a great horse and a strong desire to get it done fast." She giggled.

"So…about your father…"

She told him of Lucas' research and the DNA testing. "So…now we're just waiting."

"Are you OK?"

Josey sighed, "I don't know…I keep going back and forth on that one. Will he like me? Will I like him? Where does he live? Do I have other brothers and sisters…?"

"No matter what happens…no matter what he's like…you have family here…your happiness is here…he can't change that." Matt said. "It's the same way I thought about Nick."

"Well, that gives me hope," She grinned. "He just added to your happiness."

"Yeah…that he did." He chuckled. "But then again, it's also what Nikki said about Elena."

"Well that just burst that bubble." Josey shook her head. That didn't help!

"Well, she was, ultimately, the reason you are here now…which I kind of like."

Josey giggled softly, "Well, haven't we come a long ways since last spring?"

"That we have." He laughed. "So what part of what you told me has helped Josey come back."

"It just all added up…" She paused and looked down the arena at him. "But the biggest thing?"

"Yeah?" He said softly.

"I realized I had to regain Josey…my independence…my life back…for me…not you."

He was silent.

"I need to be strong for me…be able to stand on my own as an individual before being with you. I've spent the last few months trying to be strong for you; I needed to do it for me. I hope you understand."

"I do…and you're right. I wish we would have figured that one out months ago."

Josey laughed softly, "Me too."

"Are you there?"

"Pretty much…" She gave him a wicked giggle.

"Oh, how I missed that sound." He laughed.

She flushed again as she looked around at his family.

"Matt?"

"Yeah?"

"Everyone has missed you so much…I'm starting to feel guilty."

"Me, too."

"Can I come down and get you?"

"So I can ride on the back of Trooper and put my arms around you for support?"

"Oh, yes…" She whispered breathlessly at the thought.

"When they switch out the steers again."

"See you soon." She whispered.

"Hold you soon."

Her heart melted again as she ended the call.

She nudged Trooper through the competitors and smiled at everyone, she couldn't wait for their reactions.

Trooper was positioned next to the fence by the gate. Her heart was racing and she had to concentrate on keeping her breathing normal…patience…she told herself.

Dru, Leah, and Jordan cut their three steers, half way to the pen the steers scattered. It took them over a minute to get them rounded up and to the small round pen. The bell finally rang out.

"Well, good thing you had a good first round." The announcer laughed.

The three women pushed the steer back to the herd then returned to ride right past Josey; she grinned at all three, thinking how happy they were about to be.

"Ok, we'll take a 5 minute break while we switch out the cattle."

Josey nudged Trooper through the gate and kicked him into a run. Her heart raced as she flew across the arena.

"Josey?" The announcer's voice rang out.

She grinned when Matt appeared; crawling over the fencing. Trooper's ears perked up and he ran faster, sliding to a stop and lifting his head to his owner. Matt took a moment to greet his horse then looked at Josey.

He was pale and thinner…dark circles under his eyes. He looked so tired.

"Hello, Beautiful." He leaned in for a quick kiss, barely brushing her lips, then slid onto the saddle behind her. His arms slid under her jacket and wrapped around her; pulling her in tight. Her whole nervous system quivered and she leaned back into him…savoring the thirty seconds they would be together.

"Matt?" She heard someone yell as they trotted across the arena.

"Matt!" That was Dru.

The whole Tagger group was riding into the arena when she arrived back at the gate. The kids, Tessa, and Cora were crawling over the fence or running for the gate from the bleachers.

He kissed her quickly on the cheek then slid off the back of Trooper. His mom was off her horse and wrapping him in her arms within seconds. Tears glistened in her eyes. Tears of relief, Josey knew. Nikki was the next to wrap him in her arms.

It was fifteen minutes of tears and hugs before they moved out of the arena. Everyone there shook his hand or said something to him…every competitor knew him and where he had been.

"Matt," The announcer called out. "We are all very happy and relieved to have you back home. We have one more round, the draw round. We put all the names in a bucket and will draw out three names to create the teams. First up is; Jordan, Mike B, and Nikki.

Jordan and Nikki rode into the arena with the competitor Josey didn't know.

Patience, Josey told herself as she watched Matt mingle with family and friends; they would have their time.

An hour later, Matt was standing at Trooper's head and giving him attention while Josey removed his tack. It was so good to have him there, hear his voice, and see the laughter in his eyes.

"Who did you ride here with?" He asked softly as he shut the trailer gate.

"I drove." She smiled.

"Drove what?"

"I bought my own vehicle this week." She grinned and took his hand.

His touch, as his fingers entwined in hers, warmed her heart. He was there…he was home…she squeezed tightly and he responded. She enjoyed the quiet walk back to the parking area.

She stopped in front of the yellow Jeep.

He turned and looked at it then turned back to her. She gave him a wicked giggle and nodded her head to the Jeep.

"You bought this?" Matt turned to her with a look of surprise.

"Yes," She laughed and turned to open the door. "I saw it and couldn't keep my eyes off it. Grayson told me if I wanted it, then buy it…but I had to promise he could…"

She turned back to him and his hands came to each side of her face. She inhaled sharply as his lips lowered to hers. She had no chance to prepare for the emotions that swept over her. Her legs began shaking, forcing her to grip his jacket tightly to keep from melting to the ground. He must have noticed since one of his arms lowered to wrap around her waist and lift her upright. He pushed her back against the Jeep and increased the pressure and intensity of the kiss. She twisted one leg around his leg…just for added support.

When he finally broke the kiss, he leaned back…his very happy brownish green eyes looked into her very contented chocolate brown eyes. "Welcome back, Josey. I like your Jeep."

"Kiss me again and I might let you ride in it." She grinned and wrapped her arms around his neck and pulled him into another kiss that she had waited so long for.

And she had absolutely no inclination of breaking the kiss…even when she heard the horn honk…a long blaring obnoxious noise from a Tagger truck. Then the second which was a higher tone joined in and then the third. Matt chuckled into their kiss. Afraid he was going to move away, she clenched his jacket tighter and pulled him closer. She didn't need to worry…he leaned into her, pressing her into the Jeep.

It was the fourth horn that joined the racket that made them jump and break the kiss. Their heads turned to the Jeep's steering wheel, a mere two feet away. Grace's hand was pressing the horn, holding it steady…like the other three were.

Josey looked up at Matt and grinned at the laughter in his eyes and the wide smile spread across his face.

"OK!" Matt waved and yelled, the horns stopped and the silence was almost deafening.

They gazed into each other's eyes a moment, both understanding their futures were now entwined…they would be together…side-by-side. Matt bent down to her ear, which made her tilt her head to his. He felt so good…so safe.

"I'll see you in a couple days." He whispered.

Shock ran through her and her body stiffened…he was leaving?

"It's OK…" He assured her. "I'm exhausted…that kiss nearly took everything I had left in me." He sighed. "Mom's insisting I go to The Homestead so she can nurse me back to health. Besides, I need some rest before I take you out on a date again."

Josey relaxed and nodded against him. He leaned in for one brief gentle kiss. As he began to back away…she pulled him back for one more…just one more. Matt chuckled and all four horns started blaring again.

CHAPTER NINE

Josey paced the floor of the Circle 50 ranch kitchen…there was no lingering over the branding book today. She glanced out the window…again…searching for Nick's truck.

"When do you think they will get here?" She yelled to her sister.

"Should be any minute," Nikki answered as she walked into the kitchen with the house plans they had completed. "Mom said Matt has been eating everything in sight so I made enough lasagna and French bread to feed an army. Nick was swinging by the ranch house to see if Jessup and Kate wanted to join us for dinner."

Josey helped her sister spread the plans out on the kitchen table and stared at the house one more time…hoping that someday it would be her house too.

"What's taking Lucas so long at the barn?" Nikki peered out the window.

"Well?"

"He's talking on his phone."

"Well, there's a shocker." Josey giggled.

Nikki turned with a smirk, "True, but he promised no phone while everyone is here."

"The man would give you the world if you just asked for it." Josey smiled at her.

"I know," Nikki giggled, her eyes lighting up. "I think I might just have to marry him!"

Josey chuckled then glanced out the window for the millionth time. Nick's black truck was approaching the house, with Jessup's silver one following.

"They're here!" She could barely contain the excitement running through her…three days! It had been three long days since their kiss at the Jeep. She hoped he hadn't changed his mind…that he still wanted to see her. Why did she always doubt herself?

Nikki grinned at her, "No poker face for you?"

"NO!"

"You've talked every day."

"Not the same! Is talking on the phone with Lucas in Australia the same as having him here?"

"No…definitely not." Nikki chuckled.

As the truck stopped in front of the house, the two sisters stepped out the door.

Josey could see Matt in the passenger seat looking toward Lucas at the barn. He was wearing a black Circle 50 hat and a black jacket and he looked positively handsome sitting in the black truck. Does he still want to see her? Would he still feel the same?

Matt started opening the door, turned to her, their eyes met…and he grinned…yes!

She couldn't take it another second; her feet barely touched the steps as she ran down them. Ten running strides later she was jumping in his arms to the sound of his laughter.

Her arms squeezed tightly around his neck as his came around her waist and he leaned back lifting her feet off the ground. Just to help him support her…she wrapped her legs around his waist and giggled as his arms went under her thighs to lift her higher.

She leaned back just enough to grin into his smiling eyes.

"Feeling better?" She asked followed by a slight giggle.

"Yes," He answered; his eyes rested and looking very happy. "Between Mom's pampering and Cora's cooking, I feel much better."

"Is there anything I can do to help you feel even more better?" She tilted her head making her long dark hair slide to one side; she smiled innocently.

He chuckled, "I think there is."

"And what would that be?"

"I think…maybe…a kiss would work."

"A kiss…" She tilted her head the other direction making her long hair swish behind her and sighed dramatically. "I think…I might be up to that."

"I sure hope so," He sighed. "Because I've been thinking of nothing else for the last three days."

When she leaned back, his arms tightened around her legs so she placed a hand on each side of his neck so her thumbs could trace his jaw line. With the tip of her thumbs she tilted his head back, then just a little to the side. She looked him square in the eye and gave him a wicked giggle just before she placed her lips on his.

****

Josey sat cross-legged on the kitchen chair and watched Matt's reactions as Nikki reviewed the house drawings with him. She forced herself not to bite at her lip like she usually did when she was nervous. She really hoped he liked what she suggested.

"So, if we find the right spot to build…our wing of the house will actually have the sunrise on one side and the sunset on the other." Matt looked at Nikki then to Josey.

Josey's heart skipped a beat…he said "our"!

"Yes!" Nikki nodded. "And we'll be blocked from the morning sun but the fitness room will also have the sunrise."

"I like that it's away from the bedrooms so if I go in there in the middle of the night I won't disturb anyone." Lucas nodded.

"What's out here?" Matt asked.

Josey leaned forward to see where he was pointing. It was the crook of the L shape.

"The only thing I thought of was a door leading from the living room out to that area…maybe a patio." Nikki answered.

"This outside wall of the living room has the fireplace in the middle with windows on both sides?" Matt asked.

Nikki nodded.

"Let's put an outside fireplace on the back of the inside fireplace and put something like an outdoor living room out there too." Matt looked at Nikki. "Placed correctly it should be protected by the weather."

"Oh, Matt!" Nikki grinned. "I LOVE that idea!"

"Me, too." Lucas agreed.

Josey was staring at the drawing…picturing the outdoor room. She could visualize the four of them resting after a long day of work on soft cushy sofas with their feet up on an ottoman or watching the morning sun...

"Josey!"

She jumped and looked up at the three of them. "What?"

"What do you think of that idea?" Lucas chuckled.

"I was already sitting out there with a cup of coffee watching the morning sun light up the mountains." She grinned at him then glanced at Matt. He returned her grin which caused her heart to race.

Jessup leaned over the drawing, "Put a roof on that and it would be a great place to cuddle up with your lady and watch it rain."

Josey smiled at the foreman who held a special place in her heart. He had been a great friend and teacher the last seven months.

"You're more of a romantic than I thought." She teased him.

"And you told me to keep that a secret." Kate laughed. "Then you go and blow it."

Jessup's eyes lit up when he looked at his girlfriend. "We'll just have to swear them in on the secret too."

They all chuckled.

"I'm thinking Nick needs to look into an outdoor space." Tessa tilted her head to him. "Maybe an enclosed gazebo?"

"Anything you want." Nick grinned.

"After our house is built!" Nikki said quickly.

"We're going to keep that contractor pretty busy." Matt nodded as he concentrated on the house plans.

"You're missing something." Kate said while looking at the drawings.

"What?" Nikki and Matt said in unison.

"Guest rooms." She chuckled.

"Oh, dang!" Nikki sighed.

A phone alert rang out and nearly everyone reached for their phones.

They all smiled at each other but it was Lucas that started poking at his phone.

"You said no phone." Nikki raised a brow to him.

Lucas leaned down, kissed her on the cheek, grinned, and walked to the back office.

Within minutes he returned with a piece of paper in his hands. He walked past everyone, slid his jacket on then threw Josey her coat.

Josey caught it, "What the heck?"

Without a word he opened the door and motioned for her to step outside.

She glanced around the room at the other confused faces but did as Lucas asked. He followed her out the door and motioned for her to sit on the step of the porch…so she did.

There was only one reason he would do this, Josey thought as he sat down next to her.

"The DNA tests?" She asked.

He nodded with a grim smile.

That didn't bode well.

Josey sighed as she looked out at the ranch…or what she could see of it from the moonlight. It had been such a great night…she hadn't thought about the test all day…just Matt.

"OK, did they find a match?" She couldn't get herself to look at him. She concentrated on the silver Circle 50 brand on the side of Nikki's dark blue truck.

"Yes."

She took a deep breath and let it out slowly. "Which one?"

"Dean Hayes."

"Wow…the one we started with." She glanced at him and he nodded. "Does he know?"

Lucas hesitated again. "It's not that simple."

She frowned, "He either does or doesn't…how hard is that?"

"Josey," He took her hand and looked right in her eyes. "He died in Kuwait."

She stared…stunned. The tears started to rise; she wasn't sure if it was for the father she didn't know she had then lost, or because she was fatherless again.

"So…in ten days…I have a father…don't have a father…may have a father…then don't." She whispered.

He handed her the paper in his hand that had two pictures on it. One picture was a bull rider, the other a soldier…but they were the same man. The bull rider was grinning, young and excited with life; the soldier was serious with a stern but proud look.

She stared at the two pictures; a flash of excitement at finding him was quickly squelched when she remembered he was gone. But if he was gone…?

"How did you get the DNA for testing?" She looked back up at Lucas.

"His parents."

"Oh…" She looked back at the picture. "Do they know?"

"Yes, all the people tested were sent the results at the same time."

She nodded and stared at the pictures again. His hair was the same color as hers…their eyes the same shape and color…his jaw was more slight…like hers. "I look like him."

"That's what I thought. The part of you that doesn't look like Nikki, definitely looks like him."

He sat quietly with her as she studied and compared herself to the man in the photos.

"Where do they live?"

"Enterprise, Oregon." He answered. "I had to Google it but it's not too far from here; two hours to Lewiston then two hours from there."

He took another deep breath which made her look at him. "What?"

"He didn't have brothers or sisters…an only child. He was married just before he went into the service but didn't have any kids."

Her eyes widened again, "So his parents…they're alone?"

"Yes."

"Oh…how awful." She sighed. "How old was he when he died?"

"I think around twenty-four."

"I would have been three. So they had him for all that time…then he was gone…"

"Yeah…"

"I am the only thing they have of their son?" She looked at Lucas as the realization hit her.

"Yeah…"

"And now they know…oh, Lucas! Can you imagine what they are going through right now?" Tears sprung to her eyes for the grandparents she never knew she had.

He slid an arm around her shoulders and tucked her to him as the tears fell.

The tears started to slow down, then she thought of the mother who lost her son, and they started back up again.

"Oh my gosh…" She muttered and tried to wipe her eyes. "I can't make them stop."

"Well, let's go for a walk and see if that helps." He took her hand to help her rise and they walked down the gravel road under the moonlight.

They walked side-by-side with their hands tucked deeply in their jackets to ward off the chilly December night. Her mind finally relaxed and the tears stopped.

"Can I meet them?" She looked up at him.

"I have their number…would you like to call them?"

She walked quietly a moment…if she was them, a phone call wouldn't be enough. They needed to see their son in her. Thank goodness she looked like him! Hopefully that would help them and not be too hard.

Josey stopped and looked up at him. "Can you call and set up a meeting? I want to see them…not just talk to them."

"Where do you want to meet?"

"Can we go there? If this is too emotional for them, they shouldn't be on the road."

"When?"

"If they want…as soon as possible; it's too late today but maybe tomorrow?"

He grinned down at her and pulled out his phone. "I'll see what I can do."

"I need equine therapy..." She turned quickly and jogged to the barn. Apollo was at the other ranch so she went to the twin bay colts. They always made her smile.

It had taken Shakespeare and Romeo awhile to warm up to people but when they finally did they were just the friendliest little fellows around.

She ran her hands over the colts as she thought of the last fifteen minutes. Her eyes widened… What if they didn't want to see her? What if they weren't good? Lucas would have checked on that before calling them. But still! What if she was reading this all wrong? Just because she had this reaction didn't mean they would. The tension rolled through her body…what had she just done? What if they said no? How was she supposed to interpret that?

The barn door opened and she held her breath when Lucas stepped through.

He leaned over the stall door and a smile appeared through his whiskers, "They are over joyed."

The tears sprang up as the tension left.

"They were ready to drive up tonight but agreed to wait for you tomorrow."

With the stall door between them, Josey reached up and drew her future brother-in-law into a relieved embrace. "Thank you so much."

"Well, you're not going alone…so would you like Nikki and I to go with you?"

"Oh!" She had totally forgotten about the house full of family. "We should go tell them."

Half way to the house Lucas repeated his question, "Do you want Nikki and I to go with you?"

"Well…yes…and Matt if he wants."

"That's a silly statement."

They looked at each other and laughed as they entered the house to a half dozen very curious expressions.

Ten minutes later Matt looked at her like she was nuts, "If I want to go?"

"Well…yeah…" Josey said nervously. "I didn't want to force you to go."

He shook his head and rolled his eyes. "What time do we leave?"

CHAPTER TEN

Josey stood on the front step and watched Jessup and Kate, then Nick and Tessa drive away from the house. Nikki was showing off the twin colts to Matt in the barn and Lucas was in his office.

It had certainly been an interesting dinner, Josey thought as she stared out into the darkness. Her mind went to the grandparents she didn't know. What was the night like for them? How their hopes must have been on edge the last week waiting for the test results; a last chance of having a little touch of their son with them.

How awful was it that she took a moment to be disappointed that life never worked out right for her? She was never going to have the father that she wanted. He was gone now, taken before she even knew about him. She'd never have the loving parents that she'd dreamt about and had wanted so bad. It seemed selfish to her, even if it was in her own mind. His parents that had loved him and lost him…they had so many dreams for him.

What if she disappointed them? The thought made her heart drop. She was a good person, with a good job, and now a strong family behind her. Would her past catch up with her? Would Elena ruin this relationship like she tainted hers and Greg's and nearly destroyed any chance of a relationship with Matt?

Why did she always have to think of the bad?

"Josey?"

She felt in a haze as she turned to see Matt standing on the step just below her. Was she so lost that she couldn't think of him? She'd wanted him with her for months…the last three days had been so hard. But now he was there but she felt so lost and confused. It was nearly heartbreaking. She looked at him with tear filled eyes.

"It's OK." He smiled gently and pulled her to him. She rest her head comfortably on his shoulder and let the tension leave her body. "We'll have our time…this is more important right now."

She nodded and let his arms and warmth comfort her. "I'll go back to Tagger Ranch and sleep in my room there."

"That's probably for the best," He spoke into her hair as he leaned into her. "I don't think I could sleep with you in the next room."

She chuckled, "I couldn't either."

"I'm very proud of you Josey…thinking of his parents like you did."

"I just can't imagine what they are going through tonight."

"Every doubt you are having…they are having the same ones."

"How did you know I was doubting this?"

"The lost look on your face when I walked up here."

"Oh," She turned her face into his neck and closed her eyes. He was so warm, so comfortable, so…wonderful. "Do you think we could just stand like this all night?"

He chuckled. "We have a long drive in the morning."

"You know…if we let Nikki and Lucas win the battle of whose going to drive…then we can sit in the back seat and cuddle…and make-out." She giggled.

"I'm all for that."

"So it's settled…we plan on losing the battle?"

"Absolutely."

***

"It's OK, you can drive your Jeep," Nikki smiled innocently. "We know you've been wanting to go on a road trip since you bought it. This is a great chance."

"No, that's OK." Josey returned her innocent smile. "You know the road there…I don't. Besides your truck has more room so it should be much more comfortable."

The sister's innocent smiles quickly changed to knowing grins. They both wanted to lose and cuddle their men in the back seat.

"So how are we going to settle this one?" Nikki tipped her head inquisitively.

"Well…whoever rides in the back going over, drives on the way back?"

"Agreed…"

"Rock, paper, scissors?" Josey giggled.

"Flip of the coin?" Nikki countered.

"Hmmm…" Josey squinted her eyes at her sister. "Well, both men are in the barn doing chores."

"Yeah…"

"And they are too big to fit through the front door at the same time."

"True…"

"So, whichever one comes through the door first…without our calling them, gets the back seat first."

"Ohhh…I like that." Nikki grinned and motioned to the couch. "Shall we?"

The sisters sat on the couch and patiently waited for the door to open.

It wasn't long before they heard the men talking. Both girls giggled as they stared at the door in anticipation.

"It sounds like Lucas is closer." Nikki whispered.

"No…I think that's Matt."

The handle turned…

Josey nearly cried out when Matt's face appeared first.

"What?" He asked at the laughing sisters.

"We'll tell you on the way…right now," Josey grinned at him. "We're headed for the backseat."

He laughed and happily grabbed her hand to drag her out the door.

Matt sat behind Nikki and Josey sat in the middle, buckled her seat belt then twisted so she could lay across his lap. She looked up just as his lips came down to hers. They both giggled into the kiss.

"Remember," Lucas said from the driver's seat. "Whatever you make us listen to on the way over, we're going to times it by 10 on the way back."

They all laughed.

Josey nestled comfortably into Matt's arms and closed her eyes to think about their destination.

"Josey," Nikki's voice was distant.

Matt's left arm was draped over Josey's waist and held her into him. His right arm was wrapped around her shoulders securing her into his chest. Her forehead nestled into the curve of his neck so she could feel his pulse and hear his heartbeat. He was warm, safe…and he smelled so darn good.

No one had ever held her like he was now; a caring, secure 'you're not leaving my arms' hold. She felt…loved and didn't want to be pulled from that moment in time…she wanted to hold onto it forever.

"Josey," Nikki's voice intruded again.

"Go away." Josey whispered and Matt's arms pulled her in closer. She tried desperately to hold onto the moment. She breathed in his intoxicating aroma and nestled further into his chest and arms; the warmth surrounding her.

"Matt."

"Go away…" His voice was low…tired.

"We're five minutes out of Enterprise." Nikki said.

"What?" They said in unison as Josey opened her eyes and looked around.

"You've slept the whole way." Lucas informed them with a wry smile.

"I'm pretty glad you weren't driving if you were both that tired." Nikki smiled back at them.

Josey looked up at Matt who was smiling down at her.

"I like this view." He leaned down and kissed the top of her head.

She giggled and sat up and away from him. As awful as it was to have the moment interrupted, she needed to focus.

"How far away are …." She stopped when she saw the road ahead of them. "Oh, my!"

They were at the base of a large mountain range…the top half was covered in snow; the lower half mixed with blues and greens. It's jagged height towered over them.

"It's beautiful, isn't it?" Nikki asked.

"This place is spectacular." Lucas nodded while taking in the majestic view.

"We'll have to come back this summer…Enterprise, Joseph, and Wallowa." Matt told her. "We can climb, hike, kayak, and bring the horses for a day ride. You'll love this place."

"Oh, yes." Josey smiled at him. Future plans!

"According to the GPS, their place is about 20 minutes away." Nikki turned in the seat and looked at Josey. "The address is between Enterprise and Joseph."

"Well…I'm well rested," Josey sighed. "Hopefully I won't be as emotional."

"Let's stop and stretch for a minute before we get there." Matt suggested.

They stopped at the first gas station they found and within fifteen minutes were anxiously crawling back into the truck.

Josey stared out the side window watching the beautiful scenery go by.

"Lucas?" Josey whispered.

"What?"

"What are their names?" She was so caught up in the thought of them as Dean Hayes' parents…she didn't think of them individually.

"His name is also Dean and her name is Anna." He answered.

"What else do you know about them?" She asked nervously.

"It's all for you to learn with them." He answered.

She nodded and caught her breath when she heard the blinker turn on. She glanced around at the rolling green pasture that seemed to reach all the way to the towering mountain range. Trees covered a good portion of the area next to the road. "They're really out in the middle of nowhere."

She saw a sign but not in time to read it. "What did that say?"

"HQH…Hayes' Quarter Horses!" Nikki gasped and turned to Lucas, who grinned. "That's one heck of a secret to keep to yourself."

"I would never want to face you in a courtroom." Matt chuckled.

"I'm a corporate attorney…I don't get to court much." Lucas smiled.

"And when you do?" Josey asked.

"We usually win." He admitted. "I lost once…Nick was pissed so I do my best to win."

"What did you lose?" Nikki asked.

"A business that the corporation bought and turned around; it ended up going back to a parent company." Lucas answered.

"What did Nick do?" Josey asked. This was the most she'd heard of their work in Australia and just a little bit more confirmation that Lucas worked for Nick.

"Bought the parent company and got the original one back." Lucas laughed.

They were still smiling when the horses came into view. There were dozens of them. Then the house; it was a long ranch house built of pine and rock…it was beautiful…it looked like it should be in a magazine.

"Wow…" Josey whispered. Her heart constricted…this was too much! She suddenly felt very self -conscience, out of her league. All her doubts came rushing back to her, flooding her heart with dread.

Her gaze turned to Matt who was watching her closely. There must have been something in her expression; he quickly took her hand and squeezed. "It's OK." He whispered.

"Maybe this wasn't right." She was near tears, her heart trying to come up her throat.

"It is right, Josey." He assured her.

She turned back to the house as Lucas pulled around a circle drive and stopped. The front door of the house opened.

She turned back to Matt; fear was gripping her. What if they didn't like her? What if Elena scared them away? What if…

"We're all here…if you get uncomfortable then we can just leave." He told her. "But you need to stay strong. I know you can do this."

She nodded nervously, he was right, she could. Taking a deep breath she turned back to the house.

There was an older couple standing in front of the house…they were holding hands. That was a good sign. They had to be around 60 she guessed but they looked healthy and…hopeful.

The couple; her heart seemed to swell as she thought of them as her grandparents. They were on the opposite side of the vehicle as she stepped out of the truck. Lucas turned to her and checked on her with his eyes. She nodded and tried to smile.

Josey closed the door and took a deep breath then followed him around the front of the truck. When she stepped to the far side, she moved around him to face the couple. They had glanced at Nikki…they must have thought she was their granddaughter but when they turned to Josey they both gasped and stared.

She smiled tentatively but stared into the eyes of the man…her grandfather she told herself. His eyes…were her eyes. He wore jeans, a dark blue button up shirt and a tan ranch jacket. He had a lot of dark hair that was peppered in grey.

"Hi," She said softly and smiled.

"Josey…" The woman smiled. Her hair just touched her shoulders and curled in; it was blonde with lighter streaks. She was wearing khaki pants and a white top with a denim jacket over the top.

They looked…comfortable, Josey decided and walked up to them and held out her hand.

They both reached for her hand and grasped it tightly. She held out the other so they could all hold hands.

"You have my eyes." Josey smiled at the man, trying to release the nerves.

"Funny," He grinned. "I was going to say you had my eyes."

Josey giggled and they both relaxed; tears teetered on the edge of the older woman's eyes.

"Would you mind?" The woman asked and moved as if to hug her then hesitated.

Josey understood…she suddenly wanted to hold them, too. They were part of the family she had so desperately wanted when she was alone in Montana.

Josey took the step and the woman's arms came around her…shaky at first then she gripped tightly. The man's arms came around both of them and held them firmly.

Josey waited until his arms relaxed then took a step back. They both looked at her with happy, joyful eyes that made her heart warm.

She turned to her companions. "This is my sister, Nikki." She stepped back as Nikki stepped forward to shake their hands. "We share a mother. And this is her brother Matt, they share a father. And this is Nikki's fiancé Lucas."

"I'm Dean and this is Anna." The older man smiled as they finished the greetings.

"You have a beautiful place here." Nikki said as she looked around the property.

"Thank you," Anna nodded. "We've been here for years trying to perfect it for our retirement."

"Which will probably never happen," Dean chuckled. "Neither one of us would be able to give up the horses or our art."

"You're artist?" Josey asked in surprise.

They smiled at her then laughed softly.

"Yes," Anna nodded. "I guess we have lots of questions for each other."

"Let's go inside out of this chilly air." Dean motioned for the door.

Anna took the lead and stepped into the house. A large foyer that was elegantly decorated with brown, blue, and red tapestries against a deep cherry wood wall greeted them. A bronze of two stallions fighting sat on a pedestal against the wall. Josey caught her breath at the opulence of the room and her nerves started tingling in anticipation of the rest of the house. She took a step forward and promptly stopped...frozen in place.

The house wasn't just a house, it was a showroom for the most beautiful western art show in the world. There were paintings lining the wall showing horses, cowboys, cowgirls, wildlife; western scene after western scene. The table tops were covered in show pieces from small to large sculpted bronzes matching the paintings. In the back corner of the very large room, there was a life-size running horse bronze! Colorful Pendleton wool blankets adorned the back of the large brown leather furniture. The dark wood floors shined.

Josey stared...she couldn't get herself to move. A hand slid into her own, squeezed tightly and moved her forward. It felt like Matt's hand but she wasn't sure because she couldn't pull her eyes from the room to look.

She started to tremble at the feeling of inadequacy. This life they lead...how could they ever accept her with her history? Her shortcomings...her mother! The tears started to rise.

"Before we settle down in here, would you mind if we visited with your horses?" Matt asked politely.

He knew…she needed immediate equine therapy!

CHAPTER ELEVEN

"That would be my greatest pleasure." Anna said happily and they retraced their steps outside.

Matt pulled Josey out of the room and kept her hand tightly in his.

"I see the brand on your truck, Circle 50?" Dean asked and turned to Lucas.

Lucas grinned and nodded his head to Nikki, "That would be my bride's truck, she allows me to drive it when I'm here."

Dean and Anna looked at him in surprise.

"Your accent caught me off guard." Dean chuckled. "You live in Australia?"

"I work there, but live in Idaho with Nikki." Lucas answered as his grinning bride slid her arm around his.

"We have a ranch outside of Cottonwood." Nikki told them.

"Cattle or horses?" Anna asked.

"Cattle and farming," Matt answered. "Nikki and I own the ranch together and our family owns one adjacent to it."

A dozen young horses trotted over to the fence along the driveway leading to the large barn. Josey looked to them then to the barn. It was large and matched the house but she'd been around big barns before…they didn't scare her. She looked back at the house, THAT scared her…she didn't care if she ever went back in.

Her attention was drawn back to the horses when they whinnied a welcome to them. Just the sound and sight of them helped calm her nerves. Most were duns, a few buckskins, palominos and a number of black ones.

Matt walked her to the horses and she instantly released his hand to play with them. They gently fought for her attention which made her laugh and her muscles relax.

"So you're not afraid of horses," Anna laughed. "That's good."

"Especially since I'm a horse trainer," Josey grinned at their surprised and pleased expressions. "I actually work for Circle 50 as a horse trainer and wrangler with Nikki and Matt's uncle."

The rest of the group reached a double door entry at the side of the barn. Matt gently tugged on her jacket. She glanced at him and gave him a pouty smile which caused him to chuckle but she gave in and reluctantly left the young horses. She would have liked to have the whole visit right there next to the colts.

Just inside the barn doors and in front of the elegant long aisle of the barn was a large sitting room…a living room right there in the barn! Josey wanted one of these. There were two large leather couches facing each other with a few cushioned chairs scattered around. In the middle of the furniture was a life-sized bronze mare and foal. The mare's legs were curled under as she lay on her side; the foal standing next to her with his head leaning lovingly on his mother. They were so detailed; it looked like they were bronzed in the pasture and placed in the barn.

"That's….just…wow…" Josey whispered as she stared at the sculpture.

"That's one of our favorite pieces," Anna stopped next to her. "It is a replica of our first brood mare, Legacy and her foal Naya. Our first stallion, Mr. Marvelous, is in the house."

"The running bronze in the corner?" Nikki asked.

"Yes," Anna nodded.

"The paintings and sculptures…that's what you do…your art?" Josey looked at her in awe.

"Yes," Anna smiled. "Dean is the painter and I am the sculptor but he is a great assistant with the larger pieces."

"I've seen some pieces like this in galleries in Montana," Josey continued to stare at the bronze. "But nothing like this…nothing so real."

"Thank you, Josey." She said. "Did you go to the galleries very often?"

"Whenever I could," Josey nodded. "There were a couple of galleries I went to so much they knew me by name." She felt her face warm from the blush of embarrassment, which frustrated her. How would they know she went there to fill the emptiness inside her?

"Have you ever tried to sculpt?" Anna asked.

Josey shrugged, "Just a little in school during shop class. I really enjoyed it."

A loud whinny vibrated down the barn causing Josey's head to twirl and look.

"That would be Mr. Handsome, Mr. Marvelous' son." Dean laughed. "He likes attention and is probably annoyed we haven't gone to see him yet."

"Can we?" Josey and Nikki asked in unison.

"Let's go greet him or he'll holler at us all afternoon." Anna laughed.

The stallion was beautiful, a deep golden color that reminded them of Scarecrow. He had a long, sleek, but strong muscular conformation and he curiously nudged each one of them. From the looks on the older couple's faces, they were totally in love with the golden stallion.

"We have a second stallion, we call him Ted." Anna laughed softly at the name. "Luckily it's just his barn name, not quite as elegant but it really fits him. He likes it outside…that's probably where he is."

Anna walked to the stall across from Mr. Handsome's and tapped on the wall. Within minutes a black stallion stuck his head in the door and looked at them curiously. His ears twitched forward then back. He had a shorter mane that lay over one of the most muscular necks Josey had ever seen on a horse. His head was compact; which indicated that his body was probably a bulldog conformation. He looked at them one last time before his head disappeared.

Anna chuckled; "He is as calm and friendly as Mr. Handsome but he just prefers the outdoors."

Josey walked back to the palomino stallion and ran a hand down his nose. He was very gentle for a stallion.

Reluctantly, she left his side as they walked back down to the barn living room. Josey turned and looked at the stud's stall door. The horse was leaning out the door watching them. She smiled at him and the horse bounced his head as if waving good-bye. It made her giggle.

"He is a charmer." Anna smiled in understanding.

"It surprises me when people don't understand that horses have personalities." Josey told her.

"I agree!" Anna nodded. "I am so thrilled you love horses…just like DJ did."

"You called him DJ?"

"Dean Hayes, Jr.…so it was either Junior or DJ and neither of us liked Junior." She smiled. Her eyes lit up when she spoke of her son.

"Lucas gave me two pictures, one bull riding and one in uniform."

"Probably from our business website," She nodded. "In our bio section."

"Can you tell me about him?" Josey asked.

"Of course, but we have something for you." She said and looked up at her husband and nodded. He excused himself and walked out the door. "We tried hard this last week not to get our hopes up too much."

Josey felt her heart constrict; that must have been horrible.

They all took seats around the room; Josey in the middle of a couch with Anna on one side. When Dean returned he was carrying a large box and sat down on the opposite side of her.

"Once we got the call last night," Anna continued. "We copied every picture of DJ we had and put an album together for you…in hopes you'd want it."

"Of course!" Josey felt the tears well as she pictured their excitement and flurry to get the pictures together.

Dean opened the box and carefully pulled out a thick photo album.

For the next few hours they reviewed every picture and told her every story that went with them. Their voices rang in pride and love.

Josey's birth father rode horses before he could crawl, learned how to rope from a trick roper and was also a calf roper in the rodeo along with bull riding. His horse was a son of Mr. Marvelous; a sorrel gelding with a wide blaze named Preacher. He graduated high school with honors. A full scholarship was offered but he declined so he could go on the rodeo circuit. He just missed going to the National Finals the year before he joined the service and had planned to try again after he completed his time in the military.

He died six months into deployment to Kuwait; their Humvee ran over an IED and he was killed instantly.

They quickly moved on from the story of his death by reaching in the box and pulling out gold buckles…the ones that meant the most to him. Then, his high school ring that was looped through a chain. Much to Josey's surprise, Dean took her hand and placed the ring and chain in her palm.

"We would like you to have this." He smiled warmly at her, tears glistening his eyes.

"I…" Josey was stunned. Her first instinct was to decline but by the look in his eyes, it would have hurt him so she curled her fingers around the ring. "Thank you." She whispered.

He nodded with a smile and placed everything back in the box and slid on the lid. "This is yours."

"Thanks," She smiled at both of them.

"Now…I'm sure we'll come up with more stories over time…but it's your turn now," Anna said light heartedly. "Tell us about you."

She looked into the woman's blue eyes that were expecting a great story and her heart sunk. Josey looked away and down to the ring in her hand. She slowly slid it onto a thumb and twirled it in circles. How much to tell them without them kicking her out of the barn?

"I was raised by my father since I was five," She started and took a deep breath. "Or the man I thought was my father until last week."

Josey looked up at them and her mind raced…what to tell them? They remained quiet; they must have realized it wasn't a fairy tale they were going to hear.

"Tell us the absolute worse first," Dean said softly. "Just let it out and we'll just move on from there."

Josey fought the tears that rose from the tenderness in his voice. She didn't look at Matt or Nikki for support…she had to do this herself. She nodded, took a deep breath and told them about Elena.

When finished, she hesitantly looked up to them and was surprised to see the tenderness in their eyes was still there and something else. A flicker of…pride?

"It sounds to me like you survived some tough times and were very strong to confront her like that." Dean said making Josey catch her breath. "It's not exactly a woman that I would see DJ being with but…he was young."

Josey nodded, "Nick said that she wasn't like that with him, so maybe she wasn't with DJ."

"Well, that kind of makes me feel better." Anna chuckled.

Josey smiled at the look of relief on her face.

"Well, I'm a bit hungry," Anna said and looked around the group then back to Josey. "Would you be OK going in now? We'll have some lunch while you tell us the good things?"

Josey felt the heat run up her neck.

"It's OK," Dean said and stood. He offered a hand that she quickly took. "You're actually not the first person that didn't want to walk in there."

"Really?" Josey asked as they left the barn and headed to the art gallery house.

Her companions followed them into the house and wandered the large room looking at all the art work. Walking in the house had been much easier after telling them about Elena. If they still wanted her in their lives after hearing that then she could 'cowgirl up' and face a room full of art.

Josey watched her grandparents fix lunch as if it was a choreographed dance. They seemed to know exactly what the other was going to do. She chuckled then turned to see Lucas still staring at the large running stallion bronze in the corner of the room. He'd been there for at least five minutes.

Nikki and Matt were looking at a large painting over the fireplace of a herd of horses running through a wide open pasture, so Josey walked to her future brother-in-law.

"What is so compelling you can't pull yourself away?" Josey smiled at him.

He looked at her with furrowed brows. She could almost see his brain working overtime as she looked into his narrowed eyes.

"If you lived at Nick's place and you were looking for high-end quality quarter horses…this place is so close…wouldn't you call here?" He asked knowing that Nick had purchased his property from Cora after her husband's death.

Josey's jaw dropped in surprise, "You think one of the Tagger Herd was from here?"

"It makes sense."

"It does…" Josey nodded and turned back to the kitchen with Lucas following.

"Do you keep records of everyone you sell horses to?" Josey asked.

"Of course," Anna answered. "We have records on the computer all the way back to the first colt we sold."

"How old are they when you sell them?" Lucas asked.

"We've sold them from pre-conception up to four years." Dean answered.

"Do you know, about four years ago from this next spring, did you sell any horses to a man named Wes Smith?" Josey asked.

"What about Wes?" Matt asked as he and Nikki joined the conversation.

Lucas asked them the same question he had asked Josey.

"I've read all the registration papers," Nikki said. "I don't remember a Mr. Handsome."

"Me too and me neither." Matt added.

"Well, Mr. Handsome is his barn name," Dean said; a bit confused at the conversation. "Let's check."

He retrieved a laptop and settled into a chair at the dining room table and pulled up the information.

"Four years?" Dean confirmed.

"Yes." They all answered.

"When Mom transferred the papers on all the horses they renamed them to include the T3E brand." Nikki said.

"Well…here it is…" Dean started nodding. "Looks like two of them."

"Oh, my gosh!" Josey gasped.

"There has to be a story behind these questions. Who is Wes Smith to you four?" Anna asked as she placed a platter full of sandwiches on the table.

"Which two?" Nikki asked excitedly, "Then we'll tell you the story of the Tagger herd."

"Tagger?" Dean looked at her in surprise.

"Yes," Nikki laughed. "Matt and Nikki Tagger."

"Well you didn't say your last name the first time, for some reason I just attached Franklin to you too." Dean stood and walked to a book shelf. He flipped through a stack of magazines and pulled one out to tip towards them. "I knew you looked a bit familiar."

The magazine he showed them was from the large article written about The Tagger Herd just months after their rescue. The horses were on the cover and a picture of Matt, Nikki, Trooper and Harvey was on the inside.

"You're telling us that two of our babies went through that?" Anna gasped. "There was no mention of the original owners name or town they were rescued from in the article."

"That was done to protect Wes' widow, Cora." Matt explained quickly.

"We were shocked by the article. We were in London at an art showing when the initial news coverage happened so we missed the initial furor…they were our babies?" She asked again.

Nikki nodded hesitantly, "Yes, but…"

Anna shook her head, "It's OK…well not OK, but it wasn't your fault." She said quickly. "The article was very detailed on how much your family, including the kids, put into the saving of those poor things. Dean, which two babies came from here?"

"A palomino filly and a black colt." He answered.

"Star or no star on the colt?" Matt asked.

"No star…solid black." Dean answered.

"Scarecrow and Cooper!" Nikki told them. "Which really makes sense because Scarecrow is nearly identical color to Mr. Handsome and Cooper has the bulldog conformation like Ted."

"I just love Cooper!" Josey exclaimed. "And Scarecrow…both of them!"

"You'll be very proud of how they've turned out." Matt grinned proudly.

They spent the next hour talking about the Tagger herd rescue.

It was already dark outside when Lucas mentioned the long drive back. They all nodded reluctantly. Josey took one last look around the house she had been so terrified to enter, but now felt relaxed and comfortable. She was sure it was because of her grandparents and not the artwork. They had made her feel so welcome.

She took one last walk around the room and stared at each bronze as the others said goodbye.

Dean and Anna joined her as she was looking at a smaller bronze of a mare standing patiently as her foal seemed to be running circles around her. She had seen Matt's colt, Leroy, do the same thing to his mom, Kit. The memory of it made her smile.

"Good artwork brings back memories," Josey looked up at them and they seemed impressed by her comment. "Yours does that for me."

"I am so glad." Anna smiled, her eyes lit up in pride and happiness.

"Josey…" Dean said hesitantly.

"Yes," She smiled at him.

"We…well…do you need anything?" He finally stammered.

She shook her head in confusion. "No, I'm OK."

"You said that Elena stole your college fund…if you still want to go…we can…" Anna said and looked at her earnestly.

"I don't want your money!" Josey gasped.

"I understand," Dean said quickly. "It's just to help…"

Josey shook her head vigorously, her heart feeling dejected that they would think she needed or wanted their money, "No, I don't want your money. I will take care of myself."

"And you've accomplished that and should be very proud of yourself." Anna said. The honesty filled her voice, which made Josey feel better. "But we're here…if you need anything."

"Anything at all," Dean added; looking desperate to calm her down.

Josey shook her head, "I don't need money."

"Is there anything else we can help with?" Anna nodded in understanding.

Josey looked at their warm and friendly expressions and still felt comfortable with them. "Two things…" She finally said.

"Anything…" Anna nodded with a smile.

"I want to be able to call and talk to you…or visit you…and you come see me at the ranch."

Tears sprung to their eyes, one escaping down Anna's cheek before she pulled Josey into a strong, warm, thankful embrace. Dean's arms wrapped around the two of them and he squeezed tightly.

When they finally stepped back, Anna took in a deep breath and released it with a smile to Josey, "We'll have no problem with the first request," She grinned. "What's the second?"

Josey turned to the statue of the mare with the running foal, "Can you teach me how to do that? How to sculpt?"

Their faces lit up in delighted surprise.

"Absolutely!" Anna exclaimed. "We didn't even get out to the studio!"

"Your studio is here?" Josey asked.

"Yes…" Dean turned to the group who were waiting at the door. "It will only take a few more minutes…the studio is right behind the house, we can…"

"YES!" They all three exclaimed.

It was another two hours before they were driving away from the house and horses.

Josey waved at them one more time. She had been amazed at the studio and in awe of all the pieces in different stages of development. Her grandparents had explained to them how a bronze was created from a simple piece of wax all the way to the foundry.

They had chosen to build their horse ranch in Enterprise because of their bronze work and the foundries in Joseph that had the kilns large enough for their work. It was also close to their original home in Pendleton. Their painting and sculptures were sold all over the world!

Dean's studio for his painting was also in the large building. A large windowed wall stood between the two rooms so they could see each other as they worked.

Anna had given them each a piece of wax to try molding and they had all laughed and played. Matt and Lucas created horse shoes which actually looked pretty good. Nikki tried a bowl…it turned out a little warped.

Josey had formed the wax to a smooth cylinder then flattened it on the top and bottom. She then created four limbless trees that protruded up from the cylinder base.

"What are those?" Anna asked.

"That one is Lucas, it's the tallest." Josey chuckled as she pointed at the limbless trees. "Then Matt, Nikki, and me."

"What are they?" Matt grinned.

"The beginning of our forest," She explained with a giggle. "But since we're a little…" She moved each tree just a little in a circle so it bent as if the wind was blowing against it.

"Since we're a little what?" Lucas asked warily.

"Twisted…or bent…however you want to describe it." Josey chuckled as she twisted the four trees just a little more.

CHAPTER TWELVE

"What time did you get home?" Grayson asked.

"They dropped me off around two," Josey emptied the box of her father's memories on the ranch house table. His class ring was still on her thumb with the chain coiled around her wrist; somehow it made her feel like he was with her. From the stories her grandparents had told her, she knew she would have liked him…and he would have liked her. The thought made her smile.

"So you had a good time?" Jessup asked.

The Trio were already flipping through the photo album.

"A fantastic time; they are just wonderful." She grinned at him.

"You look a lot like him," Scott said. "Was that good or hard for them?"

"Very good," Josey sighed. "And I cannot believe how Lucas can hold a secret! He didn't let us know they owned a horse ranch until we drove into the driveway!" The Trio chuckled and nodded in understanding.

"Oh! Oh! Oh!!!" Josey nearly jumped with excitement.

They looked at her in surprise and laughed.

"I didn't tell you! Scarecrow and Cooper came from there!"

All four jaws dropped.

"I know!" Josey laughed at their expressions and quickly told them about the horses. She retrieved her laptop and looked up her grandparent's business website. The sound of the main door opening reached her and she quickly became distracted when Matt appeared with a smile.

As if they had done it a thousand times, he walked up to her, slid an arm around her waist and gave her a gentle good morning kiss. Her heart melted.

"So, you had your picture taken with them." Grayson said.

"Yeah, how did you know?" Josey asked as she turned back.

Dru had taken control of the laptop. The picture of Josey standing between Dean and Anna was front and center on their website. They were all smiling; the happiness radiating from all three.

"Let me read this to you." Dru smiled at her.

"OK…" Josey whispered in anticipation.

"A miracle came into our lives today and her name is Josey." Dru read with a crack of emotion in her voice.

Tears sprang to Josey's eyes. She leaned her head on Matt's shoulder as he tightened his arm around her waist.

"As you all know, our beloved son, Dean Junior, was lost to us seventeen years ago while he was proudly serving our country. Last week we were approached to take a DNA test for a young person who might possibly be DJ's child. Needless to say…it was a very long week.

It is with immense joy that we learned that the child is DJ's little girl. You can imagine the elation we felt at this news. But that joy escalated yesterday when we had the great honor of meeting this beautiful, strong young woman. The euphoria of having a part of DJ still with us skyrocketed as we visited with her and the wonderful family she had with her.

It was also a surprise to learn that she not only has the love of horses, just like her father, but she is a horse trainer for two cattle ranches in Idaho. These ranches are owned by the extraordinary family who rescued a dozen horses nearly four years ago, known as The Tagger Herd.

It was a bit disheartening to learn that two of our babies, one from Mr. Handsome and the other from Ted, were part of this herd. As terrible as it is to think of our babies going through the ordeal that they survived, it is heartwarming to learn what a wonderful family that they are a part of. Known as Scarecrow and Cooper, the family talks of them with great pride and love; we could ask for nothing more.

We look forward to the many hours, days, and every moment that we can spend with our miracle granddaughter, Josey."

Tears were rolling down Josey's face. Never in her life could she have dreamed that someone would feel about her the way her grandparents just described...a miracle.

She excused herself and stepped into the bathroom to splash cool water on her face. She sat on the edge of the tub and thought back to the spring before, after she met with Matt at the café. Her nerves were screaming when she walked into the hotel room that night by herself in the huge room. She had lain in bed in the darkness staring at the ceiling knowing that her life had changed forever. And now...it had changed again.

When she returned to the kitchen, Lucas and Nikki had joined the group around the table. Everyone was relaxed and happy as they looked over her father's items, pictures, and viewed the website of her grandparent's art.

"Josey?" Grayson leaned back in his chair and looked at her.

"What?" She smiled at her father's gold belt buckle in her hands.

"Do you know what they are doing for the holiday?" He asked.

She shook her head, "We never discussed it."

"Well, extend an invitation to join us here at the ranch." He smiled.

"Oh, yes!" Dru added. "I would love to visit with them and the kids would love to hear stories of the stallions."

Josey smiled at them, "I will, thank you."

Scott and Jessup cooked breakfast and they continued to talk of the coincidence of the horses, Hayes, and Josey's connection.

"Mate," Lucas stood and looked at Matt. "I'm taking Nikki to Spokane for a quick getaway and some Christmas shopping. The place is yours until tomorrow."

Matt just nodded and watched silently as the two left. When Josey stepped into the kitchen to put her plate in the sink he followed, "Josey, would you be interested in a dinner and movie date tonight at the premier location known as Circle 50?"

Josey laughed with an emphatic nod.

***

Her head bounced which made her eyes fly open. It was still dark outside but the moonlight shown in the windows enough she could see around the living room. She guessed that either Nikki or Lucas had turned the television off.

The last three nights, she and Matt had cuddled to watch TV but had fallen asleep in the comfort of each other's arms and the soft, comfortable couch.

Josey waited…knowing what was next. His shoulder, which she was using for a pillow, twitched again…her head bounced again. He was laying on his back with her curled into his side, facing him. The arm that twitched was under her but wrapped up around her shoulders.

His body had gone through the twitching all three nights. She didn't know what to do or why it was happening.

"She won't breathe…" Matt whispered.

Josey glanced up, his eyes were closed…he was still sleeping.

"No, he's gone." Matt mumbled under his breath and his body tensed.

It was the first time he'd spoken in his sleep. She wasn't sure what to do. Should she wake him or let him go through…whatever this was?

His leg twitched then his shoulder on the other side.

"Matt," Josey whispered.

"I can't get her to breathe." His voice still a whisper but there was anguish in the words. The tension in his body disappeared and he sunk into the mattress. "She's gone."

Tears welled in Josey's eyes. She didn't know who "she" was but his voice was so defeated.

"They are both gone." He whispered.

Josey looked into his face; it was white…tense. She needed to say something or do something.

"They are resting now," She whispered. "They won't hurt anymore, they are at peace."

His head nodded and turned to her, his arm tightened around her shoulders.

Silence…no more words…no more twitching.

Josey lay quietly watching his chest rise and fall wondering what she should do.

They both slept through the rest of the night and he made no mention of the nightmare at breakfast. She came to the conclusion that he didn't know it happened.

"So what are your plans today?" Dru asked as she slid her jacket on after breakfast.

"Christmas shopping," Josey answered as she zipped up her coat. "I haven't really even thought about it. I have lots of catching up to do."

They walked out of the Circle 50 ranch house and stood in the cold December air. Matt and Lucas were throwing hay to the horses.

"How is he doing?" Dru asked while she watched Matt.

"OK…" Josey said hesitantly. She wasn't sure she should say anything about his restless sleep. Would it be breaking Matt's trust?

Dru turned to her with a frown, "Spit it out."

Josey startled at the deep tone and stared at her. She just couldn't say it.

Dru watched her a moment then looked out at Matt and watched him smiling and joking with Lucas. Finally, she started to step down the few stairs but stopped and turned back, "Last year when he had problems because of the little girl that drowned…?"

Josey nodded when she hesitated.

"Kevin helped him." Dru looked into her eyes waiting for Josey's response.

Josey bit her lip and nodded slightly to let her know she understood.

She watched Dru walk out to the men then turned and entered the house. Nikki was in the barn doctoring a horse so she knew she was alone. Matt's phone was on the kitchen counter so she quickly picked it up and looked up Kevin's number. She hesitated…should she…? Nodding to herself she dialed the number with her phone so Matt wouldn't know.

"Hello?" Kevin answered.

"Kevin, this is Josey." She said quickly and stared out the window at the men and Dru.

"Matt's Josey?"

She smiled at the description. "Yes."

"How's he doing?"

"He needs you." She said bluntly.

"He…." Kevin paused. "Does he know you're calling me?"

"No, but he needs to talk to someone and he's not doing it with any of us. He's not sleeping well…he's been having twitching fits and talks about someone not breathing and then her being gone."

Kevin sighed heavily, "Well, I'm glad you guys have gotten that far in your relationship."

Josey's face blazed red. "Can you call him?"

"Is he free now?"

"Yes, but…"

"I understand, I won't say a word but delete the call when we hang up."

"I will."

"Thanks for calling me, Josey."

"Thanks for helping him."

The moment they hung up she deleted the call.

Matt's phone rang.

"Hello?" She answered and headed out the front door.

"Josey?" Kevin asked in surprise.

She chuckled. "Yeah, he left his phone in the house and I'm carrying it out to him now."

Matt heard the last part and frowned.

"Matt, it's Kevin." Josey smiled innocently and tried desperately to keep from looking at Dru.

Matt hesitated.

"Tell him to get his butt on the phone." Kevin said gruffly.

Josey grinned and repeated the words to Matt.

He nodded and held out a hand. After a deep sigh, he put the phone up to his ear and walked across the driveway to the tailgate of his truck. It was far enough away that they couldn't hear him.

Josey turned back to Dru and Lucas. Dru was watching Matt then turned to Josey, gave her a slight appreciative nod, and then turned to leave. "Cora is having a taco feed tonight. She wanted me to make sure you were invited."

Nikki walked out of the barn in time to wave good bye to her mother.

"I'm meeting with Jeremy for therapy and riding lessons with Rooster this afternoon." Nikki told her. "So we'll see you tonight at the Homestead?"

Josey nodded and waved as they drove off. She stood quietly looking around the property wondering what she should do. Matt's back was to her so she watched him. He nodded a lot…then shook his head…then his shoulder went up and he leaned his head down against it. Her heart froze when she realized he was wiping away tears. She turned and nearly ran into the barn.

Shakespeare and Romeo greeted her so she brushed the colts while watching Matt through the barn window. What to do when he finished? They hadn't really talked about the day. She knew Grayson wasn't expecting her so they had the whole day to themselves. How was Matt going to be after talking with Kevin? Should she approach him or wait?

She stayed in the barn for over an hour waiting. Finally he slid off the tail gate but he was still on the phone.

She'd brushed both colts and cleaned their stall; it made her relax. That's what Matt needed…equine therapy! And what better than a pair of eight month old colts? She quickly haltered the pair who pushed excitedly against each other.

Josey watched out the window and waited until his arm went down, indicating the call had ended. She quickly made her way through the big barn doors and led the two prancing colts out to him.

Matt turned; his face tense until he looked into her grinning face. He smiled, his shoulders relaxed, and she knew she did the right thing. He walked up to her but instead of taking the lead rope she offered, he put a hand on both sides of her face and tilted her lips to his. It was a gentle 'I'm so glad you're here' kiss and her heart melted for him again. He took a lead rope in one hand and slid his other hand into hers. Hand-in-hand, they walked down the snow covered road and took the colts for a walk.

***

"Josey, wake up."

She wiggled down into the warm covers and reached out for Matt…but he wasn't there. Her eyes flickered open enough to see him smiling down at her; the light blaring at her from the ceiling behind his head.

"What are you doing?" She whispered through her sleepiness…she could barely get her eyes to open. "What time is it?"

"Four O'clock." He chuckled and pulled the blankets off her. "Come on."

"What are we doing at this time of the morning?" She let him pull her off the bed.

"You'll see…here, you'll want these."

She got one eye open to see him holding out her snow pants and hooded sweatshirt. "We're going outside?"

"Yes." He chuckled again.

"Is one of the horses hurt?" The thought made her mind instantly wake and she looked at him in concern.

"No…they are fine…probably sleeping."

She put the warmer clothes on and walked out to the door where he helped her get her boots and heavy winter coat on. He shoved her warm hat on her head which made her giggle. Having a feeling he wasn't going to answer her questions, she just kept them to herself and followed him out of the house, across the snow covered road, then just down the top of the mountain.

Josey blinked twice…three times…yes, she told herself…she was seeing what she thought she was seeing.

Just inside a row of trees, he had fashioned a tarp to use as a roof to protect them from a light snowfall. It was over the top of one of the long deck chairs which was covered in pillows and blankets. He even had a small table set next to the chair that held a thermos and two coffee mugs.

She glanced at him in confusion but when she saw the excited grin on his face she just did what he asked. They sat on the chair together over the top of a thick blanket. Their legs were stretched out and entwined together and he placed the rest of the blankets over the top of them and fluffed the pillows. She cuddled into his side with his arms wrapped tightly around her.

The only thing that was chilly was the crisp air on her face.

"You felt the need to go camping on a snowy winter night?" She whispered, surprisingly warm and content.

"Just give it a few minutes." He chuckled.

From the comfort of his arms, she looked around at the snowy mountainside. The moon lit the night and reflected off the snow enough to see the distant mountains and the low cloud layer in the sky. Tree tops were dark jagged lines against the starless sky.

Then…she heard it and a chill ran down her spine. Her arms instinctively tightening around Matt who chuckled and pulled her in closer. The call was low, guttural and ended with a high pitch screech; an elk had bugled just below them. Another elk answered the call.

"How far away are they?" She whispered.

"Just down off the side; about 50 yards and moving up this way."

They spent the next two hours in each other's arms, drinking hot chocolate, watching the snow falling and listening to the elk bugle. As the sky grew lighter through the low cloud layer, the animals came into view. They were easily visible through the light snow fall. In silence and serenity, they watched the large elk herd wander the mountainside in front of them.

Josey was in country romance heaven.

CHAPTER THIRTEEN

"So you canceled a trip to the Bahamas to come here?" Wade said as he greeted Dean and Anna in the snow covered driveway of the Tagger ranch.

"Yes," Dean nodded. "I heard Idaho was as good a holiday place as the Bahamas."

Wade lifted a brow and tilted his head, "You should watch who you're talking to."

The family and new guests all laughed.

"I would have chosen the Bahamas last Christmas." Nora nodded with a grin.

"What happened last year?" Anna asked. By the look on her face she was already enjoying her visit.

"We were snowed-in for days!" She informed them with a grin.

"We shoveled and plowed for hours." Alex added while nodding.

"OK, you guys," Dru said with a welcoming smile, "Let's at least let them get ten feet from their truck before you start assaulting them with questions."

"One more?" Sadie asked quickly with a raise of the hand like she was in school.

"Alright…one more." Dru relented.

Sadie turned to the older couple and grinned, "Want to meet Scarecrow?"

"Yes!" They nearly shouted and laughed at the pleased expression it created on the teenager.

Josey's hand was grasped in Anna's as the whole family made their way through the snow and to the pasture holding the Tagger herd. Matt had even hauled over Trooper and Harvey so the whole group was together.

Anna lifted Josey's hand and looked at DJ's high school ring that was still on her thumb; the chain still wrapped around her wrist. She seemed pleased as she smiled tenderly.

They spent an hour with the kids introducing the horses before they finally made it back to help the couple carry their bags into the ranch house.

"You'll stay in my room." Josey smiled. She was thrilled they were there. They had said yes to the visit the second the invite was out of her mouth. "Jessup and Cora have rooms in here. The rest of us will be in the bunkhouse."

"We don't want to displace you." Dean said looking concerned.

"Oh, you aren't." Josey said. "I stay out in the bunkhouse when the whole family is here. Grayson would never let me stay in here when the family is out there."

"Good for him." Dean smiled. "We'll need a tour of the bunkhouse."

"Oh, you'll get it." Reilly laughed as he carried Anna's suitcase for her. "Christmas morning is out there. Cora always brings us special holiday cinnamon rolls when she and Jessup come in."

"What makes them so special?" Dean asked.

"Other than they're made on Christmas Eve?" Reilly grinned. "Cora made them."

They all chuckled as Cora gave him a hug.

"We have a special surprise for you." Alex said excitedly.

"For us?" Anna and Dean said in unison.

Alex grinned and nodded, "You only have a couple minutes to settle in then we need you out front."

"Ok," Dean said and turned to his wife. "I guess we best hurry, Anna."

"You bring them out when you hear the whistles." Alex told Josey and quickly limped out of the house.

"Happy young man, isn't he?" Anna watched Alex leave then turned to Josey.

"He is a long story…but now, he most definitely is." Josey nodded.

"So what are the whistles?" Dean asked as he returned from placing their bags in Josey's room.

"Nikki and Lucas have whistle competitions; they are ear drum shattering." Josey laughed.

The words were barely out of her mouth when the piercing sound echoed into the house.

"Oh, my!" Anna laughed.

Josey smiled and led them out of the house. The whole family, less Nick, Alex and Wade, were standing there waiting in anticipation.

"You are quite the herd out here." Dean grinned at them.

"Over here," Nikki said excitedly.

The couple moved to the spot she pointed then turned in the direction everyone was facing.

The ranch and distant mountains were covered in a new layer of snow. It lay beautifully on the trees, ground, fence tops, roof tops and over the equipment and vehicles. The snow sparkled in the morning sunshine.   The air was crisp.

"It is just spectacular up here." Dean smiled at Josey.

"I know," She said excitedly. "This is my first winter here. It's just amazing to wake up and walk out into this every morning."

"Are you ready?" Reilly bounced excitedly.

"For what?" Anna asked with a laugh at his bounce.

Reilly grinned and waved toward the barn. Nick waved back and nodded into the barn.

Nick's blue roan, Blue, elegantly walked the magnificent green and gold antique winter sleigh out of the barn. The red wreaths shone and the sound of the golden bells danced in the air.

Wade was driving this year with Alex grinning at his side.

"Oh, my…" Anna gasped.

"Magnificent!" Dean shouted at the boys.

Josey caught her breath, it was magnificent! She had seen it in the barn but they wouldn't let her see it decorated or moving until now.

Matt's hand slid into hers and he looked down at her with sparkling eyes.

"We're going for a ride…right?" She grinned.

"Oh, yeah…just the two of us." He whispered.

"Sadie?" Dean said.

"Yeah?" She answered from behind her camera as she clicked away.

"I need copies of those pictures. A blue horse pulling a green sleigh in a majestic white winter setting; it will make a spectacular painting." Dean said.

"And a bronze!" Anna added.

"Oh, cool! I saw your art on your website…it's awesome." Sadie said. "But only if I get a copy, too."

The couple laughed. "You drive a hard bargain but it's a deal." Dean said.

The sleigh came to a rest in front of them with the two boys beaming.

"Wade?" Dean said.

"What?" Wade grinned from his perch.

"You'd choose the Bahamas over this?" Dean asked with raised brow.

Wade laughed along with the entire family, "Not in a million years, Sir." He grinned. "So climb on board and I'll drive you on the loop."

"You're gonna love it!" Alex said excitedly.

After the couple made their way on the sleigh, Matt assisted Josey onto the sleigh so she could ride with them. Once set, she turned to him and held out her hand. Matt took it with a smile.

The two boys delighted the foursome with two trips around the loop.

***

Grayson and Leah were wrapped in each other's arms in front of the large window, swaying to the music. Dru and Jack were sitting on Matt's bed laughing at something Matt said to Nikki, who was at his side. Dru's hand firmly gripped Matt's. Lucas, Nick, and Tessa were playing cards with Jordan, Scott, Jessup, Kate, and Cora. Anna and Dean were at the kitchen table sitting in front of the branding books of Sadie's pictures. Alex, Reilly, Grace, Wade, Nora, and Sadie were excitedly telling them stories of the brandings.

Josey stood next to the Christmas tree filled with family-made ornaments and covering a mound of gifts. Her eyes turned to Grayson…her surrogate father; to Dru…her surrogate mother. She looked at her new grandparents, her sister, to Lucas; her future brother-in-law. Her eyes went to Grace, her best friend whose larger than life laugh was booming through the room. She looked to the rest of the kids…who considered themselves her cousins.

An overwhelming sense of emotion starting to rise making it hard to breath and causing tears to flood her eyes so she silently slid out the front door.

The night was crisp, a light snow falling from the black sky. The snow crunched under her feet and a fine spray of mist accompanied each breath she took as she made her way to the barn; to the sleigh inside. She stepped into the sleigh and pulled one of the blankets up around her legs.

How could her life change so much in one year? The tears started rolling so she lowered her face into the blanket to hide the evidence.

She didn't hear him but felt the sleigh tip to the side as he climbed inside and took a seat next to her. His arm came around her shoulders and she leaned into him as she tried to get the tears to stop.

"Little overwhelmed?" Nick asked.

She nodded into the blanket.

"But in a good way?"

She nodded again.

"Three years ago, I spent Christmas in Boise at the office designing a breeding program for bucking horses. I gave everyone the holiday off and took care of the animals for three days…by myself." He said. "Just days after that, my whole life changed."

Josey's tears finally stopped and she leaned up to look at him. He was smiling in understanding.

He relaxed back in the seat, his arm still around her for comfort. He stretched his legs out in front of him and Josey leaned her head on his shoulder.

"I didn't have normal Christmas' growing up. Two years ago, was my first Christmas and I did the same thing you just did." He looked down at her and chuckled. "I was watching you to see how long before you bolted."

Josey smiled, "Did I last longer than you expected?"

He nodded with a grin, "About what I expected."

She shook her head and sighed, "Last year I spent Christmas Eve in the older couple's house, in my little room, by myself. They were at their daughter's place for a week. I spent Christmas morning with Jamie and her family until they had to leave to go to her parent's house. I went for a walk downtown then went home and watched A Christmas Story three times in a row."

"You'll shoot your eye out," He said and they both chuckled.

"In there," She nodded in the direction of the bunkhouse. "I have a surrogate mother and father, grandparents, a brother and sister, uncles, aunts, cousins, and…Matt."

"Sounds like a family to me."

"Yeah…that's what I thought too." She sighed. "It just…I can't believe how much difference one year makes and I just got emotional and didn't want to cry in front of everyone."

"I understand."

"I didn't want for Matt to see me and think I was being weak…being Frankie again."

"Frankie's gone. Matt knows that and so does everyone else. You're just being…female." He grinned roguishly.

"And you didn't come out here two years ago and cry?" She giggled.

"Two years ago no," He looked down at her through narrowed eyes. "I will tell you something that I've never told anyone and if you repeat it I will deny it to my dying day."

"Ok…"

He paused and took a deep breath, "Three years ago, when I was standing in the Red Lion hotel room looking out at the river on New Year's day, the phone rang…" He stopped.

"I swear, I'll never say a word to anyone." Josey whispered sincerely.

"It was Matt, reaching out…asking me if I wanted to help put together the arena at The Homestead. It took all I had to keep my emotions in check while I was on the phone with him. When we hung up, I sat on the edge of the bed then slowly fell back to stare at the ceiling. I knew my whole life had changed forever…in a very good way. I had another chance with my kids." He took a shaky deep breath. "Sometimes…it's just almost too much…"

"I know…I understand. I did that last spring the night I met everyone…at the hotel." She nodded. Him sharing his story with her…it just meant everything. His trust in her was the best gift he could give her. "So what did you do two years ago when you came out here?"

"Went out and played with the horses until my nerves relaxed then went back in for a while, then slept in the ranch house."

"Equine therapy…"

"Second best to Nora therapy." He chuckled.

Josey laughed softly.

"Last year I was a bit more accustomed to it and stayed out in the bunkhouse with everyone."

"And I heard stories of an infamous barn dance out here." She smiled up at him.

He nodded with a light in his eyes, "That was fun. The most fun I had since I was riding bull and hitting bars that had a band so I could dance."

"And pick up girls."

"Well, yes…there was that." He grinned with a devilish laugh. "Oh, the stories I could tell you. It would keep us out here until morning."

Josey laughed, "I'll pass."

He tightened his arm and hugged her into him, "Better now?"

"Yes, thanks."

He stood and helped her out of the sleigh. After closing the barn door behind them, Josey looped her arm through his like Nikki always did.

"Josey," He said as they walked towards the bunkhouse; the crisp air biting at their skin and the snow crunching under their feet. "Someday I will call you my daughter…it will have the in-law after it but you will be my daughter."

She hugged his arm tightly and grinned at his confidence.

"I will give you some advice now, that I know will get you there."

"OK…"

"Don't live your life being afraid of showing Matt your true feelings; hiding any emotions from him in fear. Be open and honest, that will be what Matt sees…not weakness."

"Thanks," She whispered and just like that, she had another father in her life.

CHAPTER FOURTEEN

"What is this?" Anna asked in surprise as Sadie handed them a Christmas gift.

"It's called a present." Sadie grinned mischievously.

Anna chuckled and shook her head, "You didn't need to get us anything…just being here is gift enough."

"I know," Sadie shrugged. "But I wanted you to have this."

Anna sighed with a genuine smile at the girl then slowly opened the gift.

It was a framed picture.

"That's me and Scarecrow winning our first division championship when she was only three." Sadie said proudly. "We have a big copy of it in the hallway at home."

"Oh, Sadie," Anna looked at her with shining eyes. "It's just wonderful what you two have accomplished."

"That's not her best accomplishment." Leah said with a glisten in her eyes. "Sometime in the next couple days, we'll tell you how that wonderful palomino saved my daughter's life."

"Really?" Dean looked between her and Sadie. "We look forward to that story."

Reilly stepped forward and handed them another gift. It was a framed print of Cooper, Buttercup, Trooper, and Monty with two small grinning kids.

"And who are these two?" Anna asked.

"Their names are Amy and Adam…and Cooper helped us save their lives." Reilly said with a grin.

"And he saved Reilly." Jack added.

"Your babies grew up to be heroes." Wade said proudly.

"Oh, my. I can't wait to hear that story." Anna smiled.

"And I think that leads to our turn for gifts." Dean announced.

"You didn't need to do that." Josey said quickly.

"No, we didn't." Anna looked at her tenderly. "But we wanted to."

Matt leaned underneath his bunk to retrieve six boxes which he placed on top of Tessa's mattress since it was the closest to the front.

"We'll hand these to you but you can't open until we say so." Anna told them as Dean handed Lucas, Nikki, Matt and Josey a gift.

"We did that before!" Wade said excitedly. "And we got a new barn and an arena out of it."

Everyone in the room chuckled.

"Well, these aren't quite that extravagant." Dean laughed.

"OK, open!" Anna called out.

Josey carefully took the wrapping off her package and lifted the top of the box. She gasped in surprise just as she heard the other three call out in surprise.

"I can't believe this." Matt laughed and looked at Josey. He leaned over and looked into her box. "Just awesome."

Matt and Lucas held up bronze horse shoes. "We made these when we went over to Enterprise."

"Wow, that fast?" Dru turned to the grinning couple.

"We pulled in some favors." Anna nodded.

"What's yours Nikki?" Jordan asked.

Nikki started giggling, "I don't know if I should show you."

"Come on, Love." Lucas laughed. "It has character."

Nikki shook her head but pulled the little warped bowl out of the box.

"Oh, I love it." Dru laughed. "Lucas is right, it has character!"

"What's yours, Josey?" Tessa asked excitedly.

Josey lifted her bronze out of the box.

"OK…explain." Scott laughed.

"It's four trees," Josey smiled. "This one is Lucas because it's so tall…and then Nikki, Matt, and me."

"Trees…but they are…" Nick hesitated.

"Twisted!" The four of them laughed.

"Sounds just about right…" Grace nodded with a 'life is good' laugh.

Then Dean handed Nikki another box, it was a flat box but it was at least three by four feet. "I wasn't sure which one of you two to hand it too, but it's for you and Matt."

"Oh, Dean…Anna…the bronzes were more than enough." Nikki said in surprise.

They just smiled and shook their heads.

Matt slid over onto the bed next to Nikki. When the box was opened they both gasped. Nikki looked up in surprise as Matt reached in the box and lifted another bronze…a replica of the Circle 50 brand mounted on a dark wood base for hanging on the wall.

"Oh, that's just fantastic." Leah exclaimed.

"I want one…" Dru whined, which made everyone laugh.

Josey saw a pleased glance between Anna and Dean. He lifted the last box and walked to Grayson, who looked up in surprise.

"This is for your entire family," Anna said softly. "But we hand it to you because of the…what you have given Josey these last seven months."

Grayson nodded with a slight smile, "It's been a pleasure, she's a wonderful young lady."

Josey felt the tears rise as he turned and looked at her.

"Stop that." Grayson grumbled at her with a forced stern look.

She just giggled and leaned into Matt's arm that was comfortably around her.

Grayson held the box as Leah tore away the wrapping paper with such gusto she looked like a little kid.

Josey giggled again as Dru quickly made it to her brother's side to help open the box.

Again, a gasp and looks of awe to the box then up to the two guests. Grayson lifted a bronze of the T3E brand mounted for hanging.

"Yay!" Dru cried out happily and stood to wrap the couple in a hug. "I want to commission three more! This one goes to The Homestead…I need one for The Stables, the B&B and one for here."

"I think we can handle that." Anna laughed.

"OK, my turn." Matt said and reached under the bed again and handed Josey a big wrapped gift.

She smiled into his excited eyes. "Should I open now?"

"Yes." He laughed. "It's not one of 'those' gifts."

Josey's face flamed red. "Matt!" She rolled her eyes as the whole room laughed.

Shaking her head, she unwrapped the large box and lifted the lid. "Oh, how exciting!"

"What is it?" Nora asked and leaned over to look inside.

"It's my own climbing gear." Josey grinned at Matt as she lifted the blue and pink helmet out. "And shoes, harness, and rope!"

She turned very happy eyes to him and saw his eyes sparkle in happiness as he looked at her. He just made her heart go pitter-patter.

"My turn." She whispered to him.

"I hope it's one of 'those' gifts." He laughed.

Josey chuckled and turned red but turned a wicked grin to him, "Not in front of your parents."

The whole room laughed again. She loved that sound.

She retrieved the box from under Tessa's bed and handed it to him.

He chuckled as he unwrapped the gift and looked in the box. He turned confused, but amused eyes to her.

"What is it?" Alex and Wade shouted in anticipation.

"This is my rafting helmet," Matt said as he lifted it out of the box.

"You gave him his own helmet? That he already had?" Alex looked at her with wide eyes.

"Yes, Alex." Josey said in false seriousness. "It's much cheaper to give gifts that way."

Alex burst out laughing.

Josey giggled, "It's on the inside."

Matt flipped over the helmet and pulled out a flyer.

"What is it?" Nora and Sadie asked in unison.

"Skagit River Excursions; it's a rafting trip to go eagle viewing on the river." Matt said quietly then turned to Josey.

"I have an 'in' on a plane to get us to Seattle on Tuesday. We'll stay in their wilderness cabin and raft, fish, and eagle watch for a couple days. Plus, if the weather holds out, I can put this new gear to use with some awesome rock climbing areas." She looked at him with a very pleased smile.

He continued to stare at her; a smile slowly spreading across his face.

"I want to go on adventures and I thought maybe I would let you go on this one with me." She gave him a wicked giggle just before he tackled her right off the top of the bed. By the time they hit the floor, his lips were on hers and the bunkhouse was full of laughter.

THE TAGGER HERD

SERIES

REILLY MORGAN

Arenas and Corrals

Gini Roberge

CHAPTER ONE
Monday and Tuesday Expo Week

"WSU, U of I, or Montana?" Reilly asked Grace for the hundredth time.

"I don't know. Levi hasn't said what he's doing yet."

"This is about our future not his, Grace." He looked over at her as she drove her truck, Trail Boss, down The Homestead driveway. "We're supposed to be doing what's best for us; best for your future business."

"Not so much future," Grace grinned. "This is the week we sell our first project horse. Plus, Dr. Mark is selling our first client horse."

"You've just made my point," Reilly smirked.

"I know, but I really would like to know what Levi's doing too."

"Grace…"

"I know, I know…" She sighed and parked her truck. "Which do you want?"

"Since I really don't know what I want to do yet, and will only be working on the required classes, it doesn't matter to me."

They stepped out of the truck in unison and shut the doors in unison. Just like every day after school they met at the back of the truck and walked to the back of the house together. He always walked up the steps first so he could open the door for her. At his dad's insistence he treated all females with respect, which he liked to do anyway.

As part of their routine, Cora was placing their bowls of bananas and peanut butter on the small kitchen table.

"These days are numbered," Cora sighed wistfully.

The two, soon to be high school graduates, hugged her before sitting at the table.

"With the Expo every night this week and spring break next week, we only have five or six weeks left before graduation." Grace nodded.

"So twenty or thirty more bowls remaining…" Reilly sighed and hugged the older woman again.

"I hate change," Grace mumbled.

"Remember," Reilly grinned at her. "Change is what brought me here to The Homestead to haunt your every waking moment."

"Yeah…yeah…" Grace chuckled. "But this is different. Instead of bringing us together this change takes us away."

"You'll have fun…an adventure before you settle down in life and work." Cora said cheerfully then changed the subject. "What's on the agenda tonight?"

"Nikki should be here anytime with Mustang and Dr. Mark's horse." Grace answered. "Last week, she filmed us doing different things with the two horses and last night she and I created a marketing video for both of them. She posted them to the official sales website just a little while ago."

"Well, let's go take a look." Cora said and they walked to the library computers.

The first video was Dr. Mark's bay horse right after the auction where he was purchased. Sadie was in the video and explained what was wrong with his hoof. She demonstrated by making him trot away from the camera; the slight limp was visible. She explained the surgery that Dr. Mark and her parents had let her view then they let him recuperate for a month. She told the camera she had designed an exercise program for the bay that changed each week as his hoof improved.

Nikki appeared on the video and explained what feed supplement program she designed for the horse and why. This included the diet during the horse's recovery time and the diet once exercise was introduced to his program.

Then it was Nora's turn as she rode him and put the horse through all the basic training moves. He responded quickly to everything she asked.

Grace was the last on the video and was shown riding him up and down the mountains at the ranch, through creeks, around cattle, and roping off him in the corrals. The final shot was Sadie trotting him away from the camera showing there was no issue with his stride.

"That's fantastic." Cora nodded impressed. "I'd buy him after seeing that video."

"You have more than a dozen to choose from." Reilly laughed.

"IF I was looking…" Cora grinned.

"Just look as far as the barn." Grace giggled and started the next video.

It started with a close up view of the mustang named Mustang before they cleaned the mass of cockleburs out of the horse's mane and tail. Sadie then spoke of his history of being a captured wild mustang as a baby then adopted. After initial training, his owner had become ill and he remained unused in the fields for three years. She pointed out his weight loss, his physical condition and explained the exercise program she designed to help him build muscle, but not lose the needed body fat.

Then the camera focused on the doors of the barn at the Tagger ranch. The doors opened slowly and Sadie appeared out of the dark barn walking the large brown horse toward the camera. The first thing noticeable was the black, extra-long, full mane and flowing tail; then was the significant increase in the horse's weight and the amount of muscle the horse had gained. His new conformation was tremendous. Even with the power his new physique demonstrated, he walked calmly at her side.

Nikki explained the feeding program had changed over the months to compliment the exercise program. At first to put on weight, then to help the horse with his more intense training.

Nora put him through the basic training moves, then she surprised everyone with a full reining pattern on him. It wasn't perfect, but he was willing to do it all.

There was a short section showing the first endurance ride with Josey riding Cooper. The video then cut to the second ride just weeks before where he cut his time by twelve minutes on the same trail.

Grace repeated her demonstration up and down the mountain, through creeks, cows, and roping in the corrals. He was a beautiful horse to watch running across the range with the mountains as a backdrop. His lean conformation highlighted each muscle as he moved and the long mane and tail flowed around him like black silk.

The video came to an end with all four Tagger girls giving the horse a very foamy bath and the gelding biting at the water from the hose. It was quite obvious that horse and owners were enjoying themselves.

"Sold!" Cora called out. "That was fantastic. You and Nikki did excellent!"

"They did!" Reilly nodded. "I played it for everyone at school. A few were headed home to try and talk their parents into buying him."

Grace nodded, "I'm riding him in team roping tomorrow, Sadie's got barrels on him Wednesday, Nikki is doing the team penning on Thursday, and finally Nora will show him at the pre-sale show on Saturday. The auction is on Sunday before we leave to the ranch for branding week."

"What about Friday?" Cora asked.

"I'm riding my first bull!" Reilly reminded them excitedly.

He had finally gained the courage to ask his parents if he could ride a bull and was shocked when they both said yes without hesitation. Dru later told him they were expecting it and had talked it over between themselves and Nick who had ridden bulls for years. The only condition was that he had to have training, which Nick would be handling. Reilly was overjoyed. He trusted Nick more than anyone else to teach him to ride.

They spent the last three weekends at the stock contracting business in Boise that Nick worked for. They trained him on all the equipment, how to research a bull's history, judge the bull, and how to dismount safely…if possible. Reilly started riding smaller bulls that didn't buck very hard and moved up to more experienced bucking bulls that were used at high school rodeos. He didn't ride the elite bucking bulls they used at the professional rodeos. He needed more training and experience before he could ride them.

Every spare minute Reilly had he was watching videos on riding bulls. Friday was the first time any of the family would see him ride.

"I think I'll need a horse tranquilizer to be able to watch you." Cora chuckled nervously.

"I can't wait." Grace grinned.

"You just want to see me get bucked off." Reilly chuckled.

"I just want to see you do something you've wanted to do for years." Grace corrected him.

"We leave for branding right after the sale on Sunday," Cora said. With a glint in her eye she smiled at Reilly. "Hopefully, you're not broken and bruised too bad you can't help brand and ride all week."

"I won't be…it's only one ride. I did more than that with Nick in training and I'm alright…just sore." Reilly laughed. "Nick's taught me well."

"So if you do well, we'll congratulate Nick." Grace teased.

They heard the sound of a truck passing by the dining room window.

"That's Nikki!" Grace said excitedly.

They took their bowls to the sink and followed Cora out the door. Matt and Josey had also arrived in Josey's new yellow Jeep Sahara.

Surprisingly, Nora and Sadie very happily crawled out of Nikki's truck. "We just got off the bus as Nikki got here so she gave us a ride up the driveway." Sadie explained. Her and Nora's eyes were lit with excitement of the upcoming two weeks.

Nora turned to Josey, "I LOVE your Jeep!"

"Me too!" Josey and Matt said in unison and they all laughed.

Wade, with Alex in tow, arrived by bus a half hour later.

They spent the evening grooming all the horses and cleaning tack in preparation for the long week at the expo followed by the week of branding at the ranch.

******

Reilly stepped out of the horse trailer and shut the gate behind him. Dollar, Buttercup, Snickers, Mustang, and Rufio were loaded and ready for the drive to the arena for the first night of the expo. He passed Sadie as he was heading into the barn. Her hair was in the braid down her back. She was wearing her black cowboy hat and a bright blue jacket that made her blue eyes brighter.

"I could barely concentrate at school today after Nikki posted those videos." She grinned.

"Me too," He nodded. "It's gonna be terrible all week."

He stepped into the tack room to retrieve Rufio's extra boots. When he stepped out, Sadie was standing at the door of the barn looking out into the driveway. He stepped in behind her to see what she was looking at.

Levi's red truck was slowly making its way down the driveway to park next to Reilly's truck. Wade, Alex, Nick, Grayson, Scott, and Nikki were all standing in the driveway nodding a welcome to him.

"What?" Reilly asked Sadie in a near whisper.

"Watch Grace."

Reilly looked at the group again, "I don't see her."

"She's in the kitchen window."

She was standing and staring with a blank expression as she watched Levi exit the truck and greet the group in the driveway.

"She's not doing anything." Reilly said.

"Exactly," Sadie nodded. "Watch Levi…"

Reilly turned his attention to Levi. He was grinning and shaking hands with everyone. Laughter rang out. He looked relaxed, happy, and comfortable in his surroundings. Reilly looked back to Grace but barely caught a glance of her before she disappeared from view.

She reappeared through the back door in her boots and jeans, with a sparkling red shirt that was mostly covered by her official royalty jacket. She was placing a black hat adorned with her queen crown over her dark blonde hair that was now flowing down her back in large curls. Even though she was team roping with him on Buttercup and with Mustang, she was also representing the Lewiston Roundup rodeo through the week. The next Saturday night was her official queen coronation at the Horseman's Ball. She smiled at the group of people in the driveway.

Levi turned to her, his grin melting to a smile and his back straightened making his shoulders raise. He looked…Reilly wasn't sure but he wasn't relaxed anymore. If Sadie hadn't pointed it out to him though he wouldn't have noticed.

"Egg shells…" Sadie whispered and walked out to join the group.

Reilly hesitated as he watched Grace walk up next to Levi. Their hands entwined but it seemed automatic.

His attention was drawn from them to Nora and Candace walking out of the back of the house. Their grins wide and sparkling as much as the crowns on their black hats. Jordan and Leah had spent the last hour styling the hair of Grace as well as Nora and

Candace who were the queen and princess of the Northwest Youth Rodeo Association. Their hair was long and curly down their backs.

Deciding to put aside the actions between Levi and Grace, Reilly stepped out of the barn and toward the group.

Fifteen minutes later, they were stepping out of the truck at the rodeo grounds. There weren't a lot of people in the stands watching but there was a large amount of teams entered. He was riding twice with Grace and Buttercup, then twice with Grace and Mustang, then they would draw with mixed teams. Wade and Alex were riding together twice then they would ride with a mixed team. Levi was riding with one of his rodeo teammates from school.

Levi's black and white paint horse was already saddled so he rode into the indoor arena to warm up. Wade was the next in the arena followed by Grace on Buttercup and Sadie riding Mustang to warm him up too. The rest of the family had already entered the building.

Alex leaned against the horse trailer and stared at the ground. His bay horse's head was up watching the rest of the competitors preparing for the competition.

"What's up?" Reilly walked Rufio over to the thirteen-year-old.

Alex lifted worried eyes to him.

"Buttercup," He mumbled.

Reilly chuckled, that had become so automatic for everyone in their family.

"What's wrong?"

Alex took a deep breath, "I'm not good at roping and Wade is really patient with me."

"You're just not as experienced…you'll get there."

"I don't know…" Alex sighed, "It's just that I don't mind roping with Wade and you guys, but here, in front of everyone?"

"You've competed in front of other people before."

"Badly…I've never caught one in competition," Alex sighed again. "This is my first jackpot. I've only competed against kids my age not adults."

"Alex, everyone here has been a beginning roper, they all understand."

He lifted a defeated shoulder and stood to climb the mounting block and slide on his horse, Snickers. Most people in attendance would never know he limped.

"Not even all the experienced riders catch all the time…they miss too. Just ride for fun. Enjoy the night." Reilly stepped into the stirrup and up onto Rufio. "It'll be exciting to see how Grace and Mustang do."

Alex's shoulders relaxed. "Thanks, Reilly."

They entered the building just as Wade and Dollar rode by. They joined the group warming up by riding around the parameter of the dirt covered floor. The March evening was just chilly enough for coats and they had closed the outside doors to cut back on the wind.

Grayson and Scott were helping with the steer and chutes for the night. The rest of the family was huddled together on the bleachers on the north wall.

"Nora has been bringing Mustang to play nights here to get him used to the speakers," Wade said.

Reilly nodded. The horse had frozen and refused to move at the auction when he became confused by the auctioneer's voice coming from the speakers. They looked across the arena to see the two Tagger sisters riding side-by-side. The brown mustang and the cream colored quarter horse looked good together.

"They're going to do some practice runs. Do you want to do one?" Wade asked Alex.

Reilly glanced at Alex who shrugged.

"Might as well get as many throws in as we can," Alex nodded.

Reilly watched them ride away then turned his attention back to Grace. She had glanced over to Levi a few times but they were on the opposite side of the arena.

She turned her head to Sadie who was grinning and talking. Grace's 'life is good' laugh echoed throughout the building. Sadie's laugh followed and between the two, Reilly relaxed.

The announcer's voice boomed, "Let's have everyone move to the end of the arena and we'll get the practice runs going."

Grayson was standing at the chutes talking to Alex.

"Watch your rein length," Grayson said. "Keep your swing open."

Alex nodded.

"Snickers knows what he's doing so you concentrate on you this time." Grayson added. "Forget about everything and everyone else."

Again, Alex just nodded.

"You've caught dozens of steer in this building, out of that chute, when we're here for practice." Grayson reminded him. "You can do this. Just don't put so much pressure on yourself."

Alex took in a deep breath and sighed. "I'll try."

"You have to get past the 'I'll try' and get to the point you say, 'I will'," Grayson said.

Alex looked at his coach with a grimace. Grayson nodded, patted his leg and walked to the fence and out of the way.

Reilly moved Rufio against the fence next to Grace, Sadie, and Levi. He crossed his fingers as Alex backed Snickers into the box. Wade backed Dollar into the box and kept his eyes on Alex. Once Alex bounced his rope to relax his shoulders, Wade nodded and the chute was opened.

Metal clanking, horse's hooves pounding, whirl of ropes flying, and the Tagger crowd shouting; Reilly held his breath.

Wade's rope danced around the horns and he turned Dollar as he dallied. The rope pulled tight and turned the steer to give Alex access to the back legs. Alex's rope swinging…and the throw…the rope slid just above the ground and under the steer as Snickers put on the brakes and Alex pulled. The rope tightened and one back leg lifted from the ground. The Tagger crowd cheered!

Wade pumped a fist in the air and Alex grinned anxiously.

"Way to go!" Reilly high-fived Wade as he rode up next to him.

Alex rode behind them and to his grinning coach.

"Atta, Boy!" Grayson shook the excited Alex's hand.

Wade leaned over to Reilly and whispered, "Uncle Grayson told me to watch Alex and go as soon as he relaxed his shoulder. That way he didn't think about it too much."

Reilly nodded, "It worked this time but it was still just practice."

Maybe now Alex would be able to relax in front of everyone, Reilly hoped. But he and Grace would ride first.

The competition began; Reilly and Grace backed Buttercup and Rufio into the boxes.

"Ready?" Grace grinned over at him.

"Always."

Reilly watched Grace, she nodded, chute opened and they took off. The steer ran dead straight but he was fast. Grace kicked Buttercup faster and had to lean forward more to stretch the rope out. It barely tipped over the horns, Grace yanked to tighten the loop…then she was turning and twisting the rope as fast as she could to dally around the saddle horn.

Reilly's rope was whirling over his head. Rufio moved to the right so he quickly moved him back then let the rope fly. It swirled around the steer's hooves to set the trap and he slid to a stop. Both hooves rose in the air and the flag was dropped.

"That was a close one," Grace laughed as they trotted over to retrieve their ropes.

Levi and his teammate rode next and beat their time by two full seconds.

"Our steer was faster!" Grace teased her boyfriend as she and Sadie traded horses.

"And you did a great job catching him…but we were still faster…and that's what brings home the money!" Levi laughed.

The ease of Levi and Grace's relationship returned for the evening.

The announcer's voice boomed and Mustang's head rose and looked around.

"Ladies and gentlemen; the next horse up is Mustang the mustang, one of the horses up for auction Sunday. If you haven't seen the video on this horse yet take some time to take a look. Tonight, he is ridden by Grace Tagger, this year's Lewiston Roundup Queen, and a very good horsewoman as you've seen already tonight with her first run on her quarter horse Buttercup."

Grace nudged the brown horse toward the roping box and he moved with ease. They had practiced with him at the Homestead arena as well as this one. He wasn't perfect but he still did as Grace asked.

Reilly looked down at the steer they drew. Luckily it wasn't the fast one they had the first time.

He bounced his rope, backed Rufio into the corner, then tucked the rope under his arm and waited for Grace.

Mustang pranced anxiously so Grace walked him out of the box then brought him back in. Scott took his bridle and helped back him into the box then moved out of the way quickly.

Grace nodded, chute opened, steer and horses bolted. Mustang stayed up with the steer but moved to the left too far leaving Grace another long throw to reach the steer…the rope nestled around the horns. Reilly threw and barely had enough space to catch the back hooves…but he did and dallied quickly. He was so close to the steer, he had to back up Rufio to get the steer to stretch enough for the judge to drop the flag.

"Not bad for a mustang only having a couple months of training," The announcer said. "You'll have a chance to see this auction horse tomorrow night running barrels then Thursday night in team penning. He'll also be featured Saturday in the auction preview. He did a fine job tonight."

Grace and Sadie high-fived before switching horses.

Sadie excitedly stretched down the mustang's neck with both hands to congratulate him.

Wade and Alex were announced and trotted towards the box. Alex's shoulders were up as he glanced around at all the people.

"One down already," Reilly yelled out. Alex nodded slightly.

Horses ready, Wade nodded and the chute opened. Wade hit his mark and turned the steer, Alex threw and the rope bounced off the back of the steer's legs. His disappointment was clearly visible.

Nearly every competitor said something to him:

"You'll get it next time."

"I missed my first one too…nerves…"

"Good try!"

"He turned a bit on ya."

"I'm gonna blame my rope."

Alex chuckled on that one.

Mustang's second try took a second longer than the first but everyone was pleased with his efforts and composure.

Alex missed his second run with Wade.

He trotted up next to Reilly with a shake of the head, "I think Wade and Grayson are going to give up on me."

"Never…you'll get it, Alex." Reilly encouraged him. "Want to do a draw round with me?"

Alex glared at him, "I was going to go put Snickers in the trailer."

Reilly sighed in disappointment, "Alex…"

Alex held up a hand, "I'm not going to quit trying. I was only going to do the draw if someone asked me to."

Six riders asked Alex to team with him and he caught one back leg. Every rider encouraged him to continue trying.

Grace and Levi teamed together and took third place overall and won enough to pay back their entry fees. They were relaxed and seemed happy together.

Reilly and Wade teamed together and took fourth place and took home a check too.

Overall, it was a good night with the entire family having fun.

It was a good way to start the Expo week that was leading them to branding week.

CHAPTER TWO
Wednesday Expo

TEXT TO GRACE: Almost there, just getting back from running supplies to Jessup

TEXT TO REILLY: We just arrived at arena

Twenty minutes later, Reilly walked into the indoor arena and looked around for the mustang and Tagger girls. They were standing just in front of the cattle chute at the far side of the indoor arena. To his right was the arena with the three barrels in place for the race. To his left was the food wagon followed by three bleacher sections for the bystanders and, on the last day, would be for the buyers at the auction.

Deciding to sit mid-arena he took a seat on the end of the middle bleacher section and waited for Billy, Levi, Wade and Alex to join him to watch the girls compete. There were only a few people behind him but they were up higher on the bleacher. Two bleacher rows were below him and three teenage cowboys quickly took a position on those.

Reilly turned and looked down to the west door opening in time to see his parents walk through. He couldn't help but smile at how perfect and comfortable they looked together. Dru's hair was down around her shoulders just the way he and his dad liked it. It was held in place by her black cowboy that matched his dad's. They wore matching black western jackets with the T3E logo on them and it stopped at her waist. The jeans she wore accented her long legs. His dad wore a white shirt underneath and Dru had a light blue shirt that made her eyes 'pop'. She was just beautiful, Reilly thought.

"I like that one." Reilly heard one of the teenagers in front of him.

"Which one? They are all standing together." Another said.

"The one with blonde curly hair, she has her back turned to us." The middle kid said.

"Nice…but I like the tall blonde in the blue jacket." The kid on the left said. "She must be the oldest…looks like she's sixteen at least."

If Reilly had any doubt who they were talking about it became perfectly clear with the next statement.

"Nah…it's the little Indian girl with the crown. She must be a queen of something." The kid on the right said. "She looks…exotic."

Reilly still had his head turned toward his parents but closed his eyes tightly and took a deep breath to quell the sudden uneasiness in his stomach.

"Look at the one that just got there though…she has got to be related to the other tall blonde." Left teenager said. "I'd like either of them."

All three boys chuckled. Reilly's stomach turned and he opened his eyes to stare out the doors of the building. Other than Grace, whom all his friends at school had made comments about, he wasn't used to thinking of Nora, Sadie, and Candace as anything other than family.

"I wonder if they have boyfriends." Right teenager whispered.

"I think I know the one with the braid," The left one said. "She rides a palomino."

"But that's a brown horse she's holding onto," The right teenager said.

"So? Maybe she has more than one," The left one argued. "Her name is Sadie Tagger."

"Oh…yeah…the little Indian girl is Nora Tagger," The middle teenager nodded. "But who's the curly…oh look she has a crown too!"

The right teenager nodded. "I think I saw the other blonde's picture in the paper. That's Grace Tagger. She's the queen for the Roundup this year. See, she has a crown too."

"Three out of four have crowns," The middle one chuckled. "Boy, don't we know how to pick 'em?"

"Yeah, but the braid one ain't slackin' just because she doesn't have a crown." The left one added. "I'd take her any day."

Take her? Reilly cringed. She was only thirteen! Even though they thought she was sixteen…that was just…stomach clenching.

"Look at that lady!" The right teenager gasped.

"That's gotta be Sadie's mom." One of them said.

Reilly's eyes looked for Dru…even though she was Sadie's aunt and not her mom, there wasn't any doubt they were talking about her. He turned and looked out at the arena to see she had walked through and was almost to the girls.

"Wow!" The middle teenager exhaled. "I'd marry her in a second!"

Reilly's eyes nearly rolled into the back of his head as he stood and walked away from them. It was bad enough to hear things about the girls…but his mom? He sat back down at the far end of the bleachers so he couldn't hear them.

"What's wrong?" His dad asked as he stepped up the bleacher to sit next to him.

"What?"

"You look ill."

"I think I am."

"You were fine at home."

"Yeah…it's not that kind of ill." Reilly exhaled and glared at the three teenagers still looking at the girls.

"Well…back to the original question…what's wrong?" His dad asked.

"I just got a rude awakening." He sighed and looked out at Grace, Sadie, Nora, and Candace. They were laughing and talking with his mom. He nodded towards the teenagers. "I just heard those boys talking about the girls, it made me realize that they aren't just my cousins and family…that they're…"

His dad had followed his gaze, "Young women?"

Reilly shook his head, "Don't say it that way."

His dad chuckled, "How do you want me to say it?"

Reilly looked back down at the teenagers who had stood from the bleachers and were leaning against the fence panel close to their targets.

"They weren't rude were they?" His dad asked.

"Not really…but…they probably aren't the only ones talking."

"I'm sure they aren't."

Reilly thought of Billy and Nora. Even though he knew they liked each other and had witnessed their first kiss, he still didn't think of Nora like that.

"What do I do? How do I handle it?" Reilly sighed.

"Just watch out for them without trying to control them," His dad nodded in understanding. "It was the same thing we had to do with Nikki when she got that age. She and the rest of the girls were raised to have respect for themselves and others. That goes a long way."

Again, Reilly thought of Nora. She made the decision to not be alone with Billy. They both had big dreams and she was too young. Nora had made the right decision and he had no doubt that Sadie and Candice would do the same.

"I'm not gonna lie," His dad said. "It's tough watching the girls become women. Heck, it's tough watching you become a man. In a way, I want you to stay my little boy."

Reilly grinned, his heart warm, "I will always be your little boy…even when I'm thirty and two hundred pounds."

They laughed. He loved these moments with his dad even if he'd never tell anyone…except maybe Grace.

"I'm going to go drag Dru out of the arena or she'll never leave it."

His dad stood and stepped down from the bleachers. Reilly glanced at the three boys that were still staring at the group of girls and Dru.

"Do me a favor."

"What?" His dad turned back and his blue eyes seemed to beam from under his black cowboy hat.

"Go kiss mom…a really good kiss." Reilly grinned at his dad.

His dad laughed causing his dimples to deepen. "You want me to go 'mark' my territory?"

"Of course," Reilly laughed. "I can't do it with the girls…so you have to do it with Mom."

"Oh, Reilly." His dad just walked away chuckling.

Reilly reached for his phone.

Text to Dru: When Dad reaches you, kiss him

He lifted his head away from the phone and watched her lift her phone out of her pocket and read the message. Her head raised and she looked around. When their eyes connected her head tilted in question. She typed…

Text to Reilly: Why?

Text to Dru: Just this once, just do it, a really good kiss, trust me

She read the message and looked back at him. She turned and looked at her husband approaching, then turned back to Reilly and smiled.

Taking her hat off and handing it to Grace, she met her husband part way and placed a hand on each side of his face and kissed him…a long kiss.

Reilly turned to the three teenagers. They were all nodding and grinning. He rolled his eyes then looked back at his parents as the kiss ended.

Dru was grinning at his dad who was shaking his head while he spoke. She nodded and his arms moved around her waist and shoulders and he dipped her nearly to the ground for a spectacular movie kiss. The girls started laughing and everyone around them started hollering.

When his dad lifted her back up, they laughed at each other then turned to Reilly. He grinned at them, his heart soring…they were just epic.

"What was that all about?" Billy laughed as he stepped up the bleachers and took a seat next to him. The teenager was a linebacker on the high school football team and had the size to match. He had to be at least 6' 2" and over 200 pounds.

Levi, Wade and Alex sat just below them.

"Just showing the love," Reilly grinned.

"How soon before they start riding?" Alex asked.

"It starts at 6:00," Wade answered. "Sadie said there are over 60 riders and the Pee Wee group goes first."

"Fifteen minutes riders," The voice from the announcer's booth vibrated through the room. "Double check your riding order so we can make sure everything goes as smooth as possible and we're not here until mid-night. Riders come in from the south gate and exit from the north gate to keep it flowing with no collisions."

Reilly turned in time to see Nora and Candace walk behind the three teenage boys who turned and watched them walk away. Nora didn't seem to notice them, her eyes were on Billy. Candace was waving at Alex and Wade.

"Scoot," Reilly told Billy and nodded to the girls. "So they can sit between us."

Billy gave Reilly a very bland 'OK' look hiding the look of appreciation he knew he really wanted to give him.

Wade and Alex moved and the two girls climbed the bleachers with Candace sitting next to Reilly and Nora between her and Billy. Nora's eyes flickered to Reilly and she smiled slightly. Wade and Alex moved back in front of the two girls.

Reilly couldn't help himself; he snuck a look down at the three teenagers. They were looking at the girls who were now surrounded by five teenage boys, one of which looked like a mountain. They were well protected. Reilly smiled inside.

He heard a familiar laugh next to him and turned to see his dad grinning at him from the edge of the bleacher. Reilly returned the grin with a slight shrug.

Within minutes, all the Tagger family was sitting around Reilly and the bleachers filled with the barrel racers family and friends as they waited for the race to start.

"What number are the girls?" Grayson asked.

"Sadie is 5 with Scarecrow and 31 with Mustang. Grace is 11, Marla is 22, and Josey is 45." Jordan answered.

"Kinda spread out." Scott mumbled.

"OK, everyone!" The announcer called out. "Welcome to the Wednesday night running of barrels at the Lewiston Equine Expo! We're glad…"

Reilly shifted his gaze down to see Sadie and Scarecrow were waiting at the back of the group of horse and riders. Her hands were deep in her pockets and she was slumped back in the saddle as she spoke with one of her friends. His eyes went back down to the three teenagers then he looked back at Sadie as if through their eyes.

Being honest, she did look older than thirteen, but it wasn't just her height. It was something else…it was…confidence. She had an air of confidence about her that radiated maturity. It wasn't a cocky confidence, it was a 'comfortable with who she was and what she wanted' confidence. Luckily, she hadn't started wearing makeup yet but she was still a beautiful girl that always stood out in the crowd.

The confidence and the looks made her stand out…but then there was the temper.

His thoughts went to Candace who was sitting just to the left of him. When she first came to live with them, she was shy and would barely leave Nora and Nikki's sides. The longer she spent with the Taggers, the more confident Candace became. Once she went to live with her aunt he would only see her every couple weeks. She gained a little weight which got her back to a healthy weight since she had been so skinny. Her hair grew longer and her brown eyes seemed happy. When she came back from winning a place on the royalty court, her whole personality became 'bigger'. She had always been cute, but the confidence and happiness that was growing in her completed the whole girl.

Nora once asked him if she was pretty and it had shocked him. How could she not have known she was pretty? Nora had a unique look. Long black hair, high cheek bones, and almond shaped eyes. Was he the only one that noticed how thick and long her eye lashes were? She looked like she was wearing makeup when she wasn't. She wasn't just pretty, she was beautiful. It was because of that same confidence that Sadie had.

Nikki had that confidence too and, in his eyes, she was one of the most beautiful women he'd ever seen. Then there was her sister Josey. His mind was startled back to reality when Josey joined the family on the bleachers; she had a long time to wait for her run.

There were six pee wee girls to start the evening and the first one entered the arena to a round of applause. They all laughed and cheered the happy five year old who trotted a pretty white horse around the clover leaf pattern. The others came in and round the barrels with determination.

Then the open competition started and the first four riders were in and out quick with solid rides.

"Go get 'em, Pip Squeak!" Josey yelled causing Sadie to laugh as she and the palomino entered the arena.

Sadie trotted back and forth while staring at the barrels. She let Scarecrow go and they flew to the first barrel. The angle was good, the turn tight without a hesitation as the horse dug in and headed for the second barrel. Sadie shifted in her seat and by the time she was half-way around the turn both horse and rider were looking and aiming for the third barrel. The entire Tagger group stood to cheer her on.

Scarecrow fed off the yelling and after the sharp 'couldn't be closer to the barrel' turn she dug in and became a race horse to the end with the jockey riding high on her neck. Under her black cowboy hat, Sadie was grinning wide as she crossed the line. They had to make a sharp turn to keep from running into the fence.

"Dang that girl!" Leah cheered proudly.

"That was a 15.12, nice run Sadie." The announcer called out. "Next we have…"

"That looked fast." Billy looked down at Nora, "Was that good?"

Nora laughed, "I think that's her best run in this arena."

"Cool," Billy said excitedly. "This isn't as bad as I thought it was going to be."

"Scarecrow is just getting stronger and faster," Grayson added. "They'll just get better and better."

"You know she'll want to be under 15.0 at some point." Scott laughed.

"Well, she won't get it on Mustang, but the day will come with Scarecrow." Jordan nodded.

"Do you think Grace and Buttercup can beat the golden girls' time?" Cora asked.

Josey shook her head, "No, their turns are both really good but Buttercup isn't as fast as Scarecrow on the homestretch. Scarecrow's turns were near perfect tonight. I doubt any of our group will match her."

"Not even you and Apollo?" Matt asked in surprise.

Josey chuckled, "In Apollo's prime, we would have been neck and neck with her, but Apollo is eighteen and slowing down. I've started him on glucosamine supplements to help with his joints but that will never replace his speed."

The next runners came and went. Grace trotted into the back of the building and Reilly glanced at Levi; he was staring at her with a lost expression.

"Next up, Grace Tagger," The announcer called.

The whole Tagger group started cheering and a big grin spread across Grace's face and Buttercup pranced.

They took off toward the first barrel with Grace kicking wildly. The first turn was good, the second better, and the third near perfect but the final run to victory was obviously slower than Scarecrow's…15.82.

"So the horse you have really makes a difference?" Billy looked down at Nora.

She nodded, "You need a horse that loves to run…that's Scarecrow. She has Dash for Cash in her bloodlines which is one of the top lines for barrel horses. Mr. Handsome, her sire, has Poco Bueno in his bloodlines…that's a real good one too…they have heart."

"Plus you can see Scarecrow has a great form as she comes around the barrels and she always looks for the next one," Josey said. "She has a body and MIND for barrels, not just the speed."

"You have a racer and horse with the desire, determination, and talent that Sadie and Scarecrow share…that's a true team and they win." Candace added.

"Especially now in her division," Josey added. "As she gets older they will be competing with other teams that are closer to their talent and she'll have a tougher time."

"If they stay healthy, and continue to mature like they are, Sadie wants to make a run for the NFR," Wade told him proudly.

"That's the Super Bowl of rodeo…right?" Billy asked and received a dozen nods in return.

"Here comes, Marla," Josey said. They watched the brunette, with the wide brown hat, make her way into the arena on her tall bay gelding and immediately bolt for the first barrel. The angle was close on the first barrel and it tipped but didn't fall. The second barrel was good and the last turn around the final barrel tight…final run for victory…15.83.

"So close to Grace." Leah exhaled. "Those two are neck and neck at each race."

"So what do you think you'll run?" Billy asked Josey.

Josey shrugged, "I just run for the fun of it…to enjoy Apollo at this point."

"Relive the glory days?" Billy nodded with a knowing smile.

"Something like that," Josey answered. "I love everything about that horse…most of all that he's mine again." She wrapped her arm around Matt's and grinned at him. Matt leaned down for a swift kiss and to return her smile.

Reilly turned away from them and watched the next few horses complete the clover leaf pattern. Josey and Matt had been officially together since December; Levi and Grace since October. There was clear affection and emotion between Matt and Josey…not so much with Grace and Levi.

Reilly felt a hand on his leg and turned to see Marla smiling up at him as she stood next to the bleacher. Her brown hair was loose and hung just past her shoulders and her blue eyes looked happy and excited.

"Good run." He smiled while Levi, Alex, and Wade shifted so Marla could sit on the bleacher right in front of Reilly.

She leaned back into his legs and twisted to say 'hi' to everyone and accept their friendly comments. Then she turned and smiled up at Reilly.

"Sadie is so excited!" Marla told everyone. "Grace will be here before they run."

"I'll have to leave as soon as she's finished." Josey nodded.

"What is your horse's name?" Billy asked Marla.

"I thought you knew that Billy." Marla teased. "We've known each other since 6th grade."

Billy shook his head with a smile, "I've known you…not your horse."

"His name is Ricky." Nora answered quietly.

Reilly glanced at Nora; she was watching a horse and rider run with no expression.   She was good, he had no doubt she was jealous of the friendship between Billy and Marla.

"There's Sadie and Mustang!" Jordan announced and pointed.

The whole group turned to the large opening. Sadie, on the brown horse, was just inside of the building's large doors and trotting him in circles.

"I'm so excited." Nikki said from right behind Nora.

"Let me up!" Grace hollered from next to the bleacher.

Reilly and Marla stood and helped pull her up onto the bleacher. She excitedly wiggled past them and took a seat between Nora and Candace.

Nikki leaned forward and placed a hand over Nora and Grace's shoulder and her cousins quickly grasped the hands.

Grace had smiled at Levi and he returned the smile. Since she was in her royalty coat and hat with crown they didn't hold hands but the look still wasn't overly emotional. Marla leaned back into his legs again. That small move showed more emotion between them then Grace and Levi were showing. Reilly and Marla had moved back to the friendship mode…they weren't even a couple.

The announcer interrupted Reilly's thoughts.

"Next rider up is Sadie Tagger on Mustang. Sadie was our fifth rider on her palomino and is still our leader. She's now on the mustang that she and her cousins purchased at the livestock auction in October. Grace Tagger rode him last night in the team roping and he did a pretty good job for her. He can be seen again tomorrow night when Nikki Tagger rides him in team penning. And of course, there's Nora Tagger going to ride him Saturday in the sale preview.

"If you haven't seen the video the Tagger girls put together on this horse you need to check it out. He is up for sale this coming Sunday and he has quickly garnered a lot of attention. Come see the preview Saturday morning starting at ten."

Sadie walked Mustang calmly into the arena.

"Good job getting him used to the announcer's voice, Nora." Grayson said from behind them.

Scott chuckled, "Much better than the auction the first time we saw him."

Nora grinned and looked up at them. "Thanks." She said proudly.

Sadie loped Mustang in a circle at the front of the arena, the brown horse's thick black mane flew back across her leg. She turned the horse toward the first barrel. Mustang took off at a run with his head high and alert, his ears twisting between rider and the white barrel. Sadie wasn't pushing him at full speed.

The first barrel was wide but they recovered well on the second barrel. Sadie was looking at the third barrel as they turned but Mustang was looking at the crowd of Taggers who were yelling loudly. Sadie pulled his head back towards the barrels and kicked him for attention. Halfway to the third barrel the horse finally looked where they were going. Horse and rider leaned around the barrel, they were wide again but Mustang dug in and ran for the final stretch. His head was stretched out and it was obvious he was giving the rider all he had. He turned just at the last moment causing Sadie to slide slightly but she recovered quickly to pat him on the neck with a wide grin.

"19.5..." The announcer called out. "Again, check out the video on this horse on our Facebook or internet page. The Tagger girls have done a tremendous job on him."

"That was great!" Nikki called out and shook both girls' hands high up in the air causing everyone to laugh.

"I gotta get ready!" Josey stood and started making her way down the bleachers.

"Good luck, Babe." Matt called out.

"Must be time for us to head home," Grayson said loudly.

They heard her laugh as she stepped from the last bench and onto the ground. She turned and shook her head at him.

"Should we go help Sadie with Mustang?" Nora asked Grace.

"She's just gonna put him in the stall and come in and watch Josey." Grace answered.

A few minutes later, Sadie appeared at the door leading to the bleachers. Her head turned toward the bleacher at the far end and she stopped. The three teenage boys Reilly had overheard earlier appeared.

Sadie started nodding as they stepped closer to her.

Reilly frowned and looked up at her parents who were also staring at her with looks of concern. Sadie's laughter rang out which made their faces relax but Reilly couldn't release the anxiety. She shook her head with another laugh then started walking away with a slight wave behind her.

She waved excitedly when she saw her family and friends in the bleachers then made her way to the edge of the bleachers next to Reilly. He and Marla each took a hand and pulled her up onto the bleachers and she wiggled over to sit where Josey had been sitting.

"He did awesome!" Sadie said excited.

"Scarecrow didn't do too bad either," Leah laughed.

"Can you believe that?! Our best ever in here!" Sadie bounced on her seat causing them all to laugh. "She really loved hearing you guys yell. I could feel her energy double!"

Sadie talked excitedly about the two horses until the announcer called out Josey's name.

"Who were the boys you were talking to?" Leah asked.

Reilly tried really hard not to change his expression as he stared at Josey in the arena.

"At the end of the bleachers?" Sadie asked then shrugged. "Just some guys from Moscow down here watching one of their sisters run. They asked about Mustang."

"They want to buy him?" Nikki asked.

Sadie chuckled, "No…they were just flirting."

Reilly cringed and there was a low rumble of chuckles in their group.

"Seriously?" Marla asked with a smile.

"Yeah…they wanted to know what high school I went to." Sadie grinned.

"Did you tell them you were only thirteen?" Grayson asked.

Sadie rolled her humored eyes, "Of course not, Dad."

"Grayson…" Leah shook her head at him.

"You were just as concerned." He raised an eyebrow to his wife.

"I have confidence she can handle herself." Leah tried to sound confident and looked at Sadie with a raised brow.

Sadie shrugged as she watched the rider before Josey race down the arena. "I said what I usually do."

"Which is?" Grayson asked.

Sadie grinned without looking at her dad, "I tell them the one thing that stops them every time." She turned dancing blue eyes towards Reilly. "I tell them Reilly is my boyfriend."

The whole group laughed as Reilly's jaw dropped in surprise, and then he too starting laughing. That was so like Sadie!

Josey entered the arena and their laughter remained but their focus was on the brunette and the yellow horse.

"Look at her smile." Candace said and looked to Nora. "She's just enjoying herself and her horse."

Nora's eyes twinkled as she looked at her friend. When Candace's mother had given her a bad time about not winning, Nora had told her to just enjoy the time with her horse. That was the first time they spoke and had led them into being best friends.

"Here she goes!" Nikki whispered and Reilly turned in time to see Apollo bolt to the first barrel.

"Just routine for him," Sadie said as the barrel was turned perfectly. "When they relax and have fun they can do the pattern perfect."

"Just not fast enough anymore," Grace added.

After the pattern was completed Billy looked over at Grace, "17.92? That's just over a second from yours? How isn't that fast enough to win someday?"

"Every hundredth of a second counts. Tonight there are sixty riders and it could be that half of those will be between Sadie and Josey's time. Scarecrow's only six and will only get faster as Apollo slows down." Grace answered.

"Josey is only 21," Matt exhaled. "If she wants to continue, she needs a new horse."

"Nobody here mention that to Josey." Dru told everyone firmly and they all nodded. "She needs to admit that to herself first…she's pretty attached to Apollo."

"I understand that," Candace sighed. Her only friend for years had been her horse, Lola.

"Well, let's go get the horses loaded." Grace stood.

"Is Mustang staying here?" Alex asked.

"All week so people can see him." Wade answered. "We're just hauling the others back home."

Sadie, Grace, Nora, Candace, and Marla all left. The rest of the family sat patiently waiting for the other riders to finish. Sadie won the jackpot and very happily collected her check.

Reilly and Levi leaned against his truck as they watched the Tagger trucks and horse trailers make their way down the arena driveway.

"What's taking her so long?" Levi sighed as he turned and looked for Grace by the arena.

"You know Grace, she knows we're out here so she won't waste time and keep us waiting." Reilly shrugged.

"Well…I gotta go, I have a long drive." Levi stood away from the truck and looked back at him. "Tell Grace I'll see her tomorrow night."

"Just text her," Reilly said.

Levi shrugged and opened the door to his truck then turned and stared at Reilly. He was definitely trying to decide something.

"Just spit it out," Reilly sighed.

"I care a lot for Grace." Levi said softly.

"Yeah…" Reilly's gut clenched.

Levi lowered his head to look at the ground, then shook it and crawled into his truck. He nodded a final goodbye then drove away.

Reilly watched his lights as they turned onto the main road. When he looked back at the building, Grace appeared. She was watching the truck lights, too.

"You just missed, Levi." Reilly said as he opened his truck door and slid behind the wheel.

"Yep," She sighed and buckled her seat belt.

"You did that on purpose," Reilly concluded.

"Yep."

"What's going on? Why would you do that?"

"He's different the last couple weeks," Grace answered as she took her hat off and leaned her head back against the headrest.

So, she had noticed it too. How could she not?

"What are you going to do?" He asked.

She shrugged, "My controlling side says to just end it with him before he does with me."

"You think he wants to breakup?"

"Yep…and he's trying to figure out how without hurting me. So I can't decide whether to wait it out or just go ahead and do it for him."

"What about just asking him and see what's wrong…try working it out?"

After all they went through to get together it just seemed the logical thing.

Grace didn't answer; she just stared out into the night until they drove down the Homestead driveway. All the horses were already put in the barn and the lights were off. The house lights were on allowing them to see people moving around through the windows but neither made a move to leave the truck when he turned it off.

"He does care about you." Reilly said and thought of Levi's sad eyes when he said it.

"I know and I care about him."

"That's why you're considering beating him to the punch…so he doesn't look like the bad guy?"

"He's been the bad guy once already…after Alan…"

"That wasn't your fault."

"I know…" Her blue eyes looked sad. "I don't know why he changed…I just want to know why."

"To try and control it?"

"No…I'll let it happen and not try to control it because it would be trying to control him…I won't do that."

"But you are controlling it by not letting it happen naturally."

"Dang, Reilly," She glared at him. "I control it if I do something; I control it if I don't. What am I supposed to do?"

He shrugged. "I don't know. Why didn't you just come out tonight and say goodbye?"

"Because it was just a great night for everyone; Sadie won, Buttercup improved her time in that arena, Josey and Apollo…well they won't race together much more and tonight they just enjoyed it in front of the entire family. I didn't want to ruin that by being the night Levi breaks up with me…or vice versa."

Reilly nodded, "You're pretty thoughtful."

She opened the door and stepped out to look back at him. "I thought you were going to say controlling," She huffed.

Reilly stepped out of the truck to meet her behind it.

They slowly walked to the back of the house.

"What about how you feel?" Reilly asked her.

"What do you mean?"

"Do you still feel the same way about Levi as you did the last couple months?"

She stopped at the base of the steps and looked down at the hat in her hand, but she didn't speak. Sadie's laughter echoed out of the house and Grace lifted her head and looked up at the large kitchen window.

"You always say my laughter lifts you," Grace smiled. "Sadie's does for me."

Reilly nodded as the light in her eyes returned. Who wouldn't smile when either of the sisters laughed?

"Let's just go in and enjoy the rest of the night," Grace said and walked up the stairs.

Reilly stopped when his hand wrapped around the door knob. "Gracie?"

"What?"

"Montana, WSU, and U of I have everything you need for your degree."

"Yeah," She said. "Did you decide what you wanted to do?"

"No…just," He looked back at the large kitchen window. The family's voices could still be heard. "It's just…" He turned back to her. "It's just that I don't want to be 7 hours away from this…from them."

Grace smiled, "I really don't either. When we think about coming home for a weekend, with the drive both ways, it's actually 14 hours which means we probably wouldn't do it."

"But if we were only 45 minutes from the Homestead or 2 hours from the ranch then we would."

"Matt and Nikki came home a lot for brandings or gatherings," She added.

"So we agree?" Reilly asked hopefully.

Grace grinned, "Yes, we toss out Montana from the equation. It's now U of I or WSU."

"One step closer," Reilly said and opened the door for her.

"Now you just need to decide what to get a degree in," She giggled and walked into the house.

"Yeah…there is that," He sighed and closed the door.

CHAPTER THREE
Thursday Expo

"Did you tell Harvey you were cheating on her tonight?" Reilly chuckled.

He held the trailer tack room door for Nikki as she lifted the saddle off the rack.

"No," His sister laughed. "I'm afraid she would never forgive me."

"Make sure you take a shower before you go home…she may smell another horse on you."

Nikki laughed again as she set the saddle on Mustang's back. "She doesn't even like it when I take Trip out instead of her on the ranch. I couldn't imagine what she would think of me taking another horse team penning."

Reilly leaned against the horse trailer. Trip was the red dun Nikki had purchased at the Billings horse auction. He was turning out to be a pretty good horse. "You may have to change his name."

"I know. He's learned to pick up his feet after 10 months on a rocky mountain side."

"You going to let me ride him next week?"

She shrugged and slid the bit into the mustang's mouth, "You're not riding Rufio and Cooper?"

"Jordan is riding Cooper in the cutting competition next Saturday so they didn't want to take the chance of him getting hurt. They're just riding him on the upper pasture."

"Really? What about Little Ghost? Isn't Scott riding him at the competition?" She walked through the stall gate and they made their way to the indoor arena.

"Yeah, he's only riding him during branding…not during the roundup." He answered.

"I'll be on Harvey during the roundup and on the ground with vaccinations during the branding." Nikki said as she stepped into the saddle. "I think it would be good for Trip if you want to ride him too."

"I'll ride Rufio in the morning and Trip in the afternoon." Reilly opened the arena gate for her and watched her trot away.

Reilly had no idea how much that decision was going to change the course of his life.

******

"And here we have Nikki Tagger riding the mustang that has created quite the buzz this week," The announcer's voice boomed into the arena.

Nikki, Matt and Nick walked their horses into the arena for their first run of the night and stopped just inside the gate. Trooper and Blue stood quietly. Mustang pranced in excitement which caused a grin to spread across Nikki's face.

"She's enjoying this." Grace said from beside Reilly on the bleachers.

He just nodded and watched the threesome ride.

The announcer called out the color blue. Of the dozen steers in the arena, three each had the colors blue, green, yellow, or white. The riders were to separate the three cows with the blue chains and push them across the arena and into a small pen. The fastest team to corral their steers won the round and a check.

Nick and Matt were the first to find two blue chains and moved them quickly toward the pen. Nikki nudged Mustang into the small herd; the third blue chained steer and two with white chains shot up the side of the fence right in front of Reilly and the rest of the Tagger family.

"Go Nikki!" Sadie called out.

Mustang quickly moved ahead of the three steers and stopped their escape and they turned back to the herd with horse and rider right behind them.

Matt and Nick were near the small pen when the last steer with the blue chain that Nikki was chasing turned around quickly and shot back up the fence. Mustang turned to the right to follow and Nikki turned to the left…to the shock of everyone, Nikki tipped off the horse.

A gasp rang out as she hit the ground but she was back up again before Matt and Nick could turn to see what everyone had reacted to.

Both men looked surprised when Mustang joined them and Nikki didn't. She was walking briskly across the arena toward them while wiping dust off her jeans.

"What happened?" Nick asked loudly.

"Nothing!" Nikki shouted back with a grin.

"Nothing?" Matt asked with a disbelieving smirk as he leaned down to grab the reins of the loose brown horse.

The crowd that had gasped was now laughing.

"Nothing!" Nikki yelled again as she reached for the reins.

"Then why, exactly, are you on the ground and not in the saddle?" Her dad grinned.

"Because," Nikki answered as she remounted. "I wanted to show how well Mustang could work on his own."

The crowd laughed as the buzzer announced they only had thirty seconds left.

Nikki ignored the laughing crowd, father, and brother and ran Mustang back toward the blue chained steer and had him half way back when the buzzer went off.

"Sorry Nikki, time has run out but thanks for the entertainment." The announcer laughed.

Nikki turned with a grin and tipped her hat up to the announcer's booth.

******

Reilly took Grace's hand and pulled her out of the arena building. He wasn't going to let her hold back again tonight. Levi looked at them curiously when they arrived at the truck.

After making sure no one else was around to interrupt them, he took a deep breath, and just spit it out.

"You two need to talk out whatever is happening here. Now, get it out and get it over with because you both look miserable." He nodded his head confidently; hoping he was doing the right thing.

They both hesitantly looked at each other.

Levi opened his mouth to speak then closed it quickly.

"Just spit it out," Reilly and Grace said in unison,

Levi nodded, "I'm going to college in Wyoming with Alan."

Reilly exhaled slowly and looked at Grace. Her expression was…blank.

"You've been asking and I didn't know how to tell you," Levi continued.

"So you want to break up?" Grace's voice was calm.

"I figured you would want to." Levi answered.

Grace just stared…then Reilly knew what was wrong. She didn't want to be with Levi anymore, but didn't know how to say it.

"Do you?" Levi asked nervously.

"I…" Grace stopped.

"Just spit it out." Levi and Reilly said in unison.

She nodded, "You treat me different than everyone else. I thought it was just because I was your girlfriend…but I think it's something else."

Levi sighed, "I am just so worried about hurting you again."

"That's why you didn't tell me about Wyoming and Allen?" She asked.

"Yeah, in a way…and I am really sorry…but…I am choosing going to college with Allen over you and I knew you'd be hurt." He said regretfully.

"Family is family." Grace said.

"So, you understand?" Levi asked.

"About Allen…yes." She nodded. "But not the rest of it. On the phone and texting…you're fine, but when we're actually together…you…kinda…walk on egg shells around me. Like you were going to break me."

Reilly sighed, Sadie was right.

Levi stared for a moment then finally nodded. "I hurt you once…bad…and I just can't stand the thought of doing it again."

"Not just about Allen." She said.

"No…about everything." Levi admitted.

"So, if we were actually together, in person, all the time…how long do you think you could keep that up?" She asked with a slight smile.

Levi's shoulders lowered, "As long as I had to."

"That's no way to go through life, Levi" She said. "I don't want anyone to do that around me. I'm pretty dang tough…I'll never break easy."

Levi shrugged, "I can't help it."

Grace glanced at Reilly then back to Levi, "I am not breaking up with you because of Allen. But, I think we should part ways because we just…can't…see a future together in the long run."

Levi's whole body seemed to relax, "I'm sorry, Grace."

She nodded her head slowly, "So am I, but just because we can't be a couple doesn't mean we can't still be friends. I still want the best for you."

"Ahhhh, Grace, I want nothing more than the best for you." Levi said quickly.

Grace smiled and Reilly internally sighed. Levi's desire to want the best for her is the reason she was breaking it off. That was sad but true.

"Then you go and have adventures with Allen, and I will with Reilly." Her smile didn't reach her eyes, but Reilly doubted that Levi noticed.

"We'll keep in touch," Levi smiled at her then to Reilly.

"We will," Reilly nodded and stretched out a hand. "We'll see each other at rodeos."

Levi shook it and then pulled him into a quick embrace before turning to Grace. She stepped forward and they embraced as friends before Levi walked to his truck and drove away.

Reilly slid an arm across her shoulders as they watched him leave.

"I'm sorry, Gracie."

"I know…but thanks for pushing the issue. It needed to be done."

CHAPTER FOUR
Friday Expo

Reilly and Grace placed their empty bowls into the sink and hugged a somber Cora.

"Stop counting down," Grace chuckled. "It makes me sad and we're supposed to be happy today."

Cora laughed, "Alright, we put on a happy face and go watch the bull riding tonight."

"Dress warm," Reilly said as he walked to the back door and removed his cowboy hat from the hat rack and set it on his head. "It's supposed to be chilly tonight but warm up again tomorrow."

"I will," Cora called out. "You make sure you put some padding down your jeans in case you land on your backside tonight."

Reilly looked at Grace as she laughed then back into the kitchen at Cora who was grinning.

"Very funny you two," Reilly shook his head with an internal laugh and opened the back door.

He walked to his blue truck as Grace walked to her Trail Boss.

"I thought I was driving tonight." Reilly said.

Grace lifted a brow, "I hear it hurts when you 'jump off' a bull. Can you drive when you're broken, battered, and bruised?"

She giggled devilishly.

When they arrived at the arena, he stepped out of his blue truck and was met by his dad, Grayson, Scott, and Nick. The four men had been helping setup the panels in the arena to prepare for the night and were also helping with the livestock.

"You ready?" His dad asked.

The confidence Reilly had been feeling began to turn into an ache deep in his stomach.

"Yes," He answered and retrieved his chaps, vest, helmet, and bull rope from the back seat.

"Most important thing?" Nick asked.

"Stay on for 8 seconds," Reilly smirked and received a round of chuckles.

"Most important thing to get you to that 8 seconds?" Nick grinned.

"Getting forward on the jump when he comes out," Reilly answered.

"Get off your butt and go forward with the bull." Nick nodded.

They began to walk toward the bull pens.

"Then transfer my balance so I'm ready for the kick." Reilly continued.

"If you get a good bucker, you should be able to get your timing down to move back and forth…feel him and don't try to guess what he's going to do and anticipate." Nick said as they stopped in front of the pen that held Reilly's draw: Red Gus. He was a medium sized deep red bull who turned and looked at them with bored eyes and a tiny trickle of snot dripping from his nose. Deep inside his gut, Reilly was very relieved the bull didn't have horns.

"He's a decent size for you," Grayson said.

"Aaron, the stock contractor, said Red Gus would get you a check if you make it the eight," Nick said. "He's got a good drop and a twist to the left."

"I just want to make it the eight," Reilly admitted.

They turned to the building and entered through the large door. The bleachers were already filling up with spectators. Over thirty riders would ride in four different divisions. There were seven riders in Reilly's age group.

"They pay down to 4th," Nick said.

"That will help with the doctor bills," Scott teased.

Reilly chuckled.

"We're going to help with the stock," Reilly's dad said. "We'll be back before you ride."

"Go do your thing, Dad," Reilly said. "I'm fine…just another ride."

They grinned at each other just before his dad walked away with Grayson and Scott right behind him.

Nick was still standing next to Reilly, "You got this. Red Gus isn't anything bigger or meaner than you rode down south."

Reilly nodded; the confidence building.

"Reilly?"

They both turned to the man's voice.

Standing in front of him was Marla's dad, Ethan. The last time Reilly had seen him was at a team penning in the middle of December. He had made a rude comment to Josey and then left abruptly. It was the night Matt had returned from overseas.

In the years that Reilly had known Marla, he had only met her father a couple times on the night's he would pick her up for a school prom. Her father had been drunk each night making both Marla and her mother very uncomfortable and embarrassed.

Tonight, his eyes were clear, focused, and he looked sober.

"Mr. Stuart," Reilly stretched out a hand to him. "Nick, this is Marla's father, Ethan Stuart."

The men politely shook hands and nodded to each other then Ethan turned to Reilly. "Marla told me you were riding tonight and I wanted to stop and say good luck."

"Thank you, sir," Reilly said.

Ethan took a deep breath and looked at Reilly pensively. His eyes shot to Nick then back to Reilly. "I also wanted to thank you for being such a good friend to my daughter."

Nick slowly turned to the side and stepped away.

"She's a great girl," Reilly said honestly.

"She is, and she really didn't deserve what I put her through." Ethan sighed. "Or her mother…but I've been sober 14 weeks now."

"That's good," Reilly smiled but didn't really know what to say.

Ethan nodded anxiously, "I'll let you get back to getting ready but I just…wanted to say thank you."

They shook hands again and just as he turned away Ethan stopped. He looked back at Reilly with a slight smile. "Marla and I started team roping together again so I hope to see you in the arena in the future."

"I look forward to it, Mr. Stuart," Reilly grinned.

"Call me Ethan," He nodded and walked away.

Reilly watched him disappear into the growing crowd then found a corner to put on his chaps. He was stretching his legs when Nick reappeared.

Neither of them mentioned the conversation.

"Starting up in about 5 minutes," Nick said.

He was answered by the sound of small steers walking through the ally way. The Pee Wee's would be riding them.

"Maybe I should have started at that age," Reilly nodded to a couple eight year olds that were dressed in chaps, vest, and cowboy hats. Their helmets were propped next to the chutes. The boys' fast talking, high pitched voices showed their excitement.

"I was sixteen when I started," Nick said. "I had never been in this cowboy world when I walked into my first arena." He smiled at Reilly. "I've never regretted a day in one since."

"It's always a good day when you're in an arena…" Reilly started.

"Welcome to the Expo!" Boomed from the speakers. "We're minutes away from starting…"

Reilly slid on his vest and pulled his cowboy hat down tighter. He'd put the helmet on right after his bull was in the chutes. He watched the young boys on the calves and the excited fathers and mothers standing close by.   Everyone but his dad, Grayson, Scott, and Nick would be watching him from the bleachers.

A half hour later, Red Gus was walking down the ally and past Reilly. The bull walked like he didn't have a care in the world.

"Those calm ones are pretty hard to read," Nick said. "Sometimes, they are the hardest buckers in the pen."

Reilly shook his head as the butterflies danced in his stomach, "Thanks for that."

Nick chuckled as they walked behind the chute and next to the bull. "Let's get the rope on him."

Reilly was the third of the seven riders in his division. Once the first rider sprang from the chute, flew in the air, and landed in the dirt with a loud thud within seconds of the gate opening, Reilly began stretching again. It seemed as if he concentrated on his muscles and all the advice Nick had taught him then he didn't feel the tremble in his gut. The tingles of the blood rushing through his veins that made his pulse quicken and heart beat stronger would not go away.

A bit of calm filled with anticipation came over him when he removed his hat and shoved the black helmet onto his head. Time to work, he told himself. He climbed up the metal rail of the chute then stretched a leg to the opposite side; he was hovering over the bull.

"Turn your boot," Nick said.

Reilly glanced at his foot, the spur was tucked to the side and just inches from the red bull's hide. He twisted it with toe pointing to the nose and spur to the tail. Then he lowered the other boot onto the rail and straightened his boot. He took a deep breath to ease the pressure in his lungs and heart.

"Just relax," Nick said.

Metal clanging and the crowd roared as the second rider bust out of the chute. Reilly glanced up to see the cowboy rocking back and forth on top a black bull. A grunt escaped the bull with every kick. The bull's head flew up and nearly hit the rider as he went forward then began to slide to the right. He was still on and holding the rope tight when the 8 second buzzer rang out.

"Concentrate," Grayson said from behind Reilly as he held onto the back of his vest. If the bull bucked in the chute, Grayson would be able to pull him away from the head of the animal.

Reilly lowered onto the back of the bull and his full attention went to his bull rope.   He twisted it back in forth to run it around the girth of the bull then gave the end to Nick. Reilly's hand ran up and down the rope to heat the resin.

A deep breath and his hand slid into the wrap. Reilly nodded and slapped the rope to let Nick know to pull…and he did. The red bull hunched his back as the rope tightened around his sides and Reilly's hand.

No turning back now.

Reilly ran a hand under the rope to test the tightness then nodded to Nick.

"Turn your feet," Nick said again while handing him the rope.

Reilly twisted his heels back to keep the spurs from the bull's side and twisted the rope around his hand through his grip. His fingers tightened around it; the rosin on the rope was sticky and helped him from slipping.

As he positioned the rope his mind focused on the process and his pulse started to return to normal…until he looked up. Being in the chute, on top a 1500 pound bull, with the crowd anticipating the ride sent the trembles through his veins and sweat trickled down his back.

His head suddenly flew forward and he gasped. He turned quickly to look up at Nick who was grinning at him. "Get your head back on the bull."

Nick had slapped the back of his helmet startling him out of the nervous haze.

Reilly grinned, "Yeah…yeah…thanks." He nodded again as he rocked on the back of the animal to get his balance then tugged at the rope around his hand. He pushed down on each gloved finger that was gripping the bull rope tightly. His left arm went up and he took a very deep breath as he leaned his body back in anticipation of the first thrust from the bull.

"Nod when you're ready," Nick yelled.

Other people were yelling at him too:

Good luck!

Hold on tight!

Wait for the buzzer!

Reilly didn't know who said it; his mind was tuned Nick's voice.

He couldn't tighten his grip any more than it was so one more rock of the hips, deep breath, and he nodded.

Metal clanging shattered the air around him and his whole body heaved forward as the bull made his first leaping launch out of the chute.

Reilly's grip around the rope and his legs around the bull increased as he was thrust backward. He balanced and moved with the bull for a good six bucks before the scream from the crowd penetrated into his mind.

Through the commotion he could hear the buzzer echo in the building and his hand loosened its grip making Reilly's gut clench. The bull kicked out with his back legs high propelling Reilly forward…when the bull dropped forward…the force pulled on Reilly's whole body making his hand slide from the rope. The bull went forward and Reilly did too…right over the right shoulder of the bull. His arms stretched out to the ground just as the bull twisted in the middle of the buck and his hip hit Reilly's legs. The ground twirled in front of him as his legs flew in the air like a windmill. He ended the dismount with a belly flop on the arena floor with dirt flying through the thin bars of the mask and into his eyes, up his nose, and down his throat.

Reilly lifted his head and blinked the dirt out of his eyes. The bull fighter's legs appeared between him and the red bull that stopped and looked at Reilly with a snort. Then it nonchalantly turned and trotted across the arena and to the gate.

Through the bull fighter's legs Reilly could see Nick, Grayson, and his dad running toward him. His dad was staring at him with true concern, Grayson had a slight smirk, and Nick was grinning ear-to-ear. Reilly laughed and dirt flew from his mouth. He pushed himself up onto his hands and knees and grinned up at the three men and the bull fighter.

His dad's shoulders lowered and a slight relieved smile appeared just as he reached him. "You OK?" He huffed.

"Yeah," Reilly nodded and leaned up and back so he was on his knees. "I did it, Dad. I got to the eight." He said breathlessly.

"That you did, son." Pride shone in his eyes as he took an arm and helped Reilly stand.

"It went by so fast." Reilly gasped.

"That was quite the landing," Grayson smirked. "You want to do it again?"

Reilly's veins were trembling, heart pounding, breaths coming fast. Sweat tickled down his back and across his brow.
Life...energy...the excitement of danger tingled through him.

"Yeah...yeah, I do." Reilly nodded.

"You got the fever now, boy." Nick's laughter boomed.

Reilly stood between the four of them and grinned at each.

"Wave to your mother so she knows you're alright." His dad said.

"I don't know where she is," Reilly admitted and tried to blink away more of the dirt from his eyes.

Nick laughed again, "Just turn and wave to your left...she's over there somewhere."

Reilly did as he was told.

"Your other left," Grayson chuckled.

They all laughed and Reilly waved the other direction.

CHAPTER FIVE
Saturday Expo

There was a large crowd of people on the bleachers when Reilly and his parents arrived at the indoor arena for the preview Saturday morning. The four Tagger girls were already at the stall preparing the mustang for the ride and the rest of the family would be arriving from different locations.

He buttoned his black jacket. There was barely a cloud in the sky but the air was still chilly and it was always colder in the building than outside. It was supposed to warm in the afternoon in time to go to Grace's royalty coronation at the Horseman's Ball.

"You going over with the girls?" Dru asked as they walked across the dirt parking lot and into the building.

"Nah, they don't need me." Reilly answered. "I want to sit on the bleachers and listen to people."

"See if anyone is interested in Mustang?" His dad asked.

Reilly nodded, "The video on him has already been watched over two thousand times."

"Over 500 for Dr. Mark's horse." Dru added.

They stopped for coffee from the food wagon then found their seats and blocked a row for the rest of the family.

"If we were five minutes later, we would be standing all day." Reilly said as he glanced at the large crowd entering the building.

They sat quietly and watched people while they sipped their coffee. Dru was sitting in between them with her arm through her husband's and she tucked herself into him. They were always holding hands or had their arms looped together. Reilly loved that; he hoped his future wife would want that connection too. Marla didn't like to hold hands which Reilly thought was odd and it bothered him. She had a tough family life since her father was an alcoholic. He thought of the short conversation with her dad the night before and he reminded himself to talk to her to make sure she was alright. It bothered him that she didn't mention the team roping to him.

"Is there a line-up or day sheet or something that will tell us when he's going to be shown?" A man's voice asked behind them.

"Yes, he's number 14." A woman answered.

Mustang was number 14.

"Then we can leave?" The man asked. "You're not buying…"

"I'll buy what I want," The woman chuckled. "And he's the only one that I think will work."

"What makes you think…?" The man started.

"I am going to run Tevis again and the video showed them running him for an endurance race." She interrupted. "They must think he can do it if they included it…not many people would have thought of that."

Sadie had thought of it from the beginning.

"Did you go…?" The man started again but she interrupted again which made Reilly and his parents smile.

"I went out yesterday while everyone was at the rodeo and again this morning to look at him in the pen. He was very friendly and let me love on him a bit." She answered. "I talked to the vet that knows the girls that have been working with him."

"What…?" The man started.

"He said the horse was in perfect health and in pretty good condition, which was obvious in the video and him standing in front of me." The woman said. "He didn't think there would be an issue of me running him this year. Tevis isn't until August so we have months to prepare."

"I wasn't…" The man exhaled.

"Then what were you going to ask?" The woman asked impatiently.

Reilly grinned. Obviously, those two had been married a long time.

"I was going to ask what are you going to name him?" The man finished with a bit of humor in his tone.

"Oh," The woman chuckled. "I like the name the girls gave him."

"What name?"

"Mustang."

"Yeah, what are you naming the mustang?

"He is Mustang."

"I know he is, but what is his name?"

 "Mustang."

"I know Caroline, but what are you going to call him?"

"Bill, I am going to call him Mustang."

There was a pause and Reilly had to bite his lip to keep from reacting.

"You're going to call that mustang, Mustang?" Bill asked.

"Yes."

"Well, that's just ridiculous," Bill exhaled in disbelief. "That would be like calling me man because I'm a man."

"Well, I could call you a lot more than that right now."

Reilly and his parents giggled.

Caroline chuckled and Dru turned to her. She stretched out her free hand to the woman.

"I'm Dru Tagger," She said. "My daughter and three nieces own the mustang."

"Oh!" Caroline laughed. "I have questions for you!"

Reilly quietly sat watching the people in the arena prepare for the showing while Caroline pelted Dru with questions.

Is he easy to catch?

Does he bite or kick?

Has he ever foundered?

What are his hooves like and how often have you trimmed him?

Does he pick up his feet easily?

Has he ever colicked?

Who has ridden him?

Has he been dewormed lately?

Is he vaccinated for out of state travel?

Does he load easily?

What types of trailers has he been in?

Is he herd bound?

Does he get along with other horses?

They were finally saved from her inquisition when Nora rode through the back doors. Her hair was straight down her back and she wore black jeans, a crisp white western shirt, and her black hat. Her clothes and body positioning on the horse made her look like she was riding into a show ring.

Mustang's head was high and alert as he watched the other people and horses around them.

A temporary fence was installed down the middle of the arena. To the right was an area for the horses to be shown. There were obstacles setup for riders to demonstrate the horse's ability; barrels, gates, bridges, blue tarps, and long poles setup in an L shape.

To the left was the warm up area where a dozen horses were cantering, trotting, or walking in a circle. Nora joined the group and pushed Mustang into a trot. She posted perfectly on him for a dozen laps then pushed him into a canter. The horse's speed was consistent and he moved effortlessly.

"He didn't look that big when I was standing next to him," Caroline said.

"Nora is fifteen, only 5' 2" and a pencil." Dru explained.

"Well then…" Caroline's voice drifted off.

Reilly was sure that had impressed her, but the woman didn't know that Nora wasn't like any other fifteen-year-old when it came to horses.

Sadie, Nikki, Grace, and the rest of the family joined them on the bleachers.

"Alright, ladies and gentlemen," The announcer said. "We'll get this preview moving forward so we're not late for the Horseman's Ball this evening. If everyone will clear out to the back of the building, each horse will have three minutes in the large arena and then two in the obstacle course. No more than two people at a time in there and be respectful while you go through the obstacles. Number one please enter the arena."

A bay walked through the gate and spent the first three minutes doing circles in the large arena as the announcer talked about the horse then they moved to the obstacles.

"Where's Dr. Mark's horse?" Reilly asked.

"He's one of the last to be shown today, number 34." Grayson answered. "Nora will ride him, too."

"Are you buying any?" Reilly asked.

He shrugged, "Depends on the horse and what the prices are going for."

"I'm safe," Nikki giggled. "No foals in this sale."

They all laughed. Her first auction she and Nora purchased the creamelo, Bodi, for Nick then at the same auction that Mustang was purchased she brought three foals home. One was instantly sold to Leah.

"But I love my Cappuccino," Leah grinned. Now, officially a yearling, the colt's body was the color of coffee with cream mixed in. His face and legs were white face and the white trickled up his legs and into his underbelly. He was a strong, masculine colt.

"Cappy will be a real bulldog of a horse," Sadie turned to her mom.

"I'm still not sure I like that nickname," Leah wrinkled her nose. "Maybe Chino."

Sadie scrunched her nose, "Cappy."

"Here comes Nora," Grace announced to interrupt the banter.

Nora entered at a trot then quickly moved to a canter while traveling in a figure eight pattern. She demonstrated Mustang's ability to change leads correctly then moved along the long fence. She stopped him then quickly turned him back onto his haunches and performed a respectable roll back. She repeated the move three times before moving him back into the figure eight pattern.

"Very nice…" The woman behind them whispered.

Nora maneuvered the horse through the gate and into the obstacle arena. She circled the entire area then trotted up and over the bridge and stopped at the rope gate. She lifted the rope, maneuvered the horse through, then lowered the rope back onto the fence. Then she repeated in the other direction.

They moved to the long posts that lay in an L shape and she backed the horse through them…flawlessly.

"She's always been good at teaching them to back," Reilly said.

Just before the blue tarp, she did the one thing the other riders didn't do. She stepped off the horse, walked completely around him while he stood still, then she stepped into the stirrup and back onto the horse. She repeated the maneuver but on the opposite side of the horse.

Stepping off the horse again she picked up each of his hooves and tapped on the bottom of them. When she was done, she turned to the other rider in the arena. She spoke to him but they couldn't hear what she said. The man stopped his horse and nodded to her.

Nora bent over and picked up the blue tarp. Neither horse reacted when she threw it over the body of the mustang then drug it over the top of his head. He didn't care and just stood quietly.

Nora replaced the tarp and turned to smile and nod at the other rider.

He tipped his hat to her then continued his demonstration.

By the time they were done, Nora had maneuvered every obstacle. She ended in the corner nearest the bleachers and demonstrated his shoulder movement, releasing the hind quarters, then she turned him into a spin. It wasn't perfect, but she was still smiling as it came to an end and they walked out of the arena.

"That girl is a showman…a true horsewoman," Caroline whispered behind them.

Jordan and Scott turned to look at her.

"That she is," Scott said proudly.

An hour later, Nora returned to the arena with Dr. Mark's bay horse. She repeated the pattern she had ridden with mustang. The bay did just as well and Nora ended with a smile again.

CHAPTER SIX
Saturday Coronation

"You ready guys?" Sadie's voice called from the hall at the Homestead.

"I decided not to go," Reilly answered with a grin as he hooked his gold belt buckle to the belt.

Sadie's laughter echoed down the hall making him chuckle as he glanced at Wade.

Wade laughed, "Not going to Grace's coronation? Yeah, that's going to happen."

They both set their black cowboy hats on their heads and walked out of the room. Sadie met them just outside their bedroom door. Her long blonde hair was loose and hanging down nearly to her waist. Her light blue shirt made her blue eyes even brighter as the laughter made them shine. The three cousins grinned at each other then they took off at a run. Half way down they jumped into a slide down the long hallway in their sock covered feet.

They laughed as they came to a halt against the banister, then jogged down the stairs. Their parents were all standing in the kitchen looking up at them; smiles gracing all their faces.

"No dress, Sadie?" Her mother asked.

"Of course not," Sadie laughed. "I'm gonna wear my dancin' boots and plan on dancing from the time the music starts until it stops." When she stepped off the bottom step she did a quick little jig then spun in a circle making her hair fly around her.

They all laughed.

"But you look awesome in your dress, Mom," Sadie grinned. "And you too, my two aunts." She looked at Dru and Jordan.

Leah wore a long tan lace dress with light blue cowboy boots. Dru was in black jeans and black boots with red flowers that matched her red shirt, and Jordan wore a black, long sleeve dress that stopped just before her favorite black cowboy boots.

"You can dance in a dress," Jordan laughed and Scott took her hand to spin her around the kitchen for a demonstration.

They all laughed again.

"I like it when Reilly and Wade flip me over their backs and I'd rather do it in jeans," Sadie chuckled and wrapped her arms around her dad's waist and looked up at him. "You're pretty handsome, Pops."

"Pops?" He kissed her forehead and chuckled. "That one makes me feel old."

All three men wore black cowboy hats and the black leather T3E branded western jackets. The difference came in the color of shirt they wore. Grayson was in a light gray, Reilly's dad was in a red to match his wife, and Scott wore black to match Jordan.

"Let's go," Wade said and walked toward the back door. "Nora and Grace will be mad if we're late."

The three cousins stopped at the back door and slid on their boots then raced to the trucks.

Thirty minutes later they were sliding out of the trucks and walking as a family toward the entrance of the event center where the Horseman's Ball and coronation was being held.

Reilly proudly walked next to his mom with her arm comfortably resting in the crook of his arm. Her free hand was comfortably clasped in his dad's hand.

"Matt, Josey, Nikki and Lucas will be here soon," She smiled at Reilly. "Jessup and Kate are coming too."

"When did Lucas get here?" He asked.

"Just arrived an hour ago, they are picking him up and coming straight here," His mother answered.

He smiled proudly at her. No matter if she was working with cows and covered in mud or dressed up for a night on the town; she had to be the most beautiful woman he'd ever seen.

"Grace texted and said she made sure our reserved tables were right next to her table," He told her.

"You're very handsome tonight, Son."

His heart skipped a beat from the pride shining in her eyes and just how much her calling him 'son' still meant to him.

"Can't compare to you, Mom," He smiled. "You going to save a dance for me?"

She laughed and her eyes brightened. "Of course, I can't wait."

Nick, Tessa, and Alex were just inside the front doors as they entered.

Their tickets were scanned and then they walked into the main banquet area to be greeted by Queen Grace and the two princesses, Lorena and Christina.

Their ankle length dresses were dark brown leather with long black fringe across the back shoulders and down the length of their arms. The front of the shoulders and from the elbows down to the wrists were decorated with lighter buckskin brown. Blue turquoise beads were added where the two different colors of leather met and matched the necklaces and earrings they wore. Black and turquoise boots completed the outfits. Their black hats would later be adorned with the crowns during the coronation. Lorena and Christina both had dark brunette hair and were as tall as Grace.

"You three look fantastic together." Reilly grinned at Grace.

Grace lifted her arms to the sides so the long fringe dangled like wings. She grinned at him, "Fringe."

She had told him she wanted fringe on everything because when it moved it reminded her that she was wearing something special and not just another normal shirt.

She was instantly wrapped in her father's arms then her uncles.

Reilly, Wade, and Alex waved and walked away to start looking at all the items set on tables on the parameter of the room. Everything from a handmade wooden vase to baskets full of items, to wood and metal signs, gift certificates from different stores, and more. Hundreds of donated items would be auctioned off to help pay for the expenses of the Lewiston Roundup Royalty as they traveled to promote the rodeo.

"Mom said they were all getting numbers to bid on these and the live auction items." Alex said. "There's a rafting trip and a trip to the NFR to be auctioned. Man, I'd love to go to the NFR."

Wade nodded, "Every year they come home with something."

"There's Hope," Reilly said.

"Hope for what?" Alex asked with a grin. "Hope for Nick buying us that NFR trip?"

Wade and Reilly burst out laughing.

"No, Hope Quinland," Reilly chuckled and pointed.

Alex turned toward the side of the room where Reilly pointed. There was a girl standing next to a pair of red leather chaps that were on display for the auction. She was fourteen, long dark hair pulled back into a pony tail and curled in ringlets down her back. She wore a white shirt with little red flowers decorating the shoulders and a black skirt. Bright red cowboy boots peeked out of the bottom of the skirt. Around her waist was a wide leather belt tooled so horses looked like they were in a continual stampede around her.

"Hope's mom makes the chinks, that belt, and lots of other leather work," Wade told him. "She doesn't leave home though. Hope comes down with some other ranchers from Viola to attend the Ball."

"It's about the only time we get to see her since her dad left a couple years ago," Reilly told him.

"She's a dang good cowgirl," Wade nodded. "She and her little sister just about run their little ranch."

"Hope!" Sadie's voice rang out over the growing crowd of attendees. She was weaving in and out of the brightly decorated tables as she made her way across to the girl.

"We always thought she and Reilly should get married," Wade chuckled as the two girls embraced.

"Why?" Alex looked at Reilly then Wade.

Reilly laughed.

"Because," Wade grinned. "Hope isn't her first name, it's her middle name. Her first name is Morgan."

"So she would be Morgan Morgan." Alex nodded and they all three laughed.

They walked over to the two girls.

"I'll buy it right now," Sadie said with eyes furrowed in concentration and hands on hips.

"You have to bid on it," Wade chuckled.

The two girls turned and Hope smiled at the three of them. "Hey, guys." She said then looked at Alex.

"This is Alex Elliot," Reilly said. "And you're trying to buy the chinks?" He asked Sadie.

"No, I want her belt to give to Grace for her birthday next week." Sadie explained.

"She'd love that," Wade nodded and looked at Hope. "Is it even for sale or is she trying to bully you into selling it?"

They all laughed except Sadie who gave him a death glare.

"It's for sale," Hope smiled. "That's why I'm wearing it…to show it off for Mom." Her smile disappeared. "We had to sell half the herd to get us through the summer. Mom's trying to get her leather business going so we can save the other half."

"Ah, dang," Reilly frowned. "I'm sorry to hear that."

"Well, it's just the way life is," Hope said with a shrug.

"I want to buy your belt." Sadie said. "How much is it?"

"Fifty dollars," Hope said anxiously. Obviously worried it was too much.

They all four frowned at her.

"Hope," Reilly said. "There is a lot of work in those horses…they look great. It's worth a lot more than that."

"Well," She shrugged. "Mom wasn't sure so she said to try that as a start."

"My mom will know," Wade said. "She buys that stuff all the time."

They all turned but couldn't see their parents…until Grayson's hat appeared over a crowd of people.

"Good thing Dad's so tall," Sadie grinned as Wade turned and walked away.

"Sadie, I told you fifty dollars." Hope said. "It's only fair I sell it to you at that price."

Sadie rolled her eyes and shook her head. "It's only fair if I pay you a fair price for it."

"Well…let's see if Jordan even thinks it's worth that much." Hope smiled. "I'll be looking for work for the summer too if you know anyone that needs help after school is out. It can't be too far away from home."

"We'll keep our ears open," Reilly nodded. "But you just be careful who you go to work for."

Hope smiled up at him, "I will."

"Call the Taggers if you need to check on someone before going to work with them," Alex said. "They know just about everyone around."

Hope turned to him, "Thanks Alex. I will, I promise."

Alex's cheeks turned pink.

"Well, I'll buy it for $100." They heard from behind them.

Jordan was there staring at the belt.

"No, I'm buying it." Sadie said and stepped between Hope and her aunt.

Jordan looked at her in surprise, "You don't wear stuff like that so why are you buying it?"

"For Grace for her birthday," Sadie grinned.

Jordan's eye brows shot up and she nodded. "Oh yes, she'll love that." She took a step to the side to look at the belt but Sadie moved too…with a grin.

"Sadie, darling," Her aunt huffed with a matching grin. "Move."

"It's mine." Sadie shook her head.

Jordan laughed, "Yes, I'll let you buy this one but I was thinking I'd have her design three matching belts so I could donate them to the royalty so the princesses would have them too."

"That way Hope's mom's work gets seen by all the royalty parades and rodeos." Reilly added.

"That could really help," Hope nodded.

"Well…OK then," Sadie made a dramatic show of stepping to the side and swinging a hand to show off the belt at Hope's waist.

Hope laughed and her arms went behind her to unbuckle the belt. She handed it to Jordan who reviewed the horses closely.

"Very good work," Jordan nodded. "I'll step outside and call your mother. Does she have any more already finished?"

"Just one completed and another about half way." Hope said as she took the belt back then started to hand it to Sadie.

Sadie shook her head. "Wear it tonight and show it off. I'll get it from you before we leave."

Hope grinned, "Thanks."

"Let's talk about these chinks," Jordan said to Hope and ran a finger over the silver Conchos then down the red fringe on the edge.

As Reilly, Wade, Sadie, and Alex walked away, Reilly turned to Wade.

"Your mom will own those by the end of the night." He grinned.

"No doubt at all," Wade laughed.

They wandered the room looking at the donations and talking to people until the announcer told them to take their seats.

Reilly sat in the chair right behind Grace and next to a table that held the royalty for the Walla Walla Frontier Days rodeo. No one was sitting in the chairs yet so he pushed his chair back and stretched his legs under the table while he could. The tables were close together and they would be cramped together soon enough.

Wade was to his right and then Alex…who was looking over his shoulder. Reilly followed the direction he was looking and saw Hope talking to Jordan, Dru, and Leah now. Reilly grinned. So, Alex had a crush.

He heard Grace's "life is good" laugh and turned to the table where she would be sitting. Grace and the two princesses' were escorting the multitude of brightly dressed visiting queens and princesses to their tables.

"Seriously, Reilly," Grace laughed. "Make some room."

He jumped up quickly and turned to pull out the chairs for the three royalty directly behind him. He was met by dark brown eyes, straight shoulder length black hair, and a wide shining smile under a bright blue cowboy hat. It was adorned with a shiny silver crown.

"You must be Reilly then," She said with a hint of a southern drawl.

They reached for the back of the chair at the same time and her hand slid over the top of his. It was warm and shot tingles all the way up to his shoulder.

"Yes," He grinned. "I'm Reilly and you are?"

"Adaline Brewster," She said with the drawl. "My family is from Texas, therefore, you all have wonderful accents."

They laughed.

"I was born in Texas," Reilly informed her. "My dad would agree with you on the accent part…he's still holding onto his."

"You were?" She grinned. "I've been here for two years now. Maybe I can speak with your father for a few minutes and feel a little less homesick."

Reilly nodded, "He gets around Texans and that Texas drawl, and his gets more pronounced with every second that goes by."

"Well, then…you must introduce us." She giggled and looked around at the people sitting at the tables. Her eyes stopped right behind him then she looked up at him. "No guess who your father is…with them cute dimples and all."

Reilly felt the blush warm his cheeks…dang.

The announcers voice boomed in the room: "Please take your seats. I'd like to introduce you…"

Reilly and Adaline lowered into their chairs that were back to back to each other.

"Save me a dance and I'll introduce you." Reilly said.

"Well, I'll just do that." She smiled.

They reluctantly turned away from each other.

When Reilly turned and looked up. His parents, Matt, and Wade were looking at him and grinning. He rolled his eyes and couldn't help a quick glance at Grace. She grinned and winked at him then turned her attention back to the announcer.

"Where's Nora and Candace?" Reilly asked Wade…trying to distract him.

Wade started laughing. "Right across from the queen you were just talking to."

Reilly shook his head in disbelief and slowly looked over his shoulder. Nora and Candace, dressed in red leather dresses and their black hat's adorned with crowns of the NWYRA, smiled and waved at him. They were right across from Adeline. Dang.

After a brief speech, the Royalty was sent to the buffet line. Reilly stood to make room for Adeline to stand and depart. They smiled at each other. So the buffet table didn't become too crowded, only a few tables were released at a time. The Tagger tables were standing at the buffet lines when Adeline returned to her seat. She was finished eating when he returned and she smiled again as she stood and their royalty court moved to the back of the room to socialize.

As the Tagger plates were being cleared from the table the announcer asked everyone to return to their seats.

The visiting royalty were asked to come up to the stage and were all introduced. Reilly grinned when Adeline smiled and waved at everyone. She caught his eye and her smile brightened.

The last 'visiting' royalty to be introduced was Candace and Nora as the princess and queen of the NWYRA. They received a huge round of whistles and clapping; especially from the Tagger crowd.

Then the official Lewiston Roundup Royalty coronation began.

The outgoing court said their thanks to everyone then the new princesses were announced and handed their new official royalty chaps and crowns were placed on their hats. They thanked their parents and family for attending.

Grace was then announced as the new Lewiston Roundup Queen and as she walked onto the stage the three tables full of Tagger family and friends stood up and yelled, whistled, hooted and howled until she started laughing and crying at the same time.

Her official chaps were draped over her arm and crown placed on her hat then she stepped in front of the microphone.

"Obviously," She grinned. "I have a few family members here."

More shouts and whistles from the three tables and laughter from the whole room.

She continued, "I'd like to thank the royalty judges for allowing me this opportunity and the chaperones that will be guiding us through this next year." She nodded to the ones she could see. "In thanking my family, I have to start with my Aunt Jordan who has guided myself, my sister and our cousins the last couple years to rodeo after rodeo and horse shows in helping us to fulfill our dreams." Grace nodded to Jordan who began wiping away tears as she leaned back into Scott's arms. "To my mother, who is my guiding light in life, I thank you for being here…for *literally* being here." Grace wiped away tears as she looked at her mother who was doing the same thing.

Remembering the night of their accident down the mountainside and the days that followed, Reilly had a very hard time containing the tears himself. He quickly took a drink of water to wash them away.

"To Jessup," Grace continued. "Thank you for teaching me the cowgirl way of life and keeping me country driven."

"You were born with it, Darlin'," Jessup yelled with a proud grin and his girlfriend, Kate, laughing at his side.

"Thank you to my best friend Josey, and my cousins Matt, Nikki, Wade and Nora…who I expect we'll be seeing her up here in a few years." Grace grinned.

The three tables erupted again. Reilly turned to see Nora just smile at Grace. He knew it was on Nora's schedule. The roundup queen would be a year to two before her run for Miss Rodeo Idaho.

"To Jack," Grace looked at him. "Thanks for being my first boss at The Stables. Teaching me business, respect, and how to always maintain my cool around…well, let's just say not cool people. That trait will help me a lot this next year."

The room chuckled as Jack raised a glass to her.

"Nick, Tessa, and Alex," Grace smiled at them. "Thank you for believing in me one hundred percent." They smiled and nodded. "And then there is the Tagger Trio." Grace grinned. "Which happens to include my handsome, wonderful, amazing…"

"UNCLE!" Scott yelled.

They all laughed again.

"Yes," Grace laughed. "You and Dad are both all that and more. You two and my beautiful Aunt Dru…you three have enforced in us not only the country life that I will be happily promoting this next year but also the love of family and of friendships. You set that example every day by not only being brothers and sister but being business partners and friends. I thank you for that." She nodded to each of them and received nods of love in return. "Which leads me to my last thank you…to my partners, friends, co-horts in crime…the angels on my shoulders when I need them and the devils on my shoulders when I need them. To the two people that round out my heart and make me who I truly am…my sister Sadie and my Reilly. I truly cannot tell you how much your believing and loving me means." She wiped away more tears as did Sadie. Reilly nodded with a proud grin.

Grace looked around the room. "So, now let's all eat, drink, buy, dance, and have fun. Thank you all for coming out to support the tradition!"

The two new princesses stepped up to the microphone and all three made their first official holler of the round-up motto: "SHE'S WILD!"

A half hour later, Reilly finally found Grace to give her a congratulatory hug as the live auction was in progress. The silent auction for a few tables was closed so they could prepare the announcements.

"Very eloquent," He grinned at her. "They made the right choice in you."

"Thanks," Grace grinned.

"Serious, Grace," Tessa hugged her, too. "You had great self-confidence and spoke so clearly…it was such a great speech…you will represent them…"

"YOU DID NOT!"

They all turned to Jordan who was standing with hands on hips glaring at Nick.

"Well, Jordan, I did," Nick said calmly with a smirk.

"I wanted those chinks," She glared.

"Yes…well," He casually leaned back in his chair. "I was told to outbid you so you couldn't have them."

Jordan's head tilted and eyes narrowed. She slowly turned to her husband. Scott turned rolling eyes to Nick.

"Are you kidding me?" Scott huffed to Nick, who just grinned like the Cheshire cat. "You weren't supposed to tell her."

"She scares me," Nick chuckled and received a round of laughter in return.

Scott shook his head and looked at Jordan, "I saw how much you liked the chinks and remembered you said you needed new ones. So I called Hope's mother after you were done talking to her and commissioned her to make you a new pair…that were made just for you." He stopped and stared at her but she didn't move. "You know…to your…stature…or your shortness." He grinned and received a slight smirk from her. "I was going to surprise you with them…and have…you know…your Cheyenne stuff on them that you like." He smiled again. "You know…the feathers…arrows…and symbols that you like."

"Oh, shut up," She giggled and threw her arms around him.

The group laughed again.

"So who did you buy the chinks for?" Reilly asked Nick.

"I'm pretty sure there is only one person I would be buying them for." Nick grinned.

"So they're mine?" Nikki stepped up.

"No, they're mine." Nora stepped in next to her.

"Sorry, ladies, but I'm pretty sure they would be for me." Tessa stepped in next to them.

All three stood staring at Nick who just blankly looked at all three of them.

Reilly started chuckling.

Nick turned to Scott, "You wouldn't happen to have Hope's mother's number on you, would you?"

More laughter rang out.

"Well, she's getting a lot of business from this crowd." Alex beamed and looked over at Hope who was sitting at a table with older farmers. Her elbow was on the table, chin in hand and she was staring at her plate while her fork pushed the food around.

"She looks bored," Wade said.

"Sadie, go get her," Reilly said.

Sadie turned and within minutes had Hope joining them.

"Thank you," Hope smiled.

After the live auction was over, the band took the stage and the music started.

Reilly turned to look for Adeline. She was turning to him with a smile.

"Come on, Reilly!" Sadie yelled and took his arm to drag him onto the dance floor.

Reilly followed but turned to Adeline. "I'll be right back," He mouthed to her. She smiled and nodded.

He turned his attention to Sadie and swung her under his arm and around his back over and over. Wade and Nora were next to them. Alex was standing on the side with Hope.

Reilly twirled Sadie over next to them.

"Why aren't you two dancing?" Reilly asked.

"He asked, but I don't know how to," Hope shrugged.

"He's the best to start with then," Sadie said.

Alex turned to Hope, "Because of my leg, I can't move as fast as they do. I can just show you some of the spins and twirls." He motioned a hand to the dance floor. "I promise I won't hurt you and you'll have more fun than standing here or sitting at the old farmer's table."

Reilly spun Sadie away from them as Hope and Alex stepped out onto the floor. They watched as Alex showed her a couple moves.

"Over your back!" Sadie yelled.

Reilly laughed and spun her out, they connected elbows, he turned and bent at the waist then she rolled over his back to the delighted yells of the crowd. When her boots hit the floor she was laughing and grabbing for his hand. He spun and twirled through the whole song.

When the song came to an end Sadie ran for Wade as Reilly walked to Adeline.

She was wearing a blue lace dress that matched her hat and white boots with a blue trim. Her black straight hair hung down to her shoulders. Her head was twisting back and forth and her dark brown eyes were wide as he approached.

"I don't know how to do that." She said with the Texas drawl then stepped back.

Reilly laughed, "Sadie and I were taught by one of the best and we've danced together for a couple years now." He held out a hand. "I promise, I won't toss you over my back or flip you through the crowd."

"Alright," She slowly stretched out her hand. "I'm pretty darn good with the Texas two-step. Being raised in Texas, you pretty much have to be."

"Well," Reilly grinned. "I can do that too."

The song started and it was perfect so they two-stepped through the whole song. At one point, they danced next to Nick and Tessa and Nick grinned with a nod.

Reilly internally smiled. Nick had taught him to dance right after Reilly and Kelly had broken up. He'd told him it was a great way to attract a girl. This time…he was right.

The next dance was slower so they were able to talk over the music.

"You and Grace will be traveling a lot this summer to the same places." Reilly said.

She nodded, "Yes, we will. Are you traveling with her?"

"To most. We usually team rope together but she won't have time to do that at all of them. I'll be doing some with Wade but I'll stick to calf tying when she can't rope."

"From her speech, it sounds like you two are very close." Her eyes narrowed slightly.

Reilly smiled, "My dad moved us to Idaho to work at the Tagger family business when I was seven. She was seven too and we've been best friends since. Dad married her Aunt Dru so we're cousins now."

"Oh," Adeline's smile brightened. "Can I ask why he moved you here?"

"My mother passed away when I was five and he moved here to get a new start."

"Oh," Her smile diminished.

"We try to go to Texas a couple times a year to visit his parents and my mother's family." Reilly said. "Grace and I are going down after graduation for a couple of weeks to rope and ride at some of the rodeos down there."

"Oh!" She grinned. "You'll have so much fun! What an adventure!"

"That's what we wanted."

"What part of Texas?"

Reilly caught a glimpse of his parents dancing so he maneuvered her over to them. "You wanted a little taste of Texas so let me introduce you."

He bumped into his parents and they all laughed.

"Dad, this is Adeline. She's from Texas and misses talking to someone that doesn't have an accent," Reilly grinned.

His dad laughed, "I can relate!"

Reilly handed Adeline's hand to his dad and he took his mother's. The couples danced away from each other.

"She seems sweet," Dru said.

"I do believe she is," Reilly nodded.

"You know his Texas drawl is going to be off the chart when he gets done talking with her," Dru grinned.

Reilly chuckled, "That's what I told her."

They finished the dance and met at the tables.

Adeline was talking to one of the princesses from her court when he arrived.

She turned sad eyes to him, "We have ta' leave now," She said with a heavy drawl.

Her accent had increased too. Reilly kept the laugh internal.

"Thank you so much for introducin' me ta' your dad," She smiled as she pushed her chair into the table. "And thank you for sittin' behind me and dancin' with me."

"It was truly my pleasure," Reilly said. "I'll see you in the arenas."

Her brown eyes sparkled and grin widened, "Absolutely, Cowboy."

She walked away and he watched her go. At the last second, just before going through the exit doors, she turned back and looked for him. When their eyes met, she smiled again then she was gone.

"Come on, lover boy," Grace said from behind him. "I only have time for one dance before we have to start cleaning things up."

He danced for another half hour before they began preparing to leave. Nora appeared with the red fringed chinks over her shoulder and grinning broadly at Tessa and Nikki.

"How did you end up with the chinks?" Scott asked.

"A mean game of rock, paper, scissors," Nikki huffed.

"I think she cheated," Tessa smirked with a playful wink at Nikki.

Nora laughed, "I haven't figured out how to cheat on that one yet."

"Well, then," Jessup walked in behind them. "Seems my lessons for you aren't done yet."

They all laughed as they walked toward the exit with treasures in hand and a horse belt tucked away, hidden from Grace.

"Dad?" Sadie said as she walked next to Grayson and slid a hand into his. "I know tomorrow we have to sell Mustang…but would it be OK if we just bought him back?"

"That's not the way this is supposed to go," Grayson chuckled.

"I know," Sadie whined with a yawn. "But I really like him and I'm really going to miss him."

"He's quite a character," Grayson nodded. "I'll miss him too."

"Not if you buy him back," Sadie smiled.

CHAPTER SEVEN
Sunday Expo

The whole family arrived at the arena early to claim good seats for the sale. All four Tagger girls went directly to Mustang and Dr. Mark's bay horse. The older veterinarian soon joined them in preparing the horses for the sale.

Reilly, Wade, and Alex sat directly in front of Matt and Josey with the parents, Tessa, Nick, Cora, Jessup and Kate surrounding them. His dad sat to Reilly's left with Wade to right. Dru sat in front of them so she could lean back onto her husband's legs.

Right in front of their group, a small showing pen had been constructed in the arena to showcase the horse that would be selling. Behind it and facing the crowd was a long flatbed trailer with tables and chairs set on top of it for the auctioneer and helpers.

Behind the trailer was an open arena for the riders to warm up and show off the horses just prior to entering the showing pen. To their right and along the panel next to the show pen, a temporary set of bleachers was added for the growing crowd and potential bidders.

"Mustang is third out?" Nick asked while looking at the sale flyer that displayed pictures and descriptions of each horse.

"Yeah," Scott answered. "He's garnered so much attention they were going to keep him for last but then decided people wouldn't bid on any other horses in hopes they could buy him."

"The two horses before are just to warm up the crowd." Grayson added.

"Dr. Mark's bay is number 15." Dru said.

Reilly glanced around the group of family and friends. "Who has bidder cards?"

Dru chuckled, "Jack, Scott, Grayson, Nick and Jessup."

"And Matt," Josey added.

"And Dru," Nick, who was sitting next to Alex, grinned at her.

"Tattletale," Dru humorously glared at him.

Jeremy, the auctioneer, walked up the steps of their makeshift announcer stand followed by two other helpers who would keep track of bidders.

An excited murmur erupted in the building as everyone rushed to find a good position for the auction.

"Where's the couple that were sitting behind us yesterday?" Reilly asked.

"Top row on the added bleachers." Dru answered with a nod in their direction. "She was out this morning with the girls as they were saddling him."

"You think she'll get him?" Alex asked.

"From what I have heard from other bidders that know the couple, he would be very lucky to land in their stables." Reilly's dad answered. "They are very highly regarded in the industry."

"Where are they from?" Wade asked.

"Utah," Dru answered. "Sadie was still trying to get Grayson to buy him back."

"She thinks Utah is too far away," Leah chuckled. "She's going to have a heck of a time raising horses and not wanting to sell them."

"There they are," Josey said from behind them and all heads turned to the back of the arena.

Sadie and Nora were both on the horse's back with Nora in front holding the reins. Nikki and Grace walked across the back of the arena to the gate which led them down the aisle to the bleachers. They grinned proudly and took the seats right in front of Reilly.

"Someone brought in a pair of yearlings that are just beautiful. They are just about duplicates of Romeo and Shakespeare." Nikki said of the two colts she bought at the fall auction.

"You going to get a bidder's card?" Dru asked with a grin.

"No! My place is full right now. We haven't had a chance to enlarge the corrals around the barn yet." Nikki answered with a firm shake of the head.

"As yearlings, they don't need a corral," Reilly pointed out. "Just a big open field to play in and you have plenty of those at Circle 50."

Nikki turned and glared at him as everyone else chuckled, "And I'm going to get a reputation for only buying auction horses."

"Between Bodi, Romeo, and Shakespeare, I think you've done yourself well and most people recognize that." Dru argued.

"Well…" Nikki started.

"Good morning everyone," The auctioneer's voice boomed out of the speaker system. "We have twenty-nine horses on the sales block today, so let's get started." He cleared his voice then his words came out fast and furious. "Hip #1 we have a pretty little colt here…"

The sorrel two-year-old was walked in circles in the show pen. His ears were up and eyes searching the crowd staring back at him.

Reilly tried to listen to every word the auctioneer said but the words were so fast they just blurred together. Occasionally he'd catch a bidding price. One man on the trailer and a man in front of each set of bleachers watched the crowd for bids and yelled when they received them.

The colt sold for $800 and was walked out of the pen allowing a red roan three-year-old quarter horse to be ridden in. The rider rode him in the circles then demonstrated getting off, lifting the hooves, getting back on, then backed the horse around the pen.

The auctioneer's voice was booming as the horse's descriptions and bids were called out. He pointed at each of the men helping with the bids as they yelled "yep!" when they saw a bid.

"Sold for $1200!" The auctioneer yelled and looked right at Reilly.

Reilly's shoulders rose in surprise then he slowly turned to Grayson who was sitting just behind him. Grayson held up his bidder's number.

"Why that one?" Josey asked.

"He's a good young colt." Grayson huffed. "A lot of these buyers are waiting for Mustang. Once he's gone the prices will go up."

"So you think you got him for a steal." Reilly said.

"You'll see," Grayson smirked.

They turned back to the arena as Grayson's new horse was walked out and Sadie and Nora rode Mustang into the show pen.

"They bought him for $850," Grayson whispered as the two girls rode the horse in circles. "They kept track of his feed and the time they put into him that wasn't work for the ranch. They need $1400 to break even."

"Here we go with Mustang the mustang," The auctioneer called out. "These Tagger horsewomen have done a tremendous job…"

"Two thousand!" Was yelled out and the Tagger family's heads turned to the bleacher where Caroline from Utah was sitting. Sadie and Nora grinned up at the woman.

"Oh, my!" Nikki giggled.

Excitement raced through Reilly and he proudly laid a hand on Grace and Nikki's shoulders.

"Well, I think we got our money back." Grace quipped.

"Great start…" The auctioneer said.

"Twenty Five hundred!" Was yelled to the left of them and all the Tagger family and friend's heads turned to look at the man holding up his bidder's card.

"Three thousand!" Caroline yelled and their heads turned again.

Nora and Sadie were sitting quietly on the horse as he stood in the middle of the pen. Their heads swung back and forth too.

"Thirty five hundred!" The man yelled before the auctioneer could speak and their heads turned again.

"Four thousand," Caroline yelled and they turned back to her.

"Holy smokes!" Grace giggled excitedly.

Both bidders called out while the auctioneer watched and the crowd's heads turned back and forth between the two as if they were at a tennis match. Nora, Sadie, and Mustang stood quietly in the middle of the pen and watched.

The bid slowly climbed to five thousand when Caroline's husband tugged on her arm. She hesitated and looked down at him. He said something to her and she nodded then turned back to stare across the arena at the other bidder.

"Seventy five hundred," She said firmly and loudly.

The crowd gasped as Nora and Sadie started giggling.

All heads turned to the other bidder who glared back at Caroline.

"The bid is at seventy five hundred," The auctioneer finally spoke. "Do we have eight?"

The room was silent. Even the horses warming up had stopped and the riders were watching.

Reilly turned back to Caroline. From the glaring eyes, raised shoulders, and her lips rolled into a thin line, it was pretty clear to him that she was not going to lose the horse. She was ready to bid more.

He turned back to the other bidder just as the man sighed and shook his head.

The auctioneer looked around the room. "Any other bids? Do I have eight thousand?"

The room was dead silent.

Nora and Sadie turned and looked at the auctioneer who smiled back at them.

"Sold!" He yelled and tipped his head to the girls.

"Whoo hoo!" The girls yelled and looked back to the family on the bleachers.

Clapping erupted in the room as the riders in the arena began moving again. Caroline and her husband waved excitedly at the girls. They were quickly making their way down the steps of the bleachers.

As Nora nudged Mustang out of the gate, Sadie turned to the family on the bleachers and waved. Her grin couldn't have been any wider.

"You know," Dru turned a proud smile to Nikki and Grace. "Your marketing him with that video was the major part of that sale."

The two giggled in delight.

"We're a great team," Grace nodded and the pair quickly made their way out to the barn.

Another three-year-old gelding was ridden into the show pen. He was very similar to the horse Grayson had won just before Mustang sold.

The horse sold for $1500.

"Told ya," Grayson chuckled.

Leah and Jordan made their way to the cook trailer and back with coffee for everyone and a plate full of doughnuts that were quickly devoured.

Nora rode Dr. Mark's horse into the arena then into the show pen. The bidding started at $1000 and he was sold for $3500. All the girls were grinning but laughed when the winning bidder stood proudly and held up his bidder card…it was Dr. Mark!

Scott turned and chuckled, "What the heck?"

Dr. Mark just grinned through his signature mustache, "I like him, but wanted to make sure everyone saw how well those girls did with him." He shrugged. "It was worth the commission I have to pay for selling him…to myself." He chuckled.

A few horses later, a tall dark gelding with a white blaze was ridden into the arena. He was so dark he was almost black but golden highlights shone around his eyes and muzzle.

"He must be 16 or 17 hands." Alex whispered.

"At least," Wade nodded.

The auctioneer started the bidding.

"Yep!" The helper waved his hand.

Reilly barely moved his head to see Dru bid on the horse by just slightly flipping the card in the man's direction.

"Yep!" The helper yelled.

Reilly turned the other direction and could just see Grayson flip his bidding card.

"Yep!" The helper yelled out.

Reilly chuckled.

The pair each bid again and Reilly smiled. He looked for any other bidders but the "yeps" were only yelled for Dru and Grayson.

"Yep!"

"Ok," Reilly chuckled and nudged his mom.

She turned and looked at him.

"You do know that it's just you and Grayson bidding on that horse?" He couldn't help but laugh and was joined by the rest of the family.

Grayson and Dru both turned to the man yelling 'yep' at their bids. They had known him for years and he knew they were brother and sister. The man gave them a very humorous guilty grin.

Reilly laughed again.

"You buy him and I'll take him to the Stables." Dru said to Grayson.

"I'll buy him and take him to the ranch," Grayson flipped the card again.

Dru didn't and Grayson won the horse.

They sat quietly as the tall horse was walked out of the pen and another entered.

Grayson spoke from behind Reilly. "He's going to be stolen out of the ranch corrals, isn't he?"

Dru didn't turn, she just watched the new horse walk across the arena and chuckled, "First chance I get."

CHAPTER EIGHT
Monday Branding Week

"Why are we branding at Circle 50 first?" Wade asked as they rode across the meadow.

The ground was bare of snow except in those areas the sun's rays couldn't reach.

Reilly turned and looked over at him, Alex, Sadie, Josey, and Nikki who were spread out behind at least a hundred Hereford cow and calf pairs.

At the base of the mountain, his dad, Nick, Matt, the Trio, Jessup, and Leah were pushing the cows up and out of the wide ravine. Lucas, Grace, Jordan, Nora, and Cora were sitting at strategic places in the trail where the cows liked to dive off the trail to the corrals. As the cows past them, they would ride with everyone else for the push to the branding pasture.

"Because the grass over here is dried up and we need to move them to greener pasture first." Nikki answered. "We had a pretty light winter for snow, so some areas already have grass growing. Once they are on the other side, we won't have to hay anymore."

"That'll save a lot of work," Sadie added.

"So there is more time to plan the wedding," Josey laughed.

"And the new house is almost ready," Nikki grinned. "Just a couple more weeks."

"It's going to be a busy May and June," Sadie said. "Wedding, graduations, district rodeos finals, rodeo state finals, the trip to Fort Collins for me and Nora and the trip to Texas for Reilly and Grace."

"Well, I'm glad I scheduled the wedding when I did," Nikki chuckled. "We may have been at the alter with no one there."

They rode quietly for a while then Alex turned to Nikki, "Why did they pay seventy-five hundred for Mustang?"

"Well, that was out of the blue," Nikki chuckled.

Alex shrugged, "We left right after the auction and I didn't hear anything."

Sadie answered, "When we were talking to them, the Caroline lady was impressed that we had all our plans together for our super horse business."

"Grace had told her that all the money was going into the business and none of us were actually going to be spending it on anything but more horses." Nikki added.

"So she was actually, kind of, investing in your business." Wade concluded.

"Yep," Sadie quipped with a grin.

"Who was the other guy?" Reilly asked. "Did anyone ever find out?"

"Not really," Josey answered. "He bought a couple mares. I think he was just going to use them as broodmares."

"Then why would he want a gelding?" Wade asked.

They all shrugged and continued to chat as they pushed the cows into the pasture. Just as Reilly closed the gate behind them, the first cows from the other herd appeared in the distance.

"Here they come!" Alex hollered.

"Alex, Wade, and Reilly stay here," Nikki said. "We three will go join the group."

Reilly climbed the corral fence next to Rufio and sat on the top rail. Alex and Wade remained on their horses and the three watched the riders gallop across the field. Laughter rang out from the girls.

"Galloping across an open field…it just never gets old," Wade grinned and turned to Reilly.

"I agree," Alex said.

They sat quietly watching their herd of cows settle into the pasture and occasionally looked out to the approaching herd.

"Reilly?" Alex asked softly.

Both Wade and Reilly turned to him.

"What?" Reilly asked.

"How…how do you…" Alex sighed with his cheeks turning red.

"How do I what?" Reilly asked.

Alex grimaced at him and took a deep breath, "How do you know when a girl wants you to kiss her?"

Reilly smiled as Wade's eyebrows rose.

"You kissed Hope?" Wade gasped.

Alex's face turned bright red and he leaned back in the saddle as if to hide.

"You did! Didn't you?" Wade asked.

"Well…sort of," Alex admitted

Reilly laughed, "How do you 'sort of' kiss a girl?"

Alex leaned forward with an embarrassed smile. "We just kind of stared at each other for…what seemed like forever. Then when I went to shake her hand, she leaned forward to kiss me and I kinda…well…I…"

"WHAT?" Wade yelled.

"I touched her lips with mine but I didn't…you know…smack or anything." Alex explained.

"Well, that would officially be a kiss." Reilly grinned.

Alex rose in the saddle and he smiled at a gaping Wade.

"You got your first kiss before I did," Wade's shoulders slumped.

"I'm eight months older than you." Alex chuckled.

"But still…" Wade whined. "Now I'm the only guy that doesn't have his first kiss yet."

Reilly shook his head with a contained laugh, "Alex is fourteen and you're thirteen…"

"And a half," Wade added quickly.

"I didn't get my first kiss until I was fifteen," Reilly finished.

"With Kelly?" Alex asked.

"Yeah," Reilly nodded.

"How did you know?" Wade asked.

"Yeah," Alex turned in his saddle. "How did you know she wanted you to kiss her?"

Reilly shook his head as he grinned, "I didn't…she kissed me."

"First?" Alex gasped.

Wade's eyes were wide.

"Yeah, we were painting a building at the Stables and when I walked her to her car that night she kissed me on the cheek. I didn't know what to do. She did it again the next night and I at least had half a brain and was able to pucker and kiss her back." Reilly blushed.

"Both times…she did it first both times." Wade exhaled and turned to Alex. "And Hope did it first too."

"Yeah," Alex and Reilly nodded.

"What about after that?" Alex asked Reilly. "Did she kiss first all the time?"

"No…sort of…well, to start." Reilly shrugged. They both looked at him in anticipation. "Well, after our first session on the trail…"

"WHAT?" Wade gasped. "What's a session? Is that like making-out?"

"On what trail?" Alex asked.

Reilly shrugged again, "We were on a trail ride and stopped for lunch. We were standing next to each other and she leaned in…so I leaned in…and we kissed…for like ten minutes."

Both boys looked at him with lowered jaws and wide eyes.

"Ten minutes?" Alex asked softly.

"So, since guys exaggerate their experience with girls…that would be for 5 minutes?" Wade smirked.

Reilly laughed, "No, it was really like ten minutes but we did longer after that."

"Make out sessions for longer than 10 minutes?" Alex's eye brows rose. "Wow, I'd like to kiss Hope that long."

"I'd just like to kiss a girl." Wade groaned.

"Well, maybe Nora and Sadie will help you like Nikki did for Matt." Reilly said.

"What do you mean?" Wade asked.

"Matt said that Nikki used to set him up with girls all the time in college." Reilly answered.

"College?" Wade gasped. "I don't want to wait until I'm in college for my first kiss. That's five more years!"

"That would just be horrible," Alex turned a smirk to Wade. "You know…to have to wait that long for your first kiss."

Reilly burst out laughing at the glare Wade gave Alex.

"Yours was just a brushing of the lips," Wade rolled his un-humored eyes.

"Reilly said it was officially a kiss." Alex grinned with a shrug. "And when, exactly, have you had a brushing of the lips with a girl…that's not a family member."

Wade glared at both of them and turned toward the approaching riders.

Alex and Reilly grinned at each other.

Nikki trotted in and pulled Harvey to a stop next to them. She looked between the three.

"What are you three talking about?" She asked.

"Nothin'," Wade turned to the herd.

"Just brushing…" Alex chuckled.

"Age…" Reilly chuckled.

Wade kicked Dollar into a trot away from them and Alex and Reilly laughed again.

****

"We have Tuesday and Wednesday…all day," Grayson said to Jessup as they leaned against the fence. "Then half a day Thursday."

All the Circle 50 cows were in the pasture in front of them. Reilly was leaning against the fence between them as everyone else was eating dinner.

Jessup nodded, "We can get this herd done before Scott and Jordan leave on Thursday and a good portion of the Tagger herd rounded up."

"We'll get what we can after that," Grayson said. "We've done it before with a short crew; it just takes a couple more days. I'm more worried about the canyon ride."

Jessup nodded, "Scott and Monty will be sorely missed on that one."

"We have Reilly this year," Grayson said without even looking at Reilly. "He can ride Monty."

Reilly's head jerked to him, "You want me to ride Monty in the canyons?"

Grayson shrugged, "Why not? Scott said he would rather you ride a horse that has been through there a dozen or more times."

"Scott said…but…Wade…" Reilly felt his heart sink. "Wade has always wanted to ride Monty and in the canyons."

Grayson shook his head as Jessup sent a glance to them.

"Wade's a dang good cowboy…I'd trust him with everything else…just not the canyons," Grayson said.

Reilly's stomach ached. If he was going to say something then this was the time.

"I think I might wait…" Reilly managed to get out before both men turned to him.

Grayson looked at him thoughtfully, "Wait for what?"

"Wait for Wade," Reilly said firmly and straightened his shoulders.

"Wait for me for what?" Wade walked up behind them and looked between Grayson and Reilly.

"What until you can ride the canyons," Reilly said with conviction. "I'll just…"

Wade started shaking his head with a furrowed brow, "Yeah…I appreciate the thought, but no…that's not happening."

Reilly was stunned. "Why?"

"Because you can now…why would you want to wait for something so wonderful…that you've waited years to be able to do…for years longer?" Wade's lips rolled together into a thin line as he tried to stop the smirk. "Why would you want to wait?" The right side of his mouth twitched.

Reilly grinned and the chuckle rumbled out of him.

Wade looked at Jessup then Grayson and then turned and walked away.

Neither man would ever know that it wasn't about the riding…it was about the kissing.

CHAPTER NINE
Tuesday Branding

The coffee aroma woke them before the actual alarms were to go off. Reilly sat up just as Grayson, Scott, and Sadie slid from their beds. She always rose early to listen to the branding plans. He quickly joined them at the kitchen table.

"When are you going to tell her?" Scott whispered to Grayson.

"I can't say anything until everyone's awake," Grayson said.

"Tell who what?" Sadie asked as she lifted her milk filled coffee mug to her lips.

Neither man said anything and didn't look at her.

"You are not telling me I can't help brand this year!" Sadie slammed the coffee mug down on the table and the whack echoed through the bunkhouse. "I should have last year…I'm old enough now…more than enough…" Her voice rose with every word.

"Lower your voice and change your tone," Grayson growled.

Sadie stared at him…her eyes widening and face turning a deep red.

"No one is trying to keep you out of the corrals this year," Grayson said. "But if you don't breathe you may pass out and I'm going to leave you here and make you walk there."

Sadie took in a deep breath, "Then tell me what?"

"Just tell her," Leah said from behind them.

"No," Grayson sneered. "I think I've changed my mind."

"You did not," Dru chuckled as she walked by them and to the coffee pot.

"She'll never know…" Grayson leaned back in his chair as he stared at his glaring daughter.

Sadie turned and looked up at her aunt then her mother. "So, this isn't a bad thing?"

Leah shook her head. "Seriously, Sadie? When was the last time we purposely did a bad thing to you?"

"Last year when you wouldn't let me in the corrals." Sadie answered quickly. "And you made me skip two grades and go to school with Nora and not Wade." She looked at Nora who was laying in her bed watching. "Nothing personal," She smiled.

Nora just giggled.

"You were broken, battered, and bruised last year, Sadie," Grace joined the group. "Of course, you couldn't get in the corral."

"And both of those are good things," Grayson drawled.

"In your opinion," Sadie drawled back.

Grayson's eyes narrowed, "Tone, young lady, or I don't care who says what, you'll be staying here today."

Sadie leaned back in her chair and slowly lifted the mug of milk to her lips.

The room was quiet until Dru sat in her chair across from her brothers. "You tell her or I will," She said softly.

Grayson looked from his sister to his youngest daughter.

"We have decided to change how we do branding…" He started.

"Are you kidding me?" Sadie's voice shook. "Just when I get old enough…?"

"Sadie, keep quiet," Her mother ordered.

Grayson took an impatient breath then continued, "Because you are old enough and can throw a rope better than the average cowboy, we decided that we would do a pen of 30 at a time."

There was dead silence in the bunkhouse when he paused.

Sadie just stared at him.

"You help drag to the fire when we do small herds, there is no reason you can't throw a rope when we do the big herd."

Sadie's eyes widened.

"Instead of just a crew in the saddle and one on the ground, we'll have two of each," Dru said. "We'll switch every 30 calves."

"We'll get through the herds faster." Scott added.

"Does that include us?" Wade whispered and looked at Alex then Nora.

"Of course," Scott answered with a grin.

Sadie slowly rose with the coffee mug in her hands and walked to the sink. She rinsed the mug, set it down, then turned.

"Thank you father, mother, aunts, and uncles," Sadie said too politely. "I think you have made a wonderful decision."

There was silence…until Leah was the first to chuckle.

Sadie's composure exploded with a "Yee haw!", a screech, then a run at her dad. She flew into his arms with such force they nearly toppled over the side of his chair.

An hour later, with the sun barely making an appearance above the horizon, the first crew in the saddle wandered into the herd.

Sadie, Dru, Grayson, and Grace pushed a portion of the Herefords into the large corral. While Jessup and Cora prepared the branding table with ear tags, bottles of vaccines, record book, and castration tools the rest of the crew separated the calves into a smaller pen.

"How many?" Grayson hollered from on top of the buckskin, Eli.

"A good 50 to 60," Reilly answered as he shut the gate.

"We're ready," Jessup yelled as he lifted a branding iron.

Thirty of the separated calves were released into the branding corral.

Grayson turned to a grinning Sadie, "Get to work."

With matching brown cowboy hats, well-worn tan chaps, T3E branded denim jackets, Sadie on her golden Scarecrow and Dru on the black Libby wandered toward the huddled calves. Their right arms were held just to their sides with the lariat loops dangling from their fingers. They threw their first loops and two calves were pulled into the middle of the ground crew.

Cora was right in front taking pictures of the crews…with Sadie's eyes sparkling and smile beaming.

****

Astride Rufio, Reilly flicked the rope toward the brown calf's back feet and trapped it perfectly. A quick yank and nudging the horse backwards the rope tightened and he drug the calf to the ground crew.

Rufio turned and faced the corral in time for him to see Matt and Trooper drag a second calf to the ground crew.

The tall brown horse backed into the space right next to Rufio. Reilly and Matt grinned at each other.

"Look over here," Cora said to them.

They both turned and grinned at her as she clicked the shutter on the camera. She quickly turned to capture Grayson teaching Sadie how to castrate a calf.

"Not many thirteen-year-olds want to do that," Matt chuckled.

"She, most definitely, is not like any other thirteen-year-old," Reilly nodded.

"So Grace told me you guys ruled out Montana for college," Matt said.

"Just too far," Reilly nodded. "How did you decide to go to U of I?"

"Nikki was already there. They had a resort management course and that's what she originally went to college for. I was going for forestry but I just couldn't take the classrooms."

"Maybe I should do forestry. I love the mountains and don't want to work in an office."

"There is still some office work involved," Matt shrugged. "It is an option until you figure it out. There isn't really a rush."

Their calves were released and they walked into the herd while Scott and Wade pulled two more calves to the ground crew.

As Matt and Reilly drug the two calves they roped into the corral, they laughed at the very happy Wade as he grinned his way back to the calves.

Matt and Reilly turned the horses and the ground crew went to work on their calves.

"What about waiting a year?" Matt asked.

Reilly shook his head, "Not an option. Grace knows what she wants and is ready to go. I'm not going to hold her up a full year. I can do the required classes."

 "Well, something will happen, like it did for me, that will guide you."

"Buying Andy's ranch or the plane crash?" Reilly smirked.

"The plane crash," Matt nodded. "If it hadn't been for everything we did there to save the kids? I don't think I would have ever thought of search and rescue."

"So I wait," Reilly sighed.

"You're only eighteen," Matt said. "It'll…"

He stopped when Scott hollered and everyone stopped to look.

The calf Wade had roped ran underneath Scott's horse Monty. The grey gelding pranced as the ropes hit his legs.

"Let the rope go," Scott ordered.

Wade quickly released the lariat and it danced out from under Monty and the calf took it with him into the herd.

"Sorry, Dad," Wade said sheepishly and dismounted Dollar.

 "All in a day's work, Cowboy," Scott grinned.

He retrieved the rope that had released from the calf's legs and remounted.

Reilly quickly pulled out his phone and pushed the music button. He found just the right song.

He and Matt walked back for the next set of calves and Wade pulled a calf to the ground crew.

"Hey, Wade," Reilly grinned with phone in hand. "I think you need a new favorite song."

"Why's that?" Wade asked.

"I'm pretty sure this one doesn't work for you anymore," Reilly pushed the button and the song rang out in the corral; *I should have been a Cowboy*, by Toby Keith.

"I think ya are," Reilly smirked.

Laughter, then singing burst out in the corral as everyone sang with Toby.

Epic, Reilly thought, just epic.

CHAPTER TEN
Wednesday Branding

"You three don't get lost," Grayson teased with a grin. Their first morning of rounding up the Tagger herd cows was dark and the only way they could see him was from the interior light of the truck.

Reilly, Wade, and Alex stepped up into the saddle of Rufio, Dollar, and Snickers.

"We won't," Reilly laughed. "We've been on this ride before."

"But not in the dark." Grayson said in a serious tone.

"It'll only be dark for another twenty minutes or so," Wade argued.

"And we'll have the best view in the mountains for the sunrise," Reilly reminded him.

"Rider's Point will be to your left. This time of year the sunrise should be right over the top of it. Take a moment to enjoy it," Grayson said. "Then go down the mountain about half way and you'll run into the trail that takes you west. Follow it for three ridges. Josey said she thought she saw a few pairs down there."

"Once we hit the creek we move back up the mountain," Wade nodded.

"Then we cross the road into the trees and ride to Willow Ridge," Alex added.

"We should meet up with all of you once we go down the north face of it," Reilly continued.

"We have the radio so we can make contact when we hit the road and let you know we're headed your way in case you want us to do something else," Wade smiled and held up the radio.

"We tested it this morning before leaving the ranch," Alex said.

"We got this, Grayson," Reilly said confidently.

Grayson grinned, "We'll see you for lunch." The truck and horse trailer moved down the dark road leaving the three riders on the edge of the dirt road.

"Wow," Alex whispered. "It is really dark out here."

"The clouds are covering the moon," Reilly said.

"You scared?" Wade asked.

"No…" Alex whispered.

"Stay between the two of us and pay attention to Snickers," Reilly said as he looked around. He could barely see anything but the dark night. "As long as the horses are calm, we're all good."

"OK," Alex said with a stronger voice.

Reilly pulled his cowboy hat down lower and adjusted his wild rag scarf. His coat covered his body down past his knees. He was warm in the brisk April mountain air. Rufio stood quietly under him but his head was high and he was looking out into the darkness.

"We'll wait right here until the sun comes up enough we can see," Reilly told them.

"Just remember," Wade said. "The Trio has been riding this trail for over twenty years and they are all still alive."

Alex and Reilly chuckled.

"You think they would have told us if they had seen a cougar or bear?" Alex asked.

"I can guarantee if Grayson thought there would be any problems, he wouldn't have left us here in the dark," Reilly answered.

"There's the sunrise over there," Wade pointed to their left.

There was just a hint of daylight appearing over the mountains.

"It'll be a few minutes before we actually see the sun," Reilly said. "Then it will be light enough to head out."

The sun tipped over the horizon lighting the mountains. They nudged the horses into a walk across a small field then began to make their way down into the ravine.

"Look!" Alex pointed.

A pink hue highlighted the low hanging clouds. A mountain peak appeared in the middle of the rising yellow sun.

"That's Rider's Peak," Wade whispered. "My grandparents and great-grandparents' ashes were spread over the tallest peak so they could watch over all of us."

They sat quietly on the horses and watched the clouds turn a deep pink and the sun fully rise behind the peak.

The top of the mountain was fully lit when they began their descent. As the sun rose higher into the sky, the light moved down to take over the shadows in the ravine. The ground in front of them was bare of trees until half way down the mountain then trees covered it all the way to the bottom. Drifts of snow lingered in the edges of the shadows of the trees.

"There it is," Reilly turned Rufio toward the dark trail cut into the side of the mountain.

"What's that?" Alex leaned forward in the saddle to peer into the trees ahead of them.

There was a large dark mass in the middle of the trail just before the shadows of the trees.

"It's a black cow lying down," Wade chuckled.

"I guess Josey was right," Alex grinned.

"But I don't see any others." Reilly said as they drew closer to the cow.

The black cow's head turned toward them. She tucked her front legs under her chest and rose just inches. She rocked back and forth to lift the rest of her body but nothing happened. After three tries she lowered back to the ground with a groan.

"Something's wrong with her," Reilly said as he stepped out of the saddle.

Alex and Wade joined him on the ground and they slowly walked toward the cow so they didn't scare her.

"She's really boney," Wade frowned. "And old."

"Look at the brand," Alex pointed. "It's missing the 3."

"What?" Reilly and Wade asked in unison.

Reilly handed Alex his reins and slowly stepped to the cow but she didn't seem to care. He could easily see the brand was only a TE.

"Is that Martha?" Wade asked in surprise. "Does she have the scar over her right eye from the chutes?"

Reilly looked at the cow's head as she looked at him and saw the confirming faint scar. "Yeah," He nodded.

"Who is Martha?" Alex asked.

"One of the last cows from the original herd; before the accident," Wade said. "She must be close to twenty-years-old."

"Or more," Reilly nodded and stepped back away from her with a frown.

"It's weird she's out here all by herself," Alex said.

Reilly walked farther into the trees.

"What are you doing?" Wade asked.

"Looking to see if she has a baby in here," Reilly answered but he didn't see any movement.

"Is she pregnant?" Alex asked. "Is that why she can't get up?"

Wade walked over to the cow and leaned down to look under her. "She's got a pretty full bag and a big round belly but she doesn't look like she's in labor."

Reilly looked across the mountains then back to the cow. It was still early, cold out and she was susceptible to predators.

He looked over at Wade and Alex.

"Well, we can't leave her out here alone," Reilly determined.

"I agree," They answered in unison.

"I wonder how long she's been out here by herself," Wade said as he looked around the ground. "I only see a couple fresh manure piles."

Reilly turned and looked back at the trees then to Martha. "Let's tie the horses to the trees and see if we can get a rope around her and help her stand. Then we'll see if she can walk."

Alex handed Reilly the reins for Rufio then they all three walked to the trees to loop the reins over the branches.

They heard a groan and turned.

Martha was standing and staring at them as if she was ready to go, too.

Wade chuckled, "I think she thought we were leaving her."

"Think she'll follow us?" Alex asked.

Reilly shrugged, "Let's give it a try."

They mounted the horses and followed the trail into the trees. The big black cow slowly followed behind them.

Reilly turned to Alex and Wade, "Well, let's just continue with our original plan until we get up to the road. We'll go up the mountain at an angle instead of straight up. That'll be easier on her."

With agreeing nods, the three cowboys led the old black cow across the mountainside until they ran into the creek. Martha trudged past them to the water and stuck her big black nose deep into its depth.

Reilly leaned forward to rest his arms on the saddle horn to watch her drink and assess her condition. "She's pretty boney but that could just be her age. Her belly is pretty big and she's got a bag so she's gotta be pregnant."

Wade nudged Dollar into a walk behind the cow. "She's really loose back here and there's some clear goop dripping from the opening."

"So she could have it at any time?" Alex asked; his eyebrows up high in concern.

Both Reilly and Wade nodded.

Reilly looked up the mountainside. It was steep and rocky but bare of trees. "It's going to take us longer to get up the hill by going at an angle and at her pace," He turned to Wade. "Why don't you ride ahead of us? If we don't radio in when they think we should get there, then they'll get all worried about us and send someone out to check on us."

"We don't want that," Wade nodded with a wry grin. "I'll wait for you at the top."

When Wade and Dollar started to climb the mountain, Martha's head rose in concern; water drizzled from her black lips.

"We're right here with you." Alex assured the cow. Her head turned to him then lowered back to the water.

Alex and Reilly looked at each other with a smile.

"You take the lead, Alex." Reilly said and pointed toward a protruding bluff. "Head toward that then turn the other direction at about the same angle and just keep going. I'll follow her and see how it goes."

"OK," Alex nodded and turned Snickers to the bluff to begin the climb. He turned in the saddle to make sure the cow followed. She did.

They stopped three times to let the old cow rest. Reilly was thankful she didn't try to lie down but just stood and caught her breath before they started again.

Over a half hour later, when they were a good thirty yards down from the top, he could finally see Wade standing next to Dollar at the top of the hill.

"You get ahold of them?" Reilly yelled at Wade.

"Sort of," Wade answered.

What did that mean? Reilly didn't want to yell; he'd just be patient and wait until they got to the road.

"What does 'sort of' mean?" Alex asked as he walked onto the flat ground between the mountains edge and the road.

"The radio was breaking up," Wade shrugged. "They asked if we were alright and I said yeah."

"So they are going to be expecting us at any minute on the other side of the trees." Reilly sighed.

"Yeah," Wade nodded. "I've been trying but I think they are out of range still."

Reilly looked at the cow then down the road then back at his companions.

"Alright," He exhaled. "We can't take Martha into the trees with us. It would take too long. The ranch isn't that far away. You two take her to the ranch and I'll go to the other side to meet up with them. I'll ride fast to make up time for taking so long in getting to the top here."

"You going to come get us?" Wade asked with a concerned glare.

"Yeah," Reilly nodded. "There should be a truck and trailer at the top of the mountain. It'll be faster than you two trying to ride over."

"It'll probably take us that long just to get her to the ranch," Wade nodded as he stepped into the saddle.

Alex and Wade started walking down the road. The cow hesitated, looked at Reilly, then turned and followed.

Reilly pulled his water bottle out of his saddle bag and took a long drink. By the time he tucked it back in and secured the latch, the cow had positioned herself in between the two horses. It was quite the sight. He quickly took out his phone and took the picture of the two cowboys talking to each other over the back of the old cow as they meandered down the road.

He laughed as he turned and rode into the trees at a gentle rocking lope. He enjoyed the peaceful quiet of the ride as he weaved between the trees and patches of snow.

At one point they rode around a large pine tree and startled a small herd of deer on the other side. The deer scattered in different directions as Rufio's ears twitched toward them but he didn't startle or slow down. Reilly smiled…he loved this horse.

A fallen log was in front of them and Rufio made the jump over it without hesitation. Reilly just grinned.

When they burst out of the trees and onto the road, the corrals were to his right. Scott and Grayson's trucks were there as well as the large three story cattle hauler. A smaller stock trailer was connected to Scott's truck. He could see three horses in the corral along with a small herd of cows.

The Trio and Nora turned to him as he approached. They were dressed with chaps over their jeans and dark brown T3E ranch jackets. Scott and Grayson wore black hats while Nora and Dru both wore blue T3E baseball caps and had long braids out of the back of the hat.

Their eyes went from him to the trees he just rode out of then back to him.

"Where's Alex and Wade?" Grayson asked when Reilly stopped Rufio in front of them.

"We found Martha on the trail all by herself." Reilly stepped out of the saddle. "She was having a hard time so they are taking her to the ranch."

The Trio looked concerned so Reilly pulled out his phone and showed them the picture he took of her walking between the horses.

"Well, at least she's still hanging on," Scott said.

"There are only three left from the original herd," Grayson added. "The other two are down Willow Ridge."

"What's wrong with her?" Dru asked.

"She had a hard time standing," Reilly answered. "She looks like she could calf at any moment."

"Good call taking her to the ranch," Grayson said. "Cora's there and I'm sure she'll take care of her."

"We're just heading down to the leased pasture by the highway to gather the herd there," Scott said to Reilly. "Take my truck and trailer to get Wade and Alex then meet us back here."

"Can I do it?" Nora turned excitedly to her dad. "Please? It's an easy road and I need all the practice I can get with pulling the trailer."

Scott grinned at her with a nod, "Alright…but don't wreck my truck."

"I won't," Nora shouted and hugged him tightly before running for the truck.

Reilly and the Trio stood quietly and watched her until she backed the horse trailer onto the road then moved easily toward the ranch.

"At fifteen, she is better at that than a lot of adults," Scott said proudly.

"It's good for her," Grayson said and turned back to his truck. "I'll get Arcturus out of the trailer to make room for Rufio."

Reilly nodded and started to follow when he saw a flash of red hide to his left. He glanced into the corral and saw four of the ranch horses and Trip, Nikki's horse.

"Can I take Trip instead?" Reilly asked Dru. "I promised Nikki I would get some time on him this week to help her out."

"Sure," She shrugged and walked over to open the gate for him.

Once Trip was in the trailer, the four of them loaded into the truck. Reilly enjoyed moments like this when he was riding with just the adults.

"How was the sunrise?" Grayson asked as he drove down the road.

"Beautiful," Reilly smiled. "You were right. The peak was right in the middle of the sun."

"I've always wanted a picture of that," His mom said wistfully.

"I can borrow Sadie's camera and get it for you," Reilly offered.

Her blue eyes shone when she looked at him. It always warmed his heart when she looked at him that way.

"I'll go with you," she smiled. "We can do it together."

"Just the two of us?" Reilly asked hopefully.

She nodded, "It's supposed to be clear in the morning then rain in the afternoon so we should have a good sunrise."

They made plans for the morning while they drove to the Sorenson family ranch. They had leased land from the family to winter a portion of the herd. Now it was time to move them back to the ranch, brand them, and then let them loose in the mountains in the spring pasture.

Grayson turned off the highway and drove down a long driveway to the house that was nestled into a small stand of trees. The cows were in the pasture between the house and the highway. Most of the land was flat but there was a row of trees that blocked a deep ravine on the far side.

"Seems like an easy ride," Reilly said as he looked out at the black and red cows.

"Ahhh, man! You just jinxed it." Scott laughed. "Just when you think it's going to be easy, something will happen."

CHAPTER ELEVEN
More Wednesday Branding

Reilly chuckled as he stepped out of the truck and walked back to unload Trip. Since he was the last in, he was the first out of the long cattle trailer.

The Trio's horses, Monty, Eli, and Libby were already saddled and ready when they were unloaded so Reilly hurried to saddle the red dun. He was the last to step into the stirrup but all three had remained next to him until he was in the saddle. Riding younger horses could be more dangerous than older horses. If they weren't used to being ridden by themselves they didn't like to be left behind.

"Nikki has taken him out by himself before at Circle 50," Dru said. "He should be OK for you out here."

Reilly nodded and the four of them rode along the edge of the fence until they came to the back of the herd. A half hour later, they had the cow and calf pairs pushed into the corral and the gate closed.

Grayson tied Eli to the fence then moved the three story trailer to the cattle ramp. "We'll count as we load."

"Well, heck," Reilly heard from behind him. "We'll be a few short."

He turned to see Scott looking back across the pasture and followed his gaze.

At least six pairs were walking out of the ravine at the far end of the pasture. They were slowly headed toward them.

"I'll go get them," Reilly offered.

"They'll make their way here," Scott said. "Doesn't look like they want to be left behind."

"It'll give Trip some time by himself," Reilly reasoned. "It's more training for him."

Dru and Scott nodded and turned back to the herd in the corral to start loading them into the trailer so Reilly turned toward the pasture.

Twenty feet out, Trip decided he wanted to stay with the other horses and tried to go back. He took a few side steps then crow hopped; his body going straight up in the air with all four hooves off the ground. Reilly shoved his heels into the stirrups to balance in the saddle and remained seated. After a minute of encouragement, Reilly finally had the horse moving across the open pasture. He glanced back at his mother and uncles but they were loading the cows and didn't seem to see what happened.

Once he felt Trip's body relax, Reilly moved him into a trot. The cows were slowly walking parallel to the highway at the other end of the pasture. He rode at an angle toward the back of the small group so he didn't stop their movement to the corral.

Halfway across, Reilly noticed a white car on the highway slow down and eventually stop. A number of trucks and cars drove by the car.

He watched the car as he made it to the back of the herd and followed the cows along the fence. The driver stepped out as Reilly neared. By the time Reilly was level with the car, the driver had walked to the fence and was watching the cows go by.

Curious, Reilly stopped next to the older man who wore a long black wool coat with his hands tucked into the pockets. Black dress pants stuck out the bottom and led to shiny black dress shoes. The man had a thick layer of white hair that waved in the slight breeze. He looked distinguished and out of place next to the cow pasture.

The man's eyes turned to Reilly with a smile.

"Hello, young man," The man said.

"Sir," Reilly tilted his head.

The man huffed a slight laugh, "Not many people use 'sir' now days."

Reilly had to agree, "But they still do around here."

The man nodded and looked at Trip.

"I saw that beautiful horse running across the pasture and it made me think of a family I used to know around here," The man explained. "It's been a long time, but the scene of you two pushing the cows just brought back some good memories and I had to stop and enjoy the moment."

Reilly nodded slightly and patted the horse's neck. "This is Trip. He belongs to my sister. I'm just getting some saddle time on him."

The man nodded and looked out at the cows that had continued their path to the corrals and herd. "Wet saddle blanket," The man looked back at Reilly. "I believe that is what the family used to call it."

Reilly laughed, "Yes, sir. Best thing for a horse…and rider."

"The family had a ranch in the mountains, not here on the highway, but maybe you know if they are still around."

"I've been here since I was seven…eleven years now," Reilly shrugged. "I might…what's their name?"

"Tagger," The man answered. "You know if they are still here?"

Reilly grinned, "Yes, sir. Dru Tagger is my step-mother."

The man's eye brows shot up in surprise. "Well, isn't that a coincidence?"

"Well, sir," Reilly laughed. "Even more of a coincidence is that all three of them are at the corral those cows just walked to…by the house in the trees."

"The Trio?" The man's eyes jerked back to the herd. "They are there?"

"Yes, sir," Reilly nodded.

"They moved down here?"

"No, they still have the ranch in the mountains but leased this field for the winter. We just came down today to move them back to the spring pastures."

"Well, I'll be…" The man smiled and looked in the direction of the Trio.

"Do you want to come back and see them?" Reilly asked.

"I don't want to interrupt," The man started. "But I surely would like to see how they are doing."

Reilly pointed down the paved highway, "The driveway is another thirty feet. I'll ride along side of you."

"Yes," The man nodded and looked back up at Reilly and smiled in excitement. "Yes, I'll follow."

Reilly waited until the man was in the car and the engine started then he moved Trip forward and followed the car down the fence line and down the driveway.

The Trio were looking at the car curiously as Reilly approached the gate. Dru opened it and let him through.

"Who is that?" She asked; her blue eyes looking at the car.

"I don't know," Reilly chuckled as he stepped off the horse. "I didn't ask his name."

The car door opened and Reilly turned in time to see the man's head appear over the roof and a wide smile aimed at the Trio.

"Professor?" Grayson's voice rang out in surprise.

"Oh my!" Dru exclaimed and without a glance back at Reilly she jogged to the car.

Grayson was the first to the man and much to Reilly's surprise, he didn't just shake the man's hand he wrapped him in a strong embrace. Dru was right behind him and was quickly followed by Scott.

Reilly tied Trip to the trailer and joined the group.

"You three look wonderful," The man beamed. "I've thought of you many times over the years. I was praying you were able to keep the ranch."

"We did," Grayson's smile couldn't have been wider. "Nearly killed each other a couple times over it, but we were all determined to work it out."

"You look just the same," Dru laughed.

Reilly stepped in next to her and smiled at the happiness in her expression.

"Lot's more white on top," The man laughed and turned to Reilly. "And this young man said he is your step-son."

Dru turned proudly and took Reilly's arm then turned back, "Yes, he is. Reilly this is Professor Waverly. He used to teach at the University of Idaho."

"He was my professor there." Grayson added. "He put up with me for a couple years before he moved."

Reilly grinned and stepped forward to shake the man's hand.

"Put up with…" The professor laughed and looked at Reilly. "He used to argue with me nearly every day."

"Debate," Grayson corrected with a wide grin. "We had a number of pretty intense debates."

They all laughed.

"Do you have time to come up to the ranch?" Grayson asked. "Leah would love to see you."

The professor's eye brows rose again, "You managed to get her to marry you?"

Grayson chuckled with a smirk, "Yes, sir, and we have two beautiful girls that I would love you to meet too."

"Well," The professor nodded. "I don't have to be in Spokane until tomorrow morning so…yes, I would love to see the ranch again and meet your families."

"I'll load Trip," Reilly turned then stopped and looked back. "If you want, Sir, I can drive your car so you can ride with the Trio."

"Thank you," The professor nodded and looked up at the three level, long cattle hauler pulled by a semi. "I haven't ridden in one of those since I was a teenager." He turned to Reilly with a nod. "It's a rental and if your mother says it's OK, I'm fine with it."

"It's perfectly fine," Dru nodded.

Reilly loaded the horse into the trailer next to the other three. The cows were on the upper two levels and in front of the horses.

When they arrived at the corrals, everyone was there except Leah, Grace, and Sadie.

"They will be coming up the back of Willow Ridge," Jessup said after the introductions were exchanged. "Sadie spotted a small group hiding down in the creek and they have had a heck of a time getting them out."

"We were headed to help when we spotted them half way up the ridge," Jordan said and pointed to their left.

Everyone turned to see the three riders two hundred yards away trotting across a wide green pasture. They were behind a small herd of cows and their calves that were trotting toward the rest of the herd.

"With those three, from this distance, it's hard to tell who is who," Alex chuckled. "Except the sun on Scarecrow making her shine like gold."

"That is Sadie's horse," Reilly told the professor.

The man nodded but he stared out at the three riders approaching. "It reminds me of the first time I met Nora, Anne and Dru. They were riding across a field too."

"Who? Who's Anne?" Alex turned and looked up at the professor.

"Anne was our grandmother and Nora our great-grandmother," Nora answered. "That's who I am named after. Sadie's middle name is Anne."

Reilly turned to look at his mother. She was staring out at the three riders too. Her eyes shimmered and were distant as if in a memory.

"What's your middle name?" Alex asked Nora.

"Cheyenne," Nora answered. "From where Mom grew up."

"What's Grace's middle name?" Alex asked.

"Drucilla," Nora smiled at her aunt.

Dru turned and looked at the two of them then up to the professor. "It was Dry Creek Valley…thanks for that memory," She whispered to him. He nodded warmly in return.

"Where did the name Drucilla come from?" Alex asked Dru.

She smiled at him, "My mother loved romantic novels. That's were Drucilla and Grayson came from."

"What about Scott?" Alex continued his inquisition.

"That was my mother's father's name," Dru answered. "Are you going to ask where Matt came from now?" She teased with a grin.

Alex laughed, "Well…yeah."

"My father was Mathew, his father was Anderson," Dru said.

"So…Mathew and Anne were your parents, Anderson and Nora were your grandparents," Alex said.

Dru nodded, "And then Mathew and Grace were my great-grandparents who traveled here and bought the land."

"So…" Alex grinned. "All three girls are named after their grandmothers?"

"Yes," Dru nodded then held up a hand when he opened his mouth to say something. She grinned at him, "Grayson Mathew, Scott Anderson, Drucilla Anne."

Alex laughed.

"What's your middle name?" Nora asked Alex.

"It's my dad's name," Alex shrugged. "Alex Thomas Elliot."

Nora laughed, "So your initials spell 'ate'."

They all chuckled as the sound of Grace's 'life is good' laugh reached them.

Mother and daughters wore brown leather chaps over their jeans and the dark brown T3E ranch coats. Grace's dark blonde hair was pulled into a side braid that hung over her right shoulder and a black hat was perched low on top her head.   She rode Matt's large horse Jiggers with ease and comfort as he pranced to the left then right.

On top her golden palomino, Sadie's pale blonde hair was in the one braid down her back with a few tendrils loose and wisping around her smiling face. Her dark brown cowboy hat matched the color of her jacket. The bright sun made the golden pair glow.

Leah's blonde hair was loose but tucked behind her ears and fell to the top of her shoulders. It bounced slightly as she, astride Kit, trotted into the corrals. Her black hat was just over her blue eyes that were looking at her husband with a returned gaze of love.

They stood quietly for a moment then the professor turned to Grayson.

"They are quite the vision. You are a lucky man." He said.

Grayson's smile widened as he watched his wife and daughters approach. His eyes were filled with pride and love. "Yes, I am."

When the three riders stopped, Leah's eyes moved from Grayson's to the professor.

Her eyes widened in delight, "Professor!"

She quickly stepped off the horse as Wade hurried to take Kit's reins from her. In moments, Leah's arms wrapped around the professor as they shared an embrace of welcome.

Reilly really hoped he liked the professors at college as much as this group did.

"What a surprise!" Leah stepped back away from the professor and smiled at him.

"I stopped on the highway to watch a beautiful red horse gallop across a pasture." Professor Waverly explained. "As luck would have it, it was Dru's stepson."

Leah glanced at Reilly with a laugh then turned back to the professor, "Have you moved back?"

He shook his head with a sigh, "No, a friend passed away and I came in for the funeral."

"I'm so sorry," Leah sighed.

The bellow of a cow just across the fence stopped the conversation as everyone turned and looked at her.

"Look!" Wade cried out and stepped up onto the fence. "One of the cows just had a calf."

"Oh, wonderful," Professor Waverly grinned as he walked to the fence. "I haven't been around new calves since I was a teenager."

The entire crew stood by the fence to look at the small red calf.

Wade pointed again. "There's one on the other side of her too. She had twins."

"Both red," Alex added.

The second baby was curled on the ground looking over at the people at the fence. There were a hundred cow and calf pairs in the corral. Right behind the baby was a large red cow that was aggressively swinging her head back and forth at the small newborn. The new calves black mother turned with a snort at the red cow as she nudged her second calf who was trying to nurse.

"Let's get her moved," Jessup stepped to the gate.

Reilly maneuvered in front of the foreman and grinned back at him, "I'll help."

Jessup chuckled as they walked through the gate. "Watch the red cow but the black one should be fine."

"Should be?" Reilly huffed as he knelt next to the calf lying down. He looked at the black cow; her ears were perked, eyes bulging, and body tense as if to charge.

"Yeah," Jessup grinned. "She's all bluff."

The second baby laid down behind the black mother. When she turned to look at that baby, Reilly slid his arms under the first baby and quickly lifted the calf into his arms. Her curly red hair was still wet from birth. The cow turned back to him with wide eyes but didn't move. Reilly stepped quickly toward Jessup who was at the gate to the adjoining small pen but kept his eyes on the mother cow.

As the cow watched Reilly, Matt snuck in behind her and quickly lifted the second calf into his arms and walked toward the pen. The cow snorted and trotted behind her calves and into the pen.

Reilly and Matt quickly set the calves down and walked wide around the cow as she began to nudge them.

"Should be…" Reilly shook his head at Jessup and chuckled when they walked through the gate.

"Hey…you're still walking, ain't ya?" Jessup grinned.

Professor Waverly smiled at Grayson, "Are you branding today?"

Grayson shook his head, "Today we'll be gathering and doctoring those that need it. Those two newborns will stay in there for a couple of days. We'll tag them but wait until summer roundup before they're branded." He pointed to a small corral to the west of the large pasture. "We have a few in there that need medical attention. One cow must have caught a teet on barb wire, it's cut clean open so Jessup will work on her. Another is so full that the baby can't get a good suction so we'll milk her out."

"I'd like to help with that one," The professor offered.

Grayson grinned. "More than happy to have the help, but those fancy shoes are going to get dirty."

"I have mud boots in my truck," Scott offered. "And a pair of overalls."

Their visitor stayed with the Trio and Leah for the rest of the day. Reilly left with everyone else to push the cows out of Windy Meadows. It was an easy ride so he rode Trip.

CHAPTER TWELVE
And More Wednesday Branding

"Professor? Can I ask you a question?" Reilly asked as he drove the Professor down the steep grade. Nick was waiting at the bottom of the mountain to bring Reilly back to the ranch.

"Yes, please do," He chuckled. "I forgot how much I disliked this road and you can keep my mind off it."

Reilly grinned, "How did you know you wanted to be a professor of agriculture?"

He chuckled, "I'm the one that is supposed to ask you what you're going to do with your life."

"Yeah," Reilly smiled. "I get that all the time."

"Well," Professor Waverly said. "Growing up, my mother was a nurse and my father worked in a factory. I had time during the summer so I started working in the farmer's fields when I was thirteen. I fell in love with harvest…planting, fertilizing…all of it." He chuckled. "When I told my mother that I wanted to drive tractor for a living and work the fields she just about died laughing."

"Serious?" Reilly looked over at him.

"Eyes on the road!" The professor demanded with a tense grin and his grip tightened on the arm rest.

"She wasn't supportive of you?"

"As she put it, from the time I could say my first word…I never stopped," He chuckled. "I had the gift of gab."

"So sitting on a tractor all day by yourself wasn't going to work out," Reilly grinned.

"That's what she pointed out to me and I, very disheartened, agreed with her." He began to relax again. "But she suggested that I try and come up with something that would combine the two things I loved the most…agriculture and talking."

"So teaching agriculture," Reilly nodded. "That makes sense."

"And I have loved almost every minute of it. It has been my dream job. Grayson was the type of student I truly loved because we would get into those debates and just get lost in time. The other students would either hang on every word or be bored to death." He chuckled again. "Leah enjoyed the classes but she was more laid back in her studies instead of energetic like Grayson. When we started the field trips and studies out to farms, I truly was in heaven with my job," He turned to Reilly. "That is what I wish everyone could find."

"Yeah, me too," Reilly sighed. He started to turn to the professor but stopped so he didn't scare him again. "You said you almost loved every minute of it…what didn't you love?"

There was a deep sigh, "One of the worst days of my life is when I had to tell Grayson about the car accident that killed his parents and grandparents. I don't care who you are…telling someone that and seeing that raw disbelief and gut wrenching emotion in their eyes…it stays with you," He shook his head. "I can't tell you how many times I have woken in the middle of the night just from hearing the sound that escaped him…I believe I heard his heart break."

The professor sniffed and Reilly had to wipe away a tear.

"The worst day of my life," The professor repeated. "He had troubles after that and I tried to help but he just wouldn't have it. I was the person that told him so I would always be associated with it."

"He seemed fine today," Reilly pointed out.

"Leah…his recovery was all in her hands," He nodded. "That woman was an angel brought to Grayson at the right moment to save him."

Reilly nodded in agreement and thought of the story Grayson had told him of his first kiss with her.

"Leah and those two beautiful girls of his…Sadie and Grace," Professor Waverly smiled. "I cannot tell you how happy I am that I stopped this morning to watch the cowboy on the pretty red horse ride across the pasture."

"Me, too," Reilly grinned.

"Just to see how well his life has turned out…the angels he has with him now. I will forever hold the vision of the three of them riding in on the horses and the look of happiness on Grayson's face. I think I may be able to rest better now." A deep sigh released from him and he turned in the seat and looked at Reilly. "So, let's figure out what brings you great happiness."

"My dad and the Taggers and the Tagger Herd," Reilly said without hesitation.

The professor laughed, "Take them out of the equation."

"Ok…" Reilly shrugged. "I don't know what makes me happy."

"Forget about "who" and now we forget about the 'what' and go with the 'where'."

"Where am I happy?" Reilly pondered. "Corrals…like today with everyone there."

"Riding the mountains? Pushing the cattle?"

"No…not that. When you do that, you're mostly spread out and maybe have one or two people close to communicate with. In the corral, everyone comes together. Whether we're branding, sorting, doctoring…whatever… When we're all there together working or playing…that's where I like to be. It's the comradery we share."

"Anywhere else?"

"Arenas," Reilly nodded. "Basically the same thing…it's where everyone gathers. Whether it's roping with Grace or Wade…just riding and training, or even a whole jackpot with a large group of people. We're all there with the same love of horses and ropes. I have friends that I only see when I go to rodeos or jackpots. The arenas bring us back together. If we didn't have arenas…I'd never see some of them.

"In arenas…there is that possibility…the dreams we share of rodeos and shows for Nora and just…" Reilly paused as his mind took him to riding in the Homestead arena. "Even working the arena…tilling the ground and getting it ready for riders…I love that. Being the first person to plant a horse hoof in a freshly ground arena…it's…well…it's dreams of what can be…it's sweat and work and laughter."

He glanced over at the professor and saw him smiling at him with a nod.

"So, you are your happiest in arenas and corrals."

"Yeah," Reilly grinned. "I'd be happy every day of my life if I got to spend them there."

"Besides the people…what is the connection between the two?"

"Well, the animals I guess," Reilly shrugged.

"And what is that connection?"

"What connection? The animals?" Reilly asked.

"Yes…what is the connection between the animals in the corrals and the animals in the arenas?"

Reilly stared down the road as he made one of the last hair-pin turns.

"The connection would be…" Reilly hesitated. Was it really that simple? Has it been right there in front of him all along?

"What?"

"The stock contractor," Reilly grinned. "He has corrals where he raises the horses, cattle, and bulls and takes them to the arenas for the competition where everyone comes together."

"If you were a stock contractor?"

"And I was able to play in arenas and corrals all my life? I would be happy…very happy," Reilly grinned and stopped the car in the middle of the dirt road.

"Why are you stopping?" The professor asked in concern and looked out at the road then back to Reilly.

"Because I wanted to look at you and not freak you out because I didn't have my eyes on the road." Reilly laughed.

"Oh…ok," The professor chuckled.

"If I was a stock contractor, I could still work with animals…and with Nikki because she could help in their nutrition. You have to keep them in peak condition if you want them to be successful."

"I believe Sadie told me she was going into Equine Sports Medicine."

Reilly nodded with wide eyes, "Yes! She could help with the bucking stock and Wade farming would be feeding them and Grace's business and marketing."

"Sounds like you might have hit on something," The professor grinned.

Reilly inhaled and exhaled in excitement, "You did, sir. I honestly don't believe that I would have ever figured it out…even though it was right in front of my eyes." He laughed. "It's just so clear now…I just can't believe it."

Excitement tingled through Reilly's body and he found himself bouncing in the seat. He finally started down the road again with a grin and a plan for his life.

"You sure you can drive and bounce at the same time?"

Reilly chuckled, "We're only one turn from the bottom and Nick is probably already there waiting for us."

He stopped the car again and looked across the seat with wide eyes.

"Nothing's wrong…right?" The man chuckled.

"I just spent three weekends down in Boise with Nick at a stock contracting place he works for." Reilly laughed. "Even as much as I enjoyed that, I didn't put it together."

"Sometimes it takes someone from outside your bubble to see the whole picture."

"My bubble?"

"The world you surround yourself in. Sometimes you don't see anything outside of just where you are and who you are with and the rest of the world disappears."

"Yeah," Reilly nodded and started the car in motion again. "I can't thank you enough, Professor Waverly, for bursting that bubble. I don't think I would have put that together and now I can't wait to get online and see what classes I need to take and talk to Nick and the guy that owns the place to see what they suggest."

"I'm sure animal husbandry will be in there." The professor reached in his pocket and withdrew a card. "Don't let me forget to give this to you when you can take a hand off the wheel." He chuckled and Reilly laughed. "It's my business card and you call me for anything you need. Help with a class or just someone to talk to and help burst the bubble." He turned to Reilly with a serious look in his eyes. "I cannot tell you how much seeing you today and you leading me to the Trio has meant to me. It was only a short time in my life…telling Grayson, driving him to the ranch that morning, the funeral and then seeing him in pain the rest of the year…but seeing him now with his three angels in his life?" He shook his head. "There is that little piece in me that was bruised too that is now healed."

Reilly nodded in understanding as he drove around the last turn and saw Nick's black truck in the wide pullout on the side of the road.

"I am so happy for the Trio…the whole family." The professor said as the car stopped.

Reilly stretched out a hand for the card, "Thank you, sir. You have changed my life…that's for sure. Deciding to ride Trip today has been one of most life changing moments in my…our lives."

Professor Waverly grinned, "You give him a couple treats for me tonight."

"Will do, sir," Reilly said and opened his door.

He shook the professor's hand then waited next to the passenger side of the truck until the car was moving down the road before he opened the door and crawled in.

"Who was that?" Nick asked as he put the truck in drive and started the climb up the grade.

"My life changer," Reilly grinned. "I am so glad we have this time together…just us two." He chuckled.

Nick glanced at him with a confused raised brow.

Reilly told him of the conversation and with every mile that past he bounced in the seat a little more and his smile got a little wider. Nick didn't say a word. He just stared at the road until Reilly finished.

"Well, what do you think?" Reilly said excitedly.

Nick glanced at him as if he was deep in thought then he nodded slightly. "I totally agree."

"Yes!" Reilly laughed. "I'm sure Dad will too."

"He will," Nick smiled. "But…I need to tell you something and you have to keep it between us for now until I talk to a few people."

Reilly's smile disappeared, "OK…You can trust me."

"Yeah, I know," Nick said. "Or I wouldn't have said that much."

"What is it?"

"The stock contracting business you were at?"

"Yeah?"

Nick turned with a smirk, "I own it."

Reilly's jaw dropped. "No way!"

"Bought it when I moved back from Australia."

"How come everyone thinks Marvin owns it?"

"Never saw any reason to tell anyone he doesn't. He has a good reputation in this industry and we didn't want to change that."

"Oh," Reilly nodded.

"If you want, you can come to work for us for the summer and before you go to college."

Reilly turned to him with a jolt of excitement then quickly exhaled as it rushed out of him, "We have state rodeo finals the week after graduation then Grace and I were supposed to go down and spend a couple of weeks with my grandparents in Texas."

Nick nodded, "Then the day after you get back."

"Really?" The excitement rushed back in.

"Don't see why not. We have Christmas in July about that time and can use the help. We'll be busy through September."

"Are you up around here so I can work and go to school through September?"

"We'll check the schedule when we get back to the Homestead."

"Thanks, Nick." Reilly turned and grinned down the dark road. He couldn't see anything more than what the headlights reached. "What classes do you think I'll need?"

They talked all the way to the bunkhouse.

"I'd like to tell Dad about the job," Reilly said as the truck stopped.

"Jack knows I own it."

Reilly looked at him in surprise, "Really? Does Mom know?"

Nick nodded, "The three sets of parents, Nikki, Matt, and Lucas. I need to talk to Tessa and let her know before we just come out and say it to everyone else. I think she deserves that."

Reilly nodded, he was confused as to why she didn't already know. They had been dating for almost a year.

"But there isn't any reason you can't talk about your new life plan." Nick reminded him with a smirk.

"Oh," Reilly laughed. "That's true."

They opened the doors of the truck and Reilly nearly ran into the bunkhouse.

CHAPTER THIRTEEN
Thursday Branding

Just outside the horse corral, Martha lay quietly watching Reilly approach. Since herding her to the ranch, she had decided not to leave, but she did follow Cora whenever she saw her. Cora loved it and had started carrying treats in her pockets. The cow had not yet calved.

Reilly walked past her and held the halter tightly as he made his way through the dark corral. The sun was still another hour from rising and the crew riding the canyon would leave before everyone else. It took them longer to get to the canyon gate and gather the herd than it did for everyone meeting them at the branding corral.

Normally, Reilly would be looking for Rufio, this time he was looking for Monty. He'd never ridden the grey gelding, but knew he wouldn't have a problem. He'd seen the horse cover the rockiest of ground, steepest of hillside, and deepest of water. He had also seen Monty go across ground that he didn't want to take Rufio on. It wasn't that he didn't trust his roan, it was because of Monty's experience.

He found the gelding in the farthest of corners and slid the halter on with ease. But, Monty did not budge when Reilly pulled on the rope.

"Come on," Reilly whispered. "Don't make me look like a fool so early in the morning."

He would have sworn the horse shrugged as he lowered his head then rose it high to follow him.

They saddled the horses before putting them into the horse trailer. Reilly had to let out the cinch more since Monty was broader than Rufio.

"Nervous?" Matt asked Reilly as he was saddling Trooper.

"Hmmmm…" Reilly hummed.

Matt chuckled, "I was the first time…and the second."

"That bad?" Reilly asked.

"There are places that will get your heart pumping." Matt said. "This is the first year I'm taking Trooper in. I've been working with him on some of the steeper hillsides."

"Monty will take care of you," Reilly's dad said as he walked by him with one of the older ranch geldings. "We don't take the dogs in this area because of the amount of cactus. They would give it their best try but it tears up their paws."

Reilly was not surprised that his dad wasn't riding Chevy, the gruella horse that Grayson had bought at the Billings, Montana auction and Nora had trained. The horse was only four.

"Cows do stupid things," Grayson said and walked Eli into the trailer.

"They never listen to directions," Nick huffed walking his blue roan, Blue.

"And a few get the idea they are mountain goats," Jessup said and led his sorrel horse by them.

Two hours later, Reilly stared up at the three cows and four calves that were at the top of a steep hillside on a bluff and thought of those words.

"Yep," He sighed. "Mountain goats..."

Reilly turned and looked for the other riders. Grayson and Matt were across the ravine pushing a dozen pair of cows and calves down the rocky mountain. Both men were leaning far back in the saddle to remain balanced. Nick and Jessup were out of sight on the farthest ridge.

His dad was behind him with the horse slowly making his way up the steep hill toward a cow and calf that just stood and stared. His dad was leaning far forward in the saddle.

Monty pranced impatiently under Reilly so he took a deep breath and nudged him up the hill.

"Move it!" Reilly yelled at the cows in the hopes they would start down the trail without him and the horse wouldn't have to go all the way up.

The cows did not budge.

Monty slowly made the climb with Reilly's boots firmly in the stirrups and fingers gripping the reins tighter than he had gripped the bull rope. Sweat began to form and trickled down his back. A hoof slipped making Monty tilt to the left…toward the steep mountain side…Reilly tipped then gripped the saddle horn to pull himself back in the saddle.

Halfway up the rock and cactus hillside Reilly glanced up at the cows in time to see the larger black one look up the hillside.

"Don't do it." He shouted out at the animal…but she did.

All three cows and babies began climbing up farther.

Reilly's body lurched forward with Monty's lunge and he called the cow one of the words he wasn't supposed to say. His eyes instantly went to his dad who was even with the cows he was herding but he was standing still and watching Reilly and Monty.

"Dang it," The desire to impress his father caused a pressure behind his eyes and his shoulders tightened. Sweat dripped down the side of his face.

One of his favorite movies was *The Man from Snowy River* and favorites scenes when the horse, Denny, does his run straight down the mountain. Reilly had seen Scott ride the horse in a similar fashion so he knew what Monty could do.

He turned his attention back to the climb and the cows. They had been traveling at a steep angle up the mountainside until they came across the path the cows had used to climb to their perch.

The cows had stopped and were watching them climb. He pushed Monty straight up the hill and had to lean up the horse's neck to stay balanced. They passed the trail and slowly made their way up above the cows then crossed above them. The cows moved down the trail and began their descent down the mountain. Reilly sighed in relief and glanced at his dad who was now moving down with his cows. Then Monty turned.

The horse was standing on a rock ledge then turned slightly and lunged down to the trail that was a good eight feet below them. Reilly's heart nearly stopped and a loud gasp escaped him as they flew through the air. In the seconds he was in the air, he glanced down at the large boulders, clusters of cactus, and the steepness of the mountain itself. His pulse rate doubled.

When Monty's hooves hit the ground, Reilly tipped over the horse's shoulder and had to grab the saddle horn to keep from completely falling out of the saddle. His body being off balance caused Monty's to be off balance and the horse scrambled for footing to keep from sliding down the mountain. The horse twisted his front end up the mountain and his back legs slid off the trail…he lunged to get back on the trail and not tip over.

Reilly slid off the horse and his feet slid out from under him the second they hit the dirt and rocks. He went down hard on his hip and could feel cactus needles penetrating through his jeans.

Scrambling to his feet with heart pounding, he held Monty's reins until the horse got his footing and held still. The trail was so narrow, Reilly had to climb up the mountain to be able to step back into the saddle. He pasued for a moment before he looked up to the cows…who were meandering down the mountain…and then to Matt and Grayson who were now down towards the bottom of the ravine…then he turned to his dad. He was at a steep incline following his small herd down the hill.

Reilly sighed in relief that none of them had witnessed his fall.

He leaned down and patted the horse down the neck, "Sorry, big guy. That was my fault, but ya gotta warn me before you fly."

"Watch out!"

Reilly twirled in the saddle in the direction of the voice.

Across the ravine, a black calf was running along a cow trail cut between the rocks. He was running right at Grayson and Eli. Grayson turned just enough the calf ran right under Eli's belly.

The horse spun in circles. Knowing how narrow the trail was, Reilly held his breath and his fingers gripped the reins. Four turns and the horse suddenly stopped with legs spread apart. Grayson leaned down and patted the horse's neck.

THAT could have been a disaster. Reilly took a breath and looked for his dad. He was just below him and their cows were about to merge.

"How's it going?" His dad asked casually.

Reilly shrugged to match the calm tone. "Well, he knows how to fly."

"Any issues?"

"No, we made it to the top and back down; cows added to the herd."

His dad nodded and they walked down the narrow trail with the cows trotting along in front of them.

To their left, a dozen cows with babies at their sides began to appear out of the brush. They stopped the horses to allow the cows to join their herd. Matt and Grayson walked out of the brush and fell in line with them.

In a single line, thirty animals walked in front of the four men.

As the mountain began to level out into the bottom of the ravine they came across a wide creek. The cows spread out to drink.

"It's not too deep," Grayson said from behind Reilly. "It's only here this time of year as the snow melts. It's a dry creek bed in the summer."

They were quiet a moment.

"Have any issues?" Grayson asked.

"Nope, we're good," Reilly answered. "Was kinda worried when that calf went under Eli."

"Me too," Grayson chuckled. "He did well. Calmed down quick but nicked his leg on a rock."

Reilly turned in the saddle and looked down at the horse's leg. Blood was coagulated on the black hair just below his hocks. "It's not too bad."

"No, but I'll let him rest this afternoon and use the tall gelding I bought last Sunday at the auction."

"Might as well," Reilly grinned. "Before he disappears."

Grayson chuckled, "She'll lease him out for a jumper. His bloodlines and his build work for it. I'll work him to make sure he is as safe as the other lease horses."

"Where will Nick and Jessup be coming from?" Reilly asked while looking up at the tall treeless mountains on each side of them. They were covered in rock bluffs, boulders, stubble brush and cactus.

The ravine was full of wild roses that were covered in two inch long thorns.

"There should be another dozen pairs in here," Grayson answered. "If they found them it could be low about another hundred yards to our left.   They'd be hidden by the ravine. If they didn't find them, they'll probably be up high."

"They are right there," Matt said from behind Grayson.

Reilly turned and looked in the direction he pointed. Both men were sky lined high above them.

Grayson's radio crackled.

"You hear me?" Jessup asked.

"Yeah," Grayson answered.

"They took off down the gully and should be coming out to you." Jessup said.

"Then why are you up there?" Grayson asked.

"Because there are two calves laying down just below us. Almost missed them." Jessup said.

"What do you have in mind?" Grayson asked.

"Need to push them down before the mamas make a break and try to come up and get them." Jessup answered. "But it's a bit steep."

One of the riders stepped off the horse and slowly started moving down the hillside. Reilly stared hard at the hillside but couldn't see anything moving. "Do you see them?" He asked out loud to the group.

"No," They all answered.

One of the red cows standing in the shallow creek lifted her head and let out a long low bellow.

They moved the horses forward to get between the cow and the still unseen calves.

"You hallucinating?" Matt asked into his radio.

"Nah, they are tucked in pretty good." Jessup answered. "Nick's headed down to see if he can get them to budge."

There was a bluff just below Nick and as he slid down the hill a small black figure finally appeared.

"There you go." Jessup laughed into the radio.

The red cow bellowed again and the black calf walked down the edge of the bluff.

Nick stopped and they all waited for the second calf. When nothing happened Nick bent over and pitched a rock down to the bluff. Still no movement.

"Three..." Jessup said on the radio.

"Four..." Grayson said.

"Five..." Matt said.

"Two..." Reilly's dad said.

"What's that mean?" Reilly asked.

"In front of us, at the end of the ravine is a 70 foot wide opening." Grayson answered. "The right 30 feet is a clear trail for the cows to go down which leads to the pasture and the corrals. To the left is a rocky bluff that drops down about 30 feet but it has a mountain goat of a trail that the cows like too."

"So you have to guard it and make sure they don't go down." Reilly concluded.

"Yep," Grayson said. "Whoever guesses the number of throws gets to lead the cows down the good trail."

The fourth rock he tossed caused a second little black calf to appear and he followed the first down the hill.

Grayson chuckled and started moving forward and into the creek. They moved slowly as Eli's hooves slid off rocks as he walked. He disappeared down a trail and behind a thicket of wild roses.

Once the two calves reached the creek, and Nick had climbed back to the top of the mountain, they moved the cows across the water and down the trail Grayson had disappeared down. Twenty minutes later, Grayson was sitting in the middle of a trail watching them approach. Nick and Jessup had slowly moved their horses down the mountain and they all met in front of the 30 foot bluff.

As the cows followed Grayson, Nick rode up next to Reilly.

He looked at Reilly then his dad then back to Reilly. "How'd it go? Have any troubles?"

"No," Reilly shook his head. "Monty did good."

"Huh…OK…" Nick shrugged a shoulder.

They moved forward and followed the cows.

Reilly and his dad were at the back of the cows when they approached the corrals and awaiting family. His mother and Wade were at the gates when they walked through. She smiled up at him then her smile slowly faded. She looked over at his dad who was grinning then back at Reilly.

"Everything go OK?" She asked hesitantly.

His fellow riders rode up to him, still in the saddle. They were all smiling at his mom.

"You sure nothing happened?" Wade asked through a grin.

"Nothing much," Reilly looked curiously around the group.

"Well, then," Wade's eyes were dancing in humor. "How did you get the decorations on your chaps?"

Reilly looked down at his legs…nothing. When he turned to his right, he saw dozens of cactus needles sticking out of the leather chaps.

The laughter rolled across the mountains.

CHAPTER FOURTEEN
Friday Branding

"Did you remember the camera?"

"Yeah," Reilly chuckled and looked over at his mother.

"Well, that's good," She teased.

They rode Libby and Rufio across the dark hillside toward the ridge where they would take the sunrise picture of Rider's Point.

"It's been quite the two weeks," She said.

Reilly chuckled, "I don't think we've had such a full two weeks before."

"That's the life we asked for."

"Thank you, Mom."

The moonlight lit the sky just enough he could see her smile back at him.

"For what?" She asked softly.

"Hiring Dad and letting us join your life," He said honestly.

"Hmmm, it's interesting how the little decisions in your own life make such a huge impact on someone else."

"Hiring Dad?"

"Yes, we had another person we were looking at and almost hired instead of Jack."

"Why did you choose Dad?"

"Couple different reasons. The most important was because he was raised at a stable. He wasn't from town and didn't know all the people in the area and the equine political mumbo jumbo that comes with some people. He didn't seem like he would play those games."

"Nah, but he is really liked by everyone." He glanced over at her. "Were you attracted to him back then?"

"I was dating someone when we hired him but he was, and is, handsome." She chuckled. "He got along well with Scott and Grayson. In fact they acted like old friends."

"So he fit right in."

"Him and that little seven-year-old he brought with him." She wrinkled her nose at him.

Reilly grinned. "Your decision to hire him really made a difference in our lives."

"And mine…ours. I can't image what Grace would be like if you weren't there for her."

"But you really wouldn't have known a difference." He mused.

"No, that's why you try and make logical decisions in your life. You never know how that decision will change your life in the future."

"You think being a stock contractor is the right decision for me?"

"Your wanting to stay in arenas and corrals all your life makes it a perfect decision for you."

"That's what the last two weeks has been about," Reilly nodded. "Just…everything about each day was what I want."

"Even the belly flop and cactus?" She laughed.

He chuckled with a deep sigh, "Yeah, it was a lot of good natured teasing and joking but you have to have moments like that. What fun would it be if you didn't?"

"True," She said and pulled Libby to a stop.

They dismounted the horses and Reilly took the camera out of the saddle bag.

"Watching Sadie in the corrals for the first time at the big branding and she got to throw the rope instead of ear tags. That was fun." She grinned.

"So many memories and good times."

They walked to the edge of the ravine and stared at the horizon as the light brightened and the first glimpse of the sun appeared.

Sadie had helped them with the camera settings but he still took a couple quick shots and looked at the images on the screen. He wanted to make sure this image was perfect for his mother.

He glanced at her as she gazed at the horizon. The soft morning light lit her blue eyes and shone on her blonde hair.   He turned the camera and took a picture of her.

"What are you doing?" She turned loving eyes to him.

"You're beautiful," He shrugged. "Stay there."

He walked Rufio back across the field just enough that Dru and Libby were silhouetted against the yellow rising sun, pink tipped clouds, and baby blue sky. Rider's Point was just over her shoulder. He took at least a dozen pictures just to make sure he got a perfect one.

He walked back up to her then took the pictures of Rider's Point when it was centered in the sun.

"Thank you, Reilly," She whispered. "I remember coming up here with my parents when I was little. I don't know why it took so long to get the pictures."

"I'm glad I could take them for you," He said. "Now I feel like I have a little history with it."

She turned glistening eyes to him, "I love that." She turned back to the sunrise. "My parents and grandparents would have loved you and Jack. Grandpa Anderson was a tough cowboy, some people considered him mean, but he never was to us kids. My dad was tough too but everyone loved him."

"Your grandmother and mother?"

"Grandma Nora was tough…she walked and talked the tough talk right next to Grandpa. I think she had to. She also stood a good three inches taller than him. Mom was…home. She was the epitome of the rancher's wife. She made everyone feel like part of her family even if they had never met her before. She and Dad were a lot like Grayson and Leah; love just radiated from them."

The sun was high above the horizon so they turned and mounted the horses. Just before they reached the trailer and truck she turned to him.

"I wish you would have had a life with your mother." She said softly. "I'm glad you're going down to spend time with your grandparents. Enjoy every moment with them. History…family…it's important."

Tears stung at Reilly's eyes and his throat was too tight to talk so he just nodded.

After loading the horses into the trailer she turned the truck down the road toward the branding pasture.

"Dru, you there?" Leah's voice echoed out of the radio.

"We're headed to the corrals." Dru answered.

"We're still at the house. Martha is calving and everyone wants to stay." Leah said.

"Oh wonderful," Dru sighed. "We'll come there." She said in the radio then turned to Reilly. "Little bit of that history."

As they drove to the house with a rising sense of urgency, Reilly thought of the last two weeks, the numbers game the men had played in the canyons, his future, and the family that had taken in his dad and him as their own.

History…he wanted to connect their history with his future. One of the last cows from the original ranch was going to help.

When they arrived, Martha was laying down next to the gate to the horse's corral where she had been for the last few days. Cora was at her head, and the rest of the family was leaning against or in the back of Grayson's truck which was parked across the driveway from her. Everyone was quiet as Dru walked in next to his dad. Their arms wrapped around each other. She and Grayson shared a smile.

"Gracie?" Reilly said softly as he walked up to the truck.

She was sitting on the tool box with her legs dangling off the side. Sadie was on her knees behind her.

"What?" Grace looked down at him.

"If it's a bull calf, we go to University of Idaho. If it's a heifer we go to Washington State University." Reilly said with a firm tone that didn't give an option to disagree.

"Oh, Reilly." Grace grinned. "That's perfect."

"What if she has twins…one of each?" Sadie chuckled.

"She ain't big enough for twins." Jessup said. "You'll have your answer in the next couple minutes."

Reilly and his mother shared a smile then turned to the black cow who gave birth to a black calf. They waited patiently for the cow to rise and clean the baby. Cora leaned forward and lifted the calf's long black leg and peaked underneath.

She turned with a smile, "We have a bull."

THE TAGGER HERD SERIES

Nikki Tagger

Family

Gini Roberge

CHAPTER ONE

"You did not!" Nikki rolled her eyes at her mother.

"Matt suggested it at my wedding; so I thought why not?" Her blue eyes were lit with humor.

The mother and daughter burst into giggles as Grace led Buttercup, Sadie led Scarecrow, and Nora led Harvey out of the horse trailer and to the event building at the rodeo grounds. All three horses wore veils behind their ears and down their manes.

Grace's 'life is good' laughter joined their own; "This is already starting out to be one heck of a bridal shower!"

"Wait until we play the game with them!" Nora chimed in.

"What game?" Nikki asked her cousin.

"You'll see…" Nora teased, her dark brown eyes looking mischievous.

Thirty minutes later, Nikki, Josey, and Nora were wrapping Harvey's back legs with toilet paper as fast as they could. Once the back legs were wrapped together, and hoping Harvey didn't move, they wrapped the toilet paper around her chest to her hindquarters and back until the horse was covered, all except the front legs. Taking shorter pieces, they lay them across the horses back to float down her sides to create the illusion of a dress. Longer pieces were attached to the top of her tail and draped down the tail and out on the ground to create a train.

"Time!" Cora called out.

Nikki, Josey, and Nora stood back to take in the vision they created.

"Short in the front and long in the back," Nikki laughed. "It looks like a mullet wedding dress fit for a horse!"

Nikki turned to see her mother, Tessa, and Sadie viewing the toilet paper wedding dress they designed for Scarecrow.

Nikki couldn't help but laugh at the horse. She was so covered with white toilet paper there wasn't a blonde hair in sight. They had moved one of the veils from the mane down the front of Scarecrow's head, covering her eyes and down her nose. The beautiful palomino turned and looked at her with eyes that seemed to cry for help.

"Buttercup, no!" Grace's laughter boomed causing everyone to look.

The cream colored horse had lifted her tail, tearing part of her paper wedding dress, to drop her horse apples to the ground…letting them know exactly how she felt about the situation.

"Well, at least we have toilet paper to clean it up!" Leah grinned at her partner/daughter; the third toilet paper fashion designer, Jordan, cried out in false horror.

The three teams posed for pictures with their toilet paper wedding dress covered mares, while Judge Cora decided on the winner.

"Well," Cora looked out to the party revelers, "We have the pooper dress, the mummy dress, and the mullet dress."

Nikki was sure the laughter could be heard all the way back to The Homestead.

"I'm going to have to declare the winner…the mullet dress!" Cora handed the three happy contestants three apples to feed their mare brides.

Finally sitting down for the first time since she arrived, Nikki looked out to her family, Candace, Paige, friends from college, and a few friends from high school. Kate had arrived late from the vet clinic. Helen didn't join them even though Nikki had extended the invitation. They had barely seen the woman since her confrontation with Sadie and Wade over the care of Rufio's cut leg.

The party was finally slowing down…too much laughter can really drain your energy, she decided. The light flashed on her phone, indicating a message. It was a voice message from her dad.

Nikki listened to the message; the exuberance of the day was quickly taken over by the stress that crawled up her back and into her neck and behind her eyes.

***

Nikki turned into the property that was once Cora's but now belonged to Nick. Her mind went back to the first time she had traveled the long driveway. Grayson had startled her by running out of the barn at the ranch yelling at her to backup his truck to the stock trailer as he ran to the bunkhouse to get Matt. His sense of urgency had kept her from questioning him. It wasn't until they were driving down the road that he told the two of them about her mother's phone call. They met Scott a mile down the road and unloaded the horses he was hauling into the spring branding corrals. They had decided to take two trailers to have plenty of room for the horses. It turned out to be the right decision when her mom called about the other six horses she found.

Until they witnessed the condition of the horses first hand, they didn't really believe it. How does a person comprehend a dozen horses starved unintentionally without seeing it for themselves?

When the four of them had arrived, her mother and all the kids were covered in mud and manure from head to toe; the horses were skeletons with eyes that called for help.

The brown filly in the lower barn seemed to call her the loudest and Nikki went to her first. The little Harvey…she fell in love the moment her hand touched the muzzle of the little filly. Nikki was going to call her Ella until the first time Cora had seen the horses.

Needing to break the tension in the room, Nikki said the first name that came to her head that sounded ridiculous for a filly. Where the name 'Harvey' came from, Nikki had no clue but she couldn't look at the reddish brown mare now and see her as anything but a Harvey.

The horses were almost six now…so much had happened in the last four years since they came into the Tagger family. Nick, Lucas, Josey…they were all in her life now because of the Tagger Herd.

Plus, she would be running the Barn and Breakfast now, instead of Leah, if it wasn't for the herd. Her degree in animal nutrition was changed from resort management because of the time she had taken to study and learn from Dr. Mark and the staff at WSU everything it would take to get the horses back to peak health.

Nikki reached the gate that led to the house and barns. It was still locked indicating she was the first to arrive. She left the gate open since Tessa and Nick would be driving through to join her. Nick and Lucas had arrived by plane a half hour earlier; he asked Nikki and Tessa to meet them at the property. It was time; he told Nikki, time to tell Tessa and Lucas of his past and Tessa about his life in Australia.

Nikki and Lucas had battled over the story; him wanting to know to protect Nick and the family, her not willing to break her father's trust. She didn't think Lucas would have a problem after hearing Nick's story. He would understand that it wasn't Nikki's story to tell, it was Nick's.

But she had no idea how Tessa was going to take learning of her father's corporation; his net worth totaling in the hundreds of millions of dollars. It had stunned Nikki, nearly made her physically ill. She prayed that her father would be healthy for a very long time. She couldn't handle running a $300 million dollar company the way he did, even with Matt at her side or now Lucas being there.

Would Tessa see it as a betrayal? She and Nick had been nearly inseparable since they finally broke down Tessa's emotional walls and became a couple. Her dad adored Tessa and Alex, and Nikki was pretty sure that Tessa felt the same way. But would she after learning of the secret Nick had been hiding from her this last year?

Nikki parked her truck in her usual parking spot in front of the newly enlarged house. There were two more bedrooms, a larger kitchen, and an enormous office in the back of the building overlooking the pasture where Blue and Bay roamed. On many occasions Tessa's horse, Patience, and Alex's horse, Snickers, were there too. The remodel was completed during the winter, then the construction of the new Circle 50 ranch house began. It was within weeks of being completed.

The horses trotted up to the fence when they saw her. It was a warm beginning to the month of May, with blue skies filled with puffy white clouds; a beautiful day to play with equine friends. Without hesitation, Nikki went to the horses instead of going into the house and, as usual, they fought each other for the attention.

While running a hand over the noses and down their necks, Nikki glanced up to the spot where the upper barn used to be; where they had found the first six horses. Nick had torn it down right after he purchased the property. He didn't want the kids coming to visit and have to relive the experience every time they saw it. There was an apple tree planted there now because horse's loved apples and the kids could associate feeding apples to very happy horses now instead of think about the barn. And it kept Cora supplied with apples for her famous apple pies.

It was Sadie and her knack for details that pointed out how ironic it was the place where the horses nearly died from lack of food, was now providing food.

The tree was fondly called "Angel's Tree" by the entire family.

"What a sappy family I have," Nikki laughed at the two horses.

The horse's heads raised high and ears alert when the sound of another vehicle coming up the driveway reached them. Nikki turned in time to see Tessa's SUV pull in next to her truck.

She bit her lip and frowned when she saw the passenger side door open and Alex slide out. Nick wouldn't want him there when he told his story. She waved at the mother and son as Alex limped as fast as he could towards her.

"Hi Nikki!" Alex grinned. "I didn't know you were going to be here, too. Is Matt coming?"

Nikki shook her head. "No, he's at the ranch."

Alex laughed as the horse's greeted him; eagerly checking to see if the boy had treats like he usually did.

"Do you think I would have time to ride Blue?" Alex turned to his mother, brown eyes looking hopeful.

Tessa shrugged causing her light brown curly hair to bounce, "I'm not sure…" She looked to Nikki.

Nikki nodded with relief. Alex would stay on the horses for hours or until they had to pull him off. It would be a great distraction for him while the adults talked.

Alex turned and headed for the barn. He no longer wanted help saddling the horses even though Blue was pretty tall…Bay even taller.

Tessa turned and smiled at Nikki, her face relaxed and happy, "I'll have to drag him out of here tonight."

Nikki nodded…hoping she was right. She loved Tessa and Alex…couldn't imagine their lives without them now. It seemed a repeat of her mother and Jack's relationship. If that hadn't worked out then Reilly would have left with Jack…how awful would that have been?

Nikki took a deep breath to calm her nerves. They silently watched Alex saddle the horse.

Nick had built a special ramp for Alex to mount the horse. The top of the ramp had been measured to the bottom of Snicker's stirrup so Alex just had to slide into it when his horse was there. But today he had to step up to the stirrup for Blue.

Alex turned, grinned and trotted the horse across the pasture; Bay following close behind.

The sound of Nick's truck reached them and Nikki turned…and so did her stomach…

"Are you OK?" Tessa asked, looking at her in concern.

"Yes," Nikki smiled brightly. "Just anxious to see my groom and Dad."

"Six more days!" Tessa exclaimed as they walked to meet the men. "Are you nervous yet?"

The tension eased from Nikki as she imagined Lucas standing at the alter…in the middle of The Homestead driveway, "No, just totally in love."

"It radiates from you," Tessa's eyes sparkled and her smile widened when she laid eyes on Nick.

"And from you…" Nikki teased and the women giggled softly to each other.

Nikki grinned at her Dad but walked to her future husband. They had been apart for two weeks but would be together for the next three; the week before the wedding and a two week honeymoon at an undisclosed location. Nikki had arranged the wedding; Lucas was handling the honeymoon and wouldn't even give her a clue on their destination.

A hand to each side of her face and his lips to hers. It always felt like it was the first time when they reunited.

He leaned back just enough to break the kiss, his amber brown eyes looking content, "Seven more days my lovely Nikki."

"It's only six." She smiled.

"Six to the wedding…seven to the honeymoon and I have you to myself for a whole two weeks." He sealed the promise with another kiss.

When they finally broke apart, she ran a thumb across his whiskers and sighed with love at the look in his eyes.

She forced herself to turn away from him and look to her dad and Tessa. They had moved to the patio furniture at the side of the house. It was in clear view of Alex galloping Blue across the pasture.

Tessa was leaned in giving him a kiss, but when she sat back, Nick's expression was tense and concerned.

"What's the matter?" Tessa whispered, her hand resting lovingly on his arm.

Nick's eyes glanced to Nikki. She nodded, pulled Lucas behind her and joined them at the table.

"What's up, Mate?" Lucas said to Nick. "You were fine on the plane, but now you look…ill."

Nick's eyes looked out to Alex then to Tessa…back to Lucas…to Nikki…back to Lucas.

"I know you and Nikki had a battle with her holding information about my past from you." Nick told him.

Both Tessa and Lucas leaned back in their chairs…a bit stunned at the comment.

"You don't talk about your past." Tessa said, her voice showing her nervousness.

"No," Nick shook his head and looked at Nikki. "I've only spoken of it once or twice, with Nikki, Matt, and the Taggers…parents anyway." He took a deep breath and let it out slowly. "Nora knows most but not all."

"Nora?" Tessa's eyes opened wide.

He nodded slightly but didn't elaborate.

"Why now?" Tessa asked.

"It's time that both of you know," He answered.

"I am OK not knowing," Tessa assured him. "You don't have…"

"Yes…Tessa…I do." Nick leaned back in his chair and looked into her eyes. "I don't want to keep anything from you anymore."

"Nick," Lucas stood. "You can't without the signature."

"I don't want to her to sign it." Nick glared.

"I don't care." Lucas turned toward Nick's truck.

Tessa looked totally confused, "Sign what?"

Nick didn't respond so Nikki did; "A confidentiality agreement."

"What? What for?" Tessa gasped looking between the father and daughter.

"Tessa…" Nick started.

"Nick, NO!" Lucas nearly yelled at him.

Nick gave him a look that would have melted the nerves out of most men, but Nikki was sure Lucas had seen it on multiple occasions…he just ignored it.

Lucas returned with the briefcase he always traveled with and pulled out the agreement and a pen. He placed it on the table in front of the stunned woman.

Tessa stared at it then looked to Nick…who was back to watching Alex. She turned to Nikki.

"Matt and I signed the papers too," Nikki explained, "And the Trio and spouses."

"All of them?" Tessa's voice was low.

"Yes," Lucas answered with a hint of humor in his eyes, "Although Dru wasn't too appreciative of it."

"I can imagine…" Tessa reached for the pen.

"You don't have to Tessa," Nick said firmly. "I will tell you without you signing it."

Tessa's hand froze in mid-air. She looked hesitantly between the three of them.

"You don't care…but Lucas does," Tessa's hand squeezed his arm. "He's your attorney and does what's best for you…I understand that." She glanced at Nikki. "How do you stand on this?"

Nikki took in a deep breath and looked between her future husband and her father, then back to Tessa. "I love you, Tessa, but I will always do what's best for my dad and what I need to do to protect him."

Nikki ignored the turn of Nick's head toward her. Lucas glanced at her then to Tessa.

"You want me to sign it?" Tessa clarified, her brown eyes searching Nikki's for the answer. "It's best for Nick?"

"Yes," Nikki nodded.

Tessa signed the paper, handed it to Lucas then turned to Nick. "No matter what you have to say…they are two of the four people on this earth that would do anything to protect you. From what? I don't know…but I trust them."

Nick nodded, placed a hand over Tessa's that was resting on his arm, and looked out in the pasture.

"I was born and raised in New Mexico until I was sixteen…"

CHAPTER TWO

Tessa and Lucas stared at Nick while he told them briefly of his life as a child. There was nothing there that Nikki hadn't heard…he didn't touch on the details. Tessa's hand gripped Nick's arm tighter as he spoke. His story was more involved once he told of the $50 bet that led him to ride the bull in the pasture and to bull riding…his escape.

He told of his meeting with Elena, the pregnancy, the baby in the carrier left with him in Pendleton. His eyes moved from the pasture to Nikki as he told of the terrifying drive to his mother to leave the baby with her, his meeting the beautiful barrel racer who he married, then left when she was pregnant.

Tessa's hand relaxed on his arm as he told of driving to retrieve Nikki from his mother and taking her to Dru…it was best for Nikki…he wanted her to have what Dru had and be raised with her brother…then, his disappearance to Australia. His eyes moved back to Alex in the pasture.

Nikki had watched Lucas' reaction to the story she had refused to tell him two years before. His expression never changed; he didn't move. She lifted her shoulders and twisted her neck trying to release the anxiety.

Nick skipped over his seventeen years in Australia to the day he learned of The Tagger Herd which led him back to the States.

Tessa's hand rested comfortably on his arm. Lucas remained silent and still, not once had he looked at Nikki.

Nick sat up straighter in his chair as he spoke of the phone call from Elena…the New Year's Eve party…the fist from

Matt…facing Dru and his kids. His voice cracked in emotion when he spoke of the phone call from Matt to help with building the arena. Tessa's hand squeezed tightly. He looked to Nikki.

Nikki told them briefly of how Elena came into their lives, then withdrew her phone from her pocket and played the recording of her confrontation with her birth mother in The Stables. It was the first time Nick had actually heard the recording.

Tessa gasped and gripped Nick's arm tighter, but Lucas still didn't move nor show any sign of emotion.

As they listened, Nikki had turned to Alex. He was riding to the barn.

When the recording stopped and Nick didn't start talking, Tessa looked between the three of them, "I don't understand why I had to sign a confidentiality agreement to hear that."

"I'm not through." Nick sighed.

Tessa looked back at him in confusion. Nikki felt her back tense. Still Lucas didn't move.

"When I finished riding bulls…" Nick started talking while watching Alex remove the saddle from the horse.

The brush ran across Blue's back as Nick told of the first store, when he spoke of the thirtieth store, Alex had moved to brush Bay. Nick told them of Jet Development Group and the creation of the corporation as Alex released Blue from the halter. Tessa's hand fell from his arm…Nick's eyes looked to the sky…Alex opened the gate and stepped through. Nick told her of the purchase of Andy's ranch for Matt and Nikki. Tessa didn't speak but turned pale as he told her the net worth of the corporation. Alex was half way to them, his eyes full of adoration and he was grinning from ear to ear at Nick.

Nick took a deep breath…glanced at Tessa's pale face then forced a smile to Alex. "I have willed this property to Alex…it will be his free and clear with enough money to do with it what he wants."

Tessa gasped, Lucas remained silent and still.

"Lucas and I do everything we can to keep my life here separate from my business in Australia." Nick told her as Alex was just steps away.

"Hi Nick! Hi Lucas" Alex said happily, his energy and enthusiasm a stark difference than the four adults at the table.

"Hey, kid…" Nick barely got out when Tessa stood quickly…her chair falling back to the ground.

Nikki startled at the crash and they all turned to Tessa.

"Alex, come with me." Tessa ordered and reached for his hand.

Alex looked confused but obediently took his mother's hand…the fourteen-year-old's face was full of questions as he turned to the three adults that sat in bewilderment.

They quietly watched her drive away.

Nikki turned to her dad…the hurt in his eyes made her heart tremble. "Dad…"

He shook his head, stood, and walked towards the barn.

Nikki watched him until he disappeared inside the building…she turned to Lucas who was staring out into the pasture.

She reached for his arm but was stopped by the ringing of her father's phone that was sitting on the table. A quick glance showed Tessa's face… she was calling…Nikki reached for the phone instead of Lucas.

"Tessa?"

"Nikki? It's Alex…what happened…where's Nick?" His voice was shaking.

"He stepped away…where's your mom?"

"She stopped around the first corner."

"Where is she?"

"I don't know. She told me to stay here then got out and walked into the trees."

"You can't see her?" Nikki stood and jogged down the driveway.

"No! What's going on? She was so happy."

"I'm sorry Alex…there was just…"

"Nikki, did they breakup?" She could hear the desperation in his voice.

"I don't know…"

"But you were right there!"

"I know…they just…Alex, it's hard to explain."

"Does Nick still love Mom?"

"Yes!" She walked around the corner and saw the vehicle pulled over to the side of the road. Alex was standing at the back of it watching her walk toward him.

"I want Mom to be loved, Nikki."

"She is loved, Alex."

"No…" He shook his head at her. "I want her to be loved like Nick loves her. She's been so happy…what happened?"

"I don't know," Nikki said honestly, she had no idea what Tessa was doing. "Which way did she go?"

He pointed to her left.

"Go back with Lucas. I'll go talk to your mother."

"Nikki…" His voice pleaded.

"I will do everything I can, Alex." She turned and walked into the trees.

Thirty feet in, hidden behind a thick stand of brush, Tessa was sitting on a fallen log staring out into a small clearing.

"Tessa?"

"What?"

"Are you OK?"

"Circle 50…that's where you got the name…brand…the $50 bet?"

"Yes, Matt came up with it," Nikki sat on another log to the left of her. "The circle represents family…the 50 was for Nick. It was the only way we could name it after him without anyone knowing."

"I wondered why you never really gave an answer when I asked you about it," She continued to stare into the clearing, her voice calm. "Your mother's barrel horse was Jet."

"Yes, he named the company after the horse…a way to name it after Matt and I without anyone knowing."

"You were never far from his mind."

Nikki didn't respond.

"Have you forgiven him?"

Nikki shrugged, "I…well…I agreed with him."

"What do you mean?"

"I agreed that he did the right thing by taking me to Mom and Matt." Nikki leaned her elbows across her knees and sighed. "I don't need to forgive him; I've had a great life because of his decision. He needs to forgive himself and I don't think he's there yet."

Tessa turned, her eyes glazed. "I'm a bit overwhelmed."

Nikki chuckled, "Been there."

"How did you handle all this?"

"With the help of Mom, Scott, and Grayson for the past part…they helped me…us…Matt and I to understand him…as best any of us could." Nikki lifted her shoulders and twisted her neck to release the tension. "As for the money? The corporation?" Nikki shrugged. "I don't think about it...they do a very good job of keeping it separate."

"But it will be yours someday...all those jobs…people…that's a huge responsibility."

"Thanks, Tessa!" Nikki rolled her eyes which made Tessa smile. "I told him not to die for a very long time."

"I agree with that plan," Tessa nodded, the tension in her facing leaving and the color returning.

"I asked him to give me until I was thirty; then I'll start learning that part of his life."

"Matt?"

Nikki shook her head, "His focus will be here; the ranch, search and rescue."

Tessa nodded. "How much does Nora know? That has to be stressful for her."

"I don't know, that caught me by surprise…neither she nor he has mentioned it to me." Nikki sighed. "Nora wouldn't say anything to anyone, I'm sure of that."

"I agree…she wouldn't." Tessa looked across the clearing. "I guess I should get back to Alex…he's pretty upset."

"I sent him back to Lucas."

Tessa nodded and stared into Nikki's eyes, "I don't care that he kept this from me."

"I'm glad…relieved…" Nikki smiled. "Sometimes, I wish he still kept it from me…except for Lucas…he did bring me Lucas."

Tessa frowned, "What made him bring his worlds together? Why bring Lucas over?"

"I can't answer that," Nikki said honestly. "He only brought him when he purchased the ranch."

"You've never asked him?"

"Never thought about it," Nikki chuckled. "Lucas kind of befuddled my brain the moment I met him. I didn't care why he was there…I was just glad that he was."

"Befuddled?" Tessa laughed.

"Yeah…Cora came up with that one."

They sat quietly a moment before Nikki looked at Tessa. "So now what do you want to do?"

"I love your father, Nikki," she answered. "I have to accept the good and bad from his past since it created the man that he is today…the man I love dearly. I never thought…dreamed…that I would be loved again like I know he loves me. I could see that in his eyes today…the worry and concern that I would leave him."

Tessa sighed, tilted her head up to the sky and closed her eyes; a single tear rolled down her cheek. "I never dreamed that a man would come along and love my son nearly as much as I do…but Nick does…even with his past issue with kids…he loves Alex."

"Yes, he does." Nikki nodded. "But there's more to this than that…the corporation? The money?"

"That's why I'm out here," Tessa's brows creased and she looked to the ground. "I couldn't get my head to comprehend what he said…my mind was racing and I didn't want to get on the highway like that," she looked back to Nikki. "I didn't want to leave him…I know that's what he thought…thinks. But I just needed to stop and think…try to understand how it would impact us. When I'm with him he kind of…befuddles my mind…so I had to get away."

"Well," Nikki tried to smile. "He'll buy you just about anything you can imagine."

Tessa's eyes opened wide and she shook her head emphatically, "I couldn't spend a dime of that money."

"Why?" Nikki asked…a bit stunned.

"I'd feel like I was taking food out of the mouths of all those people he employed…is taking care of…" she shook her head again. "That…just can't happen… I know what it's like to be desperately looking for a job to take care of your child properly. Or to try and decide if you should pay a bill and walk to work or buy gas and plead forgiveness to a bill collector." She hesitated; her eyes darting to Nikki then to the clearing. "I've only told Nick this…" She took a deep breath. "When we moved to Lewiston, I didn't have an apartment yet… The job started a week before we could get into it. Alex and I slept in my car for the first week." Her face turned red and a tear fell, which she quickly wiped away. "Neither Alex nor I speak of it. That is a terrible thing for a parent to put a child through…but…I didn't have a choice."

Nikki nodded but didn't respond, she was stunned; this woman had been through so much in her thirty-three years.

"I couldn't touch that money…no, I couldn't do it." Tessa said breathlessly.

They sat quietly, both lost in thought before Tessa exhaled loudly. "Alex was scared to death that Nick and I broke up…I could see the fear in his eyes when I crawled out of the car."

"He is pretty worried."

"He and Nick…" Tessa stood. "Thank you, Nikki…for coming after me…helping me think this through but I need to get back to the two men in my life…to put their minds at ease."

"…and me to my groom." Nikki smiled.

The women walked to the house, it was closer than the SUV.

Nick had walked out of the barn just before they stepped out of the row of trees. He was walking toward Alex, who was sitting at the patio furniture, but stopped when he saw them. He stared…waited.

His shoulders lowered when Tessa broke into a run toward him…he took a couple steps to her then stopped and waited…engulfing her in his arms when she finally reached him.

Nikki turned away and walked to the table. Alex's smile was wide now, as wide as when he finished riding the horses.

"It's OK now?" He asked.

Nikki sat at the table and smiled into his very relieved eyes, "Better than ever."

"Good…thank you, Nikki."

"You're welcome," she sighed and looked around the property. "Where's Lucas?"

"He left."

CHAPTER THREE

Nikki turned to him, "What?"

"He said to stay here and wait for you guys…then he got in Nick's truck and left." Alex said innocently then looked out to his mother and Nick who were walking across the lawn.

Nikki turned and looked back at the vehicles…her truck was the only one there. He left?

She pulled out her phone and looked for a message or missed call…nothing. Nick's phone was sitting on the table so she picked it up. It was full of messages from business associates…one text from Greg, the pilot of his corporate plane.

TEXT TO NICK: Wheels up in ten, will return when I drop Lucas off in Sydney.

Nikki read the message again and again…he left…a week before the wedding…he left… without a word…he left… Her body seemed to freeze in place…she couldn't pull her eyes from the message…what did this mean?

"Nikki?" She could hear the voice but couldn't comprehend or react.

"Nikki!"

Her eyes slowly moved from the phone to her dad…his eyes narrowed in concern. "What's the matter?"

Somehow her hand moved…it lifted the phone to him. He took it, read it, then turned and looked to the spot his truck had been sitting.

"What?" Tessa asked and reached for the phone. She gasped and looked at Nikki in shock.

"I can stop the plane," Nick offered…his voice sounded as stunned as Nikki felt.

She shook her head, "No…if he doesn't want to be here…I would never force him." She turned and walked to her truck, she needed to escape…she needed…Lucas…

"Nikki!" He called out and quickly caught her arm to stop her. "They have to stop in Hawaii to top off the fuel. I can stop them there if you change your mind."

Nikki shook her head, her mind was replaying the conversation…Lucas' reactions were minimal…non-existent. He had glanced at her once when she asked Tessa to sign the document then he hadn't looked at her again, nor spoke to her. Normally, he would have gone with her to find Tessa to make sure she and Alex were alright…that's what Lucas did…he took care of people.

But what was he doing now?

"Nikki," Her dad shook her arm lifting her out of her haze.

"I'm, OK," She turned and wrapped her arms around his neck…holding him tightly. His arms embraced her…he squeezed…then that little bit more that made her sigh. "You have a wonderful woman there Dad, hold her close."

"I am holding a wonderful woman close." He whispered.

She turned and rested her head on his shoulder and looked out at Angel's Tree…he would do anything for her…he would stop the plane…bring Lucas back so they could talk…so she could make him understand… Understand what? SHE didn't do anything wrong…so why did he leave?

"Stay here, Nikki." He whispered.

Nikki sighed and stood back, "No, you need time with just you guys. I need to be alone for a while."

"Are you sure you're alright to drive?" Tessa asked.

Nikki nodded, kissed them both on the cheek, gave Alex a hug then nearly ran to her truck.

Her phone rang before she reached the gate…it was her mother. Nick had been fast to call her.

"I'm OK." Nikki answered.

"Go to The Homestead."

"I'm headed to the ranch."

"Jack and I are in Seattle, I'm on the next flight out."

"You drove."

"I don't care."

"Mom, stay there with Jack, drive home. I'm OK."

"He left Nikki…why did he leave?"

"I'm not entirely sure," she said truthfully.

"Nikki…"

"Mom, do not fly home, if I need you I'll call. I'm headed to the ranch…Matt and Josey are there."

There was silence. Nikki knew her mother was battling her emotions.

"Please, Mom."

"We'll be home tomorrow afternoon…I'm coming right to you."

"OK, I'm sure I'll talk to him in the morning and everything will be fine." Nikki said it…tried to believe it…but didn't. "I've reached the highway, Mom. I need to get off the phone."

"Call me if you need me."

***

Harvey, Bodi, and the twin yearling colts were waiting for her at the gate of the front pasture when she arrived. They always recognized the sound of her truck and ran to the gate to greet her. Trooper, Trip and Jiggers were missing…Matt and Josey must have gone riding. She looked at her four horses and their excitement to see her made her smile for the first time in hours. During her drive home, she kept her mind busy by thinking about diet and exercise plans in her head for the rehabilitation horses she was caring for. There were five at the ranch and one at the vet clinic with Kate. The veterinarian would be bringing that horse to the ranch in the morning.

The five rehab horses were in the pasture on the opposite side of the barn. She wanted them each in their own corral with a lean-to and large feeder but she only had a small four corral system. She needed more, especially when the sixth horse came in the morning.

Three of the horses had been at her ranch for the last two months, since they were found wandering down Highway 95 by Riggins. Their hooves were badly damaged and they were skin and bones. No owner had come forward to claim them so Sadie called the dark bay and two sorrels the Nomads.

The other two, both brown and white paints, had only been there for two weeks. Over the winter, the owner had left his horses in the charge of a woman boarding horses near Viola, a small town north of Lewiston. She boarded twenty horses and didn't have enough feed for five. They had slowly dwindled away in size and developed a bad cold. Their noses were nearly closed from the snot crusting their nostrils when she first saw them. It was mortifying seeing the horses wheezing and coughing. The dark bay horse Kate was delivering the next morning, was also from that group but belonged to a different owner. Sadie dubbed them the Violets.

While Nikki was working on their diets, Sadie was using her research and detail ingenuity to build an exercise program for the horses. Grace was working with Sadie; helping her exercise the horses and keeping journals on each. Nora was so involved in her shows and reining competitions she wasn't able to help yet.

As Nikki stepped out of her truck, she was surprised to see Grace's Trail Boss truck in front of the house and then Sadie and Grace walked out of the barn.

"Hey, Nikki." The two tall blonde sisters called out in unison. Sadie was nearly as tall as Grace even though she was thirteen to her sister's eighteen.

"What are you two doing here?"

"It's Sunday; we're always here on Sunday if we're not at a rodeo." Sadie answered.

"But it's late and you're usually gone by now. Where's Matt and Josey?"

"Dad said the lower gate at Dry Creek Valley was mangled, so this morning Matt and Josey went down to fix it…they were going to spend the night. And…we were too sick to go home." Grace smiled.

Which means Matt and Josey didn't know that Lucas was gone…they had left the house for her and Lucas to have time alone.

"Where's Mavis?" Nikki was used to the dog greeting her with a happy smiling pant.

"They took both dogs." Sadie said.

Nikki sighed, she would have liked Mavis' company to keep from thinking of Lucas. Canine therapy is as good for the soul as equine therapy. "You called home sick?"

Grace lifted a hand to her mouth and faked a cough. Sadie coughed through a grin.

"You have school tomorrow." Nikki chuckled.

"Not when we're sick," Graced answered with another fake cough. "Mom said if we were too sick we should just stay up here with you and get better."

"She did huh?" Nikki sighed. They just weren't going to let her be alone and they had sent her kid therapy.

If she had any doubt that the girls knew what was happening, it was erased when they greeted her with a rare welcoming hug. It was firm and long…sharing their love and support.

Sadie was the first to step back…she didn't look at Nikki but instead looked to the Nomad horses. "We rode the two sorrels and ponied the dark bay. Just walked this time but went up and down hills to work the muscles. There might be something wrong with the bay's back hoof though."

Right to work…they talked about the plans for the five rehab horses. They would wait and make a plan for the horse arriving in the morning until they saw him; they had only seen him in pictures.

When the sky grew dark they turned on the barn lights and continued to work; trying to come up with a stall design plan for her business. At midnight, they walked in the house to research information on the computer. While she looked over Sadie's shoulder, as her younger cousin showed her the different layers of a horse's hoof, Nikki felt her muscles begin to ache for sleep; her eyes became heavier. She looked at Grace who was asleep at the end of the couch…it made her eye lids heavier but Sadie continued to show her what she thought could be wrong with the hoof of the bay Nomad.

Nikki leaned back…trying to focus her eyes…her attention…but she lost the battle. The last thing she remembered was wondering why Lucas left.

***

Nikki opened her eyes to the sound of dishes being washed. Leaning up on an elbow she looked into the kitchen expecting to see her cousins…but it was a man…a flicker of hope rushed through her heart…she sat up from the couch quickly.

It was Dr. Mark that turned to her with a smile in his eyes. Probably on his lips too but it was unseen through his thick mustache. As much as she loved him; he wasn't who she wanted to see.

"It's about time you woke up." His low southern drawl was pleasant first thing in the morning.

She sat back and reached for her phone;

TEXT FROM MOM: We'll be there around three

TEXT FROM DAD: Call me
TEXT FROM GRACE: Felt better…went to school

Monday morning…those girls were going to be exhausted. No missed calls…nothing from Lucas.

"I brought that gelding up for Kate…she called in a favor," he smiled and brought her a cup of coffee then sat next to her and reached for the computer that Sadie had been working on the night before. "Sadie said one of the Nomads had a problem with a hoof…"

He started up where Sadie left off. Ten minutes later, they walked outside to a beautiful sunshine filled morning. The sky was sapphire blue, the air was still crisp and the pine tree aroma helped lift her energy. Spring in the mountains was just magnificent.

"Do you know anything about his history?" She asked as he lift the lever to the horse trailer.

"He's retired from the Portland police department."

"Seriously?" Nikki's voice went up two octaves.

"Yup," He stepped the horse out of the trailer.

The horse was a deep brown and had a thin blaze dropping from a star on his forehead. He had to be at least16 hands tall and was extremely underweight.

"He's Holsteiner and Morgan bred."

"That's a heck of a combination." Nikki shook her head then her eyes narrowed as she concentrated on his movement…a habit she was picking up from Sadie.

Nikki squatted on the ground, like her cousin would, and watched the hooves, hocks and knees as Dr. Mark walked him away from her then toward her.

"What's your thoughts?" He asked with a tilt of the head.

He was testing her...Nikki grinned.

She saw nothing wrong with his legs so she watched his hips move. It was easy since there wasn't enough muscle to hide the bones. Nothing wrong with his hip action either.

"I don't see anything wrong."

"That's because there isn't anything," He chuckled.

Nikki shook her head and laughed softly, "Well…I passed that test. Why was he retired?"

"Age…he's eighteen. Went back to the people that donated him to the police department and they boarded him with the lady in Viola until they could find a good home for him."

"Kate said he reacted well to the medicine…cold is gone."

He nodded and looked at the barn; to the nine horses that were staring and nickering at the newcomer.

"Where do you want him?"

"He was boarded with the two paints over there," She pointed to the horses. "I don't have another small corral so we'll put the two paints together to make room for him. I'd like to have at least another half dozen runs so they can all have their own. That way I can make sure they get the correct feed."

"What are you thinking? Wood or panel fencing?"

"I know panels would be better, but I like the look of the wood better. It blends into the rest of the barn and its history."

Dr. Mark's phone alert rang out; he checked it while they walked. "Nick wants you to call him."

Nikki nodded but kept walking to the corral. She didn't want to talk to him, she wanted to talk to Lucas.

Dr. Mark stopped and typed into his phone then slid it in his jacket pocket.

As they reached the two paint horses, the larger one swung his head out and tried to bite the newcomer…who sidestepped and bumped into Nikki. She tripped over her foot as she tried to get out of the way and hit the ground hard, landing on her butt.

"Dang it!" She hollered at the paint horse.

The newcomer's head swung down to her, sniffing her boots then looking at her. His big brown eyes were soft and gentle, looking at her as if to check on her.

Nikki chuckled and reached a hand to his nose as Dr. Mark stepped to the gate.

"You OK?" He asked with a chuckle.

"The horse is more concerned than you are." Nikki laughed as she picked herself up off the ground.

"I've seen you take harder falls than that." He smirked.

Nikki laughed, "When I was thirteen and riding along the fence during branding..."

"...and the momma cow got mad and charged your horse..."

"...went right off the horse and over the fence...flipped in the air..."

"...and landed on your butt..."

They grinned at each other.

"Right back in the saddle..." Dr. Mark looked at her proudly.

Nikki smiled, she'd hurt for days but refused to take time off riding.

They moved the horses without further incident and stood staring at the ex-Portland police mount as he checked his new home and neighbors.

"You know anything about him?" Nikki asked.

"Not really, Kate might."

"I'm curious about him." The gelding stood quietly eating the hay she had placed in the feeder. He was the tallest horse there, even taller than Matt's auction horse, Jiggers. "He must have been intimidating to a lot of people."

"Well, I'm sure we can call the department in Portland and find out some information about him."

"I think we should."

"I'll do some checking and get a name for you to contact." Dr. Mark said.

Nikki nodded. "I'd appreciate that."

"Let's check on the bay Nomad."

She haltered the bay then walked the horse for the veterinarian as he watched the horse move. He squatted on the ground like Sadie did which made her giggle.

Dr. Mark grinned. "Trying to get her point of view to see if I can see what she saw."

"See anything?"

He shook his head. "Not saying there isn't anything. Let me get a hand on him."

He lifted the foot and examined it closely; pushing, prodding, using a hoof pick. He finally stood, shaking his head.

"I don't see it." He finally muttered.

"Maybe it was after they rode for a while." Nikki suggested.

He shrugged. "Let's saddle him up. You want to ride Harvey and we'll go for a short ride and see if it shows up?"

"Silly question…" Nikki chuckled and walked the Nomad to the hitching post.

CHAPTER FOUR

Thirty minutes later they returned from a short ride to the north pasture stock tank and back. There was a pipe leading from the natural spring to the stock tank, letting nature keep the tank full. It provided water to a portion of the herd and they watched it carefully. Once the spring runoff from the mountains dried up, they would move the cows to another pasture.

Nikki followed him for thirty yards, "I don't see anything. Can you feel anything?"

Dr. Mark shook his head. "I've learned over the last couple months to pay attention to what Sadie points out…but this time…I'm at a loss."

"Wish we had an x-ray machine." Nikki sighed.

His eyebrows shot up, "I could probably get you one."

"Really?" Nikki asked in surprise and in excitement.

"It would be an older one. A clinic in the Tri-cities is going out of business and auctioning off their equipment."

"When's the auction?"

"Wednesday."

Three days before the wedding…but was there going to be a wedding? Why did he leave? Nikki internally shook the bad thought away and concentrated on the auction.

"Do they have a list or catalog?" She asked. "I'd like to boost up the equipment I have here and getting it at a discount would even be better."

"I believe they do. Let's put the horses away and go look it up. What kind of equipment were you thinking and where are you going to put it?"

While the horses were returned to the corrals, they discussed equipment and the barn conversion then moved into the house and back to the computer. Just as they finished reviewing the auction website, they could hear a truck pulling into the ranch.

Nikki stepped outside the house just as her uncles were stepping out of the truck, which was pulling a flatbed trailer loaded with wood fencing posts.

The cow dogs, Spur and Pepper, excitedly ran to her. She knelt to greet them.

"What are those for?" Nikki stood and nodded to the posts.

"And hello to you too," Grayson grinned and gave her a long comforting embrace, then stepped out of the way so Scott could too. Hugs of support...she kept herself from thinking of Lucas and concentrated on the three men.

"Good morning," Nikki smiled.

"Well, you have too many horses for the number of corrals here." Grayson nodded to Dr. Mark. "You want wood corrals, they need fencing posts."

Nikki raised a brow and turned to Dr. Mark with an accusing glance. He just smiled through his mustache.

"Nick is on his way with the lumber so let's get these planned out before he gets here." Scott lifted an arm to point to the barn and existing corrals. "Go," He grinned. "This is your chance to be the boss and tell us what to do."

Nikki laughed; she loved these men.

They staked the area for the new corrals and ran string between each stake. Nikki walked through, making sure everything was just how she wanted it before the first post hole was drilled. Jessup arrived with the auger for drilling the fence post holes just before Nick pulled into the driveway with the truck full of lumber.

Nikki met her dad at his truck and they embraced; his arms strong and comforting. He squeezed that little bit more. His eyes were anguished but he didn't mention Lucas. They just got to work on the corral system Nikki had designed.

Just before the first hole was drilled, Nikki's phone rang and her pulse raced. She reached for it…internally hoping…but it wasn't Lucas, it was Kate.

"Hello, Kate." Nikki answered trying to keep the disappointment from her voice.

"You have room for a couple more horses?" Kate asked.

"I will in a couple hours." Nikki smiled at the group of men and stepped toward the house.

"There was an accident on the Genesee-Juliaetta Road last night involving a horse trailer and a farm truck."

"How bad?" Nikki frowned and walked into the house and her small office.

"Not good, could have been worse though."

"How many horses?"

"Three, they all lived but are cut up pretty bad."

"The owners?"

"The Becks, they are OK too, really shook up. They were heading home from a horse show in Spokane." Kate said.

"All three show horses?"

"Yeah, the Becks raised one and just bought the other two last year."

"What are the horse's conditions?" Nikki asked as she sat down at her desk and picked up a pen.

"The two that were in the front of the trailer have badly cut up legs. The one in the back has a broken shoulder."

"Dang…" Nikki whispered.

"The pair with cut legs are already out of surgery and have a good chance to pull through but they'll need rehab, which is why I talked to the owners about you." Kate sighed, "The other one, it's the one they raised from a colt, the kids are pretty devastated…but there's not much you can do with a broken shoulder bone except keep the weight and pressure off it, hope and pray."

"He'll have to be in a sling for months." Nikki sighed, already envisioning the setup she would need.

"What do you have up there now? You have time for these three?"

Nikki nodded to the empty room, "Just fattening up and exercising a handful. I'll take care of them. What about the owners?"

"The mother travels a lot, Dad takes the kids around. They want to buy or lease a couple more so the kids can continue riding while these recuperate. Which means they wouldn't have time to take care of these three themselves. If you are willing to take care of them, they'll pay you of course."

"OK," Nikki nodded. "When?"

The women discussed the details.

When Nikki ended the call she looked at the clock. To her calculations, her mother and Jack would be traveling through Spokane soon. They should be able to pick up a horse sling from there.

She called her mother.

"Are you OK, did he call?" Her mother answered.

Nikki closed her eyes and sighed, "No he didn't. I'm OK, lots of company keeping me busy."

"I heard about that. We're just getting to Spokane, we'll be there in a few hours."

Nikki told her about the horses and the supplies she needed to take care of them properly.

"We'll stop and see if we can find a sling…or anything else that looks interesting." Her mother answered. "You're sure you're OK?"

"I am for now…this will keep my mind busy."

"We'll be there as soon as possible."

"Thanks, Mom."

She ended the call with a sigh and looked down at the phone. She wanted to call Lucas and tell him about the horses…he would be interested…want to help…why did he leave?

Nikki was reaching for the door knob of the front door when she saw Matt's truck and trailer pulling in. She hesitated. The doors opened with Mavis and Bart jumping out of the truck and running to the men and fellow dogs. Matt and Josey stepped out of the truck with big grins on their faces; they were looking at the barn. They were met by Nick and her uncles. Within seconds their grins disappeared and both looked at the house with stunned expressions. Nikki stepped back, hoping they didn't see her staring at them.

She waited. Wondering if she was being a coward…not wanting to face them until they knew, hoping they would follow the example of the rest of the family and not talk to her about him…about Lucas…and ask her why he left. Why did he?

How long should she stand there? How long before her mind went back to him? How long before Josey and Matt could handle the information without being too emotional to her?

They had expected to come back to a happy bride and groom preparing for a wedding…not five men trying desperately to keep the bride's mind and body busy so she didn't fall apart.

How long?

Both Matt and Josey started nodding…they were agreeing…with what?

Nikki hoped…

Taking a deep breath she stepped out of the seclusion of the house to greet them.

They embraced her without words; long comforting embraces. Josey kept a grasp on Nikki's hand.

"What did Kate want?" Josey asked; her eyes, filled with worry and tears, looked into Nikki's.

Nikki told them about the three horses.

"You'll need three small inside stalls so they can't move around; one for the sling." Matt sighed. He too, looked at her in concern. "You guys have the corral system going. Josey and I can work on building the stalls."

"Absolutely," Josey nodded emphatically and dropped Nikki's hand. "Tell us where you want them."

The inside stalls were designed and Matt and Josey got to work. Reilly and the rest of the kids would be coming up after school and bring more building supplies.

TEXT FROM MOM: Have sling…interesting thing…be there in 4 hours

Nikki looked at her watch…noon…only noon…where was he now? What was he doing? Was he thinking of her? Was he trying to figure out how to tell her it was over? Would he even tell her?

"Nikki!"

She looked up; a bit dazed. Leah was standing in front of her.

"When did you get here?" Nikki asked in surprise.

"A couple minutes ago," She answered with a quick hug. "We brought lunch."

"We?" Nikki turned to see Jordan and Tessa pulling a cooler out of the SUV.

"Nikki!" Jessup yelled from the barn.

She turned.

"What kind of latches do you want for the gates?"

She went to him as her aunts setup lunch.

"Nikki!" Matt called from in the barn.

She stepped in the barn to answer his questions.

"Nikki!" Jordan called from the front steps.

"Nikki!" Grayson called from the corrals.

"Nikki!" Matt hollered from the barn.

The onslaught continued.

***

Nikki stepped up the ladder to the top of the indoor wall Matt and Josey had built for the stall. It was an open design so they could reach over the wall to the rafter which would be the brace for the sling system.   She stretched her arm to the rafter, making sure the eye-bolts, that would be holding the sling, were within reach.

"It's good." She called to Matt.

"Good, he'll be right in front of the little door so he can look out to the ranch parking area and the back of the stall allows easy access for removing manure." He nodded up to her. "Good design, Sis."

"Not bad on short notice." She smiled.

"Well, stay up there. Mom and Jack just pulled in. You can hang the sling and try it out while you're up there."

Matt understood she was afraid to see her mother…afraid of a meltdown…she had to stay out of reach and busy…she nodded then waited.

When her mother and Jack walked into the barn they were carrying the new sling.

"Was it expensive?" Nikki asked quickly before either could speak, hopefully they would follow her lead.

"Not too bad," Jack answered with a concerned smile. "We called Kate to find out what size to buy."

"Let's check it out." Her mother's voice shook when she spoke as she stepped into the stall and lifted the sling to Nikki.

Nikki reached down, but instead of grabbing the sling, her hand slid over the top of her mother's hand. She squeezed tightly as she looked into her mother's worried blue eyes. With just a look she told her mother she loved and needed her but not right now. Her mom smiled her understanding.

"I bet it will be perfect." Nikki spoke as she let go over her mother's hand and took ahold of the sling.

"We've used those in rescuing horses." Matt said from below.

"Great, so we can strap you in and hoist you up to hang you from the rafters. Just to test it out." Nikki grinned from her perch above the stall.

"Like a piñata." Their mother smiled.

"I want the first swing." Josey laughed.

Matt shook his head at his girlfriend. "You too?"

She just gave him a wicked little giggle; her brown eyes shining.

"Nikki, come out here!" Grayson yelled from outside the barn.

As she made her way down the ladder, she realized how tired her body was becoming. She glanced at her watch…five o'clock. What was he doing? It was ten o'clock in the morning in Sydney, was he still there? Was he at Cid's ranch or the office? Maybe his mom's…

"Nikki, come on." Grayson yelled again and pulled her out of her haze.

"What?" She asked, trying to put energy into her voice.

All of the adults in her family were standing in front of her when she walked out of the barn.

"Well, aren't you a crowd." Nikki grinned at the group as Grayson swung his arm to the side of the barn.

"Go tell us which horse you want in which pen." He ordered with a smile.

Just as the horses were placed in their own corrals, Reilly's flatbed truck pulled in with Alex and Wade as passengers. Cora's car with her and Nora, Sadie, and Grace arrived right behind them.

The whole family was there…except Lucas…Nikki sighed. He liked the moments the whole family came together too.

"Nikki?"

She turned to see each of the kids unloading supplies from Reilly's truck. Cora and the girls were carrying boxes of pizza into the house.

"Nikki?" Reilly said again.

"What?" She smiled…or tried to.

"Where does this go?" He asked.

He held up a bag of cedar wood shavings for the floor of the indoor stalls.

"In the barn, left hand side." She answered.

"Nikki? Is Matt here?" Nora ran up next to her. Her black hair was pulled back into two low pony tails at the back of her neck. Her dark brown eyes shining.

"Right, here." He walked out of the barn to help unload the bags of shavings.

"Can I ride Jiggers?" She asked hopefully. "I never have before, and you guys talk about him all the time."

"Nora," Matt chuckled. "You can ride any of my horses, any time you want."

"Oh, thank you!" She grinned.

Nora returned within a half hour. She slowly cantered toward Nikki.

"Something happened to the pipe that runs into the stock pond." Nora told her from atop of the tall bay horse. "It's almost empty and the ground around it is muddy."

Nikki tilted her head in confusion, "Dr. Mark and I were just up there; it was fine."

Nora shrugged, "Not anymore." Her eyes shifted as Nick walked up to them. A flicker of delight shown in her eyes then quickly disappeared. "Nick, you want to go for a ride with us?"

"We're going for a ride?" Nikki asked in surprise.

"Sure, it has to be fixed." Nora nodded.

"Well…" Nick said.

"You can ride Bodi!" Nora said excitedly.

Any chance of Nick saying no was quickly gone when he looked up at the happy light in her eyes. She had patiently waited for him to ride the horse for the first time.

"Well, that sounds just fine." Nick nodded at her.

Ten minutes later, Nick stood next to the saddled three-year-old and looked through narrowed eyes at Nora. "You sure he's safe."

Nora rolled her eyes, "Of course he is."

"I've hit the ground enough times in my life."

"That was from bulls, not a Nora trained horse." Nora giggled.

"A Nora trained horse…" He grinned as he put a foot in the stirrup and lifted himself up on the crème colored horse with blue eyes.

"The best kind," Nikki laughed.

"Except for Uncle Grayson," Nora corrected her.

They watched him ride Bodi around the driveway, testing him out; testing out Nora's training.

He nodded and smiled at Nora, "So far so good, let's see how he does on the trail."

They walked for a few minutes, then moved to a trot and eventually finished their ride to the stock tank at a slow gallop; all three smiling.

Springtime in the mountains came with fields covered in lush green grass and yellow flowers. There was nothing like galloping across the spring fields.

"He's a whole lot different than riding Blue." Nick said.

"It's weird riding such a light colored horse after riding Isaiah and Arcturus." Nora told him.

"How is Jiggers?" Nikki asked.

"Oh, he's fun." Nora replied. "He lives up to his name. I could ride him all day."

"That's what Matt said the first time he rode him." Nikki nodded.

Nikki stepped out of the saddle and looked at the muddy ground around the stock tank. It was obvious the creek was still flowing since the ground had puddles of water and a small stream trickled from puddle to puddle. Fresh manure piles showed the cows had been in the area that day and had drained the tank since her and Dr. Mark had visited that morning.

Her riding companions had also stepped down from their horses and were tying them to a nearby tree. She followed suit with Harvey.

"The pipe is still aimed in the tank," Nick commented. "It must be broken above the brush and trees."

"Maybe in it." Nora tried to look up into the brush.

Nikki looked up the hill as if she could see behind the brush. "I'll go up." She said and unhooked her saddle bag which held the pipe repair supplies. She'd been repairing pipe since she was little. She always traveled with one of the Trio when she was younger and they let her help when they repaired fences, pipes, or anything else.

"I can do it." Nick told her.

"I will." Nikki said and turned to walk up the hillside and around the brush. She wanted to keep busy and not just sit around and wait for him or think of Lucas.

She found the break around the first thicket of brush. There were cow hoof prints all around the pipe and one over the top of the pipe which had created the break. She had it repaired in less than ten minutes.

Stepping back and looking around she found a long dead, but thick, branch and placed it along-side the pipe. Hopefully it would guard the pipe from the next set of hoofs that walked by.

Looking at the placement of the sun in the sky, she calculated they only had an hour or so before sunset. Rolling her head and shrugging her shoulders she tried to get rid of the exhaustion in her muscles but it didn't help much…she was just plain tired.

She turned and retraced her steps until she heard a noise that took her by surprise. She stopped and listened; she heard it again.

CHAPTER FIVE

With a tilt of the head and inquisitive eyes she took a step to her left and could just see her dad and Nora.

Nora was sitting causally on the edge of the stock tank. She was smiling at Nick who was sitting on a fallen tree facing Nikki, but he didn't see her.

Nick leaned down and picked up something from the ground and tossed it at Nora. She ducked and the stick missed her head. Both of them GIGGLED. Light, playful, little kid giggles. Nikki had never heard anything like it coming from her dad and she couldn't remember the last time Nora had giggled like that.

Nora leaned down and put her fingers in the mud. Nick pointed to his own nose and they both grinned. Nora held out her hand and flicked mud from the tip of her finger towards him. It hit him in the cheek and they giggled again while he wiped it off and shook his head slowly. Their faces were relaxed and eyes lit with humor; Nick looked ten years younger.

Nora touched her nose and he reached down and scooped mud on the end of his finger and flicked it at her. Nora didn't move and it hit her in the forehead. Both of them burst out in little kid giggles. Nikki stood in stunned awe as they repeated it until Nora finally hit Nick right on the end of the nose. She squealed in delight as he laughed quietly and wiped it off.

"See, he can still have fun now and then." Nora giggled and tried to wipe the mud off her hands.

The comment stunned Nikki. 'He'? Who was she talking about?

"Every now and then," Nick giggled at her then leaned to look behind her.

Nikki quietly stepped back, he would have noticed the water flowing back into the tank through the pipe and realized it was fixed.

Purposely breaking a few sticks as she made her way to them, she emerged from the brush and smiled, "All fixed."

"That was quick." Nora smiled. The little girl expression was no longer there.

Nikki glanced at her dad; no sign of the delightful giggle on his face. He smiled at her calmly and looked at her proudly.

"Aren't you just the all-around cowgirl." He teased.

Nikki laughed on the outside but was totally confused on the inside.

They remounted the horses and headed back to the ranch. Nora rode to her right and Nick was to her left.

Nikki replayed the whole scene in her head. She knew there was something special between the two of them but she never realized that it was…what? She didn't even know how to describe it.

"Nikki?"

She heard her name and looked up. They were both looking at her in concern.

"Are you OK?" Nora asked.

"Who is 'he'?" Nikki blurted.

"What?" They asked in unison.

"You said, 'He can still have fun now and then'; who is 'he'?" Nikki quickly turned to both of them to see their reactions.

Nora's jaw dropped and she looked at Nick, her eyes apologetic.

Nick's face was frozen, his lips rolled together in a tight line and he looked to Nora. He nodded at her as if to say it was OK.

They rode quietly for a few minutes. Nora had turned away from Nikki so she couldn't see her face but occasionally lifted a hand as if wiping away tears.

Nick was looking out to the mountains, his face unreadable.

The guilt was beginning to take over the confusion. Whatever she had witnessed and called them on ran deeply; emotionally.

"I'm sorry." Nikki finally whispered. "I didn't mean…"

"There isn't anything to be sorry about." Nick said but didn't look at her.

Nikki was near tears; her exhaustion started to take over her mind and body. The need for Lucas hit her strong and hard; she so desperately wanted his arms around her, comforting her. Would his arms ever be around her again? Was she doomed to never see his amber eyes again? Would she ever hear his laughter again? The tears started to fall. She tried hard to stop them but they wouldn't.

She leaned back in the saddle and cued Harvey to slow down. Once the horse's head was behind Bodi and Jigger's rumps she turned to the left and headed away from them. She didn't hear them follow so she took off at a trot. She had no idea where she was going but she just needed to get away.

Jigger's head appeared first to her left, then Bodi's to her right. They trotted along-side her without attempting to stop her. She trotted up the hillside to the main ranch road and slowed down to a walk. They remained on each side of her.

The sun was beginning to set, creating pink clouds to dot the light blue skyline.

"She was talking about the young kid I used to be before I bet on the bull in the pasture." Nick said without emotion.

Nikki glanced at him in surprise. That hadn't occurred to her. So for some reason, Nora brought out the kid in him.

"I didn't think you were like that." She said honestly. "You never talk about before you started riding."

"I wasn't like that," He sighed. "I didn't have any friends outside of school because I didn't want them to know about my parents or my house…hut…hole in the wall. I didn't have a real friend until Scott and Grayson, but I didn't really understand the friendship until after I moved to Australia. Cid is really the only longtime true friend I have ever had and we didn't meet until I was twenty-one."

"So you were a lonely kid?" Nikki asked.

He nodded.

Nikki glanced at Nora but her head was still turned so she couldn't see her face. How did that relate to Nora? Was Nora lonely too? How could you be lonely in such a close family as theirs?

Glancing at Nick, he was looking down the road with no expression.

Nikki bit her lip. So he was lonely as a child, slept in the dirt, and barely ever had a full stomach. Then he left and started riding bulls. When he finished riding, he started a business; a business that was now worth nearly 300 million dollars. The company was there to help people and he and Lucas fought for them.

"Dad?"

"What?"

"Did you ever think that if you hadn't been that lonely kid, gone through what you did with your parents, that you wouldn't have grown up to start a large corporation that helped families? A company that helps kids like you used to be?"

She glanced over at him and was surprised to see him staring at her; an odd look on his face. Even though it was hard to say it to his face, she continued, "The kid you used to be was strong enough to change his life and make it better…to go on to make other kid's lives better."

He blinked, his jaw dropped in surprise.

"If you didn't go through what you did, you couldn't have helped me." Nora's voice was so low that they barely heard it.

Nikki turned to her in confusion. Helped her with what? But Nora was still looking off the other direction. Her hand went to her face again then lowered to the saddle horn.

"Where would I be? What would I be like now?" Nora continued, her voice shaking.

"You would have been fine, you would have been OK." Nick told her with a tender voice.

Nora turned slowly, tears in her eyes and the tracks of shed tears on her face. "I would still be ugly."

Nikki was stunned at that comment.

"Nora…" He said, his voice low.

She shook her head at him, "Nikki's right, he was a strong kid, not just a lonely kid."

He didn't respond; just looked into the sunset.

"Dad, if you had a normal childhood, would you have started the business? Or been so focused to help people get to work and provide for their kids?" She asked.

He continued to stare into the sunset.

"Nick, let him admit it, let him be strong." Nora said as she too stared into the clouds turning pink and yellow.

Nikki heard him sigh heavily, "I would not have created the corporation."

She knew that was a huge step for him but she pushed a little more, "So, be proud of him."

The barn was within sight.

"Nora, can I talk to Nikki?" He asked.

Nora's answer was to nudge Jigger's into a slow canter and ride away from them.

Nikki watched her for a moment then turned to her dad before he could speak.

"You said Nora knew most but not all, how much does she know?"

He glanced at her and nodded, "She knows everything of my childhood, more than anyone else, you and Matt included. She knew about the corporation before I told you two and the Taggers but she doesn't know the dollars behind it or the inheritance. They didn't want her to know, so I've never told her."

Nikki couldn't help the hurt feeling running through her. Why had he told Nora and not her?

"Nikki, there is no way I will ever say that I am proud of leaving you behind, with my mother or with Dru." He said bluntly.

"I'm not asking you to say that. I just said to be proud of him, how he turned out. He fought to get out of the situation he was in and build a new life."

She glanced at him and saw a slightly amused look on his face.

"What?" She asked and stopped Harvey since they were so close to the barn they could see people moving around. Nick stopped Bodi next to her.

"Nora talks of 'him' as a different person than me; it's odd hearing that from you."

Nikki smiled in understanding but wasn't going to let the subject drop. "Well, 'he' was strong enough to go get me from your mother and take me to Mom and her family. I can't imagine what it took for you to face the Tagger family after leaving like you did. Let alone the inner strength it took to ask them to raise me with Matt." When he didn't answer she continued. "You don't have to be proud, but you do need to understand what that kid did for me, the life he gave me." Her throat constricted as the tears welled.

Nick rolled his lips together tightly and stared at her.

"Your secret is safe with me." She sighed. "You know that."

He nodded.

The sun had set and the sky started to darken. "We should head in."

"Nikki," He whispered.

When she glanced back at him she saw his eyes glisten.

"I block the past, it only comes up when I try to use it to help Nora through…"

He stopped.

"It's OK, I don't understand, but whatever it is, I know you two have really helped each other."

"When I was growing up, I never had the thoughts and dreams of other kids; college, family, career. I didn't see that from my parents so I never thought I would have it for myself. When I left you with Dru, if there was even a flicker of hope inside me, it was gone. I never thought I would ever be back in your life or be part of such a strong family. I never, in a million years, thought I would have the love for someone like I do with Tessa. When I look at Alex, and he looks at me with such happiness to see me…it just overwhelms me and, to be honest, there are times I feel the need to run and hide."

"Please don't," She said quickly.

"I won't, never again."

"Nora helps you with that?" She finally realized.

He chuckled, "Nora therapy."

"For you or him?"

Nick shrugged, "Both I guess. She grounds me; makes me reach into my past but not in a bad way. It helps when I can use my past to help her."

"Makes the little kid come out," Nikki smiled.

He chuckled which made Nikki laugh.

"I was floored when I heard you two giggling and flicking mud at each other."

He grinned then looked at her in concern.

"I will never mention it to her. That's between you two."

Nick nodded and sighed. "I don't know if I'll ever truly be…healed, I guess is what you would describe it. I still fight that urge to get away sometimes, when it gets overwhelming. What I have realized, with Nora's help, is when I start to feel that flight urge, it's because that 'smothering' feeling I have is just emotions. I didn't have that growing up." He paused and took a deep breath. "This may seem odd to you; but what Nora gives me…is a friend that kid never had, she helps heal him which ultimately heals me."

The tears had welled in her eyes as she listened to him. It was the most honest and 'deep' he had ever been with her.

He chuckled as he looked up into the now dark sky, "I've read a lot of psychology books."

"Self healing?" She smiled.

"Nora therapy," He smiled slightly. "The first time she got 'him' to come out was last fall. Everyone was gone, it was just me and her at The Homestead. I had taken off my boots at the back door so I was in my socks and she talked me into going upstairs."

"The long hallway?" Nikki grinned.

"Yeah," He chuckled. "She took off at a run and slid down that hallway then turned and nearly had to beg me to follow."

"You did it?" Nikki laughed at the image she created in her head.

"Took her some talking but I did it," He chuckled. "I told her I would do it once just for her."

"And how many times did you slide?"

"We slid for an hour." Nick admitted with a laugh.

"Well, next time…I want to slide with you too."

He nodded with a grin to her, "I think I could 'force' myself to do it again."

***

It was 9:00 before everyone departed into the night and to their own homes. It was going to be another late night for Sadie and Grace. Those girls were going to be exhausted again.

At 11:00 Matt, Josey and Nikki were still in the barn checking the new stalls and supplies one more time. The three injured horses would be arriving by 8:00 in the morning. Nikki wanted everything ready for them.

She turned off the lights in the barn and they walked through the crisp May evening to the house.

"Sometimes I forget just how small that house is." Matt said as they neared the building.

"And how Clara, Andy, and their three boys lived in it for so long." Nikki nodded.

"When did Clara pass away?" Josey asked as they entered the chilly house.

Matt stoked the fire and warmed the house as Nikki relaxed onto the couch and listened to him answer.

"It's been about ten years now." Matt said and looked to Nikki for confirmation.

"That's about right…." Nikki felt the warmth from the room and the softness of the couch start to drain the energy from her muscles.

"She got the flu and it just never let go of her." Matt sighed. "She just kept getting sicker and sicker until they took her to the hospital."

"She was there for three days and starting to get better when she suddenly…just died in her sleep." Nikki's mind flashed to those sad days…it drained her even more and her eye lids fought to stay up.

"Clara was a couple years older than Andy." Matt yawned, which caused Nikki to yawn…then Josey. "She was twenty-one when they got married and I think she was in her early seventies when she died."

"They had a really long life together." Josey said.

"Andy said it was a perfect life…always on the ranch. He admitted they argued a bit but neither one of them would change the life they had." Matt yawned again.

Nikki finally lost the battle with her eyelids. The last thing she remembered was thinking she and Lucas would have the perfect life …Andy would have been proud of her.

CHAPTER SIX

Nikki's eyes fluttered open and she stared at the ceiling. Another night sleeping on the couch; it was a good thing it was comfortable. Today was Tuesday...Kate would be bringing the injured horses this morning...for Lucas it was Tuesday evening...what was he doing? She just needed to know...to understand...why he left.

The aroma of coffee reached her and it pulled her from the thoughts of him. She slowly rose to look around. Neither Matt nor Josey were in sight so she stood and stretched trying to get the exhaustion out of her muscles. Coffee would help. When she took a step, she saw Matt through the window walking from the barn to the house, Mavis and Bart trotting happily beside him.

She waited, but he didn't walk through the doors so she glanced out the window to see him sitting on the front steps. She poured two cups of coffee and stepped out the door and took a seat next to him. He smiled his thanks as she handed him the coffee mug. Bart was sitting happily next to Matt; Mavis quickly lay down next to Nikki's bare feet.

They sat quietly and drank their coffee. Nikki looked out at the morning. There was a small yard that led directly to the narrow driveway and immediately blended to the dirt road. Across the road was a row of trees to her right then mountains as far as you could see to her left. The sides of the road were covered in new spring grass and the always favorite yellow and purple wild flowers.

The sky was a beautiful blue with just a few clouds on the horizon; the air was still crisp with a little bite on the skin. She took in a deep breath filled with the scent of pine trees… springtime in the mountains.

"I love this place." Nikki sighed.

"I do too. I can see why Clara's parents built their house here," Matt answered softly. "There is so much history here. It's amazing how many hours and days we spent at this ranch as kids…playing on these steps…and now…it's ours."

"I couldn't imagine the history that would have been lost if we changed the house. I love our new one and really like where we placed it."

"It's a bit more private then right on the road," He chuckled. "Have you been over there lately?"

"Not since Saturday," she admitted. "I didn't want to go see it without…"

Lucas…she thought to herself. She wanted him there.

"I was just sitting here thinking of the first time he came back." Matt nodded, knowing what she was thinking.

First time…hopefully there would be a next time…soon.

"I don't think I could have hated or loved you more in those moments." Nikki chuckled at the memory.

"You should have seen the look on your face. I wish I had a camera." He grinned.

"He had *just* told me that he had *just* got on the plane in Australia and I had a 19 hour plane ride and a 2 hour drive to wait for him…21 hours of waiting!"

"And within seconds I pulled around that corner over there with Lucas in the passenger seat of my truck." Matt laughed.

Nikki laughed and glared at her brother. "I was never so shocked in my whole life…and mad…and happy…then upset…then happy again."

"Well…if I remember right, there was a whole lot of happy after Candace and I left for the week."

Nikki chuckled and blushed.

They were quiet a moment before Matt placed his coffee cup on the steps and took her hand and squeezed.

"Everyone has been avoiding it, Nikki." He whispered and looked at her in concern. She could see in his eyes the hurt and desperation he felt for her.

Nikki nodded, the tears rushing to her eyes.

"Saturday…" He whispered.

She took in a quivering breath. For some reason…maybe it was their strong bond…the discussion needed to be with him. "I honestly can't believe he won't be here…I feel in my heart that we will be married."

"I feel the same way," Matt nodded. "You two have been connected since the first time you laid eyes on each other."

"Was it too easy, Matt?" She closed her eyes and envisioned the first moment she looked into his amber eyes.

"Easy?" Matt shook his head.

"Is that why this is happening?"

"Nikki, you two spend half your lives thousands of miles apart from each other. How is that too easy?"

"I don't know…I just don't know why he left…so I don't know what to say." Nikki wiped away the first tear.

"We will carry on as if the wedding is taking place…I believe it will." His grip on her hand was firm and his eyes mirroring the honesty in the words he said. She nodded and wiped away more tears.

"The closer we get to Saturday, the harder it will be to make decisions." He was working hard at keeping his voice calm and unemotional.

Nikki nodded; her throat was constricted and wouldn't let words escape.

"So you don't have to make the decisions, I will tell you what I think should happen and you just have to nod or shake your head."

More tears escaped as she took in a quivering breath…he knew her so well.

"Jessup was bringing the mountain flowers down Saturday morning…he just won't pick them so we don't have to worry about those."

Nikki nodded.

"The rental place will be delivering the tent, chairs, and tables on Friday…they still can, we'll just wait to set them up until Saturday morning or load them up and return them."

Nikki sighed as the tears continued.

"The food can still be cooked…everyone has to eat anyway." He smiled warmly. "I'll call the photographer and just let them know they have the day off."

Nikki nodded and wiped away the tears…he was dismantling her wedding as gently as he could.

"We'll call the cake place and have it delivered to the children's home."

Nikki lowered her head…at least someone would enjoy that beautiful cake Tessa had designed.

"The dresses will remain in the closets until later. Any gifts that arrive, we'll just return them later." He took a deep breath and let it out slowly. "The guests…we'll call those that we can…I'll bring you here, home…so you don't have to see anyone arrive that we can't get a hold of."

She leaned her head on his shoulder and nodded, tears freely flowing down her face. It just couldn't happen…Lucas would come home…he would never break her heart like this…he had to be here…this just couldn't happen…

"And if you look right here." Matt said loudly.

Nikki leaned back and looked at his arm where he was pointing at a scar.

"That's where you pushed me off these very steps…right over there…" He pointed to the corner to their right.

"You fell." Nikki whispered as she wiped away the tears.

"No…you pushed me." Matt smiled. "I remember it like it was yesterday. I…"

"…fell." Nikki's mind flashed to the day he was talking about. "We were in the house and Clara told us to go outside and get Andy for her. You rushed out, tripped on the bottom of the door and fell down the steps."

"Then how come I remember you saying 'She said me!' really loud and something hitting my shoulder which pushed me forward and down the steps." Matt tilted his head to the side and raised a brow.

Nikki chuckled…because he was right, and she had been momentarily terrified that she had really hurt him until he jumped up and yelled at her…the blood dripping from his arm. But she would NEVER admit it so she shook her head, "You were only five…you don't remember."

"Yes, I do!" He shook his head with a very amused grin.

"No…you were too young!" Nikki laughed; she could feel the tension leaving her muscles.

"What are you two arguing about?" Josey stepped out of the house.

"Nikki tried to kill me when we were little…right here on these steps."

"I did not!" Nikki shook her head. "You fell that time! I TRIED to kill you when I threw you in the stock pond."

"Oh, yeah! Except the fact we had been swimming in it for months so you didn't have a chance to kill me that time." Matt laughed and pointed at Nikki as he looked at Josey. "You have no idea how many times she tried to kill me when we were kids."

"Nuh, uh…you were just a clumsy boy!" Nikki laughed.

***

Jessup, Grayson, and Scott arrived just minutes ahead of Kate who was pulling the horse trailer containing the three injured Beck horses. All the dogs were put in the kennel so they didn't frighten the horses.

Kate backed the horse trailer right up to the double barn doors so the horses wouldn't have too far to walk.

"We'll take one out at a time and I'll go over their injuries and upkeep." Kate told them. "The first has the broken shoulder and some cuts and abrasions."

"We have the sling ready." Nikki informed her.

"To be honest," Kate hesitated by the door with a grim expression. "There is a good chance that he'll never recover and we usually suggest having the horse euthanized in these situations. It's humane for the animal, but the Beck's want to give it a try. He's twelve and they have raised him from a colt and promised the kids they would do whatever they could."

Nikki nodded, "It's no less than what we would do."

Kate nodded to Scott and he lifted the door handle.

"They wanted to bring the kids up but I told them this would be really stressful for the horses and ultimately the kids. I asked them to wait until tomorrow." Kate said.

"Josey and I will be here." Matt said. "Nikki will be at the auction with Dr. Mark."

The back of the horse trailer dropped to the ground to create a ramp for the horses so they didn't have to step up or down.

Nikki stood back and let Grayson, Scott, and Matt assist with the horse. As much as she wanted to help, she knew the men's strength would be needed if something happened.

The horse was a dark bay of average height with a thin blaze down his nose. His head was low and his eyes squinted against the morning light. Bright blue traveling boots covered his legs. There was a wide canvas band that ran under his belly and attached to the top of the trailer.

"I gave him pain killers, but not enough to knock him out. The canvas sling was put in place in hopes he wouldn't go down." Kate frowned in concern.

With Grayson on one side and Matt on the other, Scott released the sling and slowly led the limping horse out of the trailer. The side that was injured also had numerous scratches and abrasions.

"Just keeping those clean and flies away is all that's needed on his side. He has three cuts and about thirty stitches under the boots on his front leg." Kate added. "It took three of us nearly two hours to stitch all three horses."

"Dang!" Josey exhaled.

They led the bay to the stall and the horse stood patiently while Matt instructed the group on the installation of the sling. Once the horse was attached to the rafters and his weight supported, the horse's body relaxed.

"Well, I think we lucked out on that one." Nikki nodded in relief. "I was worried he wouldn't like it and we'd have a fight."

"He's probably relieved he doesn't have to support himself anymore." Jessup nodded.

The group stood patiently while Kate checked the horse. "His heart rate is up. I'll give him something for the pain."

Within minutes the horse's head hung low, his eyes drooping half closed. Matt removed the traveling boots from his legs showing three tracks of stitches on the upper portion.

"I was told he was pretty docile when handled but energetic in the pasture so you'll need to watch him closely once this wears off." Kate instructed and they all nodded. "We want to really watch his pain threshold."

"What if we put the training heart monitor on him?" Nikki asked. "We can track when he's in pain."

"Good idea." Kate nodded. "Keep track of how much and the time you give it to him. We want to document any improvement to see if this is working."

The second horse was dark brown with a flaxen mane. There was a long hairless patch across his shoulder and a few abrasions around it.

"Wow, he's a pretty one." Scott muttered as he led the horse down the ramp. The horse walked with four stiff legs so he moved at the horse's pace.

"He's Morgan bred." Nikki nodded.

"He's the daughter's show horse." Kate said. "He's the luckiest of the group; only the bald spots and scratches. The hair will grow back."

The horse was released into his new small stall, which would keep him from moving too much. He quickly headed to the feeder with the hay protruding from it.

"Now, number three here has cuts on all four legs, rump, shoulders, up his neck and across his face. He's lucky he didn't lose an eye." Kate explained as the men walked into the trailer. "They said he was in the middle of the three-horse trailer which took the brunt of the damage and this guy got banged up by the dividers on each side of his body."

"Did the truck hit the side of the trailer with their head first or towards their backsides?" Nikki asked.

"It hit the rumps and pushed their heads and front legs into the sides of the trailer." Kate said. "They walk stiff, I'm sure they all feel like they were hit by a bus…which it was a big truck anyway. They even hurt laying down."

"Did the trailer turnover?" Josey asked.

Kate shook her head, "Thankfully no, if it had they would have fell onto their heads. I don't think they would have survived."

"He doesn't want to move." Grayson called out from inside the trailer.

"Just prop open the divider and let him make his own way out," Nikki said and took a step forward to look into the trailer.

The red horse had a long wide blaze and was taller than the others; except for the lighter mane, he looked a lot like Dollar. All four legs were encased in white bandages. The gelding turned his head to look out the door as the men walked out. There was a long jagged stitch track from above his right eye, down across his nose and stopping next to his lips on the left side. The muzzle was very swollen. Lines of stitching ran down his neck, over his side, and a few on his rump.

"Frankenhorse," Matt exhaled.

Kate chuckled, "That's what we called him while we were trying to get him stitched up. We took extra care across the face to minimize scarring, per the Beck's request. There are more on his legs. We wrapped them to keep him from moving too much and tearing open the stitches. It's always a gamble with leg stitches anyway, but we gave it a shot. I'm not really hopeful that it'll work, but the Beck's were pretty insistent on trying to minimize the scarring."

"He a show horse, too?" Josey asked as she stepped into the trailer to run a comforting hand down the red horse's back.

"Was…not sure what they will do if the scarring is too bad." Kate sighed.

"Scars are signs of strength," Nikki whispered. "Just like Little Ghost."

"You're right there." Grayson nodded.

Josey took a step back and the horse leaned towards her, barely lifting a hoof he managed a step. She took another step and the horse managed to turn in the trailer. His body swayed back and forth to lift his long legs as he followed Josey all the way out of the trailer and down the ramp where they stopped. Josey gently rubbed the round jaw and the horse's body relaxed and leaned into her.

Josey's expression had changed from compassion and concern she had for the other two horses, to include protectiveness with this gelding. Nikki glanced to her uncles and brother; they returned her look with a nod…they had seen it too.

CHAPTER SEVEN

"How old is he?" Matt asked.

"This one is four, and the Morgan is ten." Kate answered.

"What's his name?" Josey asked as she caressed the soft hair just under the red horse's eye.

"Bobo," Kate answered with a smirk at the name. "The bay is Jack and the Morgan is Charming."

"Bobo…what a terrible name for such a beautiful horse," Grayson shook his head.

"Well, we already have a Jack in the family." Nikki wrote their names on the white boards just outside of each stall. Kate took her lead and wrote the medications for each horse under their names.

"He'll have to be Jack in the Sling." Matt chuckled softly.

Josey took a step back and the red horse followed her until they were in the stall where she took a handful of hay from the feeder and held it out to the horse. He barely moved his swollen lips and couldn't grab the hay.

Kate exhaled sharply. "The swelling around the stitches are really going to make him sore for a couple days."

Josey turned concerned eyes to Matt. "Do you have any alfalfa pellets or cubes?"

Matt walked to the feed room and returned with a bucket of alfalfa cubes and handed it to Josey. She broke the cube into a small portion and held it out to the horse. His lips tried, but failed to open enough to pull the cube into his mouth so Josey squeezed it in for him. The horse chewed without a problem then pushed with his nose against her.

Josey chuckled softly and pushed another chunk into the swollen mouth.

Grayson shook his head, "It's gonna take hours to feed him enough to make him happy."

Nikki glanced between the three animals. Jack was in the sling…his head still low. Charming was still eating but hadn't moved, and Bobo just stood and let Josey hand feed him.

"If you ignore their injuries and just look at their bodies, they look really good. Well taken care of." Nikki said and the rest of the group nodded. "I'll get a supplements mixture put together to mix with some oats. They'll all need a little extra to keep from losing too much weight."

"I knew you were the perfect person for the job." Kate smiled at her.

"It'll be a group effort on this one," Nikki said and turned to walk toward the feed room. "I'll be gone for two weeks on my…"

Nikki swallowed hard and gritted her teeth to keep from gasping. Instead of going to the feed room she walked out of the barn. Her feet led her to the one place she always went when she needed emotional help…she went to Harvey.

The brown mare saw her appear and started trotting to her. Trip and Bodi followed with the twin colts, Romeo and Shakespeare right behind them. They already had their grain for the morning so they knew they wouldn't be fed again. Harvey was coming to her for attention and Nikki needed it more than anything…except Lucas…she really needed Lucas.

The mare stopped right next to her and smashed her nose into Nikki's face which made the laughter bubble out of her. Two quick horse breaths of air flowed over her face and up her nose making Nikki gasp for fresh air. Oh, she loved this mare!

Bodi was next with the attention grabbing shove of the nose into her stomach pushing Nikki back into the fence and making another round of giggles escape. Trip's nose went right to her hair, the horse loved the smell of her conditioner. As the three older horses assaulted her head and neck with sniffs the yearling twins assaulted her hands looking for treats.

Now this is what you call equine therapy! Nikki couldn't help but laugh…again the muscles relaxed and her stomach eased.

Ten minutes of playfully pushing noses away, pulling manes, and scratching ears Nikki finally relaxed enough to climb over the fence and she jumped to the ground.

A horn honked and she looked up in time to wave goodbye to Kate. Jessup, Scott, and Grayson made their way to her side and each gave her a loving smile and a nod of the head before they drove away.

Nikki walked toward the barn doors, intending to check on the new additions when she stopped and stared at Jessup's truck as it drove away.

"What's the matter?" Matt asked.

Nikki frowned and looked up at her brother then back at the truck. "Jessup and Kate didn't talk to each other."

Matt was silent as he stared at the foreman's truck.

"You know something?" Nikki raised her brows at his silence.

Matt sighed and nodded, "They broke up last weekend."

"What?" Nikki gasped. "They've been together for years!"

Again a sigh and a shake of the head, "Jessup said she called it quits after her son called her."

"Her son is in Oklahoma…how could he possibly cause a breakup in Idaho?"

"I don't know…that was all Jessup knew too."

"Did Helen have anything to do with it?" Nikki asked. Kate's sister was the co-owner of the veterinary clinic. She and the Tagger's avoided each other since the dispute Helen had with Sadie and Wade over Rufio's wounded leg.

"I don't know, Nikki. That is the only thing that Jessup knew."

"Is he OK?" She asked in concern.

"I guess," Matt shrugged a shoulder. "You know him…he's not going to sit around and talk feelings with anyone."

"Yeah, I know." Nikki sighed and shook her head. There wasn't much they could do.

She and Matt returned to find Josey still feeding alfalfa cubes to the big red gelding.

"How's he doing?" Nikki chuckled at her sister.

Josey smiled at her in return, her brown eyes sparkling. "He's just a sweetheart."

When Josey looked back at the gelding, Nikki and Matt shared a look. She had just gotten attached to someone else's horse…a kid's horse…not good.

"Well, we might as well get things setup out here for us to watch over them." Matt suggested and walked to the ladder that led to the barn loft.

"We concentrated so much on the horses we forgot about us." Josey laughed. "Where are you going?"

"I saw some furniture up here that Charles and family didn't take with them." Matt called out from above. "Here…"

Nikki walked over to the hole in the ceiling and looked up. Matt handed her down a small dining room chair. It had a red and white striped round cushioned back and seat with chrome legs.

"This is Clara's old dining set." Nikki gasped in surprise.

"You remember it?" Matt laughed.

"Yes! Don't you?" Nikki looked back up in time to grab a second chair. She would have been twelve and Matt ten when she bought the set.

"Yeah…it was the last set she had. Andy hated it, so after she passed away he put it up here." Matt handed down a third chair.

"As much as he hated it, he couldn't bring himself to get rid of it because she loved it." Nikki smiled at the memory of Andy and Clara sitting in the chairs together.

"That's probably why it's still here…her boys couldn't get rid of it either." Matt said.

He handed her three more chairs then the round table. It had an oval white top and chrome legs that matched the chairs.

Matt climbed back down the ladder and jumped the last couple feet, landing with a thud.

"It was covered with a tarp so it's in pretty good shape." Matt said as he turned the chairs over to look at the safety in sitting on them.

"Wait until Mom sees these!" Nikki squealed.

A large thump echoed in the building making both of them turn. Josey quickly exited the red horse's stall and looked for the source.

Jack in the Sling stomped a back hoof and it echoed again.

"Someone woke up." Matt chuckled.

They still had the doors of the stall open. The door in front of him was split so they could shut the bottom half and keep the top half open so the horse could see into the driveway. They had kept the back of the stall open for access to clean it. Nikki quickly shut the bottom of the front door so the horse wouldn't get the idea he could just walk away.

She filled the 4-wheel garden cart with hay to use as a feeder for him. That way they could wheel it in for feeding him and wheel it out when they needed to doctor him. A water bucket was placed in the middle of the cart with the hay surrounding it.

They spent the afternoon with the horses and cleaning Clara's dining set. They placed it in front of the horses so they could keep an eye on them as they came out of sedation. Nikki fixed their lunch and served her unrelated siblings on the old dining set.

When she returned from taking their dishes to the house, she stopped at the main double doors of the barn and looked at her new rehabilitation barn.

To her left was Jack in the Sling in the new stall looking out the small door of the barn. Then there were three large stalls, the first one temporarily split for Charming and Bobo.

Bobo…what a terrible name for him…

To her right was the tack/feed room; the tack on one wall and her multiple bin feeding system on the other wall. Then there were three large stalls that opened to the inside of the building and also had a door to an outside run.

They had moved the hay from in the barn to one of the outside covered runs. There was no hay inside the building which cut down on dust that could cause respiratory issues in horses that were enclosed in the barn.

Opposite of Nikki, on the far back wall, were old wooden boards nailed up for shelving. The floor of the barn was very hard compacted dirt and inside the stalls she used black heavy rubber mats to cover the dirt then it was layered with wood shavings for bedding, except for the new inhabitants. Not knowing the extent of their injuries, she wasn't sure whether to use straw or wood shavings so she had both available.

When the flooring for the loft was built, creating the main floor ceiling, Andy had used tongue and groove boards that were firmly attached to each other and leak proof so nothing could fall onto the main area. It was old and dirty right now. There were two entry ladders to the loft on the inside; one on each end. There were also the large windows on the front of the barn, above the two main doors, that led directly into the loft. Originally, that was how they loaded the barn with hay.

Matt and Josey were sitting in the chairs, in the middle of the barn, watching her.

"What are you thinking next?" Josey asked with a knowing smile.

"Staining the ceiling," Nikki smiled as both of them and slid onto the chair that faced the back wall.

"*Hiring* someone to stain the ceiling is a great idea." Matt grinned. "What about pouring a concrete floor…or I should say *hiring* someone to pour a concrete floor?"

"Maybe in a couple months, after Jack in the Sling has gone home." Nikki nodded and glanced at the horse who was calmly eating his hay.

Not being worried about Charming or Bobo wandering out of the stall, they had left the door open. Charming was laying down sleeping and Bobo was standing at the door staring at Josey.

"I think you're wanted." Nikki giggled and nodded to the horse.

Josey quickly stood and carried her chair to the door. Cradling the bucket in her lap, she sat cross legged on the chair and slipped the alfalfa chunks through the horse's lips. The gelding nudged her shoulder with his sore nose as if to thank her then stood quietly as he was fed.

"Hopefully, I'll be bringing home some good supplies tomorrow from the auction." Nikki said. "…with no cabinets to put them in."

Matt turned and looked at the back wall. "Home Depot has cabinets; metal garage type that we can just place next to each other. We could create a whole wall of storage."

"What about a sink?" Josey asked.

Nikki looked at her in surprise. She'd never even thought about that. "It would be much handier than taking everything into the house to clean."

"There was a stainless steel one in the catalog for the auction tomorrow." Matt nodded. "It wouldn't take much to put a small septic tank out the back of the barn for it to drain into."

"You can call Jessup on that one." Nikki grinned. "He loves doing stuff like that."

They spent the afternoon designing the back wall and making a list of items for Nikki to purchase at Home Depot before leaving for the auction in the Tri-Cities. They would have to arrange for someone to deliver them to the ranch.

They took a break from inside the barn to feed and give attention to the horses outside the barn. The Nomads and the Violets were all perfectly content in the individual corrals and sunned themselves in the spring sunshine.

Grace, Sadie, Wade and Nora were due to arrive at any moment for an evening ride.

"I'm supposed to go to The Homestead tonight," Nikki frowned as Grace drove Tessa's SUV into the driveway.

"What do you mean 'supposed to'?" Matt asked.

"I'm worried about leaving the Beck horses." Nikki admitted.

"Seriously, Nikki? You don't think Josey and I can handle anything that comes up? With Jessup, Grayson, and Scott within twenty minutes away?" Matt shook his head.

"I know…" She sighed as the girls and Wade walked excitedly towards the barn.

"They all three won't be moving for a couple of days and do you really think Josey is going to let you feed Bobo even one alfalfa cube?" He chuckled. "Getting away and concentrating on supplies for your business is what you need right now."

Nikki nodded and followed the four kids into the barn.

"That's Bobo!" Nora exclaimed.

"You know him?" Josey asked in surprise.

"Yeah, he was at the show last weekend." Nora gently ran a hand down the swollen face. "They bought him last summer and have been showing him this year." She looked into the other stall. "Oh, Charming!" She instantly went to the brown horse to give him attention.

"What happened?" Grace asked as she gave Jack in the Sling attention.

Sadie and Wade were examining the injuries on Bobo's face and sides.

Nikki updated the kids on the accident and all the injuries.

"Oh, poor thing…," Grace whispered to the bay horse dangling from the sling.

"What do you know about them, Nora?" Nikki asked.

"Jack has been a really good horse for them; a really good teacher." She answered. "Charming takes after his name…he is just that. But Bobo was a bit of a challenge last Saturday."

"Why?" Josey asked.

"He grew a bit taller and stronger over the winter than what they expected. He's a bit of a handful for their daughter."

"They just do shows, no games?" Sadie asked.

"They were going to do both," Nora answered. "They originally bought Bobo for their daughter to run barrels and poles. She said he was bred for barrels not for horse shows. But, because he grew too tall and big for her, they were afraid to hype him up for games…they didn't think she could control him. He kind of intimidated her, so they use Jack for gaming."

"Do you know his bloodlines?" Nikki asked.

"No clue." Nora answered. "Just that he was bred to be a barrel horse."

"You guys better head out for the ride, we can talk after dark." Matt interrupted.

The girls saddled all three Nomads and Wade rode Jiggers. He wanted to try out the big red bay gelding with the fancy prance, too.

While the kids rode, Nikki prepared the grain rations for all the horses for the next morning. All Josey and Matt would need to do is grab a bucket and pour into the correct feeder.

She prepared an overnight bag and was ready to go when the kids returned.

A quick hug and goodbye to Matt and Josey, she let Grace drive on the way to The Homestead and updated all the kids on the horses, barn plans, and the auction. The kids kept her talking the whole ride down from the mountain.

It was 9:00 when they arrived and they were met by a large group who also wanted updated on all the horses. It was nearly midnight when Nikki lay down on the guestroom bed. She stared at the ceiling and wondered what Lucas was doing. Where was he? Why did he leave?

CHAPTER EIGHT

Nikki opened one eye and looked at the clock…6:00 in the morning…Wednesday… 11:00 at night in Australia…what was Lucas doing? She slid a hand out from the warm covers and picked up her phone…two messages. She closed her eyes tightly…hoping…she pushed the button to see who they were from…

TEXT FROM NICK: See you at Home Depot at seven

Disappointed exhale…nothing personal Dad, she thought.

TEXT FROM MATT: no message; it was a short video showing all three Beck horses resting peacefully.

She sat up with a slight smile; he had to be the best brother ever. She thought of their conversation the morning before then she quickly shook her head to rid her mind of the dismantled wedding. She nearly ran to the shower and rushed to get ready so she could find her family and wouldn't have to be alone and think of Saturday.

A half-hour later the kitchen was full of chatter as Nikki showed everyone the video Matt sent of the horses.

"That sling is quite the contraption," Cora said. "I'm going to have to ride up and check it out."

"It's pretty cool." Wade agreed. "Wait till after school, so I can go with you."

"It's a date." Cora grinned.

"Dr. Mark is here," Jack said to Nikki. "We'll need to be heading to Home Depot."

"What?" Nikki asked.

"I'm taking you to Home Depot," Jack chuckled. "Then taking your supplies up to Circle 50 and help Matt."

"Really?" Nikki asked. "I thought Dad was taking them up."

"No, he's going with you." Her mom chuckled.

"Seriously?" Nikki smiled.

TEXT TO NICK: You're going to auction?

TEXT TO NIKKI: Didn't think you were going to have that much fun without me did you?

Nikki laughed.

TEXT TO NIKKI: Tessa too, figured if Dru could play hooky she could, too.

Nikki looked at her mother, "You're playing hooky? Going up with Jack?"

Her mother laughed, "No, I'm going with you."

"Seriously?" Nikki shook her head in amazement. "Where was I during all this conversation?"

"Riding home with the kids last night." Her mother answered.

Dr. Mark entered the room and was immediately handed a travel mug of coffee. "Oh, Miss Cora, you know me well." He smiled, his eyes shone as he looked around the room. "So where's my riding partner?"

"I'm right here." Nikki grinned.

He shook his head with an amused frown, "Not you…you're Dru's riding partner."

"What?" Nikki looked at her mother in bewilderment.

"Oh, Hon." Her mother laughed. "Nick and Tessa, you and me, and Dr. Mark and…"

"ME!" Hollered Sadie as she trotted down the stairs; her loose blonde hair bouncing around her shoulders and her eyes sparkling at the older man.

"There's my Tagger." Dr. Mark grinned.

"Sadie's going?" Nikki looked at Leah.

"There are only a couple more weeks of school and she's already well ahead in every class." Leah explained. "I think it will be a good learning experience to see all the equipment up close and personal."

"With Dr. Mark teaching me!" Sadie nodded and filled a biscuit with scrambled eggs and bacon, taking a big bite then shoving a few extra pieces of bacon in her mouth. "Let's go." She managed to say around the food and then tried to grin at her mother's look of disgust.

***

"When does the auction start?" Sadie asked as the last cabinet was loaded into the stock trailer Jack was pulling to the ranch.

"Preview at 11:00 and auction at 1:00. It will take us about two and a half hours to get there so we want to be on the road by 8:30." Nick answered. "We'll check out the supplies, then go have lunch, then the auction."

"How many people do you think will be there?" Nikki asked Dr. Mark.

He shrugged a shoulder, "May not be many on site, there will be more online bidding."

"Dang!" Sadie grumbled. "We have to fight with them too?"

Nikki smiled, "Just the way life is now days."

"What are you doing with your truck?" Sadie asked Dr. Mark.

"We'll leave it here…I just have to get something out of it first." He said and opened the back door.

Nick walked up to him and took a large black brief case from him and a box.

"What's that?" Sadie asked, her eyes wide.

"It's a gift to my daughter to congratulate her on getting her business going." Nick grinned at Nikki.

"What?" Nikki gasped. "Dad, you didn't have to do that!"

"I never *have* to do anything." Nick chuckled. "I pretty much do what I want and this is what I wanted to do."

"Well, let's take a look before we head out." Her mother said. There was just enough room between the tailgate of Nick's truck and the stock trailer he was pulling to the auction to lower it so he could place the bag on it.

"What is it?" Sadie said excitedly.

With an eager excitement, Nikki unzipped the bag and looked inside. She couldn't tell what it was so she pulled out the manual and plastic enclosed paperwork.

"Dad!" She gasped in disbelief.

"What is it? What is it? What is it?" Sadie was nearly jumping beside her. She grabbed the book from Nikki and looked at it.

"A mobile wireless X-ray machine!" Sadie's jaw dropped. Her eyes turned to Nick, "That's the most awesome thing EVER!"

Nick laughed, "The day you graduate college, I'll buy you one."

"It's a deal!" Sadie shouted then turned quickly and crawled into the back seat of his truck. Her head lowered and she started reading the manuals from front to back and again. She read them four times before they arrived in Kennewick at the warehouse where the auction was to be held. She had also watched You-tube video demonstrations of the machine on her phone.

"You have that thing figured out yet?" Nikki asked. She and Dr. Mark were riding in the backseat on each side of the thirteen-year-old. Nikki's mother was sitting in front of her with Nick driving and Tessa between them.

"Yeah…I think so." Sadie nodded and finally looked up from the paperwork. "You can take the x-ray and it instantly goes to a file on The Cloud. Dr. Mark can get to it all the way in Lewiston and be able to read it for you."

"Well, that's cool." Dr. Mark said.

"I was just kinda wondering if we could test it out on you." Sadie grinned at the retired veterinarian.

"Me?" Dr. Mark laughed in disbelief.

"Sure," Sadie grinned wickedly. "You got the oldest knees here. That would make them more interesting."

Laughter erupted in the truck.

"Maybe we should wait and try it on the bay Nomad." Dr. Mark said.

"Why? What's wrong with him?" Sadie asked in surprise.

"His hoof," Dr. Mark said.

"What about it? I rode him last night, he was fine." Sadie said in concern.

"You said Monday morning that there was something wrong with it." Dr. Mark tilted his head in confusion. "That's how this whole auction thing got started…when I mentioned it to Nikki."

A slow smile crossed Sadie's face…then she started giggling. "Are you serious?"

"What's so funny?" Nikki asked.

"I didn't say there was anything wrong with it." Sadie laughed.

"Yes, you…" Dr. Mark started.

"I said, 'I told Nikki' I thought something MIGHT be wrong with it…not that there WAS something wrong with it." Sadie giggled and shook her head. "Details, people! Details!"

"Sadie," Nikki frowned. "Why did you say that?"

"So I could bore you to death looking at the hoof pictures on the internet and make you fall asleep." She grinned. "And it worked."

Another round of laughter erupted.

"I am going to have to dissect every word that comes out of your mouth!" Dr. Mark shook his head in disbelief. "I thought I was losing my touch."

"Well, it did get us here." Nick said as he pulled to a stop in front of the warehouse.

The six of them did an initial quick review of all the veterinarian supplies, cabinets, tables, office chairs, filing cabinets, an equine treadmill, large pipe stalls, IV stands, rolling carts, and the sink. Then they followed Dr. Mark around to each piece of diagnostic and surgical equipment that was on display as he taught Sadie what they were. Half a dozen other people followed them around to listen to the veterinarian.

"I think Leah was right," Tessa whispered to Nikki.

"About what?" Nikki asked.

"Sadie is learning more today than she ever would have in school. What he's teaching her, on a one-on-one classroom? This is just priceless for that girl," Tessa answered.

Nikki nodded, she had already learned a lot too.

"What about a treadmill, Nikki?" Her mother asked.

"I've thought of that," Nikki answered. "It would be really nice in the winter time if I had horses that needed exercised. The Beck's horses will be OK with rehab on their legs because it will be through summer, but I'd have problems in the winter."

"You could convert one of the stalls into a treadmill room." Tessa nodded.

"I've also considered an underwater treadmill." Nikki told them.

"Seriously? They have those?" Tessa asked.

"Yes, they are very good for not only rehabilitation, but also keeping the horses conditioned in the winter months when you can't ride them as much." Nikki nodded. "It would really benefit the kid's rodeo horses."

"I think that's a great idea." Nick nodded. "Where would you put it?"

"That's what stopped me," Nikki sighed. "It doesn't make sense to have it at Circle 50, we'd have to haul the kids' horses all the time to use it. I considered asking about The Homestead because it wouldn't take too much room, but we wouldn't want clients having to go there all the time."

"How about The Stables?" Her mother asked. "You're down quite often for hippotherapy sessions and work with Tagger Enterprises. You could schedule clients around your trips…or haul them with you as you go back and forth."

"Where would we put it there?" Nikki asked. "You're pretty limited on space."

Her mother laughed, "Nikki, the field to the west of The Stables is Tagger Enterprises, too."

"Oh, my gosh!" Nikki said excitedly. "I totally forgot that."

"It's another ten acres. I think we can take an acre to build an extension barn there for your business. You could even rent it out to people to build revenue. Jack's been after me about an indoor arena…maybe we'll look at both." Her mom smiled.

"Oh, Mom!" Nikki hugged her tightly. Things were coming together! Except for one…

***

It was early evening when they left the auction and turned down the highway toward home. The trailer was full of their winnings; the long, deep stainless steel sink, rolling tables, IV stand, a large box of miscellaneous gloves, packaged needles, tubing, plastic tubs, and surgical instruments. They even won the large metal pipe stall system and the treadmill.

TEXT TO MATT: Just headed home, see you in four hours

TEXT TO NIKKI: Not staying at Homestead?

TEXT TO MATT: No want to be home

TEXT TO NIKKI: It was a video Attachment

"What is it?" Sadie asked and pulled on Nikki's arm to see over her shoulder.

"You are so impatient!" Nikki chuckled.

"Yes, we all know that." Sadie said matter-of-factly. "So show me! What is it?"

Nikki pushed the play button and laughed.

"I'm more impatient than Sadie," Nick reminded her. "So if you don't tell me what it is, I'm pulling over and ripping the phone out of your hands."

They all laughed so Nikki explained the video. "I wanted to stain the ceiling in the barn to make it look more professional. Matt wanted to hire it out."

"They're staining the ceiling AND putting in the cabinets?" Her mother asked in surprise. "There is no way he got Jack to stain that ceiling."

"No," Nikki giggled. "It's Reilly, Grace, Marla, Brady, and Billy doing the ceiling. Nora is staining the doors to all the stalls so they match."

"What about Wade and Alex?" Tessa asked.

TEXT TO MATT: Wade & Alex?

TEXT TO NIKKI: They are here too

TEXT TO MATT: Doing what

TEXT TO NIKKI: Wouldn't you like to know ☺

"Oh, that bugger." Nikki chuckled and repeated the string of texts to everyone.

"I want to go home with you!" Sadie cried out.

"I do, too." Everyone else said in unison.

"But you guys can," Sadie whined. "I don't think Mom will let me have two days in a row out of school."

"Geez, I wish school would hurry and get out." Tessa sighed. "I want Alex to stay there, too."

Nikki chuckled to herself. In another two months, Tessa would be wishing school would hurry and start!

"I just sent a text to Jack to tell him to stay there." Her mother said. "So I'll ride up with you."

"I'm afraid if I go up, Sadie will be x-raying my knees!" Dr. Mark laughed with a teasing nudge to Sadie.

She giggled and nodded then looked at Nikki with a serious expression. "But I really want to go…I want to see how the x-ray machine works."

Nikki sighed. She remembered those days that everyone else was going to work on the ranch or something else she considered fun and she was stuck at school.

"We have so much to do," Nikki told her. "I promise not to check it out until you get there after school tomorrow."

Sadie's eyes widened, "You'd do that?"

"Sure," Nikki nodded. "I have a ton of work to do between all the stuff we bought plus I have to get the Beck horses entered into the computer so we can start tracking their progress."

"That's awesome Nikki, thank you!" Sadie grinned.

Dr. Mark was dropped off at his truck then Sadie at The Homestead; the weary travelers continued on for the next two hours.

Another late night, Nikki thought as she stared out into the dark night. By the time the business got going, she was going to need some serious sleep. But she had no desire to go to her bedroom without Lucas there. It was Thursday morning in Australia…where was he? Was he going to the office or his parents? What was he doing? Did he think about her? She just needed to understand…

"What will you need for the water treadmill?" Her mother asked. She was now riding in the backseat with Nikki.

Nikki turned away from the dark night and sadness that was descending. "I'll have to look into it a little more. I watched it on RVD-TV and did some research on it a long time ago, including going to WSU to see them."

"You only need one?" Tessa asked.

They kept her talking about work the remainder of the way to Circle 50. She knew they were distracting her…and she just loved them for it.

It was 11:00 when they pulled into the driveway. The brisk evening air was a shock to the skin when the truck doors opened.

"Yikes," Her mother giggled. "I wasn't quite prepared for that."

The house was dark, so Nikki walked directly to the barn. She pulled on the handle but it didn't budge.

"What the heck?" She gasped.

"What's the matter?" Nick asked.

"It won't open." She pulled again.

CHAPTER NINE

"Hellllooo!" They heard a sweet female voice sing on the other side of the door.

"Josey? What are you doing?" Nikki chuckled.

"Who isssss it?" The voice sang out with a bit of a giggle.

"Your worst nightmare!" Nikki's mom called out.

"I'm sorry…we don't need no magazines." The voice giggled…barely containing her laughter.

"It's freezing out here." Nick hollered with a grin. "Open up or I'll huff and I'll puff and blow your barn down."

They all chuckled.

"Oh, Honey!" The voice rose. "The Big Bad Wolf be calling."

They all started laughing and Nikki heard a metal click.

"What was that?" She stepped away from the door as another loud click rang out.

The door creaked open just enough for Josey to stick her head out. She was grinning ear to ear.

"Oh, Honey! It's The Big Bad Wolf and his three little…."

"If you call me a pig, I'll ring your neck." Tessa warned with a humored glare.

"Oh, no, nice lady!" Josey called out in false horror. "I would never do that. It's the Big Bad Wolf and his three little fillies."

Nikki rolled her eyes and pushed on the door. A blast of warm air hit them.

"What the heck?" She gasped.

"Hurry in," Matt laughed. "You're wasting the heat."

The weary travelers stepped inside and stopped as Josey shut the door.

There were two clicks which made Nikki turn. There were two locks on the door.

"We installed locks to keep the equipment safe when no one was here." Matt grinned proudly. "Scott even fortified the three outside stall doors and they can be locked also."

"Oh, my gosh!" Nikki gasped as she looked around the barn.

The back wall was now covered with the chrome and black cabinets she purchased that morning. There was a hole in the middle where the sink would slide into a countertop. A pile to the left of the shelving were the items that had been on the old shelves.

"Jessup took the measurement you sent and the plumbing is ready to go for the sink." Josey said excitedly.

The old paneled stall doors looked fresh and new from the dark red stain that matched the ceiling…that looked new, too.

"It just looks fantastic," Tessa said.

"Is that…no…it…couldn't…" Nikki turned to her stuttering mother. "That's…"

"Clara's dining set." Nikki smiled and watched her mother walk to the dining set to slowly slide onto the closest chair.

"Oh, how I miss those two." Her smile was warm from the memories and her blue eyes glistened. "Andy hated this furniture. Grayson helped him put in up in the loft the day after Clara's funeral."

"We also…" Matt grinned wickedly.

"What?" Nikki asked as she wandered to Charming who was standing at the door. She ran a gentle hand down his nose and glanced in at Bobo. He was leaning against the wall and watching the action in the barn.

Not forgetting Jack in the Sling, she quickly walked to him. His head was still low.

"We just gave him some painkiller about a half hour ago." Matt informed her.

"They're OK?" Nikki asked.

"They haven't moved much all day." Matt nodded. "Pretty much just stood and watched all the commotion."

"I put ointment on Bobo's lips, they were getting pretty dry." Josey said. "He was a bit more swollen this morning, but it's gone down this evening. I soaked the cubes in water so they weren't hard for him to chew."

"The Nomads and Violets?" Nikki asked.

"All good," Matt nodded. "If they weren't watching the commotion then they were sunning themselves."

"OK, good." Nikki smiled brightly at them. "Now, what else did you do in here?"

"Well, we started winterizing the barn." Josey grinned.

"It's the first of May and you're winterizing already?" Nick asked, he was standing next to Jack in the Sling and stroking the horse's neck.

Matt chuckled, "After you drove off this morning. Jack went back inside and bought more supplies; specifically 2x4's and a whole lot of insulation."

"Insulation?" Nikki looked to the ceiling.

"The cabinets went up pretty fast." Josey nodded. "So we cleared out the rest of the loft and put down a layer of insulation then a new floor on top of that."

"Are you kidding?" Tessa gasped. "All in one day?"

"Besides us, there was Jack, Jessup, Grayson, and Scott. The 2x4's went down pretty fast and insulation just rolls out." Matt explained. "Reilly brought up more plywood and Wade and Alex nailed down the new floor."

"Alex must have loved that." Tessa exclaimed.

Josey nodded excitedly. "We had paint brushes on the ceiling down here and hammers on the floor up there."

"That must have been quite the sight." Nick chuckled.

Nikki stepped into the middle of the barn and looked around the building. It actually looked like a business! She wanted to dance with joy and call Lucas! It was a jolt….every time…he would have loved to been a part of this.

Her eyes landed on a metal box hanging from the ceiling over the double doors. There was another one above the cabinets on the far end. "Heaters?"

"Yes!" Josey bounced. "There's no flame…they are radiant heat and should really keep it warm in here during the winter while you're working."

"Which is why we insulated the ceiling; to keep the heat down here." Matt added.

"I cannot believe how much you guys got done today." Nikki sighed. "You have to be exhausted."

"Not too bad," Josey shrugged.

"You only have to decide what to do with the walls." Matt smiled.

"Tongue and groove boards to match the ceiling…you could paint them white to keep it light in here." Her mom said and Nikki nodded.

"Then the floor?" Tessa asked.

"Concrete after Jack in the Sling goes home." Nikki told her.

"I'm headed out," Her mom said and gave Nikki a big hug. "Jack is waiting in the bunkhouse, we'll see you in the morning."

After a quick hug to Josey and Matt, she left.

"We should go, too," Nick sighed and smiled at her. "It was a fun day."

"Thanks Dad, thanks Tessa." Nikki gave them both a hug.

When his arms wrapped around her, Nikki felt a twinge of anxiety. What was that about?

Then she followed him out the door and to his truck. She didn't follow her mother out… so why was she following him? Tessa walked to the passenger side of the truck while Nikki walked her dad to the driver's side.

"You OK?" He asked with a furrow of the brow.

"Yeah," She nodded and looked out into the dark night, her mind in a haze.

"Nikki?"

"What?"

"Are you sure you're alright?"

She turned back to him…he must have seen something in her eyes…he opened his arms and she nearly ran into them. Her arms wrapped around his neck and she held as tight as she could, her eyes closed to hold in the anxiety rushing through her. His arms held her with the same intensity.

"I can stay," He whispered.

Nikki couldn't let go, she felt the need to hold him and make sure he didn't leave. Why? They had been together all day…why now?

"Have you spoken with him?" She whispered. Where did that come from? She had managed all day not to ask that question.

"No."

"At the office?" It was barely a whisper.

"He had this week and the next two weeks off…no one was expecting to hear from him and as far as I know, no one has."

"I just don't understand." She turned her face into his neck to feel the warmth, her arms tightened.

"I don't know…I wish I did." He tilted his head to hers.

"I'm sorry, Dad."

"Don't ever tell me you're sorry again." His arms tightened around her.

They stood quietly, she just couldn't get herself to let go.

"Do you want me to stay?" He whispered.

"I don't want you to go." She answered softly.

"I'm here to stay then."

She managed to loosen her grip on him so they could turn to Tessa. She wasn't by the truck, and with her overnight bag slung over her shoulder, was already walking into the house.

******

Nikki jolted awake…something had echoed through the barn…a bang or boom… or something…she couldn't get her mind to clear-up enough to figure out what it was.

She blinked, rubbed her eyes, and listened. Just sounds of horses…and Nick sleeping in the lounge chair next to her. They had kicked Josey and Matt out of the barn so they could get a good night's sleep. Hauling the lounge chairs into the barn they set them up next to the stalls and settled in. Having him there was comforting…she had fallen asleep almost immediately.

Thursday morning…for Lucas it was evening…

Nikki slowly rose in the chair and looked over at her dad who was still asleep. The noise must have been in her head…it wouldn't be the first time something in a dream woke her up.

The bang rang out again and her eyes went to Jack in the Sling. His hoof had pounded the ground. This time her dad sat straight up.

"What was that?" He asked looking around the barn.

"Jack in the Sling getting restless," She answered. "Go back to sleep. I'm going to check his heart rate and temperature. Probably just needs painkillers."

He pulled his phone out of his pocket and shook his head. "It's 6:00, I'm not getting back to sleep."

"I'm surprised Matt isn't out here already." Nikki looked at Charming. The Morgan was eating his hay and looked alert. "Well, you look good."

Bobo had walked to the back of his stall and was leaning his head against the wall.

"Oh, baby." Nikki whispered and slowly walked to the horse; gently laying her hand on his back. She was almost too afraid to touch anywhere else. "You must be hurting. First you have to deal with that terrible name and now the pain."

"What can I do?" Nick asked from behind her.

"I'm going to get him some painkillers and anti-inflammatory medication, then after they kick in, we need to change his leg wraps. If you'll go check Jack in the Sling's heart rate…he stomps when he hurts."

Nikki turned the red horse's head so she could see into his eyes. They looked clear but he looked like he was hurting pretty bad. Because of the swelling around his mouth, she was not going to try to tube him to get him the medication into him. It was going to have to be a shot. She prepared the medication as fast as she could and the gelding didn't even flinch when Nikki stuck the needle in him.

"I'm sorry, Big Guy." She whispered. "We won't let it get that bad again."

"This one's heart rate is up compared to their notes on the wall." Nick said.

"There's a tube of Bute in the feed room." Nikki retrieved the tube and the second heart rate monitor. She tossed the medication to Nick and strapped the monitor around Bobo then attached the wireless monitor to her wrist. Everything was noted on the whiteboard of both horses.

Charming didn't seem to be having any problems…he seemed happy and content.

TEXT TO KATE: You awake?

While she waited for Bobo's painkillers to kick in, she prepared all the supplies she needed to rewrap his legs.

"How is he doing over there?" She called to her dad.

"He's fine, eating now. I'm going to clean up his stall."

"I could use that rolling cart that we bought yesterday. Is it buried? Can I get to it?"

"I'll back up the trailer to the door so we can unload everything. The treadmill and metal stall racks are on the bottom, we'll worry about them later."

They met at the doors and opened them to a brisk sunny morning.

"Dang," Nikki chuckled. "I didn't realize how warm it was in there."

"Their insulation job works pretty well."

"We'll have to turn the thermostat down. I don't want the horses to acclimate to the warmer temperature."

As Nick backed the trailer up to the doors, Josey and Tessa walked out of the house with trays full of breakfast and a large thermos of coffee.

TEXT FROM KATE: I am awake, problem call me

Nikki called the veterinarian and updated her on all the horses.

"Have you heard from the Beck's?" Nikki asked.

"They called yesterday. Sorry, I didn't call…it's been hectic here." Kate answered. "They were going to come up Saturday…" She hesitated.

"It's Ok…" Nikki closed her eyes and sighed; would there be a wedding or not? She just couldn't bring herself to believe he wouldn't be there.

"I told them that wouldn't work so the parents will come up this afternoon…should be there around noon. They wanted to check the status on the horses before the kids saw them." Kate explained.

"How old are the kids?"

"The girl is fourteen and the boy is fifteen."

Nikki frowned, "If they were younger, I would understand…but at their age, and have lived with horse's basically all their lives…they should be able to handle situations like this. They should be helping take care of them. That's part of the responsibility of having animals. Look what Wade and Sadie went through at nine-years-old when the Tagger herd was rescued…Nora eleven…and Reilly and Grace fourteen."

"Not all families are like yours, Nikki." The vet said with a very irritated tone.

Nikki groaned, "I'm sorry Kate…that just sounded so judgmental…I didn't mean it that way."

"Like I said, not all families are like yours," Kate sighed.

Nikki had a feeling she was talking about more than the horses. Why had Kate broken up with Jessup? Something to do with her son…

"I've got to get to the clinic." Kate said. "Let me know if anything comes up and let's touch base after your visit with the Becks."

Nikki ended the call and looked at her three companions; Josey, Tessa and Nick. "Where's Matt?"

"He left earlier to help Scott with some of the farming equipment." Josey answered.

"Let's get the truck unloaded and I'll go see if I can help." Nick said and looked to Nikki with a concerned expression.

She nodded with a smile, "I think I can let you out of my sight for a couple hours."

Nikki's phone rang as he opened the gate of the trailer. Her heart pounded in anticipation then sighed in disappointment; it was Kate.

"Kate?"

"I'm sorry Nikki," Kate said. "And I really hate to do this to you…"

"What? What's wrong?"

"Dr. Mark said you were looking for information about the tall gelding he delivered the other day."

"Yes, the police horse."

"I got a call from one of the retired patrolmen that used to ride him…did for years…I think like five or so. Anyway, he's coming up your way today, too."

"He's in town?"

"Geez, Nikki…I really am sorry I didn't call yesterday. I told him you'd be there and he's driving over this morning…probably already on his way."

Nikki chuckled, "You need an assistant."

"I need about four or five," Kate exhaled. "I hope you're not upset with me."

"Of course not," Nikki smiled into the phone. "I've had days like that."

Nikki ended the call and informed her group of the latest news as they unloaded the trailer. Her dad left and her mother arrived.

"Cora is going over to help Leah for the day then they are coming up with the kids after school." Her mother informed them and grinned at Tessa. "You're off the hook down there so you get to help up here."

Tessa laughed, "Well, that's a real bummer." She looked to Nikki. "OK, Boss…what do you want me to do?"

Nikki rolled her eyes, "There is just so much! First is changing Bobo's bandages, I interrupted Dad with cleaning Jack in the Sling's stall, the outside horses need fed, we have to fill all the cabinets with our purchases from yesterday and the stuff that's stacked in the corner that they removed from the old shelving. That's just the beginning!"

All four women laughed and got to work. First for Nikki was Bobo's legs, with Josey at her side of course. The horse's head rose alertly as they walked towards him; a sign that the painkillers were working. His nose immediately went to Josey's hands.

"I'll feed him while you change the bandages." Josey said.

"I'd like to get pictures of them so we can monitor their progress." Nikki carefully cut the top of the bandage.

"I'll go get the camera…where is it?"

"In my desk, lower left hand drawer."

Josey returned just as Nikki was pulling the bandage from the horse's front leg.

"What's the matter?" Nikki asked from her squatting position.

"Huh?"

"You look upset? Are you OK?"

"Yeah…" Josey frowned at her, like she was trying to decide something.

"Just spit it out." Nikki said and pulled back the last of the bandage from the leg.

They both gasped. Whatever Josey was going to say was lost.

CHAPTER TEN

There were three rows of stitches, each about an inch from the top of the leg down across his knee, stopping just before the hock.

Nikki took pictures as fast as she could then cleaned the skin and rewrapped the leg before the horse had the inclination to bend it and pop all the stitches. She quickly repeated for all four legs.

Tessa ran to the house to get Nikki's laptop and they proceeded to download the pictures and examine each one. The first leg they rewrapped was actually the worse, but the others also had stitches just above the horse's knees and along the back where the divider in the trailer would have been.

"Those are ugly," Josey sighed. "But the stitching is very clean and precise. Whoever did them was VERY good; there will be very light scarring…if the stitches hold."

"How long do they have to stay?" Tessa asked.

"A minimum of fourteen days," Nikki answered. "It could be longer since it's on his knees…the longer the better. Most the time they can't get stitches on legs like that to stay." After she returned from the honeymoon would be about the right time, she thought. If there was one…

"He's going to go nuts when he's finally out in a pasture." Her mother chuckled.

"I think a well sanded round pen is next on the to-do list." Nikki nodded.

Jack in the Sling's stitches were mainly on one side of his body and because he was shorter the divider had hit him higher; missing the knees.

Nikki's morning was filled with horse inventory. She caught each of the rehab horses, weighed, measured, checked over general conditions and noted everything in her notebook to enter into the computer later.

The last horse she caught was the tall bay police horse. After tying him to the hitching post in front of the barn, she repeated the procedure by running a brush over him and noting every scratch or bump. Then the mane comb. To Nikki, the healing wasn't just in the food or medicine but it was also in the touch. The food and medicine healed the body…a gentle loving touch helped heal the soul.

"You're loving every minute of this, aren't you?" She whispered to the tall gelding. In answer, the horse turned his head to her and dipped his nose to her knee. She chuckled softly and stroked his face with her bare hand. It was such a soothing and relaxing gesture…for both horse and human.

In just the few short days he was there he looked healthier.

She lifted each hoof and inspected it; as the last hoof was lowered, she heard a vehicle approaching.

A quick glance at her watch…Nikki chuckled…it wasn't a watch…she was reading Bobo's heart rate; which looked pretty good.

Nikki stepped toward the car as it pulled to a stop in the driveway. A man and a woman emerged from the car.

"Nikki Tagger?" The woman asked.

"Yes," Nikki quickly extended a hand to greet them.

She guessed them to be in their late-thirties, both had strong confident grips and wore jeans and plain t-shirts, normal enough…except for the little details on the woman. She wore new designer cowboy boots and he wore tennis shoes. The small diamond ear rings, short brown hair sprayed heavily to keep it in place, manicured finger nails, makeup basic…but perfect, and just a hint of lipstick. She very subtly elevated herself above her husband's casual tennis shoe existence.

"Paul Beck and my wife, Tina." The man said. "Dr. Wilson said you had our horses here."

Nikki nearly chuckled out loud; she didn't often hear Kate referred to as Dr. Wilson.

"We do," Nikki nodded and turned to sweep an arm towards the barn. The upper door of the small entry was open and Jack in the Swing was clearly visible.

"Oh my!" Tina exclaimed and they walked toward the gelding who was watching them intently and nickering excitedly. It was obvious the horse knew who they were.

"That is quite the contraption." Paul said with wide eyes.

"We lucked out and had someone in Spokane when we received the call." Nikki explained. "They were able to pick it up so we could have it ready for him when he arrived."

"You bought that just for Jack?" Tina exclaimed with a worried look. "Are we getting charged for that?"

The question caught Nikki off guard and she hesitated before answering, "No…it belongs to my business."

"But you bought it just for him?" Tina asked again.

"And other horses that need it in the future," Nikki answered calmly which hid the growing irritation. "Plus my brother is involved in search and rescue so they will use it when needed."

"Do we have a day charge on it?" The woman asked.

Nikki used every ounce of her control to keep her voice calm. "No, the charge is for overall care per day plus cost of medicine and feed…not the equipment we use to help get the horse healthy."

Tina nodded, evidently satisfied with the answer. Careful to avoid the straps holding the horse in the air, she ran a gentle hand down his neck but it was the man that the horse nudged with his nose. Paul happily obliged the horse by sticking a hand in his pocket and withdrawing a mint to feed him. The small gesture made Nikki smile and some of the tension leave her muscles.

They stepped out of the small stall and into the main barn where Nikki introduced the other three women. "This is Dru Tagger, my mother, Josey Franklin and Tessa Elliot."

"Nice to meet you," Paul said eagerly. "Thank you so much for taking care of our horses."

"You nor your children were hurt?" Nikki's mother asked.

"No, it was a jolt and we're a bit sore but nothing like the horses." Paul answered as Tina greeted Charming. Again the horse took the attention but nudged Paul for the treat; which he obliged while lifting his cell phone out of his pocket. "Here are a few pictures we took at the scene for the insurance company."

Nikki cringed at the site of the truck embedded in the horse trailer.

"Luckily the horse trailer moved with the truck when it hit it and it didn't crush the trailer." Tina said off handedly as she looked around the interior of the barn.

"Would you mind sending me a few pictures for my files?" Nikki asked. "It helps document what happened to the horses and how they are treated afterwards to get them going again."

"Marketing…" Tina said curtly then turned away to look at Bobo. "Now that's just terrible."

The horse had made his way to the door of the stall and was looking for Paul's pocket.

"Oh, big Bobo Boy," Paul gasped and Nikki internally cringed at the name. "He's really swollen."

"How do you feed him?" Tina asked with raised brows.

"I soaked alfalfa cubes in water and slide them through his lips." Josey said politely. She took a cube out of the bucket and demonstrated for them.

"That must take forever." Paul grinned and took the mint from his pocket. Following Josey's lead he slipped the mint through the horse's lips. Bobo bounced his head in appreciation.

Nikki was watching Tina's expression. She stared at the horse then Josey then back to the horse…then she looked at Nikki. Nikki knew she wanted to know if she was getting charged by the hour or for the full day…but the woman frowned then turned away.

"The last time I saw him, he was so covered in blood and torn open that we thought we were going to have to put him down." Tina said.

"He'll heal fine," Nikki assured her. "The veterinarians did an excellent job so there won't be much scarring."

"But there will be scarring?" Tina asked as she stared at the zipper line of stitches that ran from above the eye to the horse's swollen lips.

"Yes, you can't go through something like that and not have scarring." Nikki answered with a calm voice. "They'll mark his battle of survival."

Tina's shoulder shrugged, "But he won't be able to show. We bought him for our daughter to focus some on barrels but she likes showing better."

"But she would be able to game or work at the ranch or trail ride or just about everything else." Josey added; taking the defensive for the big gelding.

"The kids show." Tina glared but quickly relaxed her face to remove the glare and changed it to concern.

Except for the hand that was holding the bucket handle, Josey looked perfectly calm. The knuckles on the hand were white.

"Why don't we go into my office in the house and we can discuss the horses and their treatment." Nikki said quickly and waved a hand toward the doors to encourage them to move.

It was just Nikki and the Becks walking across the driveway.

"Your office is in your home?" Paul asked casually.

"Yes," Nikki answered. "For now, we're having a house built a little ways down the road. Then it will just be my office."

"Glad we could pay for your house." Tina said under her breath.

Nikki's spine stiffened. She knew the woman didn't mean for her to hear what she said but Nikki stopped, slowly turned, and with a completely serene face, stared at her. Nikki was so glad she had practiced her mother's poker face because she really wanted to slap the woman!

Tina's eyes showed shock at first, then concern, then defiance, then finally settled on embarrassment before she turned away and looked at Nikki's truck.

"I'm sorry, Ms. Tagger." Paul said quickly with a look of disgust at his wife. "That was uncalled for. We understand the time it takes to help the horses and very much appreciate everything you're doing."

"Let's just talk horses." Nikki smiled politely to him and led the pair to her small office at the back of the house.

Before Nikki could speak, Tina did. "This is a working cattle ranch, too?"

"Yes, we ranch and farm." Nikki answered as she sat in her chair behind the desk. Then she worked on keeping her voice as professional as possible. "Our family has two ranches."

"Then you use a lot of horses." Tina leaned back in the chair.

"Yes, couldn't do it without them." Nikki answered.

"Where do you get them?" She asked.

"We raise a few, auctions, private owners, rescues…" Nikki said. "We aren't picky where we get them as long as they are good and safe."

"We paid a lot for Bobo." Tina said.

"OK…" Nikki sat back in her chair.

"You didn't seem to care that he was going to scar…but we can't use him if he's scarred across the face." Tina said bluntly.

"We have a number of horses that have been injured for one reason or another." Nikki nodded while thinking of Little Ghost and all of his accomplishments; scars or not. "There are a number of different disciplines for a horse in horse shows…they aren't limited to just being shown at halter."

"Would you be willing to trade?" Tina asked; completely ignoring Nikki's comment.

"What?" Nikki and Paul said in unison.

"You can't trade him…he's the kids' horse." Paul gasped.

"Yes I can, he's registered in my name and they don't even like him." Tina glared at him. "They ignore him and only ride the other two…that's why he was so unruly last weekend. Annabelle is scared of him."

Tina's eyes shot to Nikki. Those were little details you didn't want a potential buyer of your horse to know. Most people would use it against you to lower the price…Tina knew her mistake but Nikki kept her face composed.

"What were you thinking as a trade?" Nikki asked.

Tina tilted her head back and narrowed her eyes. "We'll pay the vet clinic bill from the accident…to the point he arrived on your property. We'll sign Bobo over to you and the rest of his treatment is your cost."

Nikki nodded slightly…so far so good…

"We'll trade him for the cost of the care of Jack and Charming." Tina finished. "We paid a lot of money for him."

"Yes, you said that before." Nikki nodded and twisted her lips as if thinking about it…she was actually jumping for joy inside.

"May I use your computer?" Tina asked. Paul sat quietly and watched them. He must be used to his wife taking charge and doing what she wanted.

Nikki turned the monitor so Tina could see it and pushed the wireless keyboard and mouse to her.

She quietly watched as the woman signed into her AQHA account and pulled up Bobo's information then hit the print button. Next was a set of transfer papers and then she typed a bill of sale detailing the conditions she had stated.

Nikki read the registration papers while the other papers were prepared. Bobo's blood-lines included Dash for Cash on his sire's side and Frenchman's Guy on his dam's side. Dang! Yes…they would have paid a lot of money for him. He was bred for barrel racing, not showing, just as Nora had said.

She calmly laid the papers on the desk and relaxed…she had to stay calm! Poker Face!

"Are you interested?" Tina asked as she started to sign the transfer papers and the bill of sale. All that was left was for Nikki to sign.

"Charming will need to be here for another week." Nikki nodded slightly as if deep in thought. "Jack could be here for months and there is no way I can guarantee he will be 100% sound in the future…I believe Kate told you that."

"She did," Paul nodded, his eyes shifting between Nikki and his wife.

"You don't think Bobo is enough?" Tina asked in surprise, a quick flash of worry in her eyes, hastily replaced with a business expression.

"I am saying that I want it on the bill of sale that you understand we will put 100% in the effort to rehabilitate him, with bi-weekly updates by Dr. Wilson's clinic for progress reports but we do not guarantee he will be sound when we're done. A time limit of three months from the accident date also needs to be added; it won't be an open ended rehab stay. One more week for Charming and our obligation to him is complete."

"That all seems fair." Tina said too quickly and retyped the bill of sale, printed it, then signed it.

Nikki read the document twice, making sure she didn't forget any detail. Lucas would shoot her if she didn't watch the details… Lucas…where was he?

Nikki signed the papers and stood to shake their hands. As they walked out of the house and to their car, Nikki was cool, calm, and collected on the outside and screaming and dancing for joy on the inside.

"Can we bring the kids up to visit them?" Paul asked as he opened his wife's door for her.

"Thank you, Ms. Tagger. I have no doubt that Bobo will have a good home here and you and your team will take good care of him." Tina said as she slid into the car.

"We take care of our horses as if they were family." Nikki said honestly to her then turned to Paul. "They can visit any time, just call in advance. We'll also send them pictures and videos on the email you gave us."

"Oh, the kids will love that." Paul grinned, waved, and drove away.

Nikki turned quickly and had to keep herself from running back to the barn.

She casually walked into the barn with a slight, 'wow, weren't they something' look on her face.

"What a pair!" Tessa chuckled.

Nikki nodded, "That was interesting."

"How did it go inside the house?" Josey asked as she slid another cube between Bobo's lips.

Nikki took a deep breath and exhaled loudly, "They wanted to trade for the rehab of the horses."

"Trade what?" They all three asked.

A loud whinny erupted in the barn. They all four looked to the Beck horses who lifted their heads and were also looking for the source.

Another whinny echoed and Nikki quickly walked out the door and to the police horse that was still tied to the hitching post. Answering whinnies from the corrals and pasture echoed in the air.

A tall man, who looked to be in his mid-sixties was quickly making his way to the bay horse, his face frowning in concern. A truck with a horse trailer was parked just behind him.

CHAPTER ELEVEN

"Can I help you?" Nikki asked with the three women right behind her. She was sure he was the police officer from Portland…but she wasn't expecting him to have a horse trailer with him.

"Are you Nikki Tagger?" He asked as he reached the now prancing gelding. The horse nearly knocked him over with an excited nose to the chest.

"Yes…and you would be the police officer who used to ride our big guy here?" She said with a smile.

"And was honored to do it." He nodded while greeting the horse.

The four women stood quietly and enjoyed watching the horse and human reconnect.

"I retired four years ago and tried to get them to retire Buster at the same time so I could take him with me." He said.

"Buster?" Nikki grinned. "We didn't have his name…but I like that."

The man chuckled as Buster stuck his nose under his arm. "He helped us 'bust' a lot of people in his day…therefore he became Buster."

They all laughed thenNikki introduced the three women.

"I'm Tyson Davis." He left the horse's side long enough to shake hands.

"You wanted him four years ago?" Tessa asked.

"I want him now." He stopped petting the horse and looked at them with a firm glare. "I told everyone when I left I wanted a call the day he was retired. Unfortunately, it was over the holidays and they couldn't get ahold of me so he went to the people that donated him. It took me forever to find him…then I heard about what happened."

"He was pretty bad," Nikki nodded. "But he's recovering well."

"I can't believe this…he's so skinny… I want to take him home with me." Tyson said bluntly.

"Well," Nikki nodded. "You have to understand that I can't just let you have him. I have to talk with the owner first."

"Can you call him?" He asked hopefully. "Dr. Wilson was a bit overwhelmed when I talked to her so she didn't have the time to look up the number. But she assured me you would have it."

"I do," Nikki nodded then frowned at the words. I do…in two days…only 48 hours… she was supposed to say those to Lucas…but was she going to? Why didn't he just call!?

"Nikki," Her mother said from beside her.

"Oh, I'm sorry," Nikki blushed. "I have the number in my office. I'll go see if I can contact him." She turned quickly and nearly ran to the house.

She was searching through the papers on her desk when her mother walked in the door.

"You OK?" She asked.

"Yes," Nikki nodded as she found the paper that had the phone number she needed.

While she punched the numbers into the phone she slid the Beck paperwork across the desk for her mother to read. She sat down, leaned back in her chair, and started reading.

"Hello?" A man's voice answered.

"Hi, this is Nikki Tagger."

"Oh, Ms. Tagger…how is my horse doing? Is there a problem?" He asked quickly.

Nikki explained the situation to the owner as she watched a grin spread across her mother's face. She glanced at Nikki with an approving nod.

"I want to make sure he goes to the right place this time." Buster's owner said.

"There is no doubt the horse knows him…he was very excited to see Mr. Davis."

"You feel this is right?" He asked.

Nikki typed in the officer's name into the computer and also Busters. There were numerous pictures of the pair and a few articles.

"I just Googled them," she said. "There is an article from about six years ago. It has a picture of Mr. Davis and Buster. He is who he says he is…and has a strong affection for the horse. He drove over from Portland, pulling a horse trailer not knowing if he was going to be able to take the horse home or not." Nikki was impressed.

"I have no problem signing him over to Mr. Davis on your recommendation," he answered. "I'll draft a bill of sale and email it to you within the next thirty minutes."

Nikki smiled, that was going to make one human and one horse very happy. They ended the call and she updated her mother on the information as she turned the monitor toward her mother.

"Buster is in the middle of a riot in this picture. Look how calm he is."

"Look at that one," She pointed. "He's so tall and proud in the parade gear."

"Well, let's go tell them the happy news." Nikki grinned.

Tyson was overjoyed and told them stories about his years riding Buster while they waited for the bill of sale. Nikki reviewed with him the supplement program for the horse and he readily agreed to continue it. Within minutes of having the bill of sale in his hands, he loaded the horse, and was on his way back to Portland.

Nikki stretched her arms in the air and bent sideways to stretch her exhausted muscles. It had been a long and busy day already…that would actually sum up the whole week. She expected to be busy this week…preparing for her wedding, not getting her business in full swing.

"I think it's past lunch time already," Tessa commented. "I'll go fix us something to eat."

"What time is it?" Nikki asked.

"Almost 1:00." Her mother answered.

Nikki nodded and slowly walked back to the barn. Her wedding was scheduled for 11:00 Saturday morning…only 46 hours away. Where was he and why didn't he call?!?

The wedding rehearsal dinner was scheduled for 6:00 at The Homestead…in only 29 hours. Her whole family would be there, the minister, photographer…the food was purchased for dinner on the back deck, all the arrangements to make it happen, time involved… Why would he do this? Where was he? She was slowly changing from being lost to being angry.

After a deep breath released slowly to relieve the tension building in her veins, she quickly checked with each of the Beck horses then gathered all the health care information for all the horses and placed it on the table, but had no inclination to get it entered into the computer.

Her mind began to focus only on Lucas sitting at the table while Nick told her of his past. He didn't look at her. She could hear Alex's innocent comment, "He left". Then the turn to see the truck gone…the text from the pilot, Greg.

Why would he just leave? He should have talked to her. Her jaw clenched and her stomach ached. She twisted her neck side to side and lifted her shoulders…the tension and rising anger did not subside.

It would do no one any good to be angry.

"I'm going to go for a ride." Nikki announced, handed Josey the wrist heart monitor for Bobo, and walked out of the barn.

She had Harvey saddled and stepped into the stirrup when her mother finally walked out of the barn.

"Do you want company?" She asked; her voice full of anguish and concern.

Nikki shook her head, then nudged her beautiful brown mare into a trot down the road. She knew exactly where she was going and it only took her 5 minutes to get there.

Harvey walked to the edge of the bluff far enough Nikki could see across the small ravine to the house that was nearing completion. The house she and Josey had designed then shown Matt and Lucas. Both men had added a few design changes so by the time the construction began, the four of them had designed the house for the four of them to live in. Hopefully, someday, Matt would propose to Josey and make it official.

All four of them had started collecting furniture and items to decorate the house. First on the list and already having a place ready for it was the bronze Circle 50 that Josie's grandparents had given them for Christmas.

Nikki didn't ride to the house; she just stared at it from afar. The outside of the house, in redwood and rock, was complete. It was only the inside that still needed work. She could see people walking in and out of the main door as they worked.

The furniture was chosen and they had used the floor plans to map out exactly where everything was to be placed. Even the furniture for the outdoor living room that Matt had suggested was ready.

Nikki hadn't been to the house in five days, she had been waiting for her fiancé to join her. The construction timeline had the building complete and they would move in right after she and Lucas came back from the honeymoon.

But if there wasn't going to be a honeymoon, then how soon could she move in? How hard would it be to move in and not have Lucas by her side? She couldn't imagine moving into the house without him but if he was gone for good, then that was that.

"His loss," She huffed.

She could survive…move on with her life…put him in her past. If she didn't mean enough to him that he would talk through whatever caused him to leave…then she would just move on.

Nikki's heart ached. Yes…she would live through it…but she didn't want to have to. Life without him…those amber brown eyes…the perfect grin through his whiskers…the touch of him when he returned from a trip…no…it couldn't happen…he just wouldn't do that to her.

She turned the horse away from the house and nudged her into a trot down the road. The need to escape was overwhelming…just leave…

Nikki leaned forward and nudged Harvey into a canter…then faster…then faster. They were running down the ranch road…the fastest they had gone in years. She wasn't wearing a hat so she unclipped the barrette that was holding her hair. The wind lifted the long strands so they flowed behind her; bouncing with each stride.

The air was fresh with a pine tree aroma that filled her lungs, the bright sun warmed her skin, the energy of the horse streamed through her veins…her breath quickened and the love of riding her horse filled her heart.

She was leaned over the horse as a jockey would ride a race horse; her hands tangled into the black mane. In the distance were trucks and tractors…the men were there. She didn't care and didn't want them interrupting her escape so she didn't look or wave…she just kept running. Around herd corner, down the road, through the flower covered pasture, past the field covered in Hereford cows with calves at their side…she ran. Her pulse pounded to the rhythm of Harvey's echoing hoof beats.

Just past the cows she slowed to a rocking canter. Both their hearts were racing as Nikki's hand slid down the sweat covered neck of her horse. Then she moved into a slow jog…the energy remained in both horse and rider. Their breathing slowly returned to normal as Nikki brought the horse down to a trot…then finally a walk when Circle 50's ranch house and barn came into view.

Her mind was clear, the anger raced out of her. The energy flowed…it was the ultimate equine therapy.

CHAPTER TWELVE

Nikki took her time with Harvey; the brush gently slid over every inch of her. The mane and tail flowed in a glistening waterfall. Special mint treats were eagerly munched down just before the horse's head dipped into the bucket of grain placed at her feet. A bare hand ran down her neck and along her back; the warmth helped soothe Nikki's heart.

She stood back away from the hitching post and looked at the horse. She was perfectly conditioned, which was a good thing for a ride like they just finished. Nikki's mind flashed to the camping trip when the mare sidestepped into her back making her fly into Lucas' arms resulting in their first kiss.

Stepping back to the horse, she leaned into Harvey's shoulder and closed her eyes. She gave herself the permission to think of him…think of every moment with him…let herself miss him. Out of everything…every moment…what she missed the most was the light in his amber eyes…the light she had seen the very first time she met him…the moment she had started to fall in love with him.

"Nikki?" Josey's whisper came from the other side of Harvey.

"Yes?"

"Is there anything I can do?"

Nikki stood and took in a deep breath and let it out slowly. Harvey was done with her grain so she stroked the long dark neck one more time.

"You can update me on your horse." Nikki answered as she opened the gate and had to push the other horses back to get Harvey into the pasture.

"Apollo?" Josey asked. "I haven't seen him in a couple of days."

"No," Nikki smiled at her confused sister. "Your other horse…the big red gelding with the white blaze and red mane and tail. And don't forget the racetracks all over his body."

"What?" Josey screeched.

"I traded him for the care on Charming and Jack in the Sling." Nikki grinned. "So you have lots of work to do this summer."

"Oh, Nikki!" Josey threw her arms around Nikki's neck and squeezed.

It felt so good to have this moment of pure happiness, she wrapped her arms tightly around her sister and enjoyed it.

"He's really mine?" Josey stepped back with excited eyes.

"Well, technically he's in my name but we'll take care of the paperwork later. And wait until you see his pedigree!"

"Oh, Nikki! I don't know what to say."

"Just say you're going to give him a better barn name." Nikki laughed.

"Preacher…" Josey whispered with tears shimmering in her brown eyes. "The first moment I saw him…he was identical to the picture Anna and Dean gave me of my real dad's rodeo horse. I felt such a draw…he just pulled at my heart."

"Preacher," Nikki pulled her into another strong embrace. "Perfect…SO much better than Bobo."

The sister's giggled as they stepped into the barn through the small door and in front of Jack in the Sling.

Nikki checked his heart rate and ran a comforting hand down his neck and back. He turned his head to her so she gave him just a little more attention. Josey had run ahead to announce to Bobo that he was no longer Bobo.

"Thank goodness!" Tessa laughed. She was at the table entering the collected health data into the laptop.

"Where's Mom?" Nikki asked.

"She got a call and said she would be back later." Tessa answered. "Grace and Reilly are on their way up with Leah. Cora will bring the rest of the kids when they get out of school."

Nikki nodded and chuckled at Josey who was nearly dancing while she fed her new horse alfalfa cubes.

"His papers are on my desk." Nikki said.

Josey ran out of the barn and to the house to return with the papers in hand and her feet nearly dancing on air. She excitedly reviewed the horse's pedigree with Tessa...letting her know what a good line it was for barrel horses.

When Leah, Grace and Reilly arrived, Josey ran to meet them to tell them about the gelding and show Grace his blood lines. They were all laughing as they entered the barn. Nikki shut the doors behind them but kept the top of Jack in the Sling's little door open so he could enjoy seeing the other horses in the pasture.

"What's on the agenda today?" Reilly asked.

"Well, since we have to wait for Sadie to play with the X-ray..." Nikki started.

"Oh, let's X-ray Preacher's legs!" Josey interrupted excitedly.

"Probably a good one to start with," Nikki laughed. "But we also have a treadmill to setup."

"Where's it going?" Leah asked.

"I don't really know yet." Nikki chuckled. "It has to fit in here somewhere."

They all walked around the barn, looking at possibilities.

"What if we..." Reilly said.

Nikki's mind went back to Lucas...this is what he liked to do...figure things out...take care of things...he should be here helping her...where was he and why didn't he call?

"Nikki..." Leah said.

She looked at her aunt and nodded...a bit absent mindedly because she had no idea what she wanted. There were only 27 hours until the rehearsal dinner...and the wedding...why didn't he just call her? Let her know if he was never coming back so she could start letting him go instead of desperately holding on. She just needed to understand…

"Nikki…" Leah repeated while putting a hand on her shoulder.

She took a deep breath and focused. "Sorry, what did you suggest?" She asked Reilly.

They were standing at the three stalls that led to the outside runs and the new corrals.

"What if we changed the separator walls in these so they are removable and place the treadmill in the middle one?" Reilly pointed. "Then you have the full length of all three stalls to use when needed and can walk horses into it from here in the barn or even from outside."

Nikki pictured his plan in her head and began nodding. She grinned at her step-brother; "You just had a brilliant moment, Mr. Morgan."

Reilly returned her grin and stepped into the stall with the rest of the crew following.

"Let's see what it will take to remove the walls." Leah said.

For the next half hour they made a list of what was needed for the remaining changes to the barn.

A familiar bang rang out through the barn. Nikki looked at Tessa and Josey. "When did you give him pain medication?"

"About an hour ago, he shouldn't be needing any yet." Josey answered.

Nikki turned and walked toward the bay horse, he was looking out the window…his ears perked. His usual stance when the other horses were in sight.

As she walked to the horse, her mind went to Lucas again. She wanted to call him, talk to him, let him know all the changes. He would love this. She wanted him to know. She wanted HIM. Suddenly feeling claustrophobic, Nikki felt a strong urge to have the large barn doors open so she pushed them open and stepped into the sunlight and froze.

Lucas was leaning against a blue SUV.

Nikki just stared; wondering if she was just imagining him there because she so desperately wanted to see him.

"Lucas?" Grace whispered from behind her.

It was him…she wasn't imagining it. So why was she just standing there staring? She had wanted him and needed him all week…now he was there.

Nikki took a few tentative steps to him and he stood away from the vehicle. She stared at him trying to read his expression…trying to understand why he was there…why he left.

"Grace, stay here." Nikki heard Leah tell her cousin.

She watched his eyes closely as she walked toward him…his amber brown eyes that always danced with laughter and love but now they looked at her in desperation…her stomach quivered.

She stopped ten feet before him but said nothing.

"You said you would always do what was best for Nick and what you needed to do to protect him." His voice was low with a slight quiver of desperation.

"Of course I would," she answered, her eyes narrowing in confusion. "I would do the same for you."

He nodded, "I came to realize that, but at the time…while he talked about his past…there wasn't anything said…" He stopped then just stared, seeming at a loss for words.

"He did nothing illegal that he would be trying to hide from you."

"So there wasn't any reason to not tell me two years ago. When Tessa asked why she had to sign the confidentiality agreement to hear of his past…it just hit me…she was right…there wasn't anything there."

"There was to him. Maybe nothing illegal but…it wasn't my story to tell." Her hands went to her hips…the same old battle.

"Yes, I remember, you said that." He inhaled deeply and let it out slowly. "But at the time, I just got angry at you…at Nick…"

"So you left?" Nikki felt her temper rising.

"I don't get angry very often…the last time didn't end well."

"So you got angry once and decided not to marry me?"

He shook his head slowly, "That's just it Nikki…"

"What?"

"Not once, in the last couple days, did I say or think that we weren't getting married."

She looked at him…stunned. "But you left…you weren't coming back for the wedding."

"When I left, I didn't consider the wedding."

"What did you consider?"

"Honestly?"

"Of course."

"Just what I needed, just the thought I needed to get away before I blew up and ruined our future. I've ruined a friendship in the past because of my anger…I couldn't take the chance of yelling at you or Nick."

"I would have preferred you yell at me." She said honestly, still trying to contain her irritation.

"I would prefer neither," He tried a slight smile but she didn't react. "Two years ago, I came up with a thousand reasons why Nick wouldn't talk about his past. A thousand felonies he was trying to hide. That's why I stopped asking; I didn't want to know if there was something there."

"You didn't just have him investigated?"

"Of course not, that's a line I wouldn't cross." He sounded insulted she asked.

"So because he didn't kill someone or rob a bank, you got mad and left?"

"He said he knew we battled about it, so the two of you spoke about the argument a couple years ago."

"Yes."

"Because there was nothing illegal in his past, the only reason he didn't tell me was because he didn't trust me…you didn't trust me. Trust means a lot to me. If you…if Nick didn't trust me… That is the reason I needed to get away…why I went back home."

"It didn't have…"

"…anything to do with trust." He nodded. "Cid told me that, too. Told me I was a fool to think that Nick didn't trust me or that I would leave without talking to you first. He actually had a few more choice words than that but I won't repeat them."

"Did Dad tell Cid about his past?"

"No, which is what Cid pointed out; as close as they were, riding bulls together for years, in the States and in Australia, and starting the business together. Cid had no idea that you and Matt existed until two years ago…after I met you. It didn't have anything to do with trust."

"It's just the way he is…it's his story…his life…that he has to come to grips with; not mine to announce it or talk about it until he's ready…if that ever happens."

He nodded, "I know that now. Cid also pointed out that Nick trusted me enough to bring me here…to open this side of his life to me. We don't know why he did…but Mom pointed out that the fact he did showed a tremendous amount of trust in me."

Nikki rolled her neck and lifted her shoulders…the tension didn't leave.

"I'm sorry, Nikki."

She didn't answer, just waited for him to finish.

"After Cid's choice words, Mom handed me the book that Sadie put together of you…your pictures from the branding. I didn't even have to open it to realize the mistake I had made by leaving and not talking to you. Once I thought of what I had put you through…just disappearing without a word, I called Greg and asked him to come back and get me…us." He smirked and shrugged a shoulder. "He was already there; Nick told him to stay in Australia and wait for me."

"Why didn't you call?"

"This wasn't a conversation to have on the phone."

Nikki nodded…she wish he'd called.

"On the way back, I thought about what you must have felt when you realized I was gone." His voice shook. "I couldn't image…what I did…hurting you…I never thought I would ever hurt you like that Nikki."

His voice…the desperation, regret… She had to swallow hard to keep the tears away.

"The worse thing Nikki…" He took a deep breath…his amber brown eyes glistened. "Was when I realized what I had actually done."

"What do you mean?"

"You've spent the last three years healing from the last time a man abandoned you and disappeared to Australia."

Nikki inhaled sharply…as if he'd stabbed her in the heart. The tears flooded to her eyes and she couldn't stop them from falling. Her mind had been running from that hurt all week…why she allowed and appreciated the entire family engulfing her time, mind, and life to help her get through. That was why she had held onto her dad so tightly the night before…she didn't want him to leave…disappear again…she had to hold on to him.

"Dang, Nikki," His voice quivered and he inhaled deeply trying to contain his emotions. "I spent most of the ride back going over every detail of the honeymoon trip I had planned…hoping that you would forgive me and still be my bride. But when I realized that I had repeated what Nick had done…I nearly lost all hope."

Nikki felt her whole body shaking and was surprised she was still able to stand. She tried to wipe the tears away with her sleeve.

"Cid had to talk me through it…keep me calm…"

"He was on the plane?"

"Yeah…and my parents. They are at the hotel." His eyebrows furrowed. "They didn't want to put any pressure on you by being here."

"Pressure?"

"They came for the wedding…" His voice shook. "If there still is…if you still want…"

She didn't speak…she just watched his eyes…

"Is there any hope, Nikki?" His eyes pleaded with her.

She had refused to believe that he was gone forever; in her heart she knew he would be back. He said he never thought of canceling the wedding…not marrying her. She had not thought of canceling the wedding…or not marrying him. She couldn't imagine him not being her husband. There was no doubt she loved him and there was no reason for him to come back if he didn't love her.

She had asked herself all week why he left…why did he leave? Now she knew, he needed his family to help him understand…*he needed his family*. It was something she could understand.

"I'm still standing here," she whispered.

He took a hesitant step to her but her legs were shaking so bad she was afraid to move.

"Please know Nikki, I will never, EVER, abandon you. When I have to fly back for work…please know…that I will ALWAYS come back to you."

She took in a deep breath and nodded.

He took another hesitant step to her.

"I love you, Nikki." Another hesitant step…she could almost touch him. "I have loved you from the moment you stepped out of the backdoor of the Homestead and I saw that laughter in your eyes. I promise to never let another day go by without telling you or showing you just how much."

"Show me." She whispered, desperately needing his arms around her.

"What?" His voice was hopeful.

"Show me."

He took the last step to her and wrapped her in his arms. There was no hesitation...just his lips to hers with an intensity filled by guilt, fear, relief, and love.

She listened to his kiss and felt all the emotions he was sharing. She gripped him tightly, returning the kiss and let him know that she had released the anger and fear...she understood...and loved him.

He rose just enough to break the kiss, "You know." His lips moved against hers.

"I know." She answered and stood on her tip toes to reseal the kiss.

When he broke the kiss, he lowered himself to one knee in front of her.

Nikki grinned, loving the light shining in his eyes.

"Nikki Tagger, will you please do me the honor of becoming my wife?" His whiskers framed the grin she had grown to love.

She lightly ran a thumb across those whiskers and was rewarded with the intense look in his eyes. "Yes."

He stood and kissed her gently then looked into her eyes, the love shining. His gaze moved from hers to the barn. "You have got to tell me about this poor Mate hanging from the rafters. I've been having a stare down with him since I arrived."

"I've wanted to call you and tell you all about them." Nikki admitted with a slight smile.

"I wish I'd been here." He sighed and slid his arm around her waist to guide her to the barn. "Introduce me."

CHAPTER THIRTEEN

The family slowly arrived over the next hour after word spread that Lucas had returned.

Nikki wasn't surprised when there were no welcoming handshakes from the men; just nods of welcome. Her family was protective of her…they weren't going to greet him with happy welcoming arms.

Nick didn't speak or nod to Lucas; he just walked to Nikki and gave her a strong embrace. She could feel the tension in his body, which confused her because he should have been relaxed. Her mother did the same thing after she placed a hand on Lucas' arm and whispered something to him. Lucas nodded and looked to Nikki; their warm smiles greeted each other.

Wade and Sadie were another matter. Neither spoke or indicated that Lucas was there.

"Can we check out the X-ray machine now?" Sadie asked politely.

The entire family was there standing either just in the barn or outside. Reilly was excitedly telling his parents the plan he came up with for the treadmill. They nodded proudly. Nikki looked around…this was better…they were all there…things were good now.

Josey was standing off to the side shifting her weight from one foot to another; her bottom lip gently placed between her teeth. Nervous excitement ran through her. She glanced at Nikki who suddenly realized why she was so nervous.

Nikki laughed, "Go ahead and tell them."

"Preacher's mine!" She squealed at Matt, her feet dancing again.

"Who's Preacher?" Matt asked with a confused chuckle.

"Bobo! Nikki traded him and I renamed him to Preacher! He's mine!" She threw her arms around his neck. Matt laughed and grinned at Nikki.

"That's awesome!" Sadie cried out with a grin. She walked with Josey to the big red gelding. "We're going to have to come up with a real good rehab program for him if you two ever think you're going to keep up with me and Scarecrow."

Sadie's laugh echoed through the barn and Josey rolled her eyes.

The whole group laughed with Lucas' arms tightening around Nikki. She leaned against him to enjoy his touch. She inhaled deeply, he smelled so good…it just seemed to fill her soul.

Sadie returned and looked at Nikki, purposely not even acknowledging Lucas. "Can we?"

Nikki nodded and Sadie walked back to the shelves. Nikki glanced at her groom with a raised brow and a shrug of the shoulders. It would take time for all the family to forgive, but Nikki was sure they would.

He returned her smile and nodded, "I'll get Little Dingo to like me again."

"At least she didn't go off." Nikki chuckled.

"I think that would have been more preferable." He sighed while watching Sadie. "Her anger is a flash, it's more superficial or visual because it's usually people not listening to her or taking something from her. This is deeper, it's gonna take time."

Nikki smiled at him and leaned in to kiss him lightly on the cheek but lingered, she closed her eyes at the touch.

"I love you, Nikki." He whispered.

Another light kiss and she turned to join Sadie.

They pulled out all the equipment and set it on the rolling table; including the iron apron that had to be worn when taking the x-ray.

"I'm sorry, Nikki." Sadie whispered and looked at her with concerned blue eyes.

"It's OK."

"No…" Sadie shook her head and glared at Lucas. Matt and Reilly were pointing out all the changes in the barn over the week. "He should have called you. He loves you and should have known what you were going through. I just don't understand that."

Nikki agreed with her and just nodded.

"He should have called, at least when he knew he was coming back. That was hours ago." Sadie lowered her head and started the monitor for the machine.

Nikki frowned at the back of her head, 'that was hours ago'. She turned and looked up at the clock on the wall above the double doors. Hours ago…

It was a 19 hour flight from Australia and just over a 2 hour drive from the airport to the ranch. The plane lifted off from Australia just over 21 hours ago. It was now 5:00, which meant, it was 8:00 last night Idaho time when the plane started its flight.

Nikki's eyes moved from the clock to the floor; her mind racing. What were they doing at 8:00 last night? They were driving home from Kennewick, from the auction.

With narrowed eyes, her gaze moved from the floor to her dad. He returned her look with an unreadable expression.

His pilot, Greg, never, EVER, left the ground without sending an email to Nick. It was standard procedure that was never broken.

Nikki's lips rolled together into a thin line and she stared at her father.

He knew…

Nikki stared at him until his eyes changed…to worry. She turned away and walked through the corner stall that led to the outside pen. She continued walking through the pen, past the corrals, and into the trees that bordered the sloping mountain side where Trooper and Jiggers were pastured.

She knew he would follow; probably Lucas too, but when she finally decided she was far enough away from the barn and turned, she was surprised to see her mother.

All three came to a stop in front of her.

"Nikki," Lucas' eyes were full of fear.

"We're OK," She assured him then turned to her dad. "You knew."

"I did." He sighed.

"Knew what?" Lucas asked.

"He knew you were on your way back." Nikki answered coldly.

"How would you know?" Lucas turned to stand next to Nikki and face her parents.

"It's standard protocol for Greg to email me any time the plane leaves the ground." Nick answered.

"Really?" Lucas' eye brows shot up. "Why didn't I know that?"

Nick shrugged and kept his eyes on Nikki.

"The text came in while we were driving back?" Nikki glared.

"It did," Nick nodded.

Nikki took a deep breath, "When I asked you if you had talked to him…or anyone in the office?

He shook his head forcefully, "I didn't know when you asked me. I was driving all night and didn't check my phone until you fell asleep."

"And you didn't want to disturb me…you let me sleep," Nikki tilted her head, the irritation growing inside her. "But why not this morning? Why didn't you tell me?"

"Because I told him not to," Her mother said firmly.

Nikki's eyes opened wide in surprise.

"After I read the message, I wasn't sure what to do so I called Dru." Nick explained.

"And you decided…" Nikki started.

"What would you have done, Nikki?" Her mother asked. "What if Nick told you first thing this morning that the plane was headed back? What would you have done?"

"There would have only been one reason for it to be coming back," Nikki glared. "…Lucas was coming back."

"And what would you have done?" She repeated.

Nikki didn't answer but turned slowly to her dad. "And you agreed with her?"

His eyes were filled with worry. "Nikki, I have only been back in your life for just over three years…which means I've only been a real father to you in that time…I don't know how to be one, I'm learning day to day. I want to do everything I can for you…but I didn't know how to this time. Dru has been there for you and has only done what she thought what was best for you…that is what she will always do. So I followed her lead."

"So you two stood together on this? No one else?" Lucas asked.

They both shook their heads.

"No one else knew," Nick said. "But when I saw you riding this afternoon, I knew you were hurting and I couldn't take it. I called Dru and told her when you returned I was going to tell you."

"So I went over there to talk him out of it." Her mother finished.

"Why?" Nikki asked gruffly.

"The actions and conversation had to play out between the two of you." Her mother looked between her and Lucas.

"It's the same as when Lucas does background checks." Nick quickly added. "He finds out the details but doesn't interfere in the learning and discovering between those involved."

"Which was why I didn't tell Josey that her grandparents owned a horse ranch or, more specifically, why I didn't tell Nick that Tessa had cancer," Lucas pointed out.

"I could have called Lucas once I knew he was coming back." Nick pointed out. "But I didn't."

Nikki nodded, she was beginning to understand. "It had to be between us."

She looked at both her parents and knew what Nick said was true, they would only do what they thought was best for her…she had no doubt about that. What would she have done if she knew he was flying back? Would it have been better to know he was on his way and not know what he was going to say? Or was it better to be a surprise and immediately see the regret in his eyes and know that he loved her? She really had no idea.

Suddenly, she felt very tired; the whole week was catching up with her. The roller coaster emotions and lack of sleep, she leaned against Lucas.

"Are you alright?" They all three asked and her parents stepped to her.

"I love you all, thanks for loving me…tell Sadie I'm sorry." She sighed and walked away.

They followed her to the house but stopped as she walked to her bedroom and crawled onto the bed. The last thing she remembered was someone pulling off her boots.

***

"So how do you decide who is going to walk you down the aisle?" Cora asked as she sat down next to Nikki on the front porch of The Homestead. They were waiting for Lucas' family to join them for breakfast.

Nikki chuckled, "I've had a year to figure that out."

Lucas, Josey and Matt led Harvey, Eli, and Trooper down the driveway. The rest of the Tagger Herd was running excitedly around the pasture greeting their friends. Kit, Libby, Zorra, and Leroy were in the opposite pasture and joined the excitement.

"I've missed seeing them together." Cora said softly. "I'm glad you wanted them all here for the wedding."

"It just seemed right." Nikki sighed. "They are the reason Dad came back and eventually brought Lucas with him."

"Do you think he would have come back if it wasn't for the herd?"

"I would like to think so," Nikki had wondered about that too. "I believe it had always weighed heavy on him and seeing the rescue was just what he needed to get him to come back."

They heard the door behind them open and lots of footsteps. Nikki turned to see the entire family pour out of the building. Their eyes were locked on the running and bucking herd of horses.

"I just love seeing that." Her mother smiled and sat down next to her.

"Evidently we all do." Nora laughed.

Just as Lucas, Matt, and Josey joined the crowd at the front porch, a white car slowed down on the road in front of the property and turned into the driveway.

"Who's that?" Alex asked.

"Lucas' parents and brother." Nikki answered.

Scott chuckled; "And here is the whole family standing on the front porch to welcome them on their arrival to The Homestead for the first time."

"This must look really odd to them." Jordan laughed.

"It would have scared me off." Nick chuckled.

"OK now," Grayson grinned. "Everyone wave."

And they did…along with a roar of laughter. Nikki chuckled at her weird family and walked to the driveway to greet her future in-laws.

"Well, that was quite the welcome." Lucas' mother, Matilda, smiled as she hugged Nikki.

Evan, his father, laughed; "I have a feeling it was more watching the horses run then it was welcoming us."

"Both," Nikki grinned. "We thought we would let you get a really good look at the herd of family…I'm glad you didn't turn the car around."

"Never, Nikki," Cid grinned and wrapped his arms around her and squeezed tightly. "Lucas is a very lucky man…and you are a very forgiving and patient woman." He whispered to her.

"Thank you for being there for him." She whispered in return.

"You just let me know if he ever does anything stupid like that again." Cid smirked with a raised brow.

Nikki grinned. "I will."

"So what's on the schedule?" Evan wrapped an arm around her shoulders and pulled her in tight.

"Breakfast first," Nikki smiled. "After, will be a tour of The Stables and Barn and Breakfast then we'll do a rehearsal of the wedding and the ladies will spend the afternoon at the spa. I wish you could have stayed at the B&B but it was completely booked for a wedding that's being held at The Stables."

"That's OK," Matilda smiled warmly. "At least we get to see your home and your work. It's just beautiful here."

"Spring time in the valley is just spectacular and Matt and Nick will take you up to the ranch tomorrow night. Spring time in the mountains…well…there's really nothing like it." Nikki said.

"Who is taking care of your rehab horses while everyone is here for the wedding?" Cid asked.

"A couple veterinarian assistants from the clinic we work with." Nikki answered.

Handshakes, hugs, and introductions were shared for the next few minutes. After breakfast on the back porch, the kids led them on a tour of the barn then out to the pasture to meet all the horses.

Nikki met her future mother-in-law in the hallway by the portrait of Lucas proposing to Nikki in front of a magnificent sunrise.

Matilda was smiling warmly at the portrait. "I am so glad he brought one of these home for us to have."

"It's just beautiful," It seemed like just yesterday Matt had taken the photo for them.

"Nikki," The older woman turned to her with a serious expression. "I'm glad we have a moment alone together."

Nikki nodded.

"Lucas said he came back home and left you because he was confused and upset. He never once said he wasn't marrying you. But, he had a friend that he'd known since they were ten. They went to the university together for the first couple years. Something happened to end that friendship, but Lucas wouldn't tell us."

"He told me that he ruined a lifelong friendship because of his anger." Nikki said. "That was why he left. He couldn't take the chance to do the same with Dad and I."

Matilda sighed, "We didn't even know that much. He just said they weren't friends anymore and wouldn't talk about him again."

"I can understand his fear, but I wish he would have stayed and talked to me about it."

"Sometimes…he just acts so grown up, well beyond his years. I sometimes forget he's only 29. People make a lot of mistakes in their 20's, Nikki. He lost a really good friend. I'm just very thankful he didn't lose the best thing that's ever happened to him. The two of you are just perfect together." Matilda's voice was full of sincerity.

"Thank you, I think we are too." Nikki grinned. "We'll both make mistakes, but if we can make it through this last week, we'll do OK."

"Come on you two!" Josey yelled down the hall. "The minister is here for the rehearsal."

The two women exchanged a warm and understanding embrace then gathered with the rest of the family in the driveway behind the house. An arch created with tree limbs from the ranch was placed where the vows would be exchanged. The next morning, Jessup would bring flowers from the ranch to decorate it.

The minister stood in front of the arch and looked for the bride. "Nikki, first things first, who is walking you down the aisle."

The whole family turned to her. Over the last year, nearly every one of them had asked her the same thing.

With a smile, Nikki walked up the five steps to the deck. She turned to her dad and held out her hand, "We start at the beginning."

When he got close enough to her, he whispered, "I told you it was OK with me if…"

"This is my wedding," she grinned. "It's my way… so if you will go to the back door please." She waved her hand to the door.

He smiled, but she could see the concern in his eyes. She ignored it for now and wrapped her arm through his. They walked from the door to the top of the stairs.

"Now we go to the next stage." She crooked her finger at her uncles. "If you will stand at the bottom of the steps, Dad will walk me this far then you'll help me down the steps and walk me to the alter."

They both grinned and took their places. She slid a hand through each of their arms and they started walking down the aisle to Matt, Cid and Lucas who were standing at the archway. Nikki grinned at her groom and was rewarded with the whisker framed grin and sparkling amber eyes.

When they reached the end and stopped, she turned to Scott who was on her left.

"And next," Nikki turned to Jack. "If you will come up and stand between Scott and I."

Jack nodded with a very pleased expression and took his place beside her.

Nikki grinned at her step-father. "You remember when I was seventeen and had a major crush on you?"

His cheeks tinted red as the crowd chuckled.

"Well, you have no idea how many times I day-dreamed about us standing at the alter together!" Nikki laughed at his grin. "Never thought it would come true!"

The whole crowd erupted in laughter.

"You are just the sweetest young lass." Jack laughed and wrapped her in a huge hug.

When the laughter eased, the minister stepped forward.

"Very good," The minister smiled.

"I'm not done yet." Nikki giggled and turned around. "Dad?"

He was at her side quickly; stepping between her and Grayson.

"After the 'who gives this woman…yada yada yada' then it is only fitting we go back to the beginning." She turned to her dad and took a deep breath as the tears started to rise. "You came back and brought me you and the love of my life." His eyes glistened, she slid her hand in his and with a slight tremor in her voice she continued. "I think it's fitting if you take my hand and place in his."

"Nikki…" His voice was barely audible.

She leaned in quickly to whisper in his ear…she hid the tear that escaped from his eye. After a moment she whispered, "You promised you would do the hallway slide with me. So after we're done here, I think we should go upstairs."

He chuckled and nodded, the tension in his body released. She leaned back and they smiled at each other.

His hand tightened around hers and he lifted it to his chest. "I don't have to do it yet, do I?"

"No," She laughed.

They turned back to the minister and the rehearsal continued.

CHAPTER FOURTEEN

"Are you going to take the robe off? Or just get married in it?" Josey smiled.

Nikki giggled as she gently slid a hand over the silky cloth of the robe; it was hiding the wedding dress underneath. Only her mother and Josey knew what the dress looked like and the wedding photographer, of course.

"Come on, Nikki," Grace whined. "Let us see you in your dress."

She shook her head at Grace, Sadie, and Nora who all looked pleading at her. Their dresses were deep sapphire blue with wide straps at the shoulders, a white ribbon wrapped around their waists and they had a flowing skirt that stopped just above their knees. The girls had spent the last hour spinning to make the skirts fly around them. Their long hair was curled and flowing down their backs.

"Not until I walk down the aisle." Nikki answered with a teasing shake of the head.

Grace's shoulders slumped in defeat but her eyes shown in humor. "Well, fine then."

"It's only minutes away," Josey laughed at them. "You three head out to the kitchen and wait so we can check the dress. We only have ten more minutes!"

All three girls excitedly left the guest bedroom as her mother entered and closed the door behind her. Only the three of them remained.

Nikki smiled at the happy glint in her mother's eyes. Her long blonde hair was slightly curled and rested down her back over a baby blue lace dress.

"You know, I would have flown all the way to Australia to kick that man's butt if he didn't come back so I could see the look on everyone's face when they saw you in that gown." Her mother said as she stepped behind Nikki to lift the robe back and way from the dress.

"I would have been there with you." Josey nodded in agreement. She stood in a deep blue form fitting satin dress that stopped just above her knees. It was sleeveless with straps that hung precariously over her shoulders and had a low, but respectable, neckline. A sapphire barrette held the sides of her hair in the back where is joined the large curls that cascaded down her back. She was stunning. Nikki wished she could see the look on Matt's face when he first saw her.

Nikki sighed contently as she turned and looked at her reflection in the full length mirror. Most of her hair was down with full curls flowing down her back. The sides were pulled up and to the top of her head then clasped together by a beautiful sapphire bejeweled barrette. A narrow veil spilled from the clasp of hair to flow softly down her back and into a slight train behind her.

The gown…they had searched for just the right one. She didn't want a typical western dress, nor one that was reminiscent of her mother's, even though it had been beautiful, too. Nikki wanted one that would shock the crowd and please her groom. After looking at hundreds of gowns they had finally found it. She had only tried on three; they stopped at the gown she now gazed at in the mirror.

It was strapless, of course, and the bodice of the gown covered her completely with the material in a crisscross pattern that emphasized her but didn't flaunt her. The waist was form fitting and more narrow than usual with the help of a tight corset underneath that gave her a spectacular hour-glass figure. It continued hugging her tightly until mid-hip when the crisscross pattern came together at her right hip and was held tightly with a blue sapphire broche that matched her barrette.   From there, the material of the gown fell in a silk waterfall all the way down to the floor.

The high healed petite white sandals with blue sapphires gems decorating the straps kept the gown from just touching the floor.

"Spectacular." Her mother whispered into the reflection.

"Walk!" Josey said excitedly.

Nikki grinned and kept from looking in the mirror as she walked to the opposite side of the room. She turned and took the first step, all three women giggled.

"He's just going to die!" Josey laughed.

With each step, Nikki's right leg protruded through a slit in the material; all the way up to the top, to the broach. The white material of the gown helped emphasize her tan and the tall slight sandals helped elongate and highlight the leg.

Nikki laughed and exaggerated the swing of her hips as she walked so the slinky material swung even wider; showing the leg with every step. It was the va-va-voom factor she had been looking for.

"He's just going to die…" Josey repeated with a sigh.

"No one out there would ever imagine this tom-boy of a girl wearing something so…scandalous." Her mother laughed.

"I just love it." Nikki whispered as she looked at the total effect of hair, veil, and gown.

"Let's get this show on the road!" Josey gave her a quick hug and air kiss so she didn't mess up her makeup.

"I'd like to talk to Dad for a minute first." Nikki said to her mother.

"He's going to have a hard time with this." She sighed with a slight shake of the head.

"I know. That's why I want to see him first." Nikki nodded.

"I'll go get him," Josey smiled brightly, clearly not understanding the emotional upheaval involved.

Her happy sister disappeared through the door. Nikki stared at her reflection as her mother stepped to her side and the women beamed at each other.

"I don't have to ask if you're happy." Her mother whispered.

Nikki just shook her head, the large curls swinging down her back.

"I couldn't have created a more wonderful man for you than Lucas."

"Me, either."

Her mom took her hand gently and squeezed; all the love and adoration for each other shone in their eyes. She kissed Nikki gently on the temple as a gentle tap was heard from the door.

"Dru," Nick smiled as he opened the door and her mother quickly stepped around him.

"Josey said you wanted a minute…" His voice stopped when he saw her, his chest rose as he took in a deep breath and his eyes instantly glistened. The breath was shaking as he released it and leaned back against the now closed door.

"It meets with your approval?" Nikki smiled, trying hard not to let the tears invade her eyes.

He just nodded and took another deep breath. They stood quietly as he took control of his emotions.

"I never would have thought I could have a day like this," He whispered and looked into her eyes…the honesty warming her heart. "I never dreamed I would ever be 'the father of the bride'. Or that I could be so…" He rolled his lips tightly together and swallowed hard.

"Happy?" She finished and he nodded slightly. Nikki hesitated then whispered, "Thank him for me."

Nick swallowed hard again and had to wipe away the tear that escaped from the lonely kid inside him.

"You OK?" She whispered. He nodded and rose away from the door to walk to her. "Not so fast." She giggled, which made him stop. "There's one more thing you should see."

Nick stepped back against the door and Nikki took a long stride and exaggerated her hip movement while she flashed her leg. His eyes dropped and he started chuckling.

"I'm not sure if I should be aghast because I'm your father, or laugh heartily because I'm a man and know exactly what that's going to do to Lucas."

Nikki beamed as she reached him and leaned in to give him a kiss on the cheek, lingering just a moment to let her touch tell him how much she cared and loved having him there.

"Let's go see." She laughed and retrieved the single white rose that she was carrying as a bouquet. "I haven't had pasta in months and I want the spaghetti that Cora made for the reception."

They both laughed as they entered the hallway.

"You two ready?" Josey asked.

"Let's get this party started." Nikki nodded.

Josey stood at the intersection of the hallway to the bedrooms and hallway of the outside door. She turned to the outside and nodded. The music started. Again Josey nodded to the cousins that waited patiently at the door to start their procession to the alter.

"Those girls are just beautiful," Josey turned with a smile at the approaching father and daughter. "Watch her in those heels." She told Nick.

"I will." He nodded and looked down at the tiny sandals and the leg that was flashing.

"He's just gonna die." Josey giggled again.

They all three laughed and Josey turned to walk down the hallway; then with one last grin, disappeared through the back door.

Nick held her arm tightly as they walked down the hall following Josey's route but stopped at the doorway to the outside.

He let go of her hand and stepped out the door first. He turned to the awaiting crowd with a grin then back to her.

His hand stretched out for her and just as she clasped his hand he spoke. "Do you want to walk normally or would you like to run down halfway and jump into a slide?"

Nikki started laughing and carefully, so the leg didn't show yet, stepped out the back door and they turned together to the family and friends gathered for the day.

Her sparkling laughing eyes went past the deck, stairs, uncles waiting at the steps, chairs, people that were rising and straight to those amber brown eyes that were beaming back at her under a new black cowboy hat and above his perfect whisker-framed grin.

Her heart swelled as she thought back to the moment, two years ago, when she had first looked into those eyes. Every time, seemed liked the first.

The music changed…she didn't have them play the typical bridal march. It was "Have I Told You Lately" by Rod Stewart that floated in the air.

"Ready?" Nick whispered and Nikki placed her hand in the crook of his arm and squeezed. They both stared in anticipation at her groom.

They took the first step and Lucas' eyes dropped and a gasp rang out from the crowd. Nikki grinned wider as she heard the low chuckle from her dad.

Lucas' eyes remained on her flashing leg as they made their way across the deck. Nikki tore her eyes from him as they reached the top of the stairs.

Grayson and Scott beamed up at her, laughter shining in their eyes.

"Little shock factor is good for the heart." Grayson chuckled.

Nikki giggled as Nick held her gently and handed her arm to Scott. Her uncles, her surrogate fathers for nearly her entire life, gently held her hands as she made her way down the steps…flashing her leg appropriately.

They turned and she placed a hand around each of their elbows and they escorted her down the aisle.

She watched Lucas' gleaming eyes as she walked down the aisle; Scott and Grayson at her sides and Nick following behind. When they stopped at the end, just a few feet away from him, Scott stepped to the left and Jack appeared at her side. She glanced lovingly at her step-father then back to her groom.

Matt surprised her by stepping away from the alter and Reilly appeared at her side. When the men stopped, she had Scott, Reilly, and Jack to her left; Grayson, Matt, and Nick to her right. All seven faced the minister and a grinning Lucas, his own brother, Cid, at his side.

Nikki felt the giggle rise inside her, followed closely by the abundance of love for the men at her sides and the one in front of her.

"This is normally when I say 'Who gives this woman…'" The minister smiled. "But I know this family better than that."

Laughter rang out from the gathered guests.

It was Matt that spoke, "We don't 'give' our women in this family; we only share them."

Another round of laughter as Lucas grinned and repeated the words that Jack had said a few years before. "I'm fine with that."

Nikki grinned and hugged both brothers and each of her fathers before Nick took her hand and placed it in Lucas'.

Her groom gently steadied her as she took the few steps to the alter; her leg flashing with each step. When she looked up at him, his eyes were watching for the next flash of leg which made her erupt in a fit of giggles. His eyes slowly rose to hers and he grinned, that wonderful grin.

"You amaze me, my lovely Nikki." He whispered softly and raised her hand to his lips for a gentle kiss.

The urge for a full kiss was strong, but she held back and waited.

They turned slightly and faced the minister together.

As the minister spoke, she kept her eyes on him but her mind went to the man at her side. She concentrated on his hands; strong hands…that seemed to be shaking. A glance to him; he glanced and smiled in return. As calm as he looked on the outside, his hands told her the truth.

"Do you Lucas Carlile take this woman to …"

"YES." Loud and firm, causing another giggle from Nikki.

"Do you, Nikki Andrea Tagger take this man to…"

"I do, forever." She smiled.

"OK, then." The minister laughed. "Do you have rings to symbolize your marriage?"

Nikki turned to Josey; tears glistened in her eyes. They smiled warmly to each other as Josey took the rose from her hand and replaced it with the ring for Lucas.

The minister spoke and Lucas repeated the words and she watched as the ring was slid onto her finger. The two outside rows of the band consisted of five diamonds each, the inside row was five blue sapphires, just a hint larger than the diamonds. It was absolutely stunning. Nearly beautiful enough to make her not notice the slight quiver in his hands as he slid it onto her outstretched hand.

The minister spoke, she repeated the words and gently slid the black etched ring onto his outstretched hand. Her hand was calm…his still shaking.

"And now, Nikki and Lucas have prepared vows to each other." The minister announced.

They turned to each other. Nikki grasped both his hands tightly as she looked into his glistening eyes.

This high-end powerful corporate attorney could face the death glare from her father, the most heartless of opposing counsel in a legal case, and a vicious judge who ruled over those cases; he faced them with nerves of steel. But now, as he faced her, that composure was slowly dwindling away.

"Lucas…" The minister said softly when he didn't speak.

He took a deep breath and his amber brown eyes entranced her as he spoke;

"I saw you first in a photograph, and thought you were beautiful. Then I saw you step out of the back door of this home…I saw the laughter in your eyes, learned the gentleness of your touch, and the compassion in your heart…and I KNEW that you were beautiful. From that moment…to the moment you descended those stairs again, just moments ago, and in that…" he took a step back and looked down at her gown…the toes just barely peeking out of the bottom…and he sighed. Nikki grinned and quickly tilted her knee to the side to swing the dress and wickedly flash him the leg again. The guests laughed as Lucas rolled his eyes to the sky then back to her. "You take my breath away, my lovely Nikki."

He stepped back to her and reconnected their gaze. "I have loved you from that moment…I have loved Harvey since we went camping."

Nikki giggled at the memory of her horse sending her flying into his arms.

"There are a few men in this family of ours, that have found the loves of their lives…they live for their wives and would, without hesitation, die for their wives." He took a deep breath and pulled her hands to rest against his chest…to his heart, a single tear escaped his. "Today, I am very fortunate to join that list, as I live for you and I would die for you."

As they gazed into each other's eyes, his hands stopped shaking and grew calm and firm in hers. Nikki took in a deep calming breath and let it out slowly.

"Lucas, not even death could end the love I have for you." She smiled. "From the moment I saw you, I knew, you were to be MY life." Another calming breath and a loving squeeze of the hands.

"I know my love for you…I feel it inside me…in my mind, my heart, my body, and in my soul. But the reason I can love you so deeply and without end is because I know how you love me." She smiled as he grinned through his whiskers. She raised a hand to his temple and ran a thumb lightly over his cheekbone. "I see it in your eyes." Her hand slid to his jawline, she slowly caressed a finger down the length of it. "I hear it in your voice." Her thumb lightly ran over the whiskers on his chin, the intensity in his eyes deepened. "And I feel it in your touch." Her arm slid around his neck as his slid around her waist. Just moments before their lips touched, she whispered, "I know…"

Somewhere in the haze, she heard laughing, clapping and the minister pronounce them man and wife. He told Lucas to continue kissing the bride.

As the kiss broke, Nikki looked into the loving eyes of her husband then they turned to their family.

***

Nikki lay quietly…only the sound of Lucas' breathing and the waves from the ocean could be heard. His chest rose and lowered in his deep sleep.

The slight breeze made its way through the open double-doors of the honeymoon suite allowing her full view to the moonlight dancing off the ocean and the waves rolling onto the beach of the private island. Their first week together, two years before, every time he kissed her they were interrupted, it wasn't happening this time on the small island. As he said, they would have two weeks together…just the two of them…literally.

His arm was wrapped around her, holding her close as her head rested comfortably on his shoulder. Never in her wildest dreams did she ever think she could love someone as much as she loved him. Her arm that lay over his stomach squeezed tighter, her fingers caressed the smooth skin on his side. It caused his head to turn; his chin nuzzling into her hair. She would tell him tomorrow and it would be just their secret for the next couple weeks…just between the two of them.

But how would her dad take it? How would he handle it? They had made great progress this week with him reconciling with his past…but how would he take this? The fear of the unknown rested slightly on her mind. She chased it away by imagining the look on her mother's and uncle's faces…The Trio. She could hardly wait to tell them that the next generation of Taggers was on the way.

THE TAGGER HERD SERIES

WADE TAGGER

Giving It Your All

Gini Roberge

CHAPTER ONE

"Sadie! Come on!" Wade yelled as he stepped into the barn.

"What we doing?" Sadie didn't hesitate as she ran to his side.

"Taking the calf for a walk," He announced proudly.

"Are we too little?"

"We're four! That's not too little."

The red orphaned calf was resting peacefully on his pile of straw, and turned to them with curiosity. Without much fuss, the calf let him slide the halter on, then Sadie clipped the lead rope onto the halter's ring.

"That was easy," Wade grinned at her.

"We're not too little!" Sadie's eyes shined as she clapped excitedly.

Wade gripped the rope and pulled; the calf didn't budge. He scrunched his face at the calf then looked to Sadie.

"I'll help!" She shouted.

Together, they gripped the rope then pulled, strained, and grunted but the calf just stretched out its neck and didn't budge.

They stopped pulling on him and looked to each other.

"How do we get him up?" Wade pouted.

Sadie put her hands to her hips and glared at the calf. Her mind was racing; then her head turned to him quickly with a bright smile. "The bottle!"

She ran out of the barn. When she returned, she stopped at the door with the large supplement bottle they used to feed the calf. The calf's head turned and looked at her, his long tongue shot out, and he started to rise.

"It worked!" Wade gripped the rope and walked the animal to the door.

Sadie turned and walked out onto the road. The calf trotted after her. Wade tried to walk faster than the calf to stay in front and actually lead it. Sadie walked faster to stay ahead of the calf; she quickly had to start running.

Sadie ran, the calf ran faster. Wade hung onto the rope as he trailed behind them both.

"Sadie! Stop!" Wade cried out as his strides were unusually long.

"I can't!" She ran faster, the calf ran faster, and Wade began to stumble.

As a last resort, Sadie threw the bottle on the ground and turned quickly. The calf stopped and she grabbed the rope. They tugged on the rope and tried to pull the calf from the bottle but it didn't work. It just turned the bottle in circles as it tried to get milk from the nipple.

Sadie looked excitedly at Wade, "Now what?"

Just as he shrugged, the calf's head rose and looked down the road to the pasture. There were a few cows in the distance and the calf took off running toward them.

"Ahh!" He yelled as the calf jerked him off his feet.

With Sadie at his side, they fell to their knees then their bellies hit the ground. Gripping the rope even tighter, they held on as the calf ran down the dirt road dragging them behind.

Wade started laughing as he bounced across the rough road. He turned to see Sadie was laughing too; her eyes shining.

Suddenly, they stopped. Wade was still laughing as he looked up to see why.

The Tagger Ranch foreman, Jessup, was gripping the calf's halter and looking very confused at the two kids.

Wade grinned, "We took him for a walk."

"Yeah, that's what it looked like," Jessup chuckled.

***

"Wade! Come on!" Sadie yelled as she ran down the fence line of the spring branding corrals.

"Where to?" He didn't even hesitate in following her.

"They said we're too young to help. We're going to show them we're not!" She hollered over her shoulder.

"Sadie, we're five-years old…that IS too young to help." Wade started to slow down but she didn't even hesitate as she disappeared around the corner. He sped back up again.

When he rounded the corner she was on her hands and knees looking through the fence at the calves waiting to be branded.

"What are you doing?" He slid to a stop next to her.

"Looking for a little one," Her blue eyes were excitedly shifting from one calf to another.

"What are you going to do when you find one?" He fell to his knees to join her search for a little calf.

"WE are going to pull it out here."

Wade spotted a little black one with a white face. The calf looked smaller than the rest of them. He hesitated pointing it out to her, but figured 'what the heck?'.

"Over there!" He stood and ran along the fence until he was next to it. He fell back to his knees to peer through the fence.

She was by him quickly, her eyes narrowed as she assessed the situation. The totally unaware calf was laying at the edge of the fence but was looking out at the action in the main corral.

"If we grab his back legs, we can pull him out real quick." She finally decided.

Wade looked back at her, "Then what?"

"Then we tackle him to get him to the ground." Her eyes were wide in anticipation.

"OK," Wade nodded; that sounded like fun.

Sadie stood and looked into the main corral then quickly lowered again. "No one's looking for us," she grinned. "You take the top leg and I'll grab the one he's lying on."

Wade nodded excitedly.

"Ready? One, two, three!" She yelled and they both grabbed a leg.

Her plan worked perfectly. They had the surprised black and white calf pulled to the opposite side of the fence before it knew what happened.

The calf let out a bellow as it tried to stand, but Wade and Sadie were on top of it before it had a chance. Sadie lay across the front shoulders while Wade lay across its hips.

"Now what…?" Wade started to say but the scared calf twisted and turned and his back half slid out from under him. He scrambled to get back on.

"Hold him, Wade!" Sadie hollered as she tried to twist her body and lay it completely over the calf.

Wade dove at the back of the calf again and managed to get it back down. He and his cousin were butt to butt with their legs fighting each other to clamp around the animal. The calf bellowed again as it rose on its front legs sending Sadie rolling back over Wade and she landed on the ground at the calf's butt.

"Sadie!" Wade cried out as the calf slipped out from under him. He dove for one of the calf's legs to hold onto it.

Sadie rolled herself back over and lunged for the other back leg. They both gripped tightly as the calf tried to run away, yanking their bodies in the process.

"Hold on, Wade!" Sadie hollered as she tried to scramble to her feet.

With both of them holding on, the calf fell to the ground then kicked repeatedly; the two five-year-olds held on as long as possible. Their arms were jerked back and forth. Somehow, the calf stood then tumbled back over and rolled right over the top of Wade.

He lost his grip and it rolled over Sadie. She also lost her grip, but tried to encircle the calf's body with her arms. A swift kick to her arm from the calf, and it was released and took off running.

It ran right into the legs of Uncle Grayson.

Wade lay sprawled on the ground, his arms sore from the jerking. He stared at his uncle in surprise. Sadie lay flat on her stomach, legs wildly behind her. When she saw the denim-covered legs, she rolled over, and stared up at her dad.

She sighed heavily, "OK, you may have been right, but we'll be big enough next year."

***

"Sadie! Come on!" Wade yelled as he ran through the corral attached to the barn.

"Where we going?" She hollered and followed without hesitation.

"I think I saw a coyote puppy!"

"I've never seen a coyote puppy!" She said excitedly and climbed through the back fence right behind him.

Wade took off at a run down the mountain then suddenly stopped; his eyes looking over the open mountainside. There was a movement to his right, but the coyote was headed downhill. He hesitated in telling her but decided 'what the heck?'.

"Over there!" He pointed.

The two six-year-olds took off running down the mountain toward the coyote. It didn't see them at first and they got within thirty feet of it before it took off. It ran up and over the ridge that ran all the way down to the river.

Wade followed Sadie another twenty feet then stopped. "Sadie, it's a big one, not a puppy."

She stopped and watched the animal disappear.

"Dang coyote," She stomped her foot then turned to Wade with a smile. "It would have been cool if it was a puppy though."

"Do you think our parents would have let us keep it?"

Her shoulders shrugged making her ponytail sway. Her eyes looked past Wade.

"Ahhh, man!" The excitement in her eyes disappeared.

"What?" Wade asked and turned to follow her gaze.

They had been so excited to follow the coyote they didn't realize how far down the mountain they were.

"We're more than halfway," She grumbled.

"I hate walking uphill," Wade's shoulders drooped.

They took a few hesitant steps before Wade saw a movement. "Look! It's Mom and Aunt Leah."

"And Aunt Dru." Sadie smiled in relief. "I bet they'll get a horse and come get us."

The two kids waited, but the three women just stood quietly looking back at them.

"What are they waiting for?" Wade whispered.

"I dunno."

They were both mortified, when the three women sat down on the mountainside and waved at them.

"They're not coming down," Wade groaned.

"Nope, they don't like walking uphill either," Sadie sighed.

Resigned to their fate, they took the first of many steps to get back to the top.

***

"Wade! Come on!" The seven-year-old Sadie used her whole arm to wave him around to the side of their neighbor, Andy's, barn.

"What?" He ran to her without hesitation.

"Andy put up a new fence back here," She said excitedly when he caught up with her.

"Cool! We have a new one to walk," He quickly climbed the corner post of the new wood fence and tried to balance on the top.

Sadie was right behind him.

"Don't fall; there are cow piles all over," Wade laughed.

"I'm not falling…I'm better at this than you are."

"No, you're not," Wade rolled his eyes at his cousin.

"Yes, I am," She declared with a frown. "I bet I can walk faster."

"Prove it!" Wade pointed down the fence. "Go down two posts and we'll race to the middle post."

"OK," She climbed down the fence and quickly ran to the second post. When she reached the top of the fence they faced each other.

The pair grinned at each other in anticipation of their race.

"Ready?" Wade asked.

Sadie nodded then counted; "One, two, three!"

They walked toward each other as fast as they could. Both slipped at the same time and tumbled off the fence and hit the ground.

"Ugh," Sadie cried out.

"Dang!" Wade hollered as he lay quietly trying to catch his breath and let the pain ease from his body.

"Oh, gross!"

He turned to see Sadie start to rise from the ground; her side was covered in cow manure. Wade laughed until she pointed at his legs which had landed in a cow pile. They were covered in the green runny manure.

Just as he turned, he felt something hit his chest. He looked down to see a pile of green and brown moist cow poop. Wade turned to Sadie in disgust. She was laughing so he sat up quickly, cupped a handful of manure in his hands and threw it at her. She ducked but it hit her forehead and slimed into her hair.

"Ewww, ewww, ewww!" She laughed and carefully swiped the glob off her forehead.

She looked at it in disgust, then quickly flicked it back at him. It caught him by surprise and hit him in the cheek. When he flicked it off, he saw another pile close to where his head had landed. He turned quickly, scooped his hand through it, and flung the whole thing at her.

Sadie screamed and turned in time for it to hit the back of her head and slid down her braid, back and to the top of her jeans.

Wade roared in laughter. When she turned back, she threw another handful of manure and it splattered against his chest and up his neck. He jumped up quickly, found another pile, and scooped more poop. When he turned to throw, she had stood and also had a handful of manure. They stared, silently challenging each other. Their hands lowered and they turned as if giving up, then both turned fast and threw; the manure splattered against their arms, bodies, and faces.

They giggled and laughed as they ran from pile to pile throwing them at each other. When they finally exhausted the fresh cow piles, they stopped and looked at each other and laughed again. They were covered head to toe.

They were still laughing as they walked along the barn and back to the house. When they rounded the corner, they came face-to-face with Wade's dad and Andy. Both men looked at them in disgust. They stood quietly giggling as Andy walked to the hose and turned it on. They screamed in delight as they were hosed off by the very cold water.

***

"Wade! Come On!" Sadie stepped into the saddle and perched proudly on top of Scarecrow.

"Go warm-up," He hollered. "I run later."

"OK, you going to watch this time?"

"I will, I promise," He waved.

Having watched her run the barrels so many times, he didn't usually watch anymore. He just listened for her time.

As he warmed-up Dollar, he saw Nora enter in her princess outfit and then Queen Grace entered with a round of laughter. He shook his head. Those two sure liked their royalty duties.

The announcer called for the first barrel racer, so he made his way to the arena fence so he could watch. The girl was at a trot when she turned the third barrel; that was odd. Why would she just trot? He shrugged and waited; he knew Sadie was the second runner.

When they called her name, he leaned up on his tip toes to see her, but she didn't appear. Where was she? They called her a second time, but still she didn't ride out.

"What the heck?" Wade mumbled. He started to lower into the saddle when her name was called the third time and she finally appeared. He heard someone yell her name just as Scarecrow slipped around the first barrel. Reilly came running out of the alley making Wade's heart race. What was going on?

Sadie pulled back on the reins. Scarecrow started a sliding stop, but her front legs slid to the side. Sadie flew forward, the horse rolled, Wade's heart stopped beating as Sadie disappeared under the horse's mane.

He had stepped off Dollar and onto the fence when the roll started. Sadie flew out of the saddle and toward the wall. Reilly was running to her, Wade jumped and landed on the arena dirt as Sadie slammed into the wall. He could hear his mother's scream over the top of the gasping crowd; then Nora and Grace screaming.

Wade ran as fast as he could to his cousin…his best friend…his co-conspirator. When he reached her, Reilly was kneeling at her side. His scared eyes looked up at Wade then turned to seek help.

Wade stared at Sadie…she looked…dead. Her face was already swelling and turning colors. His heart stopped. He tried to swallow the lump in his throat as he fell to his knees.

Scarecrow was standing with her head leaning over them, so Wade placed a hand on the horse's leg as if it was his cousin. Scarecrow was a part of Sadie. Grace and Nora appeared at his side; they grabbed his arms tightly. He barely felt them.

The ambulance was driven into the arena.

Wade sat and stared, his body and mind numb. While his mom talked to an unconscious Sadie, the paramedics rolled her onto the long board. Everything was moving through a haze…after everything they had gone through growing up…Sadie was hurt by running barrels. It wasn't right…she couldn't be gone.

"I'm going in the ambulance with her," He heard his mom but the words just floated around. He wasn't really sure what happened next or how he ended up at the hospital. He thinks Reilly drove them as one of the other barrel racer's parents tended for Scarecrow and the other horses, but it would be days before he knew for sure.

At the hospital, he stood quietly listening to the noise around him. He hadn't seen his mother yet. Nora and Grace were crying. Reilly was staring at the wall; his face white. Uncle Grayson and Aunt Leah arrived, followed by the rest of the adults. It had taken them a while to get there. Cora came directly to him and he leaned into her, but he still felt like it was a bad dream.

It may be a broken neck, she may be paralyzed. The words were thrown out, but Wade couldn't grasp it. Not Sadie, she couldn't be paralyzed. They had too many calves to wrestle still…more poop fights…too many things to get in trouble for…she couldn't be paralyzed. His head swam, everything went dark and he fell back into Cora's arms; the tears welled and fell, the sobs wracked out of his body. She had to be alright…she just had to.

He didn't leave the hospital. He absolutely refused, but he was exhausted and fell asleep on one of the couches in the waiting room. Cora was at his side. When he woke, everyone was either asleep or talking in remote corners of the hospital floor.

Wade rose, careful not to wake anyone, and walked down the hall. He stood quietly at the doorway of Sadie's room. He was terrified at what he was going to see. Was she still going to look dead?

Hesitantly, he stepped into the room. Uncle Grayson and Aunt Leah were sitting in chairs next to the bed; both had their eyes closed. One more step and he could see Sadie. His breath caught in his throat. There was a cast on her arm. Half of her face was swollen and black and blue but she looked alive…she was alive. The relief flooded through him as he walked silently to her side. He carefully walked between her sleeping parents and the bed so he could get to her good hand.

He slid his hand into hers and squeezed. There was no response. He stared at her fingers and whispered out loud but screamed in his head: "Come on, Sadie!"

Her hand twitched…he gasped and heard a noise behind him but he didn't look. She twitched again.

"Wade…" Aunt Leah whispered.

He shook his head and stared at Sadie's hand; he squeezed as tight as he could, he didn't care if he hurt her, she needed to be OK. 'Come on, Sadie!' He said harshly. Aunt Leah stood and put an arm around him.

He released his grip, only to have Sadie's fingers grasp around his and squeeze back.

His tears fell again.

***

"What are you thinking about?" Sadie asked as she nudged him back into reality.

"All the trouble we got into when we were little," Wade shook his head to get the memories away.

Sadie laughed; "The poop fight?"

He joined her laughter and the bad mojo escaped from his muscles. This was not the time to be dwelling on the bad; just the good. The two thirteen-year-olds stood side-by-side and looked around. There were horse trailers everywhere.

"We made it," Sadie sighed. "We made it to the Idaho Junior High Rodeo State Finals."

"Three days of rodeo….play hard, work hard and let's get to National Finals."

"I'm for that. I know we just have to get in the top four, but I sure would like to win."

"Me, too," Wade nodded.

"Think of all the thousands of hours of practice and competitions we've done to get this far."

"I have…that and all the ridiculous things we've done growing up to survive this long to get here."

Sadie giggled and nodded as they watched more trucks driven onto the grounds, horses unloaded from trailers, and into stalls. There were trailers already parked with camping chairs and coolers set up in front of them in preparation of the long weekend.

There was a wooden outdoor arena with bleachers and chutes down the hill to their left. There was also an indoor arena covered with white canvas. It was very large. The main arena, where the state finals would be held, was to their right; up the hill and across a parking lot.

"I know we should want everyone else here," Sadie grinned. "But I'm kind of glad it's just the two of us…plus our parents."

Wade matched her grin. "I was thinking the same thing."

Sadie sighed and started walking, she turned with a grin.

"Wade! Come on!"

CHAPTER TWO

"Get your back number out of the packet," Aunt Leah said to Wade and Sadie after they had signed in for the rodeo. "We'll go over there and have it laminated."

They walked from the office window to the picnic table where two kids were working the laminating machine. The roof of the building they were in was the bleachers to the main arena.

They had parked the two trailers and unloaded the horses just 20 minutes before. The three horses, Dollar, Little Ghost, and Scarecrow were tucked safely into their stalls for the next couple of hours.

Wade glanced up the concrete ramp that split the bleachers. He could just make out the top of the fence to the main arena.

"Can we go check it out before we leave?" Wade asked.

"We have to be at the shooting range for the two o'clock session so just for a few minutes," His mother answered.

As their back numbers were laminated, they watched other competitors with their families arrive and receive their information packets.

Just as he was turning to walk up the ramp, Wade saw two girls walk into the building at the end of the bleachers. Both wore boots, jeans, and white shirts. Their black cowboy hats had red, white, and blue flag bandanas rolled and wrapped around the crowns. The girl on the right herd long black hair down to the middle of her back. The other girl's hair was the same color but it was cut to just the top of her shoulders. They were obviously sisters.

"Come on, Wade." Sadie nudged him forward and he lost sight of the sisters as they made their way to the main arena…their playground for the next three days.

The two of them and their parents stopped just at the top of the ramp. To their left was a set of covered wood bleachers that was the roof of the lower building. To their right were another set of bleachers completing the roof. Just in front of them, after a wide cement aisle, was a long narrow arena that would be used for poles, goat tying, breakaway, and tie-down roping. Just a metal panel fence separated the narrow arena from the larger, full-size arena. The bucking chutes were across the arena with the announcer's stand setting above them.

A horseracing track ran to their right and around the warm-up area then back behind the bucking chutes. It stretched out into a distance to their left and looped around by the other warm-up arena and back in front of them. The narrow arena was actually covering the race track.

"Boy, wouldn't it be cool to just let the horses run that whole race track?" Sadie grinned.

"Cooper would love it," Uncle Grayson chuckled.

"Your chute-dogging will be out of the bucking chutes," Wade's mother said. "We may need binoculars to be able to see you from the stands."

"Scott and I are volunteered to help with the gates," Uncle Grayson said. "We'll have a real good view," He teased.

The group walked to their right and made it back to the main entrance of the building-bleachers combination. As they walked by the main doors toward the parking lot, trailers, and stalls, Wade glanced into the building and just caught a glimpse of the red, white, and blue bandanas.

ᘮᘮᘮᘮᘮᘮᘮᘮᘮᘮᘮᘮ

A half-hour later, they were sitting in the office building at the shooting range listening to the safety instructions, competition rules, and receiving their paper targets. They also received bright orange strings that were to be placed down the barrel of the guns to indicate they were empty. This was a requirement when not at the shooting benches.

Their .22 rifles were inspected, and then their group walked out to the range.

"Get on opposite sides so you don't distract each other," Wade's dad instructed.

"Now, Uncle Scott," Sadie grinned. "What would make you think we would do that?"

"History," He answered with a laugh.

After more instructions, the group of six contestants walked down the range and stapled their targets on the wooden stands then walked back. Sadie was in the #1 position and Wade was in the #6 position…totally opposite.

They were given their ammunition. They would shoot five rounds in three positions; laying on the ground, kneeling, then standing. The targets had five black numbered rings and the closest to the center was a higher number.

After putting in his ear plugs, Wade lay on the ground, propped a knee forward then lifted the rifle against his shoulder. A bang rang out from down the range; another, then another as the shooters began the competition.

He took a deep breath, positioned the rifle…finger hovered over the trigger then slowly squeezed. Bang!

They all stopped once the prone position was completed by everyone. They moved to the kneeling position, and the shooting was repeated until they moved to the standing position.

On his very last shot, Wade took in another deep breath, concentrated on the gun sites and black circle on the target, then slowly squeezed the trigger. Bang!

He stepped back and slid the long orange string down the barrel of the gun. He looked down the lane to see Sadie still shooting. Her parents were right behind her with binoculars looking down the range at the target. Wade's parents had been standing right behind him. They grinned proudly at him then walked down to watch Sadie.

Everyone completed their shooting except for Sadie. There was silence on the range except for the murmur of parents behind them.

Sadie lowered the rifle and rolled her neck.

Wade lifted his phone to aim the camera at her.

"Two more?" The range master asked her.

"Yep," She nodded and lifted the rifle again.

Seconds passed…silence on the range…whispering behind them…bang!

She lowered the rifle, rolled her neck, and then lifted it again. Her shoulders rose and fell as she took in a deep breath. Wade took a quick picture.

Bang!

Sadie instantly turned and looked down the lane at Wade with a grin. He wasn't sure if she knew she shot well, or if she was grinning because she was having fun, but he just grinned back. He quickly sent the picture to Nora.

The range was called "clear" letting everyone know that the guns were down on the tables and it was safe to walk down and retrieve their targets.

Wade smiled as he approached his target. He actually did better than he expected.

Sadie had done even better; because she is normally a better shooter than him. She and Grace could outshoot all of the kids including Nikki.

Friday- Junior High School Rodeo State Finals

Friday morning, the first official day of the rodeo, Wade sat in the bleachers and looked around at all the competitors and family members who were gathered for the mandatory meeting. There were lots of people. His eye landed on a black cowboy hat that had long black curls flowing out the back, over the top of a red shirt. It reminded him of Nora. She was going to a horse show in Pasco with Candace and her Aunt Paige. She had promised to text him with how she was doing and made him promise the same. Sharing pictures from the two events was a must.

Sadie and her parents were in front of him, while his parents were to his right. With his phone he took a quick picture that caught the back of Sadie's cowboy hat and braid in the foreground, and the two arenas in the distance. He sent it to Nora.

Within minutes he received an answer back.

Text from Nora: I like the picture of her in the shooting competition yesterday better. Keep up your standards brother. ;)

He laughed.

"What's so funny?" His mother asked.

He told her quickly and she nodded with a grin. "The girl can shoot. Second-place with all those competitors is pretty good."

"I didn't do too bad," Wade chuckled. "Ninth out of all those competitors is pretty good too."

His mother grinned, her eyes shone with pride as she looked down at the speaker. "Yes, I guess you're right," She teased.

He chuckled again as everyone around them started to stand and make their way down the wooden stairs.

"OK, here we go." Uncle Grayson said from in front of him.

Wade and Sadie smiled at each other.

"What's first for our group?" Wade's dad asked.

"Scott! We've gone over this a hundred times," Aunt Leah laughed.

He grinned at her, "You may have…doesn't mean I was paying any attention."

Wade's mom laughed and shook her head. "Steer riding, then the first section of chute dogging which Wade is fifth, then poles which Sadie is ninth out. We'll just feed you a little info at a time so you don't get confused." She teased.

ᴜᴜᴜᴜᴜᴜᴜᴜᴜᴜᴜᴜ

Wade stood patiently behind the chutes and watched the first four competitors try to wrestle the steer to the ground.   The first one lost his grip as soon as the gate opened. There were ahhh's from the crowd. The second cowboy held onto the steer out of the gate and past the white line. The line was drawn in the dirt indicating the spot the cowboy could then turn the steer's head and wrestle it to the ground. Hopefully it would fall on its side with four feet off the ground. The cowboy made it past the line but the steer fell the wrong way. He lost his grip before he could get it standing again and flipped the right way; another round of ahhh's as the steer trotted away.

The third competitor was able to hold onto the horns out the chute and across the white line, but was drug another ten feet before he managed to get the steer flipped. 11.29 brought clapping from the crowd this time.

The fourth competitor was drug across the whole arena before he tripped and the animal ran off.

Wade slid down into the chute next to his black steer.   It's back was level with his hip and he could easily drop his arm over its neck then wrap up around the horn.

"Get a good grip," His dad said. "Tuck that horn into your elbow…cradle it tight."

Wade nodded and bent his back left then right to loosen the muscles then positioned his body in front of the animal's front shoulder. He tightened his arms around the horns and took a deep breath. The steer bounced its head but didn't really move. Maybe he had the luck of the draw this time.

"You ready?" He heard someone ask him.

Wade tightened his grip. He could see the white line through the rails of the chute's blue gate. The gait opened and the steer didn't move. Wade tightened his grip even more as he saw a hand come down to hit the animal's rump.

It bolted out the door, but Wade was ready. As soon as they passed the line, he leaned down to wrap his hand around the steer's nose. Then twisting, turning, falling backwards he pushed with his legs against the ground to help turn the steer. Everything was perfect…except the darn thing didn't fall. He kicked out with his leg to push its side and the steer tumbled. Its legs went up and the flag went down; 12.15…not a bad start. He needed to improve the next day so his average time of the two days combined, would place him in the top twenty overall. Then he could compete on Sunday for one of the top four spots that would go onto National Finals.

When all the chute doggers were done competing, he walked with his dad and uncle back to the bleachers where his mom and aunt were sitting. His next event was breakaway roping, which was hours away. He'd watch Sadie run poles and then go get Dollar and warm-up.

CHAPTER THREE

Wade was sitting next to his parents watching all the people cheering for their riders, reading books and their phones, or eating. It was a bit boring. He turned to the left and watched the pole bending riders warming up…lots of them…lots of pretty girls. Maybe he'd go down there and talk to Sadie.

"I'm gonna go get Sadie's picture," Wade said. He quickly headed down the wooden steps of the bleacher but still heard the knowing chuckles of his dad and uncle.

"Amber Lefler is our next rider with Kylie Reynolds up next, with her sister Tara Reynolds on deck," The voice of the announcer rang out.

The rider was out into the arena, around the poles, and racing for home by the time he made it down by the fence. Wade leaned against it next to Sadie and Scarecrow. The red, white, and blue bandana was wrapped around the hat crown of the next rider. She was the sister with the longer hair; the dark hair was nearly invisible on the black shirt she wore.   She positioned the bay horse in front of the gates.

"Next runner in is Kylie Reynolds…" The announcer's voice boomed.

The gates opened…in a flash, the girl was at a dead run down the length of the arena next to the poles. There was barely a slow down as she maded the first turn at the end. She swayed in and out of the poles with a tight turn at the end, then weaved back through again. Rider and horse seemed as one as they moved. A final tight last turn and they were racing to the end.

"Wow!" Sadie gasped. "She's good!"

19.895 was announced as her time.

Her sister was next to ride and flew into the arena. She slid into the turn at the end then weaved, turned, weaved and the final turn was as tight as her sister's. She raced to the end.

20.513 was announced.

"Dang!" Sadie grinned at Wade and he nodded in appreciation.

They watched the pair of sisters trot down the track to cool down their horses, then walked up next to them. They wore matching black shirts, dark denim jeans, and black boots with little red stars that matched the flag bandanas.

"Great runs!" Sadie told them.

They both turned friendly brown eyes to her and thanked her.

"I'm Sadie Tagger."

"Kylie and Tara Reynolds," Kylie said to Sadie with a quick glance at Wade.

"This is my cousin, Wade Tagger," Sadie said and flipped a hand towards him.

Wade nodded politely to Tara then turned to nod at Kylie; she was smiling at him. He felt a warmth in his neck and it slowly went to his stomach. He returned her smile.

"I take it you've done this a time or two," He said to Kylie.

He was thrilled when her eyes brightened as she laughed.

"Since we could sit in the saddle," Tara answered.

"Our mother raced since she was little, now she raises and trains our horses," Kylie said and leaned down to pat the bay's neck. There was a proud glow on her face…she obviously loved the horse.

"She does a dang good job," Sadie said.

The announcer's voice rang out stating Sadie was third out.

"I'll be back," Sadie grinned and trotted Scarecrow away to warm-up.

Wade didn't move and neither did the sisters. He wasn't really sure what to say…so he said the one thing he knew cowgirls liked to talk about.

"What are your horse's names?"

Tara turned with a smile; her horse was a dark sorrel with a flaxen mane. "His name is Trigger," She said. "I'm a Roy Rogers fan."

Wade grinned and nodded, "My horse is Dollar. I'm a John Wayne fan."

Both girls laughed and Wade turned to Kylie. He liked how her eyes brightened when she laughed.

"This is Clancy," Kylie said. "I'm a *Man from Snowy River* fan."

They all three laughed as Sadie's name was called out.

"My dad's cow dog is named Spur from the same movie. Sadie's riding Scarecrow," Wade said as he climbed the white rail fence to watch his cousin. The sisters moved their horses so they were out of his way.

"A movie? Wizard of Oz?" Kylie asked.

"No…long story," Wade gave her a slight smile.

He quickly pulled out his phone and captured the moment Scarecrow leaped into action. The blonde team raced down the arena. With a silent sigh, he had to admit, Scarecrow was not as fast at the sister's horses on getting to the first turn. Her turn on the end was tighter though. They weaved in and out of the red, white, and blue poles then another tight turn…weaving away from them then a final tight turn.

Wade's breath caught as the last pole began to tip then sighed in relief when it stood back up instead of falling. Scarecrow was racing back with Sadie leaning forward like a jockey. He could hear their parents screaming for them. Sadie passed the laser beam that stopped the clock…the reader board: 20.402

Wade watched her face as Sadie trotted out of the arena and down the dirt track. She was smiling; it was a good start.   He sent the picture of her race start to Nora.

"So what else are you two doing?" Sadie asked when she returned.

"Just barrels and poles," Tara answered. "And you two?"

"Chute dogging, breakaway, tie-down, and ribbon roping with Sadie," Wade answered.

"Poles, barrels, goats, breakaway, and ribbon roping with Wade," Sadie beamed.

"Well…look at you go!" Kylie shook her head with wide eyes.

Wade's phone alert rang out.

Text from Nora: That's a good one! How did she do?

Wade sent her the time.

"Plus we both placed in the shooting yesterday." Sadie was saying as he looked up.

His phone rang out again and he looked down at the message. It was a picture showing the back of Nora's horse, Arcturus' ears and on the other side of the ears was Candace walking her red horse, Lola, into a horse trailer.

"From Nora?" Sadie asked.

Wade nodded and handed her the phone. "Loading up to head to the show."

"Who's Nora?" Tara asked.

Wade looked up at the sisters, "My sister."

Kylie's eyes looked disappointed at first then they seemed to relax. But when Sadie handed her the phone to show her the picture, her brows came together again.

Tara leaned over to look at the picture. "The blonde is your sister?" She asked in obvious surprise and looked at Wade with his black hair, dark eyes and complexion; his obvious Indian heritage showing through.

He grinned and shook his head, "No, that's Nora's best friend, Candace. Nora is behind the black ears…her horse Arcturus. We're exchanging pictures throughout the weekend."

"Arcturus?" Kylie tipped her head to the side. "That from a movie too?"

"He's black with a white star. Arcturus is the fourth brightest star in the sky and the first coolest name, as Nora says." Wade explained.

"Oh…I like that." Kylie said.

Wade took back the phone from Sadie and swiped through the pictures until he found one of Nora riding Arcturus in Western Pleasure during one of her previous competitions.

Arcturus' black hair shone in the sunlight highlighting his muscular conformation and thick neck. Nora's shimmering black and silver shirt matched the silver and black bridle and saddle. He held it up to Kylie who took the phone. Her fingers brushed his and he could feel the heat run up his fingers and his arm. He glanced up at her and she looked up quickly at him, too. They smiled, then her eyes went to the phone.

"Oh, my…they're beautiful!" She gasped and leaned the phone so her sister could see.

"Oh, wow…" Tara's eyes widened.

Wade took the phone back and swiped to a picture of Nora and both her horses posing proudly with their blue 'best of class' ribbons and Isaiah's first Grand Championship. He turned it to the sisters.

"This is her with Arcturus and Isaiah." He said proudly…of both horses and rider.

"They are both so beautiful!" Kylie said.

The announcer's voice boomed letting them all know the second section of Chute Dogging was now starting and would be followed by the first section of goat tying.

"I gotta go get my goat string," Sadie said and backed Scarecrow away from them.

"What did she draw?" Tara asked.

"She's third out," Wade answered. "Then tie-down for me and we've got until the second section of breakaway for both of us."

"I need food," Kylie said as she looked over at the bleachers.

"You always need food," Tara laughed.

Kylie shrugged which made Wade chuckle.

"I need food too and I need to get Dollar," Wade said and slid down from the fence. "But I want to watch the next round of chute-dogging and Sadie first."

"We can go tie the horses up and meet you on the bleachers to watch her, then go get food when she's done," Tara said with a quick glance at her sister then back to Wade.

Wade nodded with a smile. "Yeah…Sadie always needs food too."

ᴗᴗᴗᴗᴗᴗᴗᴗᴗᴗᴗᴗ

He made sure to sit on the opposite end of the bleachers as his parents, aunt, and uncle. The-chute dogging was nearly completed when the sisters appeared. To his surprise, they sat on both sides of him. He sure didn't want his family seeing that!

The girl's feet hit the bleacher seat in front of them, so they were sitting in the same position as him. The announcer called Sadie's name as the third rider. The three of them leaned forward and waited. The first rider ran down the arena at a good speed but she tripped and stumbled over the ten foot tether rope that attached the goat to the stake in the ground.

The second rider ran down the arena, tied the goat, and stepped back the required three feet. The goat kicked the string loose just before the required six-second rule. She received a no time.

The gate opened showing Sadie and Scarecrow prancing on the other side then they burst forward. They thundered down the arena toward the dark brown goat; the string dangling from Sadie's teeth. She lifted out of the saddle and lowered herself to the left side of Scarecrow. She hit the ground running toward the goat and managed to get the tether rope between her long legs so the goat couldn't run away from her.

In a flash, she had the goat lying on its side and the legs pulled together. Her arm was swinging the string around then looping the final tie…her hands flew up and the judge's flag went down. The clock stopped at 9.79. Sadie had stepped back away from the goat as they waited the required six seconds to make sure the goat remained tied. Scarecrow trotted up behind her.

"Great start," Wade whispered, then he yelled. "Way to go Scarecrow!"

The sister's giggled.

"We always credit our horses first," Wade explained with heat rising in his cheeks.

They sat quietly a moment…Wade wasn't sure if he should stand first or wait for them to. Then, with a sinking feeling, he realized they should have gotten up right away and left to meet with Sadie. He could see his dad and uncle walking in the aisle in front of the bleachers. His dad pulled the phone from his pocket. The motion of tipping his head to the phone caused his eyes to move into the bleachers and connect with Wade's. His dad spoke into the phone as his eyes flickered to the two girls on each side of him. Wade felt the flush of heat rise into his face as the smile crossed his dad's face. Wade didn't move.

The two men continued to walk past him. Wade didn't turn his head; he just followed them with his eyes. His dad's elbow tapped his uncle's arm and a chin motioned toward the bleachers. His uncle turned just as they rounded the corner and disappeared. Wade waited…seconds later his uncle's grinning face reappeared.

Wade couldn't help but smile. His uncle tipped his head then disappeared.

OK, so maybe it wasn't so bad that those two knew, but he sure didn't want his mom and aunt to know. He stood and the girls rose with him.

A half-hour later, the four of them were sitting on the bleachers at the very top, stuffing hamburgers in their mouths and watching the boy's goat tying then the steer riding. They still had plenty of time before Wade would compete in tie-down but they all decided they wanted to be on horseback. After retrieving their horses they walked around the track that circled the arenas and talked about rodeos until Wade rode to the chutes to get ready.

ᙀ ᙀ ᙀ ᙀ ᙀ ᙀ ᙀ ᙀ ᙀ ᙀ ᙀ ᙀ

He met with his uncle and listened intently.

"Relax first…clear your mind of everything except…"

"Rope, calf, horse…" Wade nodded.

"You got this," Uncle Grayson said and patted him on the leg. "Just another rodeo."

Wade took a deep breath and watched the rider before him bust out of the box and chase the calf to the far end of the arena then down the side back towards them. The calf stayed just far enough ahead of the rider that no throw was made within the thirty-second time limit.

Wade and Dollar walked into the arena then turned into the box next to the chute. Dollar pranced excitedly so Wade stroked his neck to calm him down as two men strung out the barrier rope. Once the horse stood still, Wade lifted his rope, swung it over his head once, then tucked it to his side. Deep breath…nods of the head.

CHAPTER FOUR

The metal clanging of the chute opening made his heart beat faster. Dollar lunged forward as Wade began to twirl the rope. They raced down the arena; one…two…three twirls of the rope and he let it fly. It wrapped perfectly around the calf's horns and Dollar slid to a stop as Wade stepped out of the saddle, gripped the rope, and ran down toward calf. He had the calf on its side and three legs wrapped together when he realized that he'd heard a groan from the crowd. He stepped back from the calf and looked back to the box as he ran to remount the horse. He'd broken the barrier…10 second penalty on top of his time. His 12.32 turned into a 22.32. Not a good start.

Deep breath…and a shake of the head in disappointment. The calf was released and he gathered his rope as he trotted to the end of the arena and out the gate. He trotted down to the end of the track and back to try and release the tension and disappointment before meeting up with Sadie and the sisters. He needed their energy to help release the nerves that were mounting.

The next event was Sadie running fifth in breakaway in the girl's section. Wade would be tenth in the boys.

He found Sadie on Little Ghost loping circles in the warm-up arena. The two sisters, minus their horses, were standing next to the fence watching her. They both smiled brightly as he trotted up to them. There…that made him feel better.

The girl's breakaway was about to start as Wade swung his rope around and tried to clear his mind of the two sisters and the broken barrier. Concentrate! He yelled silently at himself. He hoped Uncle Grayson was going to be there to help talk him through and make him focus. He turned to look for him. He was standing next to Sadie and Little Ghost while the announcer's voice said Sadie was the rider on deck.

She was leaning down off the horse toward her dad; the tips of their hats just touching and they were grinning at each other. She spoke but Wade couldn't hear what she said. They both laughed as Sadie sat back up in the saddle with a wide grin.

She turned and saw him and trotted over.

"What did you say to Uncle Grayson?" He asked.

She giggled, her blue eyes sparkling. "He said he would buy me any food I wanted if I caught the calf." She grinned. "I told him if I didn't, I'd buy him what he wanted then I told him he might as well go buy my nachos now."

She laughed as she trotted into the arena with the lariat swinging comfortably at her side. Wade really admired her sense of ease during competitions. He wished he had it.

She backed Little Ghost into the box and, out of habit, reached up and tucked her hat on tighter. She twisted her waist side to side then swung the rope back and forth then tucked it under her arm. The grey gelding danced and the blonde rider nodded her head. The clanging of the chute rang out and the calf made its escape.

They were half-way down the arena with Sadie swinging the rope before they were close enough she could make her throw. The rope floated over the calf's head and Little Ghost's haunches lowered to slide to a stop. Sadie bounced in the saddle as the rope broke free from the saddle horn. Reader board: 7.586

"Good start," Wade whispered.

Sadie started trotting down to the far end of the arena to retrieve her rope but turned in her saddle to look back at her dad.

Wade turned in time to see him grin and wave as he walked into the building to the concession stand.

Wade loped Dollar in circles until his dad and uncle appeared. They stood next to the fence and watched him. When the announcer said he was third rider out Wade walked over to the two men.

They didn't mention the girls, they just talked about roping.

Wade and Dollar walked into the arena and calmly entered the box. "Just another rodeo." He said to his horse.

He backed him in and swung the rope as the two men stretched the barrier rope across the opening. Timing…don't break it this time.   Dollar danced excitedly so Wade turned him in a circle then backed him to the corner again until the horse's rump was against the fence.

Deep breath…everything cleared…concentrating on arm, horse, rope, calf…nod…

They busted out of the chute behind the calf, three rope turns and a throw…4.30.

Wade quickly turned back to the chute…no penalty this time. He heard his dad and uncle yell over the whole crowd as he followed the calf that was dragging his rope to the end of the arena.

The man handed him his rope as Wade stepped through the gate to be greeted by Sadie.

"Way to go, Dollar," She leaned over and scratched the excited horse's ears. "Great start." She high fived Wade.

"Yep," He nodded with a huge internal sigh.

"I'm the last rider of the barrels then I'll come over for the ribbon roping."

"Last rider…"

"Yep, the last rider today makes me first rider tomorrow…and hopefully I have the fastest average so I can be the last rider on Sunday."

"I'd rather be first rider every single time." Wade admitted.

They trotted the horses down the track as Wade glanced around for the sisters.

He heard Sadie chuckle.

"I think they both like you," She grinned.

"Both?" Wade looked at her in surprise.

"Yeah," She laughed.

"What am I supposed to do?"

"Just be friends with both of them until Tara realizes you like Kylie better." Sadie shrugged.

Wade looked at her in surprise. "You can tell?"

Sadie really laughed, then tipped her chin to point behind him. He turned to see the sisters trotting their horses toward them. Wade turned back to Sadie…he knew she wouldn't say anything…Sadie was good that way.

ᴜᴜᴜᴜᴜᴜᴜᴜᴜᴜᴜᴜ

They sat on the horses next to each other and watched the end of the breakaway and the first riders in the team roping compete.

"Sadie? Why haven't we been team roping together?"

"No clue," She chuckled. "You have been team roping with Alex."

"Yeah…but there isn't a reason I can't with you, too." He said thoughtfully. "Hopefully Alex will be here with us next year…if he can get himself to relax."

"He just started with Snickers last year," Sadie said. "It took you a while to start catching during competition."

"At all…" He admitted with a smirk. "I keep telling him to relax but he just…doesn't."

"Maybe between now and when the school rodeos start again in September he'll relax."

"Yeah…maybe," Wade sighed. He really liked Alex. He'd turned into his best friend and after having this year with just him and Sadie, Wade truly did hope that Alex would be there with them next year. His dream was the pair of them roping at the World Series of Team Roping in Las Vegas someday. He just didn't know how to help Alex. Uncle Grayson was trying his best too and in practice, Alex was really good…competitions he wasn't.

"I need to go switch horses," Sadie turned toward the stalls.

∪∪∪∪∪∪∪∪∪∪∪∪

"There are 74 barrel racers and Sadie is last," Wade's dad looked at his mom. "Why am I sitting here?"

Aunt Leah chuckled, "You need a nap or something? You're getting kind of cranky."

Wade chuckled along with the two sets of parents. His eyes were looking in the distance at the two sisters warming up their horses. Tara was the 11th rider and Kylie was the 34th.

His text alert rang out and all four parents looked at him.

He chuckled again and pulled out his phone. They all four leaned in to see the latest picture from Nora.

It was a video. He pushed play and the five of them watched Candace, dressed in English attire and sitting on top of her horse, Lola. A woman walked up to her and handed her a very colorful ribbon.

"Oh, my!" Wade's mother gasped. "She got best in class."

"Good for her," Aunt Leah grinned. "That girl is really blossoming."

Another text alert and another video.

Nora was walking Isaiah over a wooden bridge then perfectly executing a gate pass-through then maneuvering into a box made of four long wooden poles. Isaiah stepped into the poles, turned two perfect slow turns to the right, then the left, then stepped out to the next obstacle. They walked over a series of poles, trotted over another group of poles, then broke into a slow lope over yet another group of poles. They came to a stop and turned to maneuver backward into a path created by more poles. They backed around a corner then broke into a slow lope forward over another bridge and out of the arena.

The camera followed Nora as she bent over and stroked the horse's neck.

A voice was heard from the phone, it sounded like someone sitting behind Candace. "I heard that horse was professionally trained. I'm going down to see who the trainer was and send Chompers to them."

Candace's giggles were heard then the video stopped.

"Oh, that's funny," Aunt Leah giggled.

"I'd love to see the looks on their faces when they find out Nora trained both horses." Wade's dad grinned proudly.

Wade chuckled again when the phone was removed from his hand and both women watched the videos again. Both men walked down the steps of the bleachers.

Wade's eyes went out to the sisters. A rider was making a mad dash from the second barrel to the third. Tara was next to run. When she entered the arena, the sorrel horse reared up then lunged forward before running for the first barrel. Three turns and Wade's eyes went to the timer.

"That was an 18.363 which takes the lead so far. Next up…"

"I'm going to go get Dollar so we're ready for the Ribbon Race." Wade stood.

"No hurry…there's only 60 riders left before Sadie." His mother grinned.

They had parked the two trailers right next to each other and set up the lawn chairs, coolers and a table in between. The awnings were stretched over the top to make a roof. His dad and uncle we're sitting on the chairs and leaning forward to the table where a phone was sitting.

"What happened to it?" Uncle Grayson asked.

"No, clue," Jessup's voice answered. "I went out this morning and the arm of the silo was on the ground. It has a split in it so it could have just been time."

"Glad no one was around to get hurt when it fell," His uncle said.

"Was there any other damage?" Wade's dad asked.

"Nah…just the arm lying on the ground," Jessup answered.

"It's Memorial Day weekend so we won't be able to get parts coming in for it," Uncle Grayson said.

"I did some checking this morning. Spokane has the parts and I can head up there tomorrow and pick it up or we wait until Tuesday and they will deliver." Jessup said.

"Your call," Uncle Grayson said. "Josey and Matt have their heads out of the islands now, so they can help."

"How do the fields look?" Wade's dad asked.

Nikki and Lucas' honeymoon was on a private island for two weeks. They were there alone the first week then Lucas flew Matt and Josey in to surprise Nikki for the second week. They were all tanned and very happy when they returned.

Wade thought Lucas was brilliant for his plan. If it was him, that's what he would want, too. Him and his bride, then Sadie and her husband or boyfriend could join them…and Reilly and then there was Alex. He'd have to make sure it was a bigger island, Wade chuckled.

Knowing he would sit and listen to them talk all day about the fields and farming, Wade made the wise decision to go get Dollar instead. Sadie would be mad if he missed her run and the ribbon race…and there was the fact he wanted to watch Kylie's run too.

He arrived on horseback just as number 25 was running.

He moved to the fence by the roping chutes. The third barrel was right in front of him so he could easily see the arena. Tara appeared to his right.

"Nice run," He smiled at her.

"Still holding on to first but there are a lot of riders to the end," She said.

They sat quietly for a while. Wade wasn't really sure what to say; it was the first time the two of them had been alone.

"So…" He finally said. "What do you do outside of rodeo?"

"Farming!" She laughed. "My parents are divorced and my mom raises horses and works in a law office. My dad is a farmer and I go with him every chance I get."

"Yeah…" Wade grinned at her. "I love farming, too."

They talked about farming equipment until Kylie appeared at the entry gate, then they were quiet.

Kylie and her bay horse bolted to the first barrel.

"Nice…" Tara whispered as the pair finished the first turn. "Nice…" She whispered as they rounded the second. As they rounded the third, Tara exhaled. "I think I got her this time."

"What did you have?" Wade asked as he watched Kylie's hair flying out behind her as she finished the run.

"18.363," Tara answered.

"18.858," Was announced for Kylie.

"I don't see how you knew that with a half-second," Wade shook his head.

"She was a little wide on the third," Tara smiled. "We run neck and neck at almost every race. My third was tighter this time."

They went back to talking about farm equipment until Kylie rode in next to them.

"I'll get you tomorrow," She teased Tara. "What are you two talking about?"

"Wade's a farmer," Tara announced excitedly.

"Really?" Kylie's eyes lit up. "Dad has potatoes and sugar beets."

They talked about crops and harvest until Sadie's name was called.

All three went silent as the golden team trotted into the arena. Wade lifted his phone and hit the record button.

Scarecrow burst into a run and flew to the first barrel. Perfect turn with Sadie's braid flying in the air as her head twirled to look at the second barrel. It was another perfect turn with both horse and rider looking for the third. Scarecrow dug deep and lunged forward with Sadie staring at their target.

With one hand on the saddle horn and the other lifting the reins up high on the palomino's neck, Sadie turned the horse with dirt flying behind them, and her eyes concentrating on the barrel. By the time they were half-way around the third barrel, Sadie's eyes lifted to the finish line.

"Go Scarecrow!" Wade yelled as loud as he could. He could hear yelling from the bleachers too. "Go! Go! Go!" He yelled.

Horse and rider flew down the arena with braid and tail flying behind them.

"Wow, she's good," Kylie whispered.

"Real good…I think she…" Tara started.

"Last rider of the day, takes the lead with an 18.037."

"Yeah…" Tara sighed. "She did."

"That's my girl!" Uncle Grayson's voice rang out over the arena.

"Sorry, ladies, but…Yee Haw!" Wade yelled with a laugh and ended the recording.

He lowered the phone and quickly sent the video to Nora and his mom.

"We have to get ready for ribbon roping now," Wade said and backed Dollar away from the fence.

"We'll be cheering for you!" Kylie called out.

He grinned his way out to the warm-up arena then turned to look down at the stalls. Uncle Grayson and Aunt Leah were there, their heads turned and watching in the distance. They grinned as Sadie appeared trotting toward them.

She slid off Scarecrow, hugged them both then turned to run to the arena as her parents walked Scarecrow to her stall.

He slowly loped Dollar in circles as he watched her cross the parking lot. She was grinning when she stepped through the gate and walked toward him. He lowered a hand from on top of the horse and they high-fived.

"You smoked 'em!" He grinned.

"She did good, but you know, I wasn't as fast on the take off today. If we start at the gate, I can get more speed to the first barrel…maybe take a bit of time off today's time."

Sadie, the wizard, analyzed every move and tried to improve on every run. Wade was always impressed with that.

He chuckled, "Well, don't tell the Reynolds sisters that. They were both a little put out you beat them."

Sadie just shook her head, "They should be looking at how they can improve their runs, not worrying about mine."

"Sadie! Wade!"

They turned to Uncle Grayson waving them to the gate.

"You're next!" He hollered.

"Oh, heck!" Sadie turned and ran to the arena.

Wade trotted behind her. He lifted his rope and swung it around a time or two.

Analyze…he thought back to his tie-down and breakaway throws. They were both good…except for leaving the box a bit too early and getting the penalty. He just wouldn't do it this time, he decided.

Wade trotted into the arena and glanced at Sadie who was walking back and forth…nearly hopping as she did. The energy of her barrel race was still running through her.

Dollar's butt bounced off the roping box and Wade looked up at Sadie. She was staring at him now. She nodded at him and did a quick animated arm swing and run in place…then she grinned.

He laughed and nodded.

The metal clang made his heart race as the calf bolted from the chute. He and Dollar flew out of the box…rope swinging…once…twice…three and a throw. Perfect catch and Wade slid from the saddle as Dollar slid to a stop. Sadie was already at the calf but she couldn't grab the ribbon from the calf's tail until he touched the animal. He ran with as long as strides as he could and grabbed the calf to try and hold it still so she could get to the ribbon. In a flash, she had it pulled off and was running back to the finish line by the chutes.

10.86!

He retrieved his rope and coiled it as he walked out of the arena.

They shared another high five as they walked to the warm-up arena and the two sisters clapping for them.

"Have you ridden bulls?" Kylie asked as the four of them sat on their horses and watched the bull riding.

Wade shook his head, "Did some steer riding but never did the bulls." He looked at Sadie. "I don't know why, it looks fun. Our cousin, Reilly, started riding bulls this last winter."

"We rode sheep when we were little," Tara said.

"Me too," Sadie said. "Just a couple of times but I think steer or the smaller bulls would be fun. I have long enough legs to wrap around them." She kicked out her legs making them all laugh.

The afternoon flew by with the four of them hanging out together. Dinner was followed by watching the three girls compete in the jackpot barrel race. Sadie and Scarecrow won with both sisters placing right behind her. Both congratulated her but neither looked really happy about it.

CHAPTER FIVE

Saturday- Junior High School Rodeo State Finals

The morning sun was bright, the air brisk, and the whole rodeo grounds bubbled in excitement. Wade slid the halter under and up Dollar's nose and buckled it. He stepped out the stall door and turned to see Sadie tying Scarecrow to the horse trailer.

He hesitated and just watched her walk back to the stalls and retrieve Little Ghost from his pen and tie him next to Scarecrow. Every move she made was routine for her as she prepared the horses for the day. When she saddled the horses, her hand was always on one or the other; running a soothing hand down their necks, sides, or rumps. She talked to them about the day and what they needed to do.

She had changed a lot in the last year; ever since her accident. There was more of a contentment and confidence about her riding.

"Wade?"

He turned to see Kylie watching him with her eyebrows drawn together. She looked out at Sadie then back to him. He chuckled with a bit of a blush, embarrassed he'd been staring.

"She's been through a lot this last year," He quickly explained. "I was just thinking about it."

"Anything you need to talk about?" She asked with a slight smile and looked at his hand. "I find myself playing with Clancy's mane when I'm worried about something."

His fingers were playing with Dollar's mane.

He chuckled, "Didn't realize I was doing that." He looked back out at the family's golden team. "She had a bad riding accident a year ago going into the second barrel. Scarecrow slid and rolled."

"On top of her?" She gasped.

"Almost…Scarecrow was able to twist away, but the force of the roll sent Sadie flying out of the saddle and she smashed into a wall head-first."

"Oh…!"

"They thought she was going to be paralyzed…I was with her the first time she moved," He took a deep breath and let it out slowly. "It was…emotional."

"Yes…I'm sure," Kylie whispered.

Aunt Leah appeared next to Sadie and untied Little Ghost. Sadie untied Scarecrow then stepped up into the saddle.

"Took her a long time to recover…longer mentally than physically," He said.

"She's doing well now."

"Yeah, that's what I was just thinking," He glanced at Kylie. "Sadie and I were born a month apart and our families live in the same big house and at the ranch house."

"Wow."

"So we were basically raised as twins."

"Just not identical twins," She laughed.

He chuckled and enjoyed the light in her eyes.

"True…but we've done some scary and stupid stuff together. We've made lots of memories."

"You still are," She pointed out.

Wade nodded. "Yep, when we grow up and I get married, if my wife happens to be a barrel racer…" He paused and blushed. "She'll just have to understand I will always cheer for Scarecrow to win."

Kylie laughed, "I thought you would say Sadie."

He grinned, "They've both been through a lot. Sadie's recovered from hers but Scarecrow and Little Ghosts' whole life are their recoveries."

"What does that mean?"

"Well, Dollar here is the first horse we found of a dozen that were unintentionally starved."

He told her the story and like most people she had to wipe away tears when he spoke of the night the brown colt, Angel, died. When he finished, she looked out at the palomino mare, gray horse, then down at Dollar.

"Just by looking at them, you can't tell."

"Nope, our cousin Nikki makes sure their feed program adjust as they need it and we make sure they are physically fit. Dr. Mark is retired now, and comes over all the time and keeps an eye out for any problems. He calls them his retirement hobby."

"Well, then," Kylie smiled. "From now on, when we run against each other in barrels and poles I will be cheering my heart out for Scarecrow to place third." She laughed. "And those days I'm mad at Tara, I'll cheer her on for second."

Wade laughed. "Scarecrow loves a cheering crowd."

"Wade!" He turned to see his mother standing at the horse trailer.

Sadie was riding Scarecrow and leading Little Ghost into the arena to warm-up the horses.

"I'll see you in the arena," Kylie smiled and walked past him.

Wade ignored his mother's grin as he tied Dollar to the trailer.

UUUUUUUUUUUUU

Wade's first event for the day was chute-dogging. He wrapped his arms around the steer's horns and took a deep breath. Bracing his legs, he ran each step through his mind.

"You ready?" He heard his dad's voice.

Wade nodded.

The gate opened and he could see the line just as the steer thrust out of the chute. He expected to see horns and dirt, but he saw horns and sky instead, and then everything went black. His feet kicked out but there was no ground. When his boots finally hit dirt, he gripped the horns tighter but had no idea where the white line was. It was still dark, so in a split-second decision, he leaned down and ran his hand down the length of the steer's face. He wrapped his hand around the nose, leaned back, and the steer fell to the ground.

In a split-second of clarity, he realized his eyes were clenched closed. They flew open in time to see the flag lower so he let go of the steer. It jumped away from him and within a blink of the eye, three men and his dad were over him.

"Stay down," One of the men said.

Wade looked at him in surprise, "Why?"

He saw a smile replace the worried look on his dad's face.

"You O.K.?" One of the other men asked.

"I passed the white line didn't I?" Wade asked nervously. "I lost sight of it."

"I'm sure you did." His dad chuckled and reached down to touch Wade's cheek then lift his fingers to show the red blood on the tips.

Wade's jaw dropped in shock. "What happened?"

"The steer went airborne as he came out of the chute. When you came down, his horn hit you in the face." His dad answered.

"Did I pass the white line?"

The answer was yes and he qualified for Sunday's rodeo.

U U U U U U U U U U U U U

Sadie's first event was pole bending and it was fast. Kylie came in first with Sadie placing second. Tara slid around the last turn and came in fifth. All three qualified for Sunday's short-go.

Wade had a long wait ahead of him but Sadie was goat tying next. He made sure he was in a good position to record her so he could send it to Nora.

Sadie and Scarecrow entered the arena at a dead run. They were aimed to the right of the unsuspecting tan and white goat. Half-way down, Sadie lifted herself out of the saddle and her right leg over the horse. Her eyes stared at the target. Scarecrow's speed declined just enough Sadie stepped out of the saddle and was already running when her feet hit the ground twenty feet from the goat.

Suddenly, her arms were flying out in front of her as her whole body fell forward and slammed into the ground. Her face sunk deep in the soft dusty dirt. She crawled toward the goat with a hand hitting the rope that was tied to the animal. She quickly made her way up the rope as she scrambled to stand, flipped the goat, grabbed her string, and had the goat tied in two wraps. Her arms flew up, then instantly to her eyes as she stumbled backward the required three feet away from the goat. Scarecrow trotted right up behind her placing her nose in Sadie's back.

Sadie's hands were still wiping her eyes as her laughter rang out to the stands. The announcer called out her time of 12.26 which qualified her for Sunday's rodeo and Sadie's laughter increased as her hands went to her knees.

Both the judge and the student director walked up to her and leaned down to look up into her face. Sadie shook her head. They joined her laughter then the judge turned and waved for someone to help.

Uncle Grayson was out the gate and running across the arena to his daughter. When he reached her, he knelt down in front of her and started laughing when he looked up into her face. He guided her to Scarecrow's side and helped her mount the horse.

They were still grinning when they passed through the exit gate. Wade and Aunt Leah were instantly at their side to see Sadie's face was completely covered in dirt; her eyes were black from the grit.

"Are you OK, Hon?" Aunt Leah asked.

"I can't see anything." Sadie laughed.

The group around them joined their laughter as they walked Scarecrow to the medics. They waited as they washed out Sadie's eyes.

"How did you tie that goat if you were blind?" The medic asked.

"We do it all the time," Sadie answered.

"We started challenging each other with our goat dummies," Wade explained. "It makes for a more challenging practice."

"I'm just lucky I went in the right direction and stumbled into the rope!" Sadie grinned.

"I can't wait to see the pictures from that one." Aunt Leah laughed.

ᘖᘖᘖᘖᘖᘖᘖᘖᘖᘖᘖᘖ

Wade watched four ropers ahead of him get times good enough to qualify for the Sunday short-go. It just made him more nervous. He truly wished he could be the first competitor in every run he ever made.

He walked Dollar into the arena and to the box. His confidence began to dwindle as he thought of the day before. He'd broken the barrier and had the 10-second penalty. He had to have a good run here or he didn't have a chance to run in the short go on Sunday.

"Stop thinking of that," Wade told himself. "One darn calf at a time…just think of the rope, arm, calf, throw." Dollar pranced excitedly. Wade knew the horse was feeling his nerves, so he took a deep breath.

"Think of Alex!" He heard his dad yell. "What would you tell him?"

"I'd tell him it was just another throw," Wade whispered and took another breath. "Just another throw." He felt his body relax and Dollar stopped fidgeting.

Wade nodded. His fear of breaking the barrier again caused a late start from the box and they were way behind the calf. He kicked Dollar and the horse responded with a sudden burst of speed. Wade threw the rope and started to stop…the rope settled around the calf's neck and Wade was flying out of the saddle. It wasn't until after he had the calf on its side and three hooves tied together before he realized there was no ahhh from the crowd this time. They were all yelling loudly.

He ran back to Dollar and stepped into the saddle and turned to look at the time. Only 11.25, he'd beaten his time from the day before and didn't break the barrier!

"Yes!" Wade pumped his fist in the air and the crowd cheered again.

He qualified for Sunday.

Now he had two chances on Sunday to make the Nationals. He wanted the other two; ribbon race and, most importantly, the breakaway.

ᑌ ᑌ ᑌ ᑌ ᑌ ᑌ ᑌ ᑌ ᑌ ᑌ ᑌ

"All you have to do is catch this one and you're in the short-go for tomorrow," Uncle Grayson told Sadie.

"Thanks, Dad. No pressure…" Sadie laughed and walked Little Ghost into the arena. She went through her normal routine of adjusting her cowboy hat, swinging the rope, and twisting at the waist to stretch her back.

Wade was surprised when she did it again. The nerves were finally getting to her. He held his breath and crossed his fingers.

One last adjustment of the hat and she looked down at the calf in the chute. She nodded…

Wade's heart raced as Little Ghost sprang from the box and chased the calf. They had a late break and she was almost all the way to the end when she finally threw the rope. It settled around the calf's neck and she had to back the horse quite a ways before the rope finally broke from her saddle horn. She was shaking her head and smiling as she trotted to the gate to fetch her rope.

She qualified for Sunday but was way down the list. Her chance of making it to National Finals in breakaway might have slipped away.

Wade was still thinking of Sadie when he entered the arena for his breakaway run.

"Stop thinking so hard," His dad yelled at him. "Remember how good it feels when you do everything right. Just do that and you've got it. Just imagine it."

Wade nodded without looking back at him. He had this…he could do it. They practiced all the time for these throws in the arena. That's why they practiced, so they could remember what a good throw felt like.

He backed Dollar into the box and swung the rope around once and tucked it under his arm. Dollar was calm this time because Wade knew he could do it.

He nodded and the calf shot out of the box with Dollar right behind him. It was a perfect run and a perfect throw for a 4.1-second run. It wasn't as fast as Friday's run but he qualified for Sunday's short-go.

Now he only had the ribbon race to run.

ᑌ ᑌ ᑌ ᑌ ᑌ ᑌ ᑌ ᑌ ᑌ ᑌ ᑌ ᑌ

Sadie was the first barrel racer to enter the arena. She had fresh dirt and an excited crowd ahead of her and Scarecrow loved both.

Wade held up the camera at his position at the third barrel and hit the record button the second the gate behind her was closed. She said she wanted to start sooner so he was ready.

Sadie leaned forward and kicked Scarecrow toward the first barrel. It was nearly flawless without a slip or a touch of the three barrels and a time of 18.002, easily beating her time the day before. There was no doubt Sadie would be running on Sunday.

Kylie and Tara both tried to beat her with Kylie running next and landing in second behind Sadie. Tara knew she had to be perfect and more…the look of pure disbelief on her face when she knocked over the third barrel was heart breaking. Even with the penalty, she qualified for Sunday but it would be a long shot for her to make Finals. That only left her pole bending to qualify.

ᴜᴜᴜᴜᴜᴜᴜᴜᴜᴜᴜ

Wade took a deep breath and readied himself for the ribbon race. All they needed was a quick catch and have a decent run to take first place.

He looked out at Sadie. She was standing to the side of the arena waiting with her ankles crossed, thumbs tucked into the back pocket of her jeans…like she didn't have a care in the world.

Dang, she was good.

The last rider finally made their exit and the announcer called their names. He backed into the box, bumping Dollar's rump against the rail.

He glanced at the calf then out to Sadie. She was in a runner's stance now.

Relaxing his arm, taking another breath then the nod…

Dollar bolted out of the box as Wade swung the rope…once, twice, throw! It sailed across the calf's head then settled down. Sadie was already running as Wade stepped out of the saddle to grab the rope connected to the black and white calf. It twisted, bucked, and turned…it was a wild one!

He touched the calf so Sadie could grab the ribbon, but the calf whipped around and caught them both by surprise as the animal hit Sadie's legs first then Wade's. The cousins both ended up butt to butt on top the calf straddling it with their legs battling against each other. He frantically tried to get off as the memory of their five-year-old selves pulling the calf from under the fence during branding so they could tackle it flashed in his mind. He couldn't help the laugh that escaped…then he heard Sadie's laughter, too. He knew she was thinking the same thing.

Finally, he reached over and grabbed her belt at her waist and using his legs to brace himself, he yanked them both off the bucking calf. When he turned, he was relieved to see the ribbon in her hand as she jumped to her feet and ran to the finish line, laughing all the way.

Time: 29.354

They were out of the Sunday short-go.

Wade ran to Dollar, who had stood till during the commotion with just enough tension on the line. The two arena helpers released his rope from the calf as Wade stepped in the saddle.

He trotted back to the gate to Sadie and their waiting parents.

He shook his head. "I'm sorry, Sadie."

"For what?" She laughed. "You caught it fast enough…it's not your fault it tripped us both up. Besides, we'll have lots of wins, Wade." She grinned with a true happy light in her eyes. "I'd rather have that memory, than that win."

"Yeah, me too," He laughed.

ᑌ ᑌ ᑌ ᑌ ᑌ ᑌ ᑌ ᑌ ᑌ ᑌ ᑌ ᑌ

"I think I'm going to walk the track one more time before putting Clancy away," Kylie said.

Wade looked over at Sadie sitting on the top rail of the fence. She nodded her head in encouragement.   He took a deep breath and looked at Kylie.

"Would you like some company?"

To his relief, her brown eyes turned to him, they looked excited.

"Yes," She smiled.

They nudged the horses forward and he was relieved when no one followed.

They were around the first turn and neither had spoken so he glanced at her.

"Are you going to the dance tonight?"

"Yes, Tara wants to go but I'm not a very good dancer."

"I can help," He grinned.

"You can teach me how to dance?" She giggled.

"Yeah," He said excitedly. "I have an uncle who used to be a bull rider and he learned how to dance so he could pick-up girls."

Wade's face turned bright red when she looked at him with a grin. Maybe he shouldn't have said that part. "Anyway…" He chuckled. "He taught us how to swing dance and two-step."

"Is it hard?"

"You kinda feel like a klutz to start," He said honestly. "But once you get the rhythm it's a lot of fun."

"Well, now I really look forward to it." She smiled.

Wade smiled back, "Me too."

They were quiet as they walked around the last corner of the track.

"Do you guys ever rodeo down in southern Idaho?" Kylie asked.

Wade shrugged, "Farthest south is usually Weiser for our high school rodeos."

"Oh," She frowned.

"You're from Nampa, right?"

"Yes," She nodded with a side glance.

"Well, my parents and sister are into cutting horses so we come down for the competitions at the Idaho Center."

She smiled brightly, pulled her phone out of her pocket, and started typing.

He turned and looked out at the low mountains just behind the house to their left. His mood plummeted. He hated it when girls found it more important to type on the phones than talk.

"Wade?" She said softly.

He turned and had to force a smile.

"Are you mad at me?" She tilted her head to the side.

He just shrugged.

"Do you have your phone on you?"

"No."

"Well, when you do, you'll have a friend request from me so we can keep in touch and I know when you'll be in town and I can come see you."

Wade's face heated from the embarrassed blush.

"Sorry…" He whispered.

She laughed which eased the tension.

When they arrived at the dance she was his first dance and his last of the night.

CHAPTER SIX

Sunday Junior High School Rodeo State Finals

Even though many of the trailers and competitors that didn't make the short-go had already left, there was an excitement in the air.

"I have three chances and you have four," Wade said to Sadie as they trotted around the arena to warm-up their horses.

Sadie was riding Little Ghost and leading Scarecrow behind her. They looked so perfectly at ease together. Wade quickly took a picture of the trio and sent it to Nora.

He hadn't completed a full circle of the arena when he received a text back.

Text from Nora: I love them…Sadie included.

Wade laughed.

Text from Nora: Good luck to all five of you.

Text to Nora: Good luck to you five also.

Wade started the day for the family chute-dogging with his dad and uncle leaning over the side talking to him.

Wade calmly stood with the shoulders of the steer next to his hip and the horns tucked into his arms.

"Grip tight, but stay relaxed," His dad said.

"A relaxed tight grip?" Uncle Grayson chuckled. "That's just stupid."

Wade laughed at the brothers as the chute behind him opened and the cowboy turned the steer just past the white line. It was a great run.

"You can do that, just keep your eyes open this time." Uncle Grayson said then turned to his brother. "That's better advice."

Wade laughed again and gripped the horns tighter as the men in the arena tied the rope to his gate.

"You ready?" The man holding the rope asked.

Wade took a deep breath, tightened his grip one more time, tucked his shoulder in and nodded. The door opened and Wade took a step with the steer…then it took a hundred more without him.

He stood in shock that his arms were empty and the steer was running away.

"What happened?" His dad gasped.

Wade slowly looked up and shook his head. He was stunned.

"It's your stupid advice," Uncle Grayson said to his brother. "Relaxed tight grip…just stupid."

They both grinned at Wade and he began to laugh. Their hands reached down to grip his arms and pull him out of the chute.

Well, he wouldn't be going to Nationals for chute-dogging.

ꓴ ꓴ ꓴ ꓴ ꓴ ꓴ ꓴ ꓴ ꓴ ꓴ ꓴ ꓴ

Four riders ran into the arena, weaved and turned before running out; all decent runs which put the pressure on Sadie and the two sisters.

Kylie was the first to ride her horse to the arena gate. Her run was as perfect as the first run on Friday. Wade and Sadie looked at each other.

"Dang," Sadie sighed.

"You can do it," Wade yelled as she trotted toward the gate. "Go Scarecrow!"

He lifted his phone to video the run.

The gates opened and the golden pair burst into the arena. She hit the end pole but caught it to stand it back up. The motion threw her timing off and she barely managed to make it through the first set of weaving without knocking down another pole. The second set in the opposite direction was better and the turn looked perfect. The run to the end was accompanied by their parents screaming from the bleachers and from Wade from on top of Dollar.

She was a full second behind Kylie and without a miracle for one of the rest of the runners, Sadie would qualify for Nationals.

Sadie was grinning with her hand patting over her heart as she trotted back to Wade.

"What an ugly run!" She laughed.

"But you're going to Nationals!" He high-fived her.

Tara was the last competitor to run.

"A decent run gets her to Nationals with us," Kylie rode up next to them. "She just has to keep the poles up."

Tara ran into the arena, a perfect turn at the end, weaving left and right then the turn to weave back. Her turn for the final run was clean until the horse's tail wrapped around the pole and pulled it to the ground as they ran for the end.

The whole crowd gasped, Kylie cried out and Tara was in tears by the time she ran past them. Kylie turned stunned eyes to Wade and Sadie then turned to trot after her sister.

"Whoa…" Sadie gasped with wide eyes. "I did not see that coming."

"Me either," Wade shook his head. "Kind of like a steer disappearing out of your arms."

ᴗ ᴗ ᴗ ᴗ ᴗ ᴗ ᴗ ᴗ ᴗ ᴗ ᴗ ᴗ

"Don't fall this time!" Wade yelled as Sadie trotted to the gate for goat tying.

He was kneeling on the walkway across from the goat so he could get a good video of her. He had sent the pole video to Nora who responded the same way Sadie did…that it was ugly.

Sadie remained standing when she jumped from the horse but had to slide to a stop before running to the goat. With a time of 8.69, she was sure to qualify for Nationals, too. They would just have to wait and see if the points added up enough from the full year of rodeos and State Finals.

ᴗᴗᴗᴗᴗᴗᴗᴗᴗᴗᴗᴗᴗ

At no point in the last few days of rodeo, had Wade been as confident as he was walking Dollar into the roping box for the tie-down. He remembered what his uncle had said the day before and it reminded him to think of that perfect run. He'd done it before and he could do it again.

"You got this!" He heard his uncle yell.

Wade nodded, in his heart, he knew he could do it so he backed into the box, twisted his waist back and forth then swung the rope once before tucking it under his arm. He looked at the calf in the chute and nodded.

Dollar bolted out of the box stronger than he ever had before. Wade was sure the horse had felt his own confidence as he twirled the rope and threw. He concentrated on every swing, the throw, the step out of the saddle and the feel of the rope as it slid in his hand while he ran to the calf.

It was a perfect flip and just a quick bobble of the legs before he had them tied together. As he ran back to Dollar, that sinking feeling ran through him again. He had concentrated so hard on the run that he had blocked out the disappointed ahhh from the crowd.

The announcer confirmed he had broken the barrier, again. With the added ten seconds from Friday and Sunday, there was no way he was going to place to make it to Nationals.

His rope was released from the calf and he trotted down the arena and out the gate. He only had one more chance.

UUUUUUUUUUU

"If you ever get around to watching the video," Sadie said from on top of Little Ghost. "You'll be really impressed with Dollar. I've never seen him break like that."

"I don't need to watch it," Wade ran a hand down the horse's neck. "I felt it when he took off. As confident as I felt, I have no doubt he was feeling it too."

"Just a split-second too fast," Kylie sighed.

"Well, those split-seconds in rodeo can kill you every time," Tara grumbled.

"Or send you to the winner's circle," Sadie said confidently.

"It's just the way rodeo is," Wade nodded. "One split-second you're up and the next you're down."

They all nodded.

"I refuse to dwell on split-seconds," Sadie declared. "I'm going to concentrate on my last run and work on improving it."

"We should all do that," Tara sighed. "But sometimes that is so hard to do."

"Well, right now I have to," Sadie chuckled. "Yesterday's breakaway run was awful. Almost as bad as this morning's pole run," She turned the grey horse. "I'm going over to rope the dummy and concentrate."

"Good luck!" The sisters called out.

Wade pulled out his phone and took a picture of Sadie walking away. He sent it to Nora.

Text from Nora: Horse butts…I think that's half of what we send each other.

Wade chuckled and wasn't surprised when he received another text from her.

This time it was a picture of Lola, Arcturus and Isaiah's big quarter horse rumps together as they were tied to a hitching post.

Wade grinned again and showed the picture to the curious sisters.

"I love quarter horse butts," Tara giggled.

They watched Sadie practice roping until her event was called by the announcer. They quickly found a good spot along the fence to watch.

Sadie remained focused from the practice dummy, to her serious talk with her dad, and into the arena.

Wade sighed. He wished she had the carefree attitude she had on Friday when Uncle Grayson lost the bet and had to buy nachos. Sadie was definitely feeling the pressure, but it seemed to make her focus more.

She backed Little Ghost into the box and swung the rope then tucked it under her arm. She adjusted her hat, swung the rope again, and tucked it again. With eyes narrowed and concentrating on the calf, she nodded.

It was a fast calf but the grey horse kept up and gave Sadie a perfect opportunity to throw…and she did. The rope settled around the calf's neck and broke from the saddle in 3.5 seconds. She quickly turned back to look at the barrier. It was a clean run and it was easy to see her shoulders relax.

She had been in third place when the Finals started and with catching 3 out of 3 calves, there was a good chance she qualified for Nationals in breakaway, too.

ᑌ ᑌ ᑌ ᑌ ᑌ ᑌ ᑌ ᑌ ᑌ ᑌ ᑌ ᑌ ᑌ

"One last walk around the track?" Kylie smiled at Wade.

"Absolutely!" He grinned. "I have time before I rope and will be putting Dollar in the stall after."

They both turned and started down the track, and talked about the horses and rodeo until they were at the farthest corner away from the bleachers.

Kylie stopped and looked back. "Lots of people have left."

"Yeah, it's a bummer it's all over," Wade nodded and turned Dollar so he and Kylie were facing each other as they talked instead of being side by side. Their knees bumped.

"I'm glad we met the first morning. You and Sadie are really fun to hang out with."

"And dance with," Wade grinned.

"That was so much fun. Tara loved it too." Kylie's eyes lit up. "But watching you and Sadie dance together was the highlight. I couldn't believe how good you two are."

Wade shrugged with a proud grin, "We've practiced a lot."

"I hope we get to do it again."

"Well, there's always the school state rodeo next year…and the three years after." Wade smiled.

She laughed, "I think I'd like more than once a year."

"Me too," Wade nodded. "We'll keep in touch on Facebook and text, plus I'll go to Nampa for the cutting competitions. Plus, we can always call each other."

She sighed and nodded. "I guess that's better than it used to be when it was just calling."

"You can send pictures of your ranch to me."

"And I've already liked The Tagger Herd Facebook page and you send me pictures of your place…The Homestead and the ranch." Her eyes looked wistfully at him.

He didn't know what else to say so he just smiled and looked into her brown eyes.

"Wade?" She said softly.

"Yeah?"

"I've never been kissed before," She smiled shyly.

His heart nearly stopped. "Neither have I," He finally admitted.

"I've always wondered who my first kiss would be with," She smiled and he could see the blush on her cheeks. "I always hoped it would be a dashing handsome cowboy who made me laugh."

"Well, I hope you find him," He grinned.

Her laughter danced in the air and her brightening eyes made his heart pound a little harder.

She sighed at the end of the laugh.

"So, you'll be my first kiss?" She asked.

"We'll be each other's first kiss," Wade said nervously.

As they leaned toward each other, Wade's mind raced wondering what he was supposed to do. Eyes opened or closed? If closed, when was he supposed to close them? They had hats on? Would they bump into each other? How long was he supposed to kiss her? Short kiss? Long kiss?

But as they neared, their heads tipped just right and the hats missed and his eyes closed just seconds before their lips met. She had soft lips and he felt his whole body tingling. They leaned back at the same time but only a few inches and looked into each other's eyes.

"Maybe the second kiss too?" Wade said hopefully.

She giggled as they leaned in for another.

As they slowly walked back to the bleachers, she took off her hat and set it in front of her. Carefully, she took off the flag bandana hat-band and handed it to him with a smile.

Wade grinned as he wrapped it around his wrist and tied it tightly. He took off his hat and removed his concho hat-band and handed it to her and watched as she slid it on her hat and looked at him proudly. She was the prettiest girl he had ever seen.

They took a quick selfie together showing their gifts to each other before she rode back to the stalls and Wade rode to the roping dummies.

∪∪∪∪∪∪∪∪∪∪∪∪

Taking Sadie's example, he threw the rope until he heard his name called out as the third rider out.

His dad and uncle were waiting for him at the gate.

"You got this," Uncle Grayson patted his knee then ran a hand down Dollar's neck. "You both got this."

Wade nodded, "Thanks…I'm feeling good."

"And so was Dollar earlier, so walk in with the confidence you had last time. Just be prepared for him to come out strong. He's feeling the energy, too." His dad added.

"I got this," Wade said and he felt it too. He needed a good clean run and he had done that a hundred times before.

Just concentrate, he told himself as he made his way into the arena. He stretched his body up and twisted at the waist to relax the muscles. Two swings of the rope and he tucked it under his arm and backed Dollar into the box. The horse's body was alert…he was ready and so was Wade.

He gave them the nod and the calf bolted from the chute.

Two twirls of the rope…throw, Wade said to himself…just a couple more steps for a solid run…throw…he said again…throw…just as he was finally going to throw, the calf darted to the right and Dollar had to run after him. It took precious extra seconds but Wade threw the loop and it settled around the calf's neck. He slid to a stop and the rope broke from the saddle.

The crowd cheered but Wade knew there was nothing to cheer about. He went for a solid run, not a winning run. He didn't try to win…he just tried for a solid run and it cost him.

He trotted down the arena and tried hard not to look at Sadie, but his eyes darted to her. She was on Scarecrow at the end of the arena, her chin on chest, and hat blocking her face. She knew he needed a faster run to place higher to get the points he needed. If he had thrown when he knew he should have, then he had no doubt he would be going to Nationals with her.

But, he didn't, and he wasn't. His stomach ached and his heart hurt. It took every bit of self-control to keep the tears from falling.

Instead, he patted Dollar down the neck then back to his rump. The horse did perfect…he did not. He did not give it his best; he did not give it his all. Their dream of going to Nationals together was lost…because of him.

Wade walked calmly through the gate then trotted down the long dirt track.

ᴗ ᴗ ᴗ ᴗ ᴗ ᴗ ᴗ ᴗ ᴗ ᴗ ᴗ ᴗ

There was plenty of time before Sadie's last barrel race so he took his time cooling down Dollar then walking him to his stall. He brushed the horse, gave him extra treats, and a couple of extra pats on the shoulder and rump. The horse had worked hard and did everything he was trained to do. Wade couldn't be happier with Dollar than he was at that moment.

He filled the water bucket in the stall, gave the horse his ration of grain and hay, then closed the gate. The pair were done competing for this State Finals and would be loading the horses after the awards were handed out. He put all his tack into the trailer then stood quietly a moment with his finger slowly circling the tooled imprint of Rooster on the saddle. He was trying to get himself in a state of mind that he could face the family's commiserations and Sadie's accomplishments.

They were waiting for him with two hamburgers, nachos, fries, and even a corndog. It made Wade laugh. He had a great family.

He sat with them as the three girls warmed their horses in preparation for their final barrel runs. He didn't want to distract them, they needed to focus. Sadie and Kylie needed clean runs to qualify and Tara needed a miracle. There was no doubt that all three of them were going to try their best to win today.

Tara would be the first to run followed by her sister. Sadie's wish came true; she was the very last rider of the barrel racers. Then they would have to wait for the ribbon roping to be run and the last of the bulls to be ridden. He was also told it would take a while for the final placing calculations to be completed.

Tara's name was announced and she ran through the gate and to the first barrel. Her two runs before, she had waited for the gate to close before she started so she had changed her path.

"Good for her," Wade whispered to himself.

Her time improved to an 18.255 but it didn't beat either of Sadie's two runs. Most importantly, the down barrel the day before lowered her in the standings and kept her from getting the points needed to qualify for Nationals.   Tara walked the horse down the track just like Wade had done. She had to be just as disappointed as he was.

They watched five more riders before Kylie ran into the arena. She had changed her pattern, too. His concho headband around her hat made him smile. He found himself watching it the 18.358 seconds it took her to run across the finish line. Tara's Friday and Sunday runs were faster than Kylie's…it was just that one barrel that cost her. Wade sighed for Tara, but was happy for Kylie. She should make the Finals for poles and barrels.

Sadie was trotting down the track then back.

"The girl has been nervous today," Aunt Leah whispered.

"Yeah," Wade nodded.

Sadie's name was called and the gate opened. Wade caught his breath when she didn't take off from the gate…she waited for it to be closed then turned three circles.

"She's trying to relax," Uncle Grayson stood.

They all stood and stared.

"Just let her run it!" Aunt Leah yelled.

Sadie turned another circle then bolted for the first barrel. With every turn, the whole family leaned with her. They all started screaming as Scarecrow rounded the second barrel and dug in deep for a powerful thrust to the third. Dirt flew as they slid around the third barrel and Sadie rose in the saddle high over the horse's shoulders for that final run. Everyone left on the bleachers were standing and cheering for the team.

"Saving the best for last again!" The announcer yelled. "Sadie Tagger has the two fastest times of the whole weekend with an 18.002 yesterday and a 17.999 run today."

The Tagger family yelled while Sadie's arm pumped in the air then dropped to run it down the horse's neck.

◡ ◡ ◡ ◡ ◡ ◡ ◡ ◡ ◡ ◡ ◡ ◡

The first award to be announced for their group was for barrel racing. Wade turned to Sadie who sat just behind her mother with her chin leaning on Aunt Leah's shoulder. Sadie's eyes were closed as if she was sleeping. With Sadie, there was a good possibility she was.

Tara was fifth, second-place went to Kylie, and Sadie was announced as the State Champion Barrel Racer.

Her eyes opened as a grin spread across her face and she quickly hugged her parents. She turned to Wade with a smile and then hurried down the steps to retrieve her buckle.

He was so proud of her but looking at his cousin and Kylie posing for their picture brought a tinge of sadness to his gut. A hand rest on his knee and squeezed. He knew it was his mom because it was a small hand. He just nodded without looking at her.

Sadie also qualified for National Finals by winning third in breakaway roping and fourth in goat tying. She barely made it up the stairs to hand her mother the goat tying prize when she was announced as the third-place finisher in pole bending. Kylie won first with Tara coming in fifth, that one tipped pole dropped her from first to fifth. The girls were broken-hearted that Tara wouldn't be competing at finals.   He knew exactly how Tara felt.

Wade was watching Kylie when Sadie made it back up the bleachers to sit down with her parents with a questioning look to Wade. He grinned at her and stretched out a hand to see the breast collar she had won for coming in third. Then he reached for the buckles. She, Little Ghost, and Scarecrow had worked hard for the awards and he wasn't going to diminish their wins by his disappointments on his losses.

They began packing the coolers and seat cushions as the final awards of the year were awarded. With the inclusion of her second-place win in the shooting competition, Sadie was announced as the All-Around State Champion Cowgirl and ran down to receive her award of another buckle and a saddle.

As Sadie was posing with Scarecrow, Little Ghost, and the awards, Wade received a text as his dad's phone started ringing.

The text to Wade was a picture of Arcturus' butt in the horse trailer. More horse butts he chuckled.

They were headed home, too.

Wade turned and listened to his dad.

"Is it ready?" He asked whoever was on the phone. "Yeah, we were stopping at the ranch tonight anyway."

Wade grinned; that made their ride home two hours shorter.

"We'll just start baling in the morning then fix the silo when we're done or after Grace and Reilly's graduation party on Saturday. Wade and Sadie are going to be wiped and sleep all the way home. Tomorrow's Memorial Day…they don't have school so Wade can drive, too."

Straight from the rodeo to farming; not bad…Wade smiled.

Wade and his parents loaded the horses into the trailer as Sadie and her parents finished the official paperwork for her trip to National Finals. Before closing the separator door in the horse trailer, he took a picture of Dollar's butt and sent it to Nora.

CHAPTER SEVEN

The long pointed tines in front of the tractor slid into the side of the large square bale of hay. Wade maneuvered the 700-pound bale up into the air then turned the tractor to slowly make his way to the large stack of bales on the edge of the field. He glanced over at his dad in the field across the road. He was stacking the bales in that field.

With a grin, Wade moved the tractor to the short end of the stack of hay and began to lift the bale on the tines up into the air. He glanced at his dad. Since he should be placing the bale on the long end, he was testing his dad to see how closely he was being watched.

His phone rang just as the bale was ready to slide onto the stack. He turned down the volume on the radio.

"Hello?" Wade chuckled.

"Buddy?"

"Yeah, Dad?"

"What are you doing?"

"Checking to see if you were watching," Wade grinned.

"Oh, you're such a smart aleck."

He could hear his dad laugh just before the call ended.

Wade turned the music up louder and maneuvered the bale to where it was supposed to be. He finished clearing the field and took a picture of the huge stack of bales to send to Kylie and Tara.

Text from Kylie: Love me some green hay!

Text from Tara: We got all ours in the barn yesterday.

He made his way to the next field to start clearing and stacking bales.

Text from Dad: Don't forget you have customers coming to pick up hay. Dru told them delivery starts at 5:00. A truck pulling a long flatbed trailer was waiting for him when he arrived at the field at 4:50.

"Afternoon, ma'am," He smiled at the woman after turning off the tractor and opening the door.

"Hi, Wade," The woman waved. "Dru said she was texting you that I was picking up four bales and they are paid for."

"She did," Wade nodded.

He quickly placed four bales on the trailer and as he waved goodbye to the woman, two more trucks drove down the road and stopped next to the field.

He stepped out of the tractor and approached the first driver in a red truck.

"Good morning, ma'am," He nodded to the woman with long red hair pulled into a ponytail.

"I'm Elizabeth Moore, I've already paid for the hay but I talked to a woman…Dru…that said a man named Scott would be here." The woman's eyes narrowed.

"That's my dad."

"Where is he?"

Wade turned and pointed to the north, four fields away. The dust of his father's tractor was barely visible.

"He's clearing the back field."

She stared for a moment then turned back to him, "When is he coming here?"

"He's not," Wade answered. "He'll finish the north fields then head back to the barn."

Elizabeth huffed, "Then who is supposed to load the bale? I don't have a trailer and Dru assured me he could get a bale in the back of the truck."

Wade looked at the truck and nodded, "Yes, ma'am, a bale will fit in there with no problem."

"Am I supposed to come back tomorrow?" She grumbled.

"No, I can put it…"

"How old are you?"

"Thirteen."

"And you're going to put that bale in my truck without damaging it?"

"Sure, it's not that hard."

The woman shook her head.

Wade looked at the other truck. It was white with one of their long-time customers sitting in the driver's seat. The man behind the steering wheel waved so Wade waved back.

"Ma'am? Do you want me to load the hay?" Wade asked patiently.

"I want your father to," She answered.

"Well," Wade said calmly even though he was getting upset. "I'll send him a text and see what he says." He looked at the other truck. "I need to load the other client."

"Fine, I'll wait for your father's answer."

Wade nodded and sent a text.

Text to Dad: Lady here doesn't want a 13-year-old loading the bale in her truck. She wants you to come do it.

He climbed into the tractor and started it. He drove to the stack and placed a large bale in the white truck then waved as the man drove away. Another truck and trailer appeared and Wade loaded one bale in the truck and four bales on the trailer.

He checked his phone but there wasn't a returned message from his dad.

Another truck and trailer appeared on the horizon and Wade recognized it. They were clients who always bought hay from them each spring while the hay was still in the field. It was cheaper that way since they didn't have to use fuel and time to take the hay to the storage barns. He maneuvered the tractor to the stack of hay.

Elizabeth, from the red truck, stepped to the side and waved at him so he drove back to her.

"Yes, ma'am?" He asked after turning off the tractor.

She smiled slightly, "I'm sorry. You're quite obviously good at what you're doing."

Wade nodded, "Been driving tractor for a couple of years now."

She chuckled softly, "Well, I'm new to this area and new with dealing with farmers and their very competent children. I just got off the phone with my husband who explained that farmer's kids learn to drive early. He kind of laughed at me." She smiled. "Thank you for being so polite when I was very rude to you."

"You have cows or horses and you're new to buying hay?"

"I married a horseman," She said. "I didn't know it when I married him but when we moved to Cottonwood he wanted to get back into riding."

Wade nodded, "I understand." He turned to look at the approaching truck and trailer. "They usually buy quite a few bales so I should get yours loaded first."

"Yes, thanks," She smiled.

He, very carefully, loaded the large bale into her truck and waved as she drove down the road. At least it ended better than it started.

Text from Aunt Dru: Scott said you were loading hay. One more coming your way but not until 6:30.

It didn't take him long to get the eight bales loaded for the next client and they stayed for a while to talk about the good quality of the hay, the weather, the predicted drought, and of course the tractor he was driving. All the typical stuff people wanted to talk about. He didn't mind when it was all about farming. If it wasn't farming then it was rodeo.

As the truck and loaded trailer drove away, Wade turned the tractor to the field. He would continue to clear more bales out of the field until the customer arrived.

Thinking of rodeo made Wade think of that last calf in the breakaway roping. He should have had it. He knew it was all his fault and couldn't blame anyone else but that didn't make it easier to stomach. Why didn't he try his best? Why did he have to hesitate and twirl the rope when he should have been throwing? His heart ached. Even if he had missed and didn't get a time, it would be better than knowing he didn't try his best and didn't get to go to Nationals with Sadie.

Someday he would tell Sadie and she would forgive him, but he didn't think he would ever forgive himself.   She hadn't talked about the trip or her disappointment of Wade not going with her. They had barely seen each other before she left for horse camp with Nora and Candace.

He managed to stack eight more bales before he saw the dust flying on the road indicating someone was coming, so he turned the tractor and drove back to the stack of hay to wait for them.

It wasn't the client that arrived, it was Jessup. The foreman grinned at Wade as he stopped alongside him. With Jessup sitting in the truck looking at him through the opened window, Wade opened the door of the tractor and turned to place his feet on the platform and his elbows on his knees. He didn't know how many times he and Jessup had talked like this, but it would never be enough.

"You have any food in there?" Jessup asked as he tipped up his slanted 'Gus' straw cowboy hat. "Drove off and forgot my bag of snacks."

The man always had whiskers covering his jaw. Each year there was a little more grey taking over the black whiskers. He was slender because he was so active and could out-walk anyone when they had to climb a hill, which everyone but the foreman hated to do.

"Always," Wade laughed and stretched behind him and retrieved his little cooler that his mom had filled that morning. "Mom's trying to fatten me up so she gives me way more than I can eat."

He handed the cooler down to Jessup.

"Or she knows I'm gonna come steal some," The foreman grinned and pulled out a bag of chips, one of the two sandwiches that remained, and an apple.

"Probably that," Wade laughed as he took the cooler back and set it on the floor. "She's been a bit of a homemaker at the ranch since everyone is gone this week."

"Where'd they all go?"

"Cora went to Seattle to visit her sister. Sadie and Nora are with Aunt Leah back at that horse camp in Fort Collins with Candace and her Aunt Paige."

"Grace and Reilly are in Texas with his grandparents," Jessup nodded and took a bite out of the sandwich.

"With Nikki, Josey, Matt, Dad, and Uncle Grayson up here putting up hay it makes the Homestead pretty darn quiet this week."

"So, basically Jack and Dru have run of the place."

"Yep," Wade nodded.

"Which horse did Sadie end up taking?"

"Little Ghost," Wade sighed and thought of Sadie on Scarecrow.

"Something on your mind?"

Wade shrugged. Maybe talking with Jessup would help ease the ache in his stomach. "It's just…"

"What?" Jessup's eyes narrowed in concern.

Wade took a deep breath and just started talking. He told him about the last breakaway run where he took the extra swings and knew he didn't need to. He spoke of Sadie's disappointment which just made him even more upset and sick to his stomach. He was honest and told Jessup that his heart ached every time he thought of Sadie leaving for the Finals without him.

Jessup sat quietly and just nodded. He listened without interrupting and didn't mention the tear Wade had to wipe away when he finished.

"Life is hard sometimes," Jessup finally sighed. "You have your ups and downs…if you didn't, how would you learn and grow?"

Wade just shrugged and sighed. He did feel better saying it out loud, but the fact that Sadie was going and he wasn't still made his stomach ache.

"Wade?"

He looked over at the foreman to see a very concerned expression.

"If you had another chance today to throw that loop again, would you do your best?"

"Of course."

"If you had that chance next week, or the week after, next month…would you do your best?"

Wade nodded with his back straightening and his stomach tightening, "Every time."

Jessup smiled, "This is just a bump in the road that taught you a mighty lesson. Give it your all. Always do your best so you have no regrets."

"I guess," Wade nodded again. "But she's still going without me."

"This year…but look where she is now. She's out horsing around without you."

"But that wasn't our dream," Wade huffed with a smirk. He didn't want to be at horse camp instead of farming, so that didn't bother him. "We wanted to go together."

"You're only thirteen," Jessup pointed out. "You didn't make it this year but the reason taught you a pretty strong lesson which is going to make you try even harder next year…and the year after."

"Yeah, it will," Wade admitted.

"And not just in getting to Finals. I bet everything you do from this point forward, you're going to be trying your hardest and giving it your all. The last thing you want, is to be feeling like you do right now."

"Everything, Jessup," Wade smiled. "I'll try my hardest cuz this feeling, well, it sucks."

They chuckled at each other.

"Life lesson, learned," Jessup said. "Be proud of Sadie, Little Ghost, and Scarecrow. Cheer them on. Give them all the love and encouragement you can. Don't let her know just how upset you are."

"I will," Wade realized how much better he felt just talking with the foreman. "Thanks, Jessup. I really needed to talk to someone besides Sadie."

"Well, you're talking," He smiled. "That's been the worst thing about raising you kids. You just hold too much in."

Wade grinned at him. Yeah, Jessup had helped raise them, too. "How come you never had any kids?"

"My ex-wife had two kids when we married," He answered.

Wade gasped in surprise. "I didn't even know you were married before."

"Before I met the Trio," Jessup huffed. "Raised the kids for a little over two years and decided I didn't need any of my own because I felt like they were mine."

"What happened?"

"Summer before I went on the skiing trip and broke my hip, she decided she wanted more in life than to live on a ranch. She wanted the city life and took the two kids and left."

"Dang, Jessup," Wade shook his head. "How old were they?"

"Molly was nine and Dan was seven. I thought of going to the city with her, but it was one of those decisions in life you have to make." He shook his head. "I would have been miserable living in the city and just made their lives miserable, too."

"Do you ever talk to them?"

"Tried to stay in contact, but they moved to Phoenix and she remarried. I moved to Idaho to help raise a bunch of farm kids."

Wade laughed at the humor in Jessup's eyes.

"Well, I'm sorry it worked out that way, but their loss was definitely our gain," Wade said honestly. "I couldn't imagine life without you being in it."

Jessup grinned, "I kinda feel that way about you Taggers, too. There was a reason it all happened the way it did. Same as you not throwing that loop quicker. It taught you a valuable lesson…it happened for a reason."

Wade nodded, "Yep, I guess."

The customer he was waiting for appeared down the road so Wade swung his legs back into the tractor. He looked back to Jessup.

"Thanks, I feel better."

"You can talk to me any time you need. I'm here for you."

With that, the foreman waved and drove away.

ᘿ ᘿ ᘿ ᘿ ᘿ ᘿ ᘿ ᘿ ᘿ ᘿ ᘿ ᘿ

"Why didn't you text me back?" Wade asked his dad at dinner.

"Did she let you load the bale?" His dad lifted the steak from the barbeque and placed it onto Wade's plate.

"Well, yeah," Wade answered. "After she watched me load a couple other trucks and trailers."

"Then there wasn't a need for me to respond." His dad smirked.

"Scott, how could you ignore a son in need?" Uncle Grayson teased.

His dad shrugged. "I knew Wade could handle it and I wasn't about to stop clearing the field until it was done. That would have taken over an hour to stop what I was doing, drive over there, load the bale, tell her Wade would have been fine, and then drive back. Besides, it would have told Wade I didn't trust him."

Wade's mom chuckled and winked at Wade, "He's such a stickler with time…hates to waste it."

"Yeah," Wade nodded with a raised brow to his dad. "It was more about that dang hour."

They all nodded.

"Which means we get going on replacing the silo arm first thing in the morning," His dad countered. "That way, if we need any other parts, Dru can still get it up here tomorrow."

"Nikki is expecting a couple of horses in the morning and Matt is going to stay with her until they leave, just in case she needs help." Wade's mom said.

"Benny will be at the silos with the crane at seven o'clock," Jessup added.

"If we're there at six o'clock, we have time to get everything ready and save him time," His dad said.

"Save Benny time…" Wade's mom whispered.

Everyone chuckled.

"How is Jack in the Sling doing?" Wade asked. Nikki was rehabilitating a horse that had spent six weeks in a sling in her barn after a truck had run into the trailer he was in.

"He is limping around," Jessup answered. "Kate said she still wasn't convinced he was going to heal completely."

Kate, Wade thought, she was the veterinarian Jessup had been dating for over a year, but she had broken up with him the month before. No one really knew why. Wade wondered if Kate had known Jessup was married. Surely he had told her. Could that have been why Kate broke up with him?

"Well, the horse couldn't be in better hands," Uncle Grayson said. "Nikki's done a great job with all the horses she's taken in."

Wade's mom nodded and stood to clear the table, "Josey and that sorrel she named after her late Dad's horse…"

"Preacher," Jessup added.

"Yeah, they just started training. His wounds all healed well and he has full movement." She continued.

"We don't need Matt to start," Wade's dad said. "With Benny in the crane, we need someone in the elevator bucket and someone holding the rope to guide the arm. We'll have plenty of people."

Wade smiled as his knife cut into the steak. His dad probably thought they were wasting time talking about horses and not the job in the morning.

ՍՍՍՍՍՍՍՍՍՍՍՍ

The next morning, Wade stood excitedly watching his dad help Benny backup the large crane next to one of the three silos on the south side of the elevator access road.

They were round silver galvanized metal containers that held their harvested grain. His dad had said they were thirty feet tall. They were so wide, Wade couldn't see his uncle's four-door truck, even though it was parked right behind it. The truck was sitting on the wide dirt access road that separated the three silos from another two. It was parked under the large tank and elevator that moved the grain from the big grain trucks and into the silos.

Long white metal tubes, they called arms, ran from the top of the elevator to the tops of the silos so the grain could be poured into the containers for future use.

Their job today was to replace one of the metal arms. It was forty foot long and heavy so they used the crane to lift it above the metal silos. His dad hend Benny attached the crane's cable to the triangle metal bar that protruded out of the middle of the long white arm.

Uncle Grayson was really tall and strong, so he held the rope that was hooked to the arm to help guide it in place. The end of the arm had to be attached to the top of the elevator and to the top of the silo. Wade's dad climbed up the metal ladder that placed him at the top of the elevator. He was over 40 feet in the air and would be in charge of the top of the arm. Jessup stood on the roof of the silo where the tube would be attached. He was in charge of the bottom of the arm.

"Wade, move Grayson's truck out of the way," His dad yelled just as Benny began to lift the arm.

Wade loved driving the big silver truck so he quickly climbed up in the seat. He had to push the button to move the seat forward so he could reach the gas pedal. He was growing taller every month but was still a long way from his uncle's 6' 4".

Just to be safe, Wade moved the truck forward thirty feet past the end of the silos. He stepped out of the truck, shut the door with a slam, and looked up to his dad at the top of the ladder.

He was stretching an arm out to grab the end of the tube, but when it was within inches of his fingers it suddenly fell away. The tube slid down and with a bang, it crashed into the roof of the silo making it vibrate. Like a teeter-totter, the top of the tube fell to the ground between the silos while the end that had hit the roof rose back up. Something went flying in the air and fell to the ground across the road from where the truck had been.

"What…?" The word barely escaped Wade when his dad started yelling and was quickly descending the metal stairs in a panic.

"What happened?" Wade ran forward toward the silos but stopped when he saw what landed on the ground. A cry of fear escaped him as goose-bumps rose on his arms.

He ran.

CHAPTER EIGHT

It was Jessup he had seen flying over 40 feet in the air off of the grain bin and landing on a leg before falling to his side. He was now lying on his back on the ground in the only small patch of grass that surrounded the silos.

"Wade! Call 911!" His father was yelling as he descended the ladder.

With a trembling hand, Wade pulled his phone from his pocket and looked at it.

"There's no service," His voice shook.

Uncle Grayson was suddenly at his side, kneeling next to an unconscious Jessup. There was blood pouring from his nose.

His uncle turned to Benny. "Get in the truck and drive to the top of the hill…or to the Anderson house…see if they have a land-line."

Benny ran for Uncle Grayson's truck.

Wade was shaking; his stomach quivering…he stood frozen in place as if a statue. His father and uncle were kneeling over the foreman.

It was clear that his leg was broken, because an inch of the thigh bone had pushed through the denim of his jeans. There was blood under his swelling nose and a streak across his forehead. When Jessup moaned, Wade fell to his knees next to his head…he felt so helpless.

"I'm afraid to move him," Uncle Grayson said. "Did you see…?"

"He landed…as if he jumped…on the leg that's broken then just crumpled to the ground," His dad's voice trembled. "He just…when the tube slid back down and hit the roof of the silo, it shook him over on top of it. Then, when the top fell to the ground the portion of the tube on the silo…that he was on…flew up and launched him out…forty feet…over forty." He exhaled in anguish. "It looked like he had wrapped his arms in front of him to protect his body and head."

Jessup moaned again.

"I didn't see anything…just heard it." Uncle Grayson said and turned to Wade. "Get in Scott's truck and get the emergency blanket."

"Get the paper towels in the back seat," His dad added.

Wade stood and stumbled, then ran for the truck. He pulled the emergency blanket from under the seat and picked up the tube of paper towels.

When he returned, Jessup's eyes were open.

"Let me up," Jessup grumbled.

"You can't get up," Uncle Grayson leaned over him and held his arms down.

"Grayson, get off of me," Jessup pushed against him. "What's the matter with you?"

"You've been in an accident and need to stay down," Wade's dad said as he bundled the towels and tried to wipe away the blood from his nose and chin. "Just stay calm."

"Let me up!" Jessup grumbled again and tried to move his head away from the white towels that were quickly red.

For ten minutes, Wade listened to Jessup yell then start swearing at his dad and uncle as his confusion and anger grew.

Benny returned with a screeching of tires against dirt and gravel.

"I called 911 and Matt. He was already coming down the mountain…he should be here any minute." Benny said. "Look at that leg…"

The blood had soaked the denim around his thigh.

"There has to be internal injuries, too," Uncle Grayson said.

"His nose is crooked and swelling," Benny added.

"He's talking well," Wade whispered. "So maybe no head injury?"

"Don't talk about me like I'm not here," Jessup grumbled and tried to sit up but was held down.

They heard Matt's engine roar before they saw the truck. He pulled all the way around so he was right next to them when he jumped out of the truck.

Wade stepped back as Matt ran to Jessup's side.

"Life Flight helicopter is already on the way and so is an ambulance," Matt said as he took a knife to Jessup's jeans and cut from the hem all the way to the hip, then pushed the material away.

The white bone had punctured through the skin by at least three inches. Wade felt sick and looked at Jessup's face in amazement. He looked mad…not like he was hurting.

Silently, Matt pointed to the tip of Jessup's cowboy boot which was turned too far to the right then to the knee that looked odd. Even through the swelling and bruising it was easy to see something was wrong.

"Good thing is, the bone missed the artery when it broke," Matt said. "It's through the muscle."

"Internal injuries?" Uncle Grayson whispered.

Matt cut the shirt to expose his chest then gently slid his hand along the sides. There was a bruise already developing along his left side. Wade guessed it was where Jessup had fallen onto the pipe.

Matt looked at his uncles in concern. Wade's stomach ached as the air left his lungs. Jessup was unconscious again…this was bad.

An ambulance with two paramedics arrived. They were friends of Matt's and worked with him to keep the foreman stable until the helicopter arrived.

It was another twenty minutes before the thumping of a helicopter's blades brought all their eyes to the sky.

Wade's dad stood and ran around the silos to a farmer's field just up the hill. The grass had just been baled in small squares. Wade and Benny ran up the hill to help clear the bales out of the way. They may have weighed a hundred pounds each but all three of them were tossing and carrying them out of the helicopters way as if they weighed ten pounds.

At the top of the hill, as the helicopter lowered to the ground, Wade pulled out his phone.

"I have one bar," Wade yelled at his dad.

Once the helicopter was down and the blades quiet, his dad took out his own phone and pushed the buttons.

"Dru…there's been an accident," He said.

Wade listened to his dad and watched the paramedics gather their supplies and backboard and make their way down to Jessup.

"Dru and Jack are calling everyone and driving up to the hospital in Spokane to meet him." His dad said.

"Why Spokane?" Wade asked.

"The extent of his injuries…"

With a sinking heart, Wade nodded and followed his dad back to the silos. They stood to the side and watched the paramedics. Ninety minutes from the moment the arm fell and Jessup was injured, the helicopter rose in the air to take him to the hospital.

"Dru and Jack are already headed to Spokane," Uncle Grayson told Matt.

"Call her and tell her to go Lewiston," Matt sighed and looked at Wade and the three other men. "They don't know if he would make it to Spokane."

Wade gasped; his whole body trembled in disbelief.

"I'll call her," His dad exhaled. "Let's go."

Benny ran for his truck while the four of them loaded into Uncle Grayson's truck.

The drive seemed to take forever.

ᴗ ᴗ ᴗ ᴗ ᴗ ᴗ ᴗ ᴗ ᴗ ᴗ ᴗ

Jack was standing alone in the lobby of the emergency entrance of the hospital when they arrived.

"They took him back for x-rays," Jack said. "Dru is with him."

"Who did you call?" Uncle Grayson asked.

"Everyone but Grace, Reilly, and Leah," Jack answered. "We didn't want to call them until we had answers."

Uncle Grayson shook his head, "Leah needs to know now. We'll let her decide what to do with the kids and horses." He took out his phone and stepped outside to make the call.

He passed Wade's mom, Nikki and Josey as they ran into the hospital. His mom instantly wrapped her arms around him. It made him feel better…a little. Nikki was on the phone with Lucas who was in Australia with Nick, Tessa, and Alex.

Aunt Dru walked out of the door to the emergency room; her face was pale, tears being wiped away.

She looked around the group of family and friends…her voice trembled, "They said to come back and say goodbye."

CHAPTER NINE

"NO!" Wade gasped; his mother's arms squeezed and her body shook with a sob.

Aunt Dru turned to him…another tear fell, "They don't know if he will make it out of surgery. They are running more tests for internal injuries but we only have until the surgeon arrives." She wiped away another tear. "He's on pain killers so he is a bit loopy."

She turned and walked through the doors with the group following behind her. Wade felt numb…as if in a dream, like the night Sadie was injured at the barrel race. It all felt so unreal.

Jessup was lying on his back on the hospital bed. His broken leg was covered with a white blanket and the blood from the swollen broken nose had been wiped away. A large white bandage covered the wound across his forehead. He looked so pale but he smiled as the group walked into the room.

A nurse was behind him adjusting the monitor that was attached to him.

"Well, the gangs all here," Jessup slurred. "I'd get up but Nurse Emily won't let me."

"You have a broken leg," The nurse shook her head at him but smiled compassionately. "You just stay down, they'll understand."

Jessup smiled at her then turned to the group, "She reminds me of Kate. Straight to the point."

Kate? Wade's hand went to his phone. Should they call her?

Aunt Dru took Jessup's hand, the tears were gone and her 'poker face' smiled lovingly at him, "This is your turn to take it easy."

"What fun is that?" Jessup huffed and his eyelids drooped long enough Wade didn't think they would open again. "I forgot my boots at Kate's house."

Everyone in the room smiled with tears glistening in their eyes but Wade. He reached for his phone as he backed out of the room. Just like the rest of the family, the vet clinic that Kate owned was on speed dial.

When the phone was answered, he didn't even let the receptionist talk.

"Is Doctor Kate there?" Wade whispered. He didn't know how his family was going to react to the call but he knew it needed to be made.

"She is…"

"This is Wade Tagger and there has been an emergency. I need to talk to her right now." Wade said forcefully.

"Just a…"

Within moments, Kate answered the phone. "Wade? What's wrong?"

"Jessup has been in an accident and they don't think he's going to make it."

She muffled a cry, "Where is he?"

"We're at St. Joes in Lewiston. He's going back for surgery soon."

"I'll be right there."

The phone call ended. Wade walked back into the room as his mother was leaning over the foreman and kissing his forehead.

"Careful," Jessup slurred. "Scott's right behind you."

Even Wade smiled on that one.

"Where did you go? You alright?" Aunt Dru whispered to him.

He looked at her…not sure he should say anything.

"Just spit it out," She frowned in concern.

"I called Kate."

She exhaled deeply and nodded as she slid an arm around his shoulders, "Good call…go talk to him now."

Wade looked at Jessup trying to keep his eyes open as he smiled at Nikki and Josey then Wade turned to Aunt Dru. He looked at her with wide eyes and spoke firmly, "I'm not saying good-bye to him."

"I didn't either," She admitted. "I told him good luck, sleep well and I'd see him after the surgery."

"OK, I can do that," Wade nodded and stepped to the bed next to his mother.

"Wade…broke the same leg as I did last time," Jessup grinned with the eyelids drooping again. The skin across his swollen nose and under his eyes was a light purple.

"Well, maybe they'll fix it better this time and you won't have a limp," Wade's mom teased.

"But I like your limp," Wade huffed but smiled at the foreman. "Alex will be mad if he still has his limp and you don't."

Jessup slowly shook his head, "Love that kid…"

"We all do," Aunt Dru said and turned to look at her brothers. "Did anyone call Nick and Tessa?"

Nikki nodded, "They are still in Australia but I spoke with Lucas. He was driving over to Nick's place to tell them."

"Jessup?" Wade touched his arm and the older man looked at him with fluttering eyelids and glassy eyes. "Remember when we talked about doing our best so there were no regrets?"

"Yeah, Boy…things happen for a reason," Jessup slurred.

"Well, now it's your turn," Wade said. "You do your best and get back from surgery…give it your all."

"Best tell the surgeon that," Jessup smirked.

"We will," Aunt Dru smiled.

"Don't be going to any white lights in the sky," Wade told him with a serious and nervous smile. "You do your best, no regrets, and we'll have you back in the saddle."

"Back in the saddle again…" Jessup sang softly then chuckled. "I always loved that song."

"We'll sing it to the mountains and back," Wade grinned.

"I`m back in the saddle again, out where a friend is a friend…" Wade and Jessup sang together then smiled at each other.

"Excuse me?" A different nurse said from the door and the whole family turned. "There is a lady out here insisting on coming back…she said you called her."

"Kate?" Wade asked.

"Yes…that's what she said," The nurse answered.

"Kate's here?" Jessup's eyes opened all the way. "Maybe she's bringing my boots, then I can get out of bed."

Wade smiled at him and sighed inside. He did the right thing by calling her.

When Kate appeared, she was still wearing the white jacket she wore at the clinic. Her hair was pulled back in a ponytail and she walked to Jessup as if no one else was in the room.

"There's my lady," Jessup smiled and his whole body relaxed into the bed.

"There's my cowboy," Kate said softly with tears brimming her eyes.

"Did you bring my boots?" He slurred.

She looked at him a moment then slowly turned her head to Aunt Dru.

"He's convinced he left his boots at your house this morning," Aunt Dru explained. "He's a bit pain killer loopy."

Kate nodded and turned back to Jessup, "I'm keeping them at my house until you can walk in and get them yourself."

Jessup sighed and his eyes closed, "Broke my leg again…they are going to fix it…probably get rid of the limp."

"But I like your limp," Kate smiled.

"That's what Wade said," Jessup whispered.

"Excuse me, but they are ready for him in surgery," A nurse stood at the door.

Everyone stepped out into the hall. Wade's mother took his hand and squeezed tightly. He needed that, it made watching them wheel the bed down the hall a little easier. The fear of never seeing Jessup again made his breathing hurt. It was all he could do to keep himself from running down the hall after them.

"If you'll follow me, I'll take you to the surgery waiting room," The nurse said.

The whole group silently walked behind her to the reception area where half a dozen friends were waiting for them.

"There are a few more people on their way," Jack told the nurse as she led them to a waiting room right outside the surgery doors.

"The receptionist will let them know where you are," She said and smiled at the family. "Dr. Mallick will be here in a few moments and let you know the extent of the injuries."

"Thank you," Jack answered.

Wade stood at the window. He could only see the parking lot from where they were. Benny was pacing just outside the doors to the hospital and talking on his phone.

"Did you contact Leah?" Aunt Dru asked from behind him.

"Yes," Uncle Grayson answered. "She is making arrangements to fly her, Sadie, and Nora home…Paige and Candace too if that's what Paige wants to do. Dr. Mark is back there with them so he will drive the horses home."

"Jessup is going to be very upset they came home," Aunt Dru said. Her jaw tightened making the muscles twitch but her eyes moved to Jack and his arm slid around her waist. He pulled her close to him.

Benny's wife had arrived as well as a half dozen of Jessup's friends.

After a half-hour of silence, an older tall man in green scrubs appeared. The doctor stood at the door and his eyes wandered over the large group of people looking back at him.

"I'm Dr. Mallick," He started and stood with back straight and spoke with a compassionate but strong voice. "Starting from the top, he broke his nose and cheekbone but, miraculously, there is no bleeding or swelling of the brain."

"Oh, thank heavens," Was sighed throughout the room.

"Also," The surgeon continued. "The large dark bruise on his side indicated internal injuries but through another miracle, he only has a few broken ribs." He paused and shook his head. "We can't guarantee there are no more internal injuries but right now it looks promising."

Another relieved sigh from the room.

The doctor continued, "That would be because his leg took the force of the fall. He has a broken pelvis, obviously, the femur, every tendon and ligament in the knee is stretched or torn in half. The knee cap is shattered as well as the fibula and tibia which will all need to be rebuilt. His ankle is a mess and we'll rebuild it also." The doctor looked around the room. "He is an extremely lucky man."

"Yes…yes, he is," Wade's dad sighed. "He landed in the only grass area in between the silos."

"It could have been so much worse," Uncle Grayson added.

"The surgery will take hours…eight or more. This will be the first of many." The surgeon said then looked around the group of people hanging on his every word. "There is a very clear possibility that he will lose the entire leg."

The room was silent.

CHAPTER TEN

The doctor nodded and disappeared behind a door.

Wade turned and looked back out the window. The numbness increased…the whole leg…his body trembled. How would Jessup be able to handle that?

A movement in the parking lot caught his attention. It was Kate's sister, Helen. They had not seen her since the day Helen had been at the Homestead to check on Rufio's injured leg. She and Sadie had gotten into an ugly argument about using a twitch on the horse. Wade had basically told the veterinarian to leave the property. They had not seen the woman since that day even though she was an owner of the clinic with her sister.

"I'm going to call Leah and see what she wants to do," Uncle Grayson walked out of the room.

"I'll call Cora," Matt said and followed him.

"I'll call Lucas and Dad," Nikki said and followed the two men.

"Has anyone called Grace and Reilly?" Aunt Dru asked and turned to Jack.

"No, I was waiting for…" Jack stopped and sighed. "I'll go call them." He left the room, too.

Kate turned to Aunt Dru, "What happened?"

"You may want to wait before answering that," Wade said.

Everyone in the room looked at him and Wade turned to look at the door. As if they had planned it, Helen walked through the door and everyone turned to her.

Helen's eyes widened as she looked around the Tagger family and friends then stopped on Wade before continuing to her sister.

"Are you alright?" Helen asked her.

"Jessup was in an accident," Kate stood and her back straightened. "I came to see him and he just went into surgery."

"Yes…Maria told me that," Helen said. "But, are YOU alright?"

Kate's shoulders lowered as her eyes began to glisten, "I will be if he is," She whispered.

"Is it alright if I wait here with her?" Helen asked Aunt Dru.

"Of course," His aunt nodded.

The room was silent as everyone took seats.

Jack appeared and stated Reilly and Grace would remain in Texas for the next twenty-four hours then decide. Jessup would be upset if they left early because of him.

Matt returned and announced Cora was already at the airport and ready to board a plane. She was coming home. Matt reported the plane from Australia carrying Lucas, Nick, Tessa, and Alex was already in the air.

Uncle Grayson returned.

"Well?" Wade's mom asked.

"She decided they will stay in Fort Collins until the end of the clinic. It's only another day and Jessup will be recovering from the surgery." He answered and sat down. "She'll decide after the clinic on flying or driving home."

The room grew quiet until Kate sat straight up again and looked at Aunt Dru, "What happened? How did he get hurt?"

Wade's dad answered since he was the only one that saw the whole accident.

After he was done, Kate frowned at him, "What do you mean the only grass spot?"

"Three silos on one side of the truck ramp that goes under the elevator and two on the other," He answered. "The dirt road is almost as hard as the cement at the base of all the silos. He could have hit it, the silos themselves, the cement footings, the elevator…anything there would have been worse, but when he came down on the leg, it tipped him over and his head and upper body landed in the grass."

"It's only about three-feet wide and at a slight slope so he had room to roll," Uncle Grayson added.

Kate exhaled loudly, "What are the odds?"

No one answered.

An hour into the surgery, the waiting room was quiet. People were looking at magazines, or reading and typing on their phones. In the silence, Wade's stomach decided to grumble…loudly. Everyone looked up at him and all he could do was shrug.

"Let's go to the cafeteria," His mom stood.

His dad stood, too. The three of them walked to the cafeteria together and filled trays with food and drinks. When they sat down, Wade's mother took his hand then one of his dad's. There were tears in her eyes.

"I am so sorry you two had to see that and Jessup is going through this," She whispered. Wade squeezed her hand. "I have been missing Nora terribly and this has just made it that much worse."

"I agree," Wade and his dad said.

They had barely begun to eat when Helen walked into the cafeteria. She glanced around and when she saw Wade she walked right to them.

"Something wrong?" His dad asked and started to rise.

"No…it's still quiet," She answered and pulled up a chair to their table. "We need to talk."

Wade just stared at the woman. He didn't really know what to say since their last meeting was so hostile with him kicking her off the Tagger property and her refusing to ever work with them again.

"What is this about?" His mother asked cautiously.

Helen turned to Wade. Kate was tender and soft…really pretty. Helen wasn't as pretty and she had a stern toughness about her…like she was always ready to yell at you.

"I'd like to apologize to you," Helen said to him in an honest soft voice.

His jaw dropped in surprise.

"I was wrong for not listening to you and your cousin," She continued. "I'd had a bad day…well, week actually and I took it out on the two of you."

Wade wasn't really sure what to say.

"I should have known one of your horses would not need a twitch, in fact, I very rarely use one. Although there are times one is needed, it was not with your horse." Helen looked to his parents then back to Wade. "Scott, Jordan…Wade…again, I apologize."

"So do I, ma'am," Wade said softly. "Maybe I could have handled it better."

Helen shook her head, "You were the calm one of the three of us. You have nothing to apologize for. I'm a grown woman and shouldn't have been taking my frustrations and anger out on you nor that horse."

"I accept your apology," Was the only thing he could think to say.

"Helen?" His mom said.

The woman turned to her, "Yes?"

"This situation…" Her hand moved between Wade and the veterinarian. "Is this why Kate broke up with Jessup?"

"Jordan…" His dad shook his head.

"No," Helen answered. "That was between the two of them and her son. Kate has been lonely and missing him terribly but nothing I could say would make her call him."

"Well, thank you for answering the question," Wade's mom said. "I've been concerned about it but he wouldn't talk to anyone."

"Well, when he comes through, hopefully, they will get back together and she can tell her son to go to…" Helen stopped, blushed slightly, and then shrugged. "She can tell him to mind his own business."

"Agreed," Wade's parents nodded.

"Would you like to have lunch with us?" Wade asked.

Helen smiled and Wade thought that she wasn't so harsh looking when she relaxed, even a bit prettier.

"Thank you for the offer. I'm going to grab something for Kate and take it to her." She stood.

Wade's phone chimed.

Text from Nora: You will tell me the truth, how is he?

Text to Nora: Broken ribs, nose, cheekbone, and disassembled leg. No head or internal injuries. Hopefully will be fine after surgery but may not limp anymore.

Wade decided not to tell her about the possibility of Jessup losing the entire leg.

Text from Nora: But I like his limp.

Wade smiled.

When they arrived in the waiting room, Cora had joined the group. Her hair was shorter than when she had left; a lot shorter, just above her ears. It made her look smaller but younger than her 72 years.

She stood quickly and walked right to him and wrapped him in her arms. He sighed into her. With just a look or a touch, she could bring tears to his eyes.

"How are you?" She whispered.

"I'm OK," He said.

She leaned back and looked into his eyes. Thankfully, he'd grown enough she had to look up at him.

"I understand you saw it happen."

"Yeah," He nodded and the image of Jessup flying through the air made his heart ache.

"I'll ask again," Her eyes were filled with concern and love. "How are you?"

He took a deep breath to hold in the emotions that swarmed through him.

"No," She said and took his arm.

They walked down the hallway and out the door of the hospital. In a secluded area behind a tree, she took his hand and looked him in the eyes.

"That is a terrible thing for anyone to see," She whispered. "Let alone a thirteen-year-old that worships the man. So…you just let it go."

Wade leaned into her and cried.

◡◡◡◡◡◡◡◡◡◡◡

It was nine hours after the doctor disappeared before he returned. Thirty people were spread out through the reception area and waiting room.

The doctor looked exhausted.

"He's in recovery," The doctor said. "At this point, we were able to save the leg…"

Wade's whole body trembled. Goosebumps rose on his arms and he was barely able to keep the tears of relief from falling.

The doctor continued, "…but he has rods, pins, staples, stitches and a brace holding him together. There is an Ilizarov apparatus around his lower leg."

"What is that?" Josey asked. Her hand was firmly wrapped in Matt's hand.

"It's a metal brace, like a cage around it to support and protect the reconstructed bones," Matt answered.

"He's going to be alright?" Aunt Dru asked the surgeon.

"As long as no infection occurs, he should be out of here in a month," The doctor answered. "There will be a couple more surgeries then he'll need somewhere to rehab and he'll need extensive physical therapy."

"Understandable," Aunt Dru nodded. "He'll be well taken care of, but when can we see him?"

"He's in the intensive care unit right now," The doctor answered. "I'm limiting visitors to two at a time to keep stimulation down for the first few days."

The Tagger Trio, Wade's mom, and Kate remained at the hospital while everyone was ordered to go home.

When he arrived at the Homestead, Wade went straight to Dollar and Rooster. He remained there for an hour brushing and talking to the horses. Within minutes of going into the house, he was sound asleep on the living room couch with Cora at his side.

It was still dark when his eyes slowly opened. He could hear Cora snoring lightly and deep breathes from other people. He leaned up on his elbow and looked around. Jack and Nikki were in the recliners. He didn't see Matt or Josey and decided they were in the guest bedroom.

He checked his phone for any missed calls or messages.

Text from Sadie: Is he really OK?

Text from Nora: I'm so depressed and worried…you sure he is OK?

Text from Aunt Leah: You OK, Hun?

Text from Grace: I've checked flights. We can be home this afternoon and hire haulers to bring the horses home.

Text from Reilly: Should we be coming home?

It was 4:30 in Lewiston and 6:30 in Colorado and Texas so Wade silently slipped off the couch and walked out the door. In the barn, he made a group call to all the kids.

"He was in recovery last night," He started.

He told them everything that happened and that he agreed with Aunt Dru; Jessup would be very upset if they all came home.

"Wade…you're sure?" Sadie whispered.

"I am," He said. "You two were headed home tomorrow anyway, and Grace and Reilly on Sunday. I will text or call if there is anything that changes."

"Anything," Reilly said.

"I will," Wade nodded. He understood how hard it was for all of them to be so far away. "I promise I will text you or call if there is anything, but Matt said Jessup would be sleeping for the next couple days."

"What about the ranch?" Reilly asked.

"I'm sure the parents have all discussed it," Wade said. "I'll text you all once I hear anything."

"OK," Grace said. "We'll keep plans the way they are…for now. We'll start the drive home Sunday after the roping jackpot."

"We start our drive tomorrow morning," Nora said.

"He'll be ready for visitors about the time you're all home," Wade said. Hopefully, he thought. "Oh, but, I forgot…"

"What?" They all yelled into the phone.

"Jessup kept talking about Kate so I called her." Wade smiled. "She came right over."

"They got to talk?" Grace asked.

"Yes…they were pretty happy to see each other but I doubt Jessup will remember." He answered.

"But, she's there," Reilly said. "Since she's the one that broke it off and now she's back…"

"It's a good thing," Nora added.

"Oddly enough," Sadie said. "That makes me feel better about staying."

Wade nodded. He thought of mentioning Helen's apology but decided to wait until Sadie was home.

He hit the end button then sent a text.

Text to Aunt Leah: I'm OK, lots of shoulders to lean on here. Love you, Aunt Leah

Immediate text back.

Text from Aunt Leah: Love you too, tell him I love him when you see him, and we'll be home soon.

Text to Aunt Leah: I will

Jack was walking out the back door of the house as Wade reached the steps.

"Have you heard anything?" Wade asked.

"He slept all night," Jack answered. "He's still on pain medicine which will keep him sleeping."

"But he's OK?"

"Yes, everything looks good but they decided to keep him on the ventilator for now."

Wade's eyes widened, "What does that mean?"

"It's the tube down his throat to help him breathe and keep the chance of infection low."

"But…he's OK?" Wade whispered and Jack nodded. The look on his face and the idea of Jessup with a tube down his throat like he'd seen in the movies scared him. "Jack…I need to see him."

"I feel the same way."

Only Cora was awake and the three of them rode to the hospital together.

The building was quiet when they arrived. Jack and Wade's boots beat loudly on the floor as they walked down the hall. The sound echoed into the silence. They shared a smile and both tried walking softer.

When they stepped into the elevator, Cora smiled, "You two will sneak up on no one today."

They chuckled.

"You know where we're going, I hope," Cora said to Jack.

"Dru sent me the room number and directions." He answered.

"Did she get some sleep?" Cora asked.

"She said all five slept on and off throughout the night," The door opened and Jack waved them through first.

They walked through another set of doors and passed numerous rooms before Wade's dad stepped out of one and looked down at them. He stepped out into the hall and closed the door behind him. He looked tired and worried which made Wade's heart race.

CHAPTER ELEVEN

"Is everything alright?" Cora whispered.

His dad nodded and looked at Wade, "I wanted to warn you before you saw him."

Wade began to tremble, "Jack said he had a tube down his throat."

"He does," He smiled slightly. "They shaved him so his face is really white but his eyes are dark purple. There is a bandage over the bridge of his nose to go along with the one on his forehead. His entire face is very swollen."

Wade stopped trembling but the nerves made his stomach hurt.

His dad continued, "He's only woken once and moaned enough they increased the pain medication." He looked at Wade. "There is a device attached to his hand to gauge his pulse at all time…also the IV and tubes up to the monitor."

Wade swallowed hard and nodded, "Like the movies…that's what I've been imagining."

"Good," His dad pulled him into an embrace and squeezed tightly then that little bit more.

"Love you, Dad," Wade whispered.

He leaned back and looked down at Wade with tired glistening eyes, "We'll talk later…you and I are the only ones that saw it happen so I want to make sure you're alright."

"Ok, Dad," Wade nodded.

When they walked into the room, there was a slight beeping and the television was on to the morning news show. Uncle Grayson and Aunt Dru were leaning against the window sill while Kate was sitting in the chair next to the bed. They all three smiled. Wade's mom wrapped him in another embrace.

Wade's eyes went to the man on the bed that was covered in white blankets on white sheets. His forehead and nose were covered in white bandages but still allowed the purple under his eyes, and a small part of very tanned skin to show. It matched the very tan arms that lay to his side.

The swelling was more than he expected…he didn't look like Jessup.

Jack walked to Aunt Dru and wrapped her in his arms.

"How is he?" Cora whispered as she placed a hand on Kate's shoulder.

"Nothing has changed since he came out of surgery," Kate answered softly.

"As long as there is no infection, he should be ok," Aunt Dru added. "They are watching closely for a fever."

With Kate and Cora in Jessup's room, Wade spent the morning in the waiting room listening to the parents talk about the ranch. Moving the cattle to summer pasture was the main project.

"You want to stay here or go with us?" Wade's dad asked him.

Wade thought of Jessup, "I'll go ride with you." He finally answered. It's what the foreman would want them to do and there would be plenty of family to be with him. There was no doubt, Kate wasn't going anywhere.

An hour later, they were at the Homestead walking Dollar and Cooper out of the barn to the horse trailers for Wade to ride during the roundup. The cow dogs, Mavis, Bart, Indy, Pepper and Spur took their places in the trucks and were anxious for the ride.

Wade quickly packed a bag and rode with his dad, uncle, and Jack. Matt, Josey, and Nikki had joined them after being updated on Jessup.

Where they were riding at the ranch, their phones had no service. Josey had drawn the short straw and was waiting at the one spot on the mountain that they could receive a phone call. If anything happened, she would fire three rifle shots in the air and everyone would meet at the ranch.

After an hour, Wade had forgotten to listen for the shots.

Riding Dollar always made him feel better and it did this time, too. He spent the time pushing cows in and out of ravines and across open mountainsides. As he rode, he thought of all the years with Jessup. The image of the foreman stopping the calf and looking down at him and Sadie as they held the lead rope and laughed would always bring a smile to his face.

"We took him for a walk." Wade had said.

"Yeah, that's what it looked like," Jessup had chuckled and helped them stand.

When the first herd of cows was grazing peacefully in the thick summer grass, the riders met at the Tagger ranch for a late lunch. Their phones worked but there was no change in Jessup's condition. He was still sleeping and there was no fever.

"Let's go to the silos," Uncle Grayson said as they walked back to the trucks.

"I agree," Wade's dad nodded. "We'll push the rest tomorrow…I need to see what happened and what needs repaired."

"It will be the first thing he asks," Matt added. "If he remembers what happened."

It took an hour and a half to get to the silos from the ranch and nothing had changed. The crane was still there, the silver truck belonging to his dad was still there, as well as the coolers and tools that had been scattered around for use.

Wade's dad explained to Nikki, Josey, and Jack what had happened. They walked over to the pole that was still resting on top of the damaged silo.

The answer to what had happened was clear; the triangle bar the cable had been attached to was broken.

While they discussed the repairs needed, Wade walked up to the top of the hill where his phone had worked the day before. After taking a picture of the whole site, he sat down on one of the remaining bales of hay and sent the picture and a text.

Text to Reilly, Nora, Sadie, Grace, Alex, Candace: Jessup is sleeping. They shaved him so his face is really white, nose and forehead covered in bandage, eyes black and blue, face swollen, leg in brace. Not sure when he'll wake. We moved a portion of the herd, came to silos to see what happened. Triangle bar broke releasing the cable. We'll move more cows in the morning.

He lowered the phone and watched his dad walk up the hill to him and pull a bale over for a chair. His dad's dog, Spur, trotted next to him and sat at Wade's feet. Stroking the dog's back and neck made Wade feel a little better.

They sat quietly for a few minutes before Wade turned to him.

"You OK, Dad?" Wade whispered.

"It scared me," He sighed and leaned his elbows onto his knees. "I'm better now than I was then."

"Cora says each day will be easier."

"…and once he is better it will seem like a bad dream."

Wade's phone alerted him to a message but he just slid it in his pocket. He wanted nothing more at the moment than this time with his dad.

"How 'bout you, Buddy? You need to talk?"

"No, I'm OK," Wade shrugged slightly. "I felt helpless…him lying there and you and Uncle Grayson helping and me doing nothing. But, watching Matt was pretty cool. He stayed so calm and was so thorough as he worked. He really impressed me but I really hope nothing like this ever happens again and we never have to see him do that again. It was terrible seeing everyone arrive. They were all so scared it made my heart ache. Seeing Kate and Jessup talk to each other…they are so in love…everyone could see it. She came so fast… and then Helen. That was real shocking to see her and have her apologize. I never expected that. I talked to all the kids this morning before we went to the hospital, and I've been texting all day and letting them know what's going on. They are worried but are going to stay…" He sighed. "Sure wish they were here…not that you guys aren't helping, but it's just a kid thing. Cora got there fast…her hair is short…different. Kind of like when Mom cut her hair after the fire a couple of years ago. It took a while but I like it now. Jessup saved her that day…he's always been there for us and when I was pushing the cows I was thinking of all the time with him. Like when he saved Sadie and me. He was…or is going to show me how to brand a calf next year. I just can't imagine what life would be like without him, and we won't have to now, but I'd sure feel better when I can talk to him again."

Wade stopped talking and looked at his smiling dad.

"So…you didn't want to talk?" He teased. "I'm not sure I'm prepared for when you actually want to talk."

Wade chuckled, "I guess I was more scared than I thought."

"Feel better?"

"Yeah, I do," Wade admitted. "What about you?"

"I had Dru and Grayson to talk to last night," He answered. "You come to me anytime you need to talk about it…or anything."

Wade's phone alert beeped again.

"You need to talk more?"

"Nah," Wade smiled.

"You answer the kid's texts, tell them I love them." He stood and placed a hand on Wade's shoulder causing Wade to look up at him. His eyes were stressed but full of emotion. "I love you, Son."

The air caught in Wade's lungs. He stood and wrapped his arms around his dad and held tightly, then squeezed a little bit more. "I love you, too."

While his dad walked back down the hill, Wade pulled out his phone and read the texts.

Text from Sadie: Is Kate still there?

Text from Nora: My heart aches, I want to be there.

Text from Candace: He'll be OK, I keep telling myself that.

Text from Reilly: Sleep is good, Dad says it heals the body

Text from Alex: Storm delayed us in Hawaii, will be there ASAP

Text from Grace: I want to see him…can you take a picture? I need to know

Text to the group: Kate is there, all night. We will all keep saying he will be OK, keep the good thoughts. You'll be here in a couple of days, in time for visitors. Maybe a picture tomorrow…I don't know on that one.

There was no way he was taking a picture with the tube down his throat or with the swollen face.

Text to Kylie and Tara: Our foreman was in a bad accident so we're working and spending time at hospital. I may not text for a while.

Text from Kylie: Prayers to all of you

Text from Tara: That is awful, I will pray for him

Wade joined the group at the silos to clean the area then rode back to the ranch with his dad. Spur sat on Wade's lap and he held the dog tightly.

It was dark and late when they arrived and after calling to check on Jessup they all went to the bunkhouse. After making plans for the morning ride, the room went quiet.

Wade woke to the smell of coffee in the air.

"Aromatherapy," Nikki whispered into the room.

Wade checked his phone but there was only one message.

Text from Cora: He is fine this morning. Less pain killers and not moaning. Looks like he will be waking today sometime.

Text to Cora: Thank you. Love you Cora.

Text from Cora: Back at ya, young man

Wade smiled and rose to start the day.

Even though he had ridden Dollar the day before, the horse had plenty of time to rest so Wade walked him into the horse trailer next to Monty. Uncle Grayson decided to ride Trip, Nikki's younger horse they had purchased at the Billings auction. Isaiah, Eli, Cooper, Rooster, and Scarecrow stood at the fence and anxiously watched with nickers of dismay they were being left behind.

Trooper and Harvey were saddled and ready when they drove into Circle 50 driveway. Matt and Nikki walked them into the back of the trailer. Josey was staying in the 'phone zone' again.

When they stopped at the corrals, they unloaded the horses while Uncle Grayson told them where to ride.

"Wade, you and Matt will ride over to the north pasture and gather that herd. Push them toward Dry Creek Valley." Uncle Grayson said.

They mounted the horses and Wade followed Matt down the road and into a ravine. Bart was Matt's dog, and he led the way as if he had understood Uncle Grayson's directions.

They found the first few cows only a hundred yards down.

"I'll go left, you head that way and we'll meet at the bottom" Matt and Bart trotted away leaving Wade by himself.

The longer he rode, the lonelier he felt. He wanted to look across the valley and see Jessup riding. The foreman never rode a particular horse like his dad did with Monty; he liked to keep three or four ranch horses in shape.

Wade sighed as he moved behind two cows with babies at their side.

"He's going to be OK," He said to Dollar. "A week or two…well months, he'll be back in the saddle…"

Wade's voice faded. Jessup had survived a broken pelvis before but his leg was in pieces from ankle to hip. Then there was the possibility of losing the leg. Would he ever be able to ride again?

Wade's fingers went to the rooster carving on the side of his saddle. Jessup had tooled the rooster and dollar emblems into the saddle Wade had received for his tenth birthday. He'd out grown that saddle and watched while Jessup had worked on the new saddle…the one he was riding now…and his finger was slowly rubbing the rooster.

Wade sighed then realized he wasn't moving.

The two cows had stopped with their calves nursing. With a shake of the head, Wade realized he was so lost in his thoughts that Dollar had stopped, too.

"Come on, ladies," Wade yelled at the cows. "It'll take us forever if we don't get moving."

The cows walked forward with another pair of cow and calves joining them. By the time he arrived at the bottom of the ravine, he had fourteen pairs in front of him and he still felt alone. He turned and looked for Matt but he was two hillsides away pushing a small herd toward the valley. Bart was majestically running up a rock hillside and chasing a cow down to the rest of the herd.

Wade leaned his head back and looked at the sky. He didn't want to be alone with his thoughts and fear anymore.

Dollar's body rose and ears tweaked as his head twirled to look up the hill. Wade expected a herd of elk or deer, maybe a bear, but it wasn't and what he saw brought a gasp of disbelief.

CHAPTER TWELVE

It was Reilly, Alex, Nora, Grace, Candace, and Sadie sitting on their horses looking down at him.

He had to hold back his cry of elation. He very quickly took out his phone and took a picture.

They waved and started their ride down the slope. Dollar pranced so he let the horse trot up the hill to meet them.

Nora was the first to meet him and her expression was a mixture of fighting off tears and trying to grin. They rode next to each other and leaned in for a hug. Wade had to fight off the tears, too.

"I can't believe you're here," He looked around the smiling faces.

"We knew you'd be surprised." Reilly grinned

"But your jackpot…" Wade exhaled in surprise.

"There are lots of jackpots," Grace said seriously. "We only have one family and we needed to be here."

Wade's body relaxed into the saddle, "Did you go to the hospital? Did you see him?"

They all shook their heads.

"Mom said not until he wakes up," Sadie answered.

Seeing her on Scarecrow, made Wade think of the rodeo…his last throw. It made his stomach ache.

"Josey had all the horses saddled and ready for us when we got to the ranch," Candace said.

"Let's get the cows moved," Alex said with a low growly voice. "Then we can get something to eat."

"You sound sick," Wade frowned.

"Yeah," Alex sighed. "Me and Nick started feeling bad on the flight but nothing was stopping me from coming up to ride."

They all laughed and spread out behind the cows for the hour ride to Dry Valley and ride out to the top. By the time they rode away from the 'knee-deep in grass' cows, each of his fellow riders had ridden to him to talk. Sadie was the last.

"How was the camp?" He asked before she could ask how he was doing.

"It was fantastic," She answered seriously. "But, between the state rodeo and going back there? I'm tired." She chuckled. "Having Dr. Mark there was really great. We didn't just do the camp. When we had time, some of his friends took the three of us on a tour." She turned and looked at him with wide serious eyes. "I cannot wait to go there and learn. I want to graduate today and go." Everyone knew she was going to love it. "They are going to review my records and if I keep with the great grades and rodeo record, they will consider a full scholarship! I'd be one of the youngest but…"

She continued to talk until they all arrived at Dry Creek Valley.

The seven of them turned to ride side-by-side up the dirt road with Wade in the middle.

"Wade," Grace said next to him. "Will it bother you to tell us again what happened?"

He shook his head because each time he talked about it, some of the anxiety left his body. He told them as they rode.

"The one thing I didn't tell you," Wade sighed. "Right before Jessup went into surgery, the doctor told us there was a chance he could lose his whole leg."

"What!?" They all gasped.

There was silence which made Wade worry if they weren't going to trust him again or if they were mad.

Grace turned and looked at Wade, "I wouldn't have told us either."

The others nodded in agreement and Wade sighed in relief. The whole accident was bad enough without having them mad at him, too.

When they rose to the long stretch to the corrals at the top of the valley, Grace pushed Eli into a trot. Sadie and Scarecrow were next, then Alex and Snickers, Nora and Isaiah, Candace and Bodi, and Reilly on Cooper. Wade nudged Dollar to keep up. They moved to a heart-pounding lope which created laughter and giggles and the rest of the anxiety to leave his body. He knew it would be back, but for the moment, he let it go and just relaxed into the ride.

Lucas was with a very happy Nikki and Matt when they arrived at the corrals. Wade's dad, Jack and Uncle Grayson were impatiently waiting when the kids rode in.

"I've missed you two," Uncle Grayson said with Sadie and Grace wrapped in his arms. He was squeezing hard and so were they.

Wade's dad grouped Candace into his hug with Nora and Jack's arm was firmly around Reilly.

There was more emotion in the embraces than just missing each other. It was that feeling Wade had when he thought of Jessup. It was a bit of desperation to hug and love family.

Wade and Alex were the only two not in a hug and they just grinned at each other.

"I'm really glad you're here," Wade told him.

"Me too," Alex said with a low grumbling voice. "We met them at the airport so they could bring me here."

"How did you all get here?" Wade asked.

Grace answered from her dad's arms. "Mom called Jordan and told her all six of us wanted to come home so, since Jordan had been on the plane before she asked Jack's parents to contact the couple from Texas that had a plane."

"A couple of years ago, when Andy died, Jordan and I were flown up here by the same couple." Wade's dad reminded them. "We offered to pay their time and fuel to get the kids, Paige and Leah home."

"They are the nicest people," Grace added.

"Where's your mother?" Uncle Grayson asked his daughters.

"Nick, Tessa, and Mom went to the hospital," Sadie answered. "She said you would understand."

"Well, let's get the work done so we can get home," Uncle Grayson sighed. "Reilly, Wade, Sadie, and Alex head to the north pastures and move the cows there through the Windy Valley gate. Shut it then head back to the ranch. Nikki, Lucas, Candace, Nora, and Scott move the young heifers to the south pasture then come back to the trailers. Jack, Reilly, and Grace will help Matt and I move the bulls then meet you there. That should take us to dark. One herd to move in the morning then we'll head to town."

The thirteen riders rode to their designated herds.

Wade and his crew trotted across the wide-open pasture toward Windy Valley. When they arrived at the top of the mountain that descended down to the valley, they stopped and took in the view. Green grass and pine tree-covered mountains, tufts of yellow flowers leading down to the creek at the bottom. The sky was bright blue with just a few wispy clouds on the horizon. A gentle cool breeze swept across their skin. Black and red cattle were grazing peacefully.

The four sat quietly a moment taking in the view.

"I'll never get tired of this," Sadie finally whispered.

"I'm so lucky Mom found you guys," Alex nodded. "I almost didn't get out of bed that morning she wanted to tour the Bed and Breakfast."

"We're glad you did," Reilly chuckled.

Wade turned and looked at the three of them.

Alex; his best friend since the morning they had met during his mother's tour of the family business.

Reilly; his cousin by marriage and brother by heart.

Sadie; true cousins, but raised as close as twins who didn't have to become friends but they did. No two people could be closer than the two of them.

His eyes went back to the expanse of mountains, trees, grass, cows, and sky.

He thought of Jessup who had come to work at the ranch before Wade was even born. This had been Jessup's home for nearly twenty years. He knew these mountains better than all the kids in the family.

"How old is Jessup?" Alex asked.

Wade smiled slightly. He knew all four of them had been thinking of the foreman.

"Fifty-six," Reilly answered.

"This is the only time I ever wished we got phone service out here," Sadie said. "So we could see if there was any news about him."

Looking to his left then right to the mountain and trees, Wade smirked, "Not a cell tower in sight."

They all four chuckled with Sadie looking up to the sky. "We would need a satellite phone out here," She said.

"Josey will fire three shots if she hears anything," Wade reminded them.

A few moments of silence passed.

"Just so you know," Wade said softly and looked down the hill to the cows. "I cannot tell you how happy I am that the three of you are here."

Without waiting for a response, he nudged Dollar down the hill.

The cows were moved onto thick green pastures and the four of them had talked about life and Jessup on their way to the Tagger ranch. It was still daylight when they rode to the barn so they tied up the horses and removed the saddles so they could rest. Then they attacked the kitchen in the house so Alex could eat.

As they fixed lunch and went outside to sit at the patio table, the three of them told Wade about their trips. Alex had a blast in Australia and even saw kangaroos. Lucas' brother, Cid, had taught him how to throw a boomerang. Sadie talked more about the university in Fort Collins than she did the week-long camp. Reilly told them he had seen George Strait at one of the team roping jackpots. Wade was really jealous of that one.

His three companions went back into the house so Wade walked out to the horses. He climbed onto the fence in front of Dollar.

"They had great adventures while we were here working," Wade said to the horse. In his heart…he was OK with that. He was where he wanted to be; at the ranch and farming.

The sound of trucks arriving brought the three out of the house just as Wade's phone chimed.

Text from Mom: He woke up, doesn't remember anything except watching you run to Grayson's truck to move it. He's very worried about you. I've asked your father to bring you to the hospital.

CHAPTER THIRTEEN

Wade jumped down from the fence and quickly untied Dollar to take him to the corrals.

"Wade!" His dad yelled.

"Mom just texted!" He waved.

"What's going on?" Sadie asked as she ran for Scarecrow.

"Jessup woke up," Wade answered.

Horse trailers were hurriedly emptied and unhitched. The dogs were put in their kennel.

Wade crawled into the truck behind his dad with Sadie and Alex next to him. Reilly rode in the front to open and close the gates.

"Did she say how he was?" Sadie asked.

"Honestly," Wade's dad answered. "He was doing OK until they told him what happened. Then, he started to get agitated and worried about Wade so they gave him a sedative."

Wade's heart hurt the whole two-hour drive to the hospital.

When they arrived, Wade didn't wait for anyone else. He opened the door and took off running across the parking lot with the thunder of cowboy boots hitting pavement behind him.

The anxiety rushing through him didn't allow him to wait for the elevator, he ran up the three flights of stairs.

Aunt Dru was standing at Jessup's door waiting for the thirteen of them to arrive. She smiled slightly at the sight.

"He's just waking up," She gave Wade a hug then stepped back to let him enter the room.

Wade passed his mom, Nick, Tessa, Aunt Leah, Cora and Kate as he made his way to the bed. The rule of only two people at a time was temporarily broken.

The tube down Jessup's throat had been removed and whiskers had grown in but the swelling remained. He stood quietly waiting for the foreman to wake.

When his eyes opened, Jessup looked confused.

"What's going on?" He whispered.

"You were in an accident," Wade said. "And we're all here so you know that all of us are OK."

"What happened?" Jessup looked around the room that was wall to wall family and friends.

Aunt Dru took his hand and leaned over the side of the bed and told him about the accident again.

Jessup didn't seem to believe her until he looked down the length of the bed. Then he slowly lifted his hand in the air to look at the needle sticking in his arm and the tube attached.

His eyes went back to Wade.

"I remember you running to Grayson's truck…that's it." Jessup whispered then looked to the other side of the bed at Aunt Dru. "Broken pelvis again?"

"Yes," She said softly. "You improved on the injury this time and shattered the rest of the leg too."

His brows came together and the beeping from the machine behind him increased.

"You going to fire me?" He asked her.

Aunt Dru grinned at him, "You can't fire family."

"Never crossed our minds," Wade's dad added.

"Would never even consider it," Uncle Grayson said.

"Jessup," Aunt Dru smiled. "Don't worry about your job. It will always be here when you're ready. You worry about getting better."

The beeping decreased again as Jessup looked at her then looked behind her. His eyes widened in surprise.

"Kate?" He gasped.

"It's me," She smiled with tears in her eyes.

Aunt Dru stepped back letting Kate move forward and take Jessup's hand.

"So, this is just a dream?" Jessup asked.

"Well, I'm relieved you didn't say nightmare," She teased.

His hand tightened around hers as if it was a life preserver but he didn't say anything. The room was quiet as they stared at each other.

"Hey, since we're all here," Nikki said and broke the silence. She stepped to the bed next to Wade and looked down at their foreman. "I was wondering if you could help me with something."

"I already helped you move into that new house," Jessup smiled tiredly. "And I don't think I'll be moving for a while."

Nikki giggled, "Well, this next project will take more effort than that." Silence filled the room again. "And it gives you about seven months to heal." There was silence again so she continued. "The first couple of months you really don't have to move around much."

"You're pregnant?" Sadie gasped.

Nikki grinned at her then to Lucas and her dad, Nick. "Yes."

"Nikki!" Aunt Dru squealed and wiggled her way through the people to wrap her daughter in her arms.

Jessup chuckled and looked at Wade, "Dru hasn't realized yet that makes her an old grandma."

Wade grinned at him as the family celebrated the news.

"She's gonna be a cool grandma," Wade told him.

Jessup sighed, smiled, and then turned to look at Kate. His eyes closed.

Wade stayed in the room with Jessup all night. They had to tell the foreman two more times what happened before he began to remember.

ひ ひ ひ ひ ひ ひ ひ ひ ひ ひ ひ

"Where's Josey?" Wade asked Matt a few nights later as they met in the kitchen of the Homestead.

"With Grayson," Matt answered.

Reilly smirked, "I thought you two were attached at the hip."

Wade and Matt chuckled.

"Some days I think we are," Matt answered with a smile then his brows rose. "And some days I'm really glad we aren't."

"Where's Alex?" Reilly asked.

Wade sighed, "Nick and Alex were sent to Nick's ranch due to their increasing illness. They were officially quarantined away from everyone…especially Jessup."

They walked into the dining room together and found Sadie, Nora, Nikki, and Grace were already sitting at the table.

"Is it just us for dinner?" Reilly asked.

"And Cora," Nikki answered. "She's in her room but will be out in a few minutes. She said to start without her. Everyone else is either quarantined, at the ranch, or with Jessup."

"Spaghetti!" Wade grinned. "I love Cora's spaghetti."

As Nikki scooped the noodles onto everyone's plates, Wade looked around the table.

"Well, this is weird," He said.

"What?" Grace asked.

"Besides Cora, it's just us kids." Sadie nodded with a knowing smile at Wade.

"Yeah…that doesn't happen very often." Matt picked up the large bowl filled with garlic bread and very un-adult-like tossed each person a piece.

They all giggled.

"Where is Lucas?" Nora asked.

"Where else?" Sadie giggled. "If he isn't with Nikki, then he's with Nick."

"And you are right," Nikki smiled and, with all plates full of spaghetti, lowered onto her seat. "But he's quarantined at the ranch too so he can't get Jessup or me sick."

Wade stared at her a moment, his eyes narrowed in thought.

"So, you're pregnant," He finally said.

Nikki's eyes brightened as she smiled, "Two months, so I'm going to be adding to all those birthdays in January."

"Well," Wade smirked. "You know what this means."

"What?" Nikki leaned back in her chair and looked at him curiously.

"You're going to the dark side," Wade said as seriously as he could.

"What does that mean?" Grace giggled.

Wade turned to her, "She's going to be a parent…you know…the dark side."

Nikki gasped as everyone else laughed.

"I am not…I'm still a kid," Nikki huffed.

"You're what? Twenty-three, married, and pregnant WITH a kid so you're NOT a kid," Wade declared with a glance around the table.

Nikki was turning red as everyone else nodded their agreement.

"Sorry, Sis, you're not a kid at twenty-three…and married," Reilly shook his head at Nikki.

"I am, too," Nikki pouted with a glare at Wade.

He shook his head slowly, "No, you're a parent now…not one of us."

Her eyes narrowed as giggles filled the room.

"I am a kid of this generation…" She started.

He just shook his head, "Sorry, Nikki," He sighed dramatically. "Twenty-three and pregnant kicks you out of our club and into the dark side."

The giggles deepened and grew louder.

Nikki glared at him, looked at her plate then her hand shot out to grab a handful of the noodles. Before he could react, the red-sauce-covered noodles hit Wade smack in the face.

He gasped in surprise as all the other kids laughed. The noodles slowly slid from his face as he stared at her in shock.

"I am too a kid," Nikki growled at him then turned to look proudly around the table.

Well, Wade couldn't let that opportunity go by. He grabbed the noodles on his plate and flung them at her.

Laughter erupted as they hit her on the side of the head, covering her dark hair and cheek. She reached for more noodles and threw them at him but he was able to swat them away in mid-air…they hit Sadie and Nora.

The girls responded by throwing their own noodles at Nikki and Wade. Reilly and Grace's hands went for their noodles as Wade gathered what he could from his lap and plate then threw them again.

Noodles flew in all directions as they laughed.

Sadie turned quickly to Matt who was un-noodled and slowly backing away from the table. Her turn got the attention of everyone else and noodles began to fly at Matt. He laughed and tried to catch them in his mouth. He only managed to get his face covered in the red sauce. He swept the noodles off his chest and plate and tossed them around the table like he was the pitcher on the baseball field. The girls screeched and ducked. Wade and Reilly returned the hard throws.

The bowl that had sat in the middle of the table was quickly emptied as all their hands went in for more. Sadie and Nora were on the floor gathering noodles that had fallen and were quickly sending them flying again.

Cora appeared at the door to the dining room and everyone froze and stared at her.

Her eyes widened as she looked at the noodle and red sauce covered group. The walls were speckled with the sauce with noodles slowly sliding down and falling to the floor.

One noodle dripped from Wade's forehead and hit the floor as he grinned at Cora, "Nikki was trying to prove she was still a kid."

Cora looked at Nikki, "Hon, you're as young as you feel. Heck, I'm only 30."

They all laughed.

"And," Cora looked around at the noodle and sauce covered wall, floor, table, and grinning kids. "…I am not cleaning this up." She turned and walked out of the room.

They all laughed, again.

An hour later, there was no evidence of the spaghetti fight. Wade, Nora, and Sadie were standing outside the barn and watching down the driveway. Their parents were bringing all their horses home from the ranch.

Sadie and Wade needed to practice for the next rodeo in Colfax before Sadie left for the National Finals. Nora and Grace were scheduled for parades and rodeos for the next five weekends in a row. Reilly was leaving in the morning to work at Nick's stock contracting business for the rest of the summer.

Two of the Tagger trucks with horse trailers attached slowly pulled into the driveway.

"I'm so excited," Sadie whispered. "I know that's just dumb."

Wade smiled but had to internally agree, he was excited to be with Dollar too. He'd spent time before dinner with Rooster and the other horses that were now trotting up the pasture fence alongside the trailers. Whinnies echoed across the property.

"That sounds like your phone ringer," Wade said to Nora.

She nodded in agreement.

"I'd want running horses if I had a phone," Sadie added.

"Why don't you have a phone?" Wade asked her.

Sadie shrugged, "I'm usually with Nora or you, so I don't need one."

The trucks came to a halt and they immediately walked to the back of the trailers to release the horses. Sadie squealed when she saw Scarecrow was the first one. After putting the horses in the stalls, they walked out to retrieve the horses in the pasture. The animals were tucked into their stalls with hay and their specific rations of grain and supplements.

Wade was walking out of the barn and toward the house when he received a text alert.

Text from Kate: Call when you have a chance, no hurry

He called immediately. When he stopped, Nora and Sadie stopped with him.

"Hello, Wade," Kate answered.

Her voice was light and airy which made him release the nervous breath he was holding.

"Hi, is he OK?" Wade asked.

"Yes, he just has a question for you," She answered.

"OK…what…?" Wade started.

"Boy," Jessup's growly voice said.

"Yeah," Wade stood up straight.

"You coming to see me tomorrow?"

"Yeah…I can come tonight if you want." Wade said nervously.

"No, Kate's keeping me entertained," Jessup chuckled.

Wade smiled.

"Bring some movies," Jessup ordered. "Don't care which ones, but make sure Lonesome Dove is in the pile."

"Of course," Wade nodded. "We're riding first thing in the morning while it's cool. Sadie and I are going to team rope together at the rodeo next weekend so we have to practice. Then I'll have someone bring me down for the day."

"Sounds good," Jessup said then paused. "You tell her yet?"

Wade exhaled with a glance to Sadie, "No."

"Talk to her…get it off your shoulders," Jessup said. "I'll talk to you tomorrow."

The call ended and Wade slid the phone into his pocket.

"He, OK?" Sadie asked as they walked up the steps to the porch at the back of the house.

"Wants me to bring movies tomorrow," He answered. "He's just bored."

"We'll go with you," Nora said. "I'll drive. I'm still on the driver's permit so we have to have someone older though."

"Cora will come," Wade opened the back door and let the two girls walk into the house first. He looked at Sadie…should he just go talk to her now?

"Why are there noodles on the ceiling?" Aunt Dru asked.

"Nikki," Matt answered.

"Nikki! You're about to be a parent…you can't be throwing noodles around," Aunt Dru's teasing voice called out.

Laughter rang through the house. No, now wasn't the right time Wade decided.

ՍՍՍՍՍՍՍՍՍՍՍՍ

"Park in the parking lot," Wade said to Nora who was driving. Sadie and Cora were with them, too.

"No," She shook her head and looked to the mass of cars in the hospital lot.

"You'll be OK," Cora assured her.

"No, a guy just got in the car by the curb so I'm waiting for him to move," Nora said determinedly. "I'll just slide right in there and not have to worry about hitting a car."

"You just need practice," Sadie added.

"And you're not going to get it if you don't try," Wade rolled his eyes.

The car she had been watching moved and Nora slowly parked the blue pickup. "After hitting that car, Dad told me if there was a junk-yard around he would take me there to practice."

They all chucked.

"You drove that winding grade up to the ranch without a problem," Cora said.

"I've driven trucks with horse trailers attached, combines, the buck-out wagon, and tractors at the ranch long enough that I'm fine with everything but parking this truck around lots of cars," Nora turned off the truck.

"You just need practice," Sadie said again as their doors opened and they stepped out.

"What if I hit a car again?" Nora slung a large bag over her shoulder then placed her hands on her hips. Her black hair was braided down her back and nearly black eyes were wide as she huffed. "That lady I hit the first time yelled at me for at least ten minutes. I don't think she was going to stop but Mom finally told her to be quiet."

"What's that got to do with today?" Wade asked and started walking to the hospital entrance.

"You want to go into the hospital to stay with Jessup this afternoon or stand here and have someone yell at me when I hit their car?" Nora smirked.

They chuckled again and were quiet until they stepped into the elevator.

"Why would you think we would wait with you and not just come in here?" Sadie whispered.

Wade grinned at Sadie and Cora's twinkling eyes.

"I was wondering which one of you was going to ask that," Nora laughed.

Kate and Aunt Dru left as soon as the four of them settled around the hospital room.

"Don't you have a rodeo to go to?" Jessup asked. His bed was lifted just enough he could look at all of them comfortably. The bandage from his forehead was gone but the one over his nose was still there. The swelling had decreased a little.

"It's Tuesday," Sadie smiled from the chair next to the bed. "We rode this morning to prepare for the rodeo in Colfax next weekend."

"We just got here," Wade smirked. "You tired of us already?"

"I'm just tired of all this," Jessup sighed. "How long has it been?"

"It's been a week," Cora answered. "It's good to see the move out of ICU and to the new room has made you a bit more alert."

He turned and glared at her, "Weren't you in Seattle?"

"With my sister," Cora shrugged. "But you know, you can only take so much family." She chuckled and looked at the three kids looking at her in disbelief. "Well, of course, I don't mean you Taggers."

Jessup chuckled then grimaced.

"We thought of something more interesting than movies to entertain you," Nora said and lifted a laptop out of the large bag she was carrying.

"What's that?" Jessup sighed with his eyelids drooping.

Wade thought he looked a little pale, but after everything he had gone through maybe it was normal.

"You like rodeos and bull riding," Sadie said. "So, we started a Cowboy Channel membership so you can lay here and watch them."

"You just said it was Tuesday," Jessup sighed.

"They have all kinds of rodeos saved so you can watch on-demand," Nora said and worked on the computer until one of the bull riding events was playing.

They watched quietly for a while but Wade kept an eye on Jessup. The foreman was watching the screen but his eyes would squint occasionally as if he was in pain. An hour into their visit, sweat appeared on Jessup's brow.

Cora stood and placed a hand on Jessup's forehead. Wade walked out the door to find a nurse.

CHAPTER FOURTEEN

"Hello, Wade. Is something wrong?" Nurse Emily asked as she stepped out of a room.

"Jessup is grimacing like he's in pain and he started sweating," He answered nervously.

She walked past him and into the room he had just left. Wade followed closely. The computer lid was closed with Nora, Sadie, and Cora standing next to the bed. Jessup's eyelids were closed and clenched in pain.

"He's running a fever," Cora said to the nurse.

Wade's stomach clenched…infection?

"Jessup, what hurts?" Nurse Emily asked as she read the monitor that was attached to him.

"My leg…low," Jessup whispered and opened his eyes then took a deep painful breath and let it out slowly.

Sadie, Nora, and Cora stood back away from the bed toward the windows and out of the way.

Jessup grimaced again with another painful breath.

Wade swallowed hard and moved over next to Cora. She put her arm around him protectively.

"I'll be right back," The nurse said as she walked out.

There was silence in the room until she returned and walked to the bedside.

"Jessup?" The nurse whispered. When he opened his pain-filled eyes she continued, "The doctor is on the way…he said to give you a pain killer so I'm going to put the shot in your IV."

Jessup nodded and closed his eyes.

More silence as the nurse disappeared then returned with a needle that she inserted into Jessup's IV.   After a moment, his body relaxed into the bed.

Nurse Emily turned, "When the doctor arrives, you'll need to move to the waiting room." She looked at Wade. "Thanks for coming to get me."

He nodded nervously.

Twenty minutes later, Jessup was beginning to doze when the doctor arrived and the four of them moved to the waiting room.

Wade sent a message in a group text to the whole family.

Text: Jessup's leg is hurting, he has a fever. Doctor is with him now

For the next thirty minutes, Wade answered incoming texts. All he could really answer was "I don't know".

Kate was the first to arrive back at the hospital. She joined the silence as they waited.

Nurse Emily appeared to talk to them.

"They are taking him to surgery," She said.

Wade's chest constricted as Sadie took his hand tightly. He squeezed back.

"It's to be expected with the leg swelling and bruising…as it heals." She continued. "It's going to be a while."

"Should we go down to the surgery waiting room?" Kate asked.

The nurse nodded, "It's going to take a while and I'll let them know where you are."

Wade sent another text to the group.

Text: He's going to surgery, we're headed to the surgery waiting room.

Aunt Dru and his mother were already in the waiting room when they arrived. His mom wrapped her arms around him making him sigh.

"We were just walking in when we received your text," She whispered to him.

"I hate this," Sadie slumped into a chair. Her sad blue eyes were glistening.

Aunt Dru sat down next to her and pulled her into a hug, "They said to expect this."

"That's why he is still in the hospital," Cora said softly. "…so they can catch these things."

"They expect him to be here for a few more weeks and more surgeries," Aunt Dru added.

"We just pray it is not an infection," Kate breathed and sat in the chair opposite of Wade.

Two hours later, the whole family was back in the waiting room listening to the doctor explaining the procedure they had completed. There was no sign of an infection.

No one wanted to leave at the end of the day until they saw Jessup back in his room. They were all there when Jessup woke; the foreman smiled at all of them and went back to sleep.

ᴗᴗᴗᴗᴗᴗᴗᴗᴗᴗᴗᴗ

The next three days were, thankfully, uneventful as they watched a dozen movies, Lonesome Dove, and lots of bull riding and rodeos.

Friday, while Jessup was sleeping, Kate and Wade worked on a secret project. He had to leave early in the afternoon to get ready for the rodeo in Colfax that ran both Saturday and Sunday.

"You give it your all," Jessup told him.

"I absolutely will…no regrets," Wade said.

"You talk to her yet?"

Wade shook his head.

"You tell her and get it out there so you two can move past it and have a good weekend," Jessup ordered.

An hour later, Wade was standing at the gate of the north pasture watching Sadie walk Little Ghost towards him.

"I think I'm just going to love on them tonight," Sadie said as she walked by him. "We've been riding all week and I don't think it would hurt to give them the night off."

"Sounds like a plan," Wade nodded. "We can just rope the dummies from the ground. Both Dollar and Rooster were already walking toward him. They walked right past him and followed Little Ghost to the barn. He loved his red horses.

Scarecrow was the only horse left in the pasture since Grace and Nora had their horses with them in Spokane. All the other horses were at the ranch. The palomino horse was standing with her butt to the gate so Wade whistled. Her head rose from grazing, she turned and looked at him. After noticing the horses were walking toward the barn, she whinnied and starting trotting to catch up.

Pure gold body, long white mane and tail…the horse was just beautiful as she made her way across the pasture. Wade found himself smiling at her. He could still remember how tiny, skinny, and covered in manure and straw she was when they first found her four years before; almost to the day. No one would guess she had nearly starved to death. The thought made him think of Kylie at the state rodeo. Her eyes had looked so sad when he was telling her how the Tagger Herd had come into their lives.

Thinking of Kylie made him think of the National Finals. Sadie and her parents were leaving in less than a week and Kylie would be there to greet them. Wade's shoulders lowered at the thought of his last run…his last throw. It made his head and heart hurt at the thought of not going with Sadie or seeing Kylie again.

Maybe, if he talked to Sadie it wouldn't hurt so much.

Scarecrow ran through the gate and toward the barn so Wade followed.

The closer he got to the barn, the more his lungs ached and his boot heels drug on the ground.

"What's your problem?" Sadie stood in the doorway of the barn. It was a warm night so she had twisted her long blonde hair and pinned it to the top of her head.

"I need to talk to you about the rodeo."

"What about it? It starts in the morning. We're doing just about everything we can. It runs Sunday too, so we'll be tired when we're done but we don't have school anymore so we can just sleep in on Monday then spend the day with Jessup."

Sometimes, she just made him shake his head.

"The State Finals," Wade corrected.

"That's in the past." She shrugged nonchalantly.

"But I need to tell you something."

"It's in the past…just let it go."

He stared at her for a moment with narrowed eyes, "Let what go?"

She sighed, "We dreamed of going to our first National Finals together. We tried really hard and it didn't happen." She shrugged. "We'll have other dreams and work to get those…we can't give up."

"Sadie, stop," Wade sighed. "We always said to try our best…"

"We can't all win, but we can all do our best. That, itself, is winning."

"Sadie, you're killing me!" Wade groaned. She and Nora had said that phrase a thousand times. Was she purposely making this worse?

"And…"

"Sadie! On the last run…I didn't try my hardest. I didn't throw when I was supposed to and didn't try my best. I didn't give it my all…at all. I just tried to catch…I was playing it safe."

"Details…" She looked at him blankly.

"Details…that's your go-to when you know…" He felt his cheeks flush. "You knew?"

"That's why I was so upset," She huffed. "It wasn't because you didn't get the time to qualify. It's because you didn't try your best."

He wasn't sure how he was supposed to feel; relieved or angry.

"I'd never be upset if you tried your best," Sadie grumbled with her cheeks turning red. "I was upset because you blew our dream and I have to go back there by myself."

Wade's jaw dropped in surprise, "But you get to go."

"By myself…" She growled. "I wanted you there."

"I tried in all the other events. I tried really hard…the best I could…I did give them my all. I just got so nervous for that last one…I wanted it so bad that it kind of scared me…made me too nervous." Wade rambled.

She just stared at him with that blank look but he could tell she was upset.

"I'm sorry, Sadie. I truly am. I can apologize to you all night long but it won't do any good."

She shook her head, "Let it go…it's in the past."

It was his turn to frown at her, "Just like that? I'm supposed to just let it go? How, Sadie? How?"

"It's in the past," She repeated gruffly. "If you don't let go of the last calf, you can't concentrate on the next calf."

"You read that on Facebook?" He huffed.

"I don't have a phone or Facebook."

He glared at her.

"Wade," She finally sighed with shoulders rising and lowering dramatically. "If I didn't let go of the accident that nearly paralyzed me, then I could never have moved forward and raced again. I had to let it go…it took a while but I had to let it go and move forward."

Wade sighed in resignation.

"If you don't let go of that last throw, then tomorrow at the rodeo, it's going to be hanging over your head. It's all you will think about and more than likely not throw again."

She was right. It had been bothering him all week and he was going to have to do it again at the Colfax rodeo.

"I promised Jessup that I would always try my best again because I didn't like the way it felt." Wade shrugged. "Give it your all…no regrets."

Sadie huffed again, "Well, at least you talked to Jessup about it."

Wade understood why she was upset. The two of them had always talked about their problems together. This truly was the first time he didn't go to her…except when he broke his arm…but that was different.

Now, he just felt so frustrated and confused. What was he supposed to do? Well…maybe just take her advice.

"The only thing we can do is 'let it go'," Wade smiled slightly. "It's in the past…just let it go."

She smirked, "On one condition…maybe two…"

"What?" He asked warily.

"You promise not to hold out on me anymore."

"Done…we'll always talk." He sighed in relief. "And the second?"

"They are awarding an All-Around Cowboy and an All-Around Cowgirl saddle for the weekend." Sadie grinned with her blue eyes sparkling. "We do our best to bring both of them home."

Wade laughed with an emphatic nod, "Oh, yeah. Give it our all…no regrets."

"Well, I wish Alex was feeling better so he could join us."

Hoofbeats echoed in the barn and they both turned to look. All four horses were in the middle of the aisle succeeding in tearing apart a bale of hay.

Wade grinned with a shake of the head, "They have been in the pasture eating all day. Then they come in here and get to a bale of hay and act like they are starving."

Sadie laughed as they walked toward the horses.

He loved her laugh. It was like Grace's 'life is good' laugh. It always lifted his spirits.

"You think Mom will let me ride a bull tomorrow?" Sadie asked over her shoulder.

"If you get to, I get to!"

CHAPTER FIFTEEN

Dollar, Little Ghost, Scarecrow, and even Rooster were unloaded from the horse trailer at the Colfax Fairgrounds and tied to the trailer. All four horses were saddled and Sadie chose to ride Little Ghost since her first competition was breakaway roping. Aunt Leah stepped into the saddle on Scarecrow. Wade was thrilled when his mom suggested bringing Rooster so she could ride too.

Wade put a boot in the stirrup and smiled at his mom as he rose into the saddle.

"I love this," She said excitedly from on top of the horse. "We need to bring him more often."

"I agree!" He quickly pulled out his phone to take their picture.

"Carrie!" Aunt Leah called out.

Wade turned to see their friend, one of the rodeo coordinators, riding toward them.

"Good morning!" Carrie laughed. "I'm so glad you made it." She turned to Wade and Sadie. "I see you two signed up for everything in your age range."

"Yes, ma'am," Wade nodded. "Even riding the bull."

"Me, too!" Sadie squealed in excitement. "Well, it's a cow, not a bull, but I still get to do it."

Aunt Leah laughed, "Her legs are so long she'll be able to just lock her ankles under it and ride all day."

"I can't wait to watch," Carrie grinned.

"Could you take a picture of the four of us?" Aunt Leah asked and handed Carrie her phone.

The four of them lined up with Wade and Sadie in the middle and the mothers on the outside.

It was a great picture that Aunt Leah instantly sent to everyone in the family.

Just before the first race, Wade called Kate to put their plan in action. She and Cora were going to be in the hospital room with Jessup.

"Good morning!" Kate answered. "Are we ready?"

"For what?" Jessup asked in the background.

Wade grinned in excitement, "Yep, I'll set up the video chat and call you back."

"The laptop is ready!" Kate answered.

Wade made the call and when they answered, Jessup's face appeared.

The foreman grinned in surprise, "Well, look at you." He said to Wade.

Wade waved into his phone, "You enjoyed the rodeo on-line so much, we thought you could ride along with me and Sadie when we're competing."

"That's great!" Jessup smiled tiredly. "I never get to see you guys compete."

Sadie nudged into Wade to look into the phone. "Wade is riding bareback first then it's a ways off before the next event…which is me on poles."

Jessup smiled, "I'll take a nap in between to make sure I'm ready for the rest of the day."

Sadie held the phone toward Wade to show him getting ready to ride the bucking horse that was waiting in the chute. He was going to be the first competitor of the day and then he and Sadie team roping together would be the very last.

Wade rode the bucking horse to the whistle and won the event for the day followed by Sadie placing second in poles, Wade placing second in chute dogging and then winning both steer riding and saddle bronc.

Something had taken over him…a grit. Pure determination that wasn't going to let him let go or fall off the animals.

Sadie was standing at the top of the bucking chute with her protective vest on and lowered the helmet over her head.

She grinned at Jessup on the phone. "Any advice?"

"Hold on and don't fall off until you hear the buzzer," Jessup answered with a smirk.

Sadie laughed. It was going to be her very first 'official' cow riding and Wade was amazed at how calm she seemed.

"But that's only eight seconds," Sadie grinned mischievously. "If I'm having fun, why do I have to get off at only eight seconds?"

Jessup laughed, "I'll give you a dollar for every second you remain on her."

"Oohhh, I love money," Sadie giggled.

She turned to the man helping her lower into the chute and onto the black and white speckled cow. Her full concentration went to the instructions he was giving her.

"Nod when you're ready," The man told her.

She wiggled her shoulders, took a deep breath then nodded.

The gate opened and the speckled cow jumped out of the chute then took off running. Every other stride was completed with a buck in the air of the back hooves. Sadie's legs were tight around the girth of the cow and both hands were holding tight onto the rope. The third buck had Sadie starting to slide off the side but the cow bucked again and set her back on top. The horn buzzed into the air with everyone on the bleachers, standing along the edge of the fence, or on top of the chutes yelling and hollering for her.

"Come on, Sadie!" Wade yelled over and over.

The cow bucked all the way across the arena then down the edge with Sadie holding on tight and her braid swinging behind her. Wade kept the phone pointed in her direction as the pickup men ran along the side of her. Wade could hear Aunt Leah yelling at her daughter to get off the cow.

As if she had done it a hundred times before, Sadie reached up to grab the arm of the pickup man and he lifted her off the running cow. The cowboy slowed his horse to a walk and Sadie dropped to the ground on her feet then jumped in the air with a fist pumping.

The crowd erupted in applause and cheers.

"That's my girl!" Aunt Leah was yelling with her own phone in the air pointed at Sadie.

Wade had no doubt that Uncle Grayson was watching on her phone. His mom had her tablet out and was recording the ride.

Sadie jerked the helmet off her head making her long braid swing wildly. She waved over at her mom then strutted over to the bucking chutes.

High fives were exchanged with everyone in her path as she made her way back to Wade. She climbed the chute and grinned into his phone. Her eyes were shining and aura trembling in excitement.

"I'll be over Monday morning to collect my money," She grinned at Jessup.

"I'll have it here for you," Jessup laughed. "I couldn't be prouder of you and you best get over to your mom."

Sadie laughed, waved and ran down the back of the chutes to her mom.

She followed the win on the cow riding with a win in goat tying with Little Ghost and barrels with Scarecrow. Wade placed third in tying his calf and even in riding his first small bull. It was as exciting as Reilly had told him it would be.

Steer daubing was next for Wade but before he stepped up into the saddle, Sadie appeared. She was carrying a roll of grey tape.

"What's that for?" Wade asked.

Sadie grinned at him then looked into the phone to talk to Jessup.

"I thought you should go along for the ride on this one," Sadie laughed and ripped off a length of the tape.

She took the phone and placed it on Wade's chest then ran a couple pieces of tape across it.

"Can you see?" Sadie asked the foreman.

"I see a cute blonde cowgirl," Jessup chuckled.

Sadie grinned at him.

"Just in case I never told you," Sadie said to Jessup. "I love you."

Her eyes glistened and it was a full minute before Jessup spoke.

"I love you, too," He said in a low voice.

"Ok, so here we go," Wade said quickly to relieve the compression that suddenly rose in his chest. He stepped up on top of Dollar.

"Can you see?" Wade asked as his hand went to the phone that was taped to the center of his chest.

"Yup," Jessup answered. "Right between the horse's ears."

He rode along with Wade as both he and Sadie competed in steer daubing then breakaway. They both won second for daubing the circle on the steer with yellow paint. Wade was second in breakaway while Sadie won her section.

Jessup even rode along with them during the team roping…which they placed second.

On Sunday, they did it all again with as much grit and determination as they had the day before. Jessup, Kate, Aunt Dru, and their fathers watched from the hospital room.

They gave every event their all and tried to win each one.

Aunt Leah held the phone while Sadie and Wade were presented with their all-around cowboy and cowgirl saddles.

"I couldn't have been prouder of you two," Jessup smiled at them from the phone.

"Doing our best so there are no regrets," Wade told him.

"And now I need a nap," Jessup winked and the phone went dark.

As they placed the trophy saddles in the tack room of the horse trailer for the ride home, Wade turned to Sadie.

"Well, I fulfilled my promise," he said.

"Then I can officially forgive you for making me go back to Finals by myself."

They chuckled and high-fived as a wave of relief swam over Wade. Now he felt he could handle her leaving without him.

Wade woke early on Monday morning. The whole house was quiet and he had no idea why he was even awake. Having no patience to lay in bed he rose and dressed to go out to the barn and move the horses from the stalls to the pasture.

He stepped out of his room and took off at a run down the long hallway then jumped into a slide. He nearly toppled over the top of the banister and it made him laugh. Dang, he was going to have to watch that.

No one was awake yet so he grabbed a muffin and a banana then made his way to the barn.

Of course, Dollar and Rooster were moved first. He took the brush with him and ran it down their red hides as they grazed. His heart was finally happy. Jessup was doing better, he and Sadie were on good terms, and they had a really great weekend.

This happy relaxed feeling was what he was going to strive for after each rodeo. Winning the saddles was a great thing, but even when he didn't have as a successful rodeo at least he would know he did his best. It was better than the regrets.

We can't all win, but we can all do our best. That, itself, is winning.

The girl's mantra was so true. He swore he was going to live by it…just like they did.

The horses were nice and shiny when he walked back to the barn for Sadie's horses. Their halters were hanging on the door of the stalls. Wade lifted Scarecrow's in the air and tucked the brush under his arm to be able to slide the handle.

The door swung open…he turned and ran with the halter and brush hitting the floor.

CHAPTER SIXTEEN

"Sadie!" He yelled as he bust through the back door of the house. He was trying to hit Dr. Mark's speed dial button with a shaking hand. "Sadie, come on!" He yelled as loud as he could while running up the stairs.

Doors were opening as he made it to the top. As the people appeared, they were pulling on jeans, shirts, and robes.

Sadie stepped out of her door in bright blue pajama bottoms and her "Tagger Drive-Team" t-shirt. Nora and Grace walked out behind her with eyes wide and curious.

"What?" Sadie asked and rubbed her eyes.

"Scarecrow…" He gasped with a trembling voice.

She didn't wait for anything else. She just took off running past him and down the stairs with everyone right behind her.

"What happened?" Matt asked as he jogged down the hallway from the guest bedroom.

"Hello?" Dr. Mark's voice came through the phone.

"Something is wrong with Scarecrow," Wade told him. "She's down."

"I'll be right there," He said and the call ended.

Sadie had already made it to the barn when the family ran down the porch then across the driveway. She was on her knees next to the palomino's head when they came to a running halt at the stall door.

Lying on her side, Scarecrow's back leg was quivering uncontrollably.

Sadie's terrified blue eyes looked at her father. "Dad?" Her chin quivered.

"Let's get her up," He answered.

All four men stepped into the stall to help lift the horse. Sadie stepped back into a corner and seemed to melt into the wall.

"Get the halter," Uncle Grayson said.

It was handed to Jack and he quickly slid it onto the palomino.

The four men encouraged and lifted the horse. She stood stiffly and her body sighed. The leg relaxed and stopped quivering.

Uncle Grayson led the horse out of the stall. There was an obvious stiffness in the leg and up into the hip. Matt had his arm around Sadie's shoulder in support as the group walked down the aisle of the barn.

"We'll keep her right here," Uncle Grayson said. "We don't want to move her too much until Dr. Mark has a chance to look at her."

Sadie stepped to Scarecrow's head and wrapped her arms around her nose. The horse leaned into her and seemed to sigh. Sadie ran a hand down her nose and covered her eye gently.

"Her eyes are all matted," Sadie whispered and wiped the green and brown gunk off her eye. "This one is swollen."

"I'll get a wet cloth," Aunt Dru said and stepped into the washroom.

Both eyes were wiped clean when Dr. Mark arrived. His truck was backed right up to the stable door.

The family parted from the horse except Sadie who stood at her head.

Wade told the doctor what he had seen when he opened the stall door.

They stood quietly as the retired veterinarian examined the horse. He finally walked her twenty feet down the aisle and back. The stiffness had eased.

Dr. Mark spoke directly to Sadie, "She seems healthy. It could have just been a pinched nerve in her hip causing the trembling since it stopped when she stood."

"She's OK then?" Sadie whispered with wide hopeful eyes.

"Give her the day off," He said and put an arm around Sadie's shoulders. "I'll come over tonight and see how she is."

"Can I call you if I see anything else?" Sadie asked.

"Of course, you can," The older vet tightened the embrace. "You can call me for anything."

"Should we take her to the pasture to stretch out the leg?" Wade's mother asked.

The vet nodded, "Maybe in a pasture by herself to start."

Sadie slowly led Scarecrow down the aisle. Grace, Nora, and Wade haltered the remaining horses and led them to the pasture.

"Well, since you're here," Aunt Dru said. "You'll stay for breakfast."

Dr. Mark nodded with a chuckle. "First, I need to call the missus and let her know how Scarecrow is doing."

"Cora is at the hospital with Jessup this morning," Aunt Leah said. "So we'll get breakfast going."

It was a quiet morning as everyone began to relax from the morning scare.

After checking on Scarecrow one more time, Grace drove Wade, Sadie, and Nora to the hospital to visit Jessup.

He and Kate had watched the video of Sadie's Saturday cow ride and timed her from start to finish. He handed her $42 dollars when they arrived.

They laughed and watched movies the entire day.

Dr. Mark arrived after dinner to examine Scarecrow as they led her to the stall for the evening. Her stiffness was still evident but it wasn't worse.

"Is it OK to give her a deep massage?" Sadie asked.

"Just be careful around that hip," Dr. Mark nodded.

They were in the barn late, and up early in the morning. Scarecrow's hip wasn't better or worse.

"We're supposed to leave on Thursday for the National Finals," Aunt Leah told Dr. Mark when he arrived.

"We'll just have to wait until tomorrow," The vet sighed and looked at Sadie. "Her eyes are still a bit dry and the right one is still swollen. I can't say why. It's pretty late in the season for allergies but that doesn't mean it isn't. Put the fly mask on to protect her eyes as much as possible. The leg could be…well…either way in the morning."

Sadie seemed calm as she nodded her head. She didn't want to leave the horse for the day so Nora stayed with her and it was Grace and Wade who spent the day at the hospital.

When they arrived back at the house, Sadie was sitting on one of the benches in the island in the middle of the pasture. Scarecrow was grazing quietly next to her.

Grace and Nora had to leave for a royalty practice so he walked out to sit with Sadie.

"How is she?" Wade asked as he sat on the bench across from her.

Sadie shrugged, "The same…I guess."

"Reilly texted me that he was on the phone with you most of the day," Wade said.

She nodded, "They are moving the horses and bulls to another town. I can't remember where."

"Me either," Wade sighed and saw Aunt Leah walk into the pasture and towards them. "Here comes your mom."

Sadie sighed.

"Hon," Aunt Leah said as she sat down. "We need to discuss the Finals."

"Tomorrow, Mom," Sadie pleaded.

Her mom nodded, "I'm going to think positive and prepare the trailer for the trip."

Sadie leaned onto her shoulder.

"But," Aunt Leah continued. "You have to consider taking another horse if Scarecrow can't go."

Tears sprung to Sadie's eyes and Wade felt his heart constrict. This truly had been one of the worst weeks he'd ever had.

"I can't go without her, Mom," Sadie cried. "I just couldn't…she's the reason…"

"No, Hon, you also qualified with Little Ghost and we can go back with him and compete in those…it's not just barrel racing."

Sadie clenched her eyes making more tears fall.

"We'll make that call tomorrow," Aunt Leah wrapped her arms around Sadie.

They sat quietly until Dr. Mark's truck appeared on the road.

Sadie rose and slid the halter onto Scarecrow and started walking toward the barn.

"Oh, dang…" Aunt Leah whispered and Wade's heart sank.

The limp was even more pronounced and Sadie had to walk very slowly to lead her. Tears were sliding down Sadie's face when she led the horse through the gate. Dr. Mark greeted her with open arms and she fell into them and cried.

"There, there, my Tagger," He whispered.

"I don't care about the rodeo," Sadie sobbed. "She just has to be alright…she has to be OK."

Tears rose in Wade's eyes and his aunt slid her arm around his shoulders and pulled him into a tight embrace.

His phone alert chimed.

Text from Reilly: How are Scarecrow and Sadie? Kills me I'm not there.

Text to Reilly: Not good, limp worse, Dr. Mark here

Text from Reilly: Let me know after he leaves

An hour later, Wade returned the text.

Text to Reilly: Hip is really sore. Picked up foot and flank quivered for ten minutes when he put it down. Dr. Mark stumped.

Text from Reilly: That is not good.

Text to Reilly: No, it's not

Sadie's tears had subsided but she sat on a bale of straw just outside of Scarecrow's stall. She just stared at the ground.

Wade returned Rooster, Dollar, and Little Ghost to their stalls.

"Sadie?" Wade sat down next to her. His heart and stomach ached.

"She has to be OK," Sadie whispered.

They were quiet until Grace and Nora returned. Wade helped take care of their horses then they all sat next to Sadie.

"You can take Buttercup," Grace whispered. "You know Nikki will offer Harvey, too. They both can run barrels."

"It's not about the rodeo," Large teardrops fell from Sadie's eyes. "She has to be OK."

Grace took her hand and squeezed.

"Sadie," Nora whispered but Sadie didn't move. "Sadie, it's not your fault." Sadie slowly turned to look at her with more tears falling. "You didn't do anything. You didn't hurt her." Nora whispered.

There was something in the way they looked at each other that made Wade feel there was more said then what was said out loud. Sadie finally nodded and leaned her head on Nora's shoulder.

It was a long quiet night and Wade barely slept. He was not surprised to find Sadie asleep on the bale of straw outside of Scarecrow's stall.

She woke when he walked closer and they both looked in at the horse who was standing with her head in the corner.

Scarecrow's flank was quivering again.

They stepped into the stall and Sadie ran a soothing hand over the horse until the quivering eased. Her hand slid up inside the horse's leg and stopped. Sadie's eyes widened then she dipped and looked underneath the horse.

"Wade, look," Sadie whispered.

Tucked into the crease of the leg was a large pocket of loose skin. It looked like there was something under the skin. The horse's underside was wet with sweat.

Sadie took a picture and sent it to Dr. Mark then called him.

"It's an edema," Sadie said into the phone. "OK…OK…"

She lowered the phone.

"What?" Wade asked.

"He's about two minutes away."

"Wow, he's up early."

"He's worried, too."

"I'm going in the house and tell them," Wade turned.

By the time Dr. Mark arrived, everyone was back in the barn looking at the pocket of loose skin. Uncle Grayson had led her back into the aisle and was inspecting the mass.

"Doing my job?" Dr. Mark teased him with a quick hug to Sadie. "Lift her leg and see how flexible it is."

Uncle Grayson lifted the leg but she couldn't bend it at the hock and the muscle began quivering again down into her gaskin and slightly up her rib cage. Scarecrow pulled it away from him and stretched it out behind her. The entire leg started to shake uncontrollably.

Sadie gasped, tears started falling, and she looked at Dr. Mark in desperation. He stepped forward and took the fly mask off the horse's head to inspect her eyes. He wiped them gently and the horse tilted her head into the hand.

"I'm going to start her on an IV to get the fluids into her. I'll add Dexamethasone…." He turned to his truck.

"You think its allergies?" Aunt Dru asked when he returned.

"The dryness and swollen eyes lead me to believe it is or is part of the issue." He answered.

Sadie was leaning into her mother's arms. Her hand was tightly wrapped in her dad's hand.

After the IV was started and the medicine given, Dr. Mark turned to Sadie. "We should see a difference within a few hours…twelve at the most. If she doesn't have any changes by morning, we need to take her into the clinic for more in-depth testing…maybe WSU."

"OK," Sadie whispered.

As Dr. Mark consoled her, Wade walked away to call Jessup and Reilly and let them know what was happening.

It was another long, quiet day and night.

CHAPTER SEVENTEEN

The sun was barely rising when Scarecrow's stall door was opened. The entire family was standing in the aisle. Nick and Alex were healthy and with Tessa had arrived early.   Matt, Josey, Nikki, and Lucas had driven down from the ranch the night before.

Sadie stepped into the stall with halter in hand and was greeted with alert ears and a soft nicker.

"The leg isn't quivering anymore," Sadie announced.

Wade was holding his breath when Sadie walked out of the stall with Scarecrow right behind her. There was no limp…her stride was perfect.

Tears brimmed Sadie's eyes as she leaned underneath the horse and her dad was next to her with a flashlight.

"The edema is the same size but she's not sweating anymore," Uncle Grayson announced.

Aunt Leah removed the fly mask, "Her eye isn't as swollen,"

"The edema and swollen eye were on her right," Jack said. "Whatever it was seemed to just affect this side."

Uncle Grayson was still looking under the horse's belly, his hand at the edema. "Sadie," He whispered. "Look at this…"

She knelt back down and almost laid on the ground to look at the odd pocket of skin.

"Are those scabs?" She asked.

"What?" Wade's mom asked and held out her phone. "Take a picture so we can see."

Uncle Grayson took the picture and handed her the phone. They all wiggled into his mother to see the picture.

There were two scab marks about an inch apart and about three inches from the swelling.

"Snake bite?" Aunt Dru gasped.

"Could be…" Wade's dad nodded. "If it was a rattlesnake with venom, I'd expect some of the skin to blacken but she could have laid down or rolled on a bull or garter snake."

Sadie stood straight up and her head flipped to her mother. "I need to call Dr. Mark."

Aunt Leah handed her the phone. They stood quietly and listened to Sadie update the veterinarian.

She paused, took a deep breath, and her shoulders rose, "So…she's going to be alright?" Her eyes were wide, hopeful, tear-filled, then the tears fell. A quivering breath released and her shoulders lowered. Her head began nodding.

"OK," She whispered into the phone. "OK…"

The phone was lowered and she looked around at everyone, "He said he was going back to bed since there wasn't anything more to do…she will be fine."

Relieved grins were shared, the palomino patted, and everyone went back to bed except Wade, Alex, Sadie, and her mom.

"I'm sorry, Mom," Sadie said with a determined stance. "We don't know when she'll be rideable and she shouldn't be traveling that far in a horse trailer and I'm not going without her and Wade."

Her mother took her hand, "I understand…it just had to be your decision."

"It is," Sadie nodded. "No one but you even talked to me about it so they didn't try to sway my decision. I know Little Ghost and I could go but he went to Colorado with me and I don't think he'll complain about riding here and not having to travel another two thousand miles." Her mother smiled lovingly. "Wade and I will be there next year and hopefully have Alex with us."

"Then I'm going to bed," Aunt Leah smiled and gave them a hug before walking out the door.

"Let's put all the horses in the pasture then go to bed too," Sadie said.

"Yeah," Wade nodded. "Between Scarecrow and Jessup, I'm exhausted."

He didn't wake until noon then Nora drove him, Alex, Sadie, and Cora back to the hospital for the day. She was excited to see a parking spot open along the curb so she didn't have to park in the parking lot.

They were in the elevator when Wade's phone alert rang out.

Text from Kylie: Just heard about Sadie and Scarecrow, can't believe it. So glad she is going to be OK. Give Sadie my best. Tara was going with me for support but we just loaded her horse, too. She is beyond grateful that she will be taking Sadie's place at Nationals. I am so sorry for Sadie but happy for Tara.

Wade handed the phone to Sadie so she could read the message. She didn't respond...not a flinch, smile, frown...nothing. After reading it, she just handed him the phone.

When they walked into the room, Helen was in with Kate and Jessup. All three smiled at the group as they entered. Wade glanced at Sadie. He had forgotten to tell her Helen had apologized to him. With narrowed eyes and shoulders high, Sadie stood to the back of the group. She didn't say anything until Kate and Helen walked out of the room.

"Sadie?" Jessup looked past everyone to see her.

"Yeah," She walked up to the side of the bed.

"Kate told me about Scarecrow," He said. "I'm really glad she's OK."

"Me too," Sadie nodded.

"And the Nationals..." He said and Sadie's shoulders rose slightly. "I'll tell you the same thing I told Wade after State. Things happen for a reason."

"Yep, I know," She nodded and sighed. "Maybe it was meant to happen with Alex, too."

"You may know, or the reason may never be clear," Jessup said. "But don't forget one thing."

"What's that?" She asked.

"You are the Idaho State Junior High Champion Barrel racer," He smiled. "No one can take that away from you and Scarecrow."

Sadie grinned, "Just in case I haven't told you…"

"Yeah…yeah…" He shook his head. "You only get one of those."

They all laughed.

ᑌ ᑌ ᑌ ᑌ ᑌ ᑌ ᑌ ᑌ ᑌ ᑌ ᑌ ᑌ ᑌ

"Sadie! Come on!" Wade yelled down the hall.

She stepped out of her room and ran down the hall to jump into a slide and come to a halt next to him. She grinned, "Where? Why? What are we doing?"

"Dad came up with an idea to help Nora practice parking," Wade said and trotted down the stairs.

She was right behind him.

"How?"

"They brought down a couple dozen of the large square bales," He answered as they walked to the front of the house.

When they stepped onto the porch, Sadie laughed.

In the front pasture, his dad had placed the bales apart from each other creating 'parking spaces' between them. There were a dozen 'parking spaces' that Nora was currently driving her little blue truck toward.

"Come on, Sadie!" Wade said and ran toward the pasture.

"What are we going to do?"

"Stand on the bales, direct her, and see if she knocks us off," Wade laughed.

As they walked through the gate, Nora hit the first of many bales.

THE TAGGER HERD SERIES

Sadie Tagger

Day of the Dingo

Gini Roberge

CHAPTER ONE

Sadie's eyes slowly opened to the dark bedroom. The moonlight filtering in through the windows created dancing shadows on the ceiling. As her body began to wake, her thoughts went to Des Moines, Iowa. She was supposed to be there, not at the Homestead. A deep sadness touched her heart. This was supposed to be the day that changed everything. This was the first day of the Junior High School National Finals Rodeo.

She had qualified with Scarecrow and Little Ghost, but when Scarecrow was bitten by a snake and became sick, Sadie made the decision not to go. Wade didn't qualify, and she wanted to go with him and her horses. It was a hard choice to make when Wade wasn't going but, it was an easy decision to make when Scarecrow couldn't go either.

That didn't make the fact she woke up at the Homestead instead of in Iowa any easier.

She turned and looked at the faint glow of the clock next to her bed. It was 4:17 in the morning, which meant 6:17 in Iowa. They would be getting the horses out of their stalls and preparing for the day. Generators were starting, horses nickering, ATV's driving-by, the smell of fresh hay, subdued laughter, and dreams still possible…that's what she was missing. She loved those mornings.

After taking a deep breath, Sadie sat up in bed. There was no chance of her going back to sleep, so she might as well go to the barn and visit her horses. Quietly, she dressed in her favorite pink shirt, jeans for riding and slid on her socks. Her hair was loose and flowing in a tangled mess to her waist. To quickly contain it, she braided it in a loose braid in the back. The top was messy, but her hat would hide it. Since her boots were in the hall closet by the back door of the house, she tip-toed out of the room so she didn't wake Grace and Nora. She made her way down the quiet hall and steps. There was no aroma of coffee, so her dad hadn't risen yet.

Placing her straw cowboy hat on her head, she picked up her boots and then stepped out onto the back porch before sliding them on. The air was crisp, so the day wasn't going to be too warm, but it was cool enough she stepped back into the house to get her jean-jacket from the closet.

Her parent's bedroom was right above the porch where she was walking, so she tip-toed across. Half-way to the barn she stopped and looked up. The sky was alive with millions of twinkling stars and a half-moon lowering to the horizon. A deep breath of fresh air made her think of Iowa and the Finals again. She sighed and continued to the barn.

Not wanting to wake all the horses, she went to the barn office first and retrieved a small flashlight. Scarecrow was already hanging her head over the stall door, so Sadie went to her first. Stepping into the stall, Sadie lowered to point the flashlight's beam under the horse and inside her back leg. It had only been a week since they had discovered the small puncture wounds. That was after three days of the leg swelling, sweats, and uncontrollable spasms. It had been terrifying to watch. The thought of her horse dying or suffering had caused sleepless nights and an abundance of tears.

The pocket of loose skin was still there, so Scarecrow would have the day off again. She took the time to brush her beautiful palomino horse and comb the nearly white mane. After a few treats were given to the horse, Sadie made her way to Little Ghost. He was standing at his feeder eating the last remnants of the hay from the night before.

"Well, good," She whispered with a smile. "You're fed and ready for a ride in the dark."

The small flashlight lit enough of the barn so she could saddle the horse. There were a few soft nickers as she mounted the horse and walked out the front of the barn. Hoofbeats echoed in the building, but the silence took over as they walked the well-worn path to the arena. The horse knew it well; she didn't have to direct him. Shutting all the gates, Sadie relaxed in the saddle and let the grey horse wander the dirt arena with no encouragement. Her body relaxed, and she just let it rock back and forth to his stride.

Leaning her hands back on the horse's rump, her eyes went to the sky again. A million stars, if not billions, twinkled down on her.

"They would already be hidden by the sun's light if we were in Iowa right now," Sadie whispered to Little Ghost.

The horse stopped in the middle of the arena with his head high and looking up into the farmer's fields. Deer and coyotes occasionally made their way past the Homestead. They had even seen an elk once, and even a badger. But, Sadie wasn't worried because Little Ghost would take care of her.

As they stood in the arena and she looked to the sky, a star shot down to her right.

"We're supposed to wish on shooting stars," Sadie told the horse. "So, what do we wish for?"

The horse didn't answer.

"Well, I will wish for…" Sadie squinted to the sky and tried hard to think of something to wish for. "I wish…"

A familiar rumble echoed into the dark morning. She sat straight up, and her head jerked to look down at the Homestead. That was her dad's truck starting. She knew he always let it run to warm-up while he went back in the house and filled a thermos full of coffee. So, she nudged Little Ghost into a trot out of the arena and to the house. They stood in the driveway next to the horse trailer. From the lights streaming from the yard light and kitchen window, she could see her dad had loaded the buckskin, Eli, into the horse trailer. Eli was her dad's favorite horse.

"Well," Sadie giggled softly. "I wish for us to hitch a ride with Dad today."

Stepping down from the horse, she opened the horse trailer's back gate and Little Ghost needed no encouragement to step into the back. Sadie removed his bridle and tied it to the saddle horn, then loosened the cinch so he could ride comfortably.

"What is Dad doing today?" Sadie asked Eli. He didn't answer, either.

With a glance to the back of the house, she shut the gate and fastened it securely. Just as she opened the passenger side door of the truck, the kitchen light turned off. She pulled the door closed and watched as the house's back door opened to reveal both her parents. Her dad stepped away from the door, then stepped back and slid an arm around her mother and pulled her in for a long kiss. Sadie turned away with a blush. Someday, she would have a love just like her parents.

Footsteps approached the truck, and Sadie could barely contain the giggle. He was going to be surprised to see her. She stared out the window to watch for him, but the back door opened first; she leaned back into the seat so he couldn't see her. The familiar pant of the cow dog, Pepper, was right behind her. The door shut as the dog plopped his front paws on the center console while his back paws rest on the back seat. He turned with a jolt of the head when he saw her. She giggled and put a finger to her lips to hush the dog. Leaning further back in the seat and remaining perfectly still, she waited until the driver's door finally opened. He slid onto the seat and was closing the door before his eyes shot to her. His blue eyes lit with humor under his straw cowboy hat and a wide grin appeared as he handed her the thermos.

"I have a stow-away," He chuckled.

"Two," Sadie grinned. "Little Ghost is keeping Eli company."

"You think we needed company today?"

Sadie giggled, "I have no idea, but the arena was pretty boring."

"You were having a morning ride in the arena already?"

The truck started moving down the driveway.

"Couldn't sleep," She shrugged. "Where are we going?"

"Paulson called last night and asked for help in locating a missing cow and calf."

"Didn't he get hurt or something?"

"He had surgery on his hip, but he's home now. His grandson is helping, but Paulson didn't want him riding by himself to go searching."

"He's not a rider?"

"From what I understand, he rides a horse but hasn't been around cows."

He stopped the truck at the end of the driveway and pulled out his phone. "Best I let your mother know you're with me, so she doesn't think you're still sleeping."

Sadie giggled, "How long do you think it would take her to notice I wasn't there?"

He smiled as he typed, "Grace and Nora would probably mention you weren't in your bed when their alarms go off at 6:30."

"Nora has practice over at her coach's place," Sadie nodded.

"And your mother is taking your sister somewhere to meet the royalty chaperone for…something," he chuckled.

"I promise, I won't tell Mom you didn't listen when she told you what she was doing today," Sadie grinned as her dad laughed.

Two minutes after he turned onto the main road, Sadie turned to him, "What food do you have?"

He huffed, "Not nearly enough for the both of us to last the whole day."

"Cora does say we're the biggest eaters in the family," Sadie grinned.

When he stopped at a stop sign, he leaned into the backseat and lifted a small cooler, and placed it on Sadie's lap.

Half the contents were gone in the twenty minutes it took to reach Paulson's ranch's entry gate. A small barn and wooden corrals set inside the gate.

"This is what they call his lower barn. He stages cattle here for pickup when he doesn't need anyone driving to his ranch house. It saves time and money. Since Little Ghost is already saddled, go to the right and look into the ravine behind the barn. I'll get Eli saddled and join you."

"OK, boss!" Sadie grinned.

When she stepped up into the saddle, she stood quietly and looked across the bare land.   Unlike the mountainous pine tree covered Tagger Ranch, this ranch barely had a tree in sight. The rolling hills, canyon, and ravines were just beginning to lighten by the rising sun.

"Look at that, Dad," Sadie whispered.

He stood next to her as the sun's first rays shot from the horizon and created an amber hue on the truck, trailer, and deep shadows in the ravines. The few clouds in the sky were tinted pink from the sunrise.

"Never get tired of sunrises and sunsets," He said as he turned back to throw the saddle on Eli.

Sadie nudged Little Ghost into a trot along the fence line behind the barn with Pepper following along next to her. She rode to the edge of the hill and looked out to the sunrise, then down the ravine. A wide creek flowed at the bottom, but still, there were no trees, just thick thistle bushes. She also didn't see an animal, so she turned back to join her dad.

They rode along the top of the hill with his binoculars pointed to the bottom of the ravine. It was the logical place for a cow and calf to be lost. In the distance was the Paulson ranch house.

"Let's ride to the bottom and follow the creek to the ranch," He said.

They both turned and followed a deer path to the bottom. At times, they were leaned far back in the saddle with boots deep in the stirrups for balance. Stopping next to the creek, they let the horses drink. She liked riding with just her dad, but she also enjoyed riding with everyone else. Chuckling to herself, she admitted she just liked riding.

She did miss Wade. Whenever he rode with his dad, they always looked happy, and Uncle Scott so proud.

"Dad?"

"What?"

Sadie turned and looked at him with curious eyes, "Did you ever wish you had a son?"

He turned and looked at her with a chuckle, "Where did that come from?"

She shrugged. "I was thinking of Wade and Uncle Scott."

They reached the base of the mountain and started walking down the ravine next to the creek.

"Well, I have two kids that love to ride horses, can rope a calf at a run, have a strong work ethic, and will lead the way if a job needs to be done. Most importantly, they are kind, have a great sense of humor, are genuine to people, intelligent, and have a strong moral code and self-respect." He turned and looked at her. "What difference does it make if they are a son or a daughter?"

She felt the love beam from his eyes, and her heart felt as if it were going to burst.

"I guess Mom raised us right," She teased.

He laughed, "And that's another point. They have the best woman in the world for a mother."

"And she has the best husband," Sadie added. "Did you want more kids?"

"Well, honestly, when we first married, we were planning on three or four, but when Leah had so many problems giving birth to Grace, then had you prematurely in the branding corral, we decided we were blessed with two and wouldn't take a chance of a third."

"Nikki and Lucas' baby is due in January, I bet him and Nick won't let her go to the ranch the last month," Sadie teased.

"You try and tell Nikki what to do. Same way when your mother insisted on just the quick trip to the ranch that day."

"Maybe Nikki will learn from Mom's stubbornness," Sadie grinned. "But, I still get to have the best birthplace in the family."

"Goes with that nickname Lucas gave you within minutes of meeting you," He teased.

"Dingo!" Sadie chirped. "I thought it was funny then and still love it."

"And the meaning behind it?"

Sadie gave him a humored glance, "I hope the cute and cuddly lasts forever, but I am working on the 'rip your throat out' part."

He laughed, and Sadie just grinned at him.

The ravine opened to a wide valley with a few trees scattered along the winding creek. They passed a shallow pond that was nothing more than a mud-hole. Cattle tracks were deep in the mud.

They passed three more mud-holes that had a small puddle of water remaining in the middle.

In the distance, they heard a low rumbling moo.

"That has to be her," Sadie said.

"And something must be wrong."

They pushed the horses into a trot and rode toward the sound with Pepper running alongside them.

The large black cow was standing next to one of the mud holes with a shallow puddle of water in the center. At the edge of what was left of the water, her red calf was stuck deep into the mud and unable to move.

CHAPTER TWO

The calf's head was resting on the ground with its tongue hanging out to the side.

"It's exhausted from trying to get out," Sadie sighed as they neared.

The cow swung around to the sound of the horse's hoofbeats with her head rising and a loud moo escaping.

"Watch yourself," He warned as they neared.

The cow ran toward them while tossing her head.

Sadie rode to the right, while her dad rode to the left and confused the cow, so she stopped. Pepper stalked the calf from the ground next to her dad. She was just waiting for him to order her to move.

Behind the puddle and calf was a fence with a wood-paneled gate open.

"Let's push the cow through the gate before trying to approach the calf," He said.

"Yehaw!" Sadie yelled and waved her arm to the cow.

With head lowering, the cow began to step back.

"Move it on, Mama, we'll get your baby out," Sadie's dad hollered and pushed Eli closer.

The cow trotted to the left then the right, but the horses continued to push her back toward the gate. Pepper was right between them with an occasional bark and a nip.

"Little Ghost and I can keep her back if you want to close the gate behind us," Sadie suggested.

He nodded, and as soon as the cow was far enough through the gate, Sadie positioned Little Ghost between the cow and her dad. When he stepped from the horse, the black cow ran toward him, but Little Ghost blocked her path. The horse pushed the cow farther into the pasture.

"He's a cuttin' horse, Mama Cow, you ain't getting past him," Sadie grinned as the horse darted in front of the cow again.

"Come through, hurry up!"

Sadie turned the grey horse and ran for the gate. It swung closed before the cow could run back, but she trotted back and forth. Her loud, high-pitched bellows filled the air.

"Let's hope she doesn't crash through it or go through the barbed wire on each side," Her dad walked Eli back toward the calf that hadn't moved since they arrived. The horse's reins were dropped and dangled to the ground. He never tied the reins because the horse wouldn't move until her dad was ready. He took off his cowboy hat, placed it on a fence post, and then removed the rope attached to the saddle.

With Sadie on Little Ghost and her dad on the ground, they walked to the mud hole and to the calf.

"I can get in about ten feet, but I'm going to sink."

"You want me to go in?"

He shook his head, "You're best staying on the horse. I'll get the rope around the calf, and between Little Ghost and me, we'll be able to pull it free without harming its legs."

Sadie walked her horse to the edge of the mud-hole, just until he began to sink in the mud. Her dad handed her the end of the rope, and she held it tightly as he carried the coils with him. His third step had him sinking ankle-deep. He pulled his leg up out of the mud with a thrust, and took a wide stride, then sunk nearly to his knees. He needed one more step before he could reach the calf.

"Dang, this is deep," He huffed, then, with a mighty pull, his leg sucked out of the mud for that last step. His right leg sunk to above the knee, and his left leg was just below the knee.

"I hope your boots stay on your feet when you walk out," Sadie grimaced.

He chuckled as he laid the lariat's coils on the mud and ran a soothing hand down the calf's side.

"He needs some water. There are a couple of bottles in my saddlebags."

Sadie walked to Eli and unbuckled the bag. Usually, when she rode in the mountains, she would have saddlebags, too. But, she didn't have them when she was just riding in the arena like she had started the morning.

With two bottles in hand, she walked back to her dad and threw one to him. He opened the bottle then lifted the calf's head to pour water into it. The tongue began shooting in and out as the calf started to swallow.

When the calf stopped drinking, Sadie tossed the second bottle on the ground.

Her dad ran his hands down the side of the calf just behind the front legs. He was able to lift just enough to get the front legs above the mud, but the backend of the calf was entirely in the mud. The rope was looped over the calf's head and under his front legs, so it was tight around his chest. Her dad dug the mud away from the back of the calf.

With the rope tightly wound around the saddle horn, Sadie moved Little Ghost so he was positioned to pull the calf forward and not to the side. The deep, thick mud could harm his back legs if she pulled him to the side.

With his arms wrapping around the back of the calf, her dad tugged to pull, but the calf barely moved.

"Tighten up and pull a bit…take it slow," he called out.

Sadie nudged Little Ghost back until the rope was tight, then just a little more until she could see the calf begin to move. A low bawl escaped the calf.

"That's a good sign," Sadie whispered and took another step back.

Between the pull of the rope and her dad's arms, the calf finally sprung out of the mud. The exhausted baby slid across the top and watched her but didn't attempt to move.

Sadie stopped with a sigh of relief.

"I'll unhook the calf; then you'll have to help pull us both out."

"Okay, Dad," Sadie nodded and waited for him to remove the rope from the calf.

With both fists tightly gripping the rope, he nodded, and Sadie moved forward. His whole body raised and his face was scrunched in a grimace as his right leg was pulled from the mud. One more step and he held the rope with one hand and wrapped the other around the calf's chest.

"One, two, three…," Sadie nudged the horse back.

One more step.

"Moo…awwhh," The bellow of the cow was getting closer. Pepper barked and growled.

Sadie's head swirled around to see the cow running through the opened gate and right at her dad. Paulson's grandson was at the gate holding his horse and smiling proudly.

Sadie's anger switch flipped as she gasped at the boy and turned to the cow. But, she couldn't react to the boy or the cow would reach her dad and trample him. The anger switch flipped back as she tossed the rope toward her dad and turned Little Ghost to face the cow. Only fifteen feet from her dad, the horse lunged at the cow, and the animals hit shoulder to shoulder. Little Ghost nearly fell over the cow that had toppled to her side. Sadie gripped the saddle horn and shoved her heels deep in the stirrup to keep from flying out of the saddle.

The cow bellowed as she scrambled back to her feet only to be met with the determined eyes of the grey horse. The cow moved to the left, and Little Ghost matched her. Back and forth, they trotted as the cow slowly began to back up. Pepper was whimpering behind her as her dad commanded the dog to hold back.

"Asa! Go get my horse and bring him here," Her dad yelled from behind her. He was still firmly stuck in the mud.

"Okay, Mr. Grayson."

Sadie's focus stayed on the cow and the horse.

"Get the rope Sadie tossed and wrap it around Eli's saddle horn," Her dad ordered.

"Who is Eli?" Asa asked.

"The horse you have a hold of," Her dad huffed.

Sadie and Little Ghost zig-zagged in front of the cow.

"Eli, back!" Her dad called out.

When the cow stopped, Sadie glanced over her shoulder. Her dad, covered in mud from his chest to his boots, had the rope in one hand and the calf's front legs in the other as he was drug from the mud by the buckskin horse.

"Good Boy, back," Her dad called out again.

Little Ghost lunged to the left, bringing Sadie's attention back to the mother cow. She stopped trying to push the cow backward and just maintained a safe distance between the cow and her dad. Pepper had crawled forward and lay on the ground, ready for the command to move the cow.

"Let her go, Sadie!"

She nudged Little Ghost to the side then turned back to watch the cow run to her calf. The little calf had been pulled twenty feet from the mud hole and was standing on wobbling legs. Her dad and Asa were safely on top of the horses. Her dad was pouring water over his hands to wash them. His saddle was covered in mud from his clothes and boots.

Sadie looked at Asa. She guessed he was a little older than her and had brown hair, blue eyes, and skin that didn't look like it had ever been touched by the sun.

"Why did you let her go?" Sadie grumbled.

"So she could help encourage her baby to crawl out of the mud," Asa shrugged. "I thought she knew you were trying to help."

Sadie just stared at him. Paulson did say his grandson had never been around cows. She let out a frustrated sigh. "You should have a hat on," Sadie mumbled. It was either that or scream at him for nearly getting her dad trampled and killed.

Her dad smirked as the boy shook his head.

"I don't like hats," Asa said.

"The sun will burn your scalp, ears, neck, and fry your face," Sadie kept from rolling her eyes and trotted over to retrieve her dad's hat from the fence.

"Your hands are a bit dirty," She teased and placed it on his head. "And I hope you have some extra clothes in the truck."

He grinned, "Let's get them through the gate and shut it…again…so they can't get back to the mud. Then we'll have to check and make sure they have water."

"I passed a big silver tank that had lots of water in it," Asa said.

"In the same pasture as we're pushing them into?" Sadie asked.

"Yes," Asa nodded and pointed across the pasture. "It's over behind that big bush and has a little stream next to it, too."

They waited until the tired and hungry calf stopped nursing, then let it dictate the pace as they began to walk. As the three of them pushed the cows slowly toward the gate, Asa looked at Sadie, down to Little Ghost, out to the cows, then back again.

He did it three times before she finally turned to him with wide eyes, "What?"

"It was pretty cool seeing you and the horse keeping that cow away," He answered with a smile.

"He's a cutting horse. He does it all the time," she explained.

His head went back, and eyes went to Little Ghost's shoulder as he huffed, "You cut that horse on purpose?"

Sadie's jaw clenched as she turned to him. He was looking at the scars on the grey horse's shoulder.

"No," She answered through gritted teeth. "Cutting horses cut a single cow out of a herd of cows. We do not cut our horses."

"Why's he got all them scars then?" Asa frowned as if she was lying.

Her breathing stopped, her mind tingled, and her body trembled at the anger she was trying to hold back. Didn't her dad just tell her she was kind? Screaming and yelling at Asa and calling him an idiot would not be considered kind.

"He…" She finally squeaked. "He hurt himself on a broken feeder in his stall when he was two. It was an accident. WE DO NOT CUT OUR HORSES."

"Oh," Asa shrugged with a big sigh dismissing the conversation.

Sadie turned away from him and looked out at the trail they were following. Taking deep breaths, she managed to calm herself.

When the cow and calf walked into the next pasture, Sadie lowered to the ground and shut the paneled gate. The chain to latch it was lying on the ground, so her dad handed her fencing pliers and a nail. She nailed the chain to the post making sure it wouldn't fall again so the next rider wouldn't have to get out of the saddle.

"There is no cell service down here," Her dad said. "Let's ride up to the top of the hill so I can call Paulson and let him know we found them."

Asa turned his horse and nudged him forward. Sadie's dad waited until she was back in the saddle and then turned to ride up the hill.

"Asa," Her dad called out.

"What?" Asa stopped and turned to him with curious eyes.

"Don't ride away from another horse and rider when the rider is on the ground," He said calmly. "Wait until they remount."

"Why?" Asa asked.

"Our horses don't fret too much if one of the other walks away, but some horses do. You could cause the horse to run away from the rider as he tries to get back in the saddle and get them hurt."

"Oh," Asa shrugged again and just kept riding up the hill.

Sadie bit her lip to keep from talking.

When they arrived at the top of the hill, Sadie turned Little Ghost so they could look across the canyons as her dad made the phone call.   It was beautiful and peaceful, with the sun lighting the green grass and the wildflowers that had begun to bloom.

"Yeah, we found them. The calf got stuck in the mud-hole, but they are on the other side of the fence now. He'll be okay," He paused. "Sure, how long?" Another pause. "We'll give you a call later."

He slid the phone in his pocket then looked down the prairie in the direction the horse trailer and truck were parked. They were too far away to see.

"Asa, you'll be sticking with us for a while," Her dad said.

Sadie held in the groan.

CHAPTER THREE

"How come?" Asa asked with wide excited eyes.

"Your mom is with your grandfather at the doctor and will call when they finish," He answered and pointed down the dirt road. "The truck and trailer are that way."

Asa nodded, turned his horse, and took off at a gallop toward the truck they couldn't see.

Sadie exhaled the irritation and looked at her dad. His eyes narrowed as he watched the teenager galloping away. Without looking at Sadie, he nudged Eli into a slow trot. Sadie followed.

Half-way to the truck, Asa had stopped, and the bay horse's sides were heaving with exertion. When they approached, the teenager started to take off again.

"Asa, STOP!" Her dad ordered, and Asa turned quickly. "Give that horse a break."

"Okay," Asa stopped alongside of them and looked at Eli and Little Ghost. "They must be in really good shape."

"They are," Sadie sighed. "But we also didn't ask too much out of them for no reason. If you go a little slower, you can go a lot farther." She repeated the words she had been taught since she was young.

"Your horse just carried you up a steep hill," Her dad added. "Give him time to rest before you take off at a gallop. Keep your horse's health in mind when you ride."

"Okay," Asa nodded and looked toward the truck and trailer that were now in sight. "Where are we going, anyway?"

They began walking the horses to give the bay horse a chance to catch his breath.

"We're going to Asotin to look at a cart for Nick," Her dad answered.

Sadie looked at him in surprise, "What kind of cart?"

"It's an old Meadowbrook cart that Tessa wants to train her horse to pull," He answered. "One padded seat and two large wheels."

"Cool," Sadie smiled. "Nick is getting a great collection of wagons and carts."

He nodded, "Craig has it for sale."

"Who are Nick, Tessa, and Craig?" Asa asked.

"Nick is my uncle, Tessa is his girlfriend, and Craig is Nora's coach," Sadie answered.

"Who's Nora?" Asa asked.

"She's my cousin," Sadie sighed.

"What does she need a coach for?" Asa asked.

Sadie took a deep breath, "Reining, Reined Cow Horse, Cutting, and some showing."

"What is…?" Asa started.

"Asa, do you have a phone?" Sadie's dad asked.

"Yeah," He answered.

"Google each one and watch them. It will be easier than describing them," He directed, and Sadie sighed in relief.

There were no more questions on the way to the trailer as Asa watched videos.

"That all looks fun," Asa smiled as he stepped from the saddle.

Eli and Little Ghost were led into the trailer with Asa's bay horse last. Then, as she and her dad were shutting the trailer door, Asa walked up to the front of the truck. She heard a door slam, and they both looked to the truck to see Asa sitting in the front passenger seat…as in her seat. Sadie huffed; he was the 'ride-along', and he should be in the back seat. She gritted her teeth to keep from grumbling.

Without a word, her dad walked to the truck and opened the door behind the driver's seat. He withdrew a shirt and clean jeans.

"So, you do have extra clothes," Sadie giggled.

He chuckled, "Not my first time rolling in the mud."

She looked out at the vast rangeland divided by canyons as he changed clothes.

"Grab me a bottle of water so I can wash these boots off before putting them on," Her dad said.

Sadie crawled up into the truck and opened the cooler they always had in the back, and handed him a bottle. He was standing in just jeans and socks as he poured the water over the mud on the boots. The clean shirt had been tossed onto the top of the toolbox with his phone resting next to it.

Sadie's hand slowly reached out to the phone and pulled it to her. As stealthily as possible, she raised the phone and swiped her finger across the front to unlock it. Tilting it up, she waited until her dad tossed the empty bottle into the back of the truck and reached for the shirt. She took a picture of him and had to hold back a giggle. As he slid the button-down shirt over his shoulders, she took another picture, and a giggle escaped. His head jerked to her with narrowed eyes.

"What are you doing?"

Sadie giggled again and started typing on the phone as fast as she could.

"Did you take a picture?" He grumbled and reached for his phone.

Sadie giggled again and leaned away from him.

"Do not post a picture…" He lifted a boot on top of the tire and pulled himself up into the back of the truck.

"Neither one of us have social media to post anything on," Sadie chuckled and hit the send button just as his fingers wrapped around the phone and pulled it away.

She laughed at his frown as he searched the phone for the message she had sent.

A smirk appeared, "You sent the pictures to your mother," he shook his head. "Your husband is hot; he may need some ice water when we get home."

Sadie's whole body shook with laughter.

"You are a laugh a minute, little Dingo," He muttered and jumped out of the truck.

"Well, you did say I had a good sense of humor," She chuckled and followed him over the side of the truck.

"Here."

Sadie turned to see him dangling the truck keys in front of her.

"Really?" She gasped with excitement welling in her.

"We're going to drop off Asa's horse at Paulson's place and it's a flat drive with just a few turns," He smiled. "It will be good practice for you."

"Yes!" She nearly danced to the driver's door.

When she opened it, Asa's eyes widened when he saw her.

"You're driving?" He gasped.

"Yes," She grinned and slid up onto the seat and pushed the button to move her seat forward. She had long legs but not near as long as her 6' 3" dad.

After letting Pepper into the backseat of the truck, her dad opened the door next to Asa.

Asa turned to him, "Mr. Grayson, you're going to let her drive? Isn't she too young?"

"Yes, and not for a ranch kid," Her dad answered. "She's been driving for a while, and there isn't anyone out here on the ranch to worry about. I also don't sit in the back seat of my own truck."

Asa stared at him a moment, then turned to look at the center console that was covered with two water bottles in the holders, gloves, a measuring tape, and fencing pliers sitting on top.

"Where do you want me to put that stuff?" Asa asked.

Her dad smiled, "It stays where it is, and you get in the back seat."

"With the dog?" Asa sat up. "Okay."

Sadie had to turn away to hide her smile.

With the confidence of many miles on the back roads of Tagger Ranch and Circle 50, she put the truck in gear and moved down the road. It was always exciting to drive. When they arrived at the ranch, she stayed behind the wheel while her dad and Asa released the horse from the trailer. Asa walked the horse toward the barn, and her dad walked to her door and opened it. She didn't move and just grinned at him.

"You plan on driving out of here?" He smirked.

"Can I? Just until we get back to the main road?"

He nodded with an amused huff and turned back to watch Asa remove the saddle from the horse and walk the bay to the corral. The horse walked to the middle of the corral and immediately dropped down to roll. Asa carried the saddle into the barn, then reappeared and walked right at them.

"Wha…?" Sadie gasped.

With a low grumble, her dad walked toward Asa and pointed him back to the barn, and they disappeared inside. When Asa reappeared, he was carrying an arm-full of hay and tossed it over the fence into the horse's feeder. One more trip inside, and they both appeared with Asa carrying a bucket to the horse. He poured grain over the hay. The horse's head disappeared into the feeder.

Sadie couldn't believe he was going to walk away without feeding the horse that had just carried him up a mountain and galloped across the prairie. If they had the time, she would have brushed the horse, too.

"How far away is the place we're going?" Asa asked as she turned the truck and trailer around in the driveway.

He chattered all the way from the ranch to the main road about him letting the cow loose, Little Ghost pushing the cow away, and their ride. Everything they had just done together. Sadie ignored him and concentrated on keeping the truck and trailer on the road. Thank goodness she had the driving to keep her mind busy. Her dad typed on the phone until she stopped at the main gate of the ranch. They quickly switched places.

"How did your horse get those scars?" Asa asked as soon as the truck began to move.

Sadie hesitated in answering. Just how many questions would he have if she told him the whole story?

"Do you have Facebook?" Sadie asked.

"Yeah, who doesn't?" Asa chuckled.

"Me," She huffed. "Search for The Tagger Herd, and you can read and see all the pictures."

It was the best thing she could have done because he was quiet the ten minutes it took to drive to Nora's coach's training arena.

When they arrived, Nora was in the arena on the dark bay horse, Isaiah. They were slowly walking into a small herd of cows. Her coach, Craig, was standing across the arena, sipping a cup of coffee.

"What are they doing?" Asa asked.

"She is going to cut one cow out of the herd then keep it from going back," Sadie answered.

"Okay," Asa said and opened the door the second the truck stopped. He was half-way to the arena by the time Sadie walked around the truck to join her dad.

"Enthusiastic, isn't he?" He drawled. Pepper took her position right next to her dad. The dog always followed right next to him when they weren't working or at home on the ranches.

"Yeah," Sadie huffed but kept herself from rolling her eyes.

They stood outside the arena as Nora and Isaiah blocked a red heifer from joining the herd. Back and forth across the arena they trotted. Both horse and rider stared hard at the cow as they focused on every move. Craig waved the cow back toward Nora each time it wandered too far away.

When Nora raised the reins higher to let the horse know to let the cow back into the herd, she looked out at her coach. He was nodding with a pleased look on his face.

"That's fun to watch," Asa said without looking at Sadie or her father.

"It's fun to do," Sadie sighed. Even though she did it with the angry momma cow not too long ago, she sure wished she could go into the arena now and do it a dozen more times.

Nora turned with a happy grin and trotted to the fence next to them. Her long black hair had been pulled back into a ponytail, and her head was covered with a T3E baseball cap.

"That's your cousin?" Asa turned and looked at Sadie in disbelief.

"Yeah…" She answered.

"But…" Asa looked between the two of them.

Sadie sighed again, "Our fathers are brothers. My mother is tall and blonde; Nora's is Native American. So I am tall, blonde, and have blue eyes, and she is short, brown eyes, and has a darker complexion. You have an issue with that?"

Asa's eyes widened, and he shook his head, "No, of course not. That wasn't what I was going to say. I was going to say she is really cute."

Sadie huffed, and her dad's head turned to Asa, but he didn't say anything.

"So, you're saying I'm ugly?" Sadie screeched and felt her cheeks warm in anger.

CHAPTER FOUR

"No," Asa shook his head with hands up as if blocking her from attacking him physically. "It's that you don't wear makeup to make yourself prettier."

Sadie stared at him in disbelief.

"Asa," Her dad drawled, "You need to learn manners and boundaries."

"I don't wear makeup because I don't want to," Sadie growled.

"Why not?" Asa asked.

"It's none of your business why," Sadie huffed. She really wanted to hit him to make his questions stop.

Asa shrugged, "I was just pointing it out."

"Pointing what out?" Nora asked as she stopped the horse next to the fence.

Her coach walked alongside her with a hand reaching out to stroke Isaiah's neck. Sadie's face flushed in embarrassment.

"This is Asa," Her dad said and turned to Craig. "Nick said you had a cart for sale and wanted me to take a look at it. While we do, do you mind if Sadie takes a turn with the herd?"

Sadie looked at her dad in surprise and felt the anger and embarrassment dissolve into eagerness.

"You have Little Ghost with you?" Nora looked at the trailer.

"Yes," Sadie chirped and turned to Craig, who was looking at her father thoughtfully. "Can I? Please?"

Craig turned with a nod, "Don't see why not."

Sadie spun around and ran for the back of the horse trailer.

Ten minutes later, Asa's rude comment was forgotten as she walked into the herd, astride her beautiful grey gelding. The cows looked at her anxiously, and her heart began to beat faster. Uncle Scott had trained the horse and taken him to competitions and won! She truly couldn't get enough of this.

She lifted the reins high as she guided the horse into the herd. Little Ghost's ears twitched back and forth as he waited for her to designate their intended target. Four heifers trotted from the main herd, and Sadie followed until three had turned back to the herd. Sadie lowered the reins to the horse's withers to signal that the black heifer was the target.   Instantly the horse's eyes and ears fixed on the cow.

Sadie and the horse followed the calf back and forth across the arena.

"Inside leg!" Nora yelled.

Sadie pressed her leg to the horse's side. He moved just enough that when the calf darted back, the horse was in the perfect position to jump back and cut him off from the herd. Another dart from the heifer and Little Ghost's front legs bounced the other way, then again, and again. The horse bounced and Sadie grinned in excitement.

The heifer trotted to the side of the arena with horse and rider following.

"Break it off and go get another," Nora instructed. Sadie turned to her, and the cousins grinned broadly. They both loved cutting.

After the third cow was cut then released back into the herd, Sadie ran a hand down Little Ghost's neck and walked to the gate.

"That was cool!" Asa called out. "That horse is awesome. Is he for sale? Can I buy him?"

The two men and Nora laughed.

"Not in a million years," Sadie answered as she walked through the gate and to the horse trailer. "He is with me forever."

"Take his saddle off this time," Her dad instructed. "Nora can take the horses back to the Homestead with her so we can load the supplies in the back of the trailer."

"What supplies? Where are we going?" Asa asked.

Sadie's dad turned and looked at him with a slight smile, "First, we're headed over to the hospital to give you back to your mother and then visit a friend."

"Oh," Asa's shoulders lowered in disappointment. "Who is the friend?"

"Our foreman at the ranch," He answered.

Nora turned to Sadie, "Hug him for me. I'd ask Uncle Grayson to do it but, I don't think he will."

Sadie laughed as her dad nodded in agreement.

Little Ghost and Eli happily grazed on a pile of hay as Sadie shut the corral gate. She waved at Nora then quickly walked to the truck in front of Asa so she could sit in the front seat.

As they drove away from the training center, Asa was quiet. Sadie guessed he was just trying to think of another dozen obnoxious questions to ask or insult her again. They were driving across the bridge over the river that separated Lewiston and Clarkston when he finally spoke.

"Mr. Grayson?"

"Yeah?" Her dad answered.

Sadie braced herself so she wouldn't overreact.

"I know how to ride a horse, but I can't ride like Sadie. Can you teach me like Nora's coach teaches her?" His voice was low, but hopeful.

Sadie turned enough she could see her father's face.

His jaw tightened, he took a deep breath, then to her surprise, he nodded, "Once your grandfather is on his feet again, you can come up to the T3E ranch and spend a week. I'll teach you how to ride and how to take care of your horse properly."

"Yes! Thank you, Mr. Grayson," Asa cheered.

Sadie looked out at the road. She had teased her dad that her mother raised her right, giving her the kind-heart, but she knew her dad, every day, set the perfect example for her.

As they parked at the hospital, Sadie turned to her dad, "Who is here with Jessup?"

"Who is Jessup?" Asa asked.

Sadie held back an exasperated chuckle.

"He's our foreman," Her dad answered.

"What happened to him?" Asa continued.

"He was working on top of a silo when a part broke, and he was tossed forty feet in the air and landed on the ground," Sadie answered. "He broke his leg and pelvis."

"That would hurt," Asa said. "When did it happen?"

"A couple of weeks ago," Sadie answered. "He'll be here for a couple more to make sure an infection doesn't set in. If it does, he could lose his leg."

"That's an awfully long time to be in a hospital bed," Asa gasped.

"That it is," Her dad said and turned off the truck. "There is Parkston and your mother."

Asa's door flew open, and he jumped out of the truck to run to them.

"You'd think he was anxious to get away from us," Sadie chuckled.

"Hmmm," Her dad mumbled and stepped out of the truck.

When they reached Asa, he was talking fast and telling his mother about 'Mr. Grayson' agreeing to coach him.

Asa's mother turned to them with a smile, "So he didn't chase you away with all the questions?"

Sadie's dad huffed, "You don't learn unless you ask questions."

Sadie just smiled politely and didn't answer. When they said their good-byes and walked to the hospital doors, Sadie turned to her dad. "So, who is here with Jessup?"

"I don't know. Usually, Wade and Alex have the morning shift."

As they stepped into the elevator, his phone alert rang, but he didn't remove it from his pocket. It rang again when he tapped on Jessup's door. He still ignored it.

"Come in," Jessup called out.

The older foreman was leaned back in the bed. The swelling and bruising on Jessup's face had nearly disappeared. He looked a lot better than the first time Sadie had seen him after the accident. She, Nora, and her mother were in Colorado when the accident happened. They had relied on text from Wade for updates.

His broken leg was surrounded by a chrome wire cage that held his leg immobile so the bones could heal together. It was called an Ilizarov apparatus named after the orthopedic surgeon Gavriil Abramovich Ilizarov from the Soviet Union, who pioneered the technique. After learning the doctors had used it on Jessup, Sadie researched it to see if it was usable on horses, too. She found it had been used on calves and was fascinated by the story.

There were three large glass windows in Jessup's hospital room. Two of those windows had been covered with a large blanket. The image on the blanket was from a picture taken from the back porch of Jessup's home at the Tagger Ranch. He could lay in bed and look out to the hillside, river, and vast mountains in the distance. He had been overjoyed when they first hung it over the windows for him. It gave him a window to home, he had said.

Wade and Alex were leaned onto each side of the bed by Jessup's shoulders. A laptop was open on the table that stretched across the bed. The noise from the machine stopped as Jessup closed the lid.

"Well, good morning," Jessup grinned at her. "I heard you hitched a ride with your dad today."

Sadie hurried to his side and leaned in for a careful hug. Then another one. Seeing him in the bed was still hard, but just *seeing* him and knowing he was going to be okay made it better.

"That one is from Nora," Sadie smiled. "We've had an interesting morning. Dad nearly got trampled by a mad momma cow."

"What happened?" Alex gasped.

"Just another day at work," Her dad shrugged. His phone alert went off again, but he ignored it.

Jessup turned to Wade, "These two will be here long enough you two can go attack the cafeteria for breakfast."

"Oh, yeah," Wade stood and grinned at Alex. "I can go for a plate of waffles and bacon."

"Me, too," Alex walked to the door with him.

"Me, too," Jessup called out. "Bring me some." The two boys disappeared, and he turned back to Sadie and her dad. "The breakfasts here barely fill the stomach."

"Good to see you're getting your appetite back," Her dad said and sat in the chair Wade had left.

Sadie sat in Alex's chair.

"You talk to Dru this morning?" Jessup asked with a smirk.

"Briefly as I was walking out the door this morning," Her dad answered. "She's been texting, but we've been busy."

"She has it in her head, you know," Jessup leaned back into the pillows.

Sadie had no idea what he meant but looked at her dad.

"Scott and I both vetoed the whole idea," He answered. "Kate said the last doctor appointment went well."

Jessup huffed at the quick change of subject. Sadie loved hearing that Kate was at the hospital. They were all happy that Jessup and Kate had gotten back together. It was the only good thing to come out of his accident.

"And Matt said you fixed the silo last weekend," Jessup nodded.

The two men talked about the ranch and what needed to be done while Jessup was in the hospital until Wade and Alex appeared with three full plates of food.

"Dang, boys," Sadie grinned and helped get the plates on the table. "They probably cringe in the cafeteria when you two show up."

They all laughed.

"Dan, the cook, said they have been making extra food for breakfast," Wade admitted.

"Especially bacon," Alex chuckled before taking a 'too big' bite of a waffle then shoved in a piece of bacon.

Sadie and her dad reached out to take a waffle off the pile.

"Community breakfast," Jessup nodded just before shoving one in his mouth.

They stayed until the last waffle, and all the bacon was gone. Sadie gave the foreman a big grin and a hug before they left. When she and her dad were in the elevator, his phone began to ring.

He pulled it out of his pocket, looked at the screen, then dropped it back into the pocket.

"Aunt Dru?" Sadie guessed.

"Yeah, she wants to plead her case, and I'm not in the mood."

She still had no idea what he was talking about but didn't ask. If he wanted her to know, he would have told her.

The phone rang again as they shut the doors to the truck. With a sigh, he connected the phone to the truck's Bluetooth system. The phone beeped, and a text appeared on the screen on the truck console.

Text from Dru: Stop ignoring me

Her dad huffed and started the engine of the truck. A shrill of an alert chimed.

"What's that?" Sadie gasped.

"She's trying to do a video chat now."

The noise ended as they drove away from the hospital.

"Where are we going now?" Sadie asked.

"Intermountain Feed to pick up mineral tubs and a case of wormer for the horses."

"We need some fly spray, too," Sadie settled back into the seat and relaxed for the drive.

When he stopped at a red light, he glanced at her, "Let me ask you something about this morning."

"Sure, what?"

"When Asa said…"

The phone beeped again, and the text message appeared on the screen.

Text from Dru: Since you wouldn't pick up, I made the decision myself. The bull needs to be at Jan's in Nezperce this morning. Landers will pick him up from there. Payment is already in the bank.

A low growl escaped her dad, and Sadie's eyes widened as she looked at him in surprise; his jaw was clenched tight.

Just as they pulled into the feed store, the phone beeped again.

Text from Scott: Got the message from Dru. You got this?

"Text him back…just type in 'yes'."

Sadie typed in the one word and hit send. She had no idea what it meant.

She stepped into the back of the horse trailer, and as her dad placed the large round mineral tubs at the end of the trailer floor, Sadie pulled it to the front.

"The order was for two," Martin, the manager, read on the paper he was holding.

"We'll take four," Her dad answered.

Sadie wiggled the extra two tubs to the back and stepped out of the trailer.

"You have any of those round-bale feeders broken-down for shipping?" Her dad asked Martin.

"They weren't on the list Dru called down," Martin said as he walked to the metal feeder.

"We'll just add to it as I feel we need to," Her dad answered. "Add four of those galvanized stock tanks, too."

With the tubs, feeders, and now the water tanks, the back of the horse trailer was full when they shut the back gate. Just inside the store's door was a table with a tray of free cookies was waiting for her. Sadie grabbed two and handed two to her dad.

He thanked her, then nodded to a display of knee-high, heavy-duty mud boots, "Go get yourself a pair."

Sadie's eyes widened, "It's summer. I don't really need mud boots now."

He shrugged and walked by her, "They are on sale now, so get a pair for Grace and your mother, too."

"Okay…" Sadie whispered to his back.

She wasn't sure what he was doing, but she enjoyed picking out the three pairs of boots.

Pepper was on her back sound asleep, when they returned to the truck. Sadie put the boots in the tack room of the horse trailer while her dad woke the dog when he set the case of horse wormer behind the seat. Pepper stood with her back paws on the back seat and her front paws on the front seat's console. The dog's eyes beamed with excitement as she looked out the front window.

Sadie giggled at the dog and scratched her neck as they drove out of the store parking lot and started down the highway.

Her dad had connected his phone to the truck system again, so when he pushed a button, the ringing echoed in the cab.

"What?" Uncle Scott grumbled.

"Nice," Sadie laughed.

"Oh, I forgot you were with him," Her uncle chuckled. "Hi, Sadie, what do you want, Grayson?"

Sadie giggled again.

"We just left Intermountain with a full trailer," Her dad answered.

"Excellent," Uncle Scott said with a bit of a smirk in his voice.

"Put the bull in your trailer and meet us in Cottonwood at the grocery store, and we'll switch trailers," her dad ordered.

"Will do," Her uncle said, and the phone call ended.

Five minutes of silence followed before her dad finally spoke. He glanced at her with narrowed eyes. "For that question I was going to ask you…"

"Yeah?"

"When Asa mentioned you didn't wear makeup and you told him it was none of his business why…is it mine?"

Sadie's chin dropped in surprise, "What?"

"I thought it was because you just didn't want to mess with it, but you made it sound like there was a reason you weren't wearing it."

"I…" She wasn't really sure what to say, nor whether she wanted to tell him.

CHAPTER FIVE

"So, is it any of my business why you don't wear makeup?" He repeated.

Sadie stared at the road in front of her with her mind spinning in confusion. No one had asked her before, and she didn't want to lie. What should she say?

"What we talk about is between us," He said firmly. "I won't even tell your mother if that is what you want."

Still, she remained silent.

"In fact," He mused. "You wear the same jeans, boots, hat, and only wear plain button-up western shirts…nothing fancy." He glanced at her then back to the road. "Is all that for the same reason?"

She didn't look at him. Her heart was racing, but there really wasn't any reason she shouldn't tell him.

"Talk to me, Sadie Girl."

There was that tender, understanding voice. He melted her every time he used it, just like when her senses shut down after she threw Nora's saddle in the ravine. He was there for her then and she had promised to always talk to him.

"There is a reason," She whispered and stared out the front window at the passing scenery. "You're my dad, so I guess it is your business. But, it sounds a bit…vain."

"It's just between us, Sadie Tagger."

She swallowed hard and took another breath, "I don't want…I was told I…" Another deep breath. "I want things, or have dreams, and I don't want anyone to think it's…" She paused. "I…I don't want anyone to think that I use what I look like to get what I want."

He was silent long enough she glanced at him. His eyes were narrowed, and lips rolled into a thin line.

"Who told you that?" He finally asked without looking at her.

"It doesn't matter," She sighed. The words were said, and she couldn't take them back, so she might as well talk to him. He would only want the best for her. "I have lots of dreams and lots of goals in life, and if I'm just me and don't do anything…special to change that, then I can't be accused of using my looks to get what I want."

"Again…" He mumbled.

Sadie shrugged. "I'm just me."

"And I love 'just you'. So does everyone that knows you. But, we would also love you just as much if you didn't…" He paused.

"Stay plain," Sadie finished for him.

He huffed and shook his head, "You, my dear daughter, are NOT just plain."

"I try to be."

"Sadie, you will never be 'just plain'. There is a light within you that makes you glow. Your laugh, grin, sparkling blue eyes, and energy, just everything about you makes you unique and not plain. There is nothing that will take that away from you no matter what you look like."

"I can't do anything about that," Sadie shrugged. "After the barrel racing accident on Scarecrow…getting to the point I could ride again, I realized that I was content with life. I was happy with being able to move, walk, ride, and race again. I know I want to learn equine sports medicine at the Colorado university, and I'm very content with that. I'm happy with life and that part I don't want to change."

"You just don't want to change the outside to match the inside."

"I hadn't thought of it like that. I just work hard for what I want, whether it is with school or with the horses. No one can say that I use anything but my wizardly talent or my horsemanship to get it." Her voice was strong and full of conviction. It was truly how she felt.

"Your brain and horsemanship will always outshine the outside of you. No matter if you wore a potato sack and kept your hair in braids and ponytails," He glanced at her again. "Is this whole not wanting to shine thing the reason you have long hair and keep it in braids and a ponytail to hide it?"

Sadie looked at him with a smirk, "My hair is long because of Reilly."

"Reilly? What did he do…or say?"

"When Wade and I were seven, my hair was just at my shoulders; just long enough I could put it in a ponytail if I wanted it out of the way. One day, Reilly comes into the bunkhouse and says, 'lets go shooting' so Wade and I jump up to follow, but Reilly says just Wade and not me because I was a girl."

His eyes widened in surprise, "And you didn't hit him?"

"Sure I did," Sadie laughed. "Then he said I was just a girl, so I couldn't go with the guys doing guy things. Because I was wearing just jeans and a t-shirt like them, he pointed out my long hair. After they left, I went into the house to find scissors to cut my hair off, but Aunt Dru stopped me."

"Well, that's good."

"When I told her what I was doing, she got pretty mad at Reilly but madder at me for letting him get away with using the 'just a girl' reason for having their guy day," She grinned at her dad. "And she was really mad at Wade for going with him. Aunt Dru told me that I needed to show Reilly that a girl could do anything he could do. So, I kept my hair long to prove it to Reilly even though he probably has no idea," Sadie giggled. "And I also practiced like crazy at shooting so I was better than him, and he had to admit it."

Her dad laughed, "You're a pretty dang good shot. You and Grace are the best shooters of the kids."

"Grace practiced with me."

"Did she know why?"

"Nope; just that I wanted to be the best shot in the family, and she wanted to be better than me, so we practiced and practiced." She turned to look at him with a raised brow. "You think I'm not the best shooter in the family?"

He grinned, "You are of the kids, and probably your mother and Jordan."

"I'm a better shot than Aunt Dru and Uncle Scott. They both admitted it after the State Finals last month." She stared at her dad in anticipation.

"You want me to admit that you're a better shot than me?" He chuckled.

"Of course, I do," She grinned.

He shook his head, "Nah, that's not going to happen." He turned the truck off the highway and into Cottonwood. Uncle Scott was already at the store and unhooked from his horse trailer when they arrived.

"Can I go in the store and buy some food for the road while you switch trailers?" Sadie asked.

"Yeah, buy me some, too," Her dad pulled out his wallet and handed her the debit card.

"Me, too," Uncle Scott called out.

In the back of the store was a small deli, and she walked right to the counter. After giving the rather large order to a grinning deli clerk, Sadie read the bulletin board's messages and flyers. With three full deli bags, Sadie walked out of the store just as they finished switching the trailers.

She handed both of the men a bag, and both pulled out a breakfast burrito to eat while they talked.

"Avoid Nikki and Matt today," Uncle Scott said just before biting half of the burrito.

"Why?" Sadie asked.

"Nikki designed a branding corral to replace the lower pasture system at Circle 50," He answered. "The dealer called the ranch to ask about one of the gates. It wasn't on her design, so she realized Matt changed the order. The two of them have been going at it all morning."

"And it's barely 10:00," Her dad chuckled.

"There isn't any hurry to unload this trailer, so I'm headed to the equipment shop to avoid them until it blows over," Uncle Scott grinned, and with a wink to Sadie, he turned to his truck.

*****

They turned off the highway toward Jan's ranch in Nezperce. Sadie turned to her dad, "So…about that shooting thing."

He chuckled, "You ready to say I'm a better shot?"

She laughed, "No, because I'm better, and I think we should have a contest to prove it."

"You do, huh?"

"Yeah, and other than bragging rights, I have an idea what I want when I win."

"And what is that?"

"When I was in the store, I saw a flyer for the Cottonwood ranch rodeo in September."

"I've seen it before."

"If I win, you, me, and two other people create a team."

"Hmm," He hummed and turned into Jan's driveway. "And when I win?"

"Oh, we don't have to worry about that happening," She laughed.

Jan appeared around the barn, hesitated, looked back in the barn, and then continued forward to greet them. She was frowning with her lips rolled into a thin line.

"She looks worried about something," Sadie whispered.

When the woman saw Sadie's grin and wave, her scowl turned to a smile.

"And that, my Sadie Girl, is the light within you that makes everyone brighter when you're around."

Sadie didn't say anything; she just glanced at him then slid out of the truck. She knew he wanted to add that it didn't matter what she looked like, but she just ignored it.   He let Pepper out of the backseat.

"I didn't know you were with Grayson today," Jan hugged her.

"Just hitched a ride before dawn and didn't give him a chance to say no," Sadie chuckled.

"Like he would even think of saying no," Jan opened the gate. "We'll put the bull in here. They won't be here for another couple of hours to pick him up."

Four younger horses trotted to the back of the corral behind the pen.

"Can I go see them?" Sadie asked.

"Of course," Jan answered. "They are my last little herd from Bubba."

Sadie sighed. Bubba had been their stallion for twenty-four years, until his death the year before.

"I just have those four; two two-year-olds and two yearlings," Jan continued.

Sadie walked down to the four horses that were trotting around their pasture. They were excited to see what was coming out of the horse trailer.

The yearlings were black, just like Bubba had been, but one of the two-year-olds was a grey and the other a palomino. All four were beautiful and greeted her with inquisitive noses; until the bull was released into the pen, then they ran around their corral while snorting and bucking.

The bull was big, muscular, red, and she was sure it was going to be 72. The bull meandered across the corral to the fence next to the colts then turned to her. The ear tag confirmed it was 72. Sadie was surprised and a bit confused. She thought he was one of the best bulls on the ranch. And Aunt Dru sold him? No wonder her dad and uncle were upset.

Jan and her dad were walking down the fence toward her. She wanted to ask her dad but knew it wasn't the right time.

"The grey horse there is the last one out of the Bubba-Misty pairing," Jan was saying.

"Isn't that Monty's sire and dam?" Sadie asked. Monty was her uncle's cherished horse. The one Aunt Dru didn't get along with, but her uncle loved. Monty had also saved Wade's life when he broke his arm.

"Yes, it is," Jan nodded. "Last full brother to him."

"Ah," Sadie sighed and looked out to the prancing colt. "Monty's little bro."

"He for sale?" Sadie's dad asked, and her heart jumped as she turned to him with wide excited eyes.

"I was considering keeping him," Jan said thoughtfully. "That's why he is still here as a two-year-old. We've had the saddle on him but haven't ridden yet. So far, he's kind-hearted." She turned and looked at the two of them. "I'm not sure I would sell him to anyone else but your family."

"Does that mean you're writing a bill-of-sale?" He grinned.

"He would always be so loved and cared for," Sadie said hopefully.

Her dad continued, "Monty is getting up in age, and his little brother would be a good backup for him."

"You want him?" Jan asked.

As her dad nodded, Sadie gasped, "I already love him just for being Monty's little bro…please don't sell him to someone else."

"Alright," Jan nodded with a shake of the head and a smile. "Didn't expect to sell him today, but while we go do the paperwork, Sadie, go ahead and get him loaded."

"Yes!" Sadie grinned and ran to the horse trailer to get a rope and halter. Uncle Scott was going to be so happy!

With halter in hand, she opened the gate into the corral. All four horses were still at the fence looking at the bull lying down in the corner of his pen. He didn't look like he had a care in the world. Sadie was still surprised that her aunt had sold the bull.

The four younger horses turned to her as she stepped into the corral. Monty's little brother was the only one that didn't walk to her as she shut the gate.

"Wonderful," Sadie sighed. "Does that mean you're going to be stubborn like your brother?" She asked the horse and greeted the three. After a few moments, the little trio of horses walked to a big round bale of hay sitting in the corner of the corral, and the grey colt still stood next to the bull.

"Well, you like cows, so that is something," She slowly walked to him. "You just being stubborn?"

He didn't move when she approached or when she slid the rope over his neck and the halter up his nose.

"So, you don't mind being caught; you're just going to make the human work for it," Sadie grinned and ran a hand down his neck. He was darker than both Monty and Little Ghost; the other two greys in the family. Although he was already almost as tall. "You may be Little Bro now, but I have a feeling you're going to be taller than your big brother."

He walked calmly next to her and loaded in the trailer without hesitation. Jan, her dad, and Pepper were walking toward her when she shut the trailer's back gate. Her attention was pulled away by a familiar truck driving down the road toward them.

"She coming here?" Her dad asked.

"Yeah," Jan sighed as the veterinarian's truck turned into the driveway. "I have a three-year-old colt needing some attention."

"Always something," He nodded.

CHAPTER SIX

Sadie waved at Jessup's girlfriend, Kate, as she drove past them and toward the front of the barn. The veterinarian's smile widened when she saw her. Sadie couldn't help it; she glanced at her dad to see him looking down at her with a knowing smirk. She shook her head and hurried to greet the veterinarian.

"Well, Miss Sadie," Kate grinned as she stepped out of the truck. "I'm pretty sure what's going on with the colt, so this is a good chance for you to test your knowledge and diagnose it."

"REALLY?" Sadie gasped. She had to keep herself from bouncing in excitement.

"Good to see you, Kate," Sadie's dad said and stretched a hand out to shake the woman's hand. "And that is a great idea."

Kate's brown hair was pulled back into a braid down her back, and a ball cap with the veterinarian clinic logo covered the top. Ever since Sadie could remember, the woman always seemed relaxed and happy unless concentrating on a patient.

"The colt is in here," Jan said and waved an arm to invite them into the barn.

Anxious to see the patient, Sadie hurried into the barn. A sorrel horse's head tipped out of one of the indoor stalls with ears perked toward them in interest.

"If you don't mind, Jan," Kate said. "Would you tell Sadie what you told me on the phone?"

"Love to help our future equine specialist learn," Jan nodded and turned to Sadie. "His name is Dragon and has been fine with no issue in his walking until this morning. When I went out to the pasture, he was dragging a back leg."

"Like it was paralyzed or could he move his hip but just couldn't bend the leg?" Sadie asked.

Kate nodded in agreement of her question.

Jan beamed proudly, "He could lift with his hip. Just not bend the leg to push it into a step."

"Was there any change when you brought him in here?" Sadie asked.

"By the time we got to the barn, he was walking correctly," Jan answered.

Sadie hesitated as her hand reached to the stall latch. "What's his demeanor? Is he safe to be with in the stall?"

"Very friendly," Jan answered. "And that was a very excellent question."

Sadie took the halter and rope into the stall and patted the horse. After placing the halter on the friendly horse, she looked back at Jan, "Which leg?"

"His back right," Was the answer.

Sadie ran a hand down the horse's side and to the back of the leg. He was standing normal and didn't seem to be in any pain, so she pulled him forward a couple of steps. The leg moved naturally.

She handed Jan the rope, "Can you walk him out of the stall toward me?"

Sadie hurried to the front of the barn, so she had a good view of the horse as he neared.

Jan began walking with the horse while Sadie's dad and Kate followed. The horse moved normally. Nothing seemed to be wrong. Sadie mentally huffed in her mind and frowned in concentration.

"Can you walk her down to your fence and back?" She asked Jan.

The horse pranced excitedly when he saw the three younger horses that were still in the pen.

Her sorrel patient looked normal until the horse took a step, and the leg didn't bend, and he nearly tipped over before he caught himself. It looked like the knee joint had locked up.

Jan stopped, and all three adults looked at Sadie.

"I've read about what I think it is," Sadie told them. "But I've never seen it in person."

"Tell me why you're drawing the conclusion and what you think it is," Kate instructed.

"Ok," Sadie nodded and took a deep breath. She visualized what the stifle or knee of the horse looked like below the hide. "The stifle is like the human knee and has a patella like our knee cap. There are a lot of ligaments and tendons that help the knee bend, or it can make the knee lock so when the horse is sleeping standing up, it doesn't fall over." Sadie looked to Kate, who nodded, so she continued. "The medial patella ligament hooks over the medial trochlear ridge on the end of the femur, which locks the joint. When the horse steps forward it normally disengages, so the knee will bend. But, Dragon's is getting stuck in the upward position which is called the upward fixation of the patella, or a locking stifle."

"Can you unlock it?" Kate asked.

"We can try walking the horse backwards," Sadie said and took the rope from Jan and had the horse back up a few steps, and then move forward. The knee bent normally.

Sadie looked up with a relieved smile.

"Very good," Kate said proudly. "How old are you?"

"Thirteen going on thirty," Sadie's dad chuckled.

"Well, I am impressed," Kate smiled at her then looked at Jan, "We can do x-rays to check for other issues, but I agree with Sadie's diagnosis."

"Is it curable, or is he going to do this forever?" Jan sighed.

Kate turned to Sadie, "Want to answer that?"

Sadie's eyes narrowed as she tried to remember everything that she read, "You can try farrier work to see if you can angle the hoof differently, so it doesn't catch. Then there is an injection you can try, or you can do a medial patella ligament…" Sadie looked at Kate for help.

"Desmotomy…" Kate nodded.

"Yeah, that's when you cut the ligament, and it lets the patella move over the medial trochlear ridge and not get caught." Sadie concluded and looked at Jan. "It almost 100% curable, and they can have a normal life without restrictions."

Jan looked at Kate.

"I agree with her diagnoses, treatment, and prognosis," Kate nodded firmly.

Sadie grinned and looked up at her dad. He was beaming in pride.

"Well, since he's just in training, and I have a few more I'm working with, I'll get the farrier up here and see if that works first," Jan said and huffed. "I've been worrying it would be a lot more expensive than that, and dang scared I was going to have to put him down."

"No worries," Kate nodded in understanding. "This time, it is a good outcome."

"He doesn't seem to be in pain, so let's put him in the smaller pen next to the younger group," Jan said, and they walked to the fence.

"Looks like you're missing the grey colt," Kate nodded to the three younger horses trotting to the fence to greet the sorrel.

"He ended up in our trailer," Sadie's dad grinned. "He's Monty's little brother."

"Oh, and I love that grey," Kate smiled. "He is a true workhorse."

"Uncle Scott is going to be excited," Sadie chuckled and slid the halter off the sorrel.

"Jessup will be, too," Kate nodded. "He said he had a chance to ride Monty a couple of years ago and wished you all had a dozen more just like him."

Sadie's dad smiled, "Scott doesn't let anyone else ride him very often. I don't think I've ridden him after initially retraining him from the barrel racer point of view. It's been almost fourteen or fifteen years now."

"He finally let Wade ride him on a trail ride last spring," Sadie added.

They walked back to the barn and to the veterinarian's truck.

"Well, Sadie," Kate said. "One of these days you need to do a ride-along with me and be my assistant."

"Really? I can do that?" Sadie gasped.

All three adults chuckled.

"Absolutely," Kate opened the door of her truck. "I love the work and teaching it. No doubt, we would both learn from each other."

"You just say when," Sadie's dad nodded. "She has parental approval."

"Good," Kate smiled at him. "I talked to Jessup on the way up here, and he said you two were there for breakfast."

"We didn't get to stay long, but he is looking better," He nodded.

"And his attitude is better and more cantankerous every day," Kate chuckled. "The better he feels, the harder it is for him to stay there. He finally kicked me out and told me to go to work during the day. I'm only 'allowed' to visit at night."

Sadie chuckled, "And sneak him in food?"

"Oh, yeah," Kate nodded.

"Well, then," Jan raised a hand. "I have some chocolate zucchini bread for him, and I made a couple of dozen molasses cookies that I know he loves. Wait here, and I'll go get them."

As they watched her walk away, Kate sighed, "He didn't need to lose any weight before the accident, so the 20 pounds he's lost so far isn't helping him regain the strength."

"But he's strong-willed and determined," He said. "He'll get through this."

"We'll all make sure he does," Sadie declared.

Jan returned carrying a bag full of Jessup's treats and a bag for Sadie and her dad. With a thankful hug, Kate said her good-byes.

As Sadie and her dad drove away from the ranch, he pushed a button on his phone, and the ringing echoed in the truck.

"Hello Sadie, what do you want, Grayson?" Uncle Scott answered.

They could hear the humor in his voice, and both chuckled.

"You unload that trailer yet?" Her dad asked.

"No," He answered.

"Where are you?" Her dad turned and smiled at her.

"I'm at the highway leased pasture with Matt," He answered.

"So, you didn't avoid him very well," Sadie giggled.

"Not at all," Uncle Scott sighed. "Matt called and said he went to the pasture to check the cows and get away from Nikki and found part of the fence down. He's out checking the herd while I'm fixing fence."

"Matt have a trailer on his truck?" Her dad asked.

"No, he had the ATV in the back," He answered.

"Alright, Sadie and I'll come help, and then Matt can take the trailer back to the ranch since we're done with it. We have to go back to Lewiston already. "

"Alright," Uncle Scott grumbled and the line went dead.

Her dad chuckled, "I'm sure Matt gave him an earful, and he doesn't like fencing."

"Well, Little Bro will make him feel better," Sadie smiled. "We should video it for history. When did Monty come to the family?"

"Hmm, I think it was right before Wade was born and Monty was three. Jan had sold him as a yearling, and the people called and said he wasn't going to work for them because he was stubborn. He didn't have the personality to make a barrel horse."

"But he's been a perfect ranch horse."

"That he has, but it took a lot of work to get him that far. He was one of the most stubborn, hard-headed horses I had ever trained."

"Have you trained all the horses?"

"Dru trained her own when she was running barrels. Scott likes to ride and push cows, but he doesn't like the training. He would rather be in a tractor or working on it."

"And you'd rather be on horseback all day," Sadie nodded.

"Given the choice, yes. I don't mind working harvest because the work needs to be done, but I'd jump on a horse quicker than I'd jump in a tractor."

"Well, I think Little Bro is going to be just as stubborn."

To keep from going back to their previous conversation of what clothes she wore, she kept him talking about horses until they turned into the lease property driveway. They also ate all the treats Jan had placed in the bag.

Her dad parked so that Matt and Scott's trucks were between them and the fence the men were working on.

Neither looked happy.

Before he opened the door, her dad turned to her, "You pay attention to Matt's reaction when he sees you."

Sadie smiled at him, but inside she just sighed. Keeping him busy talking about the horses didn't make him forget their earlier conversation. Pepper was released from the truck and met with Uncle Scott's dog, Spur. The two dogs trotted out into the pasture together.

When Matt turned, he glared at his uncle, but when his eyes turned to her, Sadie gave him her biggest smile and waved. His shoulders lowered, and a smile appeared.

"Hi, Matt!" She chirped. "What can I do to help?"

"Get some gloves on," He chuckled.

They helped stretch barbed wire and clip connectors onto the posts for a half-hour before the horse in the trailer became impatient and let out the first low whinny.

Both Matt and Uncle Scott stood straight up and looked back at the trailers.

"I didn't see any horses in that field," Matt said.

"There aren't any," Uncle Scott said. "It's not even fenced."

Sadie grinned as she looked at her dad. He nodded with a smile, and Sadie turned to run back to the trailer. All three men were walking toward her when she stepped out of the trailer with the horse behind her.

"One of Jan's horses?" Uncle Scott huffed with a smirk to his brother.

"Couldn't pass him up," Her dad nodded.

Sadie grinned at her uncle in anticipation of his reaction, "He's Monty's little brother."

Her uncle's eyes widened in surprise.

"Last full brother before Bubba passed last year," Her dad added.

"Well, he's mine," Uncle Scott declared and reached for the lead rope.

Sadie happily dropped it in his hand as her dad and cousin laughed.

"We've been calling him Little Bro," She told him.

"Good name, and I don't have to try and come up with something," Her uncle swept a hand down the horse's neck. The colt did the one thing to him that he didn't do with Sadie; he turned his head into her uncle's chest as if accepting him and returning the affection. There was an instant connection between the pair, and Sadie's smile widened.

"You can take him and the trailer to the ranch," Her dad told Matt. "Sadie and I are headed back to Lewiston."

"Weren't you just there?" Matt asked.

"Yeah," Her dad huffed.

Ten minutes later, they were driving down the highway again.

The phone alert went off, and a text appeared on the screen.

Text from Nick: Thanks for sending pictures of cart. It's paid for.

"Text him back and ask if he wants us to go get it or if he is going," Her dad instructed.

They received an immediate text back.

Text from Nick: Lucas and I are on the plane landing in Boise. If you could, that would be great.

"Text him and ask if they left town to get away from Matt and Nikki."

Sadie giggled and typed the message.

Text from Nick: I cannot confirm nor deny that in writing.

They both laughed.

"We're going to be down there anyway, so we might as well go get it. Text him and let him know."

Sadie sent the text then curiously turned to her dad, "Why are we going back to Lewiston?"

"Because I remembered something, and we're headed down to an appointment."

"What and where?"

"I remembered who made the comment to you about using your looks to get what you want in life, and I made an appointment with her at 4:30."

Sadie's heart sunk.

CHAPTER SEVEN

Sadie didn't say anything; she just melted into the seat as the memory of the argument with the veterinarian, Helen, flooded through her mind.

The audacity of the woman wanting to use a twitch on the injured Rufio when it was Sadie that had made her mad; upset enough to call her a little blonde-headed pip-squeak.

"WHAT DID YOU CALL ME?" Sadie had yelled.

"A pip-squeak," Helen had growled. "You may think you can get your way because of your looks, but I don't care about them. So give me back the horse so I can get his leg taken care of and get away from here."

"YOU'RE NOT TOUCHING THIS HORSE OR INSULTING ME AGAIN!" Sadie screamed and turned Rufio to walk away.

When Helen had tried to take the rope from her, Wade had yelled and eventually agreed that Helen would not touch the horse again. He had kicked the angry veterinarian off the property, and they had called Dr. Mark for help.

Sadie and Wade were sure they would be in trouble, but when their parents heard the truth, there was no punishment, and it had never been discussed since.

She had no desire to talk to Helen. She just wanted it all to go away.

A quick glance at the clock on the truck dash let her know it was 11:20. She had a few hours to change his mind.

"Dad…"

"You won't change my mind. We are going to see her at 4:30 after her appointments are done."

She sighed and looked out the side window. The farmer's fields passed as if unseen. How was she going to get out of this? Just the thought of talking with Helen made her stomach ache.

"Now what?" Her dad mumbled.

Sadie's head jerked forward as the truck started to slow down. There was a red truck pulled over to the side of the road. A man had started to walk away from it as her dad stopped in front of him.

"Isn't that Warren?" Sadie asked.

"Yeah," Her dad confirmed it was the foreman of the neighboring ranch.

"Stay in the truck," He said and looked over his shoulder for the traffic on the highway. "I don't want you out here…terrible place to get stopped."

A car sped by them just before he opened the door.

"Idiots can't figure out how to slow down…" The door closed.

Sadie watched as the men spoke, then turned to walk back to Warren's truck. Another car drove by but had the decency to move to the other side away from the men and truck.

A large semi-truck drove by; the pressure from the wind shook the truck. Her body shivered, and her dad's hand flew up to cover his cowboy hat to make sure it didn't fly off.

"Ohh, I hate this," Sadie whispered to herself.

The two men walked to the front of the truck and lifted the hood. Another car drove by so close it made Sadie jump. A loud ring erupted from her dad's phone, and she cried out. Taking a deep breath, she turned the phone, so she could see who was calling.

Reilly's face appeared, and it was a video chat, so she quickly hit the button.

"Well, you're not who I was expecting," His blue eyes under the dark hair and straw cowboy hat sparkled in humor. Paneled fencing and horses with noses down in a pile of hay were behind him.

"I hitched a ride with Dad today," Sadie smiled. "We've pulled off the side of the highway in a really busy spot."

"Why?"

"Warren broke down, and Dad is helping him."

Reilly nodded, then looked pensive.

"What's going on?" Sadie asked.

"I'm having an issue with one of the horses, so I was calling to talk to Grayson…see what he thought."

"You're still in charge of the saddle horses?" Sadie asked. He had just started working for a rodeo stock contractor.

"Yeah, training the younger ones and keeping the older ones in shape."

"Maybe I can help?" Her successful diagnosis with Kate and the sorrel gave her the confidence to ask.

"Worth a shot," he smirked.

Sadie chuckled, "Thanks a lot."

He shrugged, "They said the mare was four, and she's decent size, about the same as Kit, but she has a good mindset. The problem is, when I work with her, she is really stiff. She'll turn left a bit, but her head and neck are like a board when I move her right."

"On the ground or in the saddle?"

"Both…"

Sadie frowned as her mind raced to narrow down the symptoms and remedies, "Did they give you any history on her?"

"Not really, just that they trained her a year ago, but she was out on pasture for the winter. Just brought her in a week ago and gave her to me."

"Does she have any injuries? Scrapes or cuts?"

"Just the usual from rubbing against stuff," He answered. "She's standing right here. I'll show you."

The phone turned to reveal a dark brown horse with a light blonde flaxen mane and tail tied to a post. Her shoulders were broad and flowed back to a wide back and a large, quarter horse rump. The mare turned her head slightly to look at him, and a dark brown eye, which was full of curiosity, looked at her.

"My goodness, she's beautiful," Sadie gasped.

"She's pretty flashy," Reilly agreed and walked around the horse so Sadie could see all of the mare. "She's going to be a pick-up man's horse in the arena, and that's what they like for the rodeo…a flashy, standout horse. Plus, she has the size, speed, and mindset."

She sat up in the seat and leaned to the phone, "Walk around her again so I can see her closer."

Slowly, Reilly did as she asked, then turned the camera back so she could see him.

"Does she limp?" Sadie asked.

"No…here, I'll show you."

He set the phone down on something so she could see out into a corral. After a moment, Reilly appeared at the far end and was leading the horse. He walked straight at her, turned the horse, then walked away, then repeated it at a trot. When they walked away, he stopped with his body next to the horse's shoulder and had her turn her neck to him, so her nose touched his hand. Then he went to the other side, and the horse wouldn't turn no matter how hard he pulled the lead rope. Finally, the horse just stepped around so she could face him.

Reilly patted her shoulder then walked back to the phone, "Did you see anything?"

Sadie shook her head, "No, she moves pretty good. Stand to her side and using your fingertips put pressure behind her ears and then up high down her neck to the withers. See if she reacts."

He held the phone so Sadie could see his fingers press into the horse's hide behind the ears. There was no reaction. He continued until he reached the withers, then stepped on the side she didn't like to turn. There was no reaction to his fingers until just above the shoulders and before the withers. The muscles twitched.

"Do it again, start from the top," Sadie said.

The truck door opened, but Sadie was concentrating so hard on the image of the horse she didn't react. Her dad slid onto the seat and closed the door. Leaning to the side, he looked at the phone to see the horse.

"See that?" Sadie asked Reilly and pointed to the horse's shoulder. "Her muscle twitched right there. Do it again, but just a little more pressure."

She and her dad leaned closer as Reilly moved his hand down the horse's neck. The twitch was more evident, and the horse slightly moved away from him.

"Something is going on with her cervical vertebrae," Sadie declared.

"How would that happen without an injury to the outside?" Reilly asked and patted the horse's shoulder.

"She could have fallen when she was out on the range, or rolled wrong…or just anything, just like a human hurting their neck," Sadie answered.

Reilly turned the phone, and his eyes widened when he saw the two of them looking back.

"Hey, Grayson," Reilly grinned. "I was calling you for help, but Dr. Sadie stepped in."

Sadie chuckled but hearing him call her Dr. Sadie just made her chest fill with pride, "Start with a chiropractor before you ride her again. It won't just go away."

"Sounds like good advice," Her dad nodded. "Where should Dr. Sadie send the bill?"

They all laughed.

"I'll talk to Nick before he leaves," Reilly grinned.

Her dad started the engine of the truck and looked behind them.

"Let me know how she is doing," Sadie instructed.

"Will do," Reilly said with a wave then the screen went black. The truck moved out onto the highway.

Dr. Sadie…she mused. With all her heart, she wanted that to come true. It would take years of schooling and years of being away from home and at college to make it happen, but she knew it would. There was no doubt in her mind.

But then what? Was she going to stay away or come back to town? Maybe work at one of the local universities to help teach other people how to help horses. She knew that all the local veterinarian clinics worked with the universities. If she did that, she would need their support too…including Kate and Helen.

Sadie sighed; maybe her dad was right. He wanted her to face Helen for what happened in the past, but Sadie knew she needed to face Helen for her future.

She didn't mention it to him because she didn't want to talk about it. She wanted to keep his mind away from the whole thing. She looked at the road ahead of them and saw Warren's red truck; they were following him down the highway.

"What was wrong with the truck?"

"His gas gauge wasn't working, and he ran out of gas," He answered. "I had some in the back we used for the ATV, but I'm not sure it will get him to the gas station."

When the rest-stop gas station appeared, Sadie turned to her dad.

"Can we stop and get something to drink and maybe a snack?"

"Well, I never turn down a snack," He chuckled. "You go in for the food, and I'll top off the tank, so we don't end up on the side of the highway, too."

"OK," She grinned. "I still have your debit card."

"I'll use the credit card then."

He was leaning against the truck when she walked out of the building carrying a big bag of chips, licorice, and their drinks. The phone was to his ear, and he was looking out to the farmer's fields that lay behind the station.

"…gooseneck, long bed, sturdy for hay or vehicle. The cart isn't very long, but we might as well get one for hauling." He turned and looked at her as she approached. "Just have it ready, so we can just hook-up and leave. We'll need to get the cart then out to Lenore and back to Lewiston before 4:30."

Neither of them spoke of the appointment as they left the gas station and drove toward the Winchester Grade, which would lead them to the road to Lewiston. Just at the top of the grade, his text alert rang out, and they both looked at the screen.

Text from Wade: Ask Sadie if she wants updates from Kylee and Tara

Sadie silently groaned. It was the first time all day she had thought of the Junior High School National Finals Rodeo going on without her. Of the two sisters they had met at the State Finals, Kylee had qualified for Nationals; Tara replaced Sadie.

"Well?" Her dad asked.

"I didn't really want to think of it at all today," She whispered.

"Is that why you were riding so early this morning?"

"Yeah, I couldn't sleep and didn't want to lay there and think about it."

"Horses always make us feel better."

"Yeah," She sighed. "I checked this morning, the loose pocket of skin is still on Scarecrow's leg, but it doesn't seem to bother her anymore. I know it was the right decision not to go, and I didn't want to go without Wade since it was our dream to go together."

"And now what? Did you change your dream?"

"No, we're working on going next year, and hopefully Alex will be with us."

"If he can get himself to relax."

"Yeah," Sadie nodded. Alex did well team roping with Wade at practice, but once they competed, whether jackpot or rodeo, he still had issues relaxing.

"When Scott and I were team roping, we always had a backup horse in case one was hurt, and so we didn't overwork them." He glanced at her. "If you're serious about barrel racing into the future, you need a backup for Scarecrow."

"I know," Sadie sighed again. "Grace and Nikki both offered Buttercup and Harvey, but…"

"Neither mare is competitive enough in barrels or poles to match Scarecrow."

"Honestly, Dad, the only horse that we own that could keep up with her is probably Cooper. He is fast and loves to compete."

"He is good in any discipline we've put in front of him. He'd be a good backup for Little Ghost in roping, too. He does well in poles with Nora."

"And, nothing bad about Nora, but poles is not her expertise…he could be better."

"I'm sure Nora would agree with you."

"She has; we've talked about it. I try to help, and she just shakes her head and says she only competes in poles for fun and to go to rodeos with us. She even said she wasn't going to use Cooper for cutting this year and just work with Isaiah."

"Have you talked to Reilly about using Cooper?"

"He's offered him."

"Then you need to consider using Cooper with Little Ghost and Scarecrow this year, so next year, when you qualify again, you'll have a backup horse for both of them."

"Yeah…"

He glanced at her again with a smirk, "Make it official and send a text to Reilly so you can get that part off your mind and answer Wade."

Sadie picked up his phone;

Text to Reilly: This is Sadie. Dad and I were talking. Can I use Cooper this next year or two for rodeo?

She opened the message from Wade but couldn't get herself to answer. She didn't know if she wanted to hear if the sisters were doing well or not.

The phone alert popped up.

Text from Reilly: Of course, I didn't bring him to this job, so you would have him when you were ready. Besides, he needs more on his resume.

Sadie smiled and read the message to her dad.

Text to Reilly: I will do my best to make him a state champion in poles.

Text from Reilly: I know you will.

When she put the phone back in its holder, he glanced at her.

"Did you answer Wade?"

To answer her dad, Sadie pulled out the licorice from the bag and handed him a handful of the long strands.

He didn't ask her again but did glance to her, "I have to say, I'm pretty proud of your work with Jan's horse and the horse Reilly was showing you."

"Thanks, Dad," She beamed.

"It's pretty rare to find a thirteen-year-old that is so confident and dead-set on her career."

"What did you want to be when you were my age?"

"Always in agriculture, but before the accident, I was going to become a professor."

Sadie gasped, "Really? Like Professor Waverly?"

"Exactly like him," He nodded.

"Well, Dad, I think you would have been an excellent professor," She beamed. "You are so patient and thorough that it's easy to learn from you."

"Thanks, Sadie Girl."

"What about Aunt Dru and Uncle Scott?"

"Dru's dream was barrel racing into the NFR and being a rancher."

"Well, she got the one at least. And Uncle Scott?"

"He is the same as Wade."

"Born a farmer," Sadie chuckled.

"From the moment he could sit in the tractor. And, he loves tinkering with them. He's worked on so many different machines through the years that if you took one apart, piece-by-piece, he could put it back together again."

"And it would run."

"Better than it had before."

CHAPTER EIGHT

When they arrived at the North40 store, her dad parked next to the new, long flat trailers. One of the workers was there to greet him. Within minutes they had a trailer attached to the truck and were driving away from the store.

"That was quick," Sadie smiled.

"My assistant, Scott, was able to get everything done over the phone," He chuckled.

"Assistant…I'm sure he would love that," Sadie laughed.

"It's not the first time, nor will it be the last time I call him that."

She grinned, "I think six of those carts would fit on that trailer."

He just shrugged.

When they drove back into Nora's coach's ranch, not a truck was in sight.

"It doesn't look like anyone is here," Sadie mused.

"Craig said this morning just to come and get it."

He backed the trailer next to the Meadowbrook cart and, with her dad's strength, easily rolled it up onto the trailer. After securing it tightly, they were off down the road again…only to receive another text;

Text from Tessa: I heard you were bringing the cart to Lenore. Have you left yet?

Sadie picked up the phone before her dad told her to.

Text to Tessa: Just loaded the cart and leaving Craig's ranch.

The phone rang in response.

Sadie accepted the call; "Hi, Tessa. It's Sadie and Dad."

"Hello!" Tessa's voice boomed into the truck. "I heard you hitched a ride this morning. I hope you're making her earn her keep, Grayson."

He grinned, "She's already saved my hide once and is doing a great job of keeping me fed and entertained."

"Well, you'll have to tell me that story, but right now, if it isn't too late, can you pick up Alex from the hospital on your way out here?" Tessa asked.

"No problem," He answered. "With this trailer attached, he'll need to be out front waiting for us. We'll slow down, and he can jump in the back with Pepper."

"He loves that dog, so he'll enjoy that," Tessa sighed in relief. "I'll call him and let him know."

"Bye!" Sadie chirped and hit the 'end' button.

When they arrived at the hospital, Alex was already standing next to the road and waved.

"Thanks, Grayson," Alex said when he crawled into the truck and greeted Pepper with a big hug.

"Always fun to have you along for the ride," Her dad answered. "But, now that you can talk without him around, how is Jessup doing?"

"He has his good days and his bad days," Alex answered. "The big picture on the wall of the ranch will make him happy because it makes him think of home or make him grumpy because he's not there. Today was a good day. He really liked the two of you coming by and having the family breakfast."

"Wish I could do it more often," Her dad nodded.

Alex chatted about Jessup until they were just driving out of town, then the phone went off again with the shrill of an alert.

"What is that?" Alex asked.

"Video chat request from Dru," He answered and pulled the truck over to a roadside stop and stopped the truck before hitting the accept button.

The nose of a grey horse appeared on the screen, making all three of them chuckle. As the horse moved around the corral at the Tagger Ranch, it became clear it was the newest member of the family; Little Bro.

"Want to explain?" Aunt Dru's voice asked.

"Dropped off the bull and picked up a horse," Her dad stated.

"Yes, I can see that," Aunt Dru huffed.

"Bubba passed last year, and this is the last full brother to Monty, and he was grey, so he ended up in the trailer," He said flatly to his sister.

"Oh," There was a pause with the phone beginning to move as she walked, but the horse's image remained. "I would have done the same thing. Has Scott seen him?"

"Claimed him the second he knew who it was," Sadie answered with a grin.

The phone was twisted around, with Aunt Dru suddenly appearing with her blonde hair shining against the bright blue sky behind her. Sadie and Alex leaned over the phone together.

"Well, look at you two," Aunt Dru smiled. "Much better faces to look at instead of Grayson's."

Alex and Sadie laughed.

"We called the horse "Little Bro"," Sadie grinned.

"Good name," Aunt Dru nodded. "Matt dropped him off without a word and left."

"Still arguing with Nikki?" Alex asked.

"Yeah, arguing…that is one way of putting it," Aunt Dru huffed. "I understand that after the first initial blowup, they haven't talked to each other just to everyone else. Josey is in Enterprise with her grandparents, so I got an earful from Nikki, and Scott got it from Matt."

"Side to be taken?" Sadie's dad asked.

"No, they'll work it out, eventually," Aunt Dru huffed. "Scott dropped off your trailer and said they would empty it later. What's in it?"

Sadie's dad grinned. "We're on a time limit, and I need to get back on the road."

With that, he reached out and ended the call.

Sadie giggled.

When they drove up the driveway to Nick's ranch in Lenore, Tessa was standing by the front door next to a stack of boxes. She greeted them with a wave making her curly hair bounce, and the smile made her eyes shine.

"Your mom is so pretty," Sadie said to Alex.

"She's beautiful," Alex grinned. "Inside and out."

"Just in time!" Tessa grinned with hands-on hips. "UPS was just here and delivered Nick's latest round of packages."

"For Nikki's baby?" Alex laughed.

"Of course," Tessa laughed. "Are you going to the ranch today?"

Sadie's dad shrugged, "If not the ranch, we can get it to The Homestead."

"That will work," Tessa nodded.

One box took up half of the back seat, and the rest of the boxes were tucked around it, leaving half of the seat for Pepper.

"I know the big box is a baby-sized rocking horse and a little bull. It'll be a good year before the baby can use them, but Nick thought they would be good decorations for the nursery until then," Tessa grinned.

"Good thing he only has six months left to shop before that baby is due," Sadie chuckled.

"I agree," Tessa laughed. "He was thoughtful enough to ask Nikki about the bigger items before he bought them."

Sadie looked across the pastures. Nick had purchased the property from Cora after the Tagger herd were discovered and rescued. The barn where the mudslide had flowed into was now gone. Nick had replaced it with an apple tree.

From where they were standing, she couldn't see the lower barn.

"Where are the horses?" Sadie asked.

"Up at Circle 50," Tessa answered. "We were up there last weekend and will be going back up tomorrow, so we just left them there. Nikki is training Red and getting the dog busy, so he is up there, too."

Sadie turned and looked back at the old chicken coop. They had rebuilt the coop, and dozens of chickens were pecking around it and into the trees. Just up the hill from the chickens was a large piece of plywood leaning against the pine trees. Sadie knew what it was for and turned back to her dad.

"You still have that .22 rifle in your truck?" She asked him.

He turned and looked at her with blue eyes filled with humor, "Always."

"What for?" Alex asked and looked over at the coop.

"Dad thinks he's a better shot than me," Sadie huffed. "So, I challenged him, and since you have the shooting range up, I'm thinking it's time to find out."

CHAPTER NINE

Tessa and Alex looked at him in anticipation.

"You've been called out, Grayson," Tessa grinned. "You going to accept?"

He laughed, "How could I not?"

"I'll get the targets," Alex turned and limped into the house.

With a grin, her dad opened the door of the truck and pulled out the rifle. He handed it to Sadie then the box of ammunition was retrieved.

"I'll be the judge," Tessa declared. "When we compete, it's twenty yards to start, five shots each, and we'll flip a coin to see who shoots first. Of course, the tightest pattern to the center wins. If it is too close to call, we move to 30 yards."

"Sounds fair," Sadie nodded and looked up at her dad.

"Sounds fair to me, too," He walked up the hill.

Alex appeared out of the house with a handful of paper targets, a large stapler, and handed them to his mother.

She attached two targets side-by-side on the plywood; then, as she walked toward them with a grin, she pulled a coin from her pocket.

"Alex, you decide who gets heads and tails," Tessa said.

Alex grinned, "Heads for Grayson, tails for Sadie."

The coin was tossed, and everyone but her dad leaned forward to see the result.

"Grayson, you shoot first," Tessa declared and pulled out her phone to video the competition.

Sadie grinned. That is exactly what she wanted. She wasn't sure if her dad would fudge his shooting to help her win or not, but if he shot first, she would know for sure.

Without much delay, he had the five rounds in the gun and lifted it to his shoulder.

After a deep breath, he pulled the trigger the first time.

"Bull's-eye," Alex whispered.

Four more shots rang out without much hesitation between each one.

"We'll wait for Sadie to shoot before we look at the target," Tessa said.

Sadie looked at her with an anxious smile because she did not doubt his shots were in the center.

He didn't say anything to her when he handed her the rifle; he just stepped back and looked out at the target. She loaded the five rounds, positioned herself with the gun to shoulder and feet in a strong stance. Focusing down the barrel, over the pin, and to the dark center ring on the target, she took a deep breath, let it out, and squeezed the trigger.

Bang.

"Bulls-eye," Alex whispered.

Bang….bang….bang…another deep breath…bang.

"First round!" Alex called out and led the way to the targets.

Sadie's heart was racing in anticipation as they neared the targets. They had both hit the dark center ring three times. Both had one shot just to the right, but, she had to admit, her fifth hole was further out of the black center than her dad's.

"Well, this one goes to Grayson," Tessa declared. "It's awfully darn close, though. You want to go to thirty yards?"

"Yes," Sadie and her dad said in unison.

They all four chuckled.

"Sadie, you're first on this one," Tessa said and handed her five more rounds.

Alex limped to the 30-yard marker and pointed to the line while Tessa lifted her phone again to video the competition.

Sadie repositioned, took a deep breath, then…another deep breath…bang.

"I can't see that far to see where it hit," Alex chuckled.

Sadie ignored him and concentrated on the barrel, pin, target, and her breathing.

Bang…bang…a deep breath…bang…bang.

With a huff and a grin, she handed the rifle to her dad.

"That is some pretty fine shooting, Sadie Girl," He grinned. "Glad to admit you're my daughter."

Sadie laughed, "Well, that's good."

"Final five," Tessa smirked as she handed over the last five rounds.

Sadie took another breath of anticipation as he positioned himself with rifle at his shoulder, and legs spread in a solid stance. He took a breath. There was more time taken between each round as he shot. He was obviously concentrating more, and Sadie had no doubt he was trying to win.

When the last shot rang out, all four of them had wide strides to the target.

Sadie's five rounds circled the black center ring. All close, but not one in the bulls-eye. Her dad had three just outside the black circle and two side-by-side in the middle.

"Grayson is the winner!" Tessa declared.

"Dang, good shooting, though," Alex looked at Sadie.

Sadie looked up at her dad and wrinkled her nose at him.

"I got it today," He laughed and wrapped his arm around her shoulders and squeezed. "But on any other given day, you could have won."

"So what did you win?" Alex asked.

"Well, if I had won, he had to do the Cottonwood ranch rodeo with me in September," Sadie sighed.

"So? What did you win?" Tessa asked him.

Sadie's dad grinned, "Sadie has to do the Cottonwood ranch rodeo with me in September."

"Yes!" Sadie laughed and wrapped her arms around him and squeezed as hard as she could.

"And bragging rights, this time," He laughed, and they strode down to the truck. "Anything else you need to go into town," He asked as he opened the door and set the gun inside. "We have an appointment at 4:30 to get to, so we need to move along."

"No, I think that's it. Thanks for bringing Alex home and the fun competition," Tessa smiled, and the pair of them watched as Sadie and her dad drove away.

The text alert rang out before they reached the highway.

Text from Grace: I just watched the shooting video. FUN! Congrats Dad! Great job, Sadie! Mom is with me, and you have no other choice but us completing the ranch rodeo team.

"Oh, fun, Dad!" Sadie clapped and reached for his phone to answer.

"You need a phone," He stated.

She just shrugged, "I am usually with Wade, Nora, or Grace, and they all have phones."

"Does that have to do with Helen's comment?"

Sadie sighed and shook her head. She had been trying to forget about Helen and hoped he would, too. "No, I would just rather be spending time with the horses or reading."

"You still reading the college books you got from your clinic at the university last month?"

"Yeah, the second time through. I want to read and learn as much as possible from them before school starts up in the fall."

They talked about the books and clinic for the 30-minute drive back to Lewiston.

The text alert rang out as they neared town.

Text from Cora: Call me when you can.

Sadie hit the speed dial button.

"Grayson or Sadie?" Cora answered.

"Both," Sadie smiled. "You're on the speaker."

"Well, that works, too," Cora chuckled. "I saw the shooting video. Great job to both of you."

"Thanks," Sadie giggled. "Mom and Grace have already said they are joining us."

"I can't wait to watch but, right now, are you somewhere you can pick up some supplies for me?" Cora asked.

"Just driving back into Lewiston," Her dad answered.

"Can you swing into Costco for me? I'll text what I need," Cora said.

"No problem…" He started.

"Who are you talking to?" Aunt Dru's voice was at a distance on the phone.

"Grayson and Sadie," Cora answered. "And I've put you on speakerphone here, too."

"You really think we needed more round-bale feeders and water troughs?" Aunt Dru's voice was full of accusation.

"Wouldn't have bought them if we didn't," Sadie's dad smirked.

"Grayson…" Aunt Dru started.

"How did you get to the Homestead already?" He asked.

"We're both still at the ranch," Cora chuckled. "…she is avoiding her children."

Aunt Dru sighed. "Guilty."

"Reminds me of Dad and Granddad when they would go at it, and Mom and Grandma would head for the hills," He smiled.

"Well, hopefully, Matt and Nikki won't take as long as they did to get things settled," Aunt Dru huffed. "Matt is off with Scott somewhere, and Nikki is at Circle 50…I think. Where are you?"

"We are pulling into Costco for supplies for Cora and anything else I might consider we need," He continued.

"I'm hungry," Sadie grinned.

"Me, too," Her dad chuckled.

"Sending two of the biggest eaters into Costco on an empty stomach," Cora huffed with a humored lilt to her voice.

"Grayson…" Aunt Dru started again.

"And, I have a new, empty, twenty-five-foot flatbed trailer attached to the truck we can fill, too," He chuckled. "We're here; talk to you later."

His hand shot out to end the call before another word was spoken. It was another ten minutes before they actually arrived at the store.

"Grab me a couple of long sausage dogs when you get what you want," He said as they walked away from the truck. He didn't get a basket shopping cart; he grabbed the long flat cart instead.

Sadie just chuckled and walked to the deli.

He was on the phone when she found him in the aisle with all the tools, "Yeah, we have some time and can bring it out. I have boxes for Nikki you can take to the ranch. Where are you?" He paused and picked up a new tool belt, and tossed it on the cart. "I'll let you know when we leave here."

The phone was slid back into his pocket, they walked around the corner, and he stopped.

"Where are we going next?" Sadie asked.

"Bed & Breakfast, The Stables, or at the construction site for the new arena. Where ever Jack happens to be when we get out there. He wants to use the new trailer."

Sadie chuckled, "That was fast."

He was typing on his phone, so she glanced around his arm to see what he was doing. He had the calculator up and was typing numbers.

"Whatcha' calculating?" She asked.

"The square footage of the bunkhouse," He murmured and then looked up at the cases of wood flooring on the shelf.

"You mean no more splinters?" Sadie teased.

"These two are real wood and not the cheap stuff. Which one do you like?" He pointed at a grey flooring and a deep brown with golden highlights.

"Brown and gold that looks like an aged tree."

He began loading cases of the flooring onto the cart. As they walked out of the store, he glanced at his phone.

"We won't have much time," He muttered.

"We just have to drop off the trailer?"

"Trailer, groceries, and Nikki's boxes so Jack can take them to the ranch tonight," He nodded.

"And the flooring." Sadie grinned.

A mischievous twinkle appeared in his eyes.

****

When they arrived at The Stables, both Jack and Nikki's trucks were in the parking lot.

"Looks like Jack might be getting an earful now," Her dad chuckled as he turned the truck and backed the trailer in-between the two trucks. "You put Nikki's boxes in her truck, and I'll move the flooring into Jack's."

Sadie also put Cora's supplies in the back seat of Jack's truck. She scratched Pepper's ears and solemnly closed the door leaving him inside. Dogs weren't allowed loose at the Stables.

As they walked toward The Stables office, a truck and trailer pulled in the parking lot. Sadie glanced back to see two women in the truck. She didn't know them but did recognize them haven ridden at The Stables before.

"I think we're cleared of everyone else's stuff now," Sadie chuckled.

"Until the next text," He added as he opened the door to the office. No one was inside.

They continued to the back of the property where the arenas and round-pens were.

Jack and Nikki were standing outside of the fence, watching a rider lope around the arena. Both turned to them as they approached, and both smiled when they saw Sadie.

"See…" Her dad whispered, and Sadie just rolled her eyes in exasperation.

"I heard you were having a ride-along with your dad," Nikki smiled.

"Just trying to keep him from being bored," Sadie chuckled.

"With a little shooting in there," Jack nodded. "Good job on almost beating him."

"I'll get him next time," Sadie teased.

"The trailer is in the parking lot, boxes from Nick in your truck, Nikki, and for Jack, we added some ranch supplies in the back of your truck with Cora's supplies," Sadie's dad said.

"Great, good timing on the trailer," Jack nodded.

Sadie and Nikki walked behind the two men as they made their way to the trailer. Sadie told her what Alex had to say about Jessup as they watched as the trailer was released from her dad's truck and hitched to Jack's. Within minutes, Jack was driving out of the parking lot. He disappeared down the road toward the new arena.

"So, what did Dad buy this time," Nikki asked and opened the door of her truck to see the pile of boxes.

A muffled yell echoed from behind the stables, then a high-pitched scream.

Without hesitation, the three of them ran.

CHAPTER TEN

Her dad's long legs had him well ahead of her and Nikki. He disappeared around a corner just as another scream echoed. Chills rose on Sadie's arms.

Side-by-side, she and Nikki turned the corner in time to see her dad, with one hand on the top rail, effortlessly jump the fence of the smaller arena. A large bay horse was bucking and running wildly around a woman who was lying in the middle. Another woman was at the gate trying to get it opened to lead her frightened and prancing horse out of the arena.

Sadie ran for the gate to help, but her eyes were watching her father.

The bay horse was saddled and the bridle's reins were flopping around him as he bucked. The woman in the middle lifted her head to look at the horse as Sadie's dad reached her.

"Skipper!" The woman called out. "He's never done this before."

The horse jumped in the air, bucked then ran right toward the two in the arena. The woman screamed, and Sadie's dad jumped up and waved his arms at the horse making the horse veer to the side. Sadie opened the gate for the other horse to be frantically led out and Nikki started to run in the arena.

"Nikki! Get out!" Sadie's dad yelled, and Sadie grabbed her cousin's arm and pulled her back out. She quickly shut the gate as the bucking horse approached.

The horse's owner was scrambling to stand while Sadie's dad pulled her toward the gate. The horse ran toward them again, making him have to drop the woman and wave frantically again.

"I can't just stand here!" Nikki reached for the gate.

"You're pregnant!" Sadie yelled and pushed her back.

Not wanting to take a chance of the out-of-control horse going for an open gate, Sadie crawled up and over the top. She waited until the horse ran by, then jumped down to run out to the woman. While her dad waved the horse away, Sadie helped the woman to the gate Nikki held open.

"He's never done this before," The second woman cried out.

"Never," Said the owner as she stood shaking, pale, and with wide eyes looking out at her horse. "He is always so calm."

Letting Nikki take care of the shaken owner, Sadie turned back to crawl up onto the fence.

"You stay out," Her dad called out to her.

"I will!" Sadie answered.

He was now following the horse as it bucked and kicked. Although she knew he was talking to the horse, Sadie couldn't hear what he was saying. Her heart was pounding.

When the horse stepped on one of the loose reins, it began to tumble. Her dad went into action and grabbed the other rein. When the horse rose, it bucked out again. With the back hooves in the air her dad reached for the cinch. The horse screeched and ran sideways to get away from him but he ran alongside and pulled on the leather strap. Three bucks later, the cinch was loose enough the saddle and pad went flying into the air.

"Whoa, now…" Her dad whispered as the frightened horse stopped bucking and just ran in circles with only the rein's length between them. "Easy, boy. You'll be alright."

When they moved to the opposite side of the arena, Sadie slid onto the dirt and ran for the saddle and pad. If the horse took off again, she didn't want her dad tripping over the gear. Nikki and the owner had the gate open when she ran back out.

"I just don't understand," The owner mumbled. "He's never done anything like this."

Sadie threw the gear on the ground and turned back to jump on the fence again. Finally, the horse came to a sudden stop. His tail was swishing, ears twisting back and forth, eyes searching, and head up with nostrils flaring. He looked confused but not dangerous.

"That a boy…that a boy…" Her dad whispered and slowly approached.

The horse's body was at full alert and looked like it was ready to take off again, but it let her dad approach.

"There you go…there you go…you're alright…" His voice was low and smooth.

The horse's body began to relax.

"What happened to start his bucking?" Nikki asked.

"I put a boot in the stirrup and started to rise, and he just took off," The owner answered.

"He bucked and nearly took her head off," The other woman gasped. "I'm sorry, but I did scream when he went after her."

Sadie turned and looked at the woman, "He went after her, or did he run to her for help?"

"Oh," The woman gasped. "I didn't think of that."

"He would never attack me," The owner nodded nervously.

"Something was hurting him," Nikki's voice shook. "He was going to you for help."

Sadie turned back to the arena to see her dad alongside the horse and running a soothing hand down his neck.

"He was hurting," She called out to him.

He nodded without looking at her and slowly stepped back along the horse's side to begin an inspection.

They watched as he walked down each side of the horse and just looked without touching. Then, he had the horse walk a few strides.

"He's walking fine," The owner whispered.

"I don't see anything; you see anything?" Sadie called out to him.

He shook his head and began running a gentle hand down the horse's side and legs. When he went up toward the horse's back, the horse stepped away from him.

Sadie turned back to the owner, "Same gear or is there something new?"

"The saddle pad is new," The owner answered.

Nikki walked over to the pad, picked it up, and tossed it across the fence as if it was on the horse's back. It was dark grey wool underneath with a red and black pattern on the top. There was a leather patch on each side of the pad that would be at the horse's girth then another that would cup over the high withers.

Nikki looked out at the horse with narrowed eyes, then lifted the saddle pad. Her hand went to the top, which would have been over the horse's withers, it instantly flew back, and she gasped.

"What?" Sadie asked and stepped down from the fence.

"Something bit me," She grimaced and flipped the pad over. "I don't see a bug…but…"

She bent the pad, and a silver sparkle shown.

"What is that?" The owner leaned forward.

Nikki bent it further back to reveal the tip of something silver. "Do you have your Leatherman?" She called out to her uncle.

He walked the horse to the fence as he unbuckled the holster at his waist and handed her the tool. Flipping it open and adjusting it to the plier position, Nikki clipped onto the silver and pulled. It was half of a sewing needle.

"Oh, that poor horse," The owner's friend gasped.

"Oh, Skipper," The owner cried out and walked through the gate and to her horse.

"You alright?" Sadie's dad asked the woman.

"Yes, I'll have bruises, but it could have been so much worse for both of us," She nearly cried. "Thank you for coming to our rescue."

He just nodded as they inspected the horse. He gently slid his hand down the withers to the back and lifted his hand.

"Touch of blood," He sighed with a frown. "No telling how many times he was jabbed with it."

"Every time he bucked and the saddle pressed into him," Sadie grimaced.

"Take pictures of that and send it to the company," Nikki instructed. "Let them know it happened so they can check their other pads. Someone could get killed from that."

"You're so lucky you didn't," The owner's friend stated.

"Have that pad checked out before you try it again," Sadie said. "But I can't imagine they broke off more than one needle in it."

They waited until the owner had coddled the horse and walked him back to the stable.

When they were alone, Sadie's dad turned to Nikki with a serious glare, "Don't do that again. It's not just you anymore."

Nikki nodded with shoulders lowering and hand going over her stomach, "I didn't even think. Maybe once I start showing more it will remind me."

"Well, that was scary," Sadie declared.

"Yes, it was," Nikki nodded. "I wasn't going to stop in but I'm glad I did, sort of," She chuckled nervously.

"Where were you going?" Sadie asked as the three walked toward the parking lot and their trucks.

"Over to the arena," She answered.

"Well, we have a few minutes, you can ride with us," Sadie's dad said.

"I'll ride in the back with Pepper," Sadie grinned and opened the door to the excited dog.

When they arrived, Jack was driving the Tagger Enterprise's backhoe onto the new trailer, and Matt was directing him.

A loud sigh escaped from Nikki, but neither Sadie nor her dad mentioned it.

"Can Pepper get out here?" Sadie asked.

"Yes, she probably needs a good run," Her dad answered.

The dog jumped out as soon as the door was opened and ran to greet Matt. He scratched the dog and glanced over his shoulder as the three walked toward them. His eyes flickered with disinterest at his sister before he turned back to Jack.

"You have chains to secure it?" Her dad called out.

Matt turned, "No, I was going to go back up to The Stables and get some once he was up."

"There are some in the back of my truck," Her dad said, and Sadie turned back to help him retrieve the chains.

Matt and Nikki were left standing next to each other by the trailer. They did not exchange a word nor look at each other.

"Everybody in the family has been avoiding each one of them all day," Sadie whispered to her dad as she climbed into the back of the truck. "And we end up bringing them both together."

They both chuckled as she handed him the chains.

While the men secured the backhoe to the trailer, Nikki walked Sadie to the property where the new building was planned. A long wall of rocks ran down the north side of a massive dirt field.

"We used the backhoe to clear out the large boulders," Nikki explained. "Instead of finding somewhere to put it all, we decided on a rock wall between the future parking and the arena."

"It looks natural that way," Sadie nodded.

"Tomorrow, they come in and start the measuring and placing stakes for the beginning of the construction."

"You and Matt didn't have issues deciding on this one?" Sadie teased.

Nikki laughed, "No, this was me, Jack, and Mom, and since Jack and I have been playing around with the design for years, it was pretty easy to settle on one. Mom let him, and I choose since we'll be working in it the most. We decided on stalls down both sides of the arena with a wide aisle between. Bleachers will be from the ends since we're more interested in training and rehabilitation than we are event viewing."

"One level or two?"

"We're going with two, but the upper level will just be around the parameter. Since we get nothing but direct sunlight out here, then we're going with solar panels to help with the energy bill."

"Those are cool."

"I'm more excited about the water treadmills and the vibration plate stall."

"I can't wait," Sadie grinned. "I'm borrowing Cooper from Reilly for a couple of years, so I'll have three horses on the waiting list."

"Oh, that's great," Nikki smiled. "That will be one heck of a team for you."

The trailer beginning to move had them walking back to the trucks. They waved at Jack as he drove away.

Matt was already walking to his truck.

"Matt," Sadie's dad called out, making her cousin stop and turn. Her dad turned to Nikki. "Let's get the air cleared. What happened?"

Both her cousins jaw's clenched closed, and they glared at each other.

Her dad shook his head, "Alright, Nikki, you tell me your side of the story."

With a huff, she turned to him, "We both agreed the lower pasture corral system needed to be updated. I designed one and showed it to him. HE didn't agree with it and designed a different one."

"Mine was better," Matt growled.

"You'll get your turn," Sadie's dad told Matt, then turned back to Nikki.

She continued; "We discussed them, and he left when I said I was going to order the panels for my design," She shrugged. "So I did, and HE changed the order to match his design just before they were shipping."

Sadie looked at Matt, who had a 'whatever' expression.

"Alright, Matt," Sadie's dad turned to him. "What's your side of the story?"

"It's not a story," Matt glared. "It's the facts. I did not agree with that system. I liked the chute to separate better on my design, and I DID NOT agree to her ordering her design instead. So, I changed it." He glared at his sister. "If she can order without my approval, I can order without hers."

"Well, it's arguments like these that created the voting system with your mother, Scott, and me," Sadie's dad nodded. "…and why we put it in place when you became owners of Circle 50." He looked between the two of them. "It was agreed that if you two couldn't decide between yourselves that you bring it to the three of us to help guide you through. Correct?"

They both nodded.

"It's stupid arguments like this that break up families and ranches," He continued with a glare to both of them. "You've affected nearly everyone in the family just because you didn't reach out. That is why Scott, Dru, and I vote on decisions like this."

"You're right," Matt's shoulders lowered, and he nodded with a glance to his sister.

Nikki just glared in return.

Sadie's dad shook his head, "And, Nikki, you're mad because, in the end, he is getting the corral system he wanted, and you're not." When she didn't say anything, he continued. "So, what is your solution? Just stay mad?"

"I'm not mad that he is getting his way; I'm mad that he didn't stick around when we were initially talking about it so we could talk it out. Instead, he just left."

"That's because you were getting so upset, and I didn't want you so mad it hurt the baby," Matt huffed.

Nikki's eyes widened in surprise, "Nothing is going to hurt this baby just because I get mad."

"Well, I didn't know that," Matt huffed.

"So, you're just being protective," Sadie grinned and Matt shrugged.

Nikki shook her head with an exasperated smile at her uncle, "As for the solution? We're going to replace the mountain corrals, too, so we'll put my design there. Then after we use both next year, we'll all know that my design is better than his."

All four of them chuckled.

Nikki turned to Matt, "Getting mad isn't going to hurt this baby, but I'll warn you now that making me mad while I'm pregnant may hurt you."

Matt grinned, "I'll take that warning and warn Lucas, too."

"Oh, he already knows," Nikki smirked.

Sadie's dad chuckled then pulled out his phone, "Time is ticking, so we're moving on."

Nikki rode with Matt to The Stables while Sadie and her dad pulled into the parking lot of The Bed and Breakfast.

"Now what?" Sadie grinned.

"Your mother texted and said there was a package here to pick up."

As Sadie slid from the truck, she caught a glimpse of a yellow Jeep, "Josey is here. I thought she was with her grandparents."

Her dad grinned as he opened the door to the building for her, "She was probably hiding out from Matt and Nikki, too."

There were a few people standing and talking in the large foyer of the building, no one behind the registration desk, but a loud buzz of talking filtered down the long hallway. It led past the office doors on the left and guest rooms on the right and to the event center at the end of the hall.

They made their way to the room and were met by a pile of boxes, dozens of white chairs set up in rows. The large double doors on the opposite side of the room were open with a delivery truck backed up to them. More chairs were being carried out of the truck by Josey and Nora's best friend Candace.

Aunt Jordan was directing where to place a large white archway at the front of the room by the wall of windows. Paige was instructing the movers on where to place two large pedestals on each side of the archway. They would hold the large bouquets of flowers.

Sadie hurried to help setup the chairs, "I thought you were at your grandparent's today," She said to Josey.

"I was, but Jordan asked me to come back and help set up for this week's weddings."

"More than one?"

"One on Wednesday night, and then one on Saturday," Josey nodded. "Luckily, the brides know each other and are using the same chairs and archway, just different decorations."

"Wow," Sadie chuckled.

"Yeah," Aunt Jordan said from behind her. "And, believe it or not, we have twenty weddings scheduled here this year, indoor and outdoor. It would have been 21, but I wouldn't book a wedding Roundup weekend."

Paige walked to the group, "We're full of visiting rodeo guests that weekend and we'll all be going to the rodeo to support Grace."

"Aren't you a busy lady," Sadie grinned at her aunt.

Aunt Jordan shook her head, "I'm just here filling in while Leah was busy with Grace, and Tessa took a day off before all the commotion of the week. It's all theirs and Paige's after today."

"How did you get wrangled into that?" Sadie asked Candace's aunt.

Paige shook her head with a exhale, "Dru is looking at opening a Bed & Breakfast on the other side of Moscow and wants me to consider the manager position."

"I hope you do!" Candace grinned. "That would be so much fun."

"Well, we'll see," Paige cautioned her.

Josey's head turned, and a broad happy smile appeared, and her eyes began to twinkle with love. Sadie didn't have to look to know that Matt walked through the door.

He walked right up to her and gave her a welcome home hug and kiss.

"Well, we need to get out the door," Sadie's dad said. "Where's the package?"

"On Leah's desk," Josey said. "I brought it in from town for her once she heard you were coming this direction."

"And now we're out the other direction," He nodded to everyone and turned.

Sadie was right by his side as they walked to her mother's office. It was a very feminine office, painted a light blue, with framed pictures that had been taken of the spring flower fields at the ranch. Centered on the wall across from her desk was a group picture taken the fall after the Tagger Herd had come into the family. All family members and the herd, plus Monty, were in the picture. To the right was a picture of Grace twirling in a flowered field. It was the picture Matt had taken the weekend they had rescued the two kids from the plane crash.

To the left of the group picture was Sadie and Scarecrow racing across the finish line at one of the barrel races. On the desk was a picture of Sadie's parents in a relaxed moment during branding. Both were covered in a fine layer of dirt and sweat. Their clothes showed the abuse of the day's work, but they were leaning against a fence and in each other's arms. They looked right at the camera and their happiness and love shined. Sadie had taken the picture with the camera Lucas had given her after her accident at the barrel race.

The whole room made Sadie happy, and she couldn't help but smile.

Her dad walked into the room and picked up a white bag. Then, after a quick glance at all the pictures, he turned.

"On the road again," He chuckled as they walked out of the office.

Before he started the truck, he typed on his phone then set it in the carrier. Within minutes, a text alert rang out.

Text from Grace: Mom is driving, so I am answering. We should be in town by 6:30, dinner out?

Sadie picked up the phone and looked at her dad, "I'm assuming yes, but where?"

"What's your choice?"

"Anywhere with a good steak."

Text to Grace: We are hungry, meet you at steakhouse at 6:30.

Text from Grace: Dang, now I'm hungry. I want SHRIMP!

They glanced at each other and chuckled.

*****

They drove past the Homestead as they made their way back to town. All the horses were together in one corner of the east pasture. Some were laying down, while others were standing with head low.

"What a bunch of lazy horses," Sadie smiled.

"Their day of rest," Her dad nodded. "Cooper just doesn't know what he's in for with his new jockey on board."

"Yep, training starts in the morning."

"And what are your first steps to turning him into a State Champion poles horse?"

Sadie's mind raced with all the different patterns he would be worked through and the conditioning to get him back into top shape.

They discussed different training techniques as they drove through town. When they reached the river and began to cross the bridge from Lewiston to Clarkston, Sadie's mood began to darken. She knew he was keeping her mind busy, but Sadie's stomach ached more with each mile. When the clinic came in sight, she lowered into the seat of the truck with the dread swarming over her.

He turned into the parking lot, "I'll park a distance away from the main door, and she can come out here, so the clinic staff are not disturbed."

Sadie nearly groaned out loud. There was no way she wanted to talk to Helen with her dad there.

With a sigh, she relented, "Can you just let her and me talk?"

"Alright," He nodded. "I'll wait inside."

He pulled into the parking lot and stopped the truck between the blacktop and the round-pen. There was a clear view of the truck from the large window of the building. She had no doubt he parked there so he could keep an eye on them.

When he stepped out of the truck, he hesitated and looked back at her, "Sadie Girl," He whispered.

She could feel the love in his words, but when she turned and looked at him, she saw it, too.

"I'm not punishing you or asking you to do anything I wouldn't have wanted my parents to do for me," He said firmly. "You need to face the difficult times in life and not hideaway because it makes you uncomfortable. Whatever was said between the two of you needs to be cleared up, now."

"Alright, Dad," She whispered.

"And one more thing."

"What?" She sighed and looked at him.

"All day today, we have seen just about everyone in the family."

"Yeah?"

"At no time did you ask to go with any of them so you didn't have to come here today."

She frowned, "I'm with you today, Dad. That's what I wanted…I didn't even think of going with anyone else."

He smiled in encouragement, "And I'm more than happy with that. You can come with me all summer when you're not training, but there must have been something in you that realized you needed to get this over with too. Face this, head-on. You knew that as well as I did…or you would have asked to go with someone else."

"I guess," She admitted. Sometimes, he was just too dang smart.

The door closed, and she took a deep breath

CHAPTER ELEVEN

Five minutes of torturous waiting went by before the side door of the clinic opened, and the woman walked out. She wore light blue scrubs covered with a white lab coat. Her long dark hair was pulled into a tight pony-tail, and her eyes were glaring at Sadie as she walked toward her.

"Dr. Sadie, Dr. Sadie, Dr. Sadie," she whispered as the woman neared. It was easier to focus on her dream than the past.

Helen walked toward the window, and Pepper appeared on the console next to Sadie. Normally, the dog would be anxiously and happily waiting for a new visitor, but this time the dog lowered its head and watched with narrowed eyes. Sadie felt a little better that the dog had the same opinion of the veterinarian as she did.

"Your father asked me to come out and talk to you," Helen huffed. "What do you want?"

Sadie pressed her boots down onto the floor of the truck and tried hard to keep her anger switch from flipping. Her eyes flickered back to the front of the clinic and to the large pane window. With hands on hips, her dad was staring out at them.

"I don't want anything from you," Sadie started. "He wanted us to discuss what happened at The Homestead when Rufio was hurt."

"What's to discuss?" Helen said with an impatient huff. "You thought you knew more than me, I corrected you, you got upset, I got upset, and Wade came out, and I left."

Sadie wanted to roll her eyes, "That's it?"

"Yes," Helen shrugged. "There isn't anything more to say."

Sadie glared at her.

"Well, I came out and talked to you so, I guess that's it," Helen said with a nonchalant raise of a shoulder, then she turned to leave.

Anger bubbled in Sadie's stomach, causing a bitter taste in the back of her mouth. Her hand jerked to the lever, and she yanked to open the door. Helen didn't turn when the door clicked open, so Sadie slammed it closed as hard as she could. She did it to stop and startle the veterinarian, and she accomplished both. The woman spun around, and when she saw Sadie standing with shoulders high and glaring with narrowed eyes, she took a step back.

Unfortunately, her dad had seen it, too. He disappeared from the window then reappeared as the door to the clinic opened, and he walked out. Sadie didn't want him to approach; she wanted to talk to Helen by herself and on her own terms. So, Sadie lowered her shoulders and leaned against the door to make it look like she was relaxed. Her dad hesitated then came to a stop.

She looked back at Helen.

"Wade said you apologized to him," Sadie said low enough she knew her dad couldn't hear.

Helen nodded, "Yes, I did."

"And you apologized to his parents who weren't even at the barn that day."

Again, she nodded, "They had to deal with the phone calls."

Sadie's eyes narrowed, and she stood away from the truck. She was tall enough to look the woman directly in the eyes. "Did you apologize to my parents?"

Helen's jaw tightened, and her nostrils widened, but she didn't say anything.

"I haven't heard an apology for what you said to me."

The woman's jaw shifted to the right, and her head tilted back.

"If you had no intentions of apologizing to my parents and me, why did you come out here?"

The vet's shoulders rose and dropped, "Since he'll probably tell you, I may as well tell you."

Sadie huffed, "May as well…"

Helen's eyes narrowed enough that Sadie knew she had upset her…which is what she wanted.

"He told me if I didn't come out to talk to you about the incident with the horse at your barn, then Tagger Enterprises would move their entire veterinarian needs to another clinic."

Sadie was impressed by her dad but tried hard not to show it on her face. She stayed relatively calm.

"That would be a big loss," Sadie said. "Kate would be upset with that."

"So I came out here," Helen shrugged.

"And yet you didn't say anything to me about that day or what you said to me before Wade came out and told you to leave."

Helen didn't respond; she just looked at Sadie as if she was bored. The expression made Sadie mad, and she looked back at her father to try and calm her racing heart. He stood quietly, watching them closely.

She turned back to the veterinarian.

"I don't care if you apologize to me, but I do care that you refuse to apologize to my parents since you did to Uncle Scott and Aunt Jordan."

Helen didn't respond, and it fueled Sadie's anger.

"So, maybe I should call Dad over here and tell him what you said to me before you got mad and took it out on Rufio."

Helen's eyes widened.

Sadie huffed, "People have bad moments. I know I have, and most everyone I know have, but we almost always apologize once we realize what we did or said."

"Almost…"

"Yeah, those times I don't is because I'm too embarrassed to admit what I did or even face what I did…or said." Her eyes narrowed at the veterinarian. "I will apologize that I got so angry that day, but you and everyone else know that I have a temper. I'm working on that, but that doesn't mean you didn't know it. I was eleven…you're not."

"So, that is supposed to give you an excuse?"

Sadie smirked, "I didn't need an 'excuse' for getting mad. You gave me a REASON to get mad."

"You and I both know what was said, and there is no need to repeat it. What was said was said, and now we just move on with our lives," Helen stuffed her hands into the pockets of the coat. "Maybe next time you'll let the professional adult do her job and not try to tell her how to do her job." After a moment of glaring at each other, Helen continued, "Well, there were two of us to start that argument, and since you apologized, then I should also."

Sadie's stomach clenched, "Wade said you told them you had a bad week, and you took it out on US and, to clarify, you took it out on me then Rufio. Wade barely had anything to do with it."

Helen's lips rolled into a fine line, and her jaw clenched, "You are right." She finally nodded. "I had fought to keep a dog alive for a couple of days and finally lost him. His owner took his anger out on me. It's not an excuse or reason for my…mood, just a statement. Then my sister informs me she was thinking of moving to the Tagger Ranch with Jessup…so I was losing her to your family. Again, just a fact and the spark that made me angry at your family."

"She is a grown woman…"

"Yes, I know that, but we had become close since my divorce the year before, and we agreed to buy the clinic and be partners, and I was feeling neglected and financially stressed."

"What does that have to do with what you said to me…about me?"

"I should not have called you a pip-squeak. Name-calling never helps and just fuels the fire. I most certainly shouldn't have been gruff to the horse, either," Helen took a deep breath and let it out. Her neck began to turn red, and it moved up to her face. Her jaw clenched. "I have seen…," She stopped and took an angry breath with her face turning redder. "I have seen girls like you get what you want by just batting your eyes and flashing a smile and giggling right at the right moment."

Sadie's eyes widened in anger, and felt her own face turn red, "Girls like me?" She fumed. "I don't do that!" She kept her voice low, but it trembled with anger. "I work for what I want."

"You use your looks to get what you want, and if you don't win that way, you throw your temper out, and they just give it to you to stop you from unleashing on them."

Sadie stepped away from the truck and leaned toward the woman, "I have never used my looks to get what I want. I even asked Wade if I did anything like that, and he said no."

Helen huffed, "But you use your temper."

"My temper flares when people won't listen to me because of my age or they try to take something from my family or me. It's NOT to get away with anything."

"And yet, you do," Helen growled in a low voice that only Sadie could hear. "Like I said that day, I don't care about your looks, and you may think you know what you are talking about when it comes to horses, but you're just a kid, and you don't know it all. That is what I told you that day and why you got mad. If you want to tattle-tale to your dad, then fine. Throw your little fit, bat your baby blue eyes at him, and pout that you're not getting your way, and he can take his business elsewhere just like you want."

They glared at each other with eyes on fire and skin dark red. Sadie's whole body tingled in anger.

"I never said that is what I wanted. I may not like you, but I love Kate and would never do that to her."

Helen took a deep breath and stepped back as the redness subsided, "I'm not too fond of you, either."

"Yes, so we both know that," Sadie fumed.

With another deep breath, Helen's shoulders lowered, "I'll apologize to the point that I am the adult in this situation, and this should never have happened…but it did."

"Yes, it did," Sadie agreed with a sneer.

"I'll apologize to your parents, too."

With that, Helen turned and walked to Sadie's dad that had been intently watching the whole confrontation.

Too…Sadie thought as she watched the veterinarian talk to her dad. There was no 'too' because she sure didn't feel like it was an honest apology. She also knew that she never wanted anything to do with the woman again, whether now or in the future. If it weren't for Kate, she would never have to see Helen again.

Her dad shook the woman's hand, and after a slight turn and a knowing smile pointed at Sadie, Helen walked away. Sadie huffed and turned back to the truck. She stared out the window as they drove away.

"Clear the air?" Her dad asked.

"Yes, it's very clear," Sadie answered with as calm as a voice as she could muster.

Every word of the conversation was scrutinized. It definitely did not go the way she had been anticipating or dreading all day. There was no love lost between the two of them, and Sadie thought that was OK. She always wanted to be liked by everyone, but this time, she was fine just pretending the woman didn't exist.

The thought of telling her dad crossed her mind then was quickly dismissed. Maybe Wade…no, he had spent a lot of time with Kate at the hospital with Jessup, so he wouldn't be objective. Sadie sighed…maybe Nora? She was so lost in her thoughts that when the truck stopped, and the engine was shut off she was shocked they were back at the North40 store.

"What are we doing here?"

"Come with me," He said and opened the door.

As they walked toward the front doors, he glanced down at her.

"Remember last month when that lady yelled at Nora when she accidentally hit her car while she was trying to park?"

"Yeah."

"Well, for a long time, Nora would not even try to park in a parking spot and would only park on the side of the road."

"Yeah, like down at the hospital when Jessup first got hurt. But she will now."

"She practiced and can park fine now but do you think that what that woman said to Nora will ever truly be forgotten?"

"No, she was pretty rude and mean for it just being an accident."

"Nora will think of it forever."

They walked through the store's front doors, and she followed him down the aisle that lay straight ahead.

He stopped and looked down at her, "I know that whatever was said between you and Helen just now will never erase what she said to you a couple of years ago."

Or what she just said, Sadie thought, but just nodded.

"When Reilly made the comment about you 'just being a girl' and wouldn't let you go with them, you grew your hair out in spite of him."

"To show him girls can do anything he can."

"Exactly," He nodded. "You need to prove the same thing to Helen. Do not let what she said affect you for the rest of your life. Prove to her that no matter what you look like, your brains and your talent will get you what you want in life…not that someone just gave them to you." He lifted an arm to the side and waved it toward the racks of women's clothing. "Stop making yourself plain to prove a point. Let the true Sadie out. Go pick out some clothes that YOU, the true Sadie wants to wear."

Her brows rose in surprise as her heartbeat grew stronger. She looked at all the clothes.

"I want to see the outside of you match the inside," he continued. A hand went over her stomach as the butterflies flew.

"I don't know, Dad," She whispered. She had to admit; it was a bit overwhelming.

"Take your time, Sadie Girl," He said. "I'm going to the other side of the store to pick up a few things. Walk around, get your bearings, then try on some clothes."

She looked up into his blue eyes that looked lovingly at her.

"Ok, Dad," She whispered and watched him walk away.

A few hesitant steps took her between four circular clothing racks; so much summer color. She continued walking but kept her hands down and just looked as if seeing all the bright summer colors for the first time. The overwhelming feeling washed over her again. Maybe the shirts weren't the best place to start.

She found the jeans that Grace wore, so Sadie chose a couple of those to try on. Then she wandered down the boot aisle. Her boots were always brown and plain, but she found a black pair with turquoise and red stitching and were tall, all the way up to her knees. They were bright and fun, so she tried them on. When she stood and stomped down the aisle in them, the excitement finally took over the nerves. She walked back to the shirts and looked at a t-shirt that looked like amber and dark brown leather, and it had a turquoise horse running across the front. She loved that.

A bright red shirt caught her eye. The body and collar were solid, but the arms were a flowing lace, like angel wings. Right next to it was a rack of brightly colored vests that were thin and dropped to her knees. Grace and her mom always wore them, so she found a dark blue, yellow, and red Aztec pattern that matched the boots.

A saleswoman was standing by the dressing rooms, and Sadie just smiled as she walked in. She walked out in the new jeans that she had tucked into the tall boots, the red shirt, and the long vest that stopped just at the top of the boots. The vest flowed around her, and she grinned as she looked up at the saleswoman. The lady pointed behind her. Sadie turned to find a belt rack. She added a thin silver and black concho belt to hold the vest tight to her waist.

When she stepped out of the dressing room area, she passed a jewelry case, so she stopped and looked inside. Centered on the shelf was a necklace that looked like an elk horn. It reminded her of the pair of elk sheds that were attached to the outside of the Homestead library doors. Aunt Dru and Reilly had found them on one of their spring rides.

"Can I try that necklace on?" She asked the saleswoman.

"Yes, and those little earing right there look like conchos and will match your belt," She added.

"I don't have pierced ears," Sadie shrugged.

"Well, we don't do it here, but if you want them pierced, that little beauty shop up by Home Depot might do it for you or the jewelry shop at the mall."

"I don't know…"

"Sounds like our next stop," Her dad was behind her with the biggest grin as he looked at her outfit.

"What do you think, Dad?" Sadie twirled around for him.

"Now, THAT, is my Sadie," He pulled her into a hug. "We just need to replace that hat." He pulled the old straw cowboy hat off her head and turned to look for another.

Sadie laughed and followed him.

"Not very stylish for a lady," He mused as he pulled a hat down from the display. "What would be your dream hat with that outfit?"

Sadie chuckled, "I have always wanted a black 'Gus' hat."

"Perfect," He nodded and walked down the aisle, pick up and inspecting each felt hat. "And here we go…if it fits."

He placed the black hat on top of her head and grinned with a nod, "Too wide of a brim?"

Sadie looked in the mirror and nearly squealed in delight, "It's perfect!"

He turned to the saleswoman, "We'll take everything she is wearing, and she'll wear it out the door." He turned to Sadie's gasp. "Go pick out a couple more shirts."

She squealed in delight and ran for the leather looking shirt with the turquoise horse. Five shirts later, they were walking to the checkout stands.

"Didn't you buy anything?" She asked him.

"Oh, yeah," He said with a smirk. "It's upfront waiting for us."

With her new and old clothes in a bag, they walked out of the store pushing two shopping carts full of the items he had purchased: a chainsaw, extending pole saw, gas-powered weed eater, a backpack weed sprayer, feed buckets, and a handful of new lariats.

He was most definitely on a spending spree for the day, and it made Sadie laugh.

They stopped at the beauty shop, and the lady showed her how to apply mascara and eyeliner. Sadie stopped at that much, and her dad agreed. Then they had her ears pierced so she could wear the Concho earrings and the last stop was at a hair salon.

"Now, about your hair," He looked at her in concern. "Is it still long just to spite Reilly?"

"Oh, no," Sadie gasped. "I love my hair long."

"But it's always in a braid or ponytail. For this new look, for today, you get it washed and blown out and let it hang loose."

And that's what the salon did. She walked out with hair was down to her waist and in its full glory as she skipped and made it bounce out to the truck.

"That is a serious amount of hair," He laughed.

"It's pretty though," Sadie agreed.

"Beautiful blonde just like your mother's."

"Oh!" Sadie twirled to him. "I can't wait for her to see me!"

"You want to take a picture and send it to her or surprise her in person at dinner?"

"Surprise at dinner, of course, Dad," Sadie laughed.

Twenty minutes later, Sadie was standing in the steakhouse restaurant hidden behind a booth wall so she couldn't be seen by her mother and sister walking in the door. She heard Grace's 'life is good' laugh, and it made her giggle with excitement.

CHAPTER TWELVE

She counted to thirty, stood tall and confident then strode out onto the outside patio where her family was waiting. There was no way she could stop the grin when her mother's eyes moved from her father and up to her. Blue eyes widened, jaw dropped, cheeks turned pink, and she jumped from her seat.

"My Sadie!" Her mom cried out and made the dozen or so patrons turn to look at her. Grace turned, and when she saw Sadie, she squealed and bounced in her chair.

Her mom stopped just feet from her as her hands went to Sadie's full mane of hair and her eyes swept over the boots, vest, and shirt, then up to the hat. Tears filled her eyes.

"You're not supposed to cry!" Sadie laughed.

"Tears of joy!" She squealed and pulled Sadie into a hug.

"I want to borrow that vest!" Grace called out and they all laughed.

"You two have had quite the day," Her mom took her hand and led her to their seats. She kept hold of it as they talked. Sadie noticed five glasses of ice water sitting in front of her dad.

"What's that all about?" Sadie chuckled.

"He was hot and needed ice water," Her mother laughed and scrunched her nose at her husband. "I got a couple of pictures that told me so."

Sadie's head fell back, and her own 'life is good' laugh rang out. "That was after he was nearly run over by a mad momma cow."

"And a morning I thought I'd see the Dingo come out," Her dad teased.

"I heard you survived Asa," Her mom grinned.

"We did," He nodded. "And because the Dingo held back her attack, I survived to tell about it."

"It was more Little Ghost than me," Sadie chuckled. "It was all the questions after…"

"It took all the patience I could muster," He admitted with a grin.

"No way! I thought it was just me." Sadie gasped.

A horse neighing rang out from the table, and Sadie glanced at all three. Grace was on her phone, so it wasn't her phone ringer, and after a full day of hearing her dad's phone ring, she knew it wasn't his.

"Is that yours?" Sadie asked her mom.

With a wide grin, her mother bent over and lifted the white bag they had picked up at her office at the Bed and Breakfast and set it on the table. The bag was neighing and Grace started giggling.

"It is past time you had your own phone," Her mother said and pushed it toward her.

Sadie just narrowed her eyes and shook her head, "I don't want a phone."

"Well, you have one now and answer it before the horse goes hoarse," Her mom grinned.

The white bag neighed again.

"Sadie," Her dad reached in the bag. "Look at it this way. You can't carry your equine science books around with you everywhere, but you can get to them on the phone." He handed her the phone.

"OH!" She gasped. "I never thought of that. Does it come with an instruction manual I can read?"

"Yes, it's called your sister," Her mom chuckled.

*****

As they turned down the driveway to the Homestead, Sadie held the phone in her lap. She couldn't wait to download her sports medicine books onto the phone.

"What a day," She sighed.

"Yes, it has been," Her dad agreed. "I'm proud of you today."

She turned with a smile, "And I'm proud of you for agreeing to take Asa to the ranch for a week."

He grinned, "That is going to be one heck of a week."

When they stepped out of the truck, the horses were still wandering the pasture, so she slid the phone in her pocket and walked toward their gate.

"I'm going to go check on Scarecrow," Sadie called out to him.

She didn't wait for his answer and nearly ran to the north pasture and was through the gate quickly.

All the horse's heads rose to see who was joining the quiet afternoon.

"Just me," Sadie giggled as she skipped out to her horses. Fortunately, they were grazing next to each other.

First thing she did was check Scarecrow's leg. The pouch of loose skin wasn't as pronounced or tender, and the horse was moving with ease.

"What do you think of my new outfit?" Sadie asked them and twirled in circles. When neither answered or even looked at her, she laughed. Then their heads rose to look at her, then to the gate she had just walked through.

She turned to see a warm smile and twinkling blue eyes watching her as they neared.

"I heard you had a bit of a transformation today," Aunt Dru gave her a quick hug then twirled her finger in the air. "All that beautiful hair…"

Sadie laughed and twirled around, "What do you think?"

"I think…that those colors and that style are unique, which fits you perfectly because you, my mini-me, are the most unique young lady I know."

Sadie hugged her again, "Grace wants to go shopping for more."

"Of course, she does."

"With all the rodeos she is going to, there will be plenty of clothing available to be bought. I think I may need a job."

"Good thing Grayson finally got you a phone then," Aunt Dru said and looked out at Sadie's horses. "In fact, give me your phone and go stand by Little Ghost and Scarecrow. I'll take your pictures together so you can share them now."

"Cooper, too," Sadie grinned. "He gets to be mine for a couple of years."

"Well, I can't wait to see how well you and your trio of horses do."

For ten minutes, Sadie walked around the horses and posed with them. She had never done anything like it before but just pretended she was one of the women on all the magazine covers she had seen.

As they walked through the pasture toward the house, Sadie turned to her aunt.

"Can I ask you something?"

"Of course."

"Are you mad at dad and Uncle Scott?"

She chuckled, "Why would I be mad at them?"

"He never said it, but I'm pretty sure Dad was spending all the money he thought you were making off the bull…72."

Her aunt chuckled again and stopped at the gate.

"Sadie, in business, there is a fine line you have to balance on what you make, to what you owe, to the value of your company."

"Yeah, I remember that from school."

"Well, you can't not spend money and let your property and assets devaluate. You have to add value." Aunt Dru smiled mischievously. "Scott and Grayson will know what they need in their part of the business. I don't always know."

"I don't understand."

Aunt Dru leaned against the gate and smiled, "You asked if they were going to be mad because Grayson had to deliver 72 to Jan's ranch."

"Yes."

"They may have been mad today, but in six weeks, they will even be madder when they have to go get him."

"What?" Sadie gasped.

Aunt Dru chuckled; her grin was just as mischievous as her dad's had been all day, "I agreed with them that the bull was too valuable to sell, but that doesn't mean I couldn't lease him out for six weeks after our herd was covered."

"Leased?" Sadie laughed. "Why didn't you tell them."

"Because they won't spend money unless they think I tried to pull something over on them. If you think of what they actually bought, the money wasn't wasted. They bought items for the ranch that needed to be bought and kept the value of the ranch where we want it to be."

"Well, yeah," Sadie nodded. "Except maybe Little Bro and my clothes."

"As much as we love our horses, some of them are considered tools or assets on this ranch. Monty is getting up there in age, so, on paper, he isn't as valuable as he was ten years ago. Little Bro, even though the purchase was more sentimental, and I would have done the same thing, he brought value into the business portion of the horse herd."

"My clothes didn't," Sadie grinned.

"That brought value into you and who you are and will be in the future," Aunt Dru tapped the tip of Sadie's new black hat. "And that is more important than any asset on this ranch."

"I love you, Aunt Dru," Sadie grinned. "And, I want to be around when you tell them about the lease!"

"In six weeks," She chuckled and opened the gate. "We'll let them think they got something over on me until then."

Sadie's new phone began to neigh again. She looked at it and grinned, "It's Reilly on a video chat."

"Well, let me tell my son hello before I go in so you two can talk."

They stood close together, and both grinned as Sadie accepted the video chat. Reilly's smile turned to a grin when he saw them.

"Hi, Mom," He grinned.

"Hello, Son," There was happy contentment in her greeting.

It had been three years since they became mother and son, with Aunt Dru marrying his dad, but there was always something special when he called her mom.

"Have a good day?" She asked him.

His head tilted back and forth with a smirk, "Mostly."

"Every event and trip will get better," She said.

"I know, I'm still just the newbie around here," He nodded.

Aunt Dru smiled, "Well, I know you called Sadie, so I will let you two talk, but you call if you need to, and even when you don't."

"Okay, Mom. Love ya," He smiled.

"And to you," She sighed, then turned and walked away.

Sadie shut the gate and walked back into the pasture with a determined stride.

"Reilly, I need to talk to you."

"Yeah," His smile dissolved into a serious frown. "I need to talk to you, too."

CHAPTER THIRTEEN

"Where are you?" Sadie asked.

"In the back of the corrals where no one can hear me. I can see the house behind you, so you must be in the south pasture?"

"Yeah, I'm going to the pasture island so no one can hear me."

"Must be serious."

"Yours, too."

"So, this conversation is just between us?"

She walked through the gate of the pasture island and plopped down on the bench. "Yes."

"Alright, you first," He said.

After a deep breath, she told him of the conversation with Helen.

"Before she went and talked to Dad, Helen said, "If you want to tattle-tale to your dad, then fine. Throw your little fit, bat your baby blue eyes at him, and pout that you're not getting your way, and he can take his business elsewhere just like you want."

"Dang…that's rude."

"I don't want that to happen because of Kate, so I'm not sure if I should tell dad what Helen said. And now, Helen knows that, too. That's why she gave me that little sneering smile after shaking dad's hand."

"Yeah, if you tell Grayson what Helen said, he would move the business despite Kate owning half of it, and all the adults would agree," Reilly nodded.

"I don't want that to happen to Kate, so I don't want to tell him what she called me that day and what she said today…that she didn't like me. Helen knows it, and I just don't know what to do," Sadie sighed in frustration.

"No matter how good Kate is, Helen is not," Reilly huffed.

"She just isn't a good person no matter how she 'presents herself' to other people…like Wade, Uncle Scott, and Aunt Jordan," Sadie nodded. "I always want people to like me, Reilly, but I just don't think I care about her. I just don't know what to do."

"You mean about telling Grayson and Leah?"

"Or even Aunt Dru," Sadie nodded. "Learning how to deal with people like Helen is something I'm going to have to learn to do. That's just part of life in the horse world. It's just part of the business."

He exhaled heavily, "Yeah, I'm learning that, too."

"What happened?"

His eyes lifted from the phone and looked around him, then returned.

"You know Nick and Lucas came down here today?"

"Yeah."

"Well, before they got here, I talked to the boss, Anders. I told him about what you said about the brown mare, and he wanted to know if I had been talking to veterinarians or anyone like that without his permission. I told him 'no' that I had talked to my uncle and cousin and before I had much of a chance to explain, he just 'went off' on a rant about adding cost to the company without permission, and I didn't have the authority to do that."

"Did you tell him it didn't cost anything?"

"He didn't give me a chance," Reilly huffed in frustration. "He walked out the door and started complaining about me to the other men here and telling them that I wasn't going to be worth what I cost them in vet bills."

"That's awful," Sadie cringed.

"It got worse," He moaned. "I was cleaning the corral right behind the trailer when Nick arrived, and he and Anders were in there with the window open, so I heard everything. Anders started telling Nick about me costing the company money, and I wasn't going to be worth the cost."

"Oh, Reilly…" Sadie sighed. "What did Nick say?"

"He told Anders that the only uncle I would have called would be Grayson and that I had probably saved them money by going to a man with Grayson's experience instead of going to a vet or directly to a chiropractor."

"Well, that's good. But, do they know you're related to Nick?"

Reilly grinned, "I'm not sure it's related when he is my step-mother's ex-husband."

Sadie chuckled, "I always forget they were married once. I just think of him as an uncle."

Reilly nodded, then his eyes narrowed, "After Nick shut down Anders complaining about me, Nick said the one thing that really surprised me."

"What?"

"Nick told Anders that he better watch how he talks to the future owner of the company because it might just cost him his job."

"What?" Sadie gasped.

"Yeah," Reilly nodded with wide eyes. "Nick called me the future owner of the company, and he was dead serious."

"Wow, did he ever say anything to you?"

"No, just that I could go to work for the company for a few years and learn the business."

"I thought Anders owned the business."

Reilly shook his head, "No, Nick told me he owned it when he offered me the job."

"Huh," Sadie leaned back against the bench. "You know, I never really think that much about what Nick does."

"Well, he does have a private jet," Reilly smirked.

Sadie giggled, "That's true, and if someone owns their own jet, they won't be working for someone else…especially a stock contractor. Do you know what they do when they go to Australia?"

"Not a clue," Reilly shrugged.

"No matter what it is, I guess it doesn't matter to our situations now."

He shook his head, "When I sent Grace a message about the pictures she posted of your new look and joked about how much dang hair you have, she told me to call you myself. I'm glad you got your own phone so I could call you, because I really needed to talk to someone and I knew you wouldn't tell anyone else. "

"Me, too," She admitted. "But I don't think we solved anything."

"I guess, sometimes, it's more about just talking to someone than solving anything. Not really anything to solve for me anyway."

"What do I do about Helen?"

He shook his head, "Right now, nothing. She doesn't have anything to do with the Tagger horses anymore, that's all Kate."

"And if that changes?"

"Then you worry about it when it happens. Don't stress over something you can't control or may never happen."

She chuckled, "That sounds like your dad talking."

Reilly grinned, "Yeah, but sometimes those parents actually know what they are talking about."

CHAPTER FOURTEEN

When she walked through the gate to the house, Wade walked out of the front door.

"Cool hat," He grinned and sat on the front step.

"Thanks, I love it."

"Uncle Grayson told me to come out and ask you something."

"What?" She asked and sat on the step next to him. They both looked out to the horses.

"Do you want to hear how Kylee and Tara are doing?"

"Sure."

****

Her parents, Grace, Nora, Wade, Uncle Scott, Aunt Jordan, Aunt Dru, and Jack were sitting at the table at the front of the house. Each person was digging their spoons into the bowls of ice cream and quietly watching the sun lower below the horizon. The few clouds that danced in the sky were lit with the grays, oranges, and pinks of the sunset.

The horses were still grazing in the pasture, and Pepper, Indy, and Spur were trotting across the south pasture. It was peaceful…except for the clanging of spoon to dish.

One by one, the family members walked into the house until it was just Sadie and her dad sitting on the porch watching the horses roam in the brightening moonlight. Bowls and spoons were sitting on the table, both had their legs crossed with hands together on their laps, and both were looking out into the darkness. The distant town's lights and the stars sparkled in the night.

"You know," He whispered. "We've spent hours, just the two of us, in that truck today."

"Yep," Sadie nodded.

"And yet, I have one more question to ask you."

"What's that?"

"After your talk with Helen…did you need to talk? Are you alright with how it turned out?"

"That is two questions," She smiled and heard him chuckle. She leaned back and looked up into the stars for the answer.

"Well, Dad," she said softly. "I'm thirteen."

"Yeah…"

"And some days I feel thirteen, most days I feel thirty, but right now I feel…dumb."

"What?" He huffed.

The day of the argument in the barn, Helen had called her a dumb blonde child that didn't know what she was talking about when it came to Rufio's injuries, and she should go and play with her pretty little ponies. That upset Sadie, and she had told Helen that she was an ignorant brunette that didn't have a compassionate bone in her old body. That was what had escalated the argument until Wade walked into the barn and broke it up.

Of course, Sadie didn't tell anyone that, not even Wade and Reilly.

She turned and looked at her dad, "I let someone that didn't care about me, or even realize what she was doing, influence me with one sentence. I feel dumb for letting her do that."

He nodded with an understanding smile, "A lot of people say things to other people without realizing what they are doing…how that is going to negatively affect that person's future. It happens to adults and kids."

Sadie nodded, "Like the lady that called Nora names after hitting her car."

"It works the other way, too. Just one nice word or compliment to someone can change their whole outlook on life," He smiled. "I'm going to tell you one right now."

"What?"

"You are not dumb; you're thirteen and still learning in life…even on those days you feel like you're thirty."

They smiled at each other.

"Thanks for everything today, Dad."

"Thank you, Sadie Girl, it was a fun and eventful day."

"We certainly put some mileage on your truck."

"Some days are like that but are followed by a day like tomorrow."

"Which is?"

"A complete day on horseback riding the mountains."

"Hmmm," Sadie smiled. "Maybe me and Cooper should start training by just going riding in those mountains with you."

"Another full day with the Dingo? I can handle that."

They both stood and picked up their bowls and spoons. As they walked through the door, Sadie leaned into him.

"I love you, Dad."

"I love you, too."

∗∗∗∗

After hanging her new clothes in her closet, Sadie changed into her 'Tagger Drive" t-shirt and pajama shorts, then crawled onto her bed. She sat cross-legged in the middle and braided the mass of blonde hair. It was funny that her hair was so long because of Reilly. He would probably never know that fact, but she was going to make sure that he knew he was the first person to call her; 'Dr. Sadie'.

With all her heart, she wanted to be called Dr. Sadie. Not, Dr. Tagger, or Dr. whatever her married name would be. She wanted to be Dr. Sadie, just like Dr. Mark. That was her dream and her goal in life. It was her driving force to read and reread all the books she could find and keep up-to-date on all the new technology. Now, with her phone, she could read anywhere. That was thrilling to her.

She slid under the covers and rolled onto her side to look at the dim light of the clock. It was 10:03, 16 hours after she looked at the clock when she woke. She had thought, at the time, that today was the day that was supposed to change her life forever. She was supposed to be at the National finals instead of at the Homestead. But, no matter what could have happened there, it wasn't anything compared to home.

As her eyes closed, she knew her life had most definitely changed that day, just not the way she had expected.

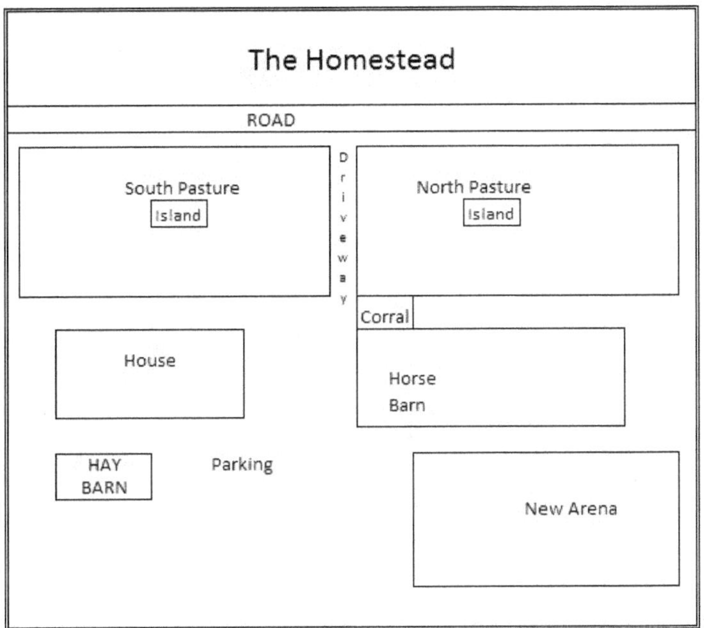

The Homestead
ROAD
Driveway
South Pasture
Island
North Pasture
Island
Corral
Horse
Barn
House
HAY
BARN
Parking
New Arena

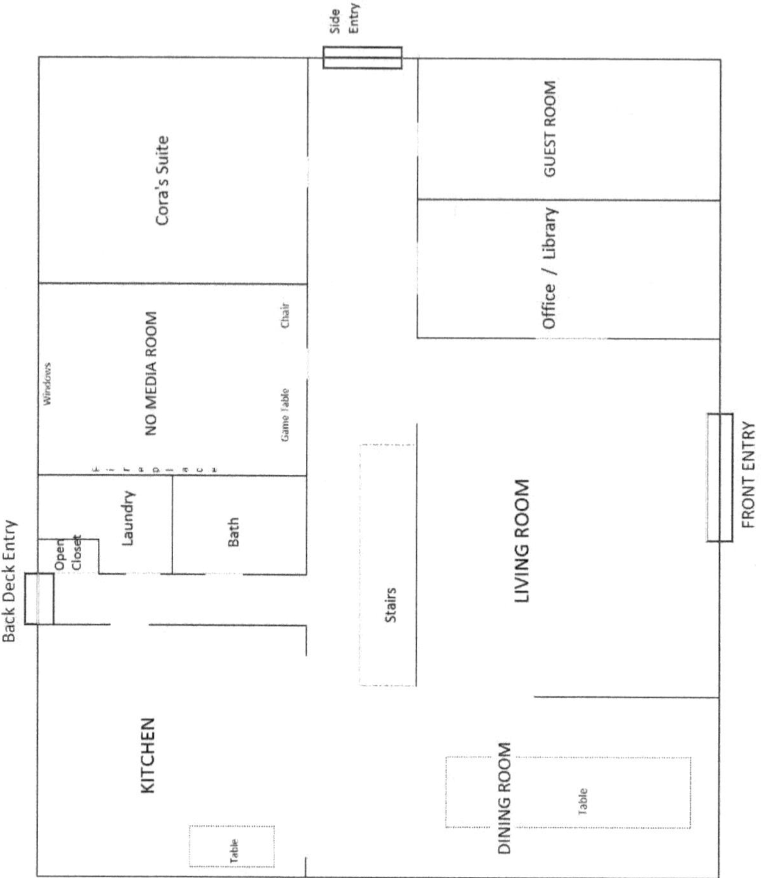

The Homestead Downstairs

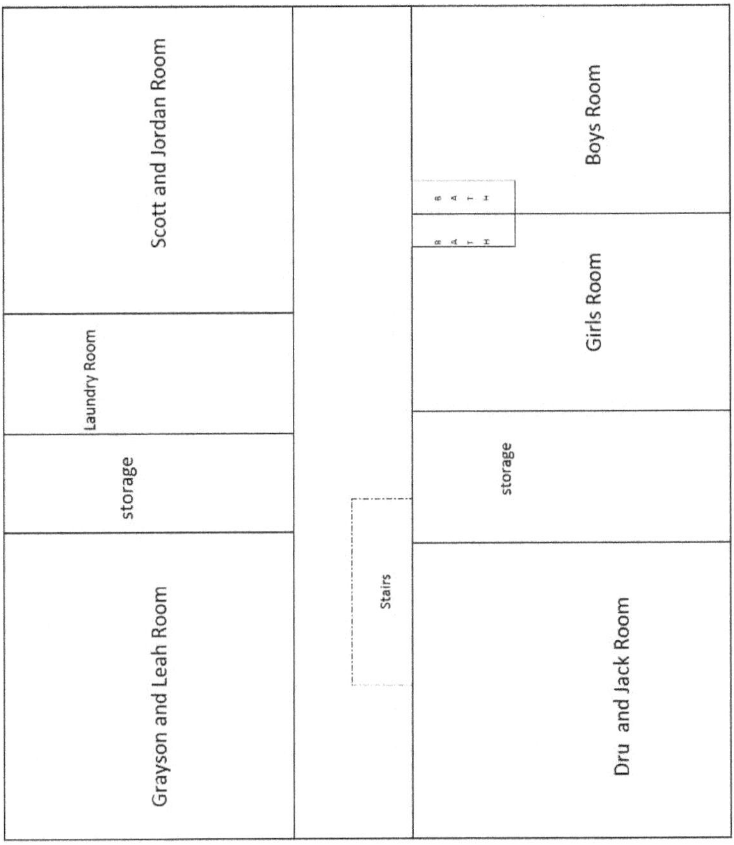

Scott and Jordan Room

Boys Room

BATH

BATH

Girls Room

Laundry Room

storage

storage

Stairs

Grayson and Leah Room

Dru and Jack Room

The Homestead Upstairs

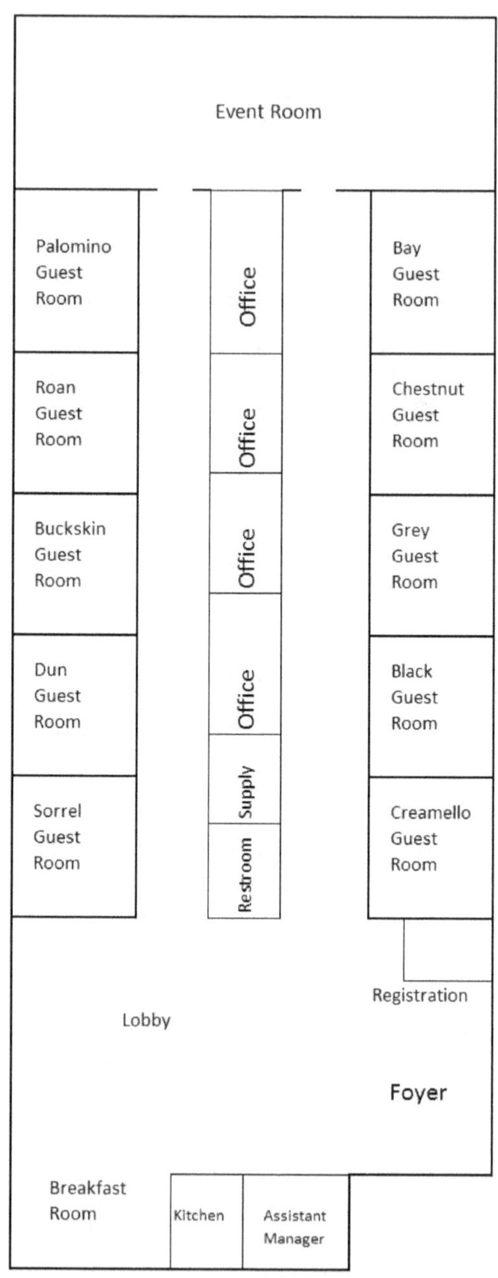

Tagger Enterprises Barn & Breakfast

The Tagger Family

Drucilla
Nikki
Matt —— Nick

Grayson
Leah
Grace
Sadie

Scott
Jordan
Nora
Wade

Jessup: Tagger Ranch

Jack Morgan: The Stables
Reilly

Cora Smith: The Homestead

Tessa Elliott: Barn & Breakfast
Alex

Tagger Property History:
Mathew and Grace
Anderson and Nora
Mathew and Anne
Grayson Mathew, Scott Anderson, Drucilla Anne

ABOUT THE AUTHOR

I was raised with Shetlands and ponies and have loved horses since I watched a Shetland colt born when I was four.

Growing up, the TV show Bonanza was my favorite. I loved that western life and wanted to be Little Joe and Hoss' little sister. I wanted to live at the Ponderosa. Watching rodeos on television and attending when I could, was the closest I could get to the cowboy way of life.

That changed when I purchased my first 'big horse' when I was twenty-one and living in Alaska. I now have the great-granddaughter of that horse in my pasture.

I am also a photographer specializing in the equine industry; shows, races, jackpots, and rodeos. With my photography, I create my own covers.

The Tagger Herd Series was my first venture into fictional writing and I love the family and horses in the series.

My first 'stand-alone' novel was Hoofbeats in the Wind which ventured into rodeo.

My next book, Coffee With Cowboys delved deeper into the rodeo world and researching for the book was an adventure. I have met wonderful people from fans, stock contractors, and competitors. I thank every one of them that have helped make that book a possibility. It will always be special to me because of the people I met.

Bijou Bay was inspired by Idaho's Black Rock Ranch and the a true story I was fortunate enough to be told.

Writing, researching, photography, my two dogs, Morgan and Tagger, and Kit in the pasture, fill my world and keep me busy.

www.ingramcontent.com/pod-product-compliance
Lightning Source LLC
Chambersburg PA
CBHW070521220726
48294CB00019B/21

9 781733 952866